Betsy's

JOURNEYS

JOURNEYS

THE ARCHERS
OF SAINT SEBASTIAN I

JEANNE ROLAND

NEPENTHE PRESS

Cover art and interior design by Nepenthe Press. *Background image*: Still Life with Poppy, Insects, and Reptiles, Otto Marseus van Schrieck, ca. 1670, in the Metropolitan Museum of Art; *Inset image*: Sant Sebastian Expiring, François-Xavier Fabre, ca. 1825, in the Fabre Museum, Montpellier, France. For a full citation of the source files for these public domain works and for all of the other artwork used herein, please see the illustration credits page located in the back of the book. Our press logo and Jeanne Roland's author logo were created for Nepenthe Press by Miblart.

ISBN 978-1-7378870-0-3 (Paperback)

ISBN 978-1-7378870-1-0 (ebook)

ISBN 978-1-7378870-2-7 (Hardback)

Published by Nepenthe Press

3195 Dayton-Xenia Rd Ste 900 PMB 120

Beavercreek, OH 45434-6390

NEPENTHE PRESS
WWW.NEPENTHEPRESS.COM

FOR MY FATHER

PROLOGUE

May 1347

O nly the faintest hint of grey light is coming in through the windows when I slip from under my covers and make my way silently between the rows of cots pushed neatly up against the walls of the long, spare room. I don't exactly sneak, but I prefer to rise before the other boys, if I can, so I can steal a few moments to wash while I'm still alone on the empty field. I never undress, so it's probably an unnecessary precaution, and I might as well admit it, I *do* like to be the first one out to the training area to get our station ready. This is the time of day I enjoy most: working off the chill of dawn by going through my meticulous, almost ritualistic preparation of our equipment — stocking the quivers, checking the arrows, and seeing to the great yew bow Tristan uses for morning practice.

But it's getting harder and harder to keep this time for myself. Some of the other boys have started getting up earlier, too, as though we're in competition amongst ourselves, or as though I'm motivated by some sort of misguided ambition to show them up and make them look lazy. They've got it all wrong, of course. I'm conscientious, but really, 'ambitious squire' is an oxymoron. Either you find satisfaction in what you do, or you don't, since there isn't really anywhere to go from here. Not for me, anyway. But there's no way to explain to them what this hour of solitude means to me, this hour safely absorbed in small tasks — simple ones, but ones in which I can take some measure of pride. On mornings like this, it all feels natural. I'm part of something bigger than myself, and I almost convince myself that I belong here.

This morning, I'm alone. No one else stirs as I make my way carefully across our dormitory. The stone floor feels like ice under my feet in the unheated room after the relative warmth beneath my blanket, but I wait until I reach the door to pull on my boots. As I step out into the corridor it's a bit warmer, since the kitchens lie just beyond and the cooking fires will have been started by now. I stop here a moment as always, partly to warm myself before the inevitable plunge into the cold outdoors, but mostly to consider my route. The shortest way out to the training ground is to cut directly across the great hall, which opens before me to the left. On the opposite side of the hall, a door leads out to a covered portico which shades a walkway between the hall and an adjacent walled garden. From there a little gate gives easy access out to the place where a row of wooden sheds stands, each one assigned to a journeyman archer for the storage of his gear. Technically we're not supposed to cut through the great hall, but all the boys do. At this hour there's no one to see, except perhaps one of the kitchen staff or old Albrecht, but he always turns a blind eye to misdemeanors of this sort.

The other route, past the Journeymen's rooms and the archives in a circuitous loop to the stables, is not only much longer, but there's always the distinct possibility of an awkward encounter in the hallway if one of the Journeymen should happen to wake early, or worse, a master. This has never happened to me, but it's happened to some of the others, and I don't relish the thought of meeting, say, Master Guillaume wandering the halls in a state of undress on his way to the veterans' lavatory, yawning and stretching, holding up his britches in one hand and scratching his hairy belly with the other. Or catching Taran unawares in a cramped corridor, still sluggish from sleep but no doubt just as brutish and unforgiving as he is when he's wide awake.

At that thought, I hesitate, my foot hovering over the threshold of the hall, and I think, perhaps this is the morning I'll take the shortcut, too.

But I know I won't.

Still, I can't stop myself from taking a quick glance into the cavernous depths of the great hall, which the thin panes of colored glass placed high along on its walls do little to light even on the brightest day. Now with only the early morning gloom pressing in, it's as black as pitch in there and a good ten degrees colder even than it was back in our dormitory. The wan streaks of blue and greenish light reaching in through the windows only add to the unpleasant atmosphere, mingling with the darkness like swirls of murky water. Above, the high ceiling of blackened wood greedily swallows what little light struggles upward, trapping it within the maze of its intricately carved coffers. The odor of musty wood and candle wax gives the air a thick quality that's slightly nauseating, as though something palpable is forming within the shadows. It would only be a matter of seconds to cross the hall, and from where I'm standing I can clearly make out the outline of the door to the portico on its opposite side, but still I hesitate. I'm not afraid of the dark, and I know there's nothing really waiting there for me. Nothing alive, anyway.

It's not the darkness that stops me, it's the painting.

The massive canvas hangs at the far end of the room, covering the wall virtually from floor to rafters. Even in the full light of day, it's a commanding presence. Now in the stark emptiness of the hall it seems to have grown to fill the space completely. Its rich background hues of sumptuous blue-blacks and deep reds bleed into the surrounding darkness, so that the huge, lone human figure bristling with arrows at its center seems suspended in agony in the middle of the room, its vast expanse of naked, rent flesh as pale and as luminous as a moon in a midnight sky. For a moment I'm as mesmerized by that tortured figure again as I was the first time I saw it, not so many weeks ago. I remember every detail of that day, but my first sight of the painting stands out most vividly. Its image has become jumbled in my mind with other images, ones I don't allow myself to see even in my mind's eye, and confused with memories of the terrible events that were quickly to follow. So much has changed since then that I can't trust the accuracy of my memories anymore, but I remember my reaction to the painting very clearly. I couldn't forget it if I tried, because I thought it was the most exquisitely beautiful thing I had ever seen. Now I can't bear to look at it.

The morbid painted figure staring past me, eyes glazed with pain, is more than a gruesome reminder. It's an accusation, a riddle I can't solve. I fight down a wave of revulsion and give myself a mental shake. I have to be sharp today; this is no time to get caught up in memories or lost in grim fancies, and Tristan's strange mood these past few days already has me on edge. Besides, perhaps it isn't the painting, after all, that keeps me now from crossing the room. Perhaps it's the plaque next to the arched doorway, which reads:

Great Hall, Archers' Guild of St. Sebastian.
Members only beyond this point. No women allowed.

I hesitate for a moment longer, then turn and proceed down the passageway along the Journeymen's quarters, as I always do. Today isn't going to be the day I try the shortcut after all. I'm lucky, though, and I make it out through the stables without meeting a single soul, except for a few stable boys still huddled asleep in one of the empty stalls. It's probably not really luck at this hour, but I feel as though I've run a gauntlet unscathed anyway. I cross out onto the corner of the field where barrels filled with water for washing are lined up under the stable's overhanging eaves. Although it's still early, I content myself with splashing some water on my face and washing my hands thoroughly. Today is the first day of the trials, and I'm understandably nervous. If everything goes as expected, we should breeze through these preliminaries, but I can't take any chances. I haven't come this far to fail now.

I run my wet hands through my hair and give my distorted reflection a quick check in the rippled glass of the empty archive window. Staring back at me is a young boy of indeterminate age. He could be anywhere from ten to thirteen, depending on what criteria you use to judge him: a little taller than you'd expect for a ten-year-old, but with a face and limbs that are still childishly soft and rounded. The facial features are small and delicate, except for the nose. That's been spectacularly broken, leaving it crooked and misshapen. Short, lank hair frames the face, either hanging down in hanks of irregular length or sticking straight up at awkward angles, as though it's been hacked off by a drunken pair of dueling barbers. It's a singularly wretched cut, but it lends an air of vulnerability at odds with the brutality of scars, old and new, that snake across the nose to adorn the left brow. In all, I see just a rather average, ugly twelve-year-old boy, nothing extraordinary.

No, nothing extraordinary — except for the fact that up until ten weeks ago, I was a fifteen-year-old girl.

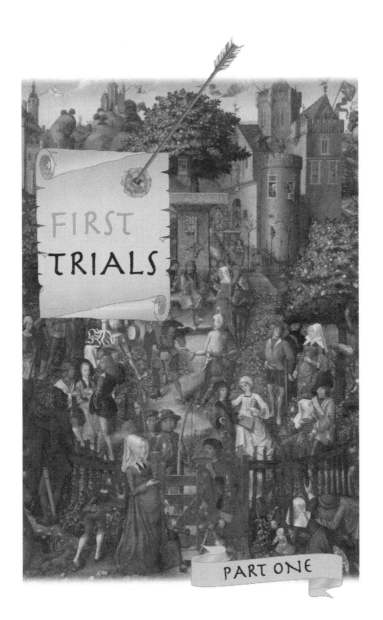

FIRST
TRIALS

PART ONE

CHAPTER ONE

March 1347, Outskirts of Louvain, in the principality of Ardennes

The sun is already streaming through my open window when I'm awoken from dreamless sleep by the sound of my father's voice just outside my door.

"Marieke," he says sharply, "Marieke, are you up?"

After a brief pause, he says flatly,

"Just bring my breakfast out to the workshop when it's ready."

His clipped tone is my father's way of letting me know that I've already let him down, even before the day has properly started. Embarrassed, I wait until I hear his footsteps on the stairs before I struggle out from under the covers. It's already late; one glance out my window tells me just how much. On today of all days, I should have been up early.

My father has promised to take me with him into Louvain this afternoon. A trip to town is a rare treat in any event, but this is to be the first time I'm allowed to accompany my father on his rounds. We're to pay personal visits to some of my father's clients, and I'm determined to prove myself useful.

My father's a fletcher, a maker of arrows and archery equipment, and I don't think I'm bragging when I say he's one of the very best. It's a highly specialized craft, and my father's skill has acquired him a loyal following. A good fletcher is always in demand, since the bow is the military weapon *par excellence* these days, but we've also got a long history of devotion to the art of longbow archery here in Ardennes. Last year, when the Welsh decisively proved the military supremacy of the heavy English-style longbow in that big battle at Crecy, it was simply confirmation of what we Ardennese have long believed (the French artillery, though armed with longer-ranged and easier to use crossbows, just couldn't keep pace with the rapid fire of the Welsh longbowmen; they say that over 4000 French knights were killed). Archery isn't just our national defense, it's our national obsession, so it's only natural that some measure of the status we afford our archers has trickled down to the fletchers who supply them. All in all, it's a very respectable and reliable living.

The only problem is, girls just don't become fletchers. No matter how useful or knowledgeable I prove today, I won't be taken on as my father's apprentice. That's out of the question, although I've been allowed to help out more in the workshop since my brother Jules died. It's just temporary, though. Sooner or later my father will have to take on a new apprentice, and my days of being treated as my father's quasi-assistant are clearly numbered. But I did hope that if on our trip today my father and I could fall into some approximation of the easy companionship he used to share with Jules, it might do something to thaw the chill that's settled between us.

I give my nightshirt an exasperated pull over my head, and I streak across the hall into the small adjacent cubicle that used to belong to Jules. The room has been largely left untouched, as though its former occupant might return at any moment. His few possessions are still where he left them after their last use, carefully arranged in his meticulous way. There's a small hinged writing case and a candle on a table by his bed, and his clothes are neatly folded in piles on a stool under the window. Worst of all, his bows are still hanging vertically from pegs on the wall above, never unstrung since he last hung them up and probably unusable now. That is, all but one. That one's resting where I left it, concealed in the woodshed at the bottom of the yard.

I slip on an old pair of breeches of Jules's and ease one of his tunics over my head. Both are too long, but I tuck the ends of the breeches down into my boots, and secure both the top of the breeches and the tunic by wrapping a long strip of linen twice around my waist. I really don't know what my father thinks about my wearing Jules's clothes, and I haven't thought too hard about my own motives, either. After Jules died, my father would go into his room every day and sit on his bed in silence. I'd see him there, unmoving, day after day. Once, when I noticed the door standing open, I found myself going in and sitting on the bed in the exact same position. I tried thinking of Jules, or of my father, or letting my mind go blank, but I felt so empty just sitting there that I had to do something. I got up and without thinking put on Jules's clothes, and I've been doing it ever since. I don't know if I was trying to bring Jules back, or to tell my father that I could take his place, but it felt oddly comforting to wrap my body in Jules's familiar things, and strangely I felt more myself dressed as Jules than I had dressed as myself.

When my father first saw me in this get-up, a disapproving look passed over his face, but all he did was raise his eyebrows slightly and go back to what he was doing. I think at first I kept it up trying to break him, to see just how long it would take him to finally comment on my attire — but he never did. Eventually it just became a habit. The clothes are comfortable, and I leave it at that; they're so much more practical than my own for the outdoor life we lead.

At the top of the stairs, I'm surprised by the sound of my father's voice calling up to me.

"*Not* those clothes today, Marieke."

He hasn't gone out to his workshop yet, after all. Instead, he's hovering near the back door, as though he's been waiting for me to come down. Apparently, today is the day he's finally decided to take issue with my dress.

"I'm not a fool," I snap, before I can stop myself. I didn't want to get in one of our arguments today, but my voice sounds challenging. "You don't really think I'd go to town dressed as a boy, do you?"

He ignores the comment.

"I put some things out on the table for you: a clean chemise, and your blue tunic. Find some clean stockings, too. And Marieke — shoes, not boots."

"I can dress myself!" I mumble, turning to the washbasin on the table outside my door to hide my sullen expression and dangling my fingers in the water half-heartedly. It's completely unlike my father to notice my clothes. "Why do you care what I wear?" I call down.

"In town, people talk," he replies shortly, with an air of finality that says the conversation is over. He's already halfway out the door when he calls back curtly,

"And for God's sake, actually wash your face!"

This last outburst is so out of character that it confirms my suspicions. When did my father ever comment on clothing, or care what people thought about it? Something's up.

As I head downstairs, I can feel myself growing unreasonably angry: angry at myself, at my father, and Jules, even, for leaving my father and me at this impasse. It wasn't always so hard between us. My father's always been reserved, at least as long as I've known him, though my aunt Berthal used to paint a very different picture of him. *"You should have seen him, Marieke,"* she'd say. *"He cut such a handsome figure, and such a flirt! All the girls were crazy for him."* I used to listen to her stories, trying to imagine my father as the light-hearted boy she'd describe, but I could never quite picture it. I know he's a loving father at heart, but he's always been just distant enough that I'm constantly torn between craving his affection and resenting his withholding of it, between seeking his approval and acting up to get his attention — between idolizing him and hating him, really.

It might have been easier growing up if my mother had been around, but she died giving birth to me, and I don't think my father ever really got over it. It was the crowning blow to a long series of disappointments. I don't think he's ever held her death against me, but some say I remind him of her and that probably hasn't helped. I can't see it myself. By all accounts, she was beautiful, and I'm anything but — and as Berthal always used to remind me, ugliness is another quality that doesn't help endear a daughter.

I think, though, that the real problem is that my father has just never really known what to do with a girl.

Out in the kitchen, I find that my father has already made a fire, so I put a heavy pot on to boil. While it heats, I head out to take care of the livestock. It has to be done every day, trip to town or not — there's no such thing as a holiday from goats.

When I've assembled our breakfast — bread, ale, and bowls of broth — I carry it out across the yard to my father's workshop. My father isn't seated at his workbench as usual; instead, he's going through his inventory to see what he'll need to restock while in town. I hesitate a moment after I place his breakfast on a long table by the door, and he beckons me to join him in a gesture that suggests our earlier conversation is to be forgotten. As we eat in silence, I try to think of something to say to make up for my sullen behavior earlier, but I can't come up with anything. I notice him rubbing his bad shoulder, so I say,

"I can help load and unload the wagon, if your shoulder is acting up."

"It's just the damp, makes it ache a bit. I'll expect I'll manage," is all he answers.

It's not just that Jules isn't here to act as a bridge between us anymore. He was very like my father in temperament; serious when working, careful, unflappable, but with an underlying sense of humor. I used to love sitting in the back of the workshop, fiddling with some bit of work of my own, but mostly watching them work together in effortless rhythm, needing few words to communicate and completely at ease with each other. Their silences were never awkward like this, but I was never jealous of them. Well, not much. It's also that Jules's death has bumped me up to the top of the list of my father's problems.

Until a year ago, I was pretty much left to the care of Berthal, my father's spinster sister, who 'did' for us as housekeeper and, I suppose, served as a sort of surrogate mother. She was sweet but scatterbrained, and what few housekeeping skills she possessed she never managed to pass on to me very successfully. It didn't help that I wasn't a very willing pupil. That never seemed to matter too much, though, since my father just assumed that when the time came, he'd pass me off with a dowry into the hands of some neighbor's son, and my poor housekeeping would become his problem. But after a well-aimed kick from a mule when I was eleven years old left my nose shattered and my face badly scarred, it soon became clear that any local interest in taking me on as a wife, even with a cash incentive, had all but dried up.

I think my father had pretty much resigned himself to the idea that I would live out my life here much as Berthal had: when he died and Jules took over his trade, I'd stay here and do for Jules as Berthal had for him. This plan suited me, too; everyone knows that a brother is often a better master than a husband. But everything changed last winter, when both Berthal and Jules contracted fever during the same epidemic and died within days of each other.

I cast a glance over at my father, bent over his bowl, and imagine that he's pondering the problem of what to do with me right now. A sobering thought occurs to me, something that would explain my father's unexpected decision to take me to town with him, and why he's even more reluctant to talk about our plans than usual. My father needs a new apprentice, and forcing one to take me as part of the bargain is the only practical solution.

Now I know why I'm to look presentable today. I'm to be shown off to my father's clients along with his other wares.

I break off a piece of bread and drop it into my bowl, but my appetite is gone. I watch it in sympathy as it floats around on the broth until it sinks to the bottom, saturated and bloated. I can't be my father's heir; legally, he can't even leave me his property, and arranged marriages are common. But somehow, I never thought of one for me. I'd just assumed the mule had ruined me for marriage, or maybe spared me from it. *Does my father already have some prospects in mind*, I wonder? Is today meant to seal the bargain? I cast a surreptitious glance my father's way, but he's as unreadable to me as ever.

Of course, I could simply ask my father, but I don't. If this is going to be my last day of freedom, I don't want to know.

To stop myself from further depressing speculation I clear the breakfast things to the side of the table. I'll take them back to the house later. While my father gets up to continue his preparations for this afternoon, I sit down at my usual place in the back of the workshop, where I've made a little workstation for myself. I never sit in Jules's empty spot though the light is better there, and I'm more comfortable here where I've always worked anyway. My father has always let me help out with the arrows, and by now, I often make whole batches by myself. I'm best at attaching the fletching, the feathers attached to the shaft of the arrow to stabilize it during flight. At first, this was all my father would let me do. I think he thought that this was more appropriate for a girl than working down the shafts, since it's quite delicate work. Anyone can do it, but it takes practice to be good. If I do say so myself, I've gotten quite proficient, and at a straight fletch, I'm almost as good as my father.

When my father notices me sitting at my worktable, he frowns, and I'm afraid he's going to tell me to go and see to my regular chores. Instead he asks,

"How far are you on the batch of broadheads?"

"I've only got a few left," I say with some pride, glad to be back on safe territory. I'd only been given them yesterday.

"If you finish them this morning, we'll deliver them today. You can tend to the yard when we get back."

I've never delivered my own products before, and the prospect begins to renew my excitement for our trip. I pick up one of the broadhead arrows from a pile by my workstation. They're almost finished, the points already attached. We produce literally dozens of these, and since they're used for mass volleys where strict accuracy isn't necessary, getting them finished quickly is more important than perfection. I can't afford to lavish too much time on a single arrow, but I'm determined to do only the highest quality work today.

I've already marked the shaft with the place where the individual vanes of the fletch will go, so I choose out three long goose feathers from the wing of a single bird from an array of materials spread out on my table. I've already cut them into a half-shield shape, so they're ready to attach. First, I position the cock feather carefully and anchor it firmly to the shaft with a length of thin silk thread whipping. Holding the thread taut in one hand, I then place the other two feathers, one at a time, as I carefully turn the shaft and wind the whipping between the individual barbs of the feathers, constantly adjusting the feathers as I go to keep them in line and to avoid any gaps forming between the barbs. As I send the thin red thread spiraling through the grey feathers, the effect is as lovely as any work of art, which seems almost wrong, since the other end of the arrow is a singularly vicious weapon:

two backward facing barbs on either side of its wide point are designed to catch in the flesh and ensure maximum bloodletting.

As I'm bent over in concentration, I sense my father pausing just behind my shoulder to watch me.

"Good, Marieke, very good," is all he says, as he places a hand lightly on my shoulder for a moment before he moves away. It might not sound like much, but this is something I appreciate about my father. He isn't lavish with his complements, so when he gives one, I know it's sincere.

When the feathers are all secure, I continue to wrap the shaft down to just above the nock, or the notch in the back end of the arrow that fits over the bowstring and secures it in place, and I make sure to bind tightly to reinforce it. If the nock splits, not only is the arrow ruined, but the archer runs the risk of serious injury from the splintered wood. When I'm satisfied, I loop off the whipping and cut it with the sharp little knife I keep with my tools.

As I take out the next arrow, I sit back for a minute and notice that my father has finished taking inventory. He's taken out a small recurve bow that I've never seen before, and has begun rubbing it with tallow. It's essentially finished. *When did he make it?* I wonder. Surely I'd have noticed something so unusual. It's small, almost delicate, a beautiful little bow with a curve so pronounced it looks positively eastern. Who could possibly have commissioned it?

"I don't think I've ever seen that before," I say casually.

"No, I don't think you have."

That's all he says. My father seems bent on keeping secrets today.

"Is it for one of your clients this afternoon?" I press.

"Not … exactly," he says, grinning.

Another infuriating answer! Now he's purposely teasing me, but it's also clear that he's not going to tell me about the bow until he's ready. *Maybe it's a bribe for my future husband,* I think bitterly. From the size of the bow, he's a little boy. Or maybe he's old and wizened.

My bitter thoughts melt away as I watch my father's hands moving lovingly over the wood of the little bow, stroking his creation gently, almost as though it were alive. He has beautiful hands, so sure and confident, and I've always loved watching them as he works. But my feelings for my father are never simple, and inevitably I begin to imagine his hands moving over the bow in another, more thrilling motion:

I picture him grasp it suddenly by the grip, raise it high in a wide arc, pull back quick and light, and let an arrow fly with deadly accuracy. I might as well admit it, this is the real reason that I idolize my father: I know he was once an expert archer, one of the best of his age, that he was in fact once a star at St. Sebastian's. Compared with this, being a fletcher, no matter how good, is nothing.

I know this about my father. It's not a secret. But I've never actually seen him take a single shot. This strange fact is, I think, what really lies behind my relationship with my father, and my confused feelings for him. Sometimes, on long evenings spent around the fire, my father did used to tell stories about the guild; funny stories that started with something like, *"Did I ever tell you about the time a pig got loose on the target range?"* or *"I remember when Alard shot his lazy squire in the foot. He claimed it was an accident, but nobody believed him …,"* but the stories were always oddly impersonal, as though he'd heard them second-hand rather than lived them, and they dried up entirely when Jules died. *"What interest can a girl have in marksmanship, in competition? These aren't proper subjects for girls"* I can almost hear my father say. But these are exactly the kinds of things I want to hear about, the kind of adventure I crave, perhaps because these are the only stories my father ever wanted to tell. His refusal to divulge any real details of his past at St. Sebastian's has only made it grow out of all proportion in my mind; I imagine it as more glorious than any possible reality, his exploits there more dashing than any folklore hero's, and his reticence has only fueled my fantasies.

It isn't possible to explain why the single fact of his membership in an archers' guild should affect me so strongly without explaining the commanding position St. Sebastian's holds not just in Louvain, but in the collective imagination of the whole of Ardennes. If archers are our stars, then St. Sebastian's is the galaxy in which they shine and where they are on most brilliant display. I'm not very good at history, but everyone knows the basics about the guild, particularly about the competitions.

It's common knowledge that St. Sebastian's started back in the 12th century as a strange combination of social club for aristocratic archers, military training camp, and commercial venture, but it quickly grew into a training ground for the country's most elite forces. Not only does it produce the mercenaries for which our country is rightly famous, it's also the origin of our Black Guard, the crack troop of archers who serve in times of peace as the prince's bodyguard and in times of war as an elite tactical fighting unit. With these skilled bowmen defending the towering fortifications which rise on a sheer rock island at the confluence of the Meuse and Sambre rivers, our capital L'île de Meuse isn't just uniquely situated to control the river trade throughout the region. It's virtually impregnable.

It's not surprising, then, that the rare appearance of one of these romantic figures in town wearing the distinctive garb of a Guardsman is often enough to cause a small riot in the marketplace. In fact, the first time I saw one of them myself I was almost trampled by a fishmonger's wife, but I'll admit that I was jostling for a better view just as hard as everyone else. It was also the day that I began to piece together how St. Sebastian's really works, and when I first learned that my own father had a past there.

It was on a trip to town about six years ago, when I was about eight or nine. Back in those days we used to go to town more often, and on the day in question we'd all gone along, making a family outing of it.

As soon as we entered town, even I could tell something out of the ordinary was happening. Louvain was packed with visitors. The inns and streets were overflowing, and there was a carnival atmosphere in the air.

"What's going on?" I asked nobody in particular. Nobody answered, so I turned to Jules. "What's all the excitement about?"

"It's almost time for the trials."

As he answered, I noticed Jules darting a glance at our father.

"Trials? Trials for what? Theft? *Murder?*" I asked hopefully. Everyone loves a good capital punishment case. I'd just seen my first man hanging in the gibbet in an advanced state of decay on our way past the town gate, and I was still feeling excitedly queasy.

"Not that kind of trials, idiot."

"What kind, then?"

"I'll tell you later," he hissed back, and I knew enough to stop asking questions. My father was looking grim.

As always, our first stop was to the blacksmith's. I was surprised, though, when instead of leaving his order with the smith as usual, my father decided to wait there, and send us on ahead.

"Aren't you coming to the square with us, Father?" I remember complaining. "Who will buy me cakes at Miraud's?"

"Run along and enjoy yourself, now, and don't whine, Marieke," he said, dropping a few coins in Berthal's hand. "Berthal will see to it that you get your cake."

So the three of us made our way through town alone, and as we got closer to the square, I could see that it was packed with tents and booths, many more than on a usual market day. In addition to the cries of merchants hawking their wares in our native French and Flemish, one often hears German on market days, since Louvain is something of a mixing pot. But that day the square was full of exotic languages I didn't recognize.

"Look, Jules!" I cried out excitedly, "There are more booths along the commons, too, and over there — more booths! I can't believe Papa would want to miss this. Should we go back and get him?"

Jules and Berthal exchanged a look over my head. "Oh, I imagine he *does* want to miss it, all right!"

"*Berthal* ..." said Jules warningly.

"What, Jules?" Berthal sniffed. "It's true. Might as well tell her. Look, Marieke, Jan doesn't want to see any of this. He doesn't want to see the trials. Most of all, he doesn't want to be seen, not today."

"Why ever not?" I demanded.

"To put it bluntly, he's hiding!"

"Hiding? Hiding from what?" I asked, upset. I couldn't imagine my father hiding from anything.

"From *everyone*! He's embarrassed. It always rakes the whole thing up again, around this time, doesn't it? People will talk. It's inevitable."

"He's *not* embarrassed," Jules interrupted, giving Berthal a nasty look, "and he's definitely not hiding. He just doesn't want to be reminded of the trials, that's all."

"Why not? What trials? What *are* you both talking about?" I shouted. "Will someone tell me what's going on!?"

By this time we'd made our way into the crowds in the market square, and before either of them could answer me someone near us exclaimed,

"There, at the cheese seller's, it's one of the Guards!"

"I see him! Now he's by the salted fish!" called out another, and suddenly everyone was pushing forward. At first I couldn't see a thing, but after a well-timed elbow in Berthal's side I caught a glimpse of a tall, handsome man surrounded by an impressively outfitted retinue. The man himself was dressed in light silver mail, a black silk hood and cloak emblazoned with silver *fleur de lis* encircling the silhouette of a castle, black hose, black boots and black gauntlets. He struck a magnificent figure. Beside him was a youth in equally fine garb, who held in his hand what was clearly the older man's huge black bow. Flung over his shoulder was a black quiver studded with silver nails.

"Oof, watch out, Marieke! Oh, it *is* a Guardsman!" squealed Berthal.

"Not just any Guardsman — that's Brian de Gilford," Jules said with interest. "He must be one of the judges this year. He doesn't usually come to Louvain for trials."

"Who is he?" I asked.

"He's one of the senior Guards. Part of the inner circle."

"Not *the* de Gilford? *Brian* de Gilford, Count Montevillier?" Berthal put in, practically foaming at the mouth, and now giving me a sharp shove out of her way. She'd never been so close to a noble before.

"What do you mean, *inner circle*?" I asked, grabbing her sleeve for support.

"Would you two stop pestering me with questions?" Jules protested, bobbing up and down and trying to keep de Gilford in view.

"I wouldn't have to ask so many questions, if once in a while you'd give me an answer!" I mumbled as the crowd swarmed past us, sweeping forward in pursuit of de Gilford and his men as they made their way on through the market. When they were out of sight, Jules turned back to me.

"Ok, Marieke. Let's get out of this crowd, and find a place to sit down. Then I'll explain anything you want," he promised.

Jules proved as good as his word. We found a shady place at the corner of the square next to the cathedral of St. Margaret to sit. When we'd settled ourselves comfortably, he sent Berthal to get the promised cakes (it was a good way to get her out of the way. Between gossiping, window-shopping, and stalking de Gilford, the smallest errand would take her forever), then he turned to me.

"All right, Marieke. Now, what do you want to know?"

Now that I had my chance, I wasn't sure what to ask first. What I really wanted to know was what Berthal had meant when she said my father was hiding, but I couldn't bring myself to start with that.

"What did you mean by *inner circle*?" I asked, picking up where I'd left off and starting with something safe. "And what are the trials you keep talking about?"

"Have you ever wondered where the Guardsmen come from, Marieke?" Jules answered.

Of course, I hadn't. For all I knew, they dropped from the moon.

"Well, they're the prince's guard, aren't they? I suppose the prince chooses them, doesn't he, from his court?"

"No — that's just it. It's the one position in this country that money and birth alone can't buy, and that's the glamour of it," he replied warmly. Jules always loved the Guards. "You have to get in on sheer skill, and the perks are enormous: fame, glory, and popularity with the ladies," he nodded toward the crowd still pressing after de Gilford, "not to mention the lands and titles granted to some of the prince's favorites. That means real power. De Gilford's not the only senior Guardsman who has used his position on the inner circle to bend the prince's ear. But you have to be the very best. And you have to prove it, through competition. That's why de Gilford is here. All the trials are held in here Louvain, since 'Guardsman' is technically the highest rank in the order of St. Sebastian."

I nodded, though I'm not sure I understood what Jules meant, then. I was still trying to figure out why anyone would want to bend someone else's ear.

"It's not just a trade guild, like the others," Jules continued. "Sure, it has a business side to it, but full membership is only for the most elite archers, and it's competitive. Every two years, only twelve of the best young archers are chosen for temporary service as Journeymen at St. Sebastian's. Even that initial contest is a huge event, since it's an open trial for boys from all across Ardennes. But there's a catch: you have to be sponsored by a full guild member. Needless to say, since most of the members are aristocrats, most of the boys they sponsor are, too." After a short pause, he added softly, "although there have been some notable exceptions." Of course, now I know he was thinking about our father. "The lucky winners live at the guild, training intensively and facing elimination in more public trials, each in a different style of archery. You've heard of the Journeymen at least, haven't you? You must have seen them around town."

I nodded again, and this time, I was sincere. Even at nine, I knew something about the Journeymen archers of St. Sebastian's, or the Journeys, as they're called around here. Since then, I've made it my business to know all about them. Young, handsome, skilled — they're our local celebrities, and for the two years they're here, they rule the town. To us in Louvain, they *are* the guild.

"That's why *everybody's* here, Marieke. The final Journeyman competition of the year is happening this afternoon, and nobody wants to miss it. Only the six best will pass, to win veteran status. That means permanent guild membership and a cut in the guild profits, so it's a big deal. And it's only the beginning. The victors advance to a second year of trials, for a shot at the ultimate victory."

"A place on Guards," I said, finally beginning to understand.

"That's right, and only one can win. It's two years of constant training and public humiliation. I can't imagine going through it, but spectators can't get enough of it, and the prize is enormous."

Jules's voice was starting to sound quite bitter, and I noticed he was looking down, drawing in the dust with the end of a stick.

"Jules," I asked quietly, "why doesn't Papa want to see the trials? What did Berthal mean?

For a moment I thought he wasn't going to answer. Then he sighed and looked up at me.

"You know the medal that Papa always wears around his neck, don't you?" he asked.

"It's a religious medal. St. Sebastian. Lots of people in town wear them."

"Yes, but Papa's isn't like all the others. It isn't just any medal. You can't buy it in a shop. It's an official medal from the guild, a member's medal."

"I know," I said. "It's his proof of certification, as a fletcher."

"No, Marieke. Papa was never certified by the guild. You can't get a medal like that by paying a fee or undergoing certification. You can only get a medal like that by winning it. Papa earned that medal, when he was a journeyman archer at the guild."

At the time, I was stunned. The Journeys! I couldn't imagine why Jules was sounding so glum about something so thrilling. Our father, a celebrity! Why hadn't anyone told me before? But it didn't make any sense.

"But — Papa, he doesn't even shoot," I said. "He's got a bad shoulder."

"He does *now*. You don't think he was born that way, do you? Didn't you ever wonder what happened to him?"

The thing was, I hadn't ever thought about it. I suppose I'd known in some vague way that he must have had an accident in the past, but it was just so much a part of him that I'd never questioned it.

"It happened right here, in Louvain, during the trials at the end of his first year, just like the ones taking place now. He fell from his horse during a mounted exercise. Right in the middle of the competition."

Unfortunately, it was just at this moment that Berthal returned, carrying the cakes.

"Accident!" she snorted, lowering herself down beside me with some difficulty. "Not just any accident. *Trampled* by his own horse, of all things! Lucky he wasn't killed. Here, Marieke — take your cake, before the honey runs all over my hand."

I took the cake dumbly, picturing the awful scene she was describing.

"Of all the stupid, arrogant stunts," she continued, licking her fingers clean, "and when he was ahead! Last competition before veterans', too. He could have made it! All he had to do was stay on his horse. Aren't you going to eat that?"

I took a bite, just to get Berthal to continue. "Everyone thought so. Why, we all thought he had a shot at making Guards! We'd have been set *then,* I can tell you. And he just threw it away! Cocky, that's what he was. There's no other word for it. Why ..."

At this, Jules stood up abruptly and cast such an angry look at Berthal that she stopped in mid-sentence, her mouth still open.

"Whatever happened, he's paid the price," he cut in icily. "He was eliminated, Marieke," he said more gently, looking down at me. "Just before winning veteran status. His shoulder on his drawing arm was virtually destroyed. You know how it is. He never bent another bow."

Jules stalked off, leaving Berthal and me nothing to do but scramble to get up and follow him. It was clear that he was done talking about the Journeys, the trials, and Father.

As it happened, I never did learn much more about it than that. Later that night, though, when we were back home, I snuck into Jules's room after he was already in bed.

"Jules?"

"What is it, Marieke? It's been a long day. You should be asleep."

"It's just that I want to understand. Why should Papa be embarrassed about having an accident? It was something great, wasn't it, to win a spot as a Journeyman in the first place, to make it that far?"

"Look, Marieke. Don't listen to Berthal," he said, propping himself up sleepily on one elbow. "It *was* something great. Remember that. It's just not often that a fletcher's son makes it into the Journeys. It's even rarer for a local commoner to be chosen. Papa was something of a hero to a lot of people from around here back then. They were all rooting for him; betting on him, too. Some of them lost money. He let a lot of people down, including himself. That's all. Now go to bed."

I did as Jules told me, but I was far from satisfied. Even then, I knew there was more to it than that. I also knew that if Jules knew more, he wasn't going to tell me. I was going to have to find out for myself.

It's true that my father's shoulder still bothers him, but as I've gotten older I've realized that since he can string a heavy bow, he could still shoot one if he tried. Something must have happened that was bad enough to make my father turn his back on St. Sebastian's entirely, something that made him want to live out here away from the talk that I know still circulates. I know Jules used to hear some of that talk from time to time when he was in town, but I never could get anything out of him, and Berthal never would talk to me about it again, either. Jules must have given her quite a scolding. Now that they're both dead, I doubt I'll ever find out exactly what happened. But whatever it was, my father's archery days were over. More than his shoulder was shattered in the fall Jules described to me that day.

CHAPTER TWO

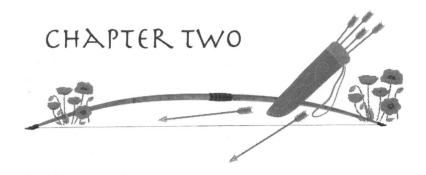

A commotion out in the yard brings me back to the present; my father's head comes up, too, and for a moment we meet each other's gaze as an unmistakable voice fills the air like a crack of thunder.

"Verbeke! Jan Verbeke! Where in the devil are you? Verbeke!"

A faint smile appears on my father's lips, and he nods slightly toward the half-open door, so we cross conspiratorially to where we can stand concealed behind it but have a clear view into the courtyard beyond. Out in the yard, a little donkey is trotting around frantically in a circle, while cabbages and other winter vegetables bounce out of the enormous sacks strapped precariously to its tiny frame. In the midst of the sacks sits an equally enormous rider, not only plump but so large of frame it would look more natural to see the little donkey riding *him*. The poor creature seems to have sensed that they've reached their destination and that his master's dismount may be imminent, and so he's begun prancing around agitatedly and giving spasmodic jerks in an attempt to hasten along his deliverance. The voice booms out again:

"Verbeke, for the love of God, come out and help me get off this confounded donkey!"

I'm ashamed to say, neither of us moves. It's much too fun to watch. It's Bellows, our nearest neighbor, a notorious gossip and freeloader. Bellows isn't his real name, of course, though I've never heard him called anything else. He's got a small truck farm just down the road, and whenever he passes by with his vegetables on market days, he always stops in — coming *and* going. It's deadly dull, and he's only got three volumes: unbelievably loud, louder, and earsplitting — hence the nickname, although I've also heard other explanations for it that I don't care to repeat.

Another problem with Bellows is that he doesn't miss a chance to hint to my father that he might be willing to take me off his hands one day — for a price. He then proceeds to spend his visit looking me up and down like a landlord waiting to take possession of a piece of property, checking to see if I've incurred any further damage that might up his price. I don't think I can face him today, now that I've been reminded that I really could end up married to someone like him.

"Well, Marieke, what do you say? Should I take pity on him?"

I pretend to consider this for a minute. "Yes ... but only for the donkey's sake."

"Why, that's who I meant, of course!" he says with a laugh, dodging a flying turnip that sails in through the door while ringing curses continue to fill the air.

I start to step forward toward the door, expecting that I'll be the one who has to pick everything up and repack it, but my father puts out his arm to stop me, and he says softly,

"It's still early, Marieke. Why don't you find something to do out back for a while? We won't be going anywhere for a while, now."

I look up, gratitude beaming on my face. I'm to be spared Bellows today! I don't wait to see if my father will change his mind. I turn and dash out of the small door leading out to the storage sheds behind the workshop and to the woods beyond. I can hear my father's voice as he makes his way out to the yard, and there's an admirable lack of irony in his tone when he says,

"Why, dear fellow, I didn't hear you. You know how I get when I'm working. You really should learn to speak up."

Smiling to myself, I reckon I've got at least a solid hour to kill, so I consider my options. I'm right next to the woodshed, so it would be the easiest thing in the world to grab Jules's bow and quiver and duck into the woods unseen. I'm always looking for opportunities to practice with it, but it seems a poor way to repay my father's kindness. It isn't that I'm not allowed to hunt. But the idea of a girl out hunting alone would no doubt seem scandalous to our neighbors, if they had any idea of it.

The thing is, my father doesn't know that I'm using Jules's bow. Not long after my run-in with the mule, I started in on one of my periodic nagging sessions, begging my father to make me a bow. He'd taught Jules to shoot, and I used to love watching him practice. It seemed only natural to me to want to try, but Jules's bows were too big for me. I'd asked before with no luck, so I didn't really expect anything, but this time my father surprised me by agreeing to make a bow to my measure. He must have been feeling sorry for me, with my freshly battered face, and after all, what did it matter, really? Even Berthal made no objection, and that's when I think I first realized just how finished she thought I was as a girl.

Jules taught me the basics of shooting out in the woods, and although I couldn't get much range with my little bow, I developed into a decent shot. I was always more careful with it than I had ever been with any other possession, but one day not long before Jules died, it cracked. Stringing a bow isn't easy. You have to apply just the right amount of pressure, and since I'm not very strong, I have to lean into the task. As soon as I heard the faint splintering crack as the wood of the arm gave way, I knew I'd done irreparable harm.

I was still trying to figure out how to tell my father I'd broken the bow when Jules died, and after that, I just couldn't find a way to tell him. Instead, one day I took down Jules's smallest, lightest bow, and stashed it out here. It's hardly ideal; it's much too long for me, and too heavy. It's ridiculous, even, but for now it gets the job done.

Out in the courtyard, I can hear Bellows warming to one of his favorite subjects, the imminent end of the world.

"Mark my words, God is already sweeping the east with terrible plagues, and we'll be next. How much more famine can we take? We'll be reduced to eating one another!"

I can't hear my father's reply, but I hope he's telling Bellows that he doesn't look like he's missed any meals.

I don't wait to hear any more, and instead I make my escape from Bellows' doomsday predictions by heading down the path that leads into the woods behind our property. It follows alongside a little stream, which soon emerges from the trees to water a meadow where I often pasture our small flock. On the other side of the meadow lies the Vendon Abbey, one of my favorite places to spend what little spare time comes my way. Jules and I used to be sent by my father to trade with the monks for beer or beeswax, but since the Cistercian order believes spirituality is best attained through manual labor, we soon found that there was always something interesting going on. I've kept on coming here even after Jules died, and the monks have never said anything to discourage me from coming alone — although admittedly, most of them don't say much about anything, period.

As I approach, I circle around to the brewery first, to visit Brother Benedict. The abbey is only of modest size, but the Cistercians are fanatic stonemasons, so the church is a spectacular gothic structure and even the humblest of its support buildings are constructed almost entirely of stone. The door is standing slightly ajar, so I let myself in. At first glance the room appears empty, but the place is warm and I can smell a mixture of smoke and hops that suggests Benedict's in the process of brewing.

Sure enough, an open fire's been kindled under the big brick cooker at the far end of the room, and the aromatic contents of a big metal pot suspended over it are boiling away merrily. The handle of a large wooden stirring paddle is sticking up out of the pot and bobbing in a lazy circle, but Benedict is nowhere to be seen.

At first the only sounds I can hear are the crackling of the fire and the bubbling of the liquid in the pot. Then I catch the sound of faint rumbling coming from somewhere among the rows of giant barrels that line the room's central aisle, and I follow the sound until I come to a stop in front of one of the larger oak casks set up about a foot or two off the ground on a low wooden platform, where two large, familiar feet clad only in stockings are sticking out from under it. It's Brother Benedict, fast asleep under the platform, snoring like an ox. *So much for the work ethic*, I think fondly.

I contemplate the monk's feet in silence for a moment. Flies are buzzing around them, and one big toe keeps twitching — he must be having a very good dream.

I look around until I find Benedict's little slippers where he's left them discarded by the door. It's a game I play with the old scoundrel sometimes. He's crazy about signs — eggs with two yolks, that sort of thing — so now and then I leave him one, and he pretends he doesn't know it's from me. At least, I think he pretends.

I cast around for a place to put the shoes, only the monks aren't big on decoration. There aren't many options, but Benedict has set up a little crucifix in an alcove near the door, so I place the shoes carefully side by side below it, toes pointing toward it, as though in an attitude of adoration. Let him figure out what *that* means!

I don't want to wake Benedict, so I go out and circle around further, past the refectory and infirmary, to the one side of the cloisters with an exterior wall. Up on the second floor is the small cubicle of Father Abelard, where he's usually occupied copying manuscripts at this time of day. There's an old chestnut tree growing right outside his window, and on warm days, I can sit on a limb by the open shutters and watch him at work through the window. He has to keep the shutters open anyway, since he's not allowed to use a candle around the delicate parchment, and he doesn't mind if I watch as long as I don't ask any questions. Unlike Benedict, Abelard usually doesn't condone idle talk, and when's he's working, he's completely absorbed.

He doesn't look up when I settle myself in my accustomed spot, but I've made something of a racket scrambling up, so I know he's aware I'm here. He's got his equipment arrayed in front of him on his desk, and I see with some excitement that along with his usual inkwell, quill, and knife, he's also got an assortment of pigment pots and brushes out as well. He must be going to work on a small square of illumination.

Usually Abelard is simply copying out lines of text from a familiar manuscript, and on such days I'm content to lie outside on my perch and watch his long, thin hands move over the paper. I can't read anyway, and he has to concentrate hard to keep from losing his place. But sometimes, if he's doing something more interesting, he'll beckon me in with a slight nod of his head. I'll slide through the window and stand beside him, watching him elaborate the first letter of a new passage or burnish gold leaf into the page. The materials are expensive, though, so they're used sparingly, and I've only rarely come across Abelard when he was actually in the process of applying one.

"You're in for a treat today, Marieke, or are you going to stay in that tree all morning?" Abelard hasn't lifted his head, but I know an invitation when I hear one, so I go in and take a place where I can see over his shoulder.

"Not in my light, Marieke, please." I move a little further away, and lean in as far as I dare.

"Malachite green, cobalt blue, saffron yellow, dragonsblood red," he says, gesturing to the contents of the row of pots lined up on his desk, "exotic names for exotic colors. They almost sound like poetry, don't they?"

"Dragonsblood?" I ask, straining to see into the pot. "Does it really have blood in it?"

"Not just any blood, but the blood of an elephant and a dragon that have killed each other in mortal combat!"

At that, I lean even closer, jostling the table.

"It's naturally very hard to come by," he says sternly, gently grabbing the pot to steady it, "so we'd best not spill any."

I jump back, but he waves me forward again.

"What do you make of her, Marieke?" He points down at his picture, and now I take a good look at it. Most often these little scenes are copied faithfully from an exemplar, but I don't see the original text anywhere. What I see is so unexpected that I wonder if it's entirely his own composition.

Usually, the scenes depict saints or illustrate prayers, but I can't see anything to suggest a religious context in this scene. Instead, in the foreground a woman dressed in elegant robes is seated sideways on a bench, so that she's looking back over her shoulder directly at the viewer with an almost coquettish expression on her face. Long golden hair streams down her back and pools at her feet. In the background rise the battlements of a grand castle.

The scene is almost finished; the only thing left to be painted is the woman's robe.

"She's breathtaking!" I say, with feeling.

"What color for her robe, do you think? Purple, for royalty, or green, for envy?" he muses.

"Blue," I blurt out, without thinking, then add, "because it will look so well with her beautiful hair," since something more seems expected. It sounds rather weak, but I don't know what blue 'means,' if anything.

Abelard dips his brush in the blue pigment and begins to fill in the woman's dress, tracing the sweep of the garment from her shoulder to the end of her trailing sleeve in one smooth motion.

He seems engrossed in his work, so his next comment takes me by surprise.

"Marieke, isn't it rather unusual for a fifteen-year-old girl to have a group of monks as her only friends?"

I'm so startled by this that I don't know what to say. Abelard has never made a personal observation like this before. I glance at him to try to read his expression, but he hasn't taken his eyes off the page.

"Well, I guess I'm not a very usual fifteen-year-old girl," I reply lightly, taking it as a joke. But Abelard's face is serious when he looks up into my face for what feels like an uncomfortably long time. Involuntarily my hand goes up to my face as though to cover my nose, as it often does when I'm self-conscious. Finally, he says:

"No. I don't suppose you are."

I'm feeling rather confused as he turns back to his illumination, so I watch him finish it in silence. It's not until he puts down his brush and puts the stoppers back on his pigments that he speaks again. I've been staring at the lovely image of the woman, when he looks up and catches me with a look of sheer longing on my face.

"Do you want to know what the text is about?" he asks after a moment, dropping his gaze and looking intently at the woman he's created. Before I can answer, he continues:

"Tell me, what do you see when you look at this picture?"

"I see a beautiful woman," I say. My voice catches a bit on *beautiful*. "I think, she must be the most beautiful woman in the world."

"Yes, she's beautiful. But beauty is a double-edged sword, Marieke." He looks up at me, and I can feel my face start burning, where the scars across the bridge of my nose still stand out like ugly welts. But he doesn't drop his gaze.

"This text is about how a woman's beauty can destroy a man. It's about a woman whose beauty is Satan's tool, an instrument of evil," he continues.

"I don't believe it!" I cry in protest, unsure why the idea upsets me so much, or why I can't bear to think ill of the woman in the picture. I suspect Abelard is just trying to be kind, that he's saying all of this to make me feel better about my shattered face, but I can't let it go.

"I don't think you believe it either! I won't believe anything so perfect is evil." I want to believe that a perfect blend of beauty, nobility, and goodness can exist. I can admit it: I want it for myself.

"Beauty is seductive, child. That's what makes it dangerous," Abelard says, but he doesn't seem to be talking to me anymore. From the way he's looking at the picture, I almost get the impression that he recognizes the lady, and it occurs to me to wonder who he used as a model for her image. I'm still wondering who he was thinking of when he was painting the woman when disaster strikes. I don't see exactly what happens, but Abelard is reaching up to put away his pen when his hand bumps the inkwell, and a stream of black ink pours out down the page.

"Oh, no!" I shout, as we both try to snatch the page out of the way of the flow of ink, but we're too late. Most of the text is either badly smeared or obliterated entirely, though the little square of illumination is relatively unscathed, with only a few scattered drops marring its perfection.

"Titivillus must have it out for me today," says Abelard, surveying the damage. "His sack should be full now."

"Titiv-*who*?" I ask stupidly, looking around, expecting to see some nemesis of Abelard's lurking in the corner.

"You can't see it, child," he says, chuckling. Curiously, he doesn't seem that upset. "Titi*villus* is the demon of the scriptorium. He gathers up all the errors we monks make, and when his sack is full, he takes them down to the Devil," he explains. "All our errors are recorded in a big book against us, for judgment day."

"Oh, Abelard!"

"You see, Marieke? What did I tell you? This lady is nothing but trouble." He laughs again. "But you see how she manages to avoid paying for her sins? There's hardly a mark on her."

"Please, Abelard," I say, "You can't let Titivillus have her!"

Abelard lifts the page and holds it up so that the excess ink drains back into the inkwell, then he hands it to me.

"Keep her, then, Marieke. As a reminder ... of a narrow escape!"

I take the page, holding it gingerly between my fingers since it's still wet. I've never been given such a lovely thing before, and I can feel tears starting to form in my eyes.

"You know, I'll miss you, when you stop visiting me." His voice is so quiet, it takes me a moment to realize he's talking to me, not his demon.

"What do you mean?" I say, confused. "Are you telling me not to come here anymore?"

"No, Marieke. But one day soon, I think, you'll find that it's time for these visits to come to an end."

When I start to protest, he waves his hand dismissively and interrupts,

"Don't fret, now. But I want you to remember this, child. You'll always have friends here, if you need them."

At the kindness of his tone and the note of finality in his voice, I feel the tears starting to run down my cheeks, and I don't brush them away. I have the unreasonable thought that maybe even Abelard knows something about a marriage being arranged for me today, but how would that be possible? He doesn't even know I'm going to town. The idea is ludicrous, but it's clear enough that I'm the only one who has been late to realize that I can't go on as I have been forever.

It's only much later, as I'm making my way home through the woods, still holding my new treasure carefully, that it occurs to me to wonder just what Abelard meant by 'a narrow escape.' At the time, I assumed he meant the narrow escape of the lady from the ink, but now I wonder if he didn't mean my own narrow escape — from the dangers of beauty.

Suddenly I realize something else. I've never seen Abelard make such a serious mistake. Usually he only makes minor errors that can be scratched out or scraped off, and the vellum is too expensive to waste. Even pages damaged by more serious errors are carefully saved, scrubbed, and used again. He must have spilled the ink on purpose to have an excuse for giving me the picture. The manuscript page is his parting gift to me. Whatever he meant by it, he must have thought the message was important.

CHAPTER THREE

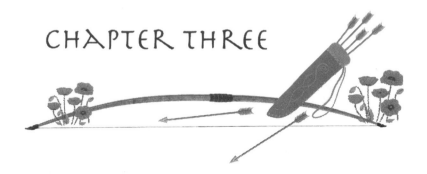

As I fall into step beside my father later that afternoon, my usual excitement at such an outing returns. I'm wearing the outfit my father laid out for me (of course), and he's changed, too. He's looking very smart, and it's easy to picture just how handsome he must have been when he was younger. My spirits are high as we ease the wagon out of the yard and onto the track that leads out to the main road. I could ride, but I decide to walk, in part to keep my father company, and also to give the mule a break (I'm not sure why I should, since it's the same one that kicked me in the face, so I don't owe it any favors). But I'll just fidget the whole way if I don't work off some of my nervous energy, and it's only about a two-hour walk to Louvain.

Our route takes us through sparse woods which gradually give way to a patchwork of open fields. At the bottom of the lane the narrow track widens out to merge into the L'île-Charleroi road, one of the main roads through Ardennes, and once we join the big road, we begin to pass an occasional fellow traveler. Since we're following the course of the Sambre, sometimes we even spot a shallow boat out on the river, so the time passes pleasantly even though we don't say much. But when we pass the ruins of the Roman tower that mark the half-way point, I start to feel anxious. My father has been so secretive about the trip that I can't help worrying why — or rather, *who*. I can't shake the feeling that I'm along simply to be introduced to a potential husband.

By the time the spires and rooftops of Louvain begin to loom on the horizon, my imagination has gotten the better of me and I'm a nervous wreck. I have a bad habit of picking at the skin around my fingernails when I'm nervous. Berthal used to get after me about it, but my father just pretends not to notice, or maybe he really doesn't. Now I've been tearing at my cuticles so furiously for the past half hour that some of my fingers have started to bleed. There are even a few stains on the sleeves of my tunic. How can I hide that?

"You're awfully quiet today, Marieke."

At the sound of my father's voice, I jump guiltily.

"*Mmm*," I say, sucking off the blood from a finger.

"Usually you're so full of questions, I can't answer one before you're coming out with the next."

He seems disappointed that I haven't been pestering him with questions (that he wouldn't answer anyway), but I can't tell him the truth: the questions are sticking in my throat, because I'm afraid of the answers. I'm trying to think of something safe to ask, when I'm saved the effort by the clatter of horses on the road behind us.

"Clear the way!" a loud voice calls out, and soon huge black horses are bearing down on us, drawing behind them a fine carriage with red trim. On either side of the carriage are more riders in fine livery. I notice they're also unusually well-armed.

"Quick, help me pull the wagon over!" my father calls. "Hurry, or you'll be trampled."

I push the old mule from one side while my father pulls it from the other, and together we just manage to get it and the cart off the road as the massive horses thunder past. As the carriage rumbles by, I look back over my shoulder to get a glimpse of its occupants. The riders on my side of the carriage partially block my view, but what I see stops me in my tracks: the flash of a bright blue sleeve, and spread over it, a flow of golden hair.

The image is fleeting; the carriage and riders are gone in an instant. Yet the impression of having just seen the woman from Abelard's picture is overwhelming. I know I'm being fanciful. It's just my overactive imagination getting the better of me, but I feel shaken.

Odd grunting noises start coming from the far side of the wagon, which strangely enough *are* real. It's my father, trying to drag the mule back onto the path.

"Damned wheel's stuck in a rut. Don't just stand there gaping. Come around this side, will you, and help me push."

"Who do you think that was, in the carriage?" I ask, not moving.

"Dunno," he grunts, pushing hard on the wagon. "Could have been anyone."

"Yes, but, who do you *think* it might have been? Just take a guess."

He straightens up and gives me an exasperated look, so I try another tactic.

"You know, like the game we used to play to pass the time," I say, coming around and rocking the wagon back and forth to help him ease it out of the mud. "Making up funny names and stories about people we met on the road."

"Well, I don't know about inside the carriage," he pants, giving a well-timed push and finally guiding the wagon free. "But the men — they looked like they might be some of Brecelyn's."

Sir Brecelyn is the local big shot around here. He's not hereditary aristocracy, but his estate lies only a few miles from Louvain. His father was knighted for service during the so-called war of the tariffs by prince Philip the XII, the current prince's father. Along with the knighthood, Brecelyn was given a large grant of land around Louvain and he even held the rights to the town itself, before it obtained a charter as a free town. I know something about him because it's always struck me as odd that my father never supplies him, though he's worked for some of his men.

"So ... if they were sir Brecelyn's men, then who might have been in the carriage?" I persist.

"Sir Brecelyn?" my father offers, with a hint of sarcasm.

"Very funny. It was a *woman*. A beautiful woman, with long blonde hair."

Suddenly my father flinches. The indulgent, slightly amused look on his face vanishes, and for a moment he looks quite sick. Instinctively, I reach out to support him on his injured side.

"Are you feeling all right? Is it your shoulder?" I ask, worried. I should have helped him more with the wagon, instead of daydreaming.

"A touch of dizziness, that's all — getting the wagon unstuck's winded me. It's nothing." He shrugs off my hand; he hates it when he needs help. "A woman with blonde hair, you say? Did you get a good look?"

"No, but she seemed quite young. A girl, really."

At this, he seems to relax. Whatever came over him has passed.

"So ... Brecelyn's daughter, maybe?" I continue.

A strange look passes over his face. "No. Sir Brecelyn has no children," he says in a tight voice. His shoulder must be hurting him more than he's admitting.

"We're past the turn-off for Brecelyn's manor here, aren't we? So whoever she is, she must be going to Louvain, too."

"Maybe, Marieke. But it probably wasn't one of Brecelyn's carriages at all. And it could be headed anywhere — the Abbey of St. Genevieve, St. Croix, or all the way to L'île."

I know he's right, still I can't help hoping that I'll see the carriage again, and that I'll get a better look at the girl, to see if she really did step to life out of Abelard's picture.

Before long the towers of Porte Charleroi come into view, temporarily pushing the girl in the carriage to the back of my mind. This massive fortified gatehouse marks the western entrance to Louvain, where its round brick towers straddle the road and support turreted battlements three stories high between them; below, they enclose portcullises at either end that can be lowered to seal off the town. The whole structure is imposing, but although the circuit wall extends forbiddingly away from the gate in either direction, it isn't complete, so the invulnerability of the town is an illusion (or a work in progress, depending on how you look at it). Still, it's more than sufficient to serve its main purpose: to make it impossible for outside merchants to come into town without paying a heavy toll. This includes us, since as I've said, my father has refused to join the association of fletchers affiliated with St. Sebastian's.

As soon as we pass through the gate, I'm so busy taking everything in that I don't think about anything else, even though the area of town right inside the gate isn't particularly remarkable.

Here humble houses with yards are widely spaced and intermixed with communal ovens and workshops. But up ahead the houses and shops are more impressive and closer together, so that they seem to grow toward each other over the streets. Some of the great buildings that mark the center of town are just visible in the distance, so I can see a maze of brick buildings of every size and shape rising up before me, all in rich hues of pink and red. Now that we're in town, I find myself on the lookout for something much less pleasant than the carriage with red trim, too. I keep starting every time I see a boy of the 'right' age — a boy who might be the right age to be my father's apprentice, and all that now seems to mean.

I'm particularly wary as we start my father's rounds, but after we make the first few stops and all the clients seem to be too old or already married, I relax. The idea that I'm along to be my father's assistant, though, now seems laughable, even to me. Everyone treats me like a useless girl, asking me patronizing questions if they talk to me at all. Even worse, if I try to help, I get pushed aside by well-meaning men who step in to take things out of my hands. By the fourth stop, I decide just to stay outside with the wagon, like the mule. It's easier that way.

On the fifth stop, I spot him.

We're still a ways from the center of town, but by this time we've reached the point where the hard-packed dirt roads give way to cobbled streets. The houses are finer here, too, rising one next to another in an unbroken line.

"Coming in this time, Marieke?" my father asks as he pulls the wagon over, signaling another stop.

I shake my head. What's the point?

"Come in with me, just one last time. You'll be glad you did." A pause. "Suit yourself, Marieke. I won't force you to come in; not today. I've got a father and son to fit here, then we can go to the square."

"All right. Good." I give a weak smile and try to summon a little enthusiasm. Visiting the square is usually my favorite part of the trip, and who knows when I'll be back to Louvain? I should have known that nobody was going to accept a girl as a fletcher. Besides, if I'm going to spot that carriage again, the square is the most likely place.

"Wait! I'm coming in, after all," I decide.

My father's already gone around back to start unloading the wagon and I'm climbing down from my perch on the wagon seat, when a youth of about eighteen comes out of one of the houses just ahead of us. He stands poised on the doorstep for a moment, looking down the street. Then he raises his hand in greeting as he catches sight of my father. A brilliant smile lights up his face, and my heart literally skips a beat and jumps up into my throat. I've heard these clichés dozens of times, but now I know what they feel like. I don't know what I expected, but it certainly wasn't anything like this! He's tall and trim, with a profile right off of an old Roman coin. He's simply dressed, but he holds himself with grace and confidence. I don't know why, but I'm particularly fascinated by the way one lock of his soft brown hair curls over his collar against the back of his neck. It isn't that he's so handsome, exactly, but there's something about him that's vibrant, radiant even. He's just so *clean*. I bet he even smells good.

At the thought that I'm about to be introduced to this incredible boy, my hands begin to sweat. I remember my bleeding fingers, and involuntarily shove my hands behind my back. I don't know whether I'm excited or petrified.

The sensation only lasts a few seconds. In a flash, the boy runs lightly down the steps to the street, and I realize with a feeling like I've just been punched in the stomach that the idea he was greeting my father was just an illusion. He passes right by our wagon without even a glance my way, to catch up with the friend he was really greeting further down the street. I'm left there wringing my hands, which I've begun picking at furiously again. Who cares if they're bleeding now? My heart drops back into place with a hollow thud.

"That must be one of the new Journeymen," my father says, straightening up and following my gaze. I'm so disappointed, I can't say anything.

"You can always tell," he continues. "There's something about them. A certain air."

This is so vague it's ludicrous, but I know what he means.

"Whatever it is, that boy certainly has it!" I blurt out before I can stop myself, but my father just laughs.

I try to imagine my father radiating that same air of confident youth, but I can't. Even today, when he's looking his best and seems happier than I've seen him in a long time, the impression that life has passed him by still clings to him.

"Monsieur Verbeke?" A deep but hesitant voice behind me interrupts my thoughts.

"Ah, Luc, isn't it? How are you? How is your father?"

"Very well, sir, and very much looking forward to seeing you again."

I don't need to turn around to see the owner of the voice to know that this, and not that glorious boy of a moment ago, is my future husband.

"Excellent, excellent," my father is saying. "This is my daughter, Marieke. Marieke, this is Luc Fournier."

I don't want to turn around. I wish I could freeze this moment and stay standing on the street forever, watching the beacon of that other boy's back receding in the distance, but I can't be that rude. I have to turn around. How bad can it be?

When I finally turn, I'm met with a shy nod from a boy who seems as reluctant to be introduced as I am. I wonder if he has any idea of what's being plotted for us by our fathers.

He's about the same age as the other boy, but the resemblance ends there. This boy is huge. He's got a large, round head topped by a fringe of lank blond hair which hangs down in the unflattering bowl cut favored by farmers. His head is slightly bowed so that his hair is falling in his eyes, although I doubt he could see me anyway, since he's looking at his feet so hard you'd think he's just noticed that he has them. He reminds me of a big old ox lumbering through the fields — slow but amiable. How can my father expect those big, clumsy hands to help him with his work?

An older man, Luc's father, appears at the gate, saving us from further conversation — or lack thereof.

"Jan! You're come at last. We'd begun to give up on you," he says, shaking my father's hand vigorously.

"No chance of that. I haven't disappointed a customer yet — not a paying one, anyway. And never an old friend."

We're ushered into a small courtyard, to a table in the shade of the house already set with mugs of ale. As we go, Monsieur Fournier puts is arm lightly around my shoulder to guide me like he knows me, but I can't remember ever having met him. I guess there's no need for formality, since we're soon to be in-laws.

I take a seat, expecting to be ignored for the rest of the visit as usual, but as my father begins taking out some sample bows, he says,

"Marieke's been a great help to me this year. She's very good with her hands." I can feel myself blushing. What is this, advertisement?

"She's been acting as my interim apprentice, and she's quite the accomplished fletcher in her own right. Take a look at this."

He pulls out one of my arrows and holds it up for the others to admire. To my embarrassment, they exclaim over it so much you'd think I just did something really amazing, like laid an egg right in the middle of the courtyard. I guess to most people, the idea that a girl could do a job as well as a man *is* as amazing as laying an egg. Or maybe even more so.

My father is really laying it on thick. He's never been so lavish in his praise. I must be an even tougher sell than I'd thought. He sounds sincere, though, and I can't help feeling some pride at his words, even if I suspect his motives. Despite myself, I'm feeling rather affectionate toward my father, when out of nowhere I hear him suggesting,

"I've just had a great idea. Marieke, why don't you measure Luc, while I measure M. Fournier?"

"What?" I say stupidly. I must have heard wrong. Put my hands all over this hulking boy while our fathers watch?

Seeing my expression, he continues quickly, "Sure! Don't be shy. You've seen me do it plenty of times, and this will give you a chance to practice, among friends. Luc won't mind, will you?"

Taking the anguished squeak that comes from Luc as a 'no,' my father takes out a knotted length of twine and puts it in my hand, smiling innocently. There's nothing for it — I have to take it. I take a deep breath and turn to Luc.

To measure up his arm, across the shoulders, and down the other arm, I have to stand so close to Luc's chest that I can feel his breath on the top of my head. His hands are trembling so much he's flapping like a feeble chicken, and to my disgust, so are mine. I look over at my father, because if I see that he's enjoying this, I really might kill him.

But he and Monsieur Fournier are deep in conversation, and he doesn't seem to be paying any attention to us. So I relax, and before long I'm absorbed in the task of finding the right fit for Luc, since it's something of a challenge. He's strong, all right. But his technique is terrible, and after a while I've become so focused on the problem that I hardly notice just when it is that Luc relaxes, too, and we begin to talk together quite easily.

When I try to measure his grip, however, saying, "Give me your hand, Luc," a terrified look flashes across his face, and I realize that for a moment he must have thought I'd gotten so friendly that I wanted to hold his hand.

"I'm not going to bite you!" I growl, irritated.

Luc's reply is so low I hardly catch it:

"Good. Then I won't have to bite you back."

My head snaps up in alarm, and for a minute I'm genuinely afraid when I see him flash his teeth at me, but there's a twinkle in his eyes. He's joking! That's the last thing I expected from him. Maybe there's more to him than I thought. He breaks into a grin, and we both laugh.

By the time we're done and I've got the bow I'm going to make for Luc all planned out, I find that we're chatting away quite comfortably. I've been unfair (as usual). Luc really is a pretty nice boy. I know I could do a lot worse.

That doesn't mean I'm not still mad at my father for the whole set-up, though. As soon as we say our goodbyes to the Fourniers and we're on our way again, I turn on him.

"That was all a bit much, don't you think?" I say angrily.

"Whatever are you talking about?" He really seems puzzled. "Fournier is an old friend."

I snort.

"I can't figure you out, Marieke," he says, giving me a stern look over the wagon. "You've been sulking all day. I can only assume it's because I haven't let you help out more. Then I give you a chance to be really useful, and you sulk even more."

I know I'm being unreasonable. But I can't help myself. I never can.

"So M. Fournier, whom I've never met, just *happens* to be an old friend," I say.

"As it *happens*, yes. I knew they'd treat you well, not like the others. I thought you wanted to be my assistant today. I thought you'd be pleased."

He's right. They *did* treat me well. Ordinarily, I would be pleased. I suppose I should just come out with it, and ask my father directly about Luc, but if he's going to marry me off, he's going to have to bring it up himself. I'm not going to make it easier for him by giving him an opening.

As we head for the center of town, I'm deep in thought. If I'm fair, it's clear that my father's done well for me. Luc seems kind, and it's pretty easy to imagine him fitting into our routine without causing so much as a ripple. Not that he could take Jules's place, exactly, but he could provide an extra pair of hands without a forceful personality behind them to disrupt the pattern of our life. We could go on basically just as before, with hardly any change (well, besides the obvious ones, which don't bear thinking about). That's what I've wanted, isn't it — for nothing really to change?

But we're passing the house where I saw that other boy appear just a little while ago. The difference between him and Luc is like a cruel jab. I imagine I see the boy standing there again, poised on the step with his hand raised in greeting, his face radiant. That single soft, brown curl tickles the back of his neck, and at the memory of it I know I wouldn't mind the idea of change so much if I thought a boy like that could be part of it.

We turn to make our way to the square via the main thoroughfare in town. We're back on what is really just a portion of the L'île-Charleroi road that bisects town, but this stretch leading to the market is known as the Street of the Guilds, for obvious reasons. Here in the heart of town the shops and workshops of like artisans are all lined up in a row, marked by matching banners displaying the crests of their guilds — weavers, dyers, masons, harness makers, a dozen others — and the buildings are truly magnificent. I love the colorful banners fluttering in the breeze against the multicolored bricks of the stepped facades, and it's easy to forget everything else in the pure joy of seeing them again.

Once in the square, although there are plenty of taverns to choose from, we prefer to make a meal out of the various wares available from the few booths that are still set up in the square. It's getting to be afternoon now, so most of the market traffic is gone and the owners of the remaining stalls are starting to pack up. But the square isn't empty. In addition to stragglers left over from the market, there's a small crowd gathered around a makeshift stage set up in a corner in front of the bailiff's office, where some traveling performers are putting on a show. I don't ask if we can go over and watch, since there are really only two kinds of shows: religious passion plays, or crude comedies about cuckolded husbands. The religious plays bore me (unless they have really fancy costumes, or involve reenacting the torture of some saint), and my father never lets me watch the sexy stuff (I've seen my fair share, though, because Berthal used to love it. Of course she pretended not to, but she'd always linger much longer than necessary at the stalls near the stage when a particularly juicy performance was going on. She'd keep up a running commentary to cover herself, muttering *what is the world coming to, with filth like this on every street corner?*," but her chuckles under her breath always gave her away. If my father and Jules left us alone in the square, she'd drop all pretense and elbow right up to the front, hooting along with everyone else). Today there's an impossibly large man up on stage, with an even more impossibly large bottom. As we go by, he bends over and starts wiggling it in the air at the audience. A tall thin woman with wild hair wearing a long strap-on nose like a carrot grabs the man's buttocks and begins grinding around in his groin with the tip of the fake nose, cackling like a banshee. I don't even want to know what that's all about, but Berthal would have loved it. I really do miss her.

By the time we've passed the stage and the woman's cries are growing fainter, we've eaten a veritable feast, and I give a loud and very un-ladylike burp of satisfaction. I've kept my eye out for the carriage with the red trim, with no luck (I doubt I have to mention that I've also been on the lookout for another glimpse of the lovely boy, with equally little success). I'm still wiping crumbs off my face as we approach the cathedral of St. Margaret, which is always our last stop on the square. It's always our last stop of any trip to town.

The cathedral is a huge gothic structure, with high arched ceilings reaching up to imitate the vast vault of heaven, but it's very austere. The only real ornament inside, besides the crucifix and a painting of the saint over the altar, is a row of stained-glass windows, each one displaying the emblem of one of the guilds. It isn't particularly beautiful, but it's impressive.

I go to light a candle in memory of my mother in a small alcove dedicated to mother Mary. It's something I've always done, but now I light two additional candles, one for Berthal and one for Jules. I always ask the blessed Virgin to help me be a better daughter, to help me to be more obedient and subservient, as is proper for a girl. I always mean it at the time. Today I add one new prayer, and I try to mean it, too: I ask for help accepting the inevitable, even if it involves Luc Fournier. I can't help it; the image of that other boy floats through my thoughts, even as I'm praying. But it would be too presumptuous to pray for a miracle.

When we come out, I feel like I've made my peace with the day. The trip is over, and it was what it was. I circle around to climb back up onto the wagon seat, but as I pass the back of the wagon, I see something that makes me stop.

"Papa, we've made a mistake somewhere."

"What do you mean?" My father is still standing on the cathedral steps. He hasn't made a move back toward the wagon and he's smiling again, that secret smile he's had all day.

"My broadhead arrows. They're still in the wagon. Look."

"I know."

"But we didn't deliver them."

"You mean, not yet."

"We're already at the square." It doesn't make sense. "There's nothing beyond here."

"Nothing?" He's positively grinning now.

"No, nothing," I say stupidly. "Nothing but St. Sebastian's." It's only when I say it that the truth dawns on me. It's taken me a ridiculously long time to process the obvious.

"That's right. We've got one more stop."

My father is smiling broadly as I fall into his open arms. I hug him tightly around the waist, just like I used to do as a child, and hide my face against his stomach.

"Happy?" he says gently, as he ruffles my hair lightly with one hand. "I know you've been wanting to visit St. Sebastian's for a long time. It shouldn't have taken me so long to take you there. Forgive me?"

"Anything, and everything," I say, but I don't let go. It's not just that we're finally going to visit St. Sebastian's. It's also that I've been all wrong about the day from start to finish. *This* is the big mystery, *this* is the big surprise my father's been hinting at. He really has been puzzled by me all day — he probably will marry me off to Luc Fournier eventually, but it isn't going to be today.

When at last I look up, my father brushes my hair back into place with his hand.

"You want to look your best, now, don't you?"

I nod. His words this morning come back to me, and I blush. I really have been a brat!

"And the broadheads?" I ask. "They're for St. Sebastian's, then?" With a little thrill, I imagine the beautiful boy I saw earlier pulling out one of my arrows, turning it over in his hands, running a well-manicured hand gently over the feathers, admiring the workmanship, but I know it's unlikely. They're the wrong kind of heads for target shooting.

"Sort of. It's complicated."

I don't ask for an explanation. Who cares, really? I'm going to St. Sebastian's!

St. Sebastian's isn't really just one place. It's a large walled compound that straddles the L'île-Charleroi road and occupies the entire northeastern quadrant of Louvain. On one side of the road is the guild hall proper, along with its offices, workshops, and barracks. On the other, open fields stretch all the way to Porte L'île. These are the exposition grounds, where the competitions are held.

The main entrance to St. Sebastian's lies at a crossroads, where a narrow alley that follows the guild wall intersects with the main road. Arched doorways at the corner of the building face both onto the main road and onto the alley, and over each door hangs a banner displaying a single silver arrow on a black field — the crest of St. Sebastian's. I've seen the doors from afar at least a dozen times, and the walls of warm pinkish-brown stone stretching away from them in both directions, but I've never been inside. I've never even *seen* inside. Under the archways are large wooden doors that are always kept shut.

My father steps inside the nearest archway and gives the door within a gentle push. I'm surprised at how easily it gives way under his touch. All this time, and it's just that easy. Any day, I could have done it myself.

In the doorway, he hesitates.

"I know how eager you are, Marieke. Don't be too disappointed."

"Why should I be disappointed?"

"Just don't set your expectations too high," he says, but it's too late for that. "You know that I can't show you much, right? Women aren't allowed inside most of the guild. It's the cardinal rule of St. Sebastian's."

As he says this, he swings the door open, and I'm stepping into the loveliest room I've ever seen.

"It's already better than I imagined!" I cry.

"This is just the vestibule," he protests, but I can tell he's pleased.

I'm not sure what a vestibule is, exactly, but the room is incredible. The high ceiling is ornately coffered, and each recess is painted with intricate designs. Tapestries hang on the walls, and closely spaced windows high overhead flood the room with colored light.

"Can I help you?"

The room is so elaborately decorated, I haven't noticed that a boy is seated at a large desk in the far corner of the room, in front of a huge set of double doors. He's about the right age to be one of the Journeymen, but I doubt he's one of them. My father was right; you can just tell. He seems more like a clerk or a scribe. His tone is bored and a bit condescending. Before my father can answer, an old man shuffles out of a door in another wall.

"François! Are you still here, my friend?" my father cries. The old man turns at the sound of his voice, and I see that his eyes are clouded by cataracts.

"Master Jan? Can it be?" The old man holds out a shaking hand in the general direction of my father. It's clear he can hardly see. My father puts his own hand into the old man's and shakes it warmly.

"Jan. Jan Verbeke. I'd know your voice anywhere. Even after all these years."

"It's been a long time, François. Too long."

"Do you have some business here?" the bored boy cuts in.

"Young whippersnappers. No respect!" grumbles François under his breath, then he barks at the boy, "Stand when you're in the presence of your betters!"

The boy rolls his eyes, but I notice that he stands up. He leans forward indolently, resting both hands on the desk.

"Do you have some business here, *sir*?" he drawls.

"Here to see the Guildmaster, no doubt. Who else? Don't just stand there! Go tell Master Guillaume that Monsieur Verbeke is here!"

The boy moves slowly around the desk and disappears through the great double doors. As soon as he's gone, François starts chuckling.

"They say I'm too old for this, Jan. But I can still get the boys moving when I want to!"

"I bet you can! You were always the best, François."

"They don't let me do much these days, Master Jan. Given most of my responsibilities to young Albrecht, of all people!" François shakes his head. "It's not like when you were here. We had real boys, then, not these insolent pups! Even the squires think they're something on a stick nowadays."

"You'll whip them into shape, François. St. Sebastian's is in good hands, as long as you're here." My father pats him affectionately on the back, as François shakes his head sadly.

I've been watching this exchange with great interest. I'm not sure why it surprises me that my father is so warmly remembered here, but it does. I'm also impressed by my father's treatment of François, whose status I can't quite make out, though he seems to be some kind of servant. I'm listening very intently, hoping that François will let something slip about my father's past, but the boy reappears at the double doors.

"Monsieur Verbeke, if you'll follow me, please," he says, a new note of respect in his voice.

I start forward, but the boy puts up his hand to stop me.

"You can't come in here. No girls allowed."

My father turns to me.

"I'm sorry Marieke, but the offices are inside the restricted area. But look, I'll ask the Guildmaster for permission to show you around the training ground afterward. That's where all the real action takes place around here anyway, and in my day, girls used to be allowed out there on occasion. I think he'll allow it." He gives a questioning look to the boy, who gives a noncommittal shrug. "There's a little chapel of St. Sebastian just through there that's open to the public," he continues, gesturing toward the adjacent wall. "You can wait for me there. François will show you, won't you François?"

"Don't worry about me, I'll be fine," I say brightly, as I watch my father disappear through the doors after the boy. I'm not really disappointed. I expected as much.

In the meantime, François has been slowly shuffling across the room, muttering *right this way, missy*. He seems to be about to crash right into the wall, and I wonder if I should put out a hand to stop him. Then I notice he's gesturing to a small door that blends in with the wall paneling so well that I hadn't noticed it.

I really do intend to go straight into the chapel. But as I turn to go in the direction indicated by François, I notice that one of the great double doors behind the boy's desk is standing slightly ajar. My father didn't pull it all the way shut behind him. Beyond lie the forbidden places of St. Sebastian's. When I take a quick look behind me to see if François has noticed, he's already vanished. I'm momentarily alone in the vestibule.

I tip-toe over to the great doors, and I peek my head through the opening. Beyond is a large hall like the interior of a cathedral, but without the arched roof. It's empty, too, except for rows of long, heavy wooden tables and benches which are pushed up against the walls. Although I've never been here before, I know what this must be. It's the actual guild hall, the room that gives the complex its name. I know I shouldn't be here, I shouldn't even be looking in. I might even get my father into trouble. But I take a step forward. Just a small one, but it's enough to cross the threshold. I can't help myself. I have to get a better look, because there's one other thing in the room, something I just have to see. It seems to be pulling me into the room against my will. It's a huge painting which covers the wall at the far end of the room.

It's like nothing I've ever seen before. The only other art I've ever seen is the miniature, jewel-like illumination of Father Abelard; this is something completely different. It's big, bold, dark — layer upon layer of rich color building to a startling mixture of sensuality and violence. I recognize the scene instantly. It's the passion of St. Sebastian, the same scene as on my father's medal, but executed and imagined so differently that it's transformed into something deeply disturbing and powerful. Here the saint is depicted not as an adult but as a provocatively attractive young man, just blooming into manhood, his body a curious combination of the lithe, lean musculature of maturity and the soft, sensuous curves of youth.

He's just the age of the Journeymen, in other words.

Plenty of both curves and muscles are on display, since he's virtually nude except for a small, strategically draped cloth just large enough to preserve modesty. He's not standing, as on the medal, but slumped at an impossible angle at the base of the tree to which he's tied. He's suspended only by the bonds restraining his arms, which wrench them up and back painfully on either side of his drooping head. Below, his legs are alternately bent and splayed, as though he has just ceased struggling to find purchase on the ground beneath him, and arrows pierce his body where it's most defenseless: in the hollow at the base of his throat, in the soft swell of the belly where it slides down toward the groin, and through the whiteness of his extended arm, along the paper-thin skin where the pulse beats at the bend of the inner elbow. These intimate places are so alluringly evoked that they seem to call out for a lover's touch; instead they're violated by the cruel penetration of arrows, traced by seeping blood rather than by soft lips.

I've never seen this much of a man exposed before, not even in an image. I've certainly never seen a man as physically beautiful. Even that lovely boy this afternoon doesn't come close. I picture the artist applying each brush stroke as a lingering caress, and I can't help imagining my own hands brushing that vulnerable, naked flesh. Even so, it isn't only his magnificent body that holds me rapt; it's also the expression on the saint's face.

A cascade of black hair falls in thick locks across his pallid cheeks and mingles with the beads of sweat forming on his brow, but his full lips are slightly parted and his gaze strains upward from under heavily lidded eyes — eyes glazed with a chilling look that's at once wild with ecstasy and hooded with pain. What could make anyone willingly endure such a gruesome torture, I wonder; what would it be like to feel a passion so great that it could be sustained through the agony of such a rending of the flesh? What must it be like to die like that, transfixed, in the slow death of a hundred cuts, of countless arrows?

Then I remember the story: arrows couldn't kill him. St. Sebastian was ultimately bludgeoned to death.

A strange feeling comes over me, like a cold finger touching the back of my neck. It's like the old expression: someone's walking over my grave. It must be guilt. I know I'm looking at something I shouldn't. Only members are supposed to be in here. The passion of that gorgeous, naked man up on the wall has also stirred up such strong and unfamiliar feelings in me that it's probably for a good reason that women aren't supposed to see it. It's almost with relief when I hear footsteps approaching, since the fear of discovery jolts me out of my reverie. I cross quickly back into the vestibule — the boy is coming back.

He gives me a suspicious look as he pulls the doors firmly shut behind him.

"Is the chapel door stuck?" His tone is calibrated to be more insulting than helpful, so I hustle across the room. He's still staring at me with a sour look on his face as I open the chapel door and go in. He's probably worried that I'll stay in the vestibule and he'll have to find some work to pretend to do. I don't think he can have seen me in the great hall.

It's quiet and cool in the little chapel. It's like a little miniature version of St. Margaret's, simple and austere. I sit down at one of the pews near the altar and look around. There's no decoration at all. The small windows that give the room its only light have red and yellow tinted glass, but no designs. Still, the windows turn the high afternoon sun shining in through them a rosy hue, and it's restful sitting here bathed in pinkish light. On the altar under the crucifix is another image of St. Sebastian, but it couldn't be more different from the picture I've just seen. This is a little wooden statue. It looks ancient, and there's nothing beautiful about it. It's crudely carved, with arrows fashioned from iron sticking out of it. Here the saint is a gaunt, older man, and his bones stick out on his ribs as though he's been starved before tortured. He's standing with his arms raised over his head in a pose that matches the one on my father's medal, which I suppose must be modeled on this statue. A normal person would probably find it much more disturbing than the painting of the saint as a gorgeous youth, but it doesn't affect me like that other image.

I sit there, lost in thought, for I don't know how long. I'm looking at the wooden statue, but in my mind's eye I'm committing every inch of the painting to memory, as though that picture can tell me all I need to know about St. Sebastian's.

I'm so lost in thought about the painting that I don't hear my father come in. I'm not even sure how long he's been there before I notice him. I just begin to sense the presence of another person in the room, and when I turn around, I see my father kneeling next to one of the pews a few rows back, his head bent. At first I think he's praying, but when after a while he doesn't move or get up, I go over and sit down next to him and put my hand on his arm.

"I'm so sorry, Marieke." He shakes his head slightly in response to my touch. "I never should have brought you here."

He sounds so defeated that I'm alarmed. He hasn't even looked up; I'm not sure what's wrong. This seems an extreme reaction to a refusal from the Guildmaster to let me look around the grounds, but I can't think what else he could be talking about.

When he continues, he seems to be talking more to himself than to me.

"I thought it would be a nice surprise. *Nice.*" He stretches out the word angrily. "I thought it would make you happy. But it was a mistake. Can you forgive me?

"But I am happy!" I cry. "I'm not disappointed. It doesn't matter if we can't see any more than this —" I blush a little at the guilty thought that I've seen more than my father knows. "Just coming here, the idea of it ..." I gesture around the chapel, "it's enough for me. More than enough!"

He still doesn't look up; his shoulders are slumped forward. All his lightness of this morning is gone.

"Thank you, Papa, for bringing me today," I say carefully, more seriously now. "I *am* happy. But if coming here made you unhappy, then I'm sorry we came, too. If it brought back bad memories, bitter memories ..." I falter, unsure how to continue. Finally I burst out, "How you must hate this place!"

At this, my father finally looks up. He looks so confused, we must be talking at cross purposes again.

"Hate it? I don't hate St. Sebastian's. I love it."

At my disbelieving look, he continues:

"I'll admit, I've been bitter sometimes, but I don't hate the guild. Not at all. I've always loved this place. You don't forget your glory days, Marieke. In fact, I had hoped that maybe, one day ..." he breaks off, but I don't need him to finish to know what he's going to say. He's thinking of Jules. He didn't teach Jules to shoot for nothing, and he taught him to shoot well. Extremely well. I don't know why I never noticed it before. Of course he intended Jules for St. Sebastian's.

"Then ... why don't you ever come here? Why won't you even work for the guild as a fletcher?"

"I've been foolish, Marieke. And proud. But that's not the only reason I've stayed away. When you're older, you'll understand, and hopefully, you'll forgive me." He pauses, searching for the right words. Talking to me has never been easy for him. "Sometimes, when your old life is snatched away from you, it's easier to cut it out root and branch. Sometimes that's the only way to make way for a new life, to make it bearable." He pauses again, struggling with some emotion I don't understand, and I put out a hand as if to stop him, to tell him he doesn't need to explain, but he waves it away, determined to go on. "I didn't try to forget St. Sebastian's because I hated it, but because remembering it was too hard. Because I loved it, too much."

He sounds so sad, I can't help myself. I reach down and ruffle his hair, the way he usually does to me. I wish I understood what was going on in his mind. I've been imagining things all day, but

I'm not imagining this. Something is wrong, and I wonder if I've disappointed him again somehow. Clearly coming here was too much for him. I shouldn't have asked it of him.

As I run my hand down the back of his head, I find the thin string he always wears around his neck. My fingers follow the string, gently pulling the little metal token hanging on it free from where it's tucked into his tunic. It's his St. Sebastian medal.

"If you want to forget St. Sebastian's, why do you always wear this?"

"Why do I wear this?" His voice sounds far away, as he looks down at the medal as though he's seeing it for the first time. "Let me show you." He slips it from around his neck and holds it out where I can get a closer look.

"Do you see what it says here?" Some tiny letters are inscribed on a banner unfurled below the saint's feet, but all I see are squiggles. They don't mean anything to me, but now isn't the time to remind my father that Jules was the one learning to read, not me. But my father doesn't wait for an answer. He still seems to be talking to himself more than to me.

"*Non me occident sagittae.* Do you know what that means?"

I shake my head. It sounds like Latin.

"It's the motto of St. Sebastian's. *Arrows won't kill me.* Now do you understand?"

"It's part of the saint's legend, isn't it? When the Romans tried to kill him for his faith, they shot him full of arrows, but he didn't die."

"That's right," my father agrees slowly. "But I think there's more to it than that. St. Sebastian survived what he shouldn't have survived. He survived what should have been fatal blows. I think that this is telling us that in life, the arrows keep coming. Life is a shower of arrows. You just have to take them. But sometimes, you can find a way to survive even a mortal wound."

I think of all the arrows my father has suffered: my mother's death, his failure at the guild, and now the loss of Jules. I wonder which of these he's thinking about right now. Of all these shafts, which was his mortal wound?

He looks up at me intently.

"Do you believe it, Marieke?"

I feel my hand start to reach up to my shattered nose, but I clench my fist to will it to stay down by my side as my father's gaze searches my face. I can't remember the last time he's looked at me this way, really looked at me. He's still holding tight onto my arm and staring into my eyes when he finally continues:

"I do. I believe it. That's why I wear this medal. It reminds me that I'm not the only one who has endured the unendurable. It reminds me to have faith that I can survive."

"You mean, anyone can be a St. Sebastian?" It sounds sacrilegious, putting it this way, and completely unlike my father. I bite my lip, wishing I could take it back, since he so clearly wants me to understand.

"Yes, no — I don't know. Not exactly. But I want you to believe it, too."

I don't know what to say, but the intensity passes from my father's face as quickly as it came, and he looks beaten down again. His head droops back into a position of defeat. When he looks up again, his face is set back in its familiar, diffident expression. But there's a bitter look that's new, too.

"Do you know what else they say about St. Sebastian's arrows? What else they can mean?"

I shake my head again.

"Some say they're arrows of plague. That they're a metaphor for illness. That's why the sick pray to St. Sebastian."

I look up at the little wooden image of the saint on the altar, pierced by arrows, and I imagine Jules's body, wracked with fever. Where was the saint then, when Jules was dying?

"It's a terrible thing to lose a child," he says, reading my expression.

He's never mentioned Jules's death to me before. I slip my hand into his, and he grips it tightly.

"There have been a lot of misfortunes in my life, Marieke. Tragedies, even. Maybe more than my fair share, I don't know. But God, in his mercy, gave me something to help me endure them. Something in exchange for the arrows. Do you know what it is?"

"The medal?" I ask quietly, turning it over in my hand.

"No, Marieke. Not the medal. He gave me you."

CHAPTER FOUR

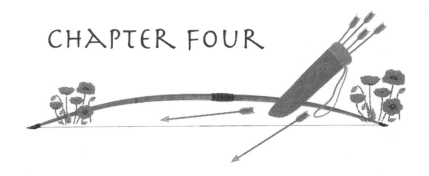

The rosy glow that surrounded us in the chapel seems to follow me all the way home. We don't say much, but it doesn't matter. The visit to St. Sebastian's upset my father more than he wants to admit. He's preoccupied with his memories, good and bad, and I don't want to disturb them. But our silence doesn't seem awkward to me anymore. All the things I wanted from the trip (and feared about it, too) no longer seem very important. Everything is going to be different from now on, I can feel it. It's going to be better. So I don't even pay much attention when I think I see a carriage with red trim parked down by Porte L'île out of the corner of my eye as we're leaving the guild, arm in arm. I'm probably imagining things, anyway. It couldn't be the same carriage, since there's nothing down that way but more outbuildings of the guild.

One little niggling thought does keep coming back to me, though. It's something about the tone of the conversations I've been having all day, first with Abelard, then with my father. Everyone seems to be saying goodbye to me today. Even now, I can't keep my imagination from being overactive, but I'd be a fool to let one of my crazy ideas spoil my contentment. So when I notice something odd as I'm climbing down from the wagon seat once we're back in our own yard, I only frown slightly and let it go.

The box of broadhead arrows is still lying in the bottom of the wagon.

At home again, I change quickly back into Jules's clothes. Up in my own room, I find Abelard's illumination right where I left it, drying on the windowsill by the open shutters. I fold it up carefully and tuck it into my waistband. I want to get another good look at it, out in what little twilight is left. It's just one of the images of the day I want to revisit while it's still fresh, now that I can get off by myself. I always do my best thinking outdoors, and my favorite spot for contemplation is out in the kitchen garden, where the poles for the climbing beans hide me from the view of the house, and the heady scent of herbs and earth paints a backdrop for my imagination.

As I come downstairs, my father is crouched by the fireplace. He's already lit a fire, but he's stayed there close, staring absently into the flames. I'm almost out the door when he calls after me,

"Don't bother about chores tonight. It'll be dark soon. We can catch up on everything in the morning."

"I know," I reply, "But there's still some light. I won't go far."

My father can probably guess that I want to be alone with my thoughts as much as he does, so he doesn't protest. He hasn't even turned around. On impulse, I run over and put my arms around his neck, something I haven't done for years. I kiss him lightly on the cheek.

"Thank you for today, Papa. For all of it," I call back over my shoulder as I run out the door. For the first time today, I'm absolutely sure I mean it.

When I wake, I feel an instant sense of alarm. I meant to close my eyes for just a moment, to relive the day more vividly in my mind, but I must have fallen asleep out in the garden. Now it's pitch dark. I'm so cold and disoriented, it takes me a moment to remember I'm outside. It's late and I'm going to be in trouble, but that's not all that's bothering me. I have a vague memory of a dream in which the interior of St. Sebastian's, the alluring painting of the saint, and the little chapel with its grotesque wooden statue swirl in disturbing combinations with Abelard's picture and Luc Fournier's bared teeth. There was something else in the dream, too, I'm sure of it, only frustratingly I can't remember what it was. For some reason, it seems important. But it's gone. The more I try to remember it, the more it flits away.

The garden is around behind the house, where little light from the interior reaches it, but it doesn't look as though my father has lit any lamps in the house. He must be content with the light from the fireplace. It's odd that he hasn't called me in, and this morning, I might have thought he was trying to punish me with silence for staying out too late, but I think I understand him better now. He's probably still lost in thought, like I was. We're more alike than I thought.

It's a night with no moon, so I have to pick my way carefully through the vegetables to keep from stumbling in the darkness. As I come out across the yard, something feels wrong, although I can't quite put my finger on what it is. The yard is just as usual, alive with the usual night sounds — an occasional cricket, the tinkling of a goat bell. Then I do hear an unexpected sound, low under the comforting murmur of country noises. A faint but distinct sound of clattering and stamping is coming from somewhere around in front of the house, as though there are horses out on the path where it joins the main road. It's odd that anyone would be out riding at this hour, and odder still for anyone to be stopping here at this time of night. It's too late for visitors, and even thieves don't usually ride when there's no moon.

I pause to listen. At first, I think I'm mistaken. Then the sounds come again. Someone's left horses and attendants out on the main path. Visitors would surely ride down into the yard, wouldn't they? I try to shake off the confusion of waking in the garden. There's no sign of a visitor in the dark house; from here, it looks empty. I'm being fanciful again, yet I feel uneasy. Afraid, even. I suppose that's why I decide on a whim not to go straight in, and instead I circle around quietly to the kitchen door that opens out on the far side of the yard.

Once I'm inside, I hear voices coming from the main room. My father is deep in quiet conversation with someone, so I begin to relax. It's someone my father knows, just a late visitor, after all. The faint glow of the dying fire my father lit earlier this evening doesn't penetrate far into the gloom of the kitchen, but after the darkness of the yard the soft light is comforting. It must be someone my father knows well, for him to have kept the lamps unlit. Only there's something intimate about a late chat at fireside that isn't my father's style. It's funny he didn't tell me he was expecting someone. For a moment, I even wonder if I'm still dreaming. Like a dreamer, I drift closer toward the beacon of the fire, curious to see the scene inside, curious to see our mysterious visitor.

The door at the far side of the kitchen is open, flung wide into the main room of the house, so that as I approach, I have a clear view into the room beyond. Through the open doorway I can see my father standing in front of the fire, not far from where I left him when I went out to the garden. He's behind the large wooden table where we eat our meals, leaning forward with both hands resting flat on the table. There's something awkward about the way he's standing, but he looks calm enough — at least, not how I'd expect him to look with thieves in the house. I can't see who he's talking to, but from the direction of his gaze, his visitor must be standing right on the other side of the kitchen wall from me. We must be standing right next to each other, though I can't see him; we're separated from each other by the open kitchen door.

They're speaking so quietly that at first, I can't make out what they're saying. For some reason, I haven't quite shaken the feeling of alarm that came over me from waking in the garden. There's something off, but I can't quite place it. My father is facing me, more or less, but he's looking intently at whoever is standing on the other side of the wall. I'm pretty sure he's seen me come in, but he if he has, he doesn't give any sign of it. He doesn't even look my way. I usually wouldn't hesitate to go in, to join my father and help play hostess for him, but tonight something stops me. There's an undercurrent in the room that tells me I've come in on the middle of something. I decide to wait for a sign from my father, when I hear the other man's voice clearly for the first time. He must be so close to me that I could reach out and touch him, if the open door wasn't between us.

"You know, I really didn't want it to come to this, Verbeke."

The voice sounds sad and tired, like an old friend reluctant to deliver bad news. Only there's something off about his tone, too. There's an edge to it that's cold and hard. It makes me glad I didn't go into the room.

"I'm sure you didn't. I'm sure things suited you just fine as they were." My father's smiling, but he doesn't look very amused.

"Yes, I've followed your 'career' with great interest — satisfaction, even! The great Jan Verbeke, fletcher *extraordinaire* ..." The voice drags the word out in a sneer. "He's got a lame shoulder, to be sure, but that hasn't stopped him from rising to the top of his *profession*." He stretches out the word unpleasantly. "You must be very proud."

"I'm not ashamed of it," my father says simply.

"You wouldn't be!" The man sounds angry, like he's frustrated that my father isn't rising to his bait, but my father doesn't reply. He's standing stock still, and I get the impression he's willing me not to move, either. The conversation is innocent enough, but my sense of alarm is growing. I feel the hairs on the back of my neck bristle, but I'm not sure why. It's clear from his tone, though, that whoever the voice belongs to, he isn't my father's friend.

"And your son," the disembodied voice behind the door continues. The man's tone is calm again, controlled and calculated, but my father looks even more wary. "He's your apprentice, isn't he? You must be so proud of him, too. Why don't you call him? I'd love to meet the son of Jan Verbeke."

I can feel my cheeks growing hot at the man's openly insulting tone. How dare he speak to my father this way?! How dare he speak to him of Jules. But my father's face is impassive, just like a mask.

"My son is dead," he replies, his voice hollow. The simple dignity of this statement makes my heart lurch.

"*Tsk tsk*. What a tragedy," the voice continues, cold as ice. I can't understand it. Why is my father just standing there so casually, letting this man insult him? "But you must be used to tragedies by now. One could almost say, they're your specialty."

"It might be more accurate to say, they're *yours*."

There's a pause, and I can almost feel the unseen man struggling to control his anger again.

"Even a man like you, with good reasons for wanting his privacy, must have some companionship here, surely?" the voice continues.

"No. I live here alone."

It's very slight, but my father puts just enough emphasis on the word *alone* that I take it as a warning to me. For whatever reason, my father doesn't want my presence known. I'm taking a slow, careful step backwards when I see it. The thing that's been bothering me, the thing that's off. I must have seen it when I first walked through the door, but it's so incomprehensible, so impossible, that it's taken this long for my mind to process it. There's an arrow sticking out of the back of my father's right hand, pinning it to the table in front of him. That's why he hasn't straightened up from that deceptively casual stance — he can't move. He's been nailed to the table.

I freeze, my foot midair, eyes riveted on the arrow. The room spins around me; I see it, but I can't take it in. Saliva fills my mouth, and I know in a minute I'll be sick. I can feel my eyes go wide, and I struggle to stifle the scream I can feel building in my throat. But my father's seen me start. Before I can make a sound, he turns his head. It's the slightest of movements, not even a turn, really, just enough of a shift to look me right in the eye. I can tell he's using all the force of his will to keep me silent, to keep me from giving myself away. His look is so intense, I can tell he's trying to tell me more, too, but I can't think. My senses are about to explode. The whole world seems to tilt off balance.

"How sad," the cold voice comes drifting through the wall again. "No one should be all alone. Killing you, then, it won't really be murder, will it? It's more like mercy."

My eyes are still locked on his when I hear the sickening twang of a bowstring, and a second arrow flies from behind the door and rips through the base of my father's throat.

"A lame horse like you; someone should have put you down a long time ago," the cold voice continues, as my father slumps to the ground, his right hand still impaled against the top of the table. As blood gurgles up from the hole in his neck, the voice laughs,

"Oh, don't try to thank me. It's my *pleasure*."

There's a scrape of wood on wood, followed quickly by another twang, and a third arrow pierces my father, straight through the heart.

I can't believe that earlier today, I thought there was anything even remotely beautiful about the sight of a man shot full of arrows.

I DON'T KNOW HOW LONG I WOULD HAVE STOOD HERE, unable to move or speak, if I weren't shocked back to my senses by the sound of a new voice coming from the other side of the wall: the man isn't alone.

"A man like that, living out here all by himself."

"He was lying, you idiot!" snaps the first voice, the one I'm sure belongs to the shooter.

"I don't know," chimes in another voice. There are at least three of them. Of course. A villain always has henchmen. "I did hear his son died a while back. I think he was telling the truth. The place looks deserted."

"I've heard the rumors, too, but we have to be sure," the first man insists. "Search the place." What he says next finally jolts me fully awake. "And he was certainly lying. There's a daughter." There are some shuffling sounds, then:

"What are you waiting for? Go find her."

"You didn't say anything about killing a girl," the third man says finally.

"What's this? Scruples? From you? That's one I didn't expect." I hear the shooter's cold laugh again, with no humor in it.

I don't wait to hear any more. I turn and run as quickly and silently as I can back out into the yard, with the men's laughter ringing in my ears. And not a moment too soon. The sound of heavy footsteps echoes through the kitchen as I hastily conceal myself behind some barrels pushed up against the side of the house. Now I'm glad for the concealing darkness of the moonless night. The men are still talking as they follow their leader out into the yard.

"I'm telling you, she's not in the house," insists the second man.

"Make sure. Then look around outside. Verbeke must have had his workshop out back somewhere. Search it, then sack the whole place. I don't want anyone asking questions. Make it look like a robbery, or looters."

"Pretty fancy shooting, for brigands," puts in the third man.

"Then take care of it. Just find the girl."

"She's not here, I tell you," the second man says again. "What does it matter, anyway? It's just a girl."

The shooter is already disappearing down the path, heading

back to the mount waiting for him out on the main road, when he answers:

"She'll turn up, sooner or later. Leave one of your men, if you don't find her. And tell him to be inconspicuous. We can't afford any loose ends. Not now."

From my spot behind the barrels I can hear the sound of gravel crunching under boots as the remaining two men cross the yard. Soon I hear the sound of splintering wood coming from the workshop. They're wrecking everything in the place. From out on the road come the fainter sounds of men mounting up and riding away, and I guess that the shooter is gone. He's left his lackeys behind to do the dirty work. But the dirtiest job is already done.

It would be easy to slip out through the garden and into the woods while the men are searching the workshop, but I can't do it. I can't leave my father. Instead, I say a hasty prayer and I creep out from my hiding place. In a flash, I circle back around to the front of the house, moving as quietly as I can, and let myself in by the front door.

By the time I reach my father, he's already dead. He's still partially upright, held in place by his hand, still transfixed by the arrow in the table. His head is bent, so that if I didn't know better, he could still be crouching by the fire, not so different from when I left him this afternoon. I crawl into his lap, and bury my face against his stomach, but his free hand is limp. He'll never reach up and ruffle my hair again.

I feel completely empty, and completely alone. My father is no longer here; wherever he is, I can't reach him. All I feel is a sickening sensation, like sand is grating through my veins instead of blood. I taste sand filling my mouth. It fills my eyes and my ears, pours out of my mouth. The side of my body nearest the fire is unbearably hot; we're dangerously close to the flames, but I don't move. The painful heat feels perversely right. I know the men out in the workshop might come back at any moment, but I don't move. What does it matter? Let them find me here with my father. Let them kill me right here, in his arms. I can still hear them out in the workshop, overturning his carefully arranged tools, breaking his beautiful creations. With a stab, I wonder which crack is the sound of that little bow breaking, the one I saw in my father's hands this morning. It's the thought of that lovely thing, its body lying broken, violated by his murderer's hands, that finally starts tears flowing from my eyes.

But I don't want to cry. It seems so inadequate. So I squeeze my eyes tightly shut, and against my eyelids I see my father's hands lovingly stroking the little bow again. That's when the obvious hits me: the bow was for me. Why didn't I realize it earlier? Of course, my father must have known about Jules's bow all along. It was probably even meant to be the final surprise of the day (what a bitter irony!), almost a promise that things weren't about to change. How unfair it is that I never really knew my father until today. How cruel that our happiest day should be our very last.

The sand flooding my veins pumps into my stomach, filling me up, weighing me down, pulling me under. I know I haven't got the strength to get up again. I sink down a little further into my father's lap, almost willing the men to return. What can the men be doing out there for so long? Surely they must come back; surely they intend to search some more. I imagine them coming back and finding me. I imagine the slit of a blade, opening me up, letting all the sand pour out over the floor, putting me out of my misery.

I don't know if I really would have waited there, unmoving, for certain death. I'd like to think that I would have, but I'll never know. Because as I'm lying there clutching my father and willing the men back, something flashes in the firelight, catching my eye. It's lying on the floor, not far from my father's outstretched hand, as though he was holding it when he died and it rolled out onto the floor when his hand relaxed in death. It seems to be dancing in the firelight, trying to get my attention. I recognize it immediately. It's his St. Sebastian medal. The string he wore it on is gone, but I can clearly see the small, raised image of the saint. The light from the fire playing over the little body makes it look alive, as though the saint is writhing in his final torment. A wave of nausea washes over me; I try to block out the arrow piercing my father's heart that I can see out of the corner of my eye.

I have no idea how his medal got onto the floor, but it can't be pure chance. I make fun of Brother Benedict and his signs, yet this can't be a coincidence. My father was holding this when he died, I'm sure of it. Staring at the medal dancing in the firelight, I see again the look on my father's face as he was dying, his eyes boring into mine, trying to tell me something. His words to me in the chapel this afternoon, his intensity about this very medal, come back to me: *"Do you believe it, Marieke?"* With startling clarity, I suddenly know what he was talking about. Somehow, he already knew it, there in the chapel. He knew he was going to die. When he was talking about surviving a mortal wound, he wasn't talking about himself. He was talking about me. And I know what I've got to do.

I've got to survive.

I snatch up the medal, even though it's burning hot. The searing heat in the palm of my hand is galvanizing, as though it's radiating strength and purpose into my body. There's no time to think — I hear the men coming back. All I can do is smooth my father's hair and give him a final kiss on the forehead before darting out the door. I don't dare to stop to take anything with me. Perhaps I can come back later for Jules's bow, but right now I need to get as far away as possible, which won't be easy.

The night is dark and cold. I'm vulnerable out in the open, but little light penetrates the woods, since it's a night with no moon. At least I don't have to think too hard about which direction to take, since there's only one place for me to go: the abbey. It isn't far, but it will be slow going in the dark. It takes me a while to find the path, though I've followed it hundreds of times, and I stumble and thrash so much trying to follow it in the darkness that I'm whipped painfully by branches and brambles. I have to feel my way along, and once or twice I'm convinced I'm hopelessly lost. I'm practically on top of the buildings before I see with relief the familiar stone spires looming out of the darkness. My next move is obvious, too — so obvious, I know I can't stay at the abbey long. If anyone is serious about finding me, this will be the first place to look. But the shooter's men didn't seem too diligent, so I'm betting no one will look for me here tonight. I make my way straight around to the brewery.

It should be empty at this time of night, but I pause at the doorway and listen for a minute before going in, just in case Benedict is testing again. I have to tell myself not to be disappointed when all I hear is silence. How comforting it would be to hear Benedict's familiar, rattling snore, to be able to run to him and tell him everything! What a comfort it would be to pass all my troubles off to him. But I know I can't. No one makes better beer, and I'd trust Benedict with my soul any day, but I don't think there's anything the old monk can do about my worldly problems. Something tells me my father's killers aren't very worried about eternal damnation. Besides, I don't want to endanger my friends.

I push the door open and creep into the room, making my way carefully between the casks of ale. The odor of ale and hops is even stronger and danker now than it was this afternoon, but the familiar smell is so strangely comforting that I feel tears prick my eyes again. In the far corner of the room is a small loft where Benedict leaves his bales to dry. I feel my way up the narrow wooden ladder, and I collapse at the top onto a makeshift bed of hops. I take a deep breath and let the smell surround me as I drift into an exhausted sleep, as though I'm enfolded in Brother Benedict's warm embrace.

I AWAKE WITH A START AT FIRST LIGHT. FOR A MINUTE I'm back in the garden, groggy and disoriented, vaguely uneasy. Then it all comes back to me in a rush, and I'm sick. My body heaves, but I haven't eaten since yesterday in the square, and there's nothing for me to bring up. With a stab of fear, I remember that men are looking for me, and I scramble up and peer down from the loft, but the brewery is quiet. Outside, morning birds are singing, and dust motes swirl peacefully in the slender rays of light coming in from between the slats of a shutter high on the wall. I feel queasy as I make my way down the ladder on unsteady legs, angry at the cool, quiet morning. I want fire and brimstone, hail and tempests, to match my mood. There shouldn't be any beauty left in the world, with my father dead.

I brush myself off and pick some stray stalks of hops that are prickling me from my tunic, and I try to quell the churning in my stomach. I'm sore, starving, scared, and I have no idea what to do next. In need of inspiration, I pull out the token that spurred me to action so effectively last night. In the cold light of day, the little medal just looks like a cheap piece of tin, not some mystical beacon from my father. The banner above the saint even seems to mock me. I can't read it, but I remember what it says: *Arrows won't kill me.* I close my eyes as the sound of a bowstring rips through my memory, followed by the sickening thud as the arrow rips through my father's throat in a flash that brings a flood of bile up into my mouth. *Arrows won't kill me.* What a joke. Of course they will. This medal never helped my father, and it won't help me now. It doesn't contain anything of him. I'm all alone.

Still, I can't take my eyes off the figure in the center. I rub my finger slowly over the raised image, feeling every contour. My mind's a blank; I'm at a complete loss. What did I accomplish by coming here? I gained one night, but what of today? And the next day? I can't stay here, and there's nowhere for me to go. I run my finger back over the saint. The roughness of it feels good against my fingertip. I should have stayed and died in my father's arms, I think. I close my eyes, letting myself imagine it, letting hopelessness overwhelm me, while my fingers keep moving over the little body of the saint in a ritualistic motion that's oddly consoling. Snatches of conversation from last night wash over me in a jumble, the cold voice pouring out like water from an icy well: *"what a tragedy," "Jan Verbeke, fletcher extraordinaire," "Someone should have put you out of your misery a long time ago,"* then my father's voice, *"my son is dead,"* then the cold voice again, *"there's a daughter."* My eyes fly open, and I look down at the medal again. *Do you believe it, Marieke?* Suddenly, I do. I've got a plan. A half-formed, wild, improbable plan, but a plan. It's better than nothing.

I've got to be quick. The abbey comes to life early, and I need to be finished and gone before the monks are dismissed from morning prayers. I know where Brother Benedict keeps his tools, on a bench against the wall behind the cooker, and I find what I need. It's a knife, a small scythe, really, used for trimming barley stalks. It's well-used, but the blade is sharp enough. As I pick it up, I whisper,

"You were right, Father. This wound is fatal. It's time for Marieke to die." Then I raise the blade, and shear off a large hunk of my hair.

The first cut is hardest; the blade isn't as sharp as I thought or hair is tougher than it looks, so I end up having to saw it off painfully, and I can't see what I'm doing. I'm sweating by the time

I'm done, but eventually I've got a halo of long brown hair splayed around at my feet. My head feels strange, light, as though someone's been pulling it back for years and has suddenly let go. I put up my hands to feel it all around. It's bristly and uneven, but I'm sure I've gotten it all. That's all that matters.

Next I quickly undo the soft fabric belt around my waist, and I slip Jules's tunic off over my head. Then I rebind my sash, not at my waist, but high and tight around my naked chest, painfully flattening out the modest curves of my breasts. I put the tunic back on, and hunt around among Benedict's things until I find a length of string. It's thick and coarse, but it will have to do. I slip the medal onto the string and tie it around my neck, then tuck it down inside the tunic. Then I gather up the discarded hair and shove it into the cooker, under the wood, where it will burn the next time it's lit. It will make an awful stench, but maybe it won't be noticed over the other smells of the brewery.

There's a trough of water against the far wall, and before I leave, I survey the results of my handiwork on the reflected surface of the water. *Not bad*, I think. It's unflattering just how little it took to transform me. I hardly recognize myself, and I was already wearing Jules's clothes anyway. I doubt anyone will look past them. And if I'm not very attractive as a boy, well, I wasn't very attractive as a girl, either, and for once my scars just might prove useful. At least, if they'll help me pass myself off as one of the delinquent ruffians who roam the streets of town, then I have to be glad of them.

I debate leaving a sign for Benedict, one that would tell him I was alive, but I don't dare. Someone else might find it first. I've half-turned to go when I notice Father Abelard's ruined page on the ground. I'd forgotten it was tucked into my belt when I undressed. I can't leave it here. As I pick up the fold of paper, the blonde woman winks up at me in all her beauty. On a whim, I bring the paper to my lips and kiss her briefly for luck before slipping it down into the binding around my breast.

CHAPTER FIVE

I know exactly where I'm going when I leave the abbey. If anyone had told me yesterday I'd be heading back to Louvain again, I'd have said he was crazy. But I'm the crazy one, because from here on, I don't have a plan. I have no idea what I'll do when I get there, but I know where I've got to go. I have to hope that the medal will guide me. I've made my decision to trust it. It was an easy decision: I haven't got much of a choice.

The trip takes me much longer today. Physically, I'm a wreck: weak from hunger, and bone cold and sore from a night in Benedict's loft, but my mental state is worse. I alternate between anxiety and emptiness, plagued by lurid flashes of memory so vivid that I'm sure I'm beginning to hallucinate. Every rustle of leaves is my father's killers, hot on my trail; every snap of a twig — *crack!* — is the shot of a bowstring. The soft breeze is my father's hand stroking my hair, the gurgling of the stream the blood welling up from the wound in his neck. The worst thing is that I'm so alone. If I had someone to talk to, to tell me what is real, even to tell me that the horrible thing last night really happened, it would be better. But I'm trapped inside my mind, and I can feel my grip on reality slipping away. It doesn't help that as I cross out into the rolling farmland, the sun is climbing in a sky that's impossibly high and blue. The morning is so crisp and clear, the rich smell of earth preparing to send forth its new crop is so sweet it's painful — one of those rare mornings in early spring that's so full of life.

I don't dare take the main road. I don't want anyone to see me, to remember a disfigured boy coming from this direction, so I stick to the woods and fields. I try to keep the road in sight, but once or twice I get turned around and lose time having to backtrack to find it again. In the freshly ploughed fields the ground is rough and uneven, so soon my ankles and legs begin to ache from stumbling over the unbroken clods of earth concealed in fresh grass along the margins of the furrows, or from tripping over roots as I force a path through the forest. By the time I finally push through the branches of a hawthorn thicket to see the walls of Louvain rising before me, my hands are scratched and bleeding and the sun is high in the sky.

Once I come across the wall, I follow it around to find a way into town. I would probably be safe using the gate — I doubt anyone would bother much about a peasant boy with no goods to sell, but I'm not sure. The wall stretches for a long way away from Porte Charleroi on this side of town, and following it isn't easy. The wall-builders have tried to maximize the efficacy of the wall by following the natural contours of the land, to the degree that a flat place like Louvain *has* contours, to make the approach more difficult. I barely have strength left, but I'm forced to scramble along the rocky slopes of the gullies and ravines that the wall follows, and thrash through the thick underbrush that's grown up against it. In the end, I don't make it all the way to one of the gaps. The wall isn't really one wall; it's a connected string of walls built in sections by different crews of townspeople using a hodge-podge of materials and methods, and when I find a poorly constructed stretch that's already beginning to crumble, I just climb over it.

I land in someone's yard. A few straggly-looking chickens are pecking in the dust and I have to be careful not to step down onto some pigs lying in the shade of the wall, but otherwise thankfully nobody's about. The pigs barely look up, their snouts twitching and trotters shivering with flies, but I reach down and pat one, thinking of our own animals with a pang, wondering what's going to happen to them. The thought that they might all die too before anyone finds them upsets me, but I'll have to trust that Bellows will turn up sooner or later and help himself to them. It's the first time I've been thankful for Bellows' freeloading habits. I guess there's a reason for everything.

As I pick my way out of the yard and onto the street beyond, I'm also glad my trips to town have been so infrequent. A face like mine is hard to forget. Even so, I'm petrified I'll run into someone who recognizes me, but who would that be? The Fourniers, maybe. I wonder what they would make of my transformation.

Now that I'm in town, I feel horribly exposed, naked, even. I must stick out. It must be clear I don't belong here, that I'm an outsider, a *girl*. I keep expecting someone to see through me, though nobody pays me much attention. It's high noon and things are relatively quiet in Louvain at this hour, but there are still plenty of people on the streets, going about the usual business of town: women lean out of windows to pour down buckets of foul water, young boys drive flocks in from morning pasture, and men chase pickpockets or gossip as they head home for the midday meal. After being alone in the fields, the noise is deafening and disorienting. Wandering aimlessly through the crowded streets, the clattering of metal and hooves and the din of voices ringing out around me, I'm dangerously dizzy. The unwashed stench of the city mingling with the smells of food — cooking meat, spices, stale ale and warm bread — makes my empty stomach roil. Louvain is much bigger than I'd realized, too. I'm in a part of town I don't recognize. I've only been on a few of the main streets with my father, never in the maze of smaller streets and alleys I find myself in now. Out here they aren't laid out in any pattern, not one I can figure out, anyway, and I go around in circles before I find my way to the canal that leads me back to the Charleroi road and through the center of town. Just when I think I can't go another step, I see my goal: St. Sebastian's. I've made it.

The big wooden doors under the archway stand closed, just as they did yesterday. Standing before them, I remember how easily they swung open for my father. It won't be that easy for me. I can't just go in, and I don't know what to do now. I haven't thought past just getting here. I stand in front of the doors, the unseasonably hot noonday sun beating down on me, dazed, unsure. I stand there so long, I can almost watch the sun rising higher and hotter in the sky. *Ten, twenty*, the minutes tick by. I don't know how long I wait, but nothing happens. The doors don't miraculously open. Nobody's about. There's nothing at this end of town but the guild, and everyone who belongs there is shut tight inside at this hour. Beyond the great wooden doors, there's nothing but the dusty Charleroi road, leading out of town and into the woods beyond. To the right, the exposition grounds lie deserted and empty. To the left, there's nothing but a dirty little alley, running along under the shade of a few trees that lean out from a garden concealed behind the guild wall.

It's the shade that first attracts my attention. Then I notice a small door further down along the wall, half in shadow. Behind the door, on the other side of the wall, a slanting roof covered in red tiles rises to a small spire. The door must lead into an interior garden directly adjacent to the little guild chapel where I waited for my father yesterday. I hear the echo of my father's voice — *"open to the public."* For the first time since I knelt in that very chapel by my father's side, I feel something like hope. It's a sign. Coming here was the right thing to do. There is sanctuary for me here, after all.

But when I try the door, it's locked. I rattle the handle in disbelief, but it doesn't budge. Deflated, I slump down onto the ground, my hand still on the iron knocker. I don't bother to pull it away. I rest my head awkwardly on some empty wooden crates stacked up against the wall by the door, and finally let my mind go blank, and drift into unconsciousness. It's almost a relief, to let it all go. There was no miraculous answer for me here, after all. I won't be the first corpse to be found rotting in an alley in Louvain.

I don't know how long I've been there, lost in a stupor of fatigue, hunger, and disappointment, but the sun is still high overhead when I come to my senses enough to be aware of voices on the other side of the wall. The voices are young and male; they're laughing and joking, loud, robust voices, happy and full of life — everything I'm not. And they're coming this way. I know I should get up, get away before they approach, but I just can't summon the will to do it. What does it matter, anyway? So I'm still there, half sitting and half lying against the crates, when a group of five or six boys comes out of the door into the alley beside me. The motion of the door opening inward jerks my arm off the knocker and pulls me partway across the threshold, so I fall directly into their path.

"Royce was really after you today, Falko. How'd you manage to get him so worked up?" one of them is saying.

"Ah, that was nothing. He was still fuming after that stunt of *yours*, Ari. One more like that, and he'll make good on his threat to pass you off to Baylen for sure."

"Scoff now, but you'll be trying something like it soon enough. You'll never get noticed without a few tricks up your sleeve."

A new voice cuts in:

"Hot air, Aristide. 'Fess up; it was a distraction, to hide the fact that you couldn't drop down on a clout the size of a wagon wheel at 350 paces if your life depended on it!"

Then others:

"Don't worry, Ari. Picture dropping down on the bottom of a pint of ale, and you'll find your mark, all right."

"Or try imagining you're aiming at the space between Gilles's eyes!"

"Or better yet, the space between Rosalinde's legs!"

"Nah, that's one mark he'll never find!"

They're all talking at once as they spill through the doorway. Their nonsensical words don't mean anything to me, but I catch the word *mark*, and it registers in the back of my mind that these must be the Journeys. Who else could it be? Still I don't bother to look up, or even try to get out of their way. What a thrill this would have been yesterday, but today I don't even care. They can't help me.

Then one trips right over me.

"Oof! What the devil …!?" he cries, as the others push on past him, laughing. The sharp point of a boot jabs me painfully in the side.

"Hey, you! What do you think you're doing there?" The boy's righted himself and turned on me. A few of the boys behind him stop, too, but those ahead continue to drift on down the alley, uninterested.

He gives me another deliberate kick.

My head lolls back and I gasp, in surprise at his cruelty as much as in pain. A tall, thin boy dressed in outlandishly elegant garb is standing over me. Lace drips from his cuffs, and he's wearing an embroidered jerkin over his tunic that looks like pure silk. It's fastened not with ties, but *buttons*, of all things. He should be ridiculous, but he has the arrogance to carry it off, and the evidence of his wealth is a threat in itself. He's not as handsome as the others, but his good looks and his athletic physique speak of privilege and power, and the whole effect is strangely impressive. Long, wavy hair frames a thin face dominated by a pointy, aristocratic nose that would look at home on a weasel. I blink my eyes a few times, trying to wake up my brain enough to process this strange sight, but needless to say, I mostly notice the smooth, hard-polished boots.

The weasel-faced boy leans down closer, his nose wrinkled in disgust.

"Another one! You there — you can't be here. How many times do we have to run you lot off? Get out of here. Get up. Get up!"

"Leave him alone, Aristide," a large boy behind him says, putting an arm on weasel-face's shoulder. "It's just a kid. Come on." The boy tries to lead him away, but Aristide shrugs him off.

"Just a kid. I'm tired of tripping over the trash out here. You chase one off, and two more come back." He leans a little closer to me. "No loitering here, GET UP!"

Another boy a few paces ahead, impatient to catch up with the others, cuts in:

"Come on Aristide. Jurian and Taran aren't waiting."

"Yeah, come on, Aristide," says the large boy again, slinging his arm back around his shoulder. "Leave him alone, he's not worth it. Let Albrecht chase him off. Look, I don't think the poor sod's all there."

"Drunk's more like it," Aristide replies wryly, giving a pull at his sleeves and smoothing down his jerkin, like a rooster smoothing his feathers. It's a signal that he's saved face enough to let it drop. He's about to let himself be led off to catch up with the others, when he turns back as an afterthought, and says very deliberately,

"You'll be gone by the time we're back, if you know what's good for you. And don't let me catch you here again." He drives home his point by delivering another swift jab with his foot that catches me right in the stomach.

I vomit quietly onto the toe of his beautifully polished boot.

There's a roar of laughter from the other boys. Even the ones who haven't waited and are further down the street stop and turn to see what's going on, as an angry flush floods Aristide's cheeks.

"Shake it off, man! Literally, shake it off!" someone calls back, then another: "This just isn't your day, Aristide! First disaster on the butts, now on the boots!" Then the big one is saying, "Easy, Aristide!" as I'm lifted up off the ground by the front of my tunic in one swift, powerful move. Weasel-face is surprisingly strong. He must be all sinew under his fancy clothes.

"To hell with Albrecht!" Aristide thunders. "I'm going to take this trash out myself!"

As I wait for the inevitable beating, I think with almost bemused detachment, *so these are the Journeys*. This bunch of fops, thugs, and bullies. After all I've been through to get to St. Sebastian's, it's just to be beaten to a pulp by the new incarnation of my father's old friends. My disillusionment is complete.

"Hey, hold up, Aristide! Wait a minute —" There's a sharp tug at the back of my neck. My father's St. Sebastian's medal has shaken free, and it's dangling down the front of my tunic. One of the boys has noticed it, and he's now tugging on the string.

"Where did you get this?" he demands, as Aristide tries to shove him aside with his shoulder.

"Get out of my way, Falko! You'll get your turn."

"No, stop, Aristide! Look at this, will you? He's got a medal," Falko insists.

A voice from down the street calls back, "What in damnation is going on back there? Are you guys coming or not? Come on or be left behind."

By now Aristide has stopped shaking me and he's taking a good look at the medal. A grin spreads across his face as he gives me a calculating look.

"Hey, Taran!" he calls out loudly. "Come back here a minute. I've got something for you."

"Come on, Ari," a voice drifts back, impatient. "I'm not in the mood. I'm not hanging around this alley until curfew."

"Trust me, you're going to want to see this. The kid's got a medal."

I can't see the boys down the path, but I hear some hesitant shuffling, like they're deciding if it's worth their effort to come back, if this joke of Aristide's is worth their time. They must decide to humor him, because before long I hear them coming back. Soon they're all crowding around me, with Aristide still holding me up in their midst like a half-empty sack of flour. Then the crowd parts as the other boys make way to let the one Aristide called Taran through. From their attitude, he must be their ringleader, the one to whom they all defer, even weasel-face.

I don't blame them. He's the size of a mountain, easily as big as Luc Fournier. But the similarity ends there. Where Luc was soft and rounded, this Taran is crystal-hard, a solid mass of rock. His features are chiseled stone, jagged crags on a cliff. He looks cruel, like an old Norse god, an Odin or a Tyr, one of those pagan savages willing to cut off his own hand in battle. As he steps up next to Aristide, he towers over me, his face impassive, bored. It looks like an expression he wears often, or rather, a cold lack of expression. But there's something false about that impassive look. There's a hint of something else beneath it. I can't place it, but it's dangerous, and I know enough to be afraid. For the first time this morning, I feel fully awake.

Then he looks down at my medal, and everything changes. It's like witnessing a creature of pure fire cracking out of a casing of ice. The bored look is gone in a flash. His eyes ignite and glow hot with rage. I think absurdly that he looks like a Viking in the grip of a bloodlust, about to plunder a village or disembowel an enemy, and maybe he is. All that's missing is the helmet.

In an instant he's snatched me roughly out of Aristide's hands. He's so big that my feet leave the ground entirely. My toes kick around feebly under me, finding nothing but air. I'm suspended entirely by the front of my tunic balled in his fist and the twine biting deep into the flesh on the back of my neck.

"Where did you get this, you dirty little thief!?!" he roars, his face inches from mine. His expression is so intense, it blots everything out. I must start hallucinating again, as I did out on the road, because for a moment I think he really is a god, awesome and terrible, swooping down and summoning lightning and thunder in his wake. He leans in closer, so close that I can feel the anger radiating from him and his hot breath on my face, and it occurs to me that this would be an excellent time to pass out. I just have time to think that he's the most terrifyingly handsome thing I've ever seen in my life before his massive fist slams into the side of my face.

I'm no stranger to pain. You can't reach the age of fifteen without being able to take some hard knocks. I've had two rotten back teeth ripped from their sockets with nothing to dull the agony but a few swigs of ale, but there's nothing to dull this punch. Even the mule was gentler. The impact throws my head back, smashing it into the wall. My skull is trapped between his fist and the bricks behind, and something's got to give. There's a sickening crack; it must be my head splitting open. A searing pain shoots from one temple to the other and it's almost more than I can endure, but the real pain will come later. Blood gushes out of a fresh gash where his knuckles hit above my left eye, and I taste the tang of iron as it floods down my face and into my mouth. A warm sensation spreads over the base of my skull where the bricks open an answering cut behind.

The sight of my blood only seems to enrage Taran more. He leans into me so that he's pinned me up against the wall with his forearm, and without loosening his grip on my shirt, he starts pulling on the twine around my neck with his other hand, trying to pull off the medal.

"*Where. Did. You. Get. This?*" he repeats deliberately, punctuating each word with a wrenching tug, frustrated that the tough twine won't break. I've lost track of the other boys; for me, the alley's shrunk down to just Taran, but they must be as frozen as I am — whether because they're shocked by the extremity of his reaction, or used to it, I have no idea. But when I remember the shrewd look on Aristide's face, I know he at least knew exactly what he was letting me in for.

"*Give it over, thief!*" Taran rages, shaking me again so that my battered head rattles against the wall, and giving the medal another violent tug. "You'll give it to me, if I have to rip your head off to get it!!"

He lets go of the medal, and I think he's about to grab me by the hair, like he's really going to try to take off my head. I don't doubt he could do it. His oversized shoulders and arms look trained for the task of ripping a grown man limb from limb. But I'm spared finding out by the sound of a new voice drifting down from above. It's a beautiful, lilting voice, tinged with amusement:

"*Tsk, tsk, tsk.* Taken to brawling in the streets now, Taran? Whatever will the masters say!"

At the sound of the voice, Taran starts in surprise. He lets out a grunt of irritation, but his grip slackens, and I slide a few inches down the wall. I'm still pinned, but I can feel some of Taran's intensity drain away as the voice continues:

"To quote from the 'code of conduct of the honorable guild of archers of St. Sebastian' — now do correct me if I get it wrong, I'm sure I've not memorized it quite as carefully as you have, but I believe the gist of it goes something like this: '*I do solemnly swear to use my skill always in defense of the Good, to protect the old and the weak, all women, his Holy Roman Catholic church ...*"

This speech goes on for some time, but I stop listening to the words, letting the sound of them flow over me. I don't know if it's the slightly absurd tone of the voice, so at odds with the scene below and with Taran's fury, or the content of the speech, but Taran's affected, too, like someone's thrown a bucket of ice-water over him. He seems to come to his senses, or at least, as the languid voice drones on, I feel it siphoning off his anger, redirecting what's left of it up to the speaker on the wall. His hand drops from my head, and although he doesn't let me go entirely, his grip on my tunic loosens enough to land me shakily back on my feet. I crane my neck to follow the direction of the look of intense dislike Taran's now casting up over my right shoulder, to get a look at my unexpected deliverer.

A boy of approximately the same age as the others, seventeen or eighteen, is perched lightly on the top of the garden wall. He's resting there so relaxed and easy, he might have been lounging there all morning. But an overhanging tree spreads out behind him, and it's apparent that he clambered up it from the garden on hearing the commotion outside. He's leaning back casually, supporting himself on one arm. One leg is bent and his free arm is resting on it, while the other long leg is stretched out in front of him along the top of the wall. He's dressed more simply than the others, in a white shirt open at the throat and black breeches tucked into black boots. The strong midday sun high overhead behind him silhouettes him against the tree, giving the illusion that he's suspended in its branches. Countless rays of sun stream around him and blend with the whiteness of his shirt, blurring his edges. The light is blinding, dazzling. Or maybe it isn't the sun that's dazzling. The boy seems to glow among the sharp shafts of light that penetrate through his shirt and between his limbs. I can't tell where his smooth, pale skin ends and the light begins; a thick lock of black hair falls across his brow. I blink furiously to clear the stinging blood from my eyes, but this time I'm not hallucinating. It's the young St. Sebastian, gorgeous and radiant, come to life directly out of the painting in the great hall.

"Mind your own business, Tristan!" Taran barks up at the vision on the wall. It's just another Journey, after all. Taran's words tell me so, and his tone tells me that this isn't his first run-in with this boy Tristan, either. But my illusion doesn't fade. St. Sebastian has appeared at last to save me.

"Hmm. At the very least," Tristan continues, ignoring Taran's outburst, "why don't you pick on someone your own size? Although I admit," he pauses, swinging one leg down and making a show of looking Taran up and down, "it might be hard to find one."

He pulls an apple out of a fold in his tunic and takes a bite. "Besides," he muses in the same ironic tone: "isn't the preservation of the precious reputation of our glorious guild precisely my business?" He pauses a moment, as though admiring the effect of his alliteration, before continuing, "More, my *solemn duty*? Or do you, with your overblown sense of decorum, have a monopoly on enforcing the rules — rather selectively, it appears, since you don't seem to think the rules apply to you. Really, Taran. I shouldn't have thought I'd need to give *you* a lecture on honor!"

Tristan's arrival has broken the spell on the other boys, too. They start talking over each other again, pressing back into my line of vision. I can't tell if they're urging Taran to let me go, telling him that it isn't worth it, or egging him on. Some of both, probably.

A blonde boy with delicate features I hadn't noticed before, bolder than the others, steps in close and puts a hand lightly on Taran's back. "Tristan's right, Taran. A Journey caught starting a fight with a commoner is out, period. It isn't worth it."

"Siding with Tristan, Jurian? That's rich." I recognize Aristide's voice, trying to stir Taran up again. He doesn't want to be robbed of his full pint of blood.

"It's not a matter of sides, Ari," Jurian replies. "We're all on the same side here, right? Tristan's just trying to keep us from making a mistake, in his way — you know how he is. This could mean real trouble. I mean, look at the poor chap. He's barely got a face left." I'm startled by this reference to me; the others seem to have forgotten all about me, and I've even forgotten about myself, I'm so absorbed in following the bizarre exchange.

Up on the wall, Tristan takes another bite of apple, then calls down merrily, "That's right, Jurian. That's me — the Good Samaritan, ever vigilant, eager to give my fellow guild *brothers* a little well-intentioned guidance." Then he looks straight at Taran, and dropping his affected tone, says flatly, "Touch that boy again and I'll call out the veterans."

The words have an immediate effect. Beside me, I can feel Taran's cold anger flare up again, but I don't dare look at him. The other boys fall into an uncomfortable silence.

"You make me sick, sitting up there spouting about honor," Taran finally says, his voice carefully controlled, but thick with disgust. His eyes haven't left Tristan since he appeared on the wall. He's quivering with such hatred, it can't just be because Tristan's interrupted his torment of me. In fact, none of this seems to be about me at all. "You, and *honor*. You make the word into something filthy!" he spits. "I'd like to rip it right out of your throat. It's lower than I expected, even from you, to threaten to rat out a member. But you'd do it, wouldn't you?"

"Gladly!" cries Tristan, seemingly delighted. He takes one last bite of his apple and tosses it back over the wall into the garden. In one easy motion, he slides down off the wall onto the stack of crates, then down into the alley, where he wipes his hands deliberately on his breeches.

"So," he says, coming over. I notice that the other boys part nervously to let him through, just as they did for Taran. "It would seem we're at what the philosophers call an impasse. It's your move, old boy."

At this, Taran seems at a loss, as though Tristan's refusal to rise to his bait and his relentlessly irreverent tone have finally worn him out. I wonder if he always runs this hot and cold. He shrugs, and lets go of me with an unceremonious shove. I fall onto the crates at Tristan's feet.

"The boy's a thief, Tristan," he says dispassionately, looking down at me. "He's got a St. Seb's medal. Laugh that off."

Tristan bends down and takes the medal in his hand. On seeing the medal, he darts me a quick look, then squares his shoulders and bends closer, making a show of looking the medal over carefully. As he turns it over in one hand, he puts his other hand lightly on my shoulder and gives it a gentle squeeze. It's a subtle movement, too slight for the others to notice, but I think it's meant to give me courage. He looks relaxed enough, but I can tell he's thinking hard. Then he looks up into my face and studies me for a minute, really seeing me for the first time. His brows are pulled together in a slight frown, like he's trying to make up his mind about something.

"I didn't steal it!" a hoarse voice cries. It takes me a minute to recognize it's mine.

"He talks!" Aristide chimes in behind Tristan, but I stumble on, my dry tongue heavy in my parched mouth and thick with blood:

"I'm not a thief. My father gave it to me." The words come out in a barely audible rasp, and as soon as they're out, I know I've made a mistake. A chorus of derisive snorts rises from the boys behind him, and the corner of Tristan's mouth pulls down in a flash of irritation. He leans down closer to me, raising his eyebrows slightly. I take the hint and shut up.

"Of course he did!" Tristan says smoothly, but there's a tense edge to his voice. "Probably spent more than a month's wages on it, too. Got it up north, I expect. It's a good copy, better than they make around here. Aristide's an idiot, but I'm surprised it fooled you, Taran. Where's it from — Ghent? Flanders? Am I right?" he says, shooting me a warning look that I hope I interpret correctly.

"That's r–r–right," I stutter. "He bought it in, um, Bruges. It's a souvenir. From the guild of St. Sebastian there."

It's a pretty good lie, just good enough that it could be true. Maybe even some of them believe it. But I doubt it. Before anyone can protest, Tristan puts out a hand and lifts me up. I can't support myself, so when I start to fall back again, he slips my arm over his shoulder, taking my weight, and hauls me to my feet.

"Well, that's that!" he exclaims with a laugh, as though it's all been a good joke. "What a lot of a good morning wasted over nothing!" Despite his carefree words, his tone is defiant, challenging the others to call him on the lie, and he's careful to slip the medal back inside my tunic where nobody else can get a look at it.

"Come on," he says to me. "Let's get you cleaned up. Aristide is right about one thing, you can't be here."

Nobody's moved, however. The boys are still standing close in front of us, hesitant, but blocking our way.

"So, what's it going to be?" says Tristan. "It's like Taran said. You going to waste the afternoon in the alley? *Or* —" his tone takes on a hard edge, "are you going to get out of my way?"

As Tristan hauls me down the alley, I can feel the boys watching us go. There's a sensation in the middle of my spine that might come from being hit against the wall, but it feels like the pressure of Taran's eyes burning a target onto my back. "Don't look back," Tristan hisses. He needn't have bothered. I'm not eager to see any of them again. I'm still marveling that they just stood aside and let him carry me through. Maybe they were just ready to be done with me, willing to accept the lie to avoid trouble without losing face. Maybe. But strange as it seems, I have the distinct impression that they're all afraid of Tristan, even more than they are of Taran.

CHAPTER SIX

Out of the towering presence of Taran, Tristan is bigger than I'd thought. He has to stoop to reach his arm down around my waist, and as it is, I'm hitched up onto his hip so that my feet drag along barely skimming the ground. He's already about the same height as my father, and strong; carrying me doesn't seem to be costing him much effort. I realize that all the boys were unusually big for their age. It was just by comparison to Taran that some of them seemed small. I wonder where the guild finds enough food to feed them. They must all eat meat every day.

As we make our way down the alley and the danger begins to recede behind us, I become increasingly aware of Tristan's nearness, since we're in what amounts to an embrace. I barely dared look at him in the alley, but now I work up the courage to cast a shy, surreptitious glance at his profile. His body is bent slightly forward to support my arm slung over his shoulders, so his head is bowed as if in concentration, a shock of black hair falling down over his forehead again, but he's got a little smile of satisfaction on his lips. Behind us I hear the sounds of the other boys finally dispersing, and we're well down the street when Taran's voice rings out:

"There's your proof that Tristan belongs in the gutter, if you needed any, boys. He finds his friends there!"

I tense, wondering how Tristan will react, but when he catches me watching him, he just winks and starts whistling lightly under his breath.

We're making for a corner up ahead, where a street branches off the alley to head through a maze of small houses toward the center of town. I know what's going to happen when we round that corner. Tristan will find a place to set me down, brush me off, and then he'll be on his way, his good deed or prank or whatever he thinks it was done. Involuntarily I clutch at him a little tighter, dreading the moment I'll have to let go. After the intense loneliness of the morning, I don't want to lose the comfort of human contact. The feel of his muscles under the soft linen of his shirt and his masculine smell are already familiar, and I let myself imagine that I'm back in my father's arms. The thought of being alone again, of losing the protection of these arms, is more than I can bear. It's even more painful than Taran's punch.

As we round the corner, Tristan does relax his grip, as he exclaims,

"Looks like we're in the clear, kid." But to my surprise, he shows no sign of letting me go. Instead, when I threaten to fall without his support, he grabs me up again.

"Steady! You're in pretty bad shape, kid, I know." His voice sounds different now, lower and more natural. "But don't give up now. Can you make it a little further?"

I nod.

"Taran packs a mean punch, all right. Your head is going to feel like the devil tomorrow."

"It feels like the devil now!" I say, with feeling.

"He talks!" Tristan laughs, giving a mean impression of Aristide's voice. "Seriously, though, you're lucky Taran just gave you a little tap" — at this, my head screams in protest — "to jog your memory. You don't want to be on the receiving end of a punch if Taran means business."

I get the impression he's talking from experience. He gives me a shrewd look.

"That punch isn't the only thing wrong with you, am I right? Have you had anything to eat today?"

I shake my head.

"I thought not," he says, hitching me back up onto his hip. "Come on, let's get some food into you, and see about stopping up that wound while some of your blood is still in you, and not all over my shirt."

As Tristan steers me through the streets, I try to apologize and to thank him all at once, but he waves off my words with a gesture.

"What's your name, anyway?" he asks. "I can't keep calling you kid."

"It's Mar … *um*, Mar …" Damn! I don't have a name ready.

"Forgotten your name, huh?" he laughs. "Taran knock it right out you?"

"It's Mar–*um* — I mean, it's Marek," I stutter, hoping it sounds like a boy's name.

"Ok, *Marek*." He stretches out the name sarcastically, to let me know he knows it's false. "You from around here? Got any family — a father maybe?" he raises an eyebrow. "Or is he on another pilgrimage to Flanders?"

"It was Bruges," I correct, laughing for the first time since I saw the first arrow hit my father. Incredibly, I haven't thought of what happened to my father since I woke up in the alley, but now it all comes back. All of a sudden, I see the arrow ripping through his flesh, and flinch.

"Easy now." Tristan grips me harder, attributing my attack to pain. "It's not much further."

When I respond, it's to his previous question. This one is easy — no need to lie. "No, there's nobody. I've got nobody left."

Tristan laughs, but before I can bristle at this unexpected cruelty, he says bitterly, "Then we've got something in common, kid. Neither do I."

We make our way through the town in silence. The effort of dragging me begins to take its toll on Tristan, and I haven't any more taste for conversation. As we come into a more populated part of town, we get some curious looks, but nobody bothers us. Finally we emerge from the warren of alleyways onto a larger street, one that follows the main canal. I can smell the tinny scent of its stagnant water even before we come out into the brightness of the open thoroughfare.

"Just a few more paces and you've made it, Marek." Tristan nods up the street, in the direction of a large, two-story building of whitewashed bricks opposite the canal. Along the street front, the building is perforated by wide openings, like oversized windows. Over them, large wooden panels swung upward and propped up on long poles form an awning, and planks set down into the bottom of the windows serve as counters that face both inside and out. A handful of old men are seated at the counters, some others at rickety wooden tables set up along the street in the awning's shade. A crudely carved wooden sign hangs over the open doorway, emblazoned with the profile of a massive goat with one great, curving horn. The goat is rearing up on its back legs, its tongue lolls out, and its one visible eye rolls back wildly in its head.

"I recognize this place," I say in surprise. "It's the Drunken Goat."

"The most aptly named tavern in town," Tristan confirms. "The name pretty well describes most of the clientele."

"My father doesn't let me come here," I blurt out, before I remember that I'm not supposed to have a father, but Tristan just laughs and doesn't call me on it.

"There's a first time for everything" is all he says, as he ushers me in.

Actually, I was here once, a long time ago, with my father and Jules. It's just a typical tavern and inn, with one long dining room below and a few rooms opening off an interior second story above. But when I asked why all of the customers in the tavern were men but all the rooms above appeared to be occupied by women, my father never brought me back again.

Inside, Tristan guides me to one of the long wooden tables that stretch the length of the room. He sits down on the bench opposite me, leaning back to rest up against one of the posts the thickness of a tree trunk that support the timbers of the ceiling. At the far end of the room, a massive cooking pot stands in a stone fireplace, but no fire is lit at this time of day. It's mostly for show, anyway; a low door in the back, half hidden under a wooden stairway, leads to kitchens and a kitchen courtyard beyond. Above the door, the stairway leads up to an interior balcony which looks down over the main room and gives access to the rooms of the second story.

At the sound of our entrance, a young girl hastens out of this door and bustles over to hover behind Tristan, all the while casting him shy glances and waiting nervously for him to notice her. I get the impression she knows him; she hasn't even bothered to look my way. I suspect this is not Tristan's first visit to the Drunken Goat.

Sure enough, without turning to look at her, Tristan raises his eyebrows and says,

"You're in luck, Marek." The slightly stagey voice he used on the top of the wall is back. He's slipping into character again. "Those dainty footsteps could only belong to Roxanne." He turns, and in a gallant gesture, takes the girl's hand lightly in his. The girl blushes fiercely, but it's hard to tell. She's about my age and might have been pretty, except for the livid red birthmark that covers one side of her face. I hate myself for wincing at the sight, but it isn't just the ugly puckering of the skin around the edges of the mark that makes me flinch, it's that it's like looking in a mirror. She's a distorted reflection of myself, the ghost of the recently deceased Marieke.

"The daintiest hands in Louvain," Tristan is continuing, bringing her hand up and planting just the trace of a kiss on her fingertips. "You could hope for no gentler a ministering angel. Be a love, Roxanne, and see what you can do about cleaning up my friend Marek here. And bring us something to eat."

Up to now, the girl's understandably had eyes only for Tristan. She's obviously crazy about him. But now she notices me, and with a little gasp at the profusion of blood on my face and clothes she rushes off obediently to fetch the food and supplies.

While we wait for the girl to come back, I press the bottom of my tunic against the cut over my eye to stop the flow of blood, and Tristan leans back again, folding his arms behind his head to contemplate me. After a while, he says, almost to himself:

"What am I going to do with you, Marek?"

I shrug. It's the same question I want to ask him.

"How old are you?"

"I don't know," I say miserably, and it's the truth — yet another thing I didn't think through. I have no idea how old I look.

"Hmm. No sign of a beard yet, pretty small. About twelve, thirteen? Sound about right?"

I just shrug. Tristan watches me a bit longer, pensive. I wonder what's he's thinking. He sits there studying me dispassionately for so long that I start to get uncomfortable, then annoyed. I stare back at him.

Some of the glow that surrounded him up on the wall is gone now. In my delirium this morning, everything was exaggerated. Taran probably wasn't even that big. But even so, Tristan is beautiful. That wasn't an illusion. And he knows how to turn on the charm. His flirtation with the serving girl was skillful. Nothing was overdone. He was teasing, but kind. I can't imagine any of those boys back in the alley noticing a girl like her, except to abuse her. I particularly noticed that he didn't insult her by calling her beautiful. But it bothers me, anyway. Partly because I know that's all it was, charitable flirting — a girl like that, like I used to be, would never seriously interest someone like Tristan. And partly, because I'm jealous.

The girl comes back with two bowls of porridge, a basin, and strips of cloth. Straddling the bench, she sits down next to me and starts to wipe the blood from my brow. I wince in pain, but the girl is careful and gentle. She does have unusually small, beautiful hands. Irrationally, it bothers me even more that Tristan's compliments were sincere.

She's just finished cleaning the wound and is in the process of binding a length of cloth around my head when there's a commotion at the door, and two more improbable young men burst in. More Journeys, of course — I can't believe I only saw my first Journey yesterday. Louvain is positively bursting with them.

For a horrible moment, I even think it's Aristide again, as a tall, elegant boy about his size scans the room. Then he catches sight of us and hurries over, the other boy trailing in his wake.

"By the Saint, Tristan! When you didn't show up back at the guild, Jerome and I thought we'd find you here."

The boy I took for Aristide leans up against the post beside Tristan with an exaggerated air of relief. On second glance, the boy looks very little like Aristide, though I can be excused the mistake. There's a definite similarity. I wouldn't have thought it possible, but this boy is even more flamboyant, so much so that he almost looks like a parody of Aristide. Or rather, Aristide now looks like a pale imitation of this boy.

He's wearing thigh-high black and red leather boots over tights of pure red silk, and a long tight-fitting jerkin of red and black striped silk that's cinched in at the waist so that it ruffles out below. Under the jerkin, a red silk shirt drips with white lace at the cuffs and sports an oversized flounce at the neck. His head is bare, to let a thick mane of wavy auburn hair that any woman would envy tumble down onto his shoulders. Jewels wink from a big ring on his finger and on the hilt of a dagger tucked into his belt. Topping off this sumptuous attire is an aristocratic face with a great aquiline beak of a nose. Somehow, it all works on him, and I have to resist the urge to bow. He could be the young prince himself, for all I know. Now I can see what Aristide was aiming for. What Aristide tried to pull off with arrogance, this boy carries naturally, with grace and charm, and something else: a look of unimpeachable nobility. But what strikes me most isn't the outrageous clothes, it's his voice. When he speaks, he draws out each impeccably accented word in an exaggerated drawl just short of a lisp. I can't believe I thought Tristan's voice was affected. This boy takes affectation to a whole new level.

"The barracks is full of it!" he exclaims. "Pascal got the whole story from Remy, who's in a positive state — you know how *he* is."

"Don't work *yourself* into a state, Gilles," Tristan replies, as the other boy Jerome plops down onto the bench next to him and chimes in:

"We came along as soon as we heard."

He's an unlikely companion for a peacock like Gilles. His broad, open face is framed by a mop of brown curls, and he's dressed simply in a brown shirt and trousers. In fact, he's so normal-looking that I might have doubted he was a Journey, except for the lute slung over his shoulders and the brown felt hat topped with a feather on his head, as though he fancies himself one of Robin Hood's companions. A Will Scarlett, maybe. I half expect him to whip out the lute and compose an extemporaneous ballad about Tristan's exploits. I have to suppress a laugh at the absurd rightness of these two as Tristan's friends. I don't think I can take meeting any more Journeys — each one is more inconceivable than the last. I wonder if I'm still asleep in Benedict's loft, dreaming.

"Who's Pascal?" I put in, feeling hopelessly lost. With a staged start, Gilles pretends to notice me for the first time.

"Gads, Tristan. Is this what you fished out of the alley? Don't tell me you've still got it with you. Whatever are you going to do with it?"

"That's just what I've been trying to figure out."

"Pascal is Gilles's boy," Jerome says, turning to answer me. "They've been together since they were kids."

"Positively worships me," Gilles sniffs. "A dear boy, but so diligent! He seems to think I need an entourage, even to the lavatory."

"How'd you duck him this time?" Tristan grins.

"Sent him off to my tailor's, as usual. It's costing me a fortune in shirts, but it's worth it for a little freedom. But look here, Tristan. Don't change the subject. Be serious, will you. Word is, Taran's furious. Thinks you made him look like a fool."

"He is a fool."

"Gilles is right, Tristan," Jerome says. "You've got to stop antagonizing him."

"Boys, boys, wherever are our manners?" Tristan replies, pointedly ignoring Jerome. "Gilles, Jerome, this is *Marek*," he stretches out the name again, like it's our joke. "Marek, may I present Gilles Lejeune —"

"That would be, the future Marquis de Chartrain, to you," interjects Jerome, laughing and bowing slightly at Gilles.

"… and Jerome Crecelle," Tristan continues, "who is …"

"At your service!" Jerome finishes for him, pulling off his hat with a flourish. Then he pretends to fish around in it for something. "Unfortunately, I seem to have misplaced my title."

"Must have left it in your other hat," Gilles says wryly, before turning back to Tristan with a frown. "All right, Tristan. Have it your way, but be careful."

"Lighten up, Gilles. Taran's harmless." At this, Gilles and Jerome exchange a glance over Tristan's head. The cut over my eye throbs in protest. Gilles makes a show of plucking an invisible speck of dust off his immaculate sleeve, as he asks quietly:

"Did you really threaten to have him disciplined?"

Tristan meets this comment with silence, looking for all the world like a sullen little boy. Then he brushes it off:

"The problem with Taran is, he's got no imagination."

"Enough to land you an arrow in the back one of these days, if you're not careful."

"Nah. That's not his style. When Taran finally goes for me, it'll be with a shot right through the eye. Besides, his exaggerated sense of duty will keep him in line."

"Seems to me," Gilles says carefully, plucking at his sleeve again, "that's exactly what nearly got young Marek here killed in the alley this morning. I hope you know what you're doing."

"No, I don't like it, Gilles," Jerome puts in, shaking his head. "He's got that look. We haven't heard the worst of it yet, I reckon. Just what are you cooking up, Tristan?"

But Tristan isn't paying attention to them. He's leaning forward on his elbows, studying me curiously. Finally he asks,

"Can you shoot?" The question is so unexpected that I answer honestly without thinking.

"A little, but I'm not very good. I'm not very strong."

"Tristan, steady …" Jerome warns, apparently catching the drift of Tristan's thinking, but Tristan puts up a hand to silence him.

"What about bows. Know anything about 'em?"

"Enough," I say, then I can't resist blurting out, "I can fletch my own arrows." The look of surprise on their faces is gratifying.

"That settles it!" Tristan cries, delighted. "Boys, meet my new squire."

Jerome lets out a low whistle, then the three of them all start talking heatedly at once. They seem to have forgotten I'm there, until I say stupidly,

"Squire?"

"Yeah, you know," Tristan laughs. "Servant, dogsbody — you take care of my equipment, fetch my arrows, carry the quiver, basically do whatever I tell you to and follow me around town, making me look good. Give me an entourage to the lavatory," he nods at Gilles, "that sort of thing."

"I know what a squire is," I say.

"And the best part — you get to call me *master!*"

"Your squire," I repeat dumbly. "At St. Sebastian's."

"Of course at St. Sebastian's." He gives me a shrewd look. "Don't tell me you don't know all about it."

I blush, remembering the look on Tristan's face when he saw my father's medal.

Gilles, who has recovered his composure during this exchange, says quietly,

"My dear boy, do you really think that's a good idea?"

"It's brilliant." Tristan beams. "More than brilliant — it's perfect. I'm in need of a squire, and one magically appears."

"What about the one on his way from L'île. From your, uh, *sponsor*, remember?" Gilles asks dryly.

"I'll simply send him back, with my compliments. Journeys choose their own squires, that's the rule. I'm within my rights."

"It's not going to be that simple, Tristan," Gilles insists. "Even if you can pull it off, it's not going to win you any friends."

"I'm not there to make friends."

"Fine, Tristan. But promise me something. Will you at least stop trying to make enemies?"

"Can't you just picture Taran's face when he hears about it?" Tristan sounds gleeful, but I notice that nobody's asked me what I think of the plan. I *do* picture Taran's face, with the look of rage on it right before he punched me. I'm in no hurry to see that look again.

"Isn't that a flaw in your plan right there?" Gilles insists. "Journeys can choose any *acceptable* squire, that's true. But, and do pardon me, dear boy," he says apologetically, glancing at me, "no insult intended, but a thief isn't likely to pass muster."

"Taran's sure to object," Jerome agrees.

"I'm not a thief!" I cry, but nobody's listening to me.

"That's the beauty of it! Taran can't object, without explaining how he knows he's a thief. And he can't do that, without explaining why he didn't bring him before the masters himself this morning. And he can't do *that*," Tristan finishes with a satisfied flourish, "without admitting that he broke the rules by taking a pop at him in the first place. He can't touch Marek now. I tell you, it's perfect."

"I don't like it, Tristan." Jerome is shaking his head. "Forcing Marek down Taran's throat like that. It could be dangerous."

Tristan looks at me expectantly. "Well, it's for him to decide, isn't it? What's it going to be, kid? Do you want to go back to the gutter, or are you coming with me?"

I hang my head. The idea is ludicrous. Me, at St. Sebastian's? A girl, at the guild? And among all those boys? At the thought of facing Taran and Aristide again, my stomach clenches. I don't relish being a joke, either, or waved like a red flag in front of a bull. But when he puts it like that, the answer's so obvious, I don't even bother to reply.

Jerome and Gilles argue with Tristan for a while longer, but when they're unable to dissuade him, they eventually depart, wanting to get in another practice session before supper. At least, that's what they say. I suspect they simply don't want to be around when Tristan takes me back to St. Sebastian's with him.

At some point during our debate, Roxanne's slipped off unnoticed, too, and I have a pang of conscience that I didn't thank her for cleaning me up. Gilles and Jerome never even acknowledged her, and after his initial attentiveness, even Tristan seemed to forget all about her. I haven't even been a boy for an entire day, and I'm already just like them: brawling and taking women for granted. How easy it is to slip into entitlement! I resolve that if I'm going to pretend to be male, I'm going to be a better man than the rest of them, and to make a point of thanking Roxanne if I ever see her again.

Now that we're alone again, Tristan visibly relaxes. His whole demeanor is different when nobody else is around. It's like he's acting all the time, even with his friends. It must be exhausting for them, playing the Journey.

He's quiet for a long time before leaning back and sighing, "I hope you've been telling me the truth, Marek."

"I'm *not* a thief!" I insist, wondering how many times I'm going to have to say it, and if this is even what he means.

"All right. I believe you. But if this is going to work, we're going to have to trust each other. For my part, I want to be clear. I *do* need a squire, and I do genuinely want to help you. That's not a lie. But I won't pretend that scoring off Taran, among others, doesn't sweeten the deal. And Jerome was right. I can handle Taran, but … it could be dangerous for you."

I nod, oddly touched by this speech.

"Now, for your part, are you going to tell me where you really got that medal? We both know your father didn't buy it. You can't buy a medal like that. We both know it's the real deal."

I don't know what to say. I want to tell him the truth, all of it, but I can't. I can't bring myself to lie to him, either, not when he sounds so sincere, so I settle for repeating: "I didn't steal it."

"Ok, Marek. But you'd better give me that medal for the time being, or at least, stop flashing it around. You'll have a hot time explaining how you got your hands on a veteran's medal. Those are damned hard to come by, and somewhere, there's a veteran out there who'll be wanting it back. If Taran had kept his head and turned you in, it would have meant a lashing, or worse. Men have lost a hand for less. St. Sebastian's punishes its own."

"You mean, it's a Journeyman's medal," I say, genuinely confused.

"No," Tristan says, shaking his head in disbelief, like he's amused that out of all his warnings, this is the comment I pick out to focus on. "It's an easy mistake to make, they're very similar. But look."

He slips his own medal off from around his neck. All the Journeys must wear them like that, just like my father did. He hands it over to me, and I recognize it right away. It looks just like the one my father showed me in the chapel. I slip the cord from around my neck, and hold my father's medal out next to it.

"Yes. It's exactly the same ..." I start, but then I really look at the medal for the first time since I picked it up off the floor next to my father's body. It's very similar to the one Tristan has in his hands, but it's not the same. The figures of the saint are identical, but on the medal in my hand, the banner is above the saint's head, and on Tristan's medal, it's below his feet. I close my eyes and concentrate, trying to call up the memory of the medal in the chapel with my father. Sure enough, I remember my father pointing to the banner, below the saint's feet. Tristan is right. I stare down at my hand in amazement. What I'm holding in my hand isn't my father's medal at all.

I sit gaping at the medal, as different images of it flash through my mind and tumble together: the medal in my father's hand, in the chapel; the medal dancing in the firelight by his body; my fingers rubbing the medal in the brewery at the abbey; the medal in

Taran's hand, as he tried to wrench it from my neck. How can this not be his?

Then snatches of my father's conversation last night come back to me, and I stare down at the medal in disbelief, as everything falls into place: the undelivered broadheads, my father's sudden change of mood after visiting the guild, even my initial impression that my father was talking with an old friend. I hear the twang of the bowstring, and remember the precise placement of the arrows. Why didn't I notice it before? My father was killed by an expert archer, one with a sick sense of humor, sick enough to get pleasure out of recreating St. Sebastian's torment. There's only one possible explanation. The medal I've got in my hand didn't belong to my father. It belonged to his killer. A killer, who was also a member of St. Sebastian's.

"So, Marek. What's it going to be?" Tristan asks me, taking my silent agitation for indecision.

Intense anger at St. Sebastian's floods over me — at my father's death, at my beating this morning, at the deceptive medal, and even at Tristan for not leaving me to die in the alley. It's impossible. A girl at St. Sebastian's. It means breaking all the codes of the guild, an institution I was raised to respect above all others. It means sacrilege, even, and it's dangerous. If I get caught, I'll surely be killed.

Before I can change my mind, I square my shoulders and say defiantly, "I'm in."

As I follow Tristan through the afternoon shadows and along the narrow streets back toward the guild, I turn the traitorous medal over in my hand, uncertain now whether it's friend or foe. *Did it lead me to a beating by Taran, or salvation by Tristan?* I wonder. Only one thing is certain: for good or for ill, it's leading me back to St. Sebastian's again, and I've got to follow it. But it'll be a relief to hand it over into Tristan's keeping, to hand everything over to him. Under my breath, I echo Gilles's words, unsure whether I'm talking to Tristan or to myself:

"I hope you know what you're doing."

CHAPTER SEVEN

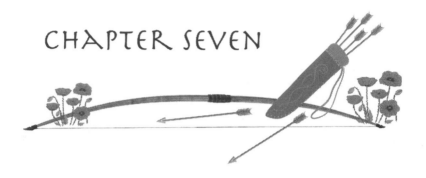

F or the second time that day, I find myself standing outside the great wooden doors of St. Sebastian's. I have a moment's panic when we enter the vestibule and the same supercilious boy is seated behind the desk who was there yesterday, but he barely looks up long enough to say, "You're late again, Tristan. Baylen's looking for you."

"Tell him I've got to see the master," Tristan calls over his shoulder, as he heads through a side door and into a dark, cramped corridor. The boy calls after him, "deliver your own messages, duBois!" But Tristan's already gone, and I have to hurry to keep up with his long strides as he weaves his way through the inner warrens of the guild. As he goes, he gestures off to the right and left and keeps up a running commentary in a tour that goes by so quickly I can't absorb any details.

"That's the kitchen, and beyond, the servants' quarters," he says as we pass the open doorway of a large, busy room with good smells emanating from it. "I'll be sending you here sometimes, but stay out of it otherwise, if you can. And be careful about flirting with the girls. It's strictly forbidden, and old Marta runs a tight ship. She'll be on you if she catches you. Anything serious, and you're out, so watch yourself."

I wonder what he'd say if he knew I'd be more tempted to goose one of the Journeys than a scullery maid, but I reply: "I wouldn't think of fooling around with a serving girl."

"Well, we'll have to fix that!" he laughs back, then points toward an arched doorway straight ahead.

"That way's the squires' barracks. You'll be in there, with the other boys. They're a pretty decent lot, but they're likely to give a new boy a bit of a hassle. Stick with Pascal in the beginning, and you'll be fine."

I hadn't thought about the living arrangements, so this comes as an unpleasant shock, but I don't have time to think about what it's really going to mean before he's already moving on. He turns a corner into a larger corridor and swings open one of a series of identical doors that open onto it.

"Journeys have their own rooms," he says, ushering me in. "It's not much, but it's home."

The room is small and stark, with no decoration. It's an interior room with no windows, so it's very dark. If I've followed the layout of the place correctly, the squires' barracks must be located right behind the back wall. All that's in the room is a cot, a small wooden bedside table, and a cedar chest, but these few items so fill the space that there's barely room for both of us to fit inside, and as it is, I have to push up against Tristan to give him room to swing the door shut. As Tristan fumbles to light an oil lamp on the table, I wonder what we're doing in here.

As if in answer, Tristan turns to me, and to my amazement he pulls his tunic off over his head in one easy motion and starts wiping his naked torso with it. All of a sudden my tongue feels thick, and I can't seem to catch my breath. All the air's been sucked out of the room, which seems to have shrunk down around us. A thin sheen of sweat flickers in the lamplight on his lean body, and as he takes a step toward me, for a wild moment I think he's about to take me in his arms. But he simply pushes past me and reaches into the chest, oblivious to my confusion. I lick my lips and put my hand against the wall, trying to compose myself, as he says, "Can't take you to the master with a bloody shirt." He takes two fresh tunics out of the chest, but it's not until he tosses one at me and it hits me in the face that the full force of what he's saying hits me.

"Here. Try that. It'll be big, but it's clean, and it'll have to do for now."

He expects me to change into it right here in front of him. And why not?

"I can't."

It takes me a minute to get the words out. What an idiot I've been! Not having a name ready, that was a mistake. Not having any idea how old I was supposed to be, that was another one. But this is so basic, there's no excuse. I can't believe it didn't occur to me before. How did I think I was going to pose as a boy, to live in a boys' barracks, of all places, if I can't undress in front of the other boys? What did I expect? Private dressing rooms? How did I expect to find myself in close quarters with half-naked men, without giving myself away? Tristan's only taken off his shirt, and I've come completely undone. My face is hotter than the lamp's flame. I'm salivating like a dog, and my hands are twitching. I have to clench my fists to keep them from reaching up to touch the places on his body where the arrows penetrate the flesh of his twin in the painting in the great hall. It's pathetic. Worst of all, how can I explain my refusal, after what Tristan's done for me? There's nothing I can say that can adequately explain such irrational behavior.

"What's the matter, Marek?" Tristan asks, misinterpreting my queasy look. Thinking I'm in pain again, he reaches out, concerned.

"Are you hurt somewhere else, too? Here, let me help you." He starts to lift my tunic up himself, and I have to snatch it out his hands.

"No! Don't!" I cry, cheeks flaming at his look of surprise. "It's not that. I can do it. I mean, I *can* do it. But — I *can't*." I drop my hands and hang my head, and add wretchedly, "I won't."

We're both silent for a moment, then Tristan puts his hand lightly up to my face and touches the place where my old scar stands out as a white welt.

"You poor kid. Was it an accident?" he asks, his voice infinitely gentle, and I get it. He thinks I'm disfigured under my clothes, too. I nod dumbly, hating myself for lying to him, even by omission, and even more, for letting him pity me.

"It can't be that bad," he says gently. "Whatever it is, I'm sure I've seen worse." He puts his hand down and takes the bottom of my tunic in his hand again, as if to lift it, but this time I wrench away from him violently.

"Don't! Don't. I just ... can't. You don't understand!" I stammer, searching for words to explain without explaining. "If I have to undress in front of anyone ... I can't do it. I'm sorry, this was a mistake." The word comes out in a sob. "I can't do it." I try to push past him, tears starting to fall down my cheeks, but Tristan puts his hands on my shoulders to stop me. He looks genuinely distraught. I can tell he's imagining something gruesome — full body burns, a goring by a boar, a brutal mutilation, even, of the kind that might explain my softness and feminine features. I've even heard that sometimes, the punishment for thievery is castration. I feel sick at the thought that Tristan might still believe I stole the medal, and that he might think I've been dismembered for a similar crime in the past. I want to tell him it isn't what he's thinking, but how can I? It has to be something. I can't tell him the truth.

He runs one hand through his hair in a motion that's half frustration, half concern. The motion sends a ripple through the muscles of his chest in the flickering light, and this time, I don't try to look away. I drink in the sight of him, since it will be my last chance. It's all over now. At least I'll have this image to take away with me. Looking at him, warm and alive, I wonder how I could ever have thought a flat canvas was sensual.

On his upper arm, not far below the shoulder, he has a small, well-defined welt about an inch and a half long in the shape of a single arrow. I know the mark; it's a Journeyman's brand. It's nothing official, but the Journeys have a tradition of branding each other with the mark as a part of their celebration after the Journeyman competition, and the guild doesn't discourage it. I was fascinated by my father's brand when I was little, even before I knew what it meant. Sometimes, he used to let me trace the smooth, raised flesh with my finger. I stare at Tristan's scar now, only inches from my face, and my fingers itch to reach out and touch it.

"Okay, kid," he says finally, with a sigh of resignation. "Have it your way. It's a complication, all right. But if it's really that bad, I guess I can't blame you. You'll have to change in here. It's not regulation, but not strictly against the rules, as far as I know.

Nobody'll bother you in here. I'll see to it. And I'll put the word out with the boys in the barracks. If anyone gives you any trouble, they'll have to answer to me." I remember the impression I had in the alley that the others were afraid of him; these aren't empty words. I still can't quite process what he's saying. Yet again, Tristan is miraculously sweeping away the barriers from my path. "You can wash in the Journey lavatory, too, if you're careful," he continues, thinking aloud. "Just don't let the others catch you. I don't have to warn you to watch out for Taran, but he's not the only one who won't like finding you in there. Better yet, use the veterans' — less traffic, and maybe I can find a way to square it with Royce. But you'll have to take care of the rest." He gives me an expectant look, and I assume he means relieving myself. I don't have any idea what this will involve, but I'm so grateful I know I'll do whatever it takes.

Tristan drapes the clean tunic over my shoulder, and wipes a tear from my cheek. "That's settled then, kid?" he asks. When I don't answer, he turns to go, to let me change in privacy. Before I can stop myself, I step into him and hug him fiercely, burrowing my face against his naked chest.

He reaches down and ruffles my hair, just like my father used to do. Before he lets me go, he whispers into my hair, "Okay, little brother."

WHO AM I KIDDING? I'M WALKING THROUGH THE MIDDLE of the squires' barracks, trailing Gilles's squire Pascal. From the moment I stepped into the room, a dozen pairs of eyes have been on me. Some are hostile, but most are just openly curious. Though the big room has a high ceiling and there's a draft coming in from under the rafters, the air is thick and heavy with the unpleasant smells of juvenile boys. The place is packed with them, and crawling with the ubiquitous dogs that seem to roam freely about the guild. Some of the boys are lying or sitting on the cots that are the dominant feature of the room, arranged in two neat lines against the wall. The heads of the beds are pushed up against the wall, so as to leave a wide aisle down the center of the room between the rows, and it's down this aisle that we're making our way now. As we pass, the boys on the cots sit up to watch us, or get up to follow us like a procession. Other boys stand gossiping in groups or gaming with dice on the floor between the cots, but they've all stopped whatever they were doing to stare at me, making no effort at subtlety.

From the looks of them, they're all at least a few years younger than I am. That may not seem like much, but with the differences between girls and boys, I feel much older than they are. With their scrawny bodies and pudgy faces, they look painfully young to me, too young even to be away from their mothers. But they've likely been on their own a lot longer than I have, so despite their age, they're probably a pretty tough lot. Tougher than I am, anyway. I feel a little bit like I'm in a twisted version of an old fairytale, a mangled princess in disguise trapped in a cottage full of malevolent dwarfs. There's a vulnerability under their toughness, though, that's unsettling; they look like they're trying to imitate the cocky confidence of the Journeys, but without much success. Having to try to fit in with them is going to be an unpleasant necessity, yet another thing I didn't anticipate. The reality of living at St. Sebastian's is going to mean spending much more of my time in close quarters with a bunch of flatulent, pimply twelve-year-olds than with gleaming, half-naked Adonises. Frankly, I'm not sure which is going to be harder to take.

It was just a few moments ago that Tristan dropped me off here without so much as a backward glance. He said he needed to talk to the masters alone, then he'd be back to present me to them once he'd smoothed the way. In the meantime, why didn't I start settling in with the boys in the barracks? He didn't seem concerned, but I got the impression that putting me over as his new squire wasn't going to be quite as easy as he was letting on, so I was happy enough to be left out of the initial interview, but I didn't relish being thrown in with the other squires quite so soon. After all the mistakes I'd already made, I wanted some time to prepare, but that wasn't to happen.

When Tristan led me in, the boys momentarily straightened up to attention, as I was to learn that they always did on those rare occasions when a Journey was in the barracks. With one motion, Tristan both waved them back at ease and beckoned to a tall, serious-looking boy who I rightly assumed was Pascal. When he'd hurried over, Tristan pulled him aside and engaged him in a low but intense conversation that excluded me and left me nothing to do but stand there awkwardly, exposed to the blunt stares of the other boys. Tristan's back was to me, but from the parade of expressions that crossed Pascal's face and his curt nods, I got the impression that Tristan was telling him some pretty interesting things about me — whether they were some new lies of Tristan's or the implied lies of my own, I don't know — and instructing him to look out for me. Then, with a quick pat on my back he was gone, and I found myself unexpectedly adrift in St. Sebastian's without him. I felt bereft as I watched Tristan's back receding down the corridor, leaving me with only Pascal for protection.

As I stumble along now behind Pascal, I start picking at my fingers again — a bit of the old Marieke resurfacing. I try to ignore the stares and fight down nervousness, but there are just so many of them! One for each of the twelve Journeys, obviously, but it feels like twice as many, with so many sets of eyes trained on me. Normally, it wouldn't occur to me to be afraid of a twelve-year-old boy, but *twelve* of them — I'm not so sure. At the very least, I'll never be able to keep them all straight, let alone match them up with the appropriate Journey — and I haven't even met all of *them* yet, either. And, needless to say, my first encounter with the Journeys wasn't particularly auspicious. It wasn't exactly the ideal way to introduce myself at the guild, and it's clear everybody here's heard about my beating in the alley. Gilles said as much, and the looks I'm getting confirm it. So do the murmurs and snickers that began as soon as Tristan left the room.

"Your bunk is down at the end, on the left," Pascal tells me in his brisk, businesslike voice as we pick our way over sleeping dogs and discarded boots. He seems older than the other squires, closer in age to the Journeys, and frankly, he seems older and more mature than Gilles. In fact, he seems to be almost the polar opposite of his master, and I wonder if this is the norm. I'd just assumed that the squires would try to mimic their masters, that I'd be able to match them up that way, but maybe a good squire complements rather than copies his master. That seems to be the case with Pascal, anyway. I can picture him reining in Gilles's extravagances with his cool efficiency, and for my part, if I have to brave this place without Tristan, I'm glad to have someone as competent as Pascal looking out for me. The only similarity I can see between Pascal and Gilles is that Pascal is also extremely well-dressed, much more so than the other squires, and as we walk along, he plucks at his cuff in a preening motion that copies exactly the one I saw Gilles execute a number of times at the Drunken Goat.

We're half-way across the room when a foot shoots out in front of me, catching me right in the shin and causing me to fall forward heavily onto the floor. My palms sting as I put out my hands to break my fall, but the kick wasn't really intended to hurt me. It was just some joker tripping me up, and the chorus of snickers turns into open peals of laughter at my pratfall. I'm caught off guard, and being made a laughing stock by these little punks is more than I can take. I'm just about to lose it, when instead of getting angry, I start to laugh, too. It's such a juvenile version of my attack this morning. *Really, is that the best they can do?* I think, as I sit there laughing like an idiot — laughing with them, at them, at myself, and at the utter absurdity of it all. Just like that, my nervousness is gone. And in that moment, I start to belong.

By now most of the boys have begun trailing us, and a few of them reach down to help Pascal get me to my feet. They must like a boy who can take a joke.

"This one's you," Pascal says, coming to a stop in front of a bunk. "That's yours, too." He points to a small table against the wall at the head of the bed, adding "for your stuff," even though he can see I don't have any belongings. Still laughing, I drop down onto the cot, having to push aside a particularly foul-looking dog to do so, and the other boys all crowd around expectantly. I guess not much goes on around here, so the arrival of a new squire is entertainment. They're probably hoping for my version of the fight this morning, too. But they seem to be waiting for something.

Mine isn't the last cot in the row. Behind me, a few more identical beds stand empty. They're fitted out with the same thin, straw-filled mattresses, and at the foot of each one, a single coarse, neatly folded woolen blanket signals that these are unoccupied, too. But in front of me, the bunk opposite is occupied, and its owner is perched cross-legged on the bed facing me. It's almost like I've been marched down here to be presented to him, from the way he's been sitting there waiting for me and the way the others press around now, to see what's going to happen.

"Uh, Marek, right?" says Pascal, making the introductions. "This is Remy. Remy, Marek." The other boys crowd in a bit closer as I put out my hand to the strange little boy.

The name's familiar. I remember Gilles or Jerome mentioning a Remy in the tavern, but I can't remember what they said, exactly. Something about a Remy being upset? But the boy across from me looks perfectly fine, so maybe I'm mistaken. He's very young, and so delicate his wrists look like twigs. His face is like a doll's, too, with huge blue eyes that bug out above a tiny red mouth. I half expect pointy ears to peak out from under the black curls of his hair, he looks so much like an elf. In fact, with a face like that, it's hard to image him ever looking anything but cheerful. But his face does look strained as he takes my hand and starts pumping it vigorously up and down. The brightness in his voice is forced, too, as he exclaims,

"Marek! Welcome! I can already tell, we are going to be the best of friends!"

"Er, um …" I say, trying to figure out the right response to this effusiveness, but Remy sweeps on, his little body bobbing up and down along with my hand:

"It's been so lonely down here, with nothing but empty cots. There's nothing more depressing than waking to a neatly folded blanket beside you, is there? But now you're come, and it's all going to be all right, isn't it?"

"I, um …" I say, still at a loss.

"And then all the unpleasantness this morning," he pushes on, not waiting for a response. "It's been very upsetting, I won't deny it. *I've* been upset." His chin wobbles for a moment, "But it's all going to be all right now, I'm sure."

I look around at the other boys for some hint of explanation, but everyone is intent on Remy, waiting to see what he's going to say.

"It's all been a big misunderstanding. A *misunderstanding*. Don't you worry, it'll all come right. Nobody's going to blame *you*, Marek."

His words have all come out in a rush, and now he falls silent. I guess he means, nobody's going to blame me for nearly getting myself killed in the alley, but he seems so earnest, and to be taking it so personally, that I resist making a sarcastic remark. Besides, I should be grateful. He seems to be saying, in a round-about way, that he's willing to believe that I'm not a thief, and for some reason, I can tell that the others have been waiting to take their cue from him. I'll never figure this place out. He looks like any of the others could knock him over with one finger.

"But, you know," he continues, putting a hand up to rub his temple as a shadow of concern clouds his face, "it is such a headache when our boys are squabbling." By 'boys,' I guess he means the Journeys. "We must put on a brave face," he says, brightening again. "They're under so much pressure, poor things! There's nothing for it, but to wait it out. They're all such good friends, really. It'll all blow over soon, you'll see. It always does."

"Good, then," Pascal breaks in, with an air of relief. "You'll be all right here, then, Marek? I'll leave you to settle in with Remy. I've got errands to attend to."

As Pascal hurries off, most of the other boys start to move away, too, after one of them says in apparent disappointment, "Nothing to see here after all, boys." From their attitude, I wonder if they expected this little elf to try to punch me, too. Or at least to give them permission to do it. Instead, I seem to have passed some kind of test.

Remy is now looking at me expectantly, but I'm not sure how to respond to his strange little speech. I can't believe anyone could be so delusional about the Journeys. All a bunch of friends. Right.

So I change the subject, and ask something I've been wondering about but haven't liked to ask.

"So, uh, Remy, just why is this bunk free?"

"Empty bunks are always moved to the end of the room, so we can stick to the middle. It's warmer if we're all closer together," Remy replies chirpily.

"Right. Only that's not what I meant. I mean, why doesn't Tristan have a squire? Don't all the Journeys have them?" I clarify.

"Sure." It's one of the other boys who answers, sitting down so close next to me he's almost on top of me. I can tell there's going to be no concept of personal space in the barracks. He's a husky boy with bright red hair and a lopsided grin. One side of his face is covered with fading bruises, and he has the hint of a black eye. I doubt he's bathed his week, either.

"I'm Auguste," he says, giving me an elbow in the ribs in lieu of a handshake. "I go with Jerome. Skinny here," he nods toward a boy standing behind Remy, "he's Benoit. He goes with Anselm, but don't bother about him — they'll be out by first rounds, so don't waste your time with them!" Benoit sticks out his tongue as Auguste continues, "And handsome here," he nods at a particularly ugly boy who's plopped down on my other side, "he's Rennie." I let this all wash over me. I'll have to sort them all out later.

"Glad to know you," I say with a gesture that takes in all of them, then I try to get Auguste back on track. "You were going to tell me about Tristan's squire?"

"He did have one, of course," Auguste replies, "Up until a few days ago."

"What happened to him?"

The boys exchange an uncomfortable glance. Auguste clears his throat before answering.

"Tristan shot him in the foot."

"What?!" I sputter, taken aback.

"Yeah, right past the ankle and down through the top, behind the toes!" laughs Rennie.

"But he was lucky," continues Auguste. "An inch to the right, and it would have got him in the Achilles tendon."

"As it was, it wasn't too bad," adds Benoit. "He'd have healed up just fine, but he'd had enough. Master Guillaume had to send him back to Tristan's sponsor."

"What happened?" I don't know what dismays me more, the thought of the boy's wound, or that Tristan might not be a very good archer after all. For some reason, I'd just assumed his shooting matched his looks.

"Well, the boy was pretty pathetic," Auguste says, as though that explains it. "*Slackjaw*, that's what Tristan called him."

"*Slackjaw, hurry up!*" Rennie says with a laugh, mimicking Tristan's voice.

"Slackjaw, more water!" chimes in Benoit, in the same mimicking voice.

"Anyway, he was always screwing up, getting foul of Tristan's shots," continues Auguste. "One day, he hadn't cleared the course when the signal for the next flight went up, and Tristan shot him."

"But it was an accident, right?" The uncomfortable memory of one of my father's stories rises up in the back of my mind, about a Journey who shot his lazy squire on purpose. The boys start talking over each other:

"So Tristan says. But it was a damned lucky shot."

"Nobody could prove it wasn't an accident, but I don't think Tristan cares if anyone believes it."

"Gets a kick out of flaunting it, more like."

Through all of this, Remy has been conspicuously silent. He hasn't said a thing about Tristan.

"Surely it was an accident!" I insist.

"Once, maybe, sure," says Auguste. "But it wasn't the first time."

"What?!"

"Yeah. He got his previous squire with the exact same shot!" Rennie crows happily. "Twice in a row — that's some beautiful shooting. You've got to admire it."

"So, Marek," laughs Benoit. "A word of advice. Better be quick out there."

"And watch your back!" At this, I'm almost knocked off my cot by a sharp blow right in the middle of my back, and for a panicky moment I think I'm being attacked again, that the squires are going to try to finish the job their masters started in the alley. Then I realize that Auguste has simply give me a jovial slap on the back. Boys. Trying to be one would be easier if the things they did were logical. They seem to enjoy hitting each other way too much.

"Just how many squires has Tristan had?" I ask, recovering my composure, but not really sure I want to know the answer.

"He's been through a fair few, considering it's only been a few months," Auguste concedes, not really answering my question. "But don't worry... he doesn't always shoot them."

"The first one was the best, remember?" Benoit says wickedly, looking around at the others for confirmation. "When Tristan first got here, Marek, he had a real prissy git, sent with him for the competition from L'île. He was always putting on airs, refusing to run errands. Tristan couldn't stand him!"

"So Tristan started shooting at the rats that go for the straw out around the targets," says Auguste, taking up the tale with relish. "Then he'd make the poor kid retrieve them and clean off the arrows. Tristan was relentless! It finally broke him down, and he ran off. The masters were furious!"

"But Tristan's careful." It's Remy, breaking his silence in a tone that makes me think he's cagier than he's let on. "There's nothing they can do, but keep sending to his sponsor for a new one. I think, he's made a game of it."

Pretty soon, the boys begin to wander off, leaving me to contemplate this sordid story. I throw myself back onto my cot in exhaustion, not wanting to think about any of it anymore. I've hit the saturation point, and all I want to do is sleep. Tristan will be back soon enough, to take me to the masters, and my trials will start all over again. So for now, I try to let my mind go blank. This six-by-two cot is going to be my new home, so I might as well start getting used to it.

The barracks has started to empty out, as some of the squires are sent for to run errands or to attend their masters, but Remy is still sitting cross-legged on his cot, watching me, as I drift off into sleep. As I'm nodding off, I mumble,

"So, Remy, what about you? Who do you belong to?"

"Do you mean, which Journey?" he asks, his head cocked to one side.

"Yeah — who's your master?"

"Why, Taran, of course," he replies, like it's the most obvious thing in the world, and I guess it is.

CHAPTER EIGHT

I t must be hours later when a hand on my shoulder shakes me awake. I'm in the kitchen garden, having a disturbing dream, something about the painting of St. Sebastian. I struggle to open my eyes, as my father leans over me, gently calling my name.

"Did I fall asleep, Papa?" I ask groggily, reaching up to rub the sleep from my eyes, trying to stop the strange pounding in my head. My hand touches something rough, unfamiliar, and it's blocking my vision. The blurred image of my father leans in closer.

"Wake up, Marek." It's Tristan, and the thing around my head is a bandage. It wasn't a dream. I'm lying on the hard cot in the squires' barracks, and the cut over my eye is throbbing so hard it feels like it's shaking my whole body.

"I'd like to let you sleep until morning, kid, but it's time to take you to the Master."

Tristan helps me sit up enough to perch shakily on the edge of the bed. I steady myself there for a while, as my head pounds a steady rhythm, first a crashing boom behind my eye, then an echoing beat on the back of my head. My tongue feels two sizes too big for my mouth. Tristan's brought me some food and a flask of ale, but all I can manage at first are some small sips.

"Eat up, Marek. You'll need your strength for tomorrow. And — this is the last time I'll be serving you, so enjoy it."

After I've choked down what I can of the meal, I find myself following Tristan down dark corridors again. The place seems deserted. It's already late evening, and everyone else must still be at mess. Even the dogs have abandoned the hallways to pack into the great hall and lurk under the long tables where the men take their common meals. I can hear the sounds of talking and dining emanating from an arched doorway leading into the hall, and from the sound of it, they're well into the meal and the ale is flowing freely. We head in the opposite direction, toward the back of the guild where the masters' offices are to be found, near the workshops and the outlying buildings where much of the real business of the guild takes place.

At St. Sebastian's, it's normal to address all members of higher rank as 'master,' as a form of courtesy. But as a true rank, *master* is the highest in residence at the guild, and there are always only three masters of St. Sebastian's, one for each of the three original founders. In theory, all share equal status, but oversee a different aspect of the guild. Master Gheeraert is in charge of the business side and of the certifications, Master Leon is in charge of training. But Master Guillaume oversees all details of the daily running of the guild, and he's really ultimately in charge. When Tristan says 'master,' he has to mean Guillaume.

"Ordinarily," Tristan explains as we go, "you'd have been sworn in with the other squires in a ceremony in the great hall. Given the circumstances, Guilly's cut his dinner short to give you an audience tonight, so you'll be able start in first thing in the morning. Then I'll present you formally to the members tomorrow night."

Great. Another thing to look forward to. When I don't reply, Tristan adds, "Don't worry. You'll be fine. It's all *pro forma*. Just say as little as possible. Master'll want to get it over quickly, as he's likely to be in a foul mood. He usually likes to linger over his port."

"How did your interview go?" I ask, broaching the subject for the first time. Tristan is in front of me, so I can't see his face, but he squares his shoulders in a motion of determination that belies the cheerfulness in his voice when he replies, "There was a terrible row! But it's all settled now."

We come to a stop in front of a door that doesn't look any different from the others. Tristan raises his hand to knock, but before he does, he pauses and says over his shoulder matter-of-factly, as though he's telling me to wipe my boots, "You'll have to have a surname. Just make something up, nobody's going to ask questions. Just nothing too fancy." Before I can reply, we're going inside.

Master Guillaume's office isn't as big or opulent as I expect, but I'm intimidated anyway. Everyone in Louvain knows Master Guillaume by reputation, the best archer of his day, and the youngest master ever appointed at St. Sebastian's. As Tristan ushers me in, the austerity of the room is more intimidating than a show of wealth and power would have been. The man himself radiates power; he doesn't need any trappings. As we enter, he's seated behind a massive wooden desk that fills the center of the room, a powerfully built man with a somber expression. There's no decoration in the room, except for wood paneling carved with simple geometric patterns that covers the walls and ceilings. A single candle is burning on the desk, illuminating his face and casting long shadows across his features. In the wan light, the dark wood of the room resembles a cave whose walls recede into shadow, so that the master's face seems to float disembodied in the center of the room, its features exaggerated and distorted by the lamplight. I can't imagine having the nerve to have a 'terrible row' with this man. Needless to say, he doesn't look very pleased to see us. I doubt it's just because he's missing his port, either.

I feel queasy, too. My legs are shaking, and it's not only because I'm nervous. The candlelight dancing over the flesh of the master's face takes me back to last night, and I'm seeing again my father's body, slumped in the firelight. It seems so much like I'm back in my own house, back in that room, that when Guillaume speaks, his voice pours over me like ice, and for a minute, I imagine it's the terrible cold voice of my father's killer drifting back to me through the kitchen wall. *Twang!* I hear the bowstring echoing again, and Tristan has to grasp me by the arm to keep me from lurching forward.

"Steady," he hisses in my ear, and the moment passes.

"This him?" Guillaume asks, his voice not really like the killer's at all. I've got to pull myself together. "He's not much to look at. He'd better be up to it."

Not waiting for a response, the master lays his hands flat on the table, a look on his face that makes me think he's going to object, to refuse to swear me in. I wouldn't blame him. Then a trace of a smile crosses his face, like he's finally gotten a joke. He throws his head back and laughs, and I can't tell whether he's fond of Tristan, or hates him.

"If this is the way it's going to be, then let's get it done. Kneel," he commands, rising to his feet, "and face Master duBois." Since there's nobody else in the room, I figure that this must be Tristan, so I get on my knees before him, and Tristan places both hands on my bowed head. Then Tristan takes me through the squire's oath, stating each phrase slowly and pausing for me to repeat it. I can't remember all the things I swear, but predictably there's a lot of stuff about honoring the guild. I'm glad it's dark, since I can feel myself blushing in shame at all the lies I'm telling already, or rather, just one lie, really. But it's a big one. It's enough.

And so I'm sworn in to St. Sebastian's as Marek Vervloet. The name means essentially the same thing as Verbeke, so I can remember it — not too fancy, as Tristan said. Besides, it seems fitting: Vervloet, *of the brook*, to accompany duBois, *of the woods*. A matched set of pseudonyms.

I'm glad, though, not to be doing this in the great hall, with the shadow of the tormented saint looming down over me on the wall. There would have been some comfort in being anonymous, just one in the group of other squires, but I'm glad the rent body of the saint isn't here to witness me being foresworn in his name. But as it is, alone in this dark office, in the light of a single flame, it feels less like an oath than a confession. It's the first oath I swear to Tristan. I hope it will be the last one that's a lie.

MY FIRST DAY AS TRISTAN'S SQUIRE IS PREDICTABLY THE hardest. I'm at a distinct disadvantage. Some of the boys have been squires for a long time, and many have been in service to their Journeys even before coming to St. Sebastian's. Even those who were newly paired with their masters for the Journeyman competition have by now had plenty of time to learn the ropes. What the other squires have had weeks or months to learn, I've got to master in a single day; I've got to get up to speed on the daily routine and the rules of the place, and I've got to sort everybody out — at least enough to know whom to avoid.

As it turns out, getting onto the routine is the easiest part, since there are really only a few fixed points in the day. I'm pretty surprised how unstructured things are at first, but Pascal explains that too much structure isn't needed, since the threat of the competitions keeps the boys in line. They don't need anyone to tell them to practice.

I learn the hard way that there's no official morning meal. The kitchen staff puts out food on a sideboard near the great hall, and the squires usually just grab something to take to the grounds with them to share with their masters during warm-up out on the field, but nobody thinks to tell me about this. Depending on when they rise, the boys are given a half-hour or so to practice on their own, before the main event of the day: a long morning drill session, which is mandatory. That first day, morning practice seems interminable to me, and by the end, even Tristan is dragging — he's not used to having to do it on an empty stomach.

But it's not the routine, or the stress of sorting out the Journeys, that makes the first day so hard. It's the actual work of being a squire. It's physically exhausting. I suppose I thought it would be easy, just standing around holding a quiver. Instead it's real work, and I find to my disgust that even the youngest boys are all much stronger than I am, and in much better shape. By the end of morning drill, I'm not sure I'm going to make it.

The day begins with Pascal waking me at what feels like the crack of dawn, although compared with the routine I subsequently adopt, it's positively late. He's tucking a fresh shirt into his breeches when I look up, eyes blurry. Tristan was right. Starting today, I'm the servant, and I'm on my own. No more being awoken to a meal at the side of my cot. I don't have time to change, even if I had anything to change into, or anywhere to change. Before I know it, Pascal is bustling me out of the empty barracks, down the Journey corridor, past the archives and out through the stables. He's come back for me; all the other squires are already on the butts.

The butts is the term for the section of the practice range where the Journeys usually do their warm-up. Technically, a butt is a kind of backstop, an earthen embankment faced with clay onto which a mark can be pinned for use as a target. Usually butts are set up in opposing pairs, so that archers can shoot, go down and pull out their arrows, turn, and shoot back in the other direction. At Sebastian's, it's different. Between volleys the squires are sent to retrieve their masters' arrows, so the Journeys don't have to move. This mimics competition, where retrieval by the squires is thought to add to the pageantry. At the thought of having to sprint up and down the length of the butts while the Journeys stand around and watch, I find the whole set-up patently ridiculous.

Actually, there *are* two long embankments stretching out before me, but they're set up in adjacent fields, at different distances — one the 'near butts,' and the other the 'far.' On both, cloth-marks are used as the targets. These are hoops about the size of a man's palm and covered in white cloth, which are pinned to the butts using a black peg about an inch and a half in diameter. The archer aims at this wooden pin at the cloth-mark's center, but hitting the white also scores.

"We always set up at the near butts first," Pascal is telling me as we come out onto the field. "The boys like to warm up with some easy shooting. But don't be fooled. Cleaving the pin at 100 yards isn't easy, though the boys will make it look that way. Then we'll work our way down the field, depending on what Royce and Baylen have in mind." These are the resident veterans who oversee the training. I've yet to see them, but I've heard the names.

"If we move down to the far butts for some longer, elevated shooting, you'll need to get out heavier equipment," Pascal continues, leading me toward a place where a row of identical upright wooden sheds is lined up against a rickety wooden wall that separates the practice field from the guild's walled garden. "We don't always use cloth-marks out there, so just follow my lead."

He stops so suddenly that I almost run into him. "Just what do you know about target shooting, anyway?" he asks, as though it just occurs to him that I might have no idea what he's talking about.

"Not much," I say, wondering if it's true. I've watched my father training Jules so often that some of it must have sunk in, but I don't know all the proper terms.

"Ok, look. We do three different basic kinds of shooting here, and we've got a different practice area for each kind," he explains. "The near butts is for close-range, level shooting — that's 'butts.' That's where you get the most precision, the real glory shots. Then we've got the far butts, for 'wands.' That's mid-range, and often we just cut saplings and set them upright in the field, hence the name. Wands is for the most versatile archers, ones who can combine distance with accuracy, since you've got to arc your shots to get the distance, but a willow wand is still a mighty narrow target. Any shot that splits the wand is good, no matter where on the wand it hits. Then there's 'clouts.' That's for the heavy shooters. We do clouts out there," he points to a huge, unmarked field beyond the far butts. "Clouts are the worst for us squires, and the hardest on the boys, too. It means sending arrows capable of penetrating armor up to 500 yards to drop down on targets set onto the ground, and it takes a lot of strength. Only the most powerful archers can get their arrows that far, let alone come close to the marks, and for us that's a long way for retrieval. We've got to measure out the field ourselves, so it's basically a nightmare."

"What are those?" I ask, pointing to a number of unwieldy wicker structures stuffed with straw lined up off to the side of the butts. Pascal laughs.

"Those are another nightmare."

I don't ask.

"This is Tristan's cabinet," Pascal says, gesturing to one of the wooden sheds. "Each of the Journeys has one. You should find everything you need in here, though it's likely to be a mess. He's not very tidy, and he's been without a squire for days. We've all set up at the 80-yard mark today. The boys all have to shoot from the same line, to avoid shooting each other, obviously. There are no set places on the line, so I've saved you a spot for Tristan between Gilles and Jerome. They usually stick together, so that's all right, and that way Auguste and I can walk you through the process today."

"Pascal, thank you," I say earnestly, as he turns to head back to Gilles's station for a last check before the Journeys show up. Then on impulse, I add, "Just why are you helping me so much?"

"Gilles asked me to, of course," he replies, then when this

doesn't seem enough, he adds, "Look, Marek. You've got the wrong idea about the Journeys. I don't blame you. You didn't meet them under the best of circumstances. There are a few bad apples, that's true, and it's a competition, but for the most part, the decent boys help each other out. Same goes for us squires. You're one of us, now. St. Sebastian's protects its own."

It's meant to be comforting, but somehow, I don't like the sound of that. It sounds too much like what Tristan said the other day, *St. Sebastian's punishes its own.* I wonder if the two things are the same.

As Pascal moves off, I open Tristan's cabinet. Pascal is right. It's a complete mess. I make a note to start setting it in order right away, and to restock it. Fortunately for me, Auguste has gotten a late start, too, and he's still rummaging around in Jerome's cabinet, which is next to Tristan's. He looks like he's got a fresh bruise on his cheek. How can he have gotten yet another bruise since yesterday afternoon? I can't believe Jerome beats him. But anything is possible, and I guess I don't really know how Journeys treat their squires. It's an unsettling thought.

At a loss without Pascal, I try to watch Auguste surreptitiously to figure out what I'm supposed to be doing. After a while, he takes pity on me.

"Grab a cloth-mark and the bucket," he says, "and follow me out." I was expecting to handle a little more glamorous equipment. But my first task as squire is hauling water from the barrels lined up against the outer wall of the stables down the field to wet down the clay on the butts. There aren't any cloth-marks in Tristan's cabinet, so I have to beg one off of Auguste. Apparently, my afternoon is going to be spent sewing new ones.

Slogging the water down the field isn't too bad. I'm used to fetching water. Once the clay is wetted and Auguste shows me how, affixing the cloth-mark is easy, and with the butts moistened, the arrows will stick better into the target. Then I dig around in the cabinet and find a stand that's similar to the ones the other squires have put up in a row facing the butts, to hold the bow and arrows. I put it up between Auguste and Pascal, copying how they array the equipment. There's also a cone mounted on a spike that I assume is used as a kind of quiver, since Auguste is planting Jerome's near the stand and filling it with arrows, point down.

I think I've got my station set up pretty well, and I'm feeling pretty good - at least I know which bow is right for this distance, and I do such a good job of sorting through the disorganized jumble of arrows in the cabinet to pick out the right diameter and weight for the job that Pascal gives me a surprised compliment. As I'm loading the arrows into the cone, he points to three red rings painted on each arrow near the base of its shaft.

"Those are Tristan's mark. See?" He takes an arrow from Gilles's cone. The arrow has two white rings. "All the Journeys have a distinguishing color and code. Their arrows have to be clearly marked. It isn't so important for practice, but sometimes they shoot at the same target, and it has to be easy to tell who made each shot. You want to handle only Tristan's arrows. Eventually, you'll want to learn everyone's mark."

Auguste holds up one of Jerome's arrows, to show me a single band of Kelly green. Tristan, red; Gilles, white; Jerome, Green: three down, nine to go.

By the time the Journeys start coming out onto the field, I'm feeling pretty good about myself. I'm eager to show off what a good start I've made, but Tristan frustratingly is one of the last to arrive. The first ones out are boys I don't recognize, but slowly the others file out and start taking their places in the line, greeting their squires, accepting the food that they've brought for them, then gradually they begin stretching and taking practice shots. It isn't long before Jerome shows up, and then Gilles, who makes something of a grand entrance. Unlike the others, who are very simply dressed in linen or wool tunics and breeches, Gilles is decked out much as he was yesterday. On sauntering up to greet Pascal, he makes a show of stripping off his jerkin and handing it to Pascal, who folds it neatly and places it carefully on the stand, next to Gilles's bow. To my surprise, Gilles next strips off his tunic, too, which Pascal also neatly folds. When he gets some good-natured catcalls, he puts up his hands and makes a general bow.

With his torso bare, he looks very different. Around his neck, he's wearing his St. Sebastian's medal on a gold chain, which rests against an impressive set of pectoral muscles. His frilly lace shirts have been hiding unexpectedly broad shoulders, and his arms are a mass of wiry, ropey sinews. Watching him warm up in his exposed state is like an anatomy lesson, the physics of archery in motion. His shooting is so graceful and effortless, he could be in the middle of a courtly dance.

When Tristan finally shows up, he looks a bit scruffy to me compared with the others, particularly Gilles. He almost looks like he's slept in his clothes. He *is* still wearing the same clothes he wore yesterday, too, and he comes loping along indolently, yawning and running his hand through his hair in a lazy way that makes me irritable. I'm annoyed that he seems like the slouch of the group. I've barely even begun being a squire, but I'm already buying in to the competition. This has very little to do with how well we do our own jobs; it's all about whose master is best.

It all starts to go wrong when Tristan asks me for his breakfast.

It doesn't take me long to recognize that I'm woefully unprepared for the necessary level of physical activity. Eighty yards may not seem far, but I have to sprint at top speed to keep up with the other boys between flights, and even then, I'm always the last one back. Archers are expected not only to be accurate, but to be fast. In competition, the Journeys are expected to be able to let fly fifteen arrows a minute at a minimum, so when the boys decide to drill for speed, I hardly have enough time to catch my breath before I'm racing down the field again. The tight fabric wrapped around my breasts certainly doesn't help. Neither does the story the boys told me about Tristan's other squires. Every time I fall behind the other boys, the top of my foot twitches. But I don't really think Tristan is going to shoot me. Not yet, anyway.

Then comes pulling the arrows out of the butts. The smooth bodkin points used for target practice penetrate deep into the clay, and it takes real strength to wrench them out. When I grip the first one and pull as hard as I can and it doesn't come out, I panic. I've worried so much about passing myself off as a boy, it never occurred to me that I might fail at being a *squire*. Auguste sees me struggling and comes over.

"Get a firm grip right up against the butt, and pull with two hands. Put your foot on the butt for leverage, if you have to."

I follow his instructions, and when the arrow finally comes out with a pop, I almost fall over backwards. My shoulders are aching and my palms are breaking out in blisters before we've been at it for even half an hour. And that's not the worst of it.

The worst is the noise. I should have anticipated it, but the first crack of a bowstring lights up my senses like a bolt of lightning. I've been hearing the sound over and over in my head, but I'm not prepared to hear the real thing. The first one comes from somewhere down the line, then they come from all sides — *twang, zing, crack!* — a shot in the hand, a shot in the neck, then one right through the heart. All around me shots are flying, followed by the sickening thud as the arrows hit the butts. At one point, Tristan lowers his bow and puts his hand on my shoulder.

"If you're going to jump every time I take a shot, this isn't going to work, Marek," he says lightly, but he's right. I force myself to snap out of it, and before long, I've heard the sound so much that I get used to it. Almost.

I'm already about all in when Royce and Baylen finally come out onto the field, signaling that the official drilling is about to begin. They're the two resident veterans who assist Master Leon with the training of the Journeys. Master Leon, it turns out, usually contents himself with making an appearance at some point during the morning to look the boys over, note their progress, and make any necessary announcements, but otherwise he leaves the veterans to oversee morning practice.

The two men couldn't be more different. Royce is the older man. He's tall and slender, with a cheerful face, and he reminds me a bit of an adult Jerome. He's simply dressed and seems to be generally good-natured: I can picture him owning a lute. Baylen looks made to play the villain in a mummery show. He can't be much older than the Journeys himself, but he's already significantly larger than Royce, with broad, powerful shoulders and a leonine mane of black hair. His face wears a permanent scowl, in part because his lip on one side is pulled down by a long, thin scar that runs from his scalp to his chin. Its jagged line is interrupted only by an eye patch, which is black to match his solid black garments. He looks more likely to own a whip. Tristan tells me that Royce is an expert on the butts, Baylen at clouts, and that you can often tell a man's specialty by his personality. Even the masters, it seems, are playing parts; all the crack shots fancy themselves Robin Hoods, and all the powerhouses let their strength go to their heads.

As they stride out onto the field side by side, the boys line up at attention, with us squires behind. I copy the stance of the others that I take as a mark of respect: legs apart, arms folded behind the back.

"Lose your shirt, LeJeune?" Baylen barks at Gilles. I freeze. It's the cold voice again, the voice of my father's killer. Or is it? I was so sure I'd recognize that voice anywhere, that I'd never be able to forget it. But this is already the second time I've thought I heard the voice. It seems that every adult male sounds like the killer to me.

"Sweat is so damaging to silk, master," Gilles replies smoothly. "I'm on strict orders from my tailor."

"Last time I checked, you take your orders from me, not your tailor! Put it on, Gilles. And remind me to give your tailor three lashes next time I see him."

And then the real work begins. At some point, as I'm running back from a retrieval, I look way down the line and catch sight of Remy. He's skipping along, far ahead of me, as bouncy and full of energy as a little jackrabbit. It's unbearably humid already, even though it's still early in the morning. Sweat is pouring down my body, itching under the wool of my pants, chaffing under the band on my chest. My head is still pounding, and I'm already feeling the effects of another day without enough to eat. But the thought of those thin little wrists effortlessly plucking out arrows makes me determined. If that skinny little sprite can do it, so can I.

Somehow, I make it through to the end of the session. It helps that Taran is set up so far away that I can't really see him, or tell if he's seen me. I'm dreading the inevitable moment when I find myself face to face with him again. I'm not eager to find out how he's taken the news that I've come to St. Sebastian's, even though I can guess. I haven't yet seen Aristide again up close, either. Apparently the 'rotten apples' stick together, and they're all at the far end of the field, where for the time being we can all ignore each other. At least that's one thing to be grateful for; I wouldn't want them witnessing my less than stellar first-day performance. As it is, the stress is enough.

Despite everything, what stands out most from my first morning on the butts isn't the exhaustion or the anxiety. It's seeing the Journeys shoot for the first time. They really are magnificent, each one better than the last. Each has his own strengths, of course, but as a group they really are all that they're cracked up to be, and more. They are the best of the best. Watching them shoot, I can forgive the Journeys anything — all their quirks, their posturing and preening, even my beating in the alley. Out on the field, I begin to fall in love with the idea of the Journeys again.

Not surprisingly, to my eyes, the most magnificent of them all is Tristan.

He is simply put the most beautiful archer I've ever seen. It doesn't hurt that he has a gorgeous body — tall, lithe, and strong, but without the overdeveloped shoulders that the clout shooters have — crowned by that splendid profile and shock of thick, wavy black hair. It's more than just his physical beauty, though, it's the beauty of this perfect form in motion. It's the archery that's breathtaking.

When he first saunters up, I'm still annoyed with him. But as he gets down to warming up, his indolence melts away. I should have known, it was part of his act. As he starts to shoot, he gets a look of determination on his face, and I know behind his indifferent air, he means business. He wants to win as much as any of them.

As I watch him bend his bow, I can't pinpoint exactly what makes him stand out from the others. The key to being a great archer is to have good technique and to have practiced it so much that it's second nature, so you can reproduce the exact same technique effortlessly on each shot: the same stance, the same draw, the same release. Over time, all the boys have thus perfected their own unique motion, but at the same time, there's a basic sameness to their technique. But Tristan has adjusted the basics in small ways that have the effect of showing off his admirable form to its greatest advantage, to make the act of shooting the bow as impressive as the shots themselves. He looks completely at ease and balanced in his stance, but if you look closely, his legs are set wider than is natural — just slightly wider than shoulder width, but enough to give him an open, exaggerated look. Everything about how he stands and how he shoots is similarly exaggerated, not enough to be noticeable unless you're closely dissecting his style as

I am, but just enough to make the overall effect overblown, larger than life.

He nocks the arrow and draws the bow in one fluid motion, but instead of pulling straight back, even for level shots he arcs upward gently, then accelerates as he drops down into his full extension. It's as though the bow itself is taking a quick inhalation of breath before catching at the hold, and as he aims, his shoulders are a little too far back, his chest a little too extended, his trigger hand pulled a little too far back. It's like what my father once told me about ancient statues of athletes, that they're frozen in a pose meant to evoke a full range of motion in a single stance, a stance that exemplifies the peak of excellence in the depicted sport in its most defining moment, but on closer inspection, the stance proves false: it's not one that ever really occurs, it's not even humanly possible. This is Tristan as he releases his bow: the impossibly perfect image of superhuman excellence.

As he releases, instead of letting his hand drop, he follows the drawing motion through, and holds his release hand up behind him for just a second or two while still holding his bow out in front of him at full extent, striking an even more exaggerated pose, as though he is still involved in sending the arrow on its way.

Every shot he makes is genuinely thrilling, and so I'm actually shocked when I go out to the target and find that all his arrows haven't hit the white. It doesn't matter, though. I can't imagine anyone watching the target when he's shooting. I wonder if this is why the others are afraid of him: he's exactly the kind of glamorous figure that the guild favors, and he must be a real crowd-pleaser. If he can learn to be consistent, he has a real shot at sweeping the competition.

CHAPTER NINE

It's noon when what I've been dreading finally happens.

"There's been a change of plan," Tristan tells me as we make our way to the great hall. Morning practice has mercifully come to an end, and we're on our way to noon mess, the main meal of the day. Attendance is mandatory for both Journeys and squires, but I have no intention of missing it anyway. I'm starving. I didn't even know there was a plan.

"I'm to present you to the members now, not this evening." Great. I'm sweaty and disheveled, and still dressed in Tristan's oversized clothes, with yesterday's festering bandage drooping around my head. I'll more than look the part of the trash Tristan's fished out of the alley.

"We've got to hang back," he continues, "to let everyone else in first." My stomach gives an impressive growl.

"I know how you feel," Tristan laughs. But I doubt he does. Waiting while all the other boys file past, even I'm beginning to feel like I'm a disgrace to St. Sebastian's, and not just because I'm really a girl, an imposter. I wish I'd been given the chance to clean up. Some veterans go past, and I feel worse. I hover around nervously behind Tristan in the doorway, watching the men seat themselves at the long mess tables that are set up the length of the hall. They're laughing and talking among themselves, but the room is huge, and it looks so formal. In the crowd, I can't see Gilles or Jerome, Pascal or Auguste; it seems full of men and boys I don't know. I suddenly feel like Marieke again, looking into this room, knowing I'm not supposed to go in.

At the far end of the room is the painting of St. Sebastian. The masters have seated themselves at a head table facing the room right under the saint's feet. When everyone is assembled, Master Guillaume raises a hand, and the room falls silent.

"Here we go," Tristan says, and he heads into the room. There's nothing for me to do but follow. I half expect a foot to shoot out in front of me, to find myself sprawling on the floor as I did in the squires' barracks, but we make it to the front of the room unmolested. With each step, the St. Sebastian on the wall grows larger, until I'm looking up at him at such a close angle that I have the unpleasant sensation that he's about to fall from the wall on top of me. I'm so focused on the painting that Tristan has to put his hands on my shoulders and physically turn me around to face the room, much to the amusement of the men.

"Gentlemen," Tristan booms. "I present for your approval the newest denizen of St. Sebastian's, my squire, Marek Vervloet."

This pronouncement is met by a deafening noise, as all the men begin to stamp their feet and pound the table at the same time, in what I take to be the traditional way to greet new members. And then it hits me. That's me. I might be dirty. I might be weak. I might even be generally despised, forced on them by Tristan. I might be a complete disgrace. But I'm a member of St. Sebastian's now. There's a Verbeke at St. Sebastian's again.

There's no more to it. Tristan and I stand there side by side for a while longer until the pounding subsides before taking our own seats. I notice as I work up the courage to scan the room that the expressions on the men's faces range from hostile to amused. And not all the members join in the greeting. I spot Aristide, who is pointedly examining his fingernails and lounging in a way designed to indicate that he's not participating, but he's actually one of the ones who looks amused.

Then I spot Taran. He's sitting stock still, the palms of his hands flat on the table in front of him. It's the thing I've been dreading — seeing the expression on his face, now that he knows I'm to be Tristan's squire. When we lock eyes, I stop breathing. The expression on his face isn't surprise. I'm sure he found out about me sometime last night, and he's had time to get over the shock. Nobody keeps a secret long at St. Sebastian's, a fact that doesn't bode well for me. His expression isn't anger, either, or even rage. It's pure, cold hatred. I don't think I've ever been really hated before. Nobody's ever felt that strongly about me. Maybe I should be flattered. But I feel a cold, sick feeling in the pit of my stomach, like I've been struck there by an arrow. I look away first, knowing I'm a coward, but not before he does something completely unexpected. Very deliberately, he closes one eye in an exaggerated wink. I have no idea what it means, but I feel the arrow in my stomach give a painful twist.

It turns out, noon mess is the biggest meal of the day, and just as formal as the evening meal. Part of the ceremony at St. Sebastian's is that squires are expected to serve their masters their meals. No women are allowed into the guild buildings further than the kitchens, not even serving girls, so male servants bring the food into the hall and place the large platters and tankards on long tables at the back of the room. As usual, nobody's bothered to tell me this, so at first, I simply sit down next to Tristan. There are no set seating arrangements; sometimes squires sit next to their masters, or as a group at the end of the same table — anywhere they can be close enough to be on call. Today, since everyone else is already seated, I squeeze in next to Tristan, and wait expectantly.

"Marek, I'm very hungry," Tristan says.

"So am I."

"No, I mean. *I'm hungry.*"

Down the table, Rennie starts to laugh. "Get him something to eat, idiot!" he calls out to me.

Embarrassed, I get up and hustle over to the serving tables, wondering exactly what to do. I come back with such a huge pile of roasted meat on a trencher that everyone at the table bursts out laughing. Humiliated, I have to follow Pascal back to the serving table, where he shows me how to load a plate appropriately. By the time I get to eat my own meal, I feel thoroughly defeated. You'd have thought I could at least do the part of the job that involved women's work. But I guess I was never very good at that.

After the meal, the Journeys usually rest back in their rooms for a while afterward to digest, before training again in the afternoon.

I'm glad to hear it, thinking I'll get a chance to recover myself, but Pascal disabuses me of this notion in a hurry. "Now's your chance to run errands," he tells me. I find that I'm expected to do everything from taking Tristan's clothes to the laundry, sewing the cloth-marks he uses as targets, restocking equipment from the workshops, and basically running any kind of errand he can think up.

When I protest at the list of chores Pascal begins ticking off, he says, "Be grateful, Marek. We're spared real drudgery. Below the squires, there are a number of servants we outrank. These are mostly very young boys and so rather incompetent, but they can be pressed into service to do the worst tasks, if you can find one."

I spend quite a bit of time the first day trying to get any of them to recognize my authority, with little success. I try to copy Pascal's efficient tone, but the boys are like horses. They can tell an inexperienced rider, and I have yet to learn how to apply the spurs.

In the afternoon, the Journeys have individual schedules. They're left to themselves to practice alone, or to arrange for individual training sessions with one of the veterans. Not all of their training is in archery, either. The Journeys are expected to be literate, so those who didn't come in already knowing how to read and write must learn, and even those who already know the basics are expected to have regular lessons. I understand now why my father was teaching Jules to read.

They're also expected to be competent horsemen, and some of the wealthier boys have brought their own mounts with them. Gilles, apparently, has a whole aisle of the stables full of his own horses, even though he doesn't like to ride. "They're just for show," Pascal says. "He hates the smell." Fortunately, the squires aren't expected to take care of the horses — there are stable boys for that. Needless to say, I don't get along too well with anything with big hooves.

I'm just wondering how I'm supposed to know what Tristan has planned for the afternoon when a little serving boy comes into the barracks with a summons for me from Tristan. He takes me along to Tristan's room, which is fortunate, since I'm not sure I remember which door is his. I don't relish the thought of finding myself in a tiny cubicle with the wrong Journey.

Tristan's sitting on the edge of his cot when I come in.

"So, Marek, ready to get back at it?" he asks, stretching and running one hand through his hair in a motion that's already becoming familiar. Without waiting for a response, he gets up and goes past me into the hall, slapping me on the back as he passes.

"Where are we going?" I ask, falling into step behind him.

"It's a surprise. But I'm sure you're going to love it." I already know Tristan well enough not to like the sound of this at all.

Tristan takes me out to a part of the guild I've never seen before. We go past the master's office, and then out of the main building. Out back, there are a whole row of outbuildings I didn't know existed.

"These are the workshops," Tristan explains, holding the door of one of the buildings open. I step in, to find myself back at home. It's a workshop just like my father's, but on a larger scale. A half a dozen fletchers and bowyers are hard at work, shaving down staves, oiling new bows, and fletching arrows.

"Sorry to interrupt, Marcel," Tristan says to an older man who looks to be in charge. "But I've got my new squire here. I'd like you boys to meet him, as he'll be seeing to my equipment from now on. Marek, this is our head fletcher, Marcel. Anything you need, he'll get it for you."

I shake the man's hand, while Tristan continues. "Seems the boy is something of a fletcher himself. I thought it might be fun to give him a chance to show us what he can do."

So that's it. I don't know whether to be grateful to Tristan or furious with him. Is he trying to give me a chance to do something right today, or is he testing me?

Marcel steps aside to let me seat myself at his workbench, and Tristan comes up behind me, grinning from ear to ear, and slaps me on the back. Why must they all keep doing that?

"What kind of fletch do you want on this?" I ask, as Marcel hands me a 30-inch arrow shaft.

"Your choice."

I stick with a straight fletch, to be safe. At first, my fingers feel clumsy. I don't like to be watched. But as I fall into the familiar routine, I relax. I've done this so often, and it feels good to be doing something I know how to do. I've got the arrow finished in no time.

When I hold it up, Tristan plucks it from my hand and says triumphantly,

"Look at that, Marcel! What did I tell you? You'd better watch yourself, or my squire here'll have your job before you know it."

"Very impressive," Marcel concedes.

To me, he says, "I knew you could do it, kid." I hope he's telling the truth.

Tristan settles it with Marcel to leave me at the workshop for the afternoon. "He can make all my arrows from now on, time allowing," Tristan declares. He means it as a compliment, but it's going to mean more work for me.

I end up not seeing Tristan again until evening mess, but by then, I'm feeling better. I may not be able to compete with the other squires yet, but I have a skill none of them have. I've decided that this was Tristan's intention — to give me some confidence. I don't want to believe he would have set me up for public failure. So when I slop the ale and accidentally take some food from the masters' sideboard when serving that evening, I shrug it off. I'll get stronger, and I'll get better. But even if I'm never as strong or quick as the others, I'll find a way to use the skills I've got that they don't have to make me a better squire than any of them.

A girl can dream, anyway.

When I finally get back to the barracks that night after my first full day at St. Sebastian's, ready to collapse, I face one final indignity. I find the same odious dog from yesterday curled up in the middle of my bunk. Auguste laughs when he sees me eyeing it distastefully.

"You're going to have to get along with Popinjay if you're going to bunk there, Marek."

"Popinjay?" I say incredulously. It seems a ridiculously spry name for a festering, flee-ridden old bag of bones like this dog.

"You know, like the little bird puppets hung up on tall poles as targets."

"Inauspicious name," I say, giving the dog a tentative prod. "You'd better watch out," I tell it, "or I might be tempted to use you as a target."

"You won't shoot old Pop, if you know what's good for you," says Auguste, reaching down to scratch the dog behind the ears. "It must have been a fine hunting dog, in its day. It was abandoned out in the woods beyond St. Seb's. Hunters do that, when the dogs get too old, or if they just can't be bothered to care for the dogs at the end of a season, heartless bastards. Anyway, some of the squires found it out on the grounds and started shooting it at. The name stuck."

"So what's it doing on my bunk?" I ask.

"Tristan caught the boys at it and put a stop to it. Busted a few heads. The dog's his slave now, follows him around everywhere, when it can find him. If it can't get into his room, it comes in here. I guess it figures Tristan's squire is the next best thing."

I look down at the dog with disgust. I don't think I have to explain why this story bothers me. Finally, I give the dog a push and climb onto the cot next to it.

"All right, Popinjay," I say. "It looks like we're going to have to share." I put my arm over the dog, and prepare to sleep. "After all," I whisper. "I guess you've got dibs. He did pluck you off the streets first."

AFTER THAT, MY FIRST FEW DAYS AT THE GUILD GO BY IN something of a blur. Except for practice, I don't even see that much of Tristan. I spend most of my time exhausted, just struggling to keep up physically. But the exhaustion helps. The night my father died already feels like a lifetime ago.

What little concentration I have left after the morning practices I use to try to start learning as much about the members of the guild as I can. I can recognize the masters and the trainers Royce and Baylen by the first day, but the guild is crawling with personnel: servants, craftsmen, stable boys, kitchen staff, veterans who live outside the guild but who come in to help with the military training, archers seeking certification, and others I can't just keep straight. Most of these stay confined in the back buildings of the guild, though, so mostly I'm surrounded by the Journeys and their squires.

I concentrate on the Journeys first. Some of them I unfortunately already recognize from the alley. With the help of

Auguste and Pascal, I soon learn to put names to faces. Within a few days, I know all their names and just enough facts about each one to keep them all straight. I know most of the squires by sight, too, but I haven't bothered to learn all their names yet or to match them up with their Journeys. That can come later. It's enough just getting through the work and trying to get a handle on the atmosphere of the place.

By the end of the week, I've begun to have the Journeys sorted out, and I think I've begun to understand the unusual relationship between them.

The Journeys are all the same rank, in theory. But it doesn't take me long to figure out that this is false, to a degree. The social differences that would have been apparent between them on the outside count here, too. A few of the Journeys are true nobility, from landed aristocratic families. There's Gilles, of course. He's got the bluest blood, and he'll come into his title eventually. But Aristide and the equally odious Falko are aristocrats, too, though I haven't figured their lineage out exactly. It seems that Aristide's family is wealthier, but Gilles outranks him, a fact that Gilles never lets him forget. I think Falko is a second son, but I'm not sure. At any rate, Gilles won't have anything to do with either of them, and Falko seems to takes his cues from Aristide.

Then there are the sons of newly elevated families, with fathers directly in the prince's service or with a plum spot at court, like Ladislaus Bowdoin, the big boy who tried to restrain Aristide in the alley that first day, and an older boy the others call Turk, for reasons that aren't obvious to me at all. He's milky pale and blonde, shorter than the others, and thin as a whip. When I ask Tristan about it, he just laughs.

It also doesn't take me long to find out that Taran is Taran Mellor. Even I've heard of his father, Lord Mellor. He was put forward for knighthood by the young prince himself and he's a recent recipient of the L'île cross for valor. But that's not the worst of it. Everybody knows of him — he's something of our national hero. He's the captain of the Black Guard.

Then come the Journeys whose fathers are in the professions: Jerome's father is a scholar at the university in Meuse, and a boy named Laurens Lefevre's family runs a tavern in Charleroi. Only one Journey comes from what might be considered a real peasant family: the older, nervous boy Anselm Mertens. He's got raw natural talent, or he'd never have made it here, but he's out of his element. An air of defeat surrounds him, like he suspects he was let in as a mistake, or as a token commoner just to show that St. Sebastian's is fair, but without a real chance of success. He seems to be biding his time until the first cut.

Somewhere in all of this is Jurian Legrand. He's got a nebulous status. I'm not sure whether he's at the bottom of the social order, or near the top. Or both, at the same time. He's a former squire. Apparently, if a squire can shoot, a Journey can put him forward for something called apprentice status if he passes Third trials at the end of his first year. If granted, the Journey then trains with his squire during the year of his veteran trials, at the end of which he can sponsor his squire for a shot at Journeys. As it happens, Jurian was Baylen's squire. If that weren't enough, it was Master Guillaume who brought him up from the stables and matched him up with Baylen in the first place. Being Baylen's protégé and the master's favorite pretty much neutralizes the stench of the stables, if anyone remembers that that's where he's from. Personally, I can't picture Jurian as a stable boy. I remember thinking he was slight when I first saw him in the alley, but that was just in comparison to Taran. And because of his features. His face is refined and angelic, as lovely as a girl's, and his golden hair curls in a shining halo on his head that makes him look positively beatific.

The only one I can't really place is the one I should know best, Tristan. Whenever I try to ask him about it, he manages to avoid giving me a direct answer. He slips into character and makes a joke of it. Once he told me he'd been captured by pirates, another that he was the son of a vagabond king. But I can tell it bothers him, so I've stopped asking. I remember his words, "I've got nobody left, either," so I don't like to ask. Besides, I haven't told him the truth about myself either, so I'm in no position to pry. I don't want to invite confidences I can't reciprocate. It would be disloyal, too, to go behind his back for answers he doesn't want to give me himself, but I'm curious. Taran said he belonged in the gutter, but that doesn't fit. He doesn't seem like a commoner. He's educated, and he knows how to handle himself. He's got the same easy confidence as the elite boys, but there's something off there, too — he holds himself apart, separate, even from his friends. But maybe that's just Tristan. If anything, he is his own creation. As I see it, my job isn't to ask questions, it's to help him with his invention.

But what of my first Journey, the boy I saw with my father, on the steps near the house of Luc Fournier? I spot him on my first or second day as squire, and with something of a shock I realize that I'd forgotten all about him. His name is Charles Urbain, and he's one of the older Journeys. The older boys, Charles, Turk, and Anselm, tend stick to together, as though a year or two has made them much more mature than the others. With Charles, it seems true, and it's entirely without condescension. Of them all, he's the only one who completely lives up to my old image of what a Journey should be, and it isn't just because I've never lost that first image I had of him, standing on the steps, arm raised in greeting. It's because Charles is the only one who doesn't seem to be trying too hard to be a Journey. He's comfortable in his skin, self-contained, never crude or assertive. Over time I get used to being around the other Journeys, but I'm always shy around Charles, although on the rare occasions when we interact, he's always kind. I think it's because he's the only Journey I saw when my father was still alive, when I was still Marieke, and I'm grateful that I can idolize him, as though he's keeping the image of the Journeys I had as a child, the image that included my father, untarnished for me. Even his relationship with his squire is a model of what I hope one day I might share with Tristan. Charles's squire is a big, friendly blonde boy named Henri, and the two of them are inseparable. They appear to be the best of friends.

In addition to these social differences between them, there are the predictable jealousies and personality clashes. But as I make a study of the Journeys, it seems that in a way, Remy is right: they are all friends, or at least, they share a bond, despite the antipathies that simmer underneath. Even Tristan and Taran practice side by side most of the time without letting whatever it is that's between them boil over. They're all under the same pressures, and the trials stand over them all equally, in a way that only they can understand. That understanding and the shared physical routine have created a strong relationship between them. I might even go so far as to say that they're a brotherhood, of sorts, forged from pride at making Journeyman and at living up to the standards of the guild — not just the physical standards, but the rules, too, and the expected, unspoken codes of conduct to which they hold themselves. Well, all of them but Tristan. He's got his own ideas.

Fortunately for me, the Journeys seem content to forget about the day in the alley, too. For the most part, they treat me decently, when they bother to take any notice of me. All except for Aristide, but he's so condescending and abusive to all the squires that after a while his treatment of me doesn't stand out as anything special. Taran in particular makes a point of ignoring me, like I'm beneath his notice, but it doesn't fool me. When he thinks nobody is looking, I catch him watching me. He studies me with that same impassive, bored look that he always wears. I know I was right about that look the first time I saw it; there's something behind it, something all the more unsettling because I can't read it. It scares me more than open hostility would. He's biding his time. He's in no hurry. But I know he'd like nothing better than to catch me alone, away from the guild. I suspect his famous sense of honor wouldn't help me much when there are no witnesses.

CHAPTER TEN

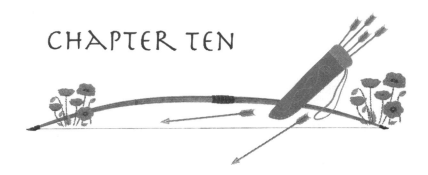

I n all, I'm surprised that I'm not subject to more harassment, and I put it down to Tristan. Nobody bothers Remy, and nobody bothers me, for the same reason. In fact, only two incidents of what might be called harassment really stand out those first few days, and one of them doesn't even happen to me.

The first incident happens on my second day. I make it a point to get up earlier this morning, so I'm pleased with myself when I get out to the field and find only a few other squires are already there. I bring my stand over to where Pascal is bent over his, but when he straightens up, I'm looking into a face I don't recognize.

"Oh. I thought you were Pascal," I say, unsure what to do. But the boy turns out to be perfectly friendly. He smiles and puts out a hand.

"I'm Armand, Aristide's squire."

At the name 'Aristide,' I involuntarily wrinkle my nose.

"He's an acquired taste," Armand agrees, "but don't tell me you're going to hold it against me." I hurriedly take his hand and he's giving me a firm shake when Pascal bustles up.

"Setting up Tristan and Aristide next to each other, are you? Interesting," he says good-naturedly, slipping his arm casually over Armand's shoulder.

"He thought I was you."

"Don't let the compliment go to your head, Armand. Marek, I thought you were more discerning."

Standing there next to each other, they could be brothers.

"You two are friends?" I'm surprised. Even I know Gilles and Aristide hate each other.

"Sure. We're the class of this place, aren't we, Pascal? We've got to stick together."

"Besides, he hates Aristide about as much as I do!"

"Well, I wouldn't go quite that far ..." Armand gives Pascal a conspiratorial smile, "but close!"

"So, Armand. What do you think?" Pascal cocks his head to one side. "Just this once, do you think they can stand it?"

"They're big boys. It'll be character-building," Armand replies, catching his drift. So Pascal brings Gilles's stand over and sets up on the other side of Armand, leaving Aristide's station sandwiched between those of Tristan and Gilles.

Gilles is the first of them out. He doesn't say anything directly about the unusual set-up. All he does is raise his eyebrows and give an exaggerated bow, saying 'Armand,' rather pointedly as he does, while shooting Pascal a questioning look.

"These things are sent to try us, master," Pascal replies, and that's that. I get the impression that the set-up rather pleases Gilles, actually. Particularly when Aristide arrives, and gives a doubletake. It doesn't take long to see that Gilles is going to enjoy Aristide's discomfort. Practicing between Gilles and Tristan could get on anyone's nerves, but once Tristan shows up, the two of them start up a routine of banter that's clearly designed specifically to irritate Aristide, who's caught in the crossfire.

At first, though, the boys seem to put up with practicing together quite well. I'm doing a little better today myself, even with the uncomfortable closeness of Aristide, who makes it a point to scoff every time I do something wrong. Once, when he catches me eyeing his boots, he grins and wiggles his foot at me. But after a while, Aristide leaves me alone. He's having troubles of his own. Either he's generally not very good, which is unlikely — he's a Journey, after all — or he's having an off day. He isn't liking being between Tristan and Gilles, who've been enjoying flustering him, and he's got to concentrate. The problem is, the harder he tries to concentrate, the more flustered he gets. But the boys are behaving themselves, more or less, and I'm just about convinced that the practice is going to come off without a hitch. Royce is leading the session by himself today, too, so it's a little more relaxed, and I'm having an easier time keeping up. I know what to expect today, so the whole thing doesn't seem quite so bad.

About halfway through drills, I'm just getting my second wind, when Royce puts up his hand to get everyone's attention.

"What about a friendly wager, boys?" he says. Unlike Baylen, Royce likes to spur on the boys with praise and incentives instead of threats. I've been at St. Sebastian's only one full day, but I already know that everything is a competition. Even the squires can make anything into a contest: pissing, swearing, spitting, you name it. So at Royce's suggestion, a cheer goes up.

"Let's make it one for the squires," he continues, and I groan. All the other squires give another cheer.

"What do you propose, Master?" Laurens asks.

"Whichever squire is back to the line first the most times for the rest of practice will win the honor of sitting with the veterans at noon mess," he has to pause to be heard over the appreciative whistles this announcement elicits. "And," he adds loudly, putting up a hand for silence, "he's to be served at table — by his own master!"

"Three cheers for Master Royce!" Armand calls out, and all the other squires cry out "huzzah!" — except me. This is just going to make my day harder. Just when I was managing to keep up, the others are all going to have a reason to push the pace. Besides, I've absolutely no chance of winning. Pascal and Armand, though, are all fired up. They've been talking and joking around with each other between retrievals all morning, and now they begin teasing each other about who's going to win, making a show of limbering up and anticipating how sweet it's going to be to be served. The Journeys are groaning and pretending that the whole thing is demeaning, but it's all an act. It's clear they all want their squires to win.

"I'm sorry," I tell Tristan, as I return dead last from the first retrieval after the competition starts.

"It's your second day, kid," he says. "You can't be king in a day." But I know, even he'd like to win.

Pascal and Armand are faring much better. In fact, I'm sure one of them is going to win. Armand was right, they are the class of the place, as far as squires go. They're older, too, about my age, so closer in age to the Journeys, and they've gotten their height. Their legs are longer, and they're both faster than the rest of us. But Pascal is fastest.

Every time Pascal gets back to the line ahead of Armand, he does a little victory dance, and he and Armand pretend to argue about it, but it's all very friendly. Gilles is keeping up a running commentary in his inimitable manner, praising Pascal in a way calculated to piss Aristide off and basically making an ass of himself. Aristide was already having a bad day, but now, as Gilles's comments get increasingly under his skin, he just gets more flustered. His shooting goes from bad to worse, which makes retrieval harder for Armand, which makes Armand lose more often — it's a vicious circle. Gilles, on the other hand, is shooting better than ever. He's enjoying himself immensely.

"Tristan, Aristide is looking thunderous," I whisper, worried.

"Good!"

"Don't you think Gilles should lay off?"

"Gilles can take care of himself. He knows what he's doing."

Hmm. They always say that.

So I drop it. But I'm not surprised when the next time Pascal's the first one back to the line, after Gilles drawls at him, "*Do* try not to kick up so much dust, dear boy! Or poor Armand is likely to choke on it," a scuffle breaks out. I miss the first part of it since I'm still hustling back from the field, but from a ways out I can hear arguing, and then Aristide comes up angrily behind Pascal.

"Ouch!" Pascal gives a surprised cry of pain.

"What the devil?!" Gilles's voice rings out, then Gilles and Aristide are shoving each other, while Armand tries to separate them, and Pascal is grabbing his own shoulder and grimacing.

"Break it up, boys!" Royce calls out, striding over just as I get back to the line. "What's the meaning of this?" The other Journeys have gathered around and succeeded in pulling Gilles and Aristide apart, while Royce barks at them.

"I've never heard of such behavior at St. Sebastian's! What in the hell happened? Pascal, out with it. What's wrong with you?" he demands. Pascal hangs his head, but he doesn't reply.

"Aristide bit him, that's what!" Gilles shrieks indignantly. "Leaned right over behind him, and bit him on the shoulder!"

"Come on, Gilles. That's a little much, even for you. Now, what really happened?"

"He *bit* him, I tell you! Look!" Gilles pulls down the tunic from the reluctant Pascal's neck, and sure enough, a set of lurid red teeth marks stand out on Pascal's shoulder.

"For the love of St. Irene!" Royce explodes. "Are you boys, or barbarians? What do you have to say for yourself, Guyenne?"

Everyone is quiet, staring at Aristide in astonishment. But Aristide looks the most astonished of all.

"Surely nobody believes I did that!" he sputters. He seems genuinely surprised by the marks on Pascal's shoulder. Either he's a better actor than I would have thought, or he's telling the truth. I entertain the thought that maybe Gilles bit Pascal himself. I have no idea which is more unbelievable.

"But I saw you, dear boy," Gilles says smoothly. "Surely Armand did, too."

"Leave me out of it!" Armand protests.

"Okay, Pascal," Royce says, getting himself under control. "That looks nasty. You're done for the day. Go get that patched up. As for you two," he turns to Gilles and Aristide. "You're lucky I have no desire to explain this to the masters. In fact, I can't imagine describing it to them!" He shakes his head, picturing the scene in his mind. He's starting to find some humor in the whole thing. "So, just this once, I'm going to pretend this didn't happen. But anyone pulls a stunt like this again, and somebody'll be out, I promise you — trials or no trials. Is that understood?"

The boys are nodding and turning to go back to their posts, but Gilles clears his throat.

"Unfortunately, master, I'm afraid I cannot forget about this just yet. Pascal is my squire, and so I must demand satisfaction. He deserves no less."

"Satisfaction?" snorts Aristide.

"It may well be a concept unknown to the nouveau-riche," Gilles sniffs.

"Hey, Aristide!" Falko calls out. "You bit the wrong boy. Next time, just go straight for Gilles!"

"I didn't bite anybody!" Aristide snaps.

"What are you on about, Gilles?" Tristan laughs.

"The squires' competition," Gilles says. "It can't be finished now, not as it started, anyway, with Pascal out. But he was surely winning." He puts out a hand to quell the half-hearted protests of some of the others. "It was down to Armand and Pascal, we all know that. Pascal has been robbed of his title. Robbed!" His voice wavers on this word, and Tristan puts an arm on his shoulder in a consoling manner while Gilles pretends to get his emotions under control, before continuing coolly: "But I propose that there is a way both to satisfy my honor on Pascal's behalf, and to decide a winner in the squires' competition. What do you say, Master?"

At the word 'competition,' the boys have all gathered around again, willing to play along, and apparently Royce is as easily suckered in as the others.

"Just what do you have in mind, Lejeune?" he asks, amused.

"Since the squires can no longer compete, I propose that the masters finish the competition for them. And, in the spirit of squires' day —" Gilles breaks off, and makes a show of scanning the crowd until he catches sight of Auguste. "Auguste — what is that little game of chance you squires are so fond of?"

"Pluck-Buffet!" Auguste shouts gleefully.

"Yes, that's it. Pluck-buffet," he draws this out, as though savoring the quaintness of the name and the way it rolls off the tongue. "I propose a game of pluck-buffet. The winner's squire will be crowned."

"Pluck-buffet? Between you and Aristide?" Royce asks, sounding uncertain. Whatever it is, it's definitely not regulation.

"Wait a minute ..." Aristide tries to protest, but Gilles is continuing.

"Thrice round, shall we say, at ten score yards? Three arrows per round. Any shot missing the white gets a buffet. What do you think, boys?"

Predictably, the other boys are all for it, and by now Royce is openly grinning. I almost wish Baylen were here instead. He'd never go along with this nonsense.

There's nothing for it. Aristide has to agree or look craven, but he looks grim as we all assemble around the 200-yard mark on the far butts. Gilles, on the other hand, looks thoroughly satisfied with himself. He's been on top form all day, a fact that can't have escaped Aristide's notice, whereas Aristide has been a mass of jitters. At the revelation of the bite marks on Pascal's shoulder, he's come completely unstrung. The probable outcome of the competition is obvious to everyone, and it can't help Aristide's mood that everyone appears to be looking forward to watching Aristide's defeat with great anticipation.

When we're all ready and the mark has been placed, Gilles steps up to the line.

"As the injured party, I'll take the first shot," he says, but he then proceeds to stretch and flex so long in preparation of his shot that Aristide lets his nerves get the better of him.

"Just take the shot already!"

"As you wish." Gilles takes a deep bow, and with no further ado and with effortless grace, he sends an arrow toward the target — an eight-inch cloth-mark, not at all an easy mark at this distance. It's hard to see exactly where on the target an arrow lands at this distance, so Armand has stayed down by the embankment, standing well off to the side, ready to send back a signal.

From here, the shot looks awfully good, so we're anxiously waiting for Armand's signal — all but Gilles, who is so composed he almost looks indifferent. He knows it was a good shot. And then Armand's arm shoots straight up. Gilles has not only hit the mark, he's hit it dead center on the one-inch square peg that holds it in place.

"What a shot! He's cleaved the pin!" Tristan whistles.

"Your turn, old boy." Gilles gestures to the line with mock courtesy. Beads of sweat have broken out on Aristide's forehead, and he licks his lips nervously as he steps up to the line. For a moment, his hands look like they're shaking so much I even think he's not going to be able to take his shot.

"You don't have to better him, Ari, remember, just make a hit," Laurens says.

"Come on, Aristide!" Falko says. "Give this peacock a plucking for us."

With that, Aristide lets his arrow fly, and soon Armand is

gesturing down and to the right. Aristide's missed. He hasn't even hit the white.

"Looks like it's going to be the peacock who does the plucking!" Gilles crows, flexing his hands.

"You know the rules, Gilles," Royce warns, as Aristide steals himself for the blow. "Open hand."

"Of course," Gilles replies smoothly. "We're all gentlemen here."

As he winds up, his face looks anything but gentlemanly. It's clear he has no intention of giving a token slap. As he strikes, Gilles says, "This is for Pascal," and when his open palm makes contact with Aristide's face, it's in a tremendously powerful blow that knocks Aristide from his feet and sends him sprawling. As Falko and Laurens help Aristide to his feet, he looks green, and there's a thin trickle of blood coming from a small cut on his lip. I quickly do the math: thrice round, three arrows at each round — that makes nine shots. That's nine blows, if Aristide keeps shooting like this, and I don't see any reason why his aim is going to get anything but worse. Eight more blows. It doesn't look to me like Aristide can take even one more. I should be pleased. I can still remember what those pointy boots felt like. Instead, I feel a little sick.

Gilles is already taking his next shot. Soon Armand's arm shoots up again — incredibly, Gilles has cleaved the pin again. I had no idea he was that good. This time, nobody bothers to encourage Aristide, and nobody's surprised when he misses the white again.

Gilles winds up for his second blow, aiming to strike Aristide again on the same side of his face. From the looks of it, he intends to show no mercy.

"Uh, Gilles," says Royce. "This time, I think you'd better give me that ring."

"An oversight," Gilles says with a shrug, slipping the ring from his finger and handing the big gem to Royce.

If anything, the blow looks intended to be harder than the first. But in the end, it doesn't matter. Aristide hits the ground before the blow can land. At the sight of that palm coming at him again, he faints dead away, much to the amusement of the crowd. I almost feel sorry for Aristide: the disgrace is going to sting tomorrow much more than his lip.

When Armand comes back from the target to see what's

happened, Royce instructs him to carry Aristide back to his room. In a (rather belated) show of sportsmanship, Gilles helps Armand get Aristide up onto his shoulder, and as he does, a look passes between them, and I wonder. Cleaving the pin with two consecutive shots at 200 yards. It's possible, I guess.

"That's two down in less than an hour. Can we get back to drilling as normal, before we lose any more?" Royce says, and that's the end of it.

It was harassment, all right. I'm just not sure who harassed whom. But Pascal tells me later that being served by Gilles at mess that noon was indeed sweet. He enjoyed every bite his master gave him that day.

"I WOULDN'T HAVE PEGGED ARISTIDE FOR A COWARD," I say to Tristan later that night, as we're talking over the incident.

"Bullies usually are. Particularly the big ones."

"Taran must be the biggest coward of them all, then," I joke.

"Taran isn't a coward, Marek," Tristan replies seriously. "Don't ever make that mistake. And, he might be a lot of things, but he isn't a bully, either."

"Really? What is he, then?" I ask, not really expecting a reply to my sarcasm. But Tristan is still serious when he answers me.

"I know what he is to me. What he is to you, well, you'll have to decide that for yourself."

Whatever Tristan says, for the time being, I'm sticking with bully.

The second incident seems to confirm it.

It might not seem like much, but it disturbs me more than I'd like to admit. It's late one night a few days later, about time for lights out, and I've gone to load a plate from the sideboard left stocked for the Journeys outside the main hall. Tristan is always hungry. They all are. But I've never seen anyone eat as much as Tristan can. He likes a little something before bed, to tide him over until morning, so I've taken to bringing some food along with me when I check in with him for instructions before retiring each evening.

There's nobody around in the dark hallway, and I'm just filling the plate, my back to the empty corridor, when I sense someone in the hallway behind me. I turn around, but it must be my imagination. No one is there. I've just turned back to the sideboard when the plate is knocked roughly from my hands, and before I know what's happening, I'm being pushed flush up against the wall in front of me. Someone leans on me heavily, using his body to flatten me against the wall and smash my face up against the cold bricks. A sharp stab of fear jabs me as two huge hands reach down and trap mine, the open palms covering them and pushing them flat against the wall on either side of my shoulders. It doesn't really hurt, but I'm immobilized, smothered under my attacker's massive body so that I can't see anything and I can barely breathe.

I can't see him, and it could be anyone — any of boys, one of the veterans, or a servant, even. But I know it's Taran. He holds me there for a while, letting me sweat while his ragged breathing pulses through me, forcing my body to rise and fall with his. It's stifling under the weight of him, and my heart feels ready to burst. Maybe he's going to search me for the medal. Or maybe he's just letting me know that he could do anything he wants, and I wouldn't be able to do anything about it. Just when I think I can't stand it any longer, that I'm going to have to scream, he leans down and puts his head so close to mine that we're cheek to cheek. His lips brush my ear as he whispers a single word into it, his breath as soft and intimate as a lover's:

"*thief.*"

And then he's gone. The whole thing is so bizarre and it's over so quickly, I might have dreamed it. But my hands are shaking as I bend to pick up the food that's fallen from my tray, and the nape of my neck is burning where his breath touched it. I don't mention any of it to Tristan.

ASIDE FROM THESE INCIDENTS, AS THE WEEKS GO BY, I begin to get used to being part of St. Sebastian's. I fall into its rigorous routine, and I find it suits me. But I never get comfortable. Always, there is the fear of being found out, and the fear of failing.

These twin anxieties keep me constantly on guard, vigilant, and combined with the physical work, they leave me little time to think, and that's what I like best. With the new name, new sex, and completely different surroundings, I can almost pretend that it was my old life that was the dream, and that I've awoken from a nightmare where I was a fletcher's daughter who saw her father shot down, to find myself safe in my bunk in the squires' barracks again. I could almost believe it, that old life seems so far away now, except of course, that I really am a girl. There's no getting around it, though by now I've figured out how to cover the practical issues of concealment pretty well.

Tristan has seen to it that changing clothes is manageable, though I do have to work at it. Using Tristan's room means changing on his schedule, so if I don't time it right, I end up stuck in wet or filthy clothes for the night, but I can put up with it. Besides, the standards of daily cleanliness in the squires' barracks are pretty low. Most of the other boys change as infrequently as I do, so nobody comments much.

Bathing is also not much of an issue, for the same reasons. In three weeks or so, even Tristan has had only two full baths, and from the looks of it, that's at least one more than some of the others (except for Gilles, of course, who seems to require a hot bath virtually every day. He's got two of his own servant boys housed in the guild, and you can hardly go down the hallway in the afternoon without running into one or the other of them carting buckets of hot water from the kitchen into the Journey lavatory to fill his tub, under the watchful direction of Pascal. For a while, I think Aristide was trying to match him bath for bath, but recently he's given up, or maybe his boys revolted — he's got more of them than Gilles, but Armand doesn't have them quite under the same level of control. At any rate, I haven't seen them at it lately, and I don't think Aristide really has that much taste for washing).

Bathing among the squires is even more infrequent, so keeping ahead of most of them isn't hard. Rennie has famously announced that he's going to bathe for first trials and not before, and he's not alone in the sentiment. Being strictly speaking female also helps me out, since I don't perspire as much as the boys do, but I do need to wash. Each time Tristan's bathed, after he finishes, he's stood watch outside the Journey lavatory and let me use his water for my own bath. I've never completely undressed — it's not that I don't trust Tristan, but even alone, I feel too exposed being completely nude. But even taking it in turns to remove my breeches and then my tunic, I've managed to do enough to keep myself as clean or cleaner than most of the others (except, of course, for Pascal, who uses Gilles's water every day). Between baths, it's not hard to get up under my tunic with a sponge now and then, either out at the barrels on the field or in the Journey lavatory when I'm refilling Tristan's splash basin.

Even relieving myself isn't turning out to be the impossibility that I thought it would be. During the day, out on the field I can find a place to slip away and do my business *au natural*, behind the butts or wicker backstops, out behind the stables, or in the garden, and all the boys do it. It's even easier at night, because the darkness helps me out. We've all got a chamber pot under our bunks, so it's a simple matter to take mine down to the end of the room and past the empty cots, where little light penetrates. Nobody is going to want to look too hard at a boy sitting on his pot. I always wait until it's pitch dark, just to be sure, and I'm careful to turn my back. Since most of the boys piss standing up, holding the pot up under them to avoid splashing, with my drop-front breeches and some careful maneuvering, I've figured out how use my pot in a standing position, too. It's tricky, but I've even been getting better at reaching up under my tunic at night to loosen my binding for sleep as much as I dare, under cover of darkness. Really, the only thing that's given me serious difficulty is dealing with some delicate feminine issues, but with a little ingenuity, you can find a way around anything.

Nobody gives me a hard time about wanting my privacy, either, though the boys all have no shame in front of each other. Whatever Tristan told Pascal has taken care of that, and so far, nobody's been too curious. Why should they be? They have no reason to be suspicious. It's amazing, really, how much people see what they expect to see. At first, I thought it was my face that was making it easy for me to pass as a boy, but I could probably take a ravishing beauty, cut her hair and plop her down in the squires' barracks, and everyone would accept her as a boy, too, because really, why in the world would any girl want to pretend to be a boy? Why would they subject themselves to this? Why would they risk it? These are questions that fortunately I don't have time or energy to think about. I just don't ask myself why I'm still here. The answer's obvious, anyway.

And so, as the days go by, I find myself slowly getting faster and stronger, and the work getting easier. My body is losing the curves that suit a woman, but I'm not very sorry to see them go. It makes running and binding my smaller but still-existent breasts easier. I'm finding I have more free time, too, as I can get my chores done faster, or at least I have the energy to make use of my down time, so I can take more part in the life in the barracks. Squires are expected to be available at all times for their masters, so unless we're sent out on an errand or actively attending our master, we hang around the guild. I spend quite a bit of my free time out in the workshop, where I'm helping Marcel out with some of the extra work in exchange for the materials to surprise Tristan with a new bow.

In the barracks, the squires without other chores to do spend most of the time gambling. As a group, we're always chronically short of cash; some of us get a small allowance from our Journey, but otherwise we have to win whatever pocket money we have from those with wealthier masters. Fortunately for everyone, Pascal is a particularly bad gamer, so he keeps most of us supplied, though he won't stoop to playing the barracks favorite, pluck-buffet. All the squires shoot, of course — there isn't much else to do at St. Sebastian's, and though none of them will say so, they all secretly hope to win apprentice status. I can tell most don't stand a chance; they're pretty bad shots.

I think that's why I finally agree one afternoon to let Auguste introduce me to the joys of pluck-buffet, even though it turned my stomach to watch Gilles and Aristide play. In the barracks, the game is a lot tamer. Nobody really tries to hurt each other, much. It's mostly a way to make some money, since you only have to take a hit if you can't pay a penny. I think girls have a higher tolerance for pain than boys, anyway, and with my damaged face, I can take an open-handed slap to the cheek better than some of the others. Plus, even without my own bow, I'm a better shot than most of them, so I get to dish out more than I get. Since I'm not very strong, my blows are particularly light, so the boys like playing with me, and they're pretty good about matching the strength of their slaps to mine. It's true — you can get used to anything. I really do feel like I'm starting to transform into a boy; it's not only my body, but I'm even beginning to acquire a taste for hitting other boys myself. A good slap is exactly what some of them need. But mostly, it's just satisfying to finally beat the other squires at something.

Sometimes, at the end of a long day, I take out the little square of illumination that I still carry with me always, tucked into my waistband. It's the only scrap of my old life I have left. I lie on my back and carefully unfold the parchment, smoothing the well-worn fold lines and running my fingers over the lovely flow of blonde hair. Sometimes I image that the woman in the picture is the mother I never knew. Or sometimes I think of her as St. Irene, the woman who tended St. Sebastian's arrow wounds, who tried to warn him to flee from Rome and escape his ultimate martyrdom. But most often, I just wonder who she is. Always, I kiss the picture for luck before folding it up and tucking it away again, as I did in the brewery, the morning Marek was born. She's become my patroness, of the narrow escape. The one thing I don't think about is my father. The image of him in my mind — well, I've folded that up and tucked it away, too, but I can't look at it now. It's still too painful.

CHAPTER ELEVEN

One afternoon not long after I first try my hand at pluck-buffet, Tristan and I are out on the clout field shooting rovers. That means setting up wands at random distances across the field, so that the archer has to switch up the elevation angle of his bow for each shot. To make it harder, I've clustered the wands back around the 300-yard mark, using the end of the far butts to gauge the distance; Tristan needs to work on his strength for the longer shots and he hates to do it, so I've learned to sneak some distance work in. He's shooting well, and it's a glorious day. After a light rain in the morning, the sky is now clear. The air is cool and crisp, carrying all the sweet smells of April that the rain has brought forth. Maybe that's why it isn't long before Tristan starts to lose his concentration. Even Popinjay, who's followed us out to the field, has tired of having to get up each time we move down the line to the next wand, and has padded off to find some shade.

"What do you say, Marek? Shall we give the rest a reprieve?" Tristan asks, putting down his bow and leaning on it.

We're only on our fourth pass down the line, and there are still five wands to go.

"We've only been shooting for about an hour," I say wryly.

"It's too nice a day to spend it drilling. Come on, don't you want to see what's beyond that wall?" He gestures to the woods beyond St. Sebastian's, and I waver. Searching my face to gauge my mood, Tristan suddenly lets out a cry.

"What the devil, Marek! Who did that to you? Why didn't you tell me!" I'm confused for a minute, then I remember. I've got the faint shadow of a fresh bruise on my face.

"Oh, that. It's nothing," I mumble.

"The hell it's nothing! Nobody's going to beat my squire and get away with it. I told those boys to leave you alone, and I meant it!"

I hate to disabuse him; his possessive tone is really quite gratifying. But I have to confess.

"Really, Tristan. It's nothing. It's just, well, the wages of losing a round of pluck-buffet."

Tristan looks nonplussed, then shakes his head.

"I can't believe it. I'd never have pegged you for a buffet man. I suppose that's what I get for introducing you to Auguste." He takes my chin in his hand, and turns my face up to the sun, to get a better look at the bruise. "It's not too bad. Who gave it to you?"

"Benoit." I hate to admit it. He's a wretched archer, and everybody knows it. "It was a lucky shot!" I add petulantly. "I wouldn't have lost, if I hadn't had to use his bow." I sound just like bratty little Marieke, talking to her father. I guess I haven't changed as much as I thought.

"Your own bow, eh?" he says, looking thoughtful. "I guess that has been an oversight."

He proceeds to strip off his gauntlet and hand it to me. "Okay, let's see what you can do."

"What do you mean? Me, shoot? Now? With what?"

"A friendly wager. Use my bow. If you can hit anywhere on the next wand in three shots, we stay here and you put me through my paces all afternoon. If you can't, we call it a day, and go see what those woods have to offer."

"But that's not fair!" I whine. "Your bow is too big for me. I won't even be able to bend it. And the wand. It's too far. You know I'm not that strong."

"All right, we'll compromise. I'll bring the wand in to 150 yards. But there's nothing I can do about the bow. Either take the wager, or not. But, if you choose to take a pass, well, then we're done. I'm going in."

He holds out the bow and gives me a 'what's it going to be' look. I hate how he has a way of putting things so as to leave me no real choice. Besides, I sense that maybe I can get myself a bow out of this.

I've handled Tristan's bows a hundred times, but I've never thought about bending one before. In my hands now, it seems extraordinarily large, though it probably isn't that much bigger than the one of Jules's I had stashed out in the woodshed. I'm stronger now than I was then, and I've been doing a bit of shooting with the squires using their bows, still I'm nervous as I slip Tristan's gauntlet over my bow arm. I've never shot in front of any of the Journeys, and while Tristan goes out to move the wand, a few other boys start gathering round to see what's going on. Everyone at St. Seb's seems to have a sixth sense for spotting when something unusual is happening. First Jurian and his squire Rennie wander over from the butts, then Charles and Henri come over from the stables. It isn't long before Anselm and Turk have materialized from somewhere, too.

"Ok, Marek. Let's see what you've got." Tristan rubs his hands together, like he's anticipating quite a show. Again, I can't tell whether he really thinks he's giving me a chance to show off or he's setting me up for failure.

"I wasn't expecting an audience," I say, looking around.

"You should be honored, squire," Jurian says. "You've got five Journeys attending your archery debut."

I don't find this very reassuring.

"You'll be fine, Marek." Charles puts a hand on my shoulder. "Just put your body into it."

I square my shoulders and give it a go. I use the same wrenching jerk and exaggerated arc I perfected on Jules's bow, but this bow is much heavier. There's a horrible moment at the top of the motion where I'm struggling so hard against the bow that I must look like Hercules wrestling the hydra, and I'm not entirely sure who's going to win. My audience breaks into hysterics, but I manage to get the bowstring pulled back just far enough and the bow leveled to aim just long enough before losing control, and I let the arrow fly. But I can't watch.

"What happened?" I ask, eyes still closed, as the group falls silent.

"Amazing!" Tristan declares.

"Did I hit the wand?"

"No. Not even close. But the shot. It wasn't half bad, given that ridiculous wind-up. Try it again!"

I open my eyes. The arrow didn't make it all the way to the target, but he's right. It wasn't too bad. The arrow is sticking in the ground about fifteen yards directly in front of the wand.

"A little more power, Marek, and you might have hit it," Charles says. "Come on, let's see it again."

So I try it again. This time I get the arrow a little further, but I pull off to the left. In all, the shot is a bit worse. My third and final arrow is a complete disaster. I try so hard to get power that my hand slips and I let go too early, before I really have time to aim. But it doesn't matter. The Journeys seem impressed anyway.

"With a smaller bow and a little practice, Marek, at a closer distance, you might make a decent butts shooter," Turk says, and the others agree.

"At least, good enough to clean up at pluck-buffet next time," says Charles's squire Henri, pointing to my face. But as the others disperse, Tristan hasn't said anything.

"What do you think?" I finally ask him.

"I think ... I'm going to have to see Marcel about getting you that bow." I'm not sure what he means, but as always with Tristan, I decide to take it as a compliment. I start to head off the field, when Tristan stops me.

"Where do you think you're going?" he asks.

"You won. I didn't hit the wand. I thought we were going in."

"We're not going anywhere now. You finish these wands, then we'll start down the line again, alternating shots. I'll have to watch myself now, won't I, to keep ahead of you." He's teasing, but it's marvelous. I roll my eyes, and he puts a hand on my arm.

"Seriously, Marek. You're young yet. Don't worry about not being strong right now. Every day, you're getting stronger. You'll get your strength. And when you do, you'll be good. I know raw talent when I see it."

I can't tell him that's he's wrong. I am getting stronger, but there's a limit. I may have some talent, and I may get better with practice. I might even get strong enough to be decent on the near butts. But I'll never be a threat to the Journeys. Even if I live to be forty, I'll never be able to send an arrow over 200 yards. I'm never going to be as strong as the others, simply because I'm never going to grow into a man.

"Just promise me something," he says. "If I do get you a bow, don't use it for pluck-buffet. I didn't save you from a beating just to have you subjecting yourself to more."

I'm touched, but by now I know Tristan well enough not to get sentimental. So I say archly,

"If you don't want me to gamble, you'd better start giving me an allowance."

"Let me revise," he laughs. "If you're going to play, just make sure you win!"

Tristan is as good as his word and we finish off another pass at the wands. But his heart still isn't in practicing, so in the end, we agree on another compromise. After shooting one last round, we quit early, while there's still a good portion of the afternoon ahead of us, and make an excursion into the woods.

There's a postern gate out by the workshops that gives access directly onto the L'île-Charleroi road, and the proper route out to the woods is to go out this business entrance and thence through the city gate beyond, but nobody ever bothers to go this way.

There's a place out past the horse pasture beyond the clout field where the wall has crumbled into a series of steps, and it's an easy thing to climb over it like a country stile. All the boys go this way to go hunting, or now that it's getting warmer, to go for a dip in a pond by an old abandoned mill about a half a mile beyond Sebastian's. I've seen others scrambling over the wall, either on their way out or coming back in again, but this is my first venture into the woods.

As I follow Tristan over the wall, I realize with a start that this is the first time I've left the guild since the morning after my father died. It's been weeks since I was outside the guild walls, and it feels strange leaving now, almost like I'm not sure if my new identity can pass beyond the barrier. This wall that once kept me out now circumscribes my whole world. How short a time it took for me to feel more at home inside the guild than outside it!

I feel something approaching real fear as we leave the safety of the guild behind. It's not exactly that I think anything will happen to us, but I'm not sure I'm ready to remember that there's a world outside the guild. I've spent the last few weeks forgetting that world — the world in which my father died. It's the first time I've been in the woods since my trek from the Vendon Abbey to Louvain, and I half expect to find the forest full of ghosts, but to my relief, I find only beauty here today. The sun streaming through the leafy canopy overhead, the sweet gurgling of the stream, the rustling and calls of birds in the thickets — none of these threaten hidden dangers as they did that day, and I think, it's because this time, I'm not alone.

Tristan's got a small bow with him, and I'm carrying his quiver, but as we make our way through the greenwood, Tristan says,

"Let's not hunt, Marek. It's too beautiful a day to kill anything." I'm happy to agree. I'd have to carry anything we caught, and he's right. It's too beautiful a day to have to carry around something dead. Instead, I content myself with calling out marks on the path ahead for Tristan to shoot at — a stump, a sapling, anything will do. Away from the guild, Tristan is relaxed, and he's shooting fabulously. I make a note of it. Maybe coming out to the woods was a good idea. I'm thinking over how I can work regular outings into a kind of training regime, when Tristan stops in front of me and I almost run into him.

"I'm sick of shooting marks, Marek. Can't we just enjoy ourselves out here? Let's give it a rest," he complains. He doesn't mean anything by it, so I think I surprise him when I answer seriously.

"Tristan, don't you want to win?"

"What a question!"

"No, seriously. I mean, you're good, Tristan! Maybe even the best. But ..." I hesitate, not wanting to go too far, not after he complimented me earlier.

"But what? Might as well be out with it."

"Well, you haven't really changed since I got here," I finally say.

"Nobody ever changes. Not really."

"That's not what I mean. I mean, you haven't really gotten any better!"

This is met with silence. So I forge on. "You never want to work on clouts, you just stick with what you're good at, day after day." I can't meet his eyes now, but I can't stop myself, either. "During drills, it's like you're playing, while the others are working." This isn't really fair. He does work hard. But his responses are making me angry. He always refuses to take anything seriously.

"Can I help it if I make it look easy?"

"Not to put too fine a point on it, you're lazy!" I huff.

I think I've probably gone too far, but Tristan just throws his head back and laughs.

"What are you laughing at?" I demand.

"I've been called a lot of things, believe me — but never that!" he replies, still amused. He's as exasperating to talk to as my father!

"Look, Tristan," I say, trying to sound earnest and not mad. "You could do it! I know you could. Don't you want to beat them? Don't you want to beat Taran? I bet he never takes an afternoon off."

At this, Tristan's smile fades. He looks around, and finds a log to sit down on. He motions me down next to him.

"Marcel tells me you've been a big help in the workshop. Is he treating you all right?"

"Yes," I say, wary. I've learned to be suspicious whenever Tristan changes the subject like this.

"I can tell he thinks you're a good worker. I think there may be an apprenticeship for you there, if you want it."

So I did go too far! "Are you getting rid of me already?" I cry, indignant. "I guess I should be grateful, that you're not just shooting me in the foot!" I'm probably not supposed to know about that, but the words are out — I can't take them back. But Tristan just laughs again.

"No, Marek. I'm not getting rid of you. Only when this is all over, when I'm eliminated — I can't keep you. I can't even afford to pay you now. As Marcel's apprentice, well, you'd be doing well for yourself. You'd be set. You'll be able to stay on, when I'm gone."

I start to protest; I can't bear the thought of St. Sebastian's without Tristan. It's unnatural, like the place is really all an extension of him. But he cuts me off.

"You might as well face it now, Marek. I'm not going to beat them all. And I'm certainly not going to beat Taran. Nobody is. Unpalatable as it may be, he's going to win."

"That's what I mean! You're defeated already!" I cry. "You could beat him, I know you could, if you'd just really try."

Tristan just pats me on the back.

"You're nothing if not loyal, eh, Marek? That's why in my book, you're already the best squire at St. Sebastian's. But — have you ever really watched Taran shoot?" When I don't answer, he says, "I thought not."

We sit there a while longer in silence.

"So, Taran's going to win!" I finally say angrily. "What are you going to do about it?"

"All I can do. I'm just going to enjoy the ride."

When we get up again and regain the path, neither of us has any appetite for shooting anymore. The woods seem humid and oppressive to me now. As we go, I call out a few more marks, just to keep up appearances. But Tristan misses them all.

After a while, we leave the beaten path and make our way uncharted through the tangled undergrowth until we come out into a meadow. It looks like a field that's been allowed to stand fallow, and there's a crumbling embankment beyond it. On the top of the embankment are the remains of an old windmill. The main structure is still standing, but only two broken arms remain. It looks like a ship that's run aground on a beach beyond the sea of grass.

In the middle of the field is a single red poppy.

"That's impossible!" Tristan exclaims. "It's too early for poppies." When I call it as a mark, Tristan says,

"I don't want to shoot it, Marek. It wouldn't be right."

"Why not? Because it's too lovely?"

"That, yes. Don't make fun of me. But also, you know what they say about the poppies."

I do. I just hadn't remembered.

"That they're St. Sebastian's blood."

"That's right. In other countries, they have other explanations — they're from the blood of the stigmata, or they grow where men have died in battle. Even the pagans thought they came from the blood of Venus's lover. But we say the poppies sprang from the blood flowing from the saint's wounds."

We contemplate the single red stain a while in silence.

"It's funny. I hadn't thought of it before. I guess it makes sense, since the flower is so red. But all the stories, they're about blood. The flower is so beautiful, Marek. Why can't anyone make up a story about it that's happy?" I cast him a quick glance to see if he's messing with me, but he's perfectly serious. Sad, even.

"I guess the stories *are* happy, in a way," I say. "Even from a wound, something beautiful can grow." I think it sounds quite good, but Tristan's response is scornful.

"Somebody should be able to do a hell of a lot better than that."

He wades into the meadow, and before I can stop him, he plucks the poppy out of the ground and presents it to me. I don't know why, but I wish he hadn't done it. I must be as bad as Brother Benedict, but it seemed somehow like a sign.

We spend the rest of the afternoon lying on the slope of the embankment under the shade of the windmill. The sun's out again, and I'm holding the poppy up to the light, twirling it in my fingers, watching the sun filter through its delicate petals.

"Do you think it's too feminine to like flowers?" I ask Tristan, for no real reason.

"On the contrary," he replies. "Being able to recognize the true beauty of things is the mark of a real man."

"Then I must be awash in masculinity!" I say, closing my eyes and caressing my face with the poppy. When I open them, I find Tristan has propped himself up on one elbow and is contemplating me.

"Do you know what I love about you, Marek?" he says. At the word 'love,' the band around my chest constricts painfully, though he's used it lightly enough. "You're completely without pretense!"

If he only knew. I blush, not only at the compliment, but out of shame, too. But Tristan doesn't notice. He rolls back onto his back.

"Admit it. Much as we may love dear old St. Seb's, it's good to be away. It's good to be able to let your guard down."

"And, to stop acting?" I venture boldly.

"Oh, I'd never do that. Not entirely!" he laughs.

"Tristan," I ask, "Just between us. Who are you, really?"

"I firmly believe, Marek, a man has two choices," he replies, crossing his arms behind his head and looking up at the sky. "He can stage his life as a comedy, or as a tragedy. Personally, I prefer comedy."

"Very clever. But that's not an answer. Besides, not even you can really laugh at everything."

"No. But I can try."

"Come on, Tristan," I say, refusing to let him brush me off this time. "Give me a real answer."

"A real answer? Ok, Marek, my friend," he says. "The real answer is, I wish I knew."

On impulse, I say, "Well, I know exactly who you are, Tristan."

"Oh really? Who's that?"

"You're the next member of the Black Guards, if I have anything to say about it." And I mean it. I resolve right then and there that I'm going to find a way to make it happen.

"Dream on, little brother. Dream on," is all he says, and I do.

We spent the rest of the idyllic afternoon dreaming side by side, under the protective arms of the old windmill.

That night, I have a real dream. It's so vivid, it stays with me all the next day.

It's night, and I'm walking alone in the woods. It's the same woods behind St. Sebastian's, and as I come out into the meadow, just as we did this afternoon, it's bathed in moonlight. The skeleton of the windmill has transformed into the trunk of a dead tree, with two thick barren limbs stretching from it in place of broken arms. Below, the pale grass is bleached as white as flesh in the moonlight, and as my eyes adjust, I see it isn't a field at all, it's a giant body stretched out on the ground. A single poppy is growing from the body, its head red as blood, its slender stalk rising from a single, gaping wound. As I watch, fresh gashes open on the body of their own accord, like hungry mouths opening, each one sending forth a new poppy, until the field is a sea of red. I run out into that sea of blood, and throw myself onto the body, clutching at it desperately, trying to cover all the wounds, to stop them up, but my arms are full of straw; the body's gone, and it's just an empty field, after all.

When I wake up, I'm clinging so hard to my mattress that some of the stuffing has worked free, and the stalks of hay are pricking my neck and face. I burrow further into the mattress, not ready to let the dream slip away, trying to remember before it fades whether the familiar body in the dream was my father's, or Tristan's.

THE NEXT DAY, TRISTAN HAS TUTORIALS IN THE afternoon, so I'm on my own until evening mess. Tristan's been threatening to start teaching me to read once I've settled in, but so far I've escaped that ordeal. I was always so jealous of Jules when my father was teaching him to read, but now I see it as just more work, and I've got enough on my plate already.

I'm coming back from restocking Tristan's cabinet, when Anselm surprises me by calling me over to where he's practicing on the butts by himself.

"Hullo, Marek," he says as I approach.

"Where's Benoit?" I reply, looking around for his squire.

"He didn't show up. He's probably asleep in the barracks." It's true. Benoit can fall asleep anywhere, anytime. One morning, Anselm even found him asleep inside his cabinet.

"Do you want me to chase him down for you? Or, I suppose I could retrieve for you for a while," I offer. I'm thinking about Tristan's comment yesterday, that I'm without pretense. But that's not me, it's Anselm. He's a Journey, but he's plain and simple. There's nothing of the snob about him, even though so many of the others are natural snobs, and Journeyman status breeds more snobbery. It almost demands it. But Anselm treats me like an equal.

"No thanks, Marek. Actually, I was hoping you could help me out, another way." He hesitates, so I give him an encouraging look, and he hurries on: "You see, I saw you shooting the other day. You were good."

"Thanks," I say, flabbergasted. I mean, Anselm may be down-to-earth, but he is a Journey.

"You seem to know what you're about," he continues. "I was hoping you'd watch me shoot, and give me your opinion."

"Are you serious?"

"Of course."

"You want *my* opinion? Shouldn't you be asking one of the other Journeys, or Royce, or Baylen, or somebody?"

"The others, well, they don't think much of me," Anselm says uncomfortably. "I don't mean it in a bad way, Marek, but you know, nobody expects much from me. And I can't really ask the boys to help me, they're competition. As for the vets, well, they don't waste much time on me, either. I mean, it's obvious I'm not going to win. Oh, don't bother to be polite and try to deny it," he says as I open my mouth, but I wasn't going to deny it. It's all true. But it's depressing to hear Anselm say it out loud.

"Look, Marek. I know it, and I don't mind. Really. But I'm not just fooling around, you know? I don't want to waste my time here. I'm older than most of the others and I don't have anything else to fall back on. It's already April, and with Firsts at the end of May, I've got to think about what comes next. I want to learn as much as I can. I want to get better, while I'm here."

"You mean, you don't want to just 'enjoy the ride,'" I say, bitterly, thinking back to yesterday.

"That's it. You do understand. I knew you would. So come on, what do you say? Will you watch me shoot?"

What can I say? The whole thing is so flattering, it goes to my head. Tristan won't listen to me, but here's a Journey actively seeking out my advice. So I agree, even though I should be remembering that he's Tristan's competition, too. But what can it hurt? It's not like I could really help him.

But when he takes his first shot, I see it right away. It's patently obvious. He takes a few more shots, then lowers his bow and looks expectantly at me over it.

"Well?"

"Not bad," I say noncommittally. "Not bad at all."

"Yeah, but not great. Come on, Marek. I'm not asking for praise. What do you think?"

"You're really serious? You really want some criticism?"

"I've said so. This isn't a trap, Marek. I'm not a hypocrite."

"Well, then," I say, hesitantly. "There is something. I think you're holding to aim too long. You're giving yourself a chance to get nervous, to second-guess yourself. This is instinctual aiming, and you've got to trust your instincts." I've heard my father say this to Jules a million times. "You wouldn't be here, if your instincts weren't good."

"Ok," he says, not offended. "So practically, what should I do?"

I find the answer easily, again hearing my father's voice in my head. I'm back in our yard, sitting on a barrel and swinging my legs, watching my father put Jules through his paces. I never realized I was paying such close attention. My father's authority is in my voice this time as I answer:

"You drop down into your full extension. That's fine. Only do it more slowly, focusing on your target the whole time. Coordinate your movement so that you sight your target and hit your full extension at the same moment, then release right away. Boom! Don't really even hold, just catch your target and release immediately. Try changing it up, too, just to see what feels better — try rising into your shot, instead of dropping down. But do it the same way, slowly, focusing on the target, coming into your aim and your release simultaneously. Don't give yourself the chance to override your instincts." When Anselm doesn't say anything, I open my eyes. I've gotten so absorbed in seeing his shots in my mind's eye, I didn't notice closing them. He's looking rather stunned.

"What?" I say.

"Wow, Marek. I thought you might have some advice, but I wasn't expecting a lecture!" He sounds so impressed, I blush. "But, I don't know, Marek. That pretty much goes against everything Royce and Baylen have been telling us."

"Well, you asked for my advice, not theirs," I say, amazed at my own arrogance. "Besides, what can it hurt? Royce and Baylen aren't here."

So he tries the next few shots, my way — or, I should say, my father's way.

"Sorry, Anselm," I say as he lowers his bow again. His shooting isn't noticeably any better. What did I expect? I feel disappointed, though, like my father's let me down. He flamed out as a Journey, after all, didn't he? "I guess I'm just talking out my ear. That's what you get for asking a squire's advice."

"No, Marek," Anselm replies slowly. "I just haven't quite gotten the hang of it. It's going to take some practice, but, do you know, I think you may just be on to something here."

When he shakes my hand warmly before I turn to go, I'm elated. I virtually strut the rest of the way back across the field. I feel like I own the place. Marieke Verbeke, doing the veterans one better at St. Sebastian's! Now, if it were only so easy to get Tristan to listen to me, I think.

Not even the sight of Taran sitting in the shadows against the stable wall, from which vantage point he's witnessed the whole thing, can put an immediate damper on my moment of triumph.

As I near the stables, though, my confidence begins to waver. I've got to go back inside through the stable door now, it's too late to change my route without making it obvious that I'm afraid of Taran. For once, I'd even be glad to have Popinjay dogging my heels, but I left him curled up at Tristan's feet back in the archives. It's ridiculous to be so petrified just to pass by Taran, but with so few people about, I feel exposed.

To make things worse, Taran suddenly gets to his feet just as I approach. I come to a complete stop, thinking he intends to block my way. I bet I'm about to find out what the wood of the stable door feels like, up close. But then Remy bounds out of the stables, babbling apologies for being late. Of course, Taran's been waiting there for Remy. He's only risen to meet his squire.

"Oh, hullo, Marek," Remy says, when he notices me. We've made friends, in a way, as he predicted. It's impossible not to like Remy. As long as we don't talk much about either Tristan or Taran, we get along just fine.

"Remy," I say, trying to slip past and make my escape, but Remy steps in front of me and we do an awkward little dance in the doorway, me trying to get past, and Remy succeeding in getting in my way.

"Come on, Remy, you're blocking his way," Taran says, not unkindly, putting a hand on his squire's shoulder to pull him gently out toward the field. To me, he adds with a sneer:

"Don't stay on our account, Woodcock." I get the implication immediately. A woodcock is a notoriously stupid bird — an easy target. "I, at least, don't need *your* advice on shooting. But, if I ever need to pick a pocket, you'll be the first to know."

"*Ha ha*, Taran!" Remy trills nervously, his little hands fluttering in front of his mouth. "You're such a tease! But poor Marek here doesn't know you like I do. He won't know you're kidding."

Taran drapes his arm protectively around Remy's shoulder, giving him a conspiratorial squeeze. "Don't worry, Remy. I'm sure Marek here knows exactly how serious I am." Our eyes meet over Remy's head, and I can't help giving an involuntary shiver. Taran's lip curls in response, and I hate myself for letting him see how much power he has over me.

"Well, that's okay, then!" Remy chirps, hustling Taran out to the field before he can say anything else, determined to keep up the charade that we're all friends here.

I watch them make their way together out to the far butts, thinking what a strange pair they make. No stranger, I suppose, than Gilles and Pascal, or beautiful Jurian and the hideous Rennie. Or Tristan and me, for that matter.

Remy starts setting up for Taran to do some mid-distance shooting, or rather, what's probably mid-distance for Taran. It looks pretty far to me. It's true that I've never really watched Taran shoot, as Tristan said, so instead of going straight in as I'd intended, I stay there under the eaves a while, and from this safe distance, I watch them.

I've heard the boys talk, so I expect Taran to be good. I know he's the strongest archer of the group. That much is obvious from his physique. His specialty is not surprisingly clouts, the powerhouse specialty — he's such a brute, it makes sense. So I think I expect him to be something of a grunt, impressive just because he's big, because he pushes himself and practices more than the others, some kind of cold, soulless automaton with no style. But I couldn't be more wrong.

He is strong, there's no doubt about that, and his body is too big to have the same graceful line as Gilles's or Tristan's, but in his own way, he's as breathtaking in motion as either of them. What's more, he's devastatingly consistent and accurate, even at this distance. But that's not really what makes an impression on me; it's the shooting itself. He combines immense strength and a kind of grace, too, with something I can't quite define, but I find it disturbingly moving. Whereas Tristan's shooting is light and high, like pure ether, glorious and joyful, Taran's seems sad to me, if that makes any sense. Watching Tristan shoot, I think of a young god, a radiant Apollo, a glorious boy at play. But Taran already looks like a man. When he shoots, he shoots like a man who's fully aware of what his arrows can do, of the violence they're meant to bring, a man who knows his target is mortal. It doesn't look like a game to him. It sounds dramatic, but if I had to put a name to that elusive quality, it might be a kind of passion, or suffering, even. He seems to suffer something with each arrow he sends, like he's letting something of himself fly, too, something that feels a kinship with the suffering of his target.

I must stand there watching him for over an hour, and with each shot, my heart sinks a little lower in my chest. I've never seen anything like it. Tristan's right. He wasn't being defeatist the other day, he was just being realistic. Tristan may be the most beautiful archer I've ever seen, but he's never going to beat Taran. Nobody is.

Getting Tristan into the Black Guards is going to be a lot harder than I thought.

THERE ARE ONLY THREE TOPICS OF CONVERSATION AT ST. Sebastian's: archery, girls, and politics. Of the three, the only one that interests me at all is archery. So I'm disappointed, when I walk into the great hall a few nights later behind Tristan and find the Journeys already in the middle of one of their heated political debates. I'll admit that these are exciting times, since Ardennes is only a very small principality, a buffer state nestled between much stronger neighbors with even stronger allies (Liege and the Holy Roman Empire on one side, Brabant backed by Burgundy on the other); with so many small independent Counties and Duchies around us, there's always something going on just across our borders. And ever since Edward of England declared himself the rightful king of France, it's become a madhouse, what with armies marching through the lowlands, and everyone scrambling to figure out how to turn the war between this pretender and the true French king to their advantage. The war hasn't come directly to Ardennes yet, but it's in our own back yard. But as a girl living out in the country, I've been woefully uneducated in politics, and half the time I've no idea who or what the boys are talking about. I'm not sure they have much idea what they're talking about half the time, either.

Gilles and Aristide are the worst offenders, though his father's university connections in Meuse make Jerome think he's got his finger on the international pulse, or some such nonsense, so he can be counted on to spout off pretty regularly, too. A popular topic of discussion is the upcoming coronation of our own young prince Philip. All princes of Ardennes seem to be named Philip, so they try to distinguish themselves from our former princes and from all the other nobles named Philip in the region by adopting epithets for themselves, like 'Philip the Bold' or 'Philip the Generous.' The current prince's father, Philip the XII, tried to dub himself 'Philip the Fair,' but everybody just called him Philip the Fat — behind his back, of course. Since the prince isn't yet 18, he's usually just known as 'the young prince' or 'Philip the Younger,' and since he's about their age and an archery enthusiast (along with everyone else in Ardennes), all the Journeys are crazy about him. There's even a rumor that his coronation next year when he comes of age is going to be timed to correspond with the final competition for Guards, so that his new Guardsman will be sworn in during the same ceremony. If true, it would be a huge honor for the boy who wins, so the Journeys understandably get quite worked up talking about it.

I'm as loyal to the prince as the next man, but frankly, Philip's uncle Reynard, who's currently ruling in the prince's stead as regent, has proven himself to be quite a savvy operator, and I don't think I'm the only one who is secretly a little worried about what's going to happen when the young prince takes over. It's like this: who would you really want in charge of defending your country against inroads by France and England — a man like Master Guillaume, or a boy like Gilles?

Tonight, there seems to be some real news.

"I tell you, Meuse is in an uproar!" Jerome is saying, as we take our places at the table. "It's pandemonium. Everyone's afraid the trouble's to spread across our border."

"Jerome's right," Falko puts in. "Guillaume's on his way to Meuse right now, to meet with the guilds." I look around; sure enough, the master's not as his place. Even the veterans' table is sparsely populated. The veterans who are there are engaged in as animated a discussion as the Journeys.

"Where *is* everybody?" Tristan asks. He's about as interested in politics as I am.

"It's Liege, duBois! Haven't you heard?" Jurian replies.

"There's finally been an uprising! They've kicked de la Marck out!" Jerome's been predicting trouble in Liege for weeks now, so he sounds pleased. Liege is a principality just north of Ardennes, not far up the Meuse river from our capital L'île de Meuse.

"What's that got to do with Guilly?" Tristan asks.

"That's just it!" cries Jerome. "Not only have they kicked their prince out, but — get this — the *guilds* themselves are now running things! The Regent sent for Guillaume himself, asked him to go and talk to the guilds in Meuse, to make sure they don't get any crazy ideas of their own."

"Guilly'll get 'em in line, that's for sure," Jurian snorts.

"It's not going to be that simple, Jurian," Gilles protests. "You know St. Sebastian's has a special status. It's exempt from all taxation and tariffs. Guillaume's going to be under a lot of pressure to support the other guilds in demanding some of the same privileges. He's going to be on the spot, between the guilds and the Regent."

"It's those weavers," Aristide says. "Mark my words. They're always causing trouble. Baylen was right — he should have whipped your tailor when he had the chance, Gilles."

"I doubt my tailor had anything to do with the uprising in Liege," Gilles replies dryly, "but much as I hate to say it, Aristide is right. What with King Edward scratching around for their support for England, the weavers and dyers are going to try to take advantage. They need English wool. Look what happened in Flanders." I have no idea what happened in Flanders, so this doesn't mean anything to me, but everyone else is bobbing their heads in agreement.

"That could never happen in Ardennes!" Turk cries. He sounds a little tipsy already, and the meal has barely started. "St. Sebastian's will never allow the guilds to get out of control! As for throwing in our lot with the English? It's laughable! I'm just as happy as the next man to have France keep its long nose out of our affairs, but not at the price of falling victim to the English claws." Getting to his feet, he raises his tankard in salute. "To our Church and to our Holy Roman Empire, nice and far away, as it should be! To an independent Ardennes! St. Sebastian's will always be loyal to the prince!"

"Hear, hear! St. Sebastian's will never allow an uprising here," Jurian agrees, as though he personally is going to do something about it.

"But if it's the guildsmen that are rising up, where will that leave St. Sebastian's?" Anselm asks seriously.

"The guilds will never rise in Ardennes. The Black Guards won't let them," Taran says solemnly, and nobody dares say anything. His father's the captain of the Guards, after all. "The Guards will never turn against the prince."

"But what of the prince himself?" It's Royce. He's wandered over and is now standing at the head of the table. "We're not going to be able to bury our heads in the sand here in Ardennes much longer. We're going to have to take sides. Concessions will have to be made, somebody's privileges curtailed. So the real question is, does anyone really know what the prince plans to do, once he's in power? St. Sebastian's may be loyal to the prince, but will the prince be loyal to St. Sebastian's? Maybe this time next year, we'll all be taking orders from Gilles's tailor."

With that, everyone loses their taste for politics, and the conversation turns general, until Master Leon calls for attention. He's a strange little man, but from all accounts he's a marvelous archer. He must be, to be in charge of training, though I've yet to see him shoot. He's got the broad shoulders of an archer, but otherwise he's terribly thin, so he looks something like a toad body grafted onto long frog legs. He's going bald, too, but he's let the hair he does have grow down past his shoulders. The effect is singularly ugly. It's unusual for anyone this blatantly unattractive to make it far in the guild; the judging is subjective enough that the judges usually find ways of cutting boys early who don't cut a fine enough figure. He must really be an exceptional shot.

"Gentlemen, it cannot have escaped your notice that Master Guillaume is absent tonight, having been called to the capital on urgent business. It will also not have escaped your notice that the date of our first trials is rapidly approaching. As you know, it is our custom here at St. Sebastian's to announce the theme of each competition well in advance and in accordance with a set schedule."

At this point, the master has to put up his hand to quiet the murmurs which have begun to echo through the hall at the mention of first trials.

"As is our tradition, each of the three Journeyman trials focuses on one of the main types of target shooting, chosen at random: butts, wands, or clouts. You can be assured that we will endeavor to set tests which interpret these themes in challenging and unexpected ways," he pauses to allow for some appreciative chuckles, "but the early announcement of the theme is meant to give you Journeys fair warning so that you can train appropriately. According to our ancestral schedule, tonight should be the night for the selection of the theme for Firsts."

Everybody's really excited now, but as the boys begin to stomp, Leon puts up his hand again. "Unfortunately, Master Guillaume is not here to preside over the selection ceremony tonight. I know this is a disappointment," he adds hastily at the cries of protest this elicits, "but we are confident that he will complete his business efficiently and quickly, and so we expect to have him back with us within the week." He pauses, letting the Journeys murmur amongst themselves, before continuing. "However, we have decided to go ahead with the ceremony as planned, despite his absence! Master Royce, will you do the honors?"

All the boys rise and stand at attention, so I follow suit. Royce takes an urn up to the masters' table and presents it to Master Leon, who makes a show of stirring the contents before pulling out an ivory token.

"The theme for first trials will be ... *Butts!*" he cries, and the boys begin to clap, some in genuine excitement, others trying to conceal their disappointment, as Master Leon holds up the token and shows the symbol on it to the room: a small, black wooden pin. "Boys!" he calls, "Let this serve as an inspiration to you to step up your training. First trials are less than a month away. And as a reminder of why you're here: leave the politics to others. You're here to shoot. And to pass butts, you've got to be in top form."

He sits down, and as the room settles down again and the boys regain their seats, all talk has turned to first trials, and the relative merits of butts as the first ordeal.

"That's good for us, isn't it?" I say to Tristan, who isn't looking very pleased.

"I don't know, Marek. I suppose. But, I rather wish it had been clouts."

"Clouts!" I say, thinking he's being defeatist again. "That's your worst. Why would you want that?"

"It's like this. At each trial, two boys are cut. I'm not bragging, but I'm pretty sure I can beat out at least two of the boys in any kind of shooting. But I'll be up against the better boys later, and we'll be competing in my worst skill. In all, I think it's an advantage to have your best skill last, not first." I hadn't thought of it this way, but maybe he's right.

"Take Anselm, for example," Tristan continues. "He's one of the weakest shooters. If clouts were first, we could count on passing him easily. At butts, I can't be so certain."

"Surely you can beat Anselm!" I say nervously.

"A few weeks ago, I'd have agreed. But he's mysteriously gotten a lot better recently. Surely you've noticed." I can't tell if he knows about my little training session, or not.

"Not enough to be a threat to you, Tristan!"

"Probably not. But competition is funny. You only get a few shots. All it takes is one lucky one for the worse man to win."

By this time everyone is starting to get up to leave, and as we rise to join the general exodus, Charles pulls Tristan aside to ask him something about a practice plan for tomorrow. I'm left to contemplate the reality of Tristan's unpleasant pronouncement as I make for the door with the others.

"Say, what's this?" All of a sudden Aristide is next to me, and before I can stop him he's pulled my little square of illumination out of my waistband. "What have you got here, Marek?"

I make a grab for it, somehow not wanting him to see it, but he's too tall. He holds the page up out of my reach.

"Give it back!"

"Been holding out on us again, eh, Marek?" My reaction was a mistake; he's interested, now. "What is it, another treasure? Another little gift from daddy?"

"It's mine! Give it back!" My voice sounds desperate. He's such a sleaze, I can't stand the thought of him looking at my picture. I don't want him to ruin it for me.

"Give the lad back his paper, Ari," Gilles says behind me.

"Oh, I will. I'm no *thief*," Aristide says. "I just want to see what it is. We all do, don't we, boys?" he says loudly, making sure he's got everyone's attention. Then he makes a big show of unfolding the page, while holding me off with his elbow. Most of the others have gathered around, curious. Even Gilles is curious, I can tell, because he hasn't made any more move to help me. Tristan has frustratingly gotten deep into a conversation with Charles back at the table, and hasn't seemed to notice what's going on.

Aristide squints at the page.

"What is it, Ari?" Jurian asks.

"Just a scrap of a book, looks like. With a mighty pretty girl," Aristide leers, turning the paper so everyone can see my blonde. I let out an involuntary moan. I feel like she's been sullied already.

"What a looker! Give it here. What's it say?" Falko makes to take the page, but Aristide sidesteps him and holds the page closer to him.

"It's pretty smudged, the kid must carry it with him all the time, but let's see: *'lying on Paris with her whole body, the beautiful Helen opens her legs, and parting his, with her mouth she … *Whoa, Marek!" he says, breaking off in delight and feigning modesty, "I can't even read this aloud! It *is* a treasure! Why, it's positively pornographic!"

The boys give a whoop and all start trying to grab the page while my face turns beet red. It can't really say that, can it? The page is so damaged, Aristide must not be reading it. He's just making up filth to embarrass me, isn't he?

By now Falko's gotten hold of it.

"What does it say, Falko?" Laurens is saying, "*You'd* say anything aloud. Come on, read it! Or give it to me!"

"*She opens her legs, and parting his, with her mouth she robs him of his seed!*" Falko reads out triumphantly, waving the page over his head, as the boys continue their catcalls, some jabbing me in the ribs appreciatively while others keep trying to grab at the parchment for themselves.

"Just a minute! There's more ... Hmm, the rest is pretty hard to make out. But there's a pretty raunchy line here about 'purple bed linens privy to their sins,' and something about stains. I can't quite make it out, but you catch the drift." By now, everyone is gathered around him, trying to make out more of the text.

So it's true. It is as sordid as Aristide claimed. I can't believe another possession has turned against me. What in the world was Abelard doing, copying something like this?

"Say, Marek, I think I'll just borrow this for the evening, whaddya say?" Falko teases, elbowing me in the ribs again. "A little reading in bed, *you* know. Just me and the purple linens. Ha!"

He makes a crude pumping gesture, and I feel so positively sick at what he's implying, I almost don't want the page back again. At this point, Tristan steps forward.

"I think I'd better take that, Falko," he says, putting out his hand. He sounds just like he did that day in the alley, so Falko just shrugs and hands it to him.

"Just having a little fun, Tristan. Don't get in a twist."

"And you," Tristan says to me, ignoring Falko and the rest, "had better come with me."

I follow Tristan back to his room in silence, my head hanging. When we're both safely inside and he's closed the door, he turns to me and says,

"So, Marek. Have you got any more 'unusual' possessions squirreled away that I should know about?"

"That was the last one," I say dismally.

"Because really, getting them back for you is starting to get tiresome." He sits down heavily on the bed, holding the parchment page out in front of him. He stares at it, lost it thought, for so long that I begin to wonder if he remembers I'm still there. He looks just like a little boy, with that one unruly lock of hair hanging in his eyes again. I have the urge to brush it away for him, but wisely I don't. I'm not sure if he's angry with me or not.

"Where did you get this?" he finally asks, not taking his eyes from the picture.

I sidestep the real question, but answer honestly enough.

"I just thought she was pretty. I didn't know what it says, honestly. You know I can't read." When he doesn't say anything, I add, "I didn't even think any of the words were legible."

"They're legible enough, all right."

"So it would seem."

There's another pause. "I swear I had no idea! It's not, *uh*, like Falko says," I add, unsure how to put it.

"I believe you, Marek. But I think, I'd better keep this, too, for the time being."

And so just like that, Tristan takes my last possession from me. But I don't really mind. I'm angry at the woman and her knowing smile. I thought she was watching over me, protecting me, but it turns out, she's been mocking me, too.

"Who is she, Tristan?" I ask. He's staring at the picture so intently, I get the impression he recognizes it. "Do you know?"

"Yes. I think I can guess," he says slowly. "From the names. This must be from Exeter's *Iliad of Darias the Phrygian*, about Helen of Troy."

"Who is that?" I ask.

"Simply put, she was the most beautiful woman in the world." He's still riveted to the picture, and I can't make out his tone. I still can't tell if he's mad at me. He sounds disappointed.

"Was she, a, um …" I falter, looking for a delicate word. "Was she a 'woman of easy virtue'?"

"A woman of easy virtue!" Tristan repeats scornfully. "What a phrase! What does that even mean? Easy virtue? Easy for whom? Not for the woman, surely. Never for the woman."

I'm not sure what he's talking about, as so often with him. But the parchment's upset him. I try again.

"I mean, was she a courtesan?"

He snorts. "Haven't you even heard of Troy?" he asks. When I just shrug, he explains. "Helen was a married woman. Married to a king of Greece. The story goes, she used her beauty to seduce Paris, the handsome young prince of Troy. It started the most devastating war in history. Because of her, both sides suffered horrible losses. Great heroes fell. Troy was burned to the ground."

"Did it really happen?"

"Oh, it happened all right. Troy burned. But I doubt it was over a woman. You might as well know now, Marek. Men love nothing better than to blame their own sins on women. It's as old as the Greeks."

I can tell he's angry now, but I don't think it's with me. So I venture one last question.

"Tristan, I might not know much, but this is from an illuminated manuscript, isn't it? Why would a monk be copying a text like this? It doesn't make any sense. Aristide was right, it is obscene."

"That's easy enough," he says, more in his usual tone. "The point of the text is to show the work of the Devil. It's a warning. You know the stuff — women's beauty as the playground of Satan. But there's a lot of relish spent listing the details. Copying a text like this adds a little spice to a monk's cold life." At this, he even chuckles, though he doesn't really sound very amused. "I bet whoever copied this had a blast."

I try to picture Father Abelard lingering lustily over the details of this sordid story, and I just can't do it. And I can't ask Tristan the real question. Why in the world would Father Abelard give this to *me*?

THAT NIGHT, I CAN'T SLEEP. I FEEL ALONE AND BETRAYED by my lady of the parchment, as I've come to think of her. It's hot in the barracks, and the band around my breasts feels so constricting I can't stand it another minute. So I decide to do something risky. I'll take it off entirely, just for the night. Once the lamps have all been put out, I reach up under my tunic and unwrap it, working it loose and wadding the long strip of material into a ball under my head. It takes some wriggling and bumping to get it off, and I don't notice how much noise I'm making until Remy says,

"Give it a rest for one night, will you, Marek?," and from down the room, Rennie cackles,

"I guess Tristan must have given him back his porn."

But for some reason, the lewd insinuations don't bother me as much from the squires as they did from the Journeys. Besides, once

I've got the band off, I feel so wonderfully cool and free, I don't mind anything, so I just say with real feeling,

"Sorry, boys. I can't help myself. It just feels so good!" And they all laugh. I instantly wish I'd kept my mouth shut. If I don't watch out, it won't be long before I'm just as crude as Falko.

I sleep fitfully, worried about oversleeping and being caught next morning with no way to get bound up again, because I won't be able to wrap the binding back on without stripping off my tunic. So when I wake at what I estimate to be a few hours before first light, I get up carefully and pick my way across the room. Even at this hour and in the dark, I don't dare undress in here. I'll just nip around to the Journey lavatory and get the band back on in there.

It all goes smoothly until I come back into the Journeyman hallway, the sash safely back in place. I haven't dared light a candle, so I've had to feel my way along, but as soon as I come out of the lavatory, I hear a door open and close softly at the far end of the hall, and candlelight appears in the hallway. I freeze, as soft footsteps approach, and a small halo of light comes closer. I suppose I could have made a run for it, but I hesitate too long, and then it's too late. I wait there, frozen in the open lavatory doorway, for the figure to approach. He's coming straight down the hall, and I expect he's headed here — there's nothing else on the hall but dormitory rooms — but the boys have pots in their rooms, so I'm not sure what anyone is doing out at this hour. With my luck, it's sure to be Taran.

It's not until he's right next to me that I can see who it is. It's Jurian, and he's not coming into the lavatory. He goes right by, and for a moment I think he isn't going to notice me. But when he's only about a foot or two away, he gives a start, and looks me right in the eye, but he doesn't stop. He keeps moving past me without a word and disappears into a room a few doors further down. His own door, as it turns out. He acts for all the world as though he doesn't see me standing there, but in that second when we lock eyes, the expression on his face is a mixture of surprise, and, I think, fear.

Once he's back in his room, I bolt down the hallway to the safety the barracks, my heart pounding. The next morning, I wait for some repercussions from my midnight stroll to hit. I'm not supposed to be out of barracks after lights out. But nothing happens. Apparently, Jurian hasn't told anyone. Could he really not have seen me? Could I have imagined that startled look? Maybe so. It was dark and I was scared, after all. And so, for the time being, I simply count myself lucky, and forget about it. It doesn't even occur to me to wonder where he'd been.

CHAPTER TWELVE

I've been at the guild for about a month when I find out why everyone is afraid of Tristan. It's perfectly simple, and it has nothing to do with archery. He's crazy.

It's the end of a particularly miserable week. Ever since the announcement of first trials, the mood at training has turned more serious. It's not really that the work is any harder, but everyone's been reminded of what's at stake, and the stress is beginning to take its toll. To make things worse, after a false spring, the weather has turned, and it's been raining steadily for days. Mostly it just drizzles enough to soak us to the skin over the course of the morning, but not enough to stop practice. Anyway, it has to be a real downpour before Baylen will call a halt to drills. It's taken me a while to realize that he's much younger than Royce, about the age of the Journeys, even. Apparently, it was just last year that it was down to him and one other archer for Guards. When he narrowly missed out, Guillaume invited him to stay on as a trainer, and I have to admit he's very good. He's got an eye for everyone's weaknesses, anyway. But I think he's too aware that he's not really much older than the boys, and so he makes up for his age by being something of a tyrant. The weather has been bringing out his famous sadistic streak, and he's decided it's the perfect time for clout shooting, hour after hour, three days in a row, even though that's not what the boys need now. First trials is butts, after all.

Everyone's exhausted, and we're all running out of dry clothes. Even Tristan's out of spares to share with me. The other squires can strip down between practices and dry their shirts by the kitchen fires, but I can't, so I was stuck in wet clothes for two days until Pascal noticed and borrowed some things for me from Gilles. Now I look a complete fool running up and down the butts with lace flopping at my neck and wrists. A day or two ago, as I slipped in the mud and fell behind, and while everyone was watching me straggle back to the line, Falko called out to me, "Watch your eye, Woodcock!" Everyone laughed, even the veterans. Even Tristan. I had to smile and pretend to be a good sport, but I didn't find it very funny. Not only do I hate the spread of the nickname Taran coined for me, but the eye is the part of the bird a hunter takes aim at. It's not just an insult. It's a threat.

Tristan just laughed at me when I said so, saying "I've shot so many squires, what do you expect? Come on, Marek, a little good-natured ribbing is a good thing. It shows they think of you as one of the boys now," but I'm not convinced. For the rest of the day, some of the Journeys took to winking at me in an exaggerated motion that recalled the one Taran made in the great hall, whenever I happened to catch their eye, emphasizing the motion with a click of the tongue. I'm sure most of them did mean it to be humorous, but by the end of the day I'd had enough of it. Some of the squires picked up on it, too, so it continued for the next few days, until it became old even to the most juvenile of them.

Between the weather, the winks, Gilles's frilly shirts, Baylen's perverse mood and the stress of first trials looming, by the end of the week I'm feeling all in, and I'm not the only one. Not even Tristan and Gilles have much taste for banter during drills, and that's saying something. So when at noon mess on Friday a free night is announced for the evening, the Journeys all get to their feet in a spontaneous toast to the master, and I'm not far behind.

Ordinarily, evening mess is mandatory. It marks the beginning of curfew, and anyone caught breaking curfew is brought before the masters. But occasionally, the boys are granted a night out on the town for relaxation. This is the first free night since my arrival, so it must not happen very frequently; the timing is pretty obvious, too.

Having the boys on display around town is advertising for the upcoming trials.

Pretty quickly, the Journeys hatch a plan to treat us squires to a round at the Drunken Goat. It turns out, this has been the traditional Journey hang-out in town for generations. It's still raining, so after noon mess most of the Journeys abandon any pretense of practicing in the afternoon, and they concentrate instead on preparing for the night out. They suddenly all want a hot bath, so there's a run on the Journeys' lavatory, and some of the braver boys appropriate the vets' lav, too. The hallways are full of squires and serving boys carrying buckets of boiling water from the cauldrons in the kitchen, and I only manage to grab one of the tubs for Tristan with difficulty. There aren't enough servants to go around and I'm still low man on the pecking order, so I end up having to haul Tristan's water myself, and I'm on my sixth bucket when Pascal comes to my rescue. He's already gotten Gilles's bath ready, so he loans me Gilles's serving boys — they're more than used to the task.

In the lavatory, it's a madhouse. Boys in various states of undress are running in and out — there are five tubs, so five Journeys can bathe at once, though I've never seen it happen before. What with Journeys and squires and servants all trying to pack into the small room, we're basically crawling around on top of each other like ants. By the time I've got Tristan's tub ready and he shows up, Gilles is already getting out and Pascal is stripping down to get into his water. Jerome is standing naked by the splash basins, using a straight razor, and Jurian and Falko are sitting in tubs while their squires pour water over them. By now I should be used to the nudity, since the boys undress in front of me all the time. I'm pretty good about trying to be discrete, though. I try hard not to look at them or see anything I shouldn't, and I'm really not at all tempted to peek at most of the squires. But we're all packed in here so tight, there's hardly a safe place to look. Somehow I've gotten backed up next to Jerome, and Auguste keeps jostling me as he attempts to fill his bath, so I keep bumping him. When my hand inadvertently skims Jerome's bare bottom, I jump about a foot in the air.

"Watch it, squire!" he says irritably. "Do you want me to take my head off?"

I mumble an apology, trying to move away, but Pascal is standing bare-chested right in front of me, and from the looks of it, he's about to take off his pants, so there's nowhere to go. Jurian and Falko are mercifully submerged, but Gilles is strutting around the room in no apparent hurry to put anything on, so it comes as a great relief when Tristan shows up and I have something to concentrate on, even though usually tending Tristan in his bath is quite stressful. Needless to say, keeping myself from peeking at him is a lot harder.

Fortunately, Tristan doesn't have as much taste for being served as Gilles does, so helping him in the bath usually just means folding his clothes and having his clean clothes ready. With a concerted effort, I can usually do this with eyes averted enough to preserve his modesty, if he knew enough to have any around me. And as I say, I make the effort. I really do. I have some dignity.

As he starts to undress, I turn my back and pretend to be busy lining up his boots, so that's all right. I reach back without looking to take each article of clothing as he discards it, and I fold it neatly on a stool, trying hard not to see Gilles swinging past right around eye level. But when Tristan climbs into the full tub and sits back, arms resting on its sides, and I turn around at his request to pour in more water, the heady atmosphere gets to me, I guess.

My guard is down, since once the boys are in the tubs, I can't really see anything. But as I watch the water I'm pouring sheet down over Tristan's head and chest, I notice a drop trickling down over the arrow brand on his arm. I can't stop myself. I reach out, and run my finger slowly over the welt, caressing its whole length, and wiping the bead of moisture from the tip of the arrow. Then all of a sudden, I remember with a jolt that inside the tub, he's completely naked. I snatch my hand away guiltily. I dart a look around the room, to see Jurian watching me from his tub. His expression is blank, but for some reason, meeting his eyes like this takes me back to the night I met him in the dark hallway. Only this time, I'm the one with the startled look. I wonder if he thinks he's caught me at something. For some reason, though, I feel like maybe it's me that's caught him again, for a second time.

"Did it hurt?" I ask Tristan, feeling the need to cover, forcing myself to touch the welt again, this time more innocently.

"No, it didn't *hurt*," he laughs. "It hurt like hell!"

"Wanna see it fly?" says Falko from behind me, and when I turn around, he flexes his muscles so the similar welt on his arm moves up and down.

"Nice, Falko," Tristan says. "About as wobbly as your usual shots."

"Girls love it," Jurian says, still looking at me curiously, and I sincerely hope he doesn't mean the comment specifically for me.

But the moment passes, as Jurian calls out to Rennie, "I'm ready to get out! Where the devil are my clothes?" As he moves to stand (and accordingly I find something very compelling to do looking the other direction), Gilles, who has finally put on some pants, exclaims:

"Ah, Jurian, you're just like Venus rising from the sea! If you were any prettier, I'd be tempted to have a go at you myself."

"I'm already prettier than any of your conquests, Lejeune."

"Too true, too true," Gilles replies, "More's the pity."

THE REST OF TRISTAN'S BATH GOES WITHOUT INCIDENT, but by the end of it, I'm feeling pretty glad that the boys don't bathe more often. I'm feeling pretty blue, to be honest. Most of the other squires are stripping down and using the water after their masters, eager to look their best tonight, but I won't get a wash. The lavatory is too crowded. It doesn't really matter — I doubt anyone will be able to smell me over the reek of the boys' perfume. All I really need to do is stand next to Gilles. It would be nice, though, to be part of the general primping, so I feel left out. I can't help it that hanging around in that crowded bath as those gorgeous boys all washed has stirred me up. That's only natural. But the thought of them all looking forward to making conquests upsets me, too. It's not even that I want the boys for myself. Not really. Well, maybe that's part of it. But it's more than that. It's that making conquests is something I'll never do. I can't overcome nature with pure will, and the path I'm on right now is destined to leave me completely alone. It's another reminder that I'll never really be one of them, no matter how hard I pretend to fit in.

So when I wander out to the stables to return the buckets, my mood is low. I'm feeling lonely, and some of the joy I had in anticipating an evening out as 'one of the boys' is gone. It's still raining steadily, but the weather's been about to break all day, so I look out to see if it shows any sign of clearing for us. Through the open stable door, I'm surprised to see there's a lone figure out on the practice field. One of the Journeys isn't taking part in the preparations, either. Instead, he's doggedly putting himself through his paces, despite the weather and the fading light. He's too far away to see clearly at this hour through the rain, but I stop and contemplate the solitary figure, feeling an odd kinship with the lone archer. From his motion, he's taking slow, powerful shots. I watch him rock far back on his legs and swing the bow in a high arc, the rain pounding down on his upturned face. His motion so matches my mood, I stand and watch him for a while, imagining I'm that boy, too, venting my sadness by sending it out as a shower of arrows into the rain. And after a minute or two, I start to feel better. Maybe I do belong here, after all.

I'm about to go when I hear a sound, and I turn to see Remy perched on top of a barrel under the eaves, watching the archer with an anxious expression.

"He insisted I stay in," he says, without looking at me. He hasn't taken his eyes off the field. "He's very protective. But I don't like leaving him out there alone."

So it's Taran. I might have known.

The idea that Remy needs to watch over him is so absurd, I don't bother to answer.

IT COMES AS SOMETHING OF A SURPRISE TO ME, THEN, when we're all assembled outside the great hall later to head off to the tavern, to find that Taran and Remy are part of the group. In the end, all the Journeys and squires come along. Everyone is so ready for a night out that all differences are temporarily forgotten, and we're a lively party.

As we make our way through town, everyone stops to watch us go past, and I'm proud to be part of such a handsome group. *En route,* the squires naturally fall behind to talk among ourselves, so we arrive at the Drunken Goat almost as two separate parties, the Journeys ahead and the squires crowding in behind. The place is packed, and the arrival of the Journeys *en masse* causes quite a stir.

"Word of our visit has clearly preceded us," exclaims Jerome, with satisfaction. "I've never seen the old Goat so stuffed!"

"Come on, boys — what are we waiting for?" Jurian chimes in. "Let's give the locals their thrill." He pushes past Jerome and heads for an empty table right in the middle of the room that looks reserved for them. How typical of the Journeys to assume that everyone is there to see them! But they're right. As soon as we come in, a cheer goes up from the crowd and everyone in the place starts craning to get a good look at the boys. As they take their seats, several of the men come up and start offering to buy them drinks. We squires sit down at a neighboring table, close enough to be technically part of the same party but separate enough to emphasize the Journeys' status. Nobody offers to buy us anything.

Even the Journeys forget their plan to treat us, until Armand calls out in mock desperation,

"Master! Master! Take pity on me! My throat is very dry," and Aristide throws a fat purse over to our table. Another general cheer goes up, and Aristide raises his hand to the room and bows slightly in acknowledgment, basking in the public appearance of generosity.

Under his breath, Armand says with amusement, "Sodding hypocrite. Oh, here come the girls, right on cue!"

A large woman with an enormous bosom has appeared on the balcony above us and is now leading a group of rather tawdry-looking women down the stairs. As she passes our table, she leans over and drapes an arm familiarly around Pascal's shoulder.

"Flush today, love?" she asks, fondling his ear.

"Unfortunately, no. An unlucky bet. I'm tapped out."

"Such a pity. But," she says, eyeing the purse in Armand's hand, "maybe later, I'll let your friend buy me a drink."

She moves on to join the others, who have wasted no time in draping themselves over the Journeys or seating themselves on their laps. They seem to know them all disturbingly well. Needless to say, it isn't long before everyone at the Journey table is having a riotously good time. Things at our table aren't much quieter, thanks to Aristide's purse, though none of the other girls bother with us.

We're all used to drinking ale, and even wine — it's usually safer than water. But whatever they're serving tonight is stronger than anything I'm used to, and it isn't long before we're all stinking drunk. I'm already quite a bit the worse for alcohol when it occurs to me that I haven't seen Roxanne anywhere. Emboldened by spirits, I grab the skirt of a passing girl, and demand to see her.

"There's nobody by that name here," she replies scornfully, working her skirt free, while the other squires laugh. I begin to insist, much to everyone at our table's amusement, when I catch sight of Roxanne darting out from under the stairs to clear an empty plate from a table in the back. She's clearly kitchen staff, not part of the entertainment.

"Gentlemen," I say, rising shakily to my feet, and steadying myself with a hand on Auguste's shoulder, "do excuse me, but I've got to go and see about a girl." Another drunken roar goes up from the table and friendly hands reach up to pull me back down to my seat, but I shrug them off and climb over the bench.

"You won't see any girls, if they see you first!" laughs Benoit, but I merely salute the table, and stumble drunkenly across the room in pursuit of Roxanne.

When I catch up with her, I try to clear my head, trying to remember why I wanted to see her in the first place. Oh yes, I want to thank her.

"Roxanne," I say, coming up behind her and clearing my throat. When she doesn't respond, I tap her on the shoulder, and she jumps like a startled rabbit. Okay, maybe I accidentally shove her shoulder. I'm having some trouble estimating my distances.

She turns around, shrinking away from me and looking frightened. She's been afraid to venture far into the room for this very reason — some drunken lout might accost her.

"Ro*sh*anne," I repeat, slurring the *x*. "It's me, um — Marek." I put my hand up in what I think is the general direction of the cut on my head, which is nicely healing now, but for some reason I slap my ear instead. "Remember me?"

Roxanne still looks stunned, so I stumble on.

"I didn't mean to *sh*tartle you, but I've been wanting to see you again." Then I falter. I'm slurring my words, and this isn't coming out right. For starters, I didn't intend to do this drunk. "I mean, to thank you, for taking care of me so e*sh*pertly." The girl still looks so thunderstruck that I grasp for something else to say. "Tri*sh*tan was right. You, uh, really do have gentle hands."

To my surprise, at this Roxanne blushes as fiercely for me as she did for Tristan. Confused, I turn to leave, but when I sway a bit, she puts out a tentative hand to steady me.

"So you're his squire now, are you, Marek?" she says. "I'm glad. It suits you." Then she reaches up and pulls a little white Jasmine flower from behind her ear, and tucks it in my waistband. "There." I look down at the flower, trying to focus my eyes, trying to remember how it got there.

"Uh, thanks."

"You clean up very nicely," she says shyly, then she darts back into the kitchen.

When I turn around to go back to my table, I find all the squires are staring at me in amazement from across the room. I shrug, and then I put a hand up in the air and give a little bow toward the table in imitation of Aristide, and the squires all give me a shout.

Who'd have thought it? Turns out, I'm the first to make a conquest tonight, even if it is only a chaste one.

Over at the Journey table, things aren't quite so chaste. There's a lot of flirting and groping going on, but I notice that none of the boys leave the table to follow the girls upstairs. I wonder drunkenly just how much of their behavior is another performance, for the benefit of each other and the crowd. It's pretty clear that the Journeys are trying hard to put on a show, like they're supposed to be real ladies' men or something, and they're trying to live up to the part. The girls seem happy to help them out, but it's a bit overdone. I wonder just how much experience any of the Journeys really have.

At little later, Turk does leave the table, but it isn't to go upstairs. He's smaller than the others and he seems to have been drinking twice as fast. He notoriously can't hold his liquor — he even gets tipsy at mess. So when he goes outside to relieve himself, it's not much of a surprise that he never comes back. We only find out much later that's he's passed out in the street.

Jurian and Laurens disappear for a while, too, but when they come back, they're leading a live goat. Somebody's had the bright idea of seeing just how much it takes to get a real goat drunk. The boys dress it up in Jerome's hat and a scarf of Gilles's, and Lad and Falko and some of the bigger boys wrestle it up onto the table. But mercifully getting a goat to drink against its will proves too hard for them in their inebriated state, and when it butts Aristide and urinates on the table, they drive it out into the street, still wearing Jerome's hat.

The only one who isn't making any effort to appear like a sport is predictably Taran. He's big and handsome (and everyone in town knows who his father is), so despite his rather dour expression, a number of the girls start out the evening by having a go at him. But he brushes them off pretty firmly. He's just short of being rude, actually. Maybe he just thinks he's too good for this lot, or maybe it's what Tristan called his overblown sense of decorum.

"Gads, Taran! Remove that ramrod from your backside and relax a little, will you?" Gilles calls down the table at one point, as Taran is trying to extricate himself from the embrace of one of the younger and more attractive girls.

"I might be tempted," Taran shoots back, "if she smelled as good as you do."

"Ah, I've seen it a million times," the girl says, fondling the neck of his tunic. "He's just shy. The big ones always are. Don't be so shy, honey." She leans in and kisses him on the ear, and Taran begins to turn a funny color. He's blushing! All the Journeys let out a whoop when they see it.

"Yeah, honey, don't be shy!" mimics Falko. Taran looks so embarrassed, I could almost feel sorry for him. But I don't.

"Here, Mellor!" cries a drunk Aristide, throwing another purse onto the table in front of Taran. "I'm feeling magnanimous tonight. She's on me!" Aristide bows around the table again, and Taran's blush deepens so much that he almost turns purple. I'm very glad I'm not Aristide right about now.

"Ah, lay off him." It's Tristan, the last person I'd expect to come to Taran's rescue. But then he says, "A girl's not as easy to handle as a bow, is she, Taran? At least, not when you haven't had any practice."

I'm not sure what might have happened, if they weren't all so drunk, and if Jurian hadn't immediately jumped in. "Yeah, come on, boys, leave him alone. There's no fun in easy targets! What about a real wager? The winner takes the purse!" And then there's a mad scramble, as they all try to grab Aristide's purse off the table, and as they shout out ideas for a wager. But I think, Tristan's had a narrow escape. Jerome was right — he really does have to stop antagonizing Taran.

It's much later, though, when the real trouble starts. I was right — Taran knows how to bide his time. Or maybe what happens doesn't have anything to do with Tristan taunting Taran about his awkwardness and inexperience with women. The worst of it is, it's actually probably all my fault.

By this point, things are winding down. Most of the girls have wandered off and the boys are slowing down. Charles even has his head down on the table, fast asleep. Next to him, Jerome and Tristan have their arms draped around each other and have started singing old, melancholy ballads, very loudly and very badly. During the commotion with the goat the boys all switched places, and somehow Taran is now sitting directly across the table from Tristan. From where I'm sitting, I can look past the back of Tristan's head, right at him.

At our table, we've switched things up, too, but I'm not sure exactly when it happened. I'm now sitting between Pascal and Armand. They're both taller than I am, and they've got their arms around each other's shoulders behind me, and I've got one arm around each of their waists. We're swaying together drunkenly and singing along to the songs Jerome and Tristan are singing at the other table. At least, I think we are. I don't recognize the songs, so I'm mostly just swaying and occasionally croaking out a phrase or two.

I'm feeling incredible. My earlier melancholy is gone, washed away in a flood of alcohol. For the first time in weeks, I'm feeling no pain at all, and no anxiety. I've got my arms around two lovely boys my own age, and I'm actually relaxed. My guard is down. I'm probably too relaxed. I've got my head resting on Pascal's shoulder, and as it bobs there, I think I even kiss Pascal on the neck. He just smells so good! I'm not sure, though, and it doesn't matter anyway, we're all so drunk.

"Pascal, my man! Has anyone ever told you," I gush boozily into his ear as it sways past me, "that you're a helluva handsome devil?"

"And you, Marek, are one ugly son of a bitch!" At this, we all three laugh so hard we almost fall off the bench. I'm having a great time.

When Pascal and Armand switch to drinking songs, right in the middle of the rousing chorus of a song I actually know, I catch sight of Taran, watching us. Taran hasn't been drinking as hard as the others, or he's so big that it takes more to get him drunk, because he's noticeably more sober than the rest of us. He's recovered from his ribbing earlier and he's got the same unreadable expression on his face he always has when he's watching me, and it annoys me just as much as ever. But as I said, I'm relaxed. *Very* relaxed. And so I make a big mistake. I open my mouth very slowly and deliberately, and give Taran a great big, exaggerated wink. Let's see how *he* likes it!

And then Armand really falls backwards off the bench next to me, and in the hilarity that follows, I temporarily forget all about it.

The evening might have ended soon thereafter without further excitement, if it weren't for the arrival of someone new. As Pascal and I struggle to get Armand back into his seat, a door bangs on the balcony above us, and from the Journey table, Laurens calls out "*Ros!*"

Above me, a striking middle-aged woman, older than the others, appears at the railing. Her lush hair and dark eyes are arresting, and she's very handsome. She looks like she must have been a real beauty when she was young, and she's still what they call 'well-preserved.'

"Ros! Ros! Ros! Ros!" The Journeys start calling up to her, stamping their feet and pounding on the table in a St. Sebastian's style salute.

"Who is that?" I ask.

"That's Rosalinde. She runs the place," Pascal says dreamily.

"My beautiful Journeys!" She calls down, leaning over the balcony but not moving to descend.

"Where have you been, Ros?" Falko demands, as Jurian cries

"Come down, Ros!" and the other Journeys all clamor to add their pleas. But Tristan outdoes them all. He jumps up onto the bench and turns around, head back and arms wide, striking a dramatic pose. His tunic is so open it looks about to fall off, and his hair is disheveled. He would look the perfect picture of young ardor if his eyes weren't so glazed over.

"Fair damsel!" he cries, swinging his arm in such a sweeping gesture that he almost falls over backwards, and Jerome has to push him back onto his feet to keep him from falling. But Tristan doesn't seem to notice. "What is this mysterious affliction that ails me?" he continues, struggling to stay upright.

"You're drunk!" yells Falko, but Tristan swings his arm to brush the comment aside, swaying dangerously again.

"No! I have been drinking, my lady, I admit it. But in vain!" He's using his best 'top of the wall' voice, as I've come to think of it, and we can all tell we're in for a show. "I cannot quench the terrible thirst that consumes me!" he cries in mock agony. "Take pity on me! Descend, fair one! For only on your lips may I find the draught to cure this malady. A kiss! I demand a kiss!"

The boys all begin to stomp again, and chant *"a kiss!,"* until the woman begins to come down, pretending to consent only reluctantly. Even I've gotten swept up in the scene and am chanting "a kiss!" too, as she makes her way past our table.

By the time Rosalinde reaches the Journey table, Jerome and Jurian have pulled Tristan back to his seat, and so as she comes up behind him, she blocks my view and I can't really see what's happening. But she appears to slide one arm over Tristan's shoulder and down inside his tunic. With the other hand, she pulls his head gently back to rest between her breasts.

"Whatever ails you, Tristan my love, is in here," she says fondly, stroking his head, and smoothing the lock of his hair that's always falling into his eyes back from his forehead with the palm of her hand. "And so, it's here you'll take your medicine!" She bends over and gives him a lingering kiss on the forehead. The boys laugh, and Tristan grins up at her. There's really nothing sexual about it; it's sweet, and the two of them resting against each other look natural, like they're old friends.

"As always, Rosalinde fair," Tristan sighs, "your lips are an elixir for a fevered brow. Come, cool my brow again!"

"What a flirt you are! And such a gallant." She gives him a playful shove, and says coquettishly, "Why are you so good to me, Tristan? I'm too old for you. You could have any of the girls here. Why do you trifle with me?" Up close, she does look more haggard than I'd thought. A hard life or an addiction, or probably both, have ravaged what must have once been an unusually beautiful face. But it's clear they've bantered like this before.

"Why do I adore you so?" Tristan asks rhetorically, then he pauses dramatically. We're all so riveted by the performance, we lean in expectantly, eager not to miss Tristan's next flight of fancy. He's clearly working himself up to deliver a masterpiece of purple prose, and nobody wants to miss any of it.

Into that unfortunate hush of anticipation, Taran's quiet, sober voice drops like a stone:

"You must remind him of his mother."

The whole room freezes, as though we're caught for a moment in a tableau arranged for a painting. Then all hell breaks loose.

Tristan's back is to me, so I can't see his face, but it must be pretty impressive, because all the boys except Taran jump instantly to their feet. Jerome's grabbed Tristan by the shoulders and is saying "Steady, Tristan, Steady!" while the others are all backing up, trying to distance themselves from what's about to happen. At the same time, Charles yells "Look out, boys! He's about to blow!," and in one swift movement, Tristan shrugs off Jerome and leaps onto the bench, making a horrible sound like the bellowing of a wounded beast that reverberates so loudly it seems to shake the tavern to its very foundations. In a feat of superhuman strength, Tristan gives a violent wrench and overturns the entire solid oak table the Journeys have been sitting at, and it goes over with a massive crash, sending Taran scrambling to get out of its way. Before Taran can recover, Tristan leaps onto the upturned table and launches himself at him, and I lose sight of them as they roll onto the floor beyond.

The sleepy tavern comes awake in a flash. Everyone who is still there is now on their feet, either crowding around to see what's happening, or making for the door, eager to get away before getting involved in real trouble. By the time I get around the table and push through the crowd of squires and Journeys, Taran is flat on his back, with Tristan sitting straddled on his chest. Tristan's hands are around Taran's thick neck and he's throttling him like a bull. Taran's already turning blue and his eyes are bugging out of his head dangerously, and as he twists and turns under Tristan's relentless grip, he rains blow after blow on Tristan's head and chest. Each blow looks even harder than the one Taran gave me in the alley; he isn't pulling any punches, but Tristan doesn't even seem to notice them. He doesn't duck the blows or try to defend himself. Instead, his eyes are wild and he's raving like a lunatic, not using words but forming inarticulate noises that hardly sound human. Taran lands another bone-crushing blow, and blood gushes out of Tristan's nose. The worst of it is, Tristan just absorbs the blow, apparently oblivious to it. When foam starts coming out of Taran's mouth, I cry out:

"Isn't somebody going to do something?!"

Nobody's made a move to stop them. It all happened so fast, and everyone's too stunned or too drunk to know what to do.

"Can't you see they're going to kill each other!?" I scream, really believing it. Jurian, Gilles, and Charles are the first to come to their senses. They rush forward, trying to pull Tristan off, but with Taran still swinging wildly and Tristan adding his own blows to anyone who tries to separate them, they can't do it. Even when some of the biggest boys, Lad and Laurens and Falko, join them, they still can't get them apart. It's not until Jerome finally resorts to breaking his lute over Tristan's head that they manage to pull him off, but not before Taran's left lying dead on the floor.

I hardly have time to process this horrible sight before I'm swept outside with the crowd as the Journeys carry Tristan out into the street. He's still struggling and raving inarticulately, so it takes five or six of them to drag him along, and the whole tavern seems to be following. "Throw him in the canal!" somebody suggests. But he's putting up such a fight, they end up dropping him in a watering trough on the street instead.

It does the trick. After a roar when he hits the water, Tristan sobers up immediately. But he looks terrible. His eyes are unfocused, and all the violent color that flooded his face in his frenzy has drained away. My stomach is in a knot. I don't know what's worse; the horrible thing that came over Tristan, that wretched body lying in the tavern, or what's going to happen to Tristan now.

Feeling all too sober, I help Gilles and Charles get Tristan back into the tavern. Acquiescent now, he lets us sit him down at the squires' table like a child, but he's dazed and confused. I stroke his head as he sits, staring with unseeing eyes in front of him. I feel dazed, too. What is to become of us now?

At the far end of the table, I catch sight of Remy. He's hovering protectively around a seated figure, who's hunched over, rubbing the back of his neck. It's Taran. So he isn't dead after all, he'd just passed out. I should have known he'd be hard to kill. But at the sight of him, I feel something like pure joy. I would never have thought I could be so glad to see Taran safe and sound, but all I can think is, "*Thank God*, thank God Tristan didn't kill him, *thank God!*"

Tristan himself doesn't seem to notice Taran at all, or even really know where he is.

"Well," says Jerome, sitting down next to Tristan and putting an arm around him. "That's that. No harm done. But, my boy, you are all in. I think we'd better call it a night."

At this point, Ladislaus comes in, followed by the rest and carrying Turk, still passed out, over his shoulder. "Look what we found outside!"

"Well, boys, we've outdone ourselves!" Charles declares in a loud voice, rising to his feet and surveying the room. "A drunken brawl, a trashed tavern, a stolen goat, and two Journeys passed out before the third hour! It must be a new guild low."

"We've given the townspeople their money's worth," Jerome agrees. "I do believe our work here is done!"

"Come on, Tristan. Let's get you home," Gilles says gently, as he and Jerome lift Tristan to his feet.

"And, by the way, old boy," Jerome says, as they lead Tristan out the door, "you owe me a lute."

It takes a few of the boys to help Taran to his feet, too, and we all stagger home, a sorry shambles of the handsome party we made earlier in the evening. On the way, I can't help casting glances back at Taran, just to reassure myself that I really saw right, that he's really still alive. He's a little green, and ugly bruises are already blossoming on his neck, but he's got a look of grim satisfaction on his face. I'm not surprised. He may have been the one pinned to the floor, and I really believe that if it weren't for Jerome's quick thinking, Tristan would surely have killed him. But if anything, he won this round, and he knows it.

CHAPTER THIRTEEN

The very next day, everything changes, but it has nothing to do with the Drunken Goat.

Predictably, when I get up in the morning, I feel the worst I have since the morning after my father died and I was beaten by Taran. I have a massive headache, but this time, I can't complain. I did it to myself. When I first wake, even before I've opened my eyes, I can tell I'm in for a hard day. The smell in the barracks is even worse than usual, since most of the boys have been sick during the night. Some of the servants are already hard at work swabbing the floor around me, and Remy's snoring like a horse in the next cot. As I'm gingerly maneuvering myself into a sitting position, pushing aside old Popinjay to do so, Armand appears out of nowhere and hands me a cup of something foul.

"What's this?"

"A special concoction of Albrecht's." Albrecht is the general factotum of the guild; he oversees the servants and the kitchen. I was surprised the first time I met him, since on the day I visited the guild with my father, the old servant François called him a young man. But that was just by comparison. Albrecht is actually quite old and crotchety, but he has a soft spot for the squires.

"Hair of the dog, that sort of thing."

"I've already got the hair of the dog in my mouth," I say, giving Popinjay a shove.

"Just drink it, Marek. You're going to need it. Then take one to Tristan. He's going to need it even more."

At the memory of the wreckage of Tristan that I helped deposit in his room last night, I sit on my bunk, hold my nose, and take a drink. As they often do, unpleasant memories start filtering through the throbbing in my head, but for once, they aren't memories of my father. They're memories of last night, vague at first, then coming into sharper focus. Was I really flirting with Roxanne? I shudder. Even worse, did I really make a pass, at *Pascal*? It's time to sober up, I think, taking another swig of the thick, disgusting liquid. Really sober up. I could have given myself away a dozen times last night!

Then I remember it with a wince. That wink. What was I thinking? Did I really antagonize Taran into baiting Tristan? Then it comes vividly before my eyes, the worst memory of them all: Taran's body lying on the tavern floor with Tristan wild-eyed on top of him, his hands around his neck.

Armand's right. Tristan's going to need one of these.

When I get to Tristan's room with his tonic, I'm surprised to find him sitting up on the edge of his cot. He looks terrible, but better than I'd expected. I didn't expect to find him conscious.

"Marek," he groans, as I came in. "Do I look as bad as you do?"

"Worse," I say, and for once, it's true.

"God. It must have been quite a night. My whole body is aching."

He reaches up and touches the side of his face, then with a surprised look he holds out his hand for me to see. "Somehow, my ear seems to be bleeding. I must have taken a nasty fall somewhere."

It's not his most convincing performance, but I get it. He's going to pretend he can't remember what happened last night. I'm not to get any explanation. I don't think I want to hear it, anyway. I'm just as eager to forget all about the Tristan I saw last night, too. But maybe he really doesn't remember. From the state he was in last night, I wouldn't be surprised.

"Thank God for Albrecht," Tristan says, taking the drink from my hand, and I help him up. "Practice is going to be hell this morning, kid. Just do me a favor, will you? Run quietly."

As we help each other down the hallway, Gilles's door pops partway open and Gilles appears in the doorway, stark naked but otherwise looking none the worse for wear.

"Help me out in here, will you, boys?"

"Gilles, haven't you forgotten something?" Tristan asks, putting a steadying hand to his head.

"What?" Gilles asks, looking around innocently.

"Your pants."

"Oh, I always sleep in the nude." Of course. "It's not that. It's Pascal. I can't open my door."

"What are you talking about?"

"Pascal. He fell asleep in the middle of my floor last night, and I can't wake him up. He's blocking the door."

So Tristan and I drag the still sleeping Pascal out of Gilles's room between the two of us, so Gilles can dress. It's pretty rough going, since Tristan's hindering more than helping. He really needs someone to carry him almost as much as Pascal does. But the effort does Tristan good, and by the time we've gotten Pascal out of doors, Tristan's revived some. We don't bother taking Pascal back to the barracks — we just drag him out to the field and stick his head in one of the rain barrels. When we pull his head out and I wipe off his face, Pascal mumbles to me,

"I'm all tapped out, love. Maybe next time."

Tristan pats him on the back, looking almost his old self. "All right Pascal, you're good to go."

As we move to join the bodies of the other Journeys lined up in the shade of the butts, Tristan turns to me. "Marek, best not mention to anyone that Pascal was out of the barracks last night. Everyone's pretty understanding about the occasional bender, but still — nobody's supposed to be wandering around the guild after lights out. Gilles and Pascal could conceivably both get in trouble."

I nod, worried. Not about Pascal. I'm sure he'll be fine. But after all, there is somebody who knows I've been out after dark myself, and I have no excuse.

"CHEER UP. NOTHING'S BROKEN. YOU'RE STILL beautiful," Gilles announces, after delicately examining Tristan's swollen nose. "Your profile is just going to be a little more Roman than usual for a few days."

Slowly, everybody's gathered out on the field, Journeys and squires, and now we're all lined up, propped against the embankment, like men waiting for an execution. Nobody's made any move to set up or start practicing. Just getting out to the field took effort enough. So now we're waiting for the axe to fall. At any moment, Royce or Baylen will come striding out onto the field, and though I'm sure they're aware of our state, there won't be any mercy. Particularly if it's Baylen — he's likely to enjoy putting us through a particularly grueling workout.

I look down the line to see who looks the worst: Gilles, of course, looks as fresh and spry as a spring rose. I don't know how he does it. Turk, on the other hand, still hasn't shown up, and despite my constant prods, Pascal has fallen asleep again. The rest of the boys all look about the way I feel. Tristan is suffering more than most, but I suspect that's more from Taran's fists than from the ale.

The only one not accounted for is Taran. He's never this late, and since he was relatively sober last night, it can't be because he's hung over. Remy's nowhere to be seen, either, and so I start to worry. The terrible image of Taran's dead body keeps rising before my eyes. What if Taran didn't make it through the night? What if Tristan did more damage than we'd thought? It's happened before. As the minutes tick by with no sign of Taran, and as even the remains of Turk stumble out onto the field, I become convinced that something's really wrong. So I surprise everyone by being the one to ask,

"Where's Taran?"

"I don't think he's coming out today," Aristide replies, his head resting in his hands.

"What's wrong with him?" I cry, alarmed.

"Do you miss him so much, Woodcock?" Falko sneers.

"Nothing's wrong with him," Aristide snaps. "Well, he'll be wearing a size or two smaller shirt around the neck, no doubt,"

Aristide says, shooting a glance at Tristan, "but otherwise, he's fine."

"Then where is he?" asks Anselm, echoing my thoughts. "It's not like him to be late for practice."

"We had a hard time waking Remy this morning, that's all," Aristide replies. "Taran was concerned. When Remy finally came to, Taran told him he couldn't come out to the field today. But you know Remy. He insisted, said he wouldn't let Taran come out alone. So Taran's staying in, too."

"Very touching!" I snort. A likely story. Taran must really be feeling the effects of his throttling. He'd never miss practice. Certainly not for someone else's sake.

"What'll happen to him if he doesn't show?" Anselm asks.

"The vets will die of shock!" says Gilles. "Other than that, probably just a reprimand, not much else. He's Mellor's son, after all. And God knows, he doesn't really need the practice."

With this depressing thought, we all try to forget about Taran again. But I'm still worried. I won't feel safe until I see Taran with my own eyes. I can't help feeling that maybe Tristan has done some permanent damage. What goes on inside a human body is a mystery, after all.

It's not long afterwards that the stable doors bang open, signaling that the dreaded practice is about to start. Only to everyone's surprise, not one master stalks out onto the field, but all three. Master Guillaume himself is leading the pack, with both Master Leon and Master Gheeraert behind him, and our usual trainers Royce and Baylen follow at a respectful distance. I've never seen anything like it. As we're making a disorderly attempt to get to our feet and at attention as quickly as possible, Aristide hisses,

"Uh oh, boys. Looks like we're in trouble. I told you stealing the goat was a bad idea."

"I didn't even know Guilly was back!" Laurens shoots back. "It looks bad. He never comes out this early."

"They're all in full regalia. We're in for it now!" Jerome observes, and it's true. All the men are wearing ceremonial dress and cloaks, and I notice they've all got on black armbands.

As the men approach, the boys fall silent, and Master Guillaume steps forward, adopting the same formal stance as the boys.

"Gentlemen," he booms. "I'm sorry to have to announce that practice will be cancelled this morning." We're all too shocked even to rejoice at this unexpected reprieve. It can't bode anything but ill. Did we really make such a mess of the tavern last night? I wonder if all the Journeys have ever been kicked out of St. Sebastian's *en masse* before first trials.

"What's more," Guillaume continues, "All regular guild activities are to be suspended for the day."

An uncomfortable murmur goes through the crowd.

"What is it, Master?" Aristide asks respectfully. "Is there trouble in Meuse?"

"Is it the bloody English?" somebody calls out, maybe Lad.

"What? No. Of course not," Guillaume snaps, "Nothing like that." He seems exasperated for a minute, then regaining his composure, he adds, "It is true, I won't lie to you boys. Although I left things stable in Meuse, there is trouble brewing, and if it comes, here at St. Sebastian's we'll be in the thick of it. And I think we should prepare ourselves for the eventuality that the regent may be forced to make overtures to King Edward in the weeks ahead. But," he raises his voice as the boys forget themselves at this and start calling out heated protests, "when and if that happens, St. Sebastian's and all its members will be expected to support the crown," he says pointedly, and the boys quiet down. "Be that as it may, I'm not here this morning to talk politics. We've had some devastating news, and it's much closer to home."

At this, the silence deepens, as we all expect to be chastised for our behavior last night. But what Guillaume says next is worse than any admonition.

"We found out early this morning that one of our own members is dead. We don't have all of the details, but from the looks of it, there is a possibility of foul play."

Panic squeezes my chest. I don't think I really believed it, but it's true. Taran's not here, because he's dead! He didn't make it through the night. Now not only do I have to face that Tristan really is that horrible thing he was last night, that he's killed a man with his bare hands, but now the masters will arrest him. *St. Sebastian's punishes its own.* I can't imagine what they'll do to him for killing Lord Mellor's son. I look wildly at Tristan, but he doesn't look panicked at all. He's frowning, looking upset by the news, but only dispassionately so. Surely he must remember! Can't he see the danger?

Incredibly, Tristan raises his hand in the air, to get the master's attention. I grab at his arm — what is he doing? He can't be so foolish as to confess, can he? But all he does is ask quietly,

"Master, who was it?"

"His name," Master Guillaume says solemnly, "was Jan Verbeke."

The name hits me like a punch in the gut. I sway forward, and I clutch Tristan's arm harder, so hard that my fingers are digging deep into his flesh.

"None of you boys will have known him," Guillaume is continuing. "Though a master fletcher, in recent years, for personal reasons he chose not to work at the guild. But he was a man much beloved by the guild, duBois." He sounds so genuinely distressed, I feel tears pricking my eyes. "Many of our members were privileged to call him a friend, and many on our staff remember him fondly. He was long before Baylen's time," he says, nodding back at the veteran trainer, "but he served as a Journeyman here with Royce, and to us masters," he pauses, his voice thick with emotion. "Well, to us, he was more than a friend. But I," his voice breaks, and he has to clear his throat before going on. "I shared a special bond with him, a bond you boys will understand well. To me, he was like a brother. He was *my* squire, when I was a Journey here. It was I who sponsored him at St. Sebastian's."

The boys have been listening to this personal speech in awed silence, but nobody is more stunned than I am. I shouldn't be shocked. After all, I've been waiting for this since I got here, haven't I? Waiting for the news to arrive, steeling myself to hear my father's name? Isn't that why I came, because he was known here, because I hoped to find out something about my father? But so much time has passed, without a word. Did I really let myself forget? It's unbearable, to be blindsided by this now, in this fragile state. When I was out carousing last night, was this message on its way? It's too gruesome to contemplate. I never expected anything like this, either — to hear that these men I've been living with all knew him so well, better than I did, even. I never expected to hear them so casually make a public announcement of the facts of his life that were secrets from me. Royce served with him as a Journey? He was *Guillaume's* squire? I can't process it. I can't bear their show of grief, either, when I'm not allowed to show any myself, as though I've got no more rights to him than Falko or Aristide. It's even more unbearable, too, because for someone, the show of grief is a lie.

"What happened to him?" Falko is asking, and I don't think I'll make it through any more. I have to get away. Tristan has begun to sense my agitation, and thinking I'm still feeling the effects of last night, he whispers to me,

"Just make it through this announcement, Marek. Just hold on a little longer."

"His body was found at the bottom of his own well two days ago," Master Leon responds for Guillaume, who looks too upset to go on. "There was, *er*, some question of identity at first, since from the looks of it, the body had been there for quite some time." I slump against Tristan, dangerously close to passing out, as Jerome asks,

"Was it an accident?"

"That's the official line, yes. Though it's damned odd. There are some questions, of course. But please —" Master Leon gestures to stop the flood of questions that threatens to start, as the boys begin to get curious. "You'll understand, boys, the news is fresh, too fresh for us to wish to talk more of it now. I assure you, we *will* get to the bottom of it, and you will be informed of any new information as we have it. For the time being, St. Sebastian's will remain closed for regular business today as a sign of the high regard in which we all held M. Verbeke, and there will be a special mass in the chapel this afternoon, which you are all encouraged to attend. That is all — you may return to your, *er*, individual practice." It's a sigh of how upset he is that he doesn't even sound sarcastic as he says this, even though it's clear nobody's been practicing.

"Regular drills will commence again tomorrow morning. Dismissed!"

Before the masters have even turned to go, I drop Tristan's arm and bolt off the field, running in the first direction that offers concealment. I don't care what it looks like. I just have to get away.

Tristan finds me five minutes later, vomiting behind a rosebush in the garden.

"Come on," he says, putting a hand on my arm and pulling me gently but firmly in the direction of the chapel. "In here."

I follow him in, wiping my mouth on my sleeve, and I drop heavily onto the seat of a pew, steeling myself to sit through a lecture on the sins of overindulgence. To my surprise, once we're inside and he's carefully closed the door behind us, Tristan puts a hand on my back and says,

"Want to tell me about it, Verbeke?"

I dissolve instantly into tears, and I wrap my arms around his waist shamelessly, burrowing my face against his stomach. He reaches down, as I knew he would, and ruffles my hair with one hand. What does it matter if I act like a girl now? Tristan knows everything. He's figured it out.

I'm Marieke again.

And it feels so good finally to weep openly for my father after all this time, with someone to comfort me. We stay like that, my body wracked with sobs, until I'm so worn out I can't cry any longer. I can feel Tristan swaying a little, too, not only from the violence of my grief, but because he's still weak from his ordeal last night. So finally, I push away shakily, wiping my nose.

"How did you know?" I ask sheepishly.

"The running. The vomiting. The medal. The *fletching*," he says. "It was pretty obvious. Besides, you've got to be somebody."

"Do you think anyone else noticed?"

"Nah, they're all too hung over."

"Tristan," I whisper, not daring to look him in the eye. "Don't be angry with me."

He sits down heavily next to me. "I'm not angry. But I wish you'd told me. I wish, you'd felt you could trust me."

"I do trust you!" My voice sounds guilty, remembering that I'd just been convinced he was a murderer a few minutes ago. "I just wanted to come with you to St. Sebastian's, so much," I say, still looking down at my hands. "If you'd known, you'd never have brought me. And once I was here, well, it was too late."

"I'd still have brought you, kid."

"No, you wouldn't have! Not if I'd told you the truth, at the tavern. You couldn't have. You know it."

"Why not?" he says, looking confused. And then I see my mistake. Tristan's not from Louvain. He doesn't know anything about Jan Verbeke. I'd just assumed that he knew it all. But just knowing I'm Jan Verbeke's child hasn't really told him anything. He thinks I'm Jan Verbeke's son.

"Because," I say, thinking fast. "There's still something you don't know." I pause, and Tristan looks at me expectantly. I lick my lips, choosing my words carefully. "My father was a Journey here, that's true. But he never made veteran status. That medal — it wasn't his. I found it by his body. That day in the tavern, when you told me it was a veteran's medal, that's when I figured it out. It must have belonged to the man who killed him."

Tristan frowns. "You found his body? I don't understand, Marek. He was killed? By a member? This is all pretty far-fetched."

"He was killed the night before you found me, Tristan! I was hiding, so I didn't see who it was. And nobody saw me. But I was there. I heard them talking. I saw the whole thing. Someone shot him full of arrows. A master archer. A veteran of St. Sebastian's."

"That's a pretty serious accusation, Marek."

We sit in silence for a while. Finally, Tristan says,

"You poor kid. Is that what made you come here, that day?"

"I guess so. I didn't have anywhere else to go. And there's more." And now I have to be very careful, to get this just right. "The men, the killers. I overheard them. They were looking for me. I mean, not me exactly, but for children of Jan Verbeke. They were worried, that if there was any of his family left, they might know something. Something about the reason that they killed him."

Tristan turns and looks at me intently. "If this is true... do you know something, Marek? Do you know why he was killed?"

"No," I say miserably. "All I know is, he was here at St. Sebastian's the day he died. Oh, you do believe me, don't you, Tristan? I'm not making this up."

"It *is* far-fetched, Marek. But, I believe you. I can tell you're scared, and frankly, you're not a very good liar."

Hmm. I don't challenge this, I'm just so grateful he believes me.

"This is very serious, Marek. I think you should tell the master. We should go to Master Guillaume."

"No! I can't!" I jump to my feet in alarm.

"You heard Guilly. You saw how upset he is. He was his friend. He'll help you. You don't seriously suspect Master Guillaume, do you?"

"No, I don't think so," I say, "but I can't know who might be involved."

I've got to think of something else, though, to convince Tristan. I don't really suspect the master, not anymore, but how can I explain why I don't want to come forward now as Verbeke's child? I doubt anyone is going to talk about my father's personal life enough for it to come up in front of Tristan that Jan Verbeke had a daughter with a broken face, or that his one son is dead. But if I start openly claiming to be Verbeke's son, it will all come out right away, and I'll be found out.

"I can't tell anyone, not now. Don't you see? It's not just that it could be dangerous for me. At the least, I've been lying. I swore the squires' oath as Marek Vervloet."

"That's true." Tristan runs his hand through his hair in frustration. "Marek, I wish I'd known! We've bungled this business badly, and I have to admit, it's partly my fault. Foreswearing that oath, that was a mistake. Oh, it was all right when you were nobody," he waves his hand at me as I open my mouth to protest, "No insult intended. But now that you're somebody, it's a real problem. Oh, Marek — if we'd just gone to the masters right away, we wouldn't be in this fix. I should have known that medal meant trouble."

"I'm sorry." What else can I say?

"It's dangerous, Marek. Damned dangerous. You're somebody now, all right. And I've brought you in under false pretenses. This'll mean both our skins, if you're found out."

Tears start down my cheeks again, and Tristan softens. "You've had one nasty blow on top of another, haven't you? Come on, we'll figure it all out later. It's been a rough night, and a rougher morning. Let's get you cleaned up, and get some sleep. We're neither of us in a state to sort it out now."

"Do you mean, I can stay?" I say incredulously.

"Of course you're staying. Don't be ridiculous," he says.

"Tristan, I —" but I don't know what to say. Nothing seems adequate. Tristan stops me anyway.

"Look, Vervloet," he raises his eyebrows, "it is going to be Vervloet, isn't it?"

"Yes," I agree firmly.

"Good. Then we'll proceed as we were. Well, almost as we were. You're going to have to tell me everything, eventually. We'll figure it out as we go." He's being so gentle, I almost start crying again, but his voice loses some of its kindness when he adds, "But, there will have to be some changes."

"Anything."

"If this is going to work, from now on you've got to be completely honest with me."

He pauses, and when he continues, he sounds more serious than I've ever heard him. "Master Guillaume was right, about the master–squire bond. It doesn't mean much to some of them. But what the master said, it's true. Imagine Gilles without Pascal. Or look at Charles and Henri. Even Taran and his little rat." Tristan seems to be the only person who genuinely dislikes Remy. "And you and I, well ..." he breaks off, not looking at me, but the air in the room has gone very still. Tristan isn't very good at serious sentiment. "But we have to trust each other. Really trust each other. No more lies. Agreed?"

I know what Tristan's offering me, and I know what I have to do to take it. He's right. There can be no more lies. So I look him right in the eye, and say:

"Agreed."

"So, before we leave here. Is there anything else you need to tell me?"

"No," I say levelly, and I mean it.

"Good. That's settled. Come on." He puts out a hand to pull me to my feet, but I shake my head.

To his questioning look, I say, "Go on ahead, I'll be along soon. I'll be all right, I promise. I just need a minute here, alone. There's something I need to do, by myself."

He nods, thinking I want to pray for my father. And when he's gone, I do get up and go to the altar, but I'm not thinking of my father now. The midmorning sun is streaming through the colored glass high on the walls, just as it did that afternoon I was first here. The little wooden effigy of the saint on the altar casts a long shadow on the floor, and I drop to my knees in its shadow. It's time to be honest, but I can't tell Tristan the truth. So I'll have to change the truth. It's time for me to swear a real oath to Tristan, with God and the Saint to witness it. An oath that will make what I've told Tristan not a lie. Not really.

And so I swear: I will never be a girl again. No matter what happens, I will never tell Tristan, and I'll do whatever it takes to keep him from ever finding out, or I'll die trying. It's true, I can't change my nature by will, but I can bend it a little. Maybe this just sounds like more lies, but to me, it feels different. I feel different. And I think, Tristan would agree. He'd see it my way, if he knew. I think he'd believe that you can decide who you're going to be. And now I've decided. There's no going back, it can't be temporary, or it's a lie. From now on, I'm a boy, and for Tristan's sake, I'll stay that way — permanently.

As I finish my vow, I have a vision worthy of Brother Benedict. The sun comes out from behind a cloud and floods the chapel, filling it with reddish light. The shadow from the effigy on the altar grows deeper around me, and shafts of red light like bloody arrows stream through the windows, striking my body. This is one sign I understand instantly. It's a blessing; the saint has accepted my vow.

But it's even more. Because in that moment, I have a revelation. I know why the medal brought me to St. Sebastian's, and it wasn't for my father. It wasn't even for myself, either. The saint brought me here for Tristan. He said it himself, didn't he? *I'm in need of a squire, and one magically appears.* And so I add a second vow, a real squire's vow to replace the one I swore in Guillaume's office. I swear to be the squire that Tristan needs. Tristan *will* win veteran status, I swear it. Then he'll be set. And if I can, I'll move heaven and earth to see him in the Black Guards. Because now I know how I can help him. I couldn't do it as Marieke, or even as Marek Vervloet. But now I can, and I'm the only one — because from now on, I am the son of Jan Verbeke.

CHAPTER FOURTEEN

W hen I wake, it's early afternoon, and I'm starving. But miraculously, I feel better. The worst of the hangover is past, and somehow, finally hearing about my father has had the effect of starting to put him to rest. After all, I've known he was dead for a long time. I've had a chance to get used to it. But I do feel different, and it's my oath. I feel like I've put something else to rest, too, and now I have a real purpose. It's time to sober up, all right. It's time to concentrate on being a good squire, and on first trials.

When I wander out into the hall, I find that all the food that's been put out is already gone. With the suspension of regular business there's no official noon mess, but we haven't been left to fend for ourselves entirely. Except for me, apparently. I'm just debating foraging for something in the kitchens when Tristan, Gilles, and Jerome appear, followed by Auguste.

"Missed your meal, too?" Jerome asks, as he looks over the dregs on the empty platters. "Come along with us, then, to the Drunken Goat."

I can't believe it. How can they stand to be going there again?

"We're, uh, on our way to make amends," Tristan says sheepishly, when he sees the look on my face. "Seems we might have done a bit of damage to the place."

"Gilles has generously offered to foot the bill," Jerome adds. "We're going to apologize to Ros."

"All right," I say. "But if I see a goat, I'm leaving."

As soon as we get there, Tristan and Jerome disappear into the back looking for Rosalinde and Auguste wanders off to join some local boys dicing in a corner, so I find myself temporarily alone at a long table with Gilles. Gilles is occupied cleaning nonexistent dirt out from under his fingernails with his dagger, but I feel awkward sitting there alone with him, so I say,

"Where's Pascal?"

"I got rid of him. Sent him out to the workshops on some errand or other. He'll be missing his lunch, but that can't be helped." When I make a critical noise, Gilles continues. "I try to keep him out of the Goat if I can. It's for his own good, poor boy. He has an unfortunate weakness for prostitutes. Just adores them."

I digest this disagreeable piece of information for a moment, but I see an opening. Trying to sound casual, I say, "So, do all the boys, *er*, frequent prostitutes?"

"Gads, Marek. What a question! Of course not. It's so *common*."

"But last night ..." I prompt.

"What? Oh, a bit of fun. Harmless flirtation. Boys will be boys. But I daresay the Journeys all fancy themselves too good to have to pay for companionship. Well, I can't speak for the likes of *Aristide*, but the rest of us, surely, wouldn't stoop. Particularly for the rather low level of company on offer here. I try to tell Pascal, but ..." Gilles sniffs.

"Would it be safe to say, then," I continue, trying even harder to sound casual, and making sure to exclude Gilles himself from my remarks, "that the Journeys, as a group, might not have as much experience, then, as they let on?"

"Gentlemen, Marek," Gilles says, looking at me reprovingly over his dagger, "do not discuss their sexual exploits."

I wait. Gilles loves to hear himself talk, and if you just wait him out, he'll usually talk about anything. It works. After a minute, he laughs. "Well, we all know now there's at least one with absolutely no experience at all!" He chuckles, remembering Taran's embarrassment, but I don't care about him.

"But the others?" I press.

"Well, if you're asking me to speculate," he muses, and I give him an encouraging look meant to tell him that I'm doing just that, so he continues in a gossipy voice. "I'd say it's probably a mixed bag. At least a few have probably been around the pasture once or twice, if you know what I mean. We're a pretty appealing bunch, after all. There's the matter of Jurian, of course," he says sternly, and I have no idea what he means, "but for most, opportunity is rather a problem. Not everyone has had the advantage of growing up in a manor, with rather obliging servants. Girls, Marek, as you may know, have an unfortunate habit of having so many fathers and brothers. And then, there's just no accounting for sensibilities. I'd have thought Falko, for example, was a terrible slut. But according to him, he's sworn a vow of chastity to some unattainable lady, so there you have it. I rather suspect this is a convenient way of explaining his spectacular lack of success, but if Falko can be chaste, then anything's possible. Speculation is meaningless."

"A chivalrous oath to an unrequited love. Sounds more in Tristan's line," I say leadingly, hoping to turn the conversation to my real objective before the others get back. But mocking Falko's vow makes me uncomfortable. In a way, I suppose what I did this morning in the chapel could be interpreted as the exact same thing.

"Quite."

We stare at each other for a minute, but I'm the first to break. He's going to make me ask.

"Okay, Gilles. What about Tristan?"

"My dear boy, I really couldn't say. He's a bit of a dark horse, isn't he? If you want to know about Tristan, you'll have to ask him yourself. Just don't expect a straight answer." Gilles's tone is light, but he looks up and holds my gaze steadily as he continues: "I can tell you one thing. Tristan loves prostitutes, too. But he'll never sleep with one. And after last night, if I have to tell you why, you're even stupider than I thought."

The others haven't been back long and we're in the middle of our meal when I see Roxanne coming toward us. As she approaches, Tristan sits back and opens his mouth to start in on one of his flowery greetings, but much to his surprise, she sweeps right past him without a look and comes around to sit down next to me. Gilles and Jerome exchange amused glances as she says,

"Hullo, Marek. I didn't expect to see you back again so soon."

"I couldn't stay away," I say, wryly. "Roxanne, look," I turn my back to Jerome, trying to shield our conversation. "I'm sorry about last night, if I said or did anything I shouldn't have. I was a little drunk."

"You were a lot drunk!" She laughs. "And, you were a perfect gentleman."

"Is it like that in here every night?" I ask. "How can you stand it?"

And just like that, we're talking like old friends. Despite my new vow, I forget I'm supposed to be a boy, nervous about talking with girls, so we chat away effortlessly, and I don't think anything about it. But when she gets up to go, she leans over and gives me a quick kiss on the cheek before rushing away.

"My God, he's stolen her right out from under your nose!" Jerome crows at Tristan when she's gone. "I'd never have thought it possible!"

"He's even appropriated your name for her," Gilles says.

"What do you mean?" I demand.

"Her name isn't really Roxanne," Jerome explains. "It's just Anne. Only Tristan calls her Roxanne. And now you, apparently," he laughs.

"So, Marek," Gilles says. "You've been holding out on us. A bit of a dark horse yourself, eh?" he says, alluding to our earlier conversation. "What's your secret? Do tell us."

"Yes," says Tristan, amused. "Just what do you know about women, Marek?"

"Nothing," I answer glumly, and it's true. What do I know about women? I was raised without a mother, and I lived with a father and brother. The only woman I've known at all was Berthal. I don't know anything about women at all.

"Out with it! How did you win over that girl so quickly?" Gilles insists. "Anyone who can win a girl's affection away from Tristan must have something to teach us."

"She's not stupid, just because she's female," I say, angrily. "She knows she's got no real chance with him, that's all. She can see, we're alike." My hand goes up to my face, and when the boys shift in their seats uncomfortably, I lighten my tone. "I just talk to her normally. Like anybody else. I don't know why you all think girls want some fake show. I'm just myself." I blush then, not only at my presumptuous words, but at how patently false they are. I've been anything but my real self with Roxanne.

Gilles shudders. "I, for one, intend never to let any girl see the real me."

"And they thank you for it, Gilles!" says Jerome.

"Come on, Marek," Tristan says. "Do you really believe that? That girls want to be treated like one of the boys? You don't want to be loved for the poor thing you really are, do you? Not when you could be loved for the man you aspire to be."

It's a fair question. I don't know the answer.

But I'm gratified. I knew in the chapel this morning that Tristan would agree with me that it's fair to invent yourself.

IT'S MIDAFTERNOON BY THE TIME WE LEAVE THE Drunken Goat, so I'm surprised when we get back to the guild, and Tristan pulls me straight out onto the field. I'd just assumed it was too late to practice, and that he still wouldn't be up to it today.

"We're not practicing. Come on, we've got somewhere else to be," he tells me, and soon he's leading me back over the wall and out into the woods. At first I'm not sure where we're going, but with each step our destination becomes more inevitable, so I'm not surprised when we come out into the same meadow in which Tristan picked a single red poppy for me.

In just over a week, the meadow has transformed. It's now filled with poppies, and it spreads out in front of us as a sea of red, just like in my dream. But today, I don't see wounds. All I see is beauty, and I run out into the field and throw myself down onto the huge, fragrant body of the meadow and hug it to me, the poppies and the earth and the grass, all of it together. As I do, I hear my father's voice in my head, *"he gave me something in exchange for the arrows. He gave me you."* And so when Tristan catches up to me, he finds me rolling among the poppies, laughing, and as he puts out a hand to help me up, I put into it a single red poppy.

"Let's go in," Tristan says, gesturing to the windmill. "It looks sound enough." And he's right. Inside, the main structure is intact. A wooden staircase leads up past the huge grinding stones and the central shaft that once moved the mechanism. We try the steps, and they creak but hold our weight. The stairs lead to a small room, where the shaft attaches to the arms, and when Tristan throws open the shutters of a small window, the room is flooded with light. It's dank and dusty, but the warped floor is sturdy enough. The only things in the small room are a wooden table with no chairs, a few moldering sacks of flour, and some straw. It's only possible to stand completely upright near the middle of the room, since we're at the apex of the windmill, but Tristan seems delighted. He gestures me over to look out the window; over the tops of the trees, in the distance, I can see the buildings of St. Sebastian's.

"What are we doing here, Tristan?" I ask.

"It seems to me," he says, in the teasing, melodramatic tone I've come to love, "that a man with a secret identity needs a hide-out." I'm not sure if he means me, or himself. I've noticed that the new complete honesty between us hasn't extended to him telling me anything more about himself. But I don't mind. The idea of a secret place just for us more than makes up for it.

He seats himself on the window ledge and says more seriously, "Tell me all about it, Verbeke." And for the rest of the afternoon, I tell Tristan everything. I tell him all about my father — the good, and the bad. I do as little editing as possible, determined not to lie. I even tell him the worst: about my father's failure, his accident, and our life in virtual self-imposed exile from Louvain. I even tell him about the arrow through his throat. And when I'm done, I have put my father to rest. We get back so late, we miss the special mass for him in the chapel, but I'm glad. I think Tristan planned it that way, to spare me. And I think my father would have preferred our private eulogy, there in the windmill, overlooking the field of poppies.

THAT NIGHT, EVENING MESS IS INFORMAL, BUT THERE'S A crowd in the great hall anyway. Everybody's revived after a day of rest, and eager for conversation. There are only two topics tonight: upcoming trials, and the mysterious Jan Verbeke. Even some of the servants are hovering around in the hall, hoping to hear some of the talk, so there's even more of a din in the room than usual. When Tristan and I take our seats, Jurian is holding forth.

"I've had some serious insider information from Baylen," he's telling everyone in a stage whisper, "only you didn't hear it from me. About trials. You know, each Journey is usually given the chance to do a shot of his own devising, something special to set him apart. But Baylen says Guillaume's planning to scratch that from first trials, to make way for an exhibition in mounted archery. He wants to show off Turk to the crowds early." From this, I gather Turk is something of a horseman.

"But that's not fair!" cries Anselm. "That'll mean those of us who are good at butts don't have a fair chance to show our stuff."

"And, I bet you can't ride. Probably never seen anything but a plow horse!" Aristide says cruelly. He never misses a chance to remind Anselm that he's a peasant.

"Don't worry. Turk'll show you which end of a horse is the front," Falko laughs.

"I already know which end you are," Anselm replies smoothly.

"Do you think it's true, Tristan?" I ask. This will hurt us, too, and not only because I'm not sure how well Tristan can ride. Butts is Tristan's specialty. I know he'll pass the trials easily, but the judging is subjective. He can't afford just to pass; he's got to wow the crowd, to make an impression that will help carry him over through the next trials. We'd been counting on him having a chance to make some trick exhibition shots, to give him an edge in the rankings going into Seconds.

Before Tristan can answer, Charles says, "The mounted shooting can be dangerous, too, for the rest of us. I've been hearing a lot of talk today about this man Verbeke. It seems he had a bad accident during a horseback stunt. Right in competition." And just like that, everyone is talking about my father. I'm glad I've already told Tristan, but I'm still not prepared to hear them all laughing over ugly rumors about him. Everyone's heard something different, and none of it is pleasant. Finally Jurian calls out to the veterans' table,

"Hey, Royce! Join us. Come on! We want to hear about M. Verbeke." To my surprise, Royce obliges, and Jerome and Lad scoot over to make room for him. Everybody's curious, so some of the other veterans who don't keep rooms at the guild come over, and even some of the servants crowd around. In the background, I see even old François has made his way out of the kitchens, eager to hear some word of my father. I'm torn. This is what I wanted, wasn't it? To learn more about him? But I didn't want to do it like this, with a running commentary of crude comments by Falko. Maybe it would be better not to know, after all.

"What was he like?" Taran, of all people, asks.

"What was Jan like?" Royce muses, enjoying having an audience. "He was a joker, you know? Charming, handsome. Popular with the ladies. Irreverent. You know the type," he says, and not a few of us glance at Tristan. "Gave Guilly a hell of a time, even back then. He had his own ideas, about everything. He wasn't very good with authority."

"Sounds like a real jerk," says Taran. He would think so.

"He could be," Royce admits. "But we were young. He was a lot of fun. Actually, he reminds me of your own father, Mellor. He was around back then, you know. You should ask him about Verbeke. He'll have some stories. I'm surprised you haven't heard some of them."

"I have heard the name, yes," Taran admits, and I blink in dismay. Does even Taran know more about my father than I do?

"Can you imagine Taran having a charming, irreverent father?" I whisper rudely to Tristan, but he simply replies tonelessly,

"Yes. Yes, I can."

"I heard he did something stupid and blew his shot at Vets," Falko is saying.

"Yeah, Royce, we've been hearing all sorts of things. What really happened? Did you see it?" Gilles asks, and I'm on the edge of the bench. Now we're getting down to it. But now, I don't want to know. I'm ready to let my father go. I don't want them to ruin him for me, the way they did my beautiful blonde.

Royce is shaking his head ruefully, as though he's remembering something both sad and funny.

"Of course I was there! It was at our last Journeyman trials. The regular tests were all completed. There'd been no official ranking yet, but it was clear he'd made it through. And then we mounted up for some routine equestrian maneuvers, and Jan got some crazy idea of doing his own stunt. It was ludicrous! He didn't need any more stunts. It was just an exhibition. All he had to do was stay on his horse, and he was set. He blew it all to do some stupid grandstanding." I know he's telling the truth — Royce's version sounds just like Berthal's.

"Tristan," I whisper. "Can we go, please? I don't want to hear any more." Squires are expected to stay at meals with their masters unless expressly dismissed, so I can't go if he doesn't. Tristan turns his back to the group, and whispers back to me,

"Whatever the truth is, isn't it better than not knowing?"

"The truth? That he was an idiot? A jerk? A disgrace, even? No. It isn't better. I don't want to know. I don't want to hear any more," I repeat. To my immense annoyance, Tristan ignores me and turns back around, and then proceeds to ask in a loud voice,

"What exactly was the trick?" When I try to get up to leave without him, Tristan puts a restraining hand on my leg, and hisses loudly, "Sit down." So I have to stay. But I want to cry at his betrayal. After this afternoon, I thought he'd understand.

"Well," Royce ponders, getting a faraway look as he casts himself back in time. "It was a long time ago, and of course, it didn't quite come off, did it?" he laughs ruefully. "But if I remember correctly, he swung both legs over onto the same side of the horse, so only one foot was in the stirrup, on the side away from the target."

"But what was the trick? What was the shot?" Tristan insists, ignoring my discomfort.

"I think, he was trying to bend over backwards, perpendicularly over the back of the horse, to shoot upside down over his head at the target." At this, Royce can't contain himself and he starts to laugh, and all the boys join in. I feel tears burning behind my eyes, and I try to slap Tristan's restraining hand away from my leg.

"That's insane!" Jerome exclaims.

"What a fool," Taran says dryly. "That's an impossible trick. Even if he hadn't fallen from his horse, there's no way he could have hit a target that way."

Behind me, I hear a strangled cry. It's old François.

"That's not true!" his old voice quivers with age and emotion. "I won't have you whippersnappers saying these things about Master Jan. You were all jealous of him, that's all."

"All right, François," Royce says soothingly, indulging the old man. "We meant nothing by it. Jan was a good friend of mine."

"I saw him do it, a dozen times! I saw it with my own eyes. Master Jan could do that trick easily. He could do anything."

"Of course he could, François," Royce says again soothingly, gesturing to one of the serving boys hovering in the doorway to come over and lead François back to the kitchen. When he's out of earshot, Aristide says insultingly,

"There you have it. *François* saw it! I'd never doubt *his* eyes." And everyone laughs.

"What happened when he fell?" Tristan's voice cuts through the laughter, trying to extract more of the grisly details before Royce can call an end to the reminiscence. "How did it happen?"

"That's the funny part. The trick was strange, all right, and it happened so fast, nobody could believe it. Just one minute, he was on the horse, the next, he slid right off, like the single stirrup couldn't support all of his weight. But there really wasn't a reason for him to fall, not that way. I never understood it. Anyway, his horse spooked, and it trampled him. He was never the same." At this, the humor goes out of Royce, and I can see that he really did like my father, after all. He's been laughing with my father, not at him.

I think it's finally over, but Tristan just can't leave it alone.

"But the shooting, Royce. Jan Verbeke — was he any good?"

"Was Jan Verbeke any good?" Royce repeats, still looking very far away. "No, he wasn't good," he says, and I almost want to kill Tristan for forcing me to hear it. But Royce isn't finished. "No, Jan Verbeke wasn't just good. François was right about one thing. We were all jealous of him. So if you tell anyone I said so, I'll deny it, but, I think it's fair to say, he was one of the best shots that's ever been at St. Sebastian's."

As we make our way out of the hall, Tristan smirks at me, raising his eyebrows and asking archly, "Still mad? Still sorry I made you hear about it?," and I know he's teasing me. I *should* still be mad at him. After all, he couldn't have known what Royce was going to say. Instead, I'm walking on air. And it's not just because of Royce's high praise for my father. Let Tristan have his moment of fun at my expense, because now I know, I have him. He's delivered into my hands the very thing I needed to convince him to go along with a plan I've been formulating since this morning. He just doesn't know it yet.

WHEN I WAKE THE NEXT MORNING, MY FIRST THOUGHT is, "It's time to start living up to my new squire's vow. It's time to put my plan into action." So I'm the first one out on the field, and I'm determined it's going to be this way from now on. When Tristan saunters out among the last of the Journeys, I'm waiting for him by the garden gate, and I pull him aside.

"Tristan," I say, sounding so serious Tristan looks concerned. "I'm going to ask you one more time. Do you want to win?"

"What are you on about so early, Marek?" Tristan replies, treating it like a joke, but I insist.

"Really, Tristan. Answer me! Do you want to win? I need to know if you're serious."

"Ok, Marek. Yes," he says, looking at me steadily. "I want to win. More than anything. Happy?"

"Then listen to me, Tristan. There is something I have to tell you. Not a secret, or a lie," I add hastily, "Just something I didn't tell you about before." And I tell him about Anselm, about how I helped him.

"I'm sorry, Tristan. He's competition, and I wasn't thinking clearly. I didn't think he could challenge you, or that I could really help him. But I'm thinking now. You heard Royce. My father was good. And this is the thing," I rush on at the frown on Tristan's face, "My father did have his own ideas. And I've realized, they were good ones. When I was watching Anselm, I could hear my father's voice, in my head. I could hear what he would have said, how he would have trained him. And it's helped him. You've seen it. And ever since then, well, when I look at you, I hear what my father would have said, to help you. Just little things, but I think I could do it. Let me try to train you, Tristan, his way."

"Was he training you, Marek? Did he mean you for St. Sebastian's?" Tristan asks unexpectedly.

I answer honestly. "I think he would have, if I'd been different.

Physically." He nods, but he doesn't say anything. I don't know if I've offended him.

"What can it hurt? I'm not talking about anything drastic. You're too good to need that, and I wouldn't touch anything about your style. But he had training ideas, drill ideas — things I think might help build your strength and consistency more than what the vets have been telling you. It could be a way I could repay you," I add, as he hasn't responded and I can't read his expression. "Let me pass my father's skills on, to somebody."

"Okay, Marek," he finally says. "This afternoon, we'll start practicing. Your way. I'll give you a week to convince me, for your father's sake." I can't ask for anything more. I start to head onto the field, but Tristan stops me. He isn't done yet.

"Don't you think, though, Marek, your father would want you to pass some of those skills on, to yourself?"

"What do you mean?"

"I mean, I'll try training your way, but only on one condition. You have to try it yourself. I got you a bow, didn't I? It's time for you to start using it, and not just for gambling. After Firsts, I want you to start training, too. If it goes well, I'll put you up for apprentice status."

What he's saying is so ridiculous, I think he's joking at first, or using it as a ploy to turn me down.

"That's impossible," I say.

"Who's being defeatist now?"

"Tristan, this isn't a game!" I reply heatedly. He isn't taking me seriously at all. "You know I'm not strong enough for the long shots. Without them, it doesn't matter what else I can do."

"Apprentice trials are at Thirds, Marek. That's a long time. Even then, all you've got to do is pass. Then you'll have another whole year to train during my veterans' competitions before the Journey trials. Of course, that's providing you get me into Veterans with the 'Verbeke method.'" He's teasing me, but it hurts. Is this all a round-about way of telling me how little he thinks of my chances for actually helping him?

"Tristan," I say sternly. "Even if I could manage to shoot clouts, which I can't, I can never be a Journey. I'm too ugly, and you know it!"

"You're no Jurian, that's true," he says, smiling. "But I think 'not traditionally handsome' is more charitable. Who knows? In a year, you'll be older. Maybe you could go for 'rugged.' We could get you an eye-patch, like Baylen."

"Stop teasing me, Tristan!" I say in real exasperation. "Haven't you ever wanted something so badly, it ached, but you knew you could never have it?" I'm getting rattled, so this just slips out. I'm not even sure what I'm talking about. He thinks I mean Journeys, and maybe I do.

"Of course, Marek. Everyone has." He's starting to sound annoyed himself. "There's nothing we want more than the things we know we can never have. That's probably why we want them in the first place. But I don't have much sympathy for that. You've got me all wrong, kid, if you really think I'm a defeatist, and I won't tolerate one."

"Don't tell me," I huff. "Next you're going to tell me that anything's possible. I just have to try hard, and believe in myself."

To my surprise, Tristan starts laughing.

"God, no. You'd never catch me saying anything so patently ridiculous. Of course everything isn't possible! Most things aren't, actually. And of the things that are possible, most aren't probable, either. The sooner you accept that, the happier you'll be. I have no patience for wasting time pining over impossibilities. But that shouldn't stop you from going for the things that are just possible. The key is to know the difference: what's impossible, what's possible, what's probable, and what's inevitable. Then find a goal within the realm of the possible," he says, reaching past me to pluck a jasmine flower from a vine that's trailing down the garden wall behind me and twirling it in his fingers, "and find a way to make it all extraordinary."

"That's easy for you to say. Everything about you is extraordinary," I grumble uncharitably.

"Yes, it is!" he laughs, "But only because I make it so. You can, too. Look. I'll grant it, for you, even with years of practice, making it into Guards, or Veterans: it's impossible. You're right, you'll never be strong enough. And you're right, you're not handsome enough. Getting you into Journeys, that'll take something impressive. But look at Master Leon! He did it. You making it into

Journeys, well, that's *just* possible. It's a stretch, sure, but you're a good shot with the lighter bows, and all you need is a little more style, some of that Verbeke flair of your own, to get you noticed."

I start to protest, but I want Tristan to agree to train my way, so I can't really object to his throwing my father back at me. I close my mouth again sulkily.

"Now, you making apprentice, though, that's more than possible — with some hard work, that's even probable! There's no excuse for not trying to make that happen."

I can't think of any answer, so I say,

"You've left out inevitable."

"That's easy — eventually, you'll die," he laughs.

I'm not going to let him win this easily.

"What's the point of being an apprentice, of trying to make Journeys, when it's inevitable that I'll fail? Even if I could pass the apprentice test, and if by some miracle I made it into Journeys, you've said yourself, I'll never make it past Firsts. I'd just be setting myself up to fail, just like my father did."

"That's where you don't know anything about your own father, Marek!" he exclaims, and the comment stings all the more because it's true. But Tristan is just being Tristan. "Maybe it isn't about winning, maybe it's about failing, but with style! He knew how to try something extraordinary."

"But that's meaningless, isn't it? He could have won. Failing spectacularly isn't better than winning; it's only worthwhile if you're going to lose."

"Ha!" he says, as though he knows he's got me, "and that's why you have an advantage over your father. You *do* know you'll lose."

I still just don't get it.

"I'm sorry, but I just don't relish the idea of being humiliated."

"Look," he says, dropping the dramatic tone, as though he's really trying to convince me of something important. "I'm not talking about being humiliated. I'm talking about finding some technique, some shot, that's all your own, and working to execute it brilliantly, so that even when you lose, you'll have made your mark. The performance of it will be worth it, the performance itself will be the prize. So what if you don't make it far? You can have your moment. Something that will make everyone sit up and take notice of you, if only for one day. It only took Guillaume Tell one shot to become immortal, after all. Why not you?"

"Don't tell me you want to shoot an apple off my head," I say dryly.

"Don't be silly. You've got to shoot it off of mine."

Honestly, I just can't tell when he's serious. But I think I'm beginning to see his point. Maybe he isn't teasing me, after all. Maybe he really does think I've got a chance to make a mark of my own on St. Sebastian's.

Still I don't like it. All this talk of failing with style. He seems more focused on going down in glory himself than on winning.

In the end, I agree. What choice do I have, and what can it hurt, really? And I don't have to worry about it, until after Firsts. I'd have agreed to anything, to get him to try things my way.

And so that afternoon, we begin to train. Really train, for the first time. As always, Tristan is as good as his word. He tries whatever I suggest, even when it seems clear it isn't working, and he works hard. We put in such long hours we put even Taran to shame. At first, I'm relentless. I've got a million ideas, and I wear Tristan out jumping from one to the other, but I learn to pace myself, and we fall into a pattern. We start on the field, and I make Tristan do the exercises that I remember my father devising for Jules. Tristan and Jules are similar in body type, so I think they'll work for Tristan, too. Then we do drills. I was serious about not changing Tristan's style. It's his single greatest weapon. But I make him work on distance and strength, and he doesn't complain, even though it would be fair to say he should focus only on accuracy with butts coming up. Then I take him into the woods, and we practice there, where he's always more relaxed. We start to make it a habit to end the day at the abandoned windmill, where we can unwind and recap the progress of the day. It's a great place to get a little perspective.

I bring along the bow Tristan's gotten for me, and at first, I'm surprised that I'm almost as good a shot at moving game as he is. Tristan explains that when you focus on an unmoving target as much as he has, it throws you off to try to hit something in motion. None of the Journeys are very good at it, but I know my father thought hunting was important for Jules, so I make a point of adding some hunting into our routine. I've got the idea that we can use it for his exhibition trick at Seconds — I can throw objects into the air, and he can shoot them down out of the sky. It'll be fantastic, something none of the others can do. Tristan's naturally the better shot, so within a few days he's already shooting at birds much more accurately than I am, and I think practicing on moving targets is helping him overall, too. When the trial week comes to an end, I don't bother to ask Tristan if I've passed the test, if we're going to keep doing things my way, and Tristan doesn't say anything, either. He's no fool. I haven't transformed him, or anything. But he's shooting better than ever.

CHAPTER FIFTEEN

I t's only about a week before first trials that the sincerity of my
new vow gets its first real test.

We've been training hard now for a few weeks at what Tristan
still jokingly calls 'the Verbeke method,' and I'm pleased with
Tristan's progress. He's been working diligently — I don't know if
I've really done anything specific that's helped him, but the whole
idea that we have a plan of action and that we're working on it
together has an effect. The only breaks he's been taking in the
afternoons are for the required tutorials, and he's been holing up
with Turk out behind the stables regularly right after morning
practice, too, but that's understandable. Everybody's got to worry
about Jurian's rumor of mounted shooting at first trials, and my
goal isn't just for Tristan to shoot well, it's for him to win. But I'm a
little hurt that he doesn't seem to want me to accompany him. He
always sends me on errands instead, saying, "It's better this way.
You get your work done while I ride, then we'll both be free to train
later." What can I say to that?

Today Tristan's infuriatingly decided to extend his horseback
lessons into the afternoon, so right after noon mess he sends me
into town to the cobbler to get a boot fixed. It's only the second or
third time I've ever run an errand in town, and I still feel exposed
and awkward whenever I venture outside the guild walls,
particularly alone. But I manage the task well enough, and I'm

coming down the alley to let myself back in by the garden door, when I spy Pascal.

His back is to me, and he's resting one arm against the wall over his head to lean down over a girl he's got backed up against the wall. The girl is young and pretty, and she's got a basket over her arm, as though she's in the process of running errands herself. But she's not one of our serving girls. I'm pretty sure I've never seen her before. Pascal's got his head down by hers and as I pass, he whispers something in the girl's ear that makes her giggle. He doesn't look up or acknowledge me at all, but I don't mind. I bet he's got the girl convinced he's a Journey himself, so I don't want to spoil it for him. Besides, Gilles would be thrilled that Pascal is finally showing some interest in free entertainment.

About half an hour later, though, Gilles comes bustling up to me looking for Tristan as I'm depositing the boot in Tristan's room. He seems annoyed, too, when I tell him Tristan is out riding.

"For the Saint's sake, what bloody timing!" he says. "Come on, Marek. We've got to chase him down. Pascal's gone to get Jerome. Cancel practice for the day. We're going hunting!"

I have no idea what can be so important about an afternoon hunt, but he's very insistent, so I follow him out through the stables. On our way, we pass Charles and Falko, and Gilles calls out to them,

"Pascal's got intelligence, boys! Tristan's quarry has been spotted in the woods. A hunting party is in order!" This is met with more enthusiasm than I would have thought, and grinning, they fall in line behind us.

We cross the yard, and when we've circled around past the rows of outbuildings to the place where the boys usually exercise their horses, we come across Laurens in the process of mounting up. Nobody wants to fall off their horse at trials, so they've all been putting their horses through their paces much more frequently since my father's story came out. Tristan is riding at the far end of the pasture, so Gilles asks Laurens to ride out and get him for us.

"Should we let some of the others in on this?" Laurens asks before he goes, having decided to come along with us himself.

"Nah, let 'em find their own game!" Charles replies, and they all laugh. Everybody's unaccountably fired up over the outing.

"Come on, let's get mounted up, boys," Gilles says as Laurens disappears over the field.

"We're not riding, are we?" I say, incredulous. I hate horses. But nobody answers, and in a minute it's clear that we are, since a pair of stable boys has appeared from the direction of the yard leading out some of Gilles's horses, and as soon as Pascal and Jerome show up, they too disappear for the stables.

"I don't ride," I say sullenly, to nobody in particular. What kind of a hunt is this, anyway? Most of the boys aren't even carrying bows.

Before long, three riders appear, coming back from the far end of the pasture. Pretty soon I can make out Tristan and Laurens trotting toward us, but the third rider has broken away from the pack and now he's racing across the pasture alone. It's Turk, riding bareback on a small tan horse with a streaming, cream-colored mane. He's stripped to the waist, and his light-colored breeches blend into the color of the horse, so it's hard to tell where the boy ends and the horse begins.

"Won't he fall?" I ask Tristan, as he reins to a stop next to me.

"Turk can stick to anything. Look at him go! Don't worry about him. He could outride the four horsemen of the apocalypse."

Turk is making his way back and forth across the field in a zigzag motion, each dangerously fast turn bringing him a little closer, and as he draws nearer, I see he's got a small, light bow slung over his shoulder. When he comes by for his last pass, he slips the bow into his hand and in a fluid motion he brings an arrow up from a leg quiver and nocks it. As he speeds by, he bends the bow, and the arrow whizzes past to stick into the fencepost a few feet in front of us.

"Quite a trick, eh, Marek?" Tristan says. "You can see why Guilly wanted him on display early. The crowd's going to love it."

"If he doesn't shoot any of them by mistake," Laurens says.

"Where in the world did he learn to do something like that?" I ask.

"His mother's Hungarian," Tristan replies, as though that explains it.

"Looks more like his mother was Genghis Khan," Laurens says dryly.

Turk joins us, slowing to a trot.

"What's up, boys? All these weeks I've been all alone, and now everybody's out on my field." I notice the appropriative way he talks about the pasture, but by the looks of it, it's deserved.

Gilles trots up, freshly mounted, and says, "Pascal reports there's game afoot in the forest. You know I can't resist the call of the horn."

"Why didn't you say so?" Turk says brightly. "Give me a minute to clean up, will you, and I'll come along."

"Hurry up, then!" Tristan calls after him, as he dismounts and goes in search of a shirt. "Or all the partridges will have flown."

When everyone is assembled again and mounted, and as Turk returns with his hair freshly slicked down and sporting a clean tunic, the party is ready to set out. But I'm still on the ground.

"Aren't you coming, Marek?" Tristan asks.

"I don't ride much," I repeat miserably, so Tristan sighs, "Okay, kid. Climb up." He reaches down and pulls me up into the saddle in front of him, putting one arm around me to steady me. Instantly, I revise my opinion of horses. But I try not to be too aware of Tristan's practical embrace. After all, I have to remember, we're all just boys together.

We head out the guild service entrance and into the L'île-Charleroi road. Once we've passed through the L'île gate and we're out beyond the wall, we turn into the woods, and follow a well-worn bridle path. I see signs of plenty of game, but the boys don't seem to pay any attention. In fact, they're all laughing and talking so loudly, I'm sure every bird and beast in a five-mile radius can hear us coming. Instead of quieting down as we go, after a while Jerome pulls out a new lute (courtesy of Gilles) and starts strumming it as we ride along. It's the strangest hunting party I've ever seen. But I don't worry about it. I lean back against Tristan and listen to the sound of his voice as he babbles along merrily with the others, and I enjoy myself.

After a while, though, it's pretty clear we're headed somewhere specific, and curiosity gets the better of me.

"Tristan, just where are we going?" I ask.

"We're here!" he says, reining the horse to a stop, and I look around. Up ahead through the trees, I see some stone buildings.

The closest one has a distinctive arched doorway and a stone spire.

"Are you telling me we came all this way to attend a mass?" I ask. "We could do that any time, back at St. Seb's."

It's true. There's mass in the chapel at least twice a day, and we're encouraged to attend regularly. None of the boys goes every day — at least, none but maybe Ladislaus, who does seem to be quite devout, and maybe Taran; I don't really know what he does. But Journeys are required to attend at least three times per week, though I'm not sure who keeps count. I know Tristan makes his quota, though, because I'm always with him. I quite enjoy it, really.

Except for confession.

"Not just any mass, Marek," Gilles replies as he helps me down from the saddle. "Don't you know where we are?" When I shake my head, he says:

"This is the convent school of St. Genevieve, Marek. What does 'convent' mean to you?"

"Nuns?"

"Convent *school*, Marek." And then I get it. Of course.

"Girls," I say sullenly. I should have known.

"Bingo!" Gilles trills, as Jerome slaps my back. And then we're all crowding through the open church door.

"A special service this afternoon. Some saint's day or other," Pascal explains.

"All praise be to our blessed saints!" Falko chimes in. He sounds ready to forget his famous vow of chastity to me.

Inside, the boys have timed it perfectly. The service proper has just ended, and the priest and altar boys have already disappeared into the vestry. A few older women are still kneeling in prayer at side alcoves, but the pews are almost empty. The little chapel has two aisles, dividing the pews into three banks. In the bank of pews along the right side of the church, there is one larger party, consisting of five or six well-dressed girls sitting in a line. Behind them are more girls who look to be their servants, and I think I spot among them the girl Pascal had cornered outside the guild. Behind these handmaidens is a larger group of older women. The nuns, keeping a watchful eye over their wards. The girls haven't made a move to leave yet, and I wonder if the information hasn't been flowing two ways. I get the impression they're stalling, waiting for us to show up.

In the center of the girls is a figure more impressive than the others. From her clothing, she must be from a family of rank. Her head is covered with a filmy veil, but she has a graceful line and I can tell without really seeing her two things at the same time: she's lovely, and she's the real reason we're here.

As we cross the narthex, Tristan grabs a single white rose from an arrangement under the chapel icon, strips the leaves and thorns, and tosses them away. At the font, he stops for holy water, but to my surprise instead of dipping his fingertips into the water, he sticks his whole hand into the basin.

"What is he doing?" I ask the boy next to me, who turns out to be Gilles.

"Watch and learn, Marek. Watch and learn," he says.

"Give the master some room to work, boys!" Jerome exclaims, putting his hands out as though to hold us all back from crowding Tristan, who is sprinkling the water all over his face and neck, and pulling the unruly lock of his hair down from his widow's peak and over his forehead. I *knew* he did that on purpose!

He untucks his tunic from its waistband and pulls the neck open, and splashes more holy water onto his chest.

"What's with all the water?" I ask.

"The fever of love, Marek!" Jerome says with admiration. "If you thought he was good drunk, wait until you see him sober."

When he looks artfully disheveled, Tristan squares his shoulders and heads down the aisle, turning back before he goes just long enough to say,

"Just follow my lead, Marek."

Having no idea what this means, all I can do is plunge in after him. We all follow as Tristan stumbles down the aisle as though in a daze, and falls dramatically on one knee next to a pew a few rows ahead of the girls. He doesn't even glance their way as he passes them, so I don't, either, but I don't need to see the girls to know that our arrival has caused quite a stir. I'm about to follow suit and kneel, when Gilles pulls me down onto a pew a row behind Tristan, whispering,

"Not there, kid! You'll block their view."

As if on uncontrollable impulse, Tristan suddenly gets to his feet and stumbles on, right up to the front of the church. In front of the altar, he throws his head back and flings his arms wide, and falls onto both knees as though in some ecstasy of religious fervor. It's really such a good move, I almost start clapping. I'm wondering what he's going to do next, when Gilles jabs me in the shoulder.

"Get up there, squire! That's your cue." I look around, and see that Tristan is turning back slightly, trying to catch my eye, while making a surreptitious beckoning gesture with his head. I get up hastily and hurry clumsily down the aisle, aware of all the eyes on me — all the Journeys, all the girls, and, of course, the nuns. I've got stage fright — I didn't know I was going to be part of the performance.

As I approach him, Tristan whispers "The *other* side, Marek!" I'm blocking the view again, so I move around hastily to his far side, so I'm not between him and the girls. But I don't have any idea what to do. Tristan reaches up an unsteady hand to me, and I play along as best I can. I reach down and support his shoulders as he pretends to swoon, and he says out of the corner of his mouth, "Say something, kid."

I lick my lips. "Master! Master!" I cry, and he gives me an encouraging look, so I continue, "Come away, please! Let me help you. Oh, come away, do! You'll make yourself ill!"

"Not bad, not bad," he whispers back, pretending to resist, and we struggle there a minute. Then he wriggles free, and flings himself flat onto the ground, spreading himself so he's prostrate right under the altar. I feel like giving him a kick. What a ham! What am I supposed to do now?

"Will no one help me?" I cry back to the Journeys who are still on the pews, only partly joking. "My master is ill!" My voice is completely unconvincing and stilted, but the boys are loving it and having a hard time not laughing out loud. I don't know which they enjoy more — Tristan's hysterics, or my discomfort.

By this time the nuns have all gotten to their feet and are trying to get the girls away, without much success. The girls are putting up a pretty good fight, using their best passive resistance, but it's clear we don't have too much time to finish the performance.

"What's wrong with him?" Falko calls out, in a voice not at all appropriate for chapel.

"What's wrong with you?" I hiss at Tristan in a loud whisper.

"I'm dying of love!" he hisses back. Oh brother.

I put on my best dramatic voice, and call back to the Journeys, "He's been struck down, boys, by the cruelest archer of them all! Love, an even surer shot than he! Love's arrow has pierced my master, straight through the heart!" I think it's pretty good myself. Jerome and Turk were already having a hard time controlling themselves, but at this, they start shaking so hard I think they might slip off the pew.

The nuns have managed to get the girls to their feet, so to expedite things Gilles jumps up, and he and Charles come down to the front. We hurriedly get Tristan to his feet, who is now supposedly so weak he can't walk, and Gilles and Charles drag him down the aisle between them, with me following obediently after, wringing my hands in mock distress.

When we reach the row where the girls are still hovering, Tristan puts up a hand, as though he can't bear to go on, and we stop.

"Gilles, my friend," he says weakly, still not looking at the girls. "Is it true, what they say? That you can die of love?" I roll my eyes. He's going to use this line if it kills him.

"Undoubtedly," Gilles replies smoothly. "But only if it isn't returned. There's no cure for unrequited love."

Tristan raises the white rose to his lips, kisses it fervently with a deep sigh, then for the first time looks directly at the girl in the veil.

"Then, I must surely die," he groans, giving her a searing look, and tossing the rose at her feet. Before the nuns can protest, he collapses onto Gilles, and we sweep back up the aisle as the other Journeys scramble out of the pews to follow us, giggling almost as much as the girls still behind us in the church.

We don't make it far into the woods after spilling out of the chapel before the boys all break out laughing.

"That was priceless, duBois!" Charles says. "Priceless!"

"And Vervloet, you're a natural!" Turk says to me. "That stuff about Love the Archer. Inspired."

"Next time don't be such a hog, though, Tristan. Leave something for the rest of us!" Falko complains jovially.

"Come on, Falko. You should thank him. He did us all a favor. Ripened 'em all up for us! They'll be ready to fall right off the tree next time they see a Journeyman," Jerome declares. "Even you should be able to gather one up."

"If there is a next time. Blasted few saints martyred at this time of year," Gilles says. He's still supporting Tristan, who hasn't yet dropped the act. He's still staggering, and since we left the church, he hasn't said anything.

"Who is she?" I venture, glancing at Tristan's profile. He looks quite stunned.

"Isolde!" he whispers rapturously.

"Actually, it's Melissande," Gilles corrects dryly. "She's the daughter of some local lord or other. A famous beauty around here. Tristan's been trying to get a look at her for weeks. Pascal finally came through."

"So," chimes in Falko, rubbing his hands together. "Is she as beautiful as they say? I couldn't get a good look."

Tristan doesn't respond. He's lost in a reverie, like he's just seen the Holy Grail. So Falko turns inquiringly to me.

"I didn't get a good look, either," I say. And it isn't a total lie. I didn't get a good look. But as we paused next to her pew, I saw enough. An extraordinarily lovely face, and a fall of long, golden hair. By this time we're almost back to where we left the horses, but I can't help looking back and scanning the woods, half expecting to see a carriage waiting. A carriage with red trim.

As the boys mount up, they keep up teasing me about my part in the drama, since Tristan is lost in his own thoughts and generally being no fun. In fact, he's so distracted, he doesn't even remember about me, and he's mounted up and started to ride away before I notice I'm in danger of being left behind.

"Come on, I'll take you," Gilles says, but Falko reaches down a huge hand and pulls me effortlessly up onto his horse with him first. He seems to think we bonded over his teasing of me about the manuscript page, and when he heard about my supposed quick work with Roxanne, he's decided we should be buddies. I still think of him as 'the odious Falko,' but I guess he's not that bad. I hated him as a girl, but now that I'm a boy, I can stand him better. I guess you really can get used to anything.

The ride back seems interminable. To any observer, we must seem an even merrier party now than we did on the ride out, but a shadow has passed over the sun and blotted out all the light from the day. Trapped under Falko's huge arm and bouncing against him in the saddle, I feel claustrophobic. I hate horses again. By the time we get back to the guild, my face is bright red, but it isn't from riding close to Falko, or even because I'm embarrassed by all the comments about 'Love the Archer.'

It's because it's true. Love's arrows really are the cruelest. Watching Tristan's back as he rides ahead, oblivious to my suffering, I wonder why it was easier to suffer them when I was the only one who'd been struck.

WHEN I GO TO HIS ROOM TO COLLECT TRISTAN FOR evening mess, I find him sitting on the edge of his cot. In his hand, he's holding my little square of illumination out in front of him.

"She could have stepped right out of this page, Marek," Tristan says, running his hand through his hair in that distracted way of his and not bothering to look up.

"I know," I say dismally, trying not to let my face grow hot again.

"You, too?" he says quietly, finally looking up at me.

I start to open my mouth to argue, but what can I say to that? Now's the time for chivalry, so I clench my fists and say,

"She's perfect. Perfect for you, Tristan."

"She *is* perfect," he says, absorbed in the page again. "She's perfectly beyond my reach."

"But in the chapel," I say, trying not to let my voice crack. "No *girl* could have resisted that. Could have resisted you." I emphasize the word girl, for my own benefit. I've got to remember that I can't let myself feel like one anymore.

He shakes his head ruefully. "It was good, wasn't it? The grand gesture! But that's all it was."

"I don't believe it," I say loyally. "I won't." Now's the time to prove something, to myself. So I add, "I'll help you win her, Tristan. Like I did today! We'll win her for you, together. Your charm, her beauty. It's right. It's perfect. It's —" I break off, swallowing hard, before I can continue. "It's what I want. For you. I swear you'll get it!" I drop spontaneously to one knee, and Tristan laughs. But he isn't laughing at me. There's warmth in his voice as he puts a hand affectionately on my shoulder and says,

"I'm a bad influence on you, Marek. You're getting to be as bad as I am!" Then when he sees the misery on my face, he adds gently,

"I appreciate the gesture, little brother. All the more, because I know how you really feel. Oh, I saw the way you looked at her, back at the chapel, so don't bother to deny it. I don't blame you for wanting her, too. But we might as well face it. I've told you, I don't approve of self-pity over what's impossible. She's a noble, Marek. She's too high for either of us ever to reach."

"Not if you stand on my shoulders," I say bravely, and with that melodramatic pronouncement I get up and leave before he can say anything else.

And I mean it. I have to, don't I? I swore an oath, and I'm going to keep it, if it kills me.

But as we make our way out to the abandoned windmill as usual after practice the next day, when we come through the field of poppies, all the beauty is gone, and I see each one as a fresh wound again. And this time, they're all mine.

CHAPTER SIXTEEN

It's only days before first trials when things start going wrong with Tristan. I think if I weren't so distracted by Tristan's unaccountable change of mood, I might have been more attentive to what happens next. I might have taken warning. As it is, Tristan's unravelling so close to trials is a crisis of such magnitude that I can't focus on anything else.

At first, I'm just annoyed. I assume that he's got a predictable malady — he's mooning over Melissande. But at heart, Tristan's a pragmatist, and I doubt he'd really let a girl, even one like her, keep him from the goal he's worked so hard to achieve. I know he really does want to win. And we have been working hard, and it's been paying off. Tristan was already good, but I like to think it's my drive that's put him in top form. He's been cool and confident, and we've both begun to look forward to his performance at trials. He's sure to sweep the competition. At least, that's what I would have said, just a few days ago. Now, I'm not so sure.

I first notice a change in him after evening mess, just three days before Firsts. With the preparations for trials well underway it's been a madhouse around the guild, and now the hall is packed. The hallways have been full of visitors for the past few days: vendors, armorers, sponsors, garland makers, you name it, and Master Gheeraert is so busy getting everything organized he hasn't appeared at mess all week.

Otherwise, as we take our seats, everything seems normal

enough. We've been a little late getting back and the table's already crowded, so Tristan squeezes in amongst the Journeys, and I find a place by Auguste among the squires at the opposite end of the table. With Firsts looming and so much activity around the guild, there's more tension among the boys than usual, but nothing that's not to be expected. Gilles and Aristide aren't speaking, since Aristide's let it be known he's placed a sizable bet at one of the seedier taverns in town that Gilles will be cut in the first round. Nobody really thinks he expects Gilles to fail this early, but Aristide's willing to lose the money to get under Gilles's skin. Gilles pretends to be gleeful at the prospect of being the cause of emptying Aristide's pockets, but the tension is getting to all of them, and I doubt he's as sanguine as he pretends.

The only one not showing outward signs of stress is Taran. He's his usual self, cool as a cucumber, unreadable.

About halfway through the meal there's a commotion at the door, and Master Guillaume rises from the masters' table and puts up a hand in greeting. A tall, well-dressed man with a small entourage returns the greeting, and we all watch him as he makes his way to the front of the room. He isn't particularly handsome, but he's distinguished-looking, with a fine head of hair greying at the temples. There have been many unfamiliar faces around the guild lately, what with trials coming up, but this is clearly someone of substance. The elaborately embroidered cloak slung over his shoulder alone looks like it cost a fortune, and he carries himself with the easy arrogance of a man who's important and knows it. When he reaches the masters' table, the two men share a hearty handshake, and before they sit, Master Guillaume calls for attention.

"Gentlemen!" his voice booms. "We are very fortunate today to have an honored visitor. Join me in giving a St. Sebastian's welcome to one of our very own, Sir Hugo Brecelyn." We all stomp our feet and pound the table as expected, while Gilles says in a loud whisper,

"Gads! The father. You don't suppose he heard about the other day at the chapel and is here to round you up, eh, Tristan?" Before Tristan can answer, Guillaume is continuing:

"Not only is sir Brecelyn a distinguished veteran of our guild, but he has been a generous benefactor these many years. Very generous. I'm exceedingly pleased to announce, this year, he is doing us a great honor indeed. Not only is he personally sponsoring the trials, but he has also agreed to serve as one of the judges for Firsts. Unfortunately, he is a very busy man and cannot stay and join us tonight, but I'm delighted he could stop by so that I could present him to you in advance of trials."

We meet this announcement with a polite increase in applause, but when Guillaume turns to Sir Brecelyn and the two begin talking together, we sit down, and I don't think much more of it. I'm curious, though, since I've heard of Sir Brecelyn all my life, but I've never seen him before. Gilles has confirmed what I suspected at the chapel of St. Genevieve about Melissande, too, so I study him with some interest. It isn't long, however, before Master Guillaume is leading his guest over to our table, and I have the opportunity of observing him from close up.

"Journeymen, may I present sir Hugo Brecelyn," he says, and the boys all nod.

"That Mellor's boy?" he asks, pointing at Taran.

"Taran," Guillaume barks, and Taran rises to his feet with military precision. "Sir Hugo has expressed particular interest in meeting you."

"Sir," Taran says with a little bow, and Brecelyn makes his way around the table until the two of them are standing side by side.

"Yes, indeed!" Brecelyn slaps Taran on the back. Taran's already the same height as Brecelyn or a little taller, so he has to reach up to do it. "A fine figure of a boy! Just like your father, aren't you? Looking forward to doing him proud at the trials, no doubt."

"I certainly hope so, sir," Taran replies respectfully.

"Well, just between us, I've got a little good news for you. I wanted to be the one to tell you myself. I've had word that Lord Mellor is on his way to Louvain as we speak, with a number of the other Black Guardsmen. They'll be here for Firsts! Now what do you think of that?! I don't think I've ever heard of Guardsmen making the trip for Firsts before. What an occasion for St. Sebastian's! It'll be a great day. That's got to be welcome news, for all of you," he nods to the table, before turning back specifically to Taran. "And just think how you'll feel, showing off what you can do with your father looking on! I've heard good things about you already. Word is, you're the cream of the crop this year. Oh yes, I'm looking forward to seeing you perform, my boy."

Through all of this, Taran's wooden expression hasn't changed. He doesn't have the grace to look embarrassed, but at least he isn't gloating, either.

"And boys," Brecelyn adds heartily, turning to the table to include all the Journeys. "I have a little special treat of my own planned for you at the competition. My very own daughter, Lady Melissande, will be presenting a garland to one of you lucky lads." At this, he slaps Taran on the chest, making it clear he expects that lucky lad to be Taran. "What a crowning moment that will be! This is going to be a Firsts Louvain will long remember. I'm anticipating quite a show, and I, for one, can hardly wait to see you in action." At this, he's turned to Taran again, and now he adds meaningfully, "and to seeing much more of you in Louvain in the near future."

"Great!" Aristide grumbles, as Sir Brecelyn moves away with Sir Guillaume to take his leave, and Taran takes his seat again, as impassive as ever. "Taran's already got one of the judges in his pocket."

"With Lord Mellor and the Guards there, the judges are all going to fall all over themselves to give Taran high scores," Ladislaus agrees.

"Oh, what does it matter?" drawls Gilles, probably just to be disagreeable to Aristide. "Taran wasn't going to be cut at firsts. We all knew that. Get over it."

"But that garland would have been sweet," Jerome says, glancing at Tristan, who hasn't said anything. That's when I first notice that Tristan has been uncharacteristically silent, and he's got a funny look on his face. But before anyone can say anything else about the garland, Master Guillaume is on his feet again, and we fall silent as he calls us to attention once more.

"Gentlemen!" his voice booms out again. "It is important to emphasize here and now that St. Sebastian's does not traffic in rumors. We hold honor in very high regard. Let me be perfectly clear that there is absolutely no favoritism shown at St. Sebastian's, not in training, and not in the trials."

"If that were true, he wouldn't have to say so, would he?" Gilles hisses, and I'm afraid he's right.

"Speaking of honor, there is another matter that must be raised tonight, but for reasons which will soon be obvious, I've waited until our guest had departed to broach the subject. A very unfortunate matter, particularly right before trials. It seems that some cakes left out cooling on the masters' sideboard disappeared during the night last night. This may seem a trifling matter, and I am prepared to assume that there is a simple explanation. Some oversight, a mistake. I fully expect this to be the end of the matter. *However*," he says ominously, "I must take the opportunity to stress that thievery will not be condoned at St. Sebastian's. Nor will rule-breaking. No one is to roam the hallways after lights out. We do not deal in rumors at St. Sebastian's," he repeats, and I get the impression he's looking particularly at Aristide. "But if anyone has real information about this incident, I must impress upon you all that it is your duty to report it to the masters. And let me repeat: we will not tolerate a thief at St. Sebastian's." He breaks off, his voice hanging in the air, without having to voice the threat that we all know so well: *St. Sebastian's punishes its own.*

Throughout this speech, I've sensed eyes on me from the Journey end of the table, and I don't have to turn around to know whose they are. I try not to look, but I can't help myself. When I lock eyes with Jurian, he's contemplating me with such a curious expression, I sense I'm in trouble.

By the time I pull myself together, I find Tristan's already left without me. I didn't notice him go; he must have been one of the first to leave. Auguste and Turk's squire Andre corner me on my way out, trying to convince me to join them at dice back in the barracks, but I know I've got to see Tristan as soon as possible. It's time for confession.

When I get to Tristan's room, I have to knock twice before he answers, and even then I almost assume he must not be there when his voice calls out a sharp "Come in, if you must."

He's lying on his cot, facing the wall. Even though it's dark in the room, he has one arm over his eyes, as though to shield them from the light.

"What is it, Marek?" he asks, without turning around. "Whatever it is, can't it wait until morning?"

"There's something I've got to tell you, Tristan," I say urgently, putting my candle down on his bedside table. "Something I didn't tell you before. I just, well, forgot about it. But I've got to tell you now."

He sits up resignedly on the edge of his bed, looking impatient. The candlelight casts dark shadows under his brows, making him look tired and angry. So I'm nervous, picking at my fingers abstractedly, as I tell him as quickly as I can about seeing Jurian in the dormitory hallway after curfew.

His immediate response is as I expected.

"And just what were *you* doing out after lights out?" he asks, not smiling.

"I just had to get away from the barracks, Tristan. Just for a minute." It's true enough. "I swear, there was nothing more to it. You don't know what it's like in there, with all the boys, all the time. I just had to get away."

"To the Journeyman lavatory?" he says sarcastically.

"It was foolish, I know."

"It was damned stupid, Marek!" he explodes. "What if someone had seen you?"

"Someone *did* see me," I say, reminding him of Jurian.

"I don't have to tell you how serious this is, do I? Things already don't look good for you. If you're pegged for the thief, Marek, there won't be anything I can do to help you."

"About that," I say urgently. "Jurian never said a word. Do you think, *he* could be the thief?"

"Don't be an idiot," Tristan says dismissively. "Jurian doesn't have to steal."

"But he was out. And he didn't say anything."

"That was weeks ago, Marek. Jurian's no thief. You're just lucky he was the only one who saw you. If it had been anyone else, you'd be out now. As it is, watch yourself, will you?" He seems suddenly worn out. "I can't be worrying now about you getting yourself into trouble." He lies back down on his cot, signaling that our interview is over. It's not the just the candlelight; he really is in a foul mood. I put it down to exhaustion and stress, so I turn to let him get some sleep. Tristan's got his arm back over his eyes, so I don't think he even notices that I'm leaving, but as I open the door, he says:

"I shouldn't have to warn you not to breathe a word of this to anybody else, Marek. And not just because you can't explain your own actions adequately. Jurian's all right. But don't let his looks fool you. He's no angel. And remember: nobody likes having their secrets aired, even when they're open secrets."

I make my way back to barracks, as perplexed by Tristan's words as I am by his mood. It's only as I'm drifting off to sleep, letting my mind go blank, that a vague memory of my father's voice echoes in my head. I must be remembering wrong, or maybe I'm even imagining it. So much has happened. But it sounds very real, and if anything, it only leaves me feeling more confused:

"Brecelyn has no children."

THE NEXT MORNING, TRISTAN IS LATE FOR MORNING drills. When he finally does show up, he looks like he's had a bad night, and some of his old indolence has returned. I might even think he was hung over, if I hadn't been with him last night. His shooting during practice is mediocre at best, and when I try to encourage him, he's so rude I give up. His mood doesn't improve at noon. He's sullen and silent through mess, and when I try to make a plan for afternoon practice, he announces calmly that he's skipping our usual workout and going riding with Turk instead. It's the last straw.

"You can't hide out in the horse pasture all day!" I explode, even though we're right outside the great hall and anyone could hear us. Tristan just stares at me with a cool expression, arms folded across his chest.

"That's all you want to do these days, prance around behind Turk. That's not going to get you past Firsts!" I can't keep my voice down, but Tristan doesn't rise to the bait. He just leans back against the wall without changing expression.

"I've made up my mind, Marek. One or two days, more or less, what does it matter at this point?" He pushes off the wall with his foot and moves to go around me, but I block his way.

"Look, Tristan," I say, getting worried. What has gotten into him? There's only one explanation. "I'm not going to stand by while you throw away all our hard work, because you're mooning over some girl!"

"What in the hell are you talking about?" he says angrily, trying to pushing past me.

"The garland!" I say. "You've been sulking ever since Brecelyn brought it up last night."

"Don't be ridiculous," Tristan says, so scornfully I feel really hurt. Somehow we're talking at cross purposes, just like I used to do with my father. But if he's not upset about the prospect of watching Melissande crown Taran, what is going on with him?

"Tristan, please," I say gently, putting out a hand to try to stop him, but he's already gone.

I have no idea what to do now. I can't follow him out to the stables, and even if I did, what would I say? I have no idea what's wrong. I consider going out to the workshops, to put the finishing touches on Tristan's bow. I'd meant to surprise him with it for Firsts, but I couldn't quite get it done in time. He'd have to have time to practice with it before using it in competition, and it's too late for that now, so I'm saving it for second trials. That is, if there are Seconds for us, at this rate. I should have had the bow finished long ago, but I've been having trouble making myself work on it. Whenever I start, as soon as my hand runs over the wood, I can't help thinking of my father's hands, smoothing that little bow I know was for me. I imagine him pouring himself into the work, putting the emotion he was never good at showing me into the bow, and I have to stop, and put the bow aside for another day. It isn't just that I miss my father. It's that I miss having that bow, having one thing from him — one thing that's really mine.

Today, with Tristan so distant, I can't face it. I'm already too lonely. So I wander out onto the practice field, hoping to find one of Tristan's friends, Gilles or Jerome. It's tricky, asking anyone for advice so close to trials, but I'm getting alarmed now and I need some help.

The field is busy, but there's nobody about that I can ask about Tristan. So I sit down in the shade by Tristan's cabinet to wait. Surely they'll come out to practice eventually, with Firsts only days away. I sit there quite a while, and despite my nerves the heavy midday meal and the warm sun begin to work on me, and I start to get drowsy. I'm just about to drift off to sleep when I catch sight of Jurian, coming in from the field. I watch him lazily for a while, thinking over what Tristan said about him last night. He's at a safe distance, over by the stable door, stripping off his tunic by the rain barrels to cool down after practicing. He *does* look heavenly, bronzed and glowing in the noonday sun, from the golden cap of his hair to his tanned torso. But I wonder what Tristan meant, he's no angel. Why hasn't he told on me, then?

I watch him splash water over himself, as flies drone around me and the sun beats down overhead, and I examine him dispassionately. Or rather, I think I do. I don't think I'm ogling him. Not really. He is magnificent, but it's the architecture of him I'm thinking about. Maybe I'm being defeatist, as Tristan said, but looking at Jurian, it's clear why I'll never be able to compete with boys. The idea I could ever be a Journey is absurd. Without his shirt on, Jurian's shoulders look ridiculously wide and strong. He's about Tristan's height, but his body is exaggerated. He's got the shoulders of a heavy shooter, but the slender waist and hips of younger boy, so he looks like an inverted triangle. His chest is smooth and hard, and my eyes follow it down to the belly, where a solid triangle of muscle slopes down between his jutting hips. I've gotten leaner and harder from training, but my belly will never be a flat, thick muscle like that. It hasn't lost its soft, feminine roundness. Tristan's negative mood is probably infecting me, but the idea that I should be training at all, even just to 'fail spectacularly,' seems more laughable than ever.

Below Jurian's belly button, there's a soft, delicate line of golden hair that I've never noticed before, and without thinking, I let my eyes follow it, fascinated, thinking how it resembles the fletch of an arrow. It looks like it would feel like a fletching feather, too, and I image running my finger down over it and feeling it spring back in place behind, the way I do sometimes when I'm working on an arrow in the shop. I follow it with my eyes down until it plunges below the line of his breeches, then I work my way back up over his chest. He really is gorgeous, I'm feeling sleepy, and there's only so tight a control over your thoughts you can keep.

But when my eyes reach his face, to my horror I find that he's watching me now, too, with an amused look on his face. I feel just like I did, when he caught me touching Tristan in his bath. He gives me an exaggerated leer, then he sticks out his long tongue at me. It gives me a sinking feeling in my gut, but I'm completely taken aback by what he does next. Not taking his eyes off me, he bends his head and slowly licks the wet arrow welt on his own arm. It's so disturbing, I feel like I've been licked myself from my toes to my fingertips.

As obscure threats go, even Taran's wink was preferable.

It's with great relief, then, that at just this moment I spot Gilles in the distance, climbing over the back wall. He looks to be on his return from a hunting trip in the woods, since he's got a rabbit slung over his shoulder. I hustle to my feet and hurry across the field, eager to meet him, and even more eager to get away from Jurian. Tristan was right, I think, as I make my escape from Jurian's mockery. I should have watched myself better with him.

But as I near Gilles, I come to a full stop. Someone else is behind him, coming over the wall. It's Taran. I stand there halfway across the field, gaping as the two of them exchange some banter that I can't make out. Catching sight of me, Gilles puts a hand on Taran's back and says something to him, then breaks away to come over to me, while Taran makes his own way back to the stables.

"What are you doing with Taran?" I ask accusingly when Gilles approaches, though I'm not sure what I'm accusing him of.

"Whatever do you mean, Marek?" Gilles replies smoothly. "I often go hunting with Taran."

"I've never seen you with him."

"That's because you're always with Tristan," he laughs. "He and Tristan don't get on, in case it has escaped your notice. But Taran's all right. I've got nothing against him, personally."

This is the first I've heard of it, but I suppose it's true. I guess I don't know what Gilles does when we aren't around. But somehow I feel betrayed, for Tristan's sake. It feels like Taran is now the golden boy, what with his famous father coming to trials and sir Brecelyn salivating over him at mess last night, and Tristan's friends are abandoning him for more glamorous company. Irrationally, I feel like Tristan's ship is sinking, and the rats are all jumping overboard. It's not fair, but I can't bring myself to ask Gilles about Tristan, not now. Not when he's one of the rats.

Jerome's my last chance, and I finally track him down in the chapel. I wait respectfully while he lights a candle in an alcove and finishes his prayers, and I can't help but notice that he doesn't look much better than Tristan. The stress of the upcoming competition is getting to him, and up until a few days ago, I would have said he had more to worry about than Tristan. He's an all-around shooter, best at wands, but he isn't in the same class at mid-distance as Gilles or Aristide. At butts, accuracy is going to be an issue for him. It isn't very tactful of me, then, to approach him about Tristan, but I'm desperate. We sit in the back of the chapel, and I tell Jerome my fears. To his credit, he seems as concerned as I am when I tell him that I think Tristan is coming unnerved.

"I wouldn't have thought he'd collapse under pressure. You know, Jerome," I say, trying to be tactful, but I'm so upset, I can't worry about it too much, "he should be confident now! He's one of the best, probably *the* best, at butts. I don't understand it."

"I was afraid this might happen, Marek, after last night." He doesn't explain, and he's going on before I can question him. "Look, even if he's not at his best, no matter what, he'll be able to do well enough to pass. He's that good. Just get him out on the field. He'll pass all right. That is, if he shows up."

Jerome means well, but this doesn't comfort me at all. And it's only one more day until Firsts.

THE DAY BEFORE TRIALS, ALL MY TIME IS SPENT ON preparations, and there's so much commotion at the guild I hardly see Tristan. We've been given a list of the equipment each Journey will need, and so I've got to assemble it all and check it over, then double-check it. I oil up Tristan's bows, fletch the arrows, and polish up everything until it shines. Then I've got to get Tristan's clothes and my own ready, which means quite a bit of back and forth to Gilles's tailor with Pascal. Ceremonial regalia is expected, and I'm responsible for making sure everything is clean and in good repair. With all these chores, there's no question of me practicing with Tristan, and for once, I'm glad. I don't even bother to urge him to practice alone. I would never have thought it a few days ago, when Tristan was on top form, that my expectations would shrink down so far that my whole goal would be just to get him to show up, as Jerome said. I try to stay optimistic: Tristan should be fine. He can't lose at butts, can he? Not unless he really tries. But at this point, I have no idea what he's capable of doing. We haven't really spoken more than to exchange clipped instructions since our quarrel in the hallway yesterday.

When I'm sure I've got everything in order, I can't sit still. I'm a bundle of nerves, so I decide to force myself to go to the workshop and work on Tristan's bow. He can't use it tomorrow, but maybe if I present it to him, the gift will do something to shake him out of his gloom. It can't hurt, and I've got to do something constructive. So that afternoon, I finish the bow. By the time I'm done my arms are aching, and I'm exhausted. I feel as though I've worked into the bow all my concern for him. And so I say a prayer that Tristan will pull himself together, so that he'll have a chance to use this bow for the next trials, in a way I never got to use mine. As the hour for evening mess approaches, I wrap the finished bow in a cloth and leave it in the workshop until tomorrow. There's nothing I can do now but wait for morning.

As I'm milling around in the hallway waiting for Tristan to show up so I can follow him in to supper, Turk passes me.

"He should be along in a minute, Marek. We just came in a few minutes ago. Tristan's really been putting in the work for trials, eh?" he says annoyingly, and I don't disabuse him. When I just make some noncommittal noise, he puts an arm on my shoulder, and says,

"I think he's really going to surprise you tomorrow, kid!"

I don't like the sound of that at all. A surprise tomorrow is the last thing I want.

CHAPTER SEVENTEEN

When the morning of Firsts finally dawns, I'm the first to wake in the squires' barracks. I haven't slept well during the night, and from the sounds from the other cots, neither have most of the boys. We're all too nervous. For two of us, this is our last night together.

I slip out of my cot to head out to the practice field. There will be no morning drills today, but I've got to check Tristan's equipment again, and to set it up out on the exhibition grounds before coming back to make my own preparations. We're all expected to look good today and I know I won't get a real wash, so I also want a chance to clean up out at the barrels before anyone else is stirring. At the entrance to the great hall I stop, and I think to myself, maybe today will be the day I take the shortcut. Yet even after all these weeks, I can't bring myself to do it.

The trials are set to begin mid-morning, so it isn't long before the other squires start making an appearance. Auguste joins me by the boys' cabinets, and we get our first load to cart over to the exhibition grounds together. I haven't been over yet; some of the other boys have been going over to get a look now and then over the past few days, but I've been too nervous. From all reports, Firsts is going to be a real circus.

Even with everything I've heard, I'm not prepared for the sight of the exhibition grounds. It's very early, but it's already crawling with activity as Auguste and I drag our stands across the L'île-

Charleroi road and through one of the makeshift gates in the temporary barricades that are now in place around the perimeter of what was until a few days ago essentially just a huge empty field. A whole army of local women are hard at work on the towering wooden bleachers that have been set up facing the open area in the middle of the grounds where the trials are to take place, festooning them with garlands of flowers. Booths and tents stretch as far as the eye can see, and everywhere people are unloading goods from wagons and carts and into the booths. Men in St. Sebastian's regalia of various rank swarm around the trials area, some setting up the field, and others milling around, waiting to serve as security once the trials begin. Spectators are already gathering; they're either peeking through the gates or openly wandering around between the booths and out by the trials field, trying to guess what the tests are going to be. Auguste and I have come to a stop and are gawking at all the activity when Baylen spots us and directs us with a sharp bark to the proper place to set up the stations for the first test.

Each of the Journeys has his own small tent, a sort of miniature pavilion for the storage of gear between tests, and from which he can make a formal entrance onto the competition field. The bright tents make an impressive array, arranged as they are in a row facing the grandstands but on the opposite side of the trials field. Each one is a solid color, the identifying color of the Journey, and at the top, they all fly the flag of St. Sebastian's: the single silver arrow on a black field. Tristan's color is red, so it's easy to spot his tent, and I bustle the extra equipment not on the list for the first test into it. It takes me a few trips to get everything over and organized inside the small tent, and on a whim I make one extra trip, to bring the bow I've made for Tristan over from the workshop.

By the time I'm done, most of the other squires have already headed back to bathe or get dressed themselves, and townspeople and visitors are starting to stream through the gates and into the stands. It isn't long now, and I haven't even seen Tristan yet today. My stomach heaves, and it isn't just because I've forgotten to eat anything. I'm a bundle of nerves, and I'm not even competing. I can't imagine what this scene is going to do to Tristan, particularly the way he's been acting.

I literally run back across the street to the barracks, and I grab up my outfit for trials. It's a sort of simplified version of the Journey's costume: all black, with a black cloak. Mine isn't silk, but thanks to Gilles's infamous tailor, it all actually fits, and I think I do look quite good in it. Maybe I *can* go for 'rugged.' I hurry with it to Tristan's room, but when I knock, there's no answer. He's not in his room. When I open the door, all I find is Popinjay, sound asleep. Where can he be? I close the door and hasten into my clothes, so worried that I don't bother to smooth them down. As soon as I'm inside them, I throw the door open, and command the old dog:

"Find him for me, Popinjay!" I have a sinking feeling that maybe he's gone out to the windmill. Or maybe he's really run away. Why did I let him out of my sight this morning?

But Popinjay simply pads down the hall, and slinks through the doorway into the great hall. Tristan's there, standing below the painting of St. Sebastian. His back is to me, but when I see he's in his full regalia, I'm so relieved, I could cry. He didn't run away! He intends to compete, after all. Of course, he never said he wouldn't. Maybe the whole thing has been in my mind. I've gotten myself worked up over nothing.

Standing there in the long black cloak emblazoned with a single silver *fleur de lis*, his magnificent head of thick black hair held high as he contemplates the painting, he looks resplendent. The contrast between his dark, draped figure and the white naked flesh above him is striking, but he and the boy in the image could still be twins, twin luminaries, the pale moon waxing above as the dark star of vespers rises before it. Seeing him like this, looking every inch the hero, I know he can't lose. We're going to be all right.

But then he opens his mouth.

"What am I doing here, Marek?" he asks, sensing my presence but not turning around.

"I don't know! We should be getting out to the exposition grounds. Most of the others are probably already there."

"That's not what I mean. What am I doing, at St. Sebastian's?" he asks.

I blink. This is no time for riddles!

"Tristan," I plead. "Can we talk about this tomorrow? Whatever's gotten into you, we can sort it out later, after trials. Just come out to the field with me, please!"

"How can you stand it, Marek?" he says, ignoring me, and still staring intently at the painting. "Day after day, how can you stand it, this picture, looming over you noon and night, like that?" I force myself to look up at the painting, to really see it. I wonder if he can see it, too, the resemblance. Is he seeing himself in that painting? But then he says quietly, "Fathers cast such long shadows."

When I don't respond, he says, "No one's here. I could rip it right off the wall. Pull it down for you, right now. Tear it to shreds. We could do it. We could pull this whole place down, brick by brick."

For a minute, I think he finally has gone insane. It's even worse than I thought. But then he turns around, and as he does, the red lining of his cloak swirls around him like a cloud of blood. Seeing my expression, he laughs.

"What's the matter, kid?"

"You *are* going to compete, aren't you, Tristan?" I cry a bit hysterically, relieved by his laughter but still unsure.

"Of course. What did you think? That I'd bolted?" At my guilty look, he says grimly, "Oh, I'm going to compete, all right."

Somehow, this doesn't reassure me as much as it should. He still seems dangerously unstable. The stress of competition has unhinged him. I keep saying Jerome's words over in my head to reassure myself as I follow him out, "Just get him to the field. He'll pass all right, as long as he shows up."

Tristan seems confident enough as he strides through the eager crowds that have gathered around the booths lining the field to get some refreshment before the trials begin. But when I notice that he isn't heading toward the row of Journey tents, I start worrying all over again.

"Tristan, we're supposed to go that way!" I say, motioning toward the trial field.

"I said I was going to compete, but you don't expect me to do it sober, do you?" he says, and I groan. He's heading for a tent selling ale, and before I can stop him, he's pushed to the front of the line and is demanding a pint. When I start trying to grab his arm, he turns to me with a grin that looks almost like his old self.

"I'm kidding, Marek. I'm not going to get drunk. But I'm thirsty. One ale isn't going to make any difference."

I'm about to respond, when I hear something so unexpected, I freeze. It's a familiar voice from my old life.

"One of our own Journeys! Good luck out there today, young man! For one of our valiant boys, the ale is on the house!" the voice is saying to Tristan.

It's Brother Benedict. This booth must belong to the Vendon Abbey.

I drop down instantly, as though in need of inspecting something on my boot. There's nothing for it. I can't help how strange it looks. I've got to crawl away, around behind the booth; short hair or no, and despite the squire's costume, Benedict knows my face very well. I can't let him see me. My heart gives a lurch, and I wonder if Father Abelard is somewhere nearby, too, and not for the first time I think how comforting it would be to be able to turn to the old monks for help. The thought that someone who could help me is so close strangely makes me feel even more alone and helpless.

By the time I've gotten myself up again behind the booth and brushed myself off, I've lost sight of Tristan. So I hurry to his tent, but he's not there. Where can he be *now*? I curse myself for letting him out of my sight again. It's getting close to starting time; the bleachers are full, and a huge crowd of people who couldn't find a seat are jostling for standing room behind the barricades set up at the edges of the field, while veterans on security duty do their best to keep them in line. On the field, the Journeys and squires are mingling with various dignitaries — greeting their sponsors, and other guests who've made the trip specifically for the trials.

But Tristan isn't among them. Since all the boys are dressed the same, it's hard to tell at first. They're all in black from head to foot, with black leather jerkins with silver studs, and matching black cloaks. The only difference is the color of the cloak's lining, which matches each boy's color. ("White!" Gilles exclaimed in despair when trying on his cloak yesterday. "Why did it have to be white? Such a bland color. It does nothing for my complexion," to which Jerome responded, "If it'll make you feel better, next time, tell your tailor to line it in pure ermine!") But there's no sign of that distinctive red lining anywhere. I plunge back among the booths. Benedict or no, I've got to find Tristan, and despite his declaration I suspect I'll find him at the bottom of a pint of ale.

Finally I do find him among the booths, but it's not as I expected. He's leaning heavily up against the back of a booth, in its shadow. His back is pressed against the booth, but he's craning his neck at a painful angle, so that he can see out to the field without being seen. He looks a little green. I follow his gaze out to the field, to where Sir Brecelyn is standing, talking with Taran and his father. Lord Mellor is an imposing man, and he's in his full Guards regalia. Since the Journey costume imitates that of the Guards, he and Taran make a matched pair. Taran's color is black, so the two of them are dressed almost identically, and with his size and physique Taran looks for all the world like a member of the Guards already. I can see what's upsetting Tristan. It looks like a vision of the inevitable future, all right. Lord Mellor and Sir Brecelyn look like they could be swearing Taran in as the next Guardsman already.

"Come away, Tristan, you're making yourself ill," I say gently. For an absurd moment, I'm reminded of the scene we played in the chapel of St. Genevieve not so long ago, only now I'm deadly earnest. "Come away. Forget about Taran."

"How can I?" he says simply. "When nobody will let me."

"You don't have to beat him, Tristan. Not today."

"Why did *he* have to be here?" he asks unexpectedly, and for a confused minute, I think he's still talking about Taran. Of course Taran is here. What did he expect? Then I get it.

"Look, Tristan. I know, it's an advantage. But Gilles was right. Nobody expects Taran to fail today. It can't hurt you any, not really, that the Guardsmen are here. And by all accounts, Lord Mellor is a very fair man. He won't let the judges show favoritism."

"He's a bastard!" Tristan spits with so much venom, I'm shocked. I know he hates Taran, but I've never heard anyone say anything against Lord Mellor.

"Come away, Tristan, please!" I plead. "The competition is about to begin. You should be out there, greeting your sponsor, if he's here." When Tristan gives a start at this, I hurry on: "I know you don't like your sponsor very much, but it's expected. Come on, let's forget about Taran and look for him."

"I don't have to look for him," he says bitterly, looking back at the field. "I know exactly where he is. But he won't want me to greet him. Not publicly, anyway."

"What are you talking about? Where is he?" I ask, confused, and Tristan nods out at the field, toward the group around Taran.

"I don't understand. Sir Brecelyn?" I ask, and Tristan snorts in derision. Then I really get it.

"Lord *Mellor* is *your* sponsor, too?" I say, incredulously. It doesn't make any sense. "Why would Taran's father sponsor you for Journeys, and against his own son?"

"You might as well know. Everyone will be talking about it soon enough," Tristan says, pushing himself off the booth, and leaning in close to me. Inches from my face, his own face red with rage, he says violently,

"It's time you knew *my* open secret, Marek. I'm that bastard's bastard son!"

And from the look on his face, I think Lord Mellor is very lucky he isn't standing where I am right now, or he'd know what it felt like to have Tristan's hands tight around his neck.

I follow Tristan across the field in stunned silence. What can I say? I'm not even sure I can really believe what he's just told me. I can't fully process the ramifications of it, either. But somewhere in the back of my mind, wheels are turning, and some of the pieces of the puzzle that is Tristan start to fall into place. But I can't think about it now. We've got trials to worry about, and now I finally understand what's gotten Tristan so unstrung. He must have known he'd have to perform in front of his father eventually, but he didn't expect it to happen so soon.

When we're safely inside his tent and waiting for the fanfare that will call us out onto the field, Tristan's hands as he picks up his bow are shaking, and I don't know if it's from nerves or rage, or both. He looks defeated, and suddenly I have an image of him as my father, as he was that last day in the chapel, beaten down, knowing the end was near, and I can't bear it. I make a quick decision. It's risky, but I have to do something. I pick up the bow I made for him, still wrapped in cloth, from where I stuck it in the corner of the tent, and I present it to him.

"Tristan," I say, my voice full of sentiment even though I know he usually hates it. "I have something for you, for good luck, at Firsts. It's a bow. I made it myself."

He takes it with a frown, and as he starts to unwrap it, I rush on. "I know you should never use new equipment in a competition, but I thought, maybe, under the circumstances, you'd try it. You know, a Verbeke bow, for the unveiling of the Verbeke method."

"You made this, Marek?" he says, running his hand appreciatively over the bow. "Where did you get the money to pay for the materials? It looks expensive. Like Venetian yew."

"I worked for them, for Marcel, in the shop. I swear it wasn't pluck-buffet!" I joke, embarrassed now, trying to lighten the moment.

He raises the bow, and stretches it a little, but not bending it all the way since there's no arrow in it.

"It's a real beauty, Marek. I've never seen the like." His voice is so quiet, I can hardly hear him.

"Tristan," I say, putting my hand on the bow, too, so we're holding it together between us. And now I don't care if it's sentimental, maudlin even. It's my chance to speak. "You're my family now. You're my father. You're my brother. You're all I have left in the world to love. To hell with all of them. A minute ago, you were ready to pull this place down brick by brick. So what are you waiting for? Go out there and do it, with this. Show them what you can do. Show them what extraordinary really means."

At that moment, the trumpets blast. Firsts are upon us, ready or not. But when I take my hand away and Tristan lifts my bow to his shoulder, his hand is steady enough.

AT THE SOUND OF THE TRUMPETS, I OPEN THE TENT flaps just a sliver to see what's going on. Master Guillaume has risen from a long table set up on the field before the bleachers, and he's addressing the crowd. I can't hear what he's saying from here, but he looks to be introducing the panel of judges, who are seated on either side of him. I recognize the masters, of course, and Sir Brecelyn, and Lord Mellor, but five or six other men I don't recognize also take their turn to rise and face the audience as Master Guillaume gestures to them. There look to be about twelve judges in all, to match the number of Journeys. When Guillaume finishes his introductory remarks, applause rings out from the stands, and there's another fanfare. It's time for us to take the field.

A single bugler closer to the tents blows a note on his horn, and a loud voice calls out *"Ladislaus Bowdoin!"* And then Lad is striding out from his tent, his cloak billowing from his broad shoulders, with his squire following him, both of them puffed up with pride. As they step up and take their places on the line next to their station, the bugle sounds again. *"Jerome Crecelle,"* the voice calls, and I hardly recognize Auguste as he struts out behind Jerome, he looks so grown up and dignified. And then we're next, and I'm plunging out behind Tristan, blinking into the blaring midmorning light. All those hundreds of eyes in the stands are on us, and I feel my heart beating so hard in my chest it feels like it's trying to escape, but at the same time my chest expands with pride so far I think I might break the tight binding around my breasts. I stand beside Tristan, reveling in the glory of the moment, as Falko next makes his way across the field. His head is thrown back and there's a huge grin on his face, and my heart expands again until I think it must burst, as I feel a rush of pride for him, too. When the loud voice calls out "Percival Ghant," I have a moment's confusion; there must be some mistake. Then I see Turk making his way regally across the field toward us, and I realize that this preposterous name must belong to him. No wonder he lets everyone call him Turk.

It goes by in a flash, but I think this moment is one of the best in my life, standing there watching as the rest of the Journeys and squires step up to the line one by one, each one more magnificent than the last, and knowing I'm one of them. Whatever else happens, no one can take this away from me. When we're all lined up and the audience is on its feet, shouting and clapping in anticipation, I look down the line, and I love them all: Gilles, elegant as ever, Charles, refined and dignified, even Aristide looks transformed into something fine and noble. And when Taran appears, towering over the line, formidable and proud, I even love him, too. How could I ever have thought of them as fops and bullies? But shining out among them all in my eyes is Tristan, and I can barely contain my joy at basking in his reflected glory.

It's only when we're lined up and ready to go that we learn the exact nature of the first test. And to my dismay, I find that the squire's skill is going to be almost as important in it as his master's.

"Our first exercise," Baylen is announcing, "will test both precision and speed. Each Journeyman will shoot five rounds of five arrows each toward a mark of six inches square, set four score yards from the line. All men will shoot at the same time, at their own target."

I look down the field, and sure enough: individual wicker butts stand 80 yards down the field from each station, and I can make out the small cloth-mark targets already pinned in place. But five times five is twenty-five, and we've only been given five arrows each. There's more to it.

"Gentlemen, let me stress, the speed of firing will be judged as closely as the accuracy of the shots. You are to shoot your arrows as quickly as possible, while maintaining accuracy. After each flight of arrows, the squires will retrieve before the next flight can begin. You are therefore required to shoot the same five arrows in each round, and the faster your squire is back to the line with your arrows, the faster you can begin your next round. So be quick out there, boys — and good luck. When the signal sounds, you may begin."

I gulp. I've gotten faster, but I'm still slower than most of the squires. I know the judges will probably be most concerned with how fast the Journeys can actually shoot the arrows, but the crowd is going to care most about which Journey finishes all his rounds first. It's a race, and I'm a liability.

I hasten to get into position, and before I can work myself up into too much of a panic, the horn is blaring and the competition has started. When Tristan shoots his first arrow, I'm sure the new bow was a big mistake. With speed being a factor, it will be even harder for him to get a feel for how the new bow shoots, and his first arrow misses the mark. So does the second. But by the third arrow, he's in the white, and I think, "We're going to be okay," as long as I can find some speed. His last shot is good, too, and I'm off, racing down the field.

A few of the other boys are already ahead of me; Pascal is already at the butts and pulling out arrows like a madman — Gilles must have gotten his arrows off in record time. I have no time to worry about the others, though. I put my head down and run like I've never run before. When I get to the butts, I give the first arrow such a violent tug that I tumble backwards and lose time. I've never retrieved from wicker before, and it's much easier to pull out the arrows from straw than from clay. I curse as I right myself, but in the long run, this will help me. I won't be at such a disadvantage because of my relative weakness, and I'll be faster on the next retrieval.

When I get back to the line with Tristan's arrows, I'm near the back of the pack. But the next flight goes much better; most of Tristan's arrows are in the white, and it looks like he may have even cleaved the pin with one of them. I get back to the line faster, too, and it looks like I even gain some ground against the slower boys. I begin to relax a little; I can't afford to trip and fall or to damage an arrow, but I push myself as hard as I dare. I'll never be fast enough for Tristan to win this round, but he's shooting well, and it's like Jerome said; he's too good even for my deficiencies to trip him up. We end up finishing the task seventh, thanks to Tristan's speed, with all but four arrows in the white and two in the pin. It's a decent showing, considering, even though I'm not sure exactly where this leaves us overall in the standings. Jerome was right; I was a fool to worry about Tristan passing butts. He's just too good, and I should be happy; I haven't completely ruined things for him.

Between tests, there's a break to allow the field to be set up for the next exercise, and to allow time for people to spend money on goods and refreshments at the booths. St. Sebastian's never misses a trick when it comes to turning a profit, and the trials are no exception; in addition to charging a hefty rental fee to the lucky vendors who've secured a coveted spot out on the exhibition grounds for their concessions, at the end of the day the guild takes a big cut of the earnings. Since there's only so long that the actual competition can take, intervals between each test allow for the trials to be stretched out over the course of the morning, making them more of an event — and giving the spectators plenty of time to empty their pockets. We're expected to go back to our tents while the field is being changed up, and as musicians and jugglers take the field to entertain the crowd.

"You did well, Marek. Really well. Thank you," Tristan says as we head off the field, and I should be happier at this praise. After all, I think it's the first time I've ever heard Tristan say thank you to me. But he doesn't sound very happy, and I know he's thinking the same things I am. Tristan is shooting just fine. Well, even. But seventh is terrible, when he should have been first, and his usual flair is gone. Tristan needs to be brilliant today, to get noticed and to set himself up as a crowd favorite to influence the subjective judging in the competitions ahead, where he'll be at a disadvantage. He really does need to be extraordinary today, and so far, he's missing that mark. I've got to figure out a way to turn his mood around, to get the old Tristan back.

Just passing Firsts now feels like failing.

Once the competition is underway, the Journeys are supposed to stay sequestered, so I set out alone to get us some refreshments. As I go, I wrack my brain for ideas. It even occurs to me to do something outrageous, like look for Brother Benedict, reveal myself, and demand a sign. But I can't come up with anything, and I have to content myself with bringing back some ale and bread. When I get back, I find Tristan looking out from behind the tent flap, scanning the audience. His expression is sad, and I can't tell if he's looking at his father, or at Lady Melissande, whose golden head I now spot in a special box in the bleachers right behind the judges' bench.

The second test is all about accuracy, and I'm relieved to find that my part in it extends no further than the traditional squire's role of adding pomp to the proceedings. The butts have been moved back to five score yards, and now each wicker backstop has five marks on it, arranged to form the corners of a large square, with one mark dead in the center. The Journeys again have five flights of five arrows, but this time speed is not a factor. On each round, the boys are to send one arrow toward each of the marks in a pattern, crossing the square in diagonals before hitting the center mark with the last arrow. The goal is to try to hit the white with each shot; a good archer should be able to cleave the pin on some shots, too. It's a deceptively simple test, made more difficult by the need to change up by only a little the focus of each shot.

Tristan is so accurate at this range that I'm not worried. His arrows all hit the white. Yet with each shot, I lose heart. His shots are good, but his shooting is flat, rote, and even though he's getting the pin regularly enough to make an impression, he's not going to turn any heads, and too many of the other boys are good at this range, too. I look down the row, and I catch sight of Gilles. He's having a great day, striking a pose with each shot, and he's clearly already a crowd favorite. With Lord Mellor and the Guards present, the crowd is also predisposed to favor Taran, who's proving himself deadlier at close range than I would have thought. Each time he shoots a shout goes up from the crowd, and I wince. Tristan needs to do something to distinguish himself soon, but I have no idea how to fire him up.

And before I know it, the second test is over and it's too late. Tristan's done well again and probably pulled himself up in the rankings, but our chances for showing what he can really do are slipping away.

It's when we're back in the tent, waiting for the final test, that I get an idea. A wild idea. But it just might work. The last test in the competition is the one for Melissande's garland. All the boys will be shooting at a single target, and I'm watching through the tent flaps as men are dragging all but one wicker backstop off the field. It will mean that all eyes are on each boy individually as he shoots: this will be our chance. I've just got to figure out how to get Tristan back on form, so we can take advantage of it. It's when I see Sir Brecelyn take the small garland of flowers from his daughter's head and hand it over to the men to attach it to the butt that the idea hits me, and I know what I have to do. I have to find Pascal.

I mumble some excuse to Tristan, and rush out of the tent. I hope there's still time! It's easy to find Gilles's tent because of the color-coding, and when I pop my head into the white tent, I find Gilles lounging, with Pascal massaging his back.

"Marek! What a delightful surprise!" Gilles drawls. "But isn't this a little irregular? You know, I wasn't expecting any social calls."

"It's a great day, Gilles. You've been stupendous," I say, really meaning it. And now it's tricky, because of course, Gilles and Tristan are competitors. But Gilles has been doing so well, I figure he'll be magnanimous. "Only now I need your help. It's Tristan."

"Why, the dear boy has been doing just fine. A little lower, Pascal," Gilles says, clearly pleased with himself. I doubt he expected to be doing better than Tristan at butts.

"You know he's off, Gilles," I say. "Oh, please! You're doing so well, you can afford to help a friend, can't you, Gilles? It's not just the pressure. It's, well, I can't explain, but Tristan needs help," I beg.

Gilles shoots me a shrewd look. "I thought this might happen. It's damned unfortunate the old man is here."

"You *know*?" I croak, while Pascal looks on, confused.

"Of course. Oh, Tristan didn't tell me, either," he says to my accusing look. "But Jerome's from Meuse. Apparently, everybody knows all about it there. Jerome had heard about it long before he'd ever met Tristan. I suppose the whole guild will be talking of it here now, too. No wonder the poor boy's lost his edge."

"About that," I say, and I tell them my plan. "But we've got to work fast. And, I'll need to borrow Pascal." Before either of them can object I've grabbed Pascal by the wrist, and I'm hauling him out of the tent.

We work our way across the field, trying not to be observed by any of the masters, and before long we're scooting around behind the judges' bench, so we're directly under the box where the ladies of rank are seated. I hang back a bit while Pascal catches the eye of Melissande's serving girl, and when he gestures to her, she excuses herself and comes down. I watch them as they put their heads together, and Pascal motions to me and to Melissande. Soon the girl is making her way back into the box, and I see her talking urgently to her mistress. The beautiful girl turns to look down at me, and we exchange a look for a long minute. Then she smiles, and it's not long before the serving girl is coming back and putting something into Pascal's hands. The entertainers are already leaving the field; time is running out, so when Pascal rejoins me with the acquired object, I merely bow deeply toward the shining girl in the stands, and rush with it back to Tristan's tent. It's only when I'm there that

I really see what it is: it's a single white rose, dried and pressed flat. She kept it all this time.

"Where the devil have you been, Marek?" Tristan says when I burst into the tent. "You had me thinking *you'd* bolted!"

"Tristan!" I say eagerly, anxious to get it out before the trumpet summons us to competition again and it's too late. "Do you remember what you told me, about going for the thing that's *just* possible?" When Tristan looks blank, I rush on. "Well, this last test, it's for the garland. You can win this one! You can be the one crowned. It's possible! It's more than possible. It's probable. Because, you see, *she* wants it to be you! Don't let her down."

"What are you babbling about?" he says, not unkindly, but without much interest.

"Don't you remember, Tristan? *You* told me it was worth going for a moment that would make everyone sit up and take notice, a moment that's spectacular, that nobody can take away from you. Imagine it! Melissande, crowning *you*, in front of all of them. Do you remember what Brecelyn said? It's the moment they're all waiting for, and it can be yours! Don't let *him* have it, don't let anyone else have it. Take it!"

"It's not that simple, Marek."

"It is! Because, imagine how much more spectacular, to be crowned by her, in front of them all, when they see it on her face, that she loves you!" I cry.

"What are you talking about?"

I pull out the rose with a flourish. "Look! It's your rose, Tristan. She's kept it all this time. Kept it with her, always. She brought it with her, today, when she knew she'd see you. And she gave it to me, now, out there, for you to carry into the competition, as a token. Why would she do that, if she weren't in love with you? If she didn't want to crown *you*, if she didn't want *you* to win?!" Tristan has been looking at the rose in astonishment, thunderstruck, and I can see it's working. So I embellish, a little. "And she told me to tell you, if you win the garland, you can claim a real reward: a kiss!"

At this, a huge grin breaks across Tristan's face, and he throws his head back and laughs, and the sound fills the whole tent. He sweeps me up in his arms and swings me around, still laughing.

"Marek, you've done it!" he cries. For the first time in days, the old Tristan is back. He lifts me completely off my feet, and swings me around again. "I could kiss you!" he crows. "In fact, I think I will!" and he bends down and plants a big kiss of pure joy right on my mouth.

When he lets me go, I'm so dizzy I stumble, and he has to steady me as he takes the rose from my hand, still laughing with delight. As he tucks in into his jerkin over his heart, he ruffles my hair.

I don't even have to see the final test to know that he's going to be brilliant, now. As he leaves the tent at the bugle, he looks like he could do anything: storm the fortifications of L'île de Meuse single-handedly, slay a dragon, maybe even face down his father. I should be ecstatic; it's what I wanted, isn't it? And I am happy. I really am. But I've just had my first kiss, and from Tristan, no less. Only it wasn't for me at all. It was for her. And I can still feel it on my lips as I follow Tristan out onto the field.

"For the final test," Baylen announces when we're lined up again on the field, "each Journey will have only three shots. Each man will take one shot, in order, at a single target: a garland, mounted at ten score yards. The upshot of each round will stay in the target, and at the end of three rounds the arrow closest to the center will win. All shots will be scored, but the owner of the lucky arrow will have the honor of being crowned with the garland, and by the hand of Lady Melissande Brecelyn herself."

The applause that meets this pronouncement is deafening. Now that they're shooting one at a time, the tension is thick; not only is the whole crowd watching the boys as they take each shot, but they're watching each other. The tests have been carefully arranged to build to this moment, both for the audience and for the boys. So it isn't surprising that some of them crack. Ladislaus is first, and his shot is far wide. It hits about a foot from the garland. Jerome is next, and he doesn't fare much better, though his arrow comes closer and misses only by about four inches.

And then it's Tristan's turn, and as he steps up and nocks his arrow, I hold my breath. But I was right; he's ready for anything now, and as he takes his shot, I imagine I can hear the sound as the audience collectively catches its breath. It's all there again: that exaggerated motion, the overextension that's almost too much, the thrill as he reaches the top of his arc and plunges down into his aim. The shot is good, inside the garland. But that hardly matters. Just like the first time I saw him shoot, the audience isn't looking at the target. He's mesmerized them with the pure beauty of his form.

At the end of the round, it's Gilles's arrow that's judged best and left for the next round as the upshot. He's put it dead in the center. It's a shot that can't be beaten, and I have to tell myself that it doesn't matter. It doesn't matter if Tristan is really crowned or not; I just needed him to have a goal, to spur him on, to get him to show his style, and he's done that. As long as his next shots are beautiful, too, he'll have made a mark on the competition, and he's sure to pass the trials. That's what counts, isn't it? Still I worry that he'll slump again now that the garland is out of reach. But as he steps up for his second shot, he turns to me and grins,

"Okay, Marek, you wanted me to show them what extraordinary means!"

And as he bends the bow, it's with such exhilaration that the crowd is swept up too, and it's on its feet in expectation. He doesn't disappoint them, either. He splits Gilles's arrow right down the middle. At this distance, it's not an impossible shot. But it's damned close.

The applause from the bleachers is deafening, and even the Journeys forget themselves and crowd around to congratulate Tristan, slapping him on the back and adding their voices to the din. But Tristan puts up his hand, and all the noise stops. He's nocking another arrow — he means to take his final shot. It isn't regulation — the other boys haven't all had their second shots yet, but nobody stops him. He's earned the right. The competition is really over, anyway. The boys will get their shots, but Tristan's won the garland. Before he takes his last shot, he turns to me.

"Shall we really do it, Marek? Shall we take this place down?" he laughs.

"Brick by brick," I say, and he shoots. And he does it. Incredibly, he splits his own arrow. He's done it again.

They'll remember him now, all right.

When later Tristan falls to one knee before Lady Melissande to receive his prize, with all of St. Sebastian's watching, and all of

Louvain, they make a splendid pair. His dark head lifts in ecstasy to gaze up at her golden beauty, as his cloak swirls a pool of red around him, and her hair cascades down around him like a flood of brilliant light. They make a scene worthy of illumination, an illustration from a work about the rapturous vision of a young saint, or the apotheosis of a god. And the expression on Tristan's face as the garland touches his brow, I can't describe it. But I recognize it. It must be the exact expression I had on my face, when I first laid eyes on Tristan up on the garden wall. Sir Brecelyn was right. It's a moment Louvain will long remember. And I'll remember it, too. I can't forget it; it's seared into my memory, as though Father Abelard painted every meticulous detail there himself, and sealed it with Melissande's kiss, still burning on my mouth.

I don't know where Tristan will end up in the final rankings after all the tests are correlated, but it doesn't matter. The day is his now. And I'm glad. Still I can't help but feel hurt, that it was Melissande's rose and not my bow that won it for him.

When I meet him back in the tent for the last time, he's still walking on air.

"Tristan!" I say, overcome by so many conflicting emotions that I don't know what to say. To my credit, joy for him wins out, and as he sweeps me into a warm embrace, all I feel is relief that it's all come right, that Tristan's all right. That he's back.

"You're sure to be first, after that!" I say, when he releases me.

"Nah, Marek. You're always so sentimental! It was three tests, remember. The judges aren't as easily swayed as the crowd. But I'm through, all right. That's the important thing. I've got to be in the top four, which is where we need to be for Seconds."

"The top four!" I snort. "You're king for the day, after that coronation!"

"Maybe," he says, grinning. "But it's not over yet." I'd forgotten about the horseback exhibition. "Turk's still going to show his stuff. We may have to pass the crown, after you see what he can do."

"Oh, Turk," I say dismissively. It's just an exhibition, after all. "Nothing can touch you now, Tristan. Let Turk be brilliant. I hope he is," I add generously. "It can't hurt your standings."

"Unless I fall off my horse," he says jokingly, and a bit insensitively, it seems to me, and he slaps me on the back.

THERE'S A LONGER BREAK BETWEEN THE FINAL TEST AND the mounted exhibition, since the field has to be reorganized, and the horses brought over from the stables and warmed up. I'm really done for the day, since squires aren't part of this exhibition for obvious reasons, and I'm so flooded with relief that everything has come off so well that I'm finally able to enjoy myself. I catch up with Auguste, and we wander around checking out all the booths and sampling some of the wares, but he isn't in as good of a mood. Jerome hasn't done very well, and he knows it. There hasn't been an official announcement about the standings, yet. There won't be a final decision until after the exhibition, since a good showing in the mounted shooting could conceivably affect the final outcome, but it's possible Jerome's done badly enough to be out. I hadn't really thought about it, but by this time tomorrow Auguste could be gone. The thought of the barracks without him just doesn't seem right. He's understandably a bundle of nerves, and so I try to be supportive, and not feel too smug about not being in his position anymore.

"Can Jerome ride?" I ask, trying to encourage him.

"I don't know. Probably not very well. I can't ride at all, so I never go out with him," Auguste replies miserably.

"Me, neither," I say. We've wandered over to the part of the field where the riding will be done, wanting to stake out a good place to watch from the sidelines. "I don't even know what they're going to do, exactly."

Auguste points out to the field, where five of the wicker butts have been lined up at intervals of about twenty yards. "I think the boys just ride past and shoot at the marks, with smaller bows. Pretty simple stuff, but shooting from horseback is an entirely different skill. I don't know how well any of them can do it, except for Turk."

It turns out to be just as Auguste said. It is pretty simple stuff, but it's pretty thrilling, too, particularly when some of the boys really put on the speed. They don't have the same accuracy that they do on the stationary targets, but it's not expected, and after all, it's just for show. It's considered good simply to hit the butt itself, let alone the target, when passing at a full gallop, and I find I'm enjoying the exhibition immensely. It just feels so good to be completely relaxed, not having to worry about Tristan anymore. The horses look beautiful (from a safe distance), the boys look good on them. Most of them can ride well enough to make a decent showing, though poor Anselm has to go past at a trot, and I think of Aristide taunting him about not knowing how to ride. It's clear that the elite boys have a big advantage. Gilles and Aristide are among the best riders, and of course Jurian the ex-stable boy is perfectly at home on horseback. But everyone is really waiting to see Turk, and I'm looking forward to it, too.

Finally, his turn arrives. All the other boys are still wearing their Journey costume *sans* the cloak, but Turk's changed into a get-up that has to be Master Guillaume's idea. He's notorious for doing everything he can to make the competitions into a spectacle, and he's really going to milk this exhibition for all its worth. He's had Turk dress all in brown leather, in something that looks like Gilles's tailor's idea of what Seljuk Turks might have worn. On his small, lithe body, though, it looks right, and when he trots out onto the field, I see that alone of the boys, he's going to ride bareback. His horse isn't even wearing a bridle. He commands it entirely by squeezing his knees against its sides, so again I have the impression I did on the day of the St. Genevieve hunt that the boy and the horse are virtually one.

He's got a small recurve bow, but no quiver. Instead, he's holding a whole fistful of arrows in one hand, and the bow in the other. A hush goes over the crowd at his appearance, and I'm as caught up in the anticipation as everyone else as Turk begins to lead his horse in a wide elliptical motion around the field, at first very slowly, then gathering speed. Before long the little horse is going like the wind, and they race back and forth in front of the line of targets, executing a stunning series of hairpin turns, before Turk finally raises his bow. I can't figure out how he's going to shoot, since he's got no quiver.

"How is he going to nock the arrows?" I ask Auguste.

"Watch this, Marek. Jerome told me about it. He's going to back-load them! It'll be sensational." he says, and I see Turk lift the whole bunch of arrows in his hand up at the same time, to the left side of his bow. He slips one of the arrows onto the back of his left hand, which is holding the bow shaft, so it's resting on the part of his hand between the knuckle of his thumb and his forefinger, on the opposite side of the bow from where right-handed archers usually shoot. I've never seen anything like it. And he proceeds to race past the targets, drawing the bowstring with only two fingers and sending arrow after arrow with great precision into the marks, all the while loading the arrows from his full fist onto the back of his hand. I wouldn't have believed someone could reload a bow that quickly if I hadn't seen it myself.

"And that, Marek,' Auguste says, "is how the Mongols ruled the steppes. You've just witnessed it. A horde of one." He's right. Turk has shot ten arrows in less than a minute at five targets spread out over 100 yards, and all the arrows stuck. It's a good trick all right. It's going to make a hell of an impression. But I smile inwardly at the memory of that golden girl placing the garland on Tristan's head; it's a good trick, but it's not enough to overturn the throne. Tristan is still the king of the day.

"Tristan's next," Auguste is saying, and I see he's right. I can see him climbing into the saddle of his large black mount. But he's still got my huge bow over his shoulder. What is he doing with a longbow for this? I wonder. Auguste is wondering the same thing.

"So, what's he going to do?" he asks, and I realize with a start that I don't know. He's never let me come out to watch him practice. Just what *has* he been up to, all that time he was with Turk?

"It doesn't matter," I say, trying to cover my confusion, trying to sound casual. But something feels wrong. So I make a joke. "After all, all he's got to do is stay on his horse."

And suddenly, I feel a stab of worry. What made Tristan say that, back in the tent? And what made me say it now? I have a horrible sense of foreboding, before Tristan even comes out onto the track.

After his performance with the garland, Tristan is now the audience's darling, so his arrival on the field is met with great enthusiasm. He sits well on his horse, too, and I can see he's an experienced rider, so there's really no reason to panic. *Please, please,* I say to myself anyway, please don't let him try something crazy. And I think that's the moment when I know that he's going to do just that. It's the moment when I know exactly what he's going to do. But it's too late to stop him.

As he trots past the place where Auguste and I are standing, he swings the bow off his shoulders and lifts it in my direction with a grin, in a kind of jovial salute. I try to call out to him, but he can't hear me over the crowd, even if he'd be willing to listen.

And then he reins his horse to a stop at the far end of the field. He's got a quiver on his leg, but there's only one arrow in it. He raises the bow to the crowd, which has started to murmur. Everyone else is starting to wonder what he's going to do, why he's got a longbow on horseback. And then he spurs the horse to motion, and he gallops across the field. All the other boys except for Turk did three passes at the targets, so the murmuring increases in the stands when Tristan makes his first pass without bending his bow at all. He turns, and heads back for his second pass, but again, he makes no move to shoot. By the time he starts his third and final pass, the crowd has fallen silent, perplexed, but as he passes the first target, he swings one leg over the saddle, so both legs are on the far side of the horse from the target. Out of the corner of my eye, I see Master Guillaume rise to his feet in alarm, and pretty soon all the judges are on their feet, and shouts have started coming from the crowd. I'm not the only one who knows now what he intends.

But Tristan isn't paying any attention. He's got only one foot in the stirrup, and with a sudden swoop he bends over backwards, draping himself perpendicularly over the back of the horse so his face is toward the targets, but bobbing upside down along the horse's flank. At the same time, he's lifted the bow up in a wide arc to sweep it up the line of his body and down over his head, the single arrow nocked. The other Journeys have run over to the railing, too, and everyone in the stands is on their feet. Master Guillaume is running toward the field, with Royce and some of the others not far behind. But they'll never get there in time. As the horse thunders past the central target, from his position hanging there like a bat, Tristan lets the arrow fly: my heart is in my throat, petrified he'll fall, seeing my father's shattered shoulder — but to my shame, even more, every fiber of my being is straining for that arrow, willing it to hit. When it sticks with a sickening thud dead center in the mark, it's too much for me. As Tristan pulls himself back upright into the saddle with a fluid motion and a careless grin to the astounded crowd, I faint dead away.

"Marek!" When I wake, I'm all wet, and Tristan is leaning down over me in concern. Someone's thrown a bucket of water over my head, and a bunch of squires and Journeys have gathered around to help revive me. I must have been out for quite a while, because some of the commotion caused by Tristan's outrageous trick has died down, though the bleachers are still buzzing, and the masters are huddled in a heated conference around the judges' bench. I get the impression that Tristan's had another 'terrible row' with Guillaume, too, from the murderous glances the master keeps sending our way. But I don't care. I only have eyes for Tristan.

"Why did you do it, Tristan?" is all I can say, when I've recovered my voice. I don't care that everybody is listening.

"It was nothing. It wasn't really that hard," he grins. "Old François was right." Seeing my expression, he adds more seriously, "I wouldn't have tried it, kid, if I wasn't sure I could do it. And after all," he adds, "I owed it to you. I had to do it, after you got me that rose."

But I know better. He didn't just decide to do it. He's been working on it, every day, with Turk, since the day my father's body was found, since the day I was humiliated at mess over my father's failure. He risked everything, at Firsts no less, to prove to me that my father wasn't a fool. And he didn't prove it just to me. After all the talk, everyone at St. Sebastian's could recognize that move. They all know exactly what he did, and he did it flawlessly, effortlessly. And it *was* spectacular! He redeemed my father, to all of Louvain. In a flash, he eclipsed even Melissande's garland. The day is all mine again, and much more: with one arrow sent from my bow, Tristan's given me back my father.

THE MASTERS HAVE ANNOUNCED A FREE NIGHT IN honor of Firsts, but nobody's going anywhere. This is our last night all together, and there's nowhere else anyone wants to be tonight. Nobody has changed out of regalia, either, but as we walk into the great hall that night, Tristan puts Melissande's garland on his head and struts into the room, stretching his arms wide. I'm behind him, but he's grinning so broadly, I can sense it from the back of his head. He's timed it so the others are already there, and as we enter, Turk jumps up onto the Journey table and raises his tankard in a salute.

"Look, boys, if it isn't Tristan *Verbeke!*" he shouts, and all the boys, even Taran, spontaneously rise and join in the salute. Tristan embraces Turk, and they stand at the head of the table, arm in arm, the princes of the night. They did the big tricks today, and everyone knows it. Nobody is going to deny them their moment.

I squeeze in among the squires, while the Journeys continue to congratulate each other. The mood is exuberant, and nobody settles down until Master Leon calls for attention.

"Gentlemen, let me be the first to congratulate you all," he says, rather belatedly. "There were no losers today." At this, the mood turns somber, as we all remember that this is not true. Two boys are about to be cut. "You all did St. Sebastian's proud, and I am particularly proud to have been your trainer." I haven't noticed him out on the practice field much, but nobody says anything. "The time has come, however, to announce the standings after first trials." A hush falls over the room, as Master Leon reaches for a list on the table. "In first place, for his overall performance in all three tests and in the mounted exercises: Gilles Lejeune!"

A roar goes up from the Journey table, and Tristan gleefully pulls the garland from his head and puts it ceremonially onto the head of his friend. I'm stomping as loudly as everyone else. Gilles deserves it, and he did it without any tricks.

Nobody's much surprised when Taran is ranked second, though I personally think this just proves that Master Guillaume's pronouncements the other day about favoritism were a bunch of rot. I guess I wasn't watching Taran's performance closely, though. Tristan's third, followed by Turk in fourth; his horsemanship pulled him up in the ranking, and I understand why Guillaume wanted the mounted exhibition at Firsts. I'm not sure Turk would have even made it to seconds without it, and it would have been a shame not to get his trick into the trials.

As might have been expected, the two lowest ranking boys are some of the heavy shooters: Ladislaus and Laurens. For once, I'm glad Tristan was wrong. Having butts first helped him immensely — not only did he pass, but two clout shooters are down, and he won't have to face them later. Falko, another heavy shooter, narrowly made the cut, just ahead of Jerome, who was right to worry. He was ranked 10th; that will leave him the lowest ranked boy now, with Lad and Laurens out. We all feel bad for them; it's no disgrace being out in the first cut, and we all know it could have been Tristan or Turk who was in their position now, if the theme had been clouts. But it isn't easy being the first to go down. I'm pleased, though, that it's two of the boys I know the least, and whose squires are boys I don't particularly care for. But as I look down the table, I know the next cut is going to be deep, and not just because it could well be us. I can't bear to see any more of them go.

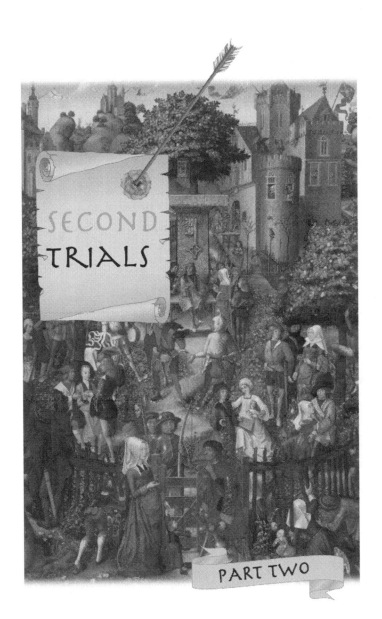

SECOND
TRIALS

PART TWO

CHAPTER EIGHTEEN

I n the early summer days immediately following Firsts, indolence settles over the guild. No one wants to move on, not yet. We all prefer to spend our time going over the competition and reliving its triumphs to practicing, and even the vets seem inclined to run drills more like reviews of Firsts than preparation for Seconds. The mood should be congratulatory, exuberant, but even though Seconds is a full two months away — too far to really worry about yet — nobody's forgotten them. It's as though we've entered a doldrums, and we're content to drift here because we're all too sure there are stormy seas ahead.

On that first morning, we're all acutely aware of being four men short on the line, too, and of the two Journeys who are packing up inside the guild and not out on the field with us. I'm also thinking of the two empty cots that will be carried down to my end of the barracks, and how we squires will all move our cots closer to the middle: the survivors huddling together.

Of everyone, I'm probably the one who wants to let go of Firsts the least, and it's not only because I haven't figured out how to help Tristan through Seconds yet. It's because of Tristan's trick. With one move he's changed my whole perception of my past and my father's legacy, and so I reasonably don't want to move on from it. I want to hold on to this moment as long as I can, when Tristan is golden and I'm standing in his reflected light, and when we're the closest we've ever been — when I'm closer than ever to being what he sometimes calls me: his little brother.

That afternoon, Tristan and I skip practice all together, and instead by unspoken consent we make our way out to the windmill as soon as noon mess is over. We make the trip in companionable silence, only breaking it periodically to catch each other's eye and laugh aloud, still caught up in the glow of yesterday's triumphs. But when we take our accustomed seats in the little room at the top of the windmill, and as Tristan opens the shutters to look out far across the woods to St. Sebastian's, the silence between us begins to grow oppressive, as though there's something there with us in the room that has to be said. It's the revelation Tristan made to me out on the field, forgotten in the stress of competition, but not so easily forgotten now, though I think we'd both like to. But I know we can't go back, so this time, I'm the one who says, "Tell me about it."

And he does. Not all of it. Not even much of it, really. But enough. Somehow, I suspect it's more than he's ever told anyone else.

He tells me about growing up a laughingstock in Meuse, and about how proud his father was of impregnating two women at virtually the same time.

"Tristan and Taran," he says derisively, spitting out the names like he can't stand the taste of them in his mouth. "What a conceit! Matched Welsh names for the sons of the self-proclaimed 'master of the Welsh longbow'! Do you know what they called us, Marek? Twins by different bitches! And he was proud of it!"

What seems to gall him the most is how everyone thought his father was a great man for openly claiming and supporting him.

"And I let him, Marek. I took his money. I let him pay for tutors and trainers, I let him sponsor me. I took his money with both hands. What does that make me?" he asks bitterly.

"It makes you practical," I say levelly. "It makes you smart. Only a fool would have turned down his help, out of some misguided sense of honor."

"Taran would have," he says simply, and I think he really believes it.

"That's ridiculous," I reply, and when he shakes his head in frustration, I snap, "Then he's a fool!"

But Tristan doesn't respond, and I sense he's done talking about the past. He hasn't mentioned his mother, and I don't ask. But there is one thing I have to know.

"Taran," I say hesitantly.

"What about him?"

"Well," I say gingerly, "He's your brother. *Half*-brother," I correct quickly as he casts me a hideous scowl. "Don't you think you could …?"

"He'll never be my brother!" Tristan cuts me off vehemently, but I can't leave it alone.

"Okay, Tristan," I pause, looking for the right words. "You told me once that you knew what Taran was to you. Can you tell me, now? If he's not your brother, what is he?"

I don't really expect him to answer, and he's quiet so long, I start to get up to go. It's getting late, and we've got to get back for mess. But as I reach past Tristan to close the shutters, slowly blocking out the view of St. Sebastian's, Tristan replies, still looking out through the closing gap.

"I guess, Taran's my impossibility."

All the way back through the woods, I try to figure out what Tristan means. Sure, Taran's obviously everything Tristan can't be: the legitimate son, and all that entails. Or maybe he's thinking about Taran winning Guards. But I sense he means more than that, and not for the first time, I have the disturbing impression that one of the reasons Tristan hates Taran so much is that for reasons unfathomable to me, he admires him, too.

We've been walking along in silence, Tristan in front and me behind, but when we get to the wall of St. Sebastian's, instead of climbing over it, Tristan comes to a stop. He turns to me, and leans against the wall.

"Marek," he says soberly, "there's something else." He sounds so serious, I imagine all sorts of gruesome revelations, but what could really be worse than what he's already told me about his past, and what I've already figured out for myself? Whatever it is, I'm not sure I want to hear it, but when I make some demurring noises to try to put him off, he continues:

"It's about your father."

All I can do is gape. It's the last thing I expected.

"I've been debating whether or not to tell you, but I think I must. I'm just worried it will upset you, all over again. So it's up to you. Do you want to hear it?"

After that introduction, of course I don't. But I have to.

"Tell me," I say, swallowing hard.

"It's about the trick. I wasn't lying yesterday when I said it wasn't all that hard. I know you want to think of me as the hero, but I was telling the truth, too, when I said I wouldn't have tried it if I hadn't been sure I could do it. Old François *was* right. Once I got on to the motion of the horse, it wasn't really that hard to hit the mark, every time. I'm sure he did see your father do it often, just as he said."

I'm not sure what he's getting at. Is this really so bad, that my father's trick wasn't actually that spectacular? For me, the important point is, he wasn't a fool to try it. This just seems to confirm it.

"So it wasn't that hard," I say. "It looked hard, and that's what matters. It looked impossible." But Tristan still looks serious, and I suspect there's more to it.

"There was some risk, I'll admit. If I'd have missed, I would have looked the fool, and all the more so, since after all the talk everyone could tell what I was trying to do. They would have said I was a fool to try a fool's trick. But the thing is," and here he pauses, and I sense we're coming to it, "missing the shot was really the only risk. I can't be sure, since there's no way of knowing if I was doing the trick exactly the same way your father did — after all, I only had some pretty vague descriptions of it — but I can't see for the life of me how he managed to fall off the horse. It's like Royce said, it just doesn't make sense. To me, that's the part of the trick that's impossible. I just can't believe he fell."

"What are you saying? Obviously, he did fall."

"Yes, but that's it. I don't see *how* he fell."

"Tristan, just what are you getting at?"

"I think, he must have had some help," he says finally.

"Are you saying it wasn't an accident?" I ask, as I feel sand start to sift through my veins again, the way it did as I lay in my father's arms for the last time. As soon as I say it, I know it's true.

"Was I right to tell you?" he asks soberly.

"I don't know."

And just like that, the glow of Firsts begins to fade. I wouldn't have thought it could happen so soon, but now our victory tastes like dust, as I realize that someone murdered my father, only it wasn't with arrows. It happened long ago, when someone tampered with his saddle, and I remember Royce's tone when he said of my father, "we were all jealous of him." I was wrong: I haven't put my father to rest at all. I even wonder if in some way I've put Tristan at risk, since somewhere there's at least one person who can't be at all happy at the prospect of the specter of Jan Verbeke rising again at St. Sebastian's.

"Do you still think about trying to find out what happened to him?" he asks carefully, and I'm not sure how to respond.

"I don't know," I say again. "How can I? And even if I could find out what happened, what could I do about it?"

"I've been thinking. We might ask around; a few well-chosen questions to François or Royce, even Albrecht, might tell us something," he says.

"I don't know, Tristan. I think it might be worse, to think I know something and not to be able to do anything about it. Can't we leave things as they are now, with my father redeemed? Isn't that good enough?"

"You tell me," he replies. "Can you leave it at that?"

It's a simple question, but to me, it sounds like an accusation. Maybe I should want to know, but I'm not sure I can stand any more revelations. I haven't even been able to make myself think about what I've already learned. I haven't tried to picture my father's life as a young Master Guillaume's squire, or as Royce's friend, or imagined him getting into mischief with Lord Mellor, of all people. What I want is to have the father I knew back, not to find out he was someone I don't recognize. I can't imagine what it would be like to know who killed him and why, and be powerless to do anything about it. Particularly if the knowledge would make it unbearable for me to stay at St. Sebastian's.

Maybe I'm a coward, but I do want to leave it at that, and I'm unreasonably angry at Tristan for casting a shadow over the image he created for me of my father's trick fully realized.

"What would you do, if it were your father?" I ask petulantly.

"Don't ask me. If someone killed my father, I'd probably just be sorry I couldn't thank him," he replies bitterly, and I'm instantly sorry I brought up his father. But he can't fool me. I know why Tristan is at St. Sebastian's, even if he pretends not to. And I haven't forgotten what Royce said about the young Lord Mellor. It isn't a coincidence that the personality Tristan has chosen for himself is so like my father's must have been.

I don't say so. And I don't add what I'm really thinking. Vengeance isn't something that particularly appeals to me. It doesn't achieve anything. At least, not vengeance as it's traditionally imagined. If I can get Tristan through trials using my father's methods, so he can win veteran status as my father never did, that will be my way of avenging my father. If I can save Tristan where I couldn't save my father, that will be better than vengeance, and unlike vengeance, it's 'just possible.' I just have to figure out how to do it.

AND SO, AS WE DRIFT INTO JUNE, THE JOURNEYS ARE still exhausted from Firsts, and the warmer weather seems designed to fit our mood. We've turned a corner. Things have changed. Not only are we fewer now, but the reality that we will only become a smaller group as the months progress has begun to set in. Tristan is particularly preoccupied, and when I ask him about it, he says,

"My prize, Marek! How the devil am I supposed to claim it?" I don't bother to tell him that the kiss was a little white lie. I have no doubt he'll get it, if the opportunity presents itself. Who could deny him anything now?

I let him have his rest. He deserves it. But I also know that soon, it will be time for Tristan to start working on his strength and endurance, if we're to have a shot at Seconds. With Tristan's precision we ended up sailing through butts; next time, it could well be clouts. It's going to take more than 'the Verbeke method' and some tricks to put him past that, since it's all about distance. I promised Tristan I'd start training seriously after Firsts, too, and soon it'll be time to keep my promise. So I'm in no hurry.

At night, I take to pouring over my illumination again as I lie in bed. Not the page Abelard gave to me; Tristan's never given that back, and it's unlikely he'll ever return it now. But I close my eyes and see before me the scene that's now painted vividly in my memory: the scene of Tristan kneeling before the teeming grandstands, while Melissande places the garland triumphantly on his head. Sometimes, I see it as I really did, standing on the sidelines and watching. Other times, I'm looking down at Tristan's upturned face, radiant and transfigured as it searches mine, while my long blonde hair falls in billows around my shoulders.

I don't have to think hard to know what Melissande is to me. She's *my* impossibility.

Something else is different in those days immediately following Firsts, too. Now, I'm the one who's watching Taran. It's partly because I need to study his technique if I'm going to help Tristan improve his distance. Or at least, that's what I tell myself. If I'm honest, I have to admit I've become increasingly curious about him, ever since Tristan told me about his father. I know what Taran is to Tristan, but what about Taran? Just what is Tristan to him?

But Taran is as unreadable to me as ever.

I have my first run-in with him only a few days after Firsts. It's a warm afternoon, and a bunch of the squires decide to make an excursion to the mill pond beyond the wall for a swim. At first just Auguste, Rennie, and Benoit are going, so I decide to tag along. I like to sit in the sun and dangle my feet in the water, and since Tristan's at tutorials it doesn't feel too decadent. But as we get going, the group swells: first Pascal and Armand decide to join us, and I start feeling uncomfortable. Ever since my last encounter with Jurian, I've got to be very careful about ogling, and I'm not sure I can trust myself when the older boys are around. I try to beg off, but it's too late, and my heart isn't really in it. I want to go along.

As we cross the field, though, we pass Falko and Taran practicing with Remy and Pruie, Falko's squire. To my dismay, when Armand calls out to them to join us, they agree, and I can't back down now. I find myself climbing over the wall between the hulking forms of Falko and Taran, and I can't help but feel I'm leaving safe territory behind.

The pond itself is not very large, but it's set in a lovely little glade in a clearing in the woods, and there's plenty of room around the bank for me to find a spot to sit that's not too close to where the Journeys are stripping down. The boys are already splashing around and laughing, and as I pull off my boots and roll up my breeches, I begin to relax. What could happen to me here? I take a step or two into the pond and let the cool mud at the bottom slide between my toes, while the warm sun beats down on my back. A few of the boys, Rennie and Pruie, make some half-hearted attempts to talk me into bathing, too, but it's just polite. They all know I don't undress, and nobody's going to make an issue out of it. After a while I stretch out on the bank, close my eyes, and pull my feet up out of the water to let them dry in the sun.

I'm not sure how long he's been standing there before I notice that someone's blocking my sun. But I start to feel cold, and so I put up a hand to shade my eyes and open them. Taran is standing over me silently, staring down at me. From this extreme angle, he looms over me like a colossus, and even his muscles seem to have muscles. For a horrible moment, I think he's completely nude. The sun is behind him and it's in my eyes, and even with a hand up before my face it's hard to see properly, but as he comes into focus, I see with a rush of relief he's still got his breeches on. They're slung low and rolled up high, so I'm still seeing a lot more of him than I care to, but he isn't looking at me. He's standing there wordlessly, expressionless, staring — at my feet.

It's so odd, I don't even feel scared.

"Tristan's gotten stronger," he says finally. "A lot stronger." I'm not sure where this is leading, but the way he says it, it's an accusation. Is he mad at the idea that I've proved to be of some real help to Tristan? "But you haven't. You haven't gotten any stronger."

"I'm not very strong," I say.

"You haven't gotten any stronger," he insists, still not looking at me, still not taking his eyes off my feet. Then he laughs. "Maybe he should get you a crossbow."

And he's gone.

I'm sure it's an insult, and it doesn't take me long to figure it out. It doesn't take nearly as much strength to wield a crossbow, and none of the boys at St. Sebastian's would be caught dead using one. We're a guild that prides itself on the use of the longbow. He's suggesting I don't belong here, that I can never make the cut. The thing that makes it worse is that he's right. Even after months at the guild, I still can't send an arrow over 200 yards.

I lie immobile a while longer, letting my arm come down and cover my eyes, trying not to let Taran get to me. I already knew I could never handle the heavy shooting, didn't I? It was obvious. Why should it matter that Taran knows it, too? They all do. But everything Taran says sounds like a threat.

So strangely enough, when Falko plops himself down on the bank and stretches out next to me, it's almost comforting. Maybe a few crude jokes are just what I need to change my mood, to forget about myself. It's like Tristan says — there's no point pining over impossibilities.

"You're missing out, Woodcock," Falko says, but from him, it sounds rather affectionate. "The water feels great!" He gives a big stretch and rolls onto his back. I close my eyes again, for obvious reasons, but as we're lying there companionably side by side, on a whim I say:

"Tell me about your girl, Falko."

"What do you want to know?"

'Whatever you'll tell me." When he doesn't reply immediately, I ask, "Is she beautiful?"

Then I lie back and wait for the inevitable rhapsody on her charms. I'm looking forward to being amused by his fulsome description of huge breasts and flowing hair, the kind of thing the boys are usually spouting, but to my surprise he says simply,

"You probably wouldn't think so. But she is, to me."

"Who is she?" I ask, really interested now.

"You wouldn't know her. She's the daughter of my father's steward. She's just, well, easy to be around. It's not that easy for me to talk to girls. I never know what to say. But she's different. We grew up together." He's been talking slowly, but he starts talking faster, his voice warming up. "She's really small, Marek. Delicate, you know? And she likes how big I am," he says, puffing up. "She'd tease me about it. I just assumed we'd get married."

"What happened?"

"When my father was elevated to knighthood, he decided she wasn't good enough for me. When I came here for the Journeyman competitions, while I was gone, he arranged with her father for her to marry someone else. He put up the money. By the time I found out, she was already married."

I digest this awful story in silence, sneaking a look at Falko. He's turned his head away, but I think I see a tear forming in the corner of his eye.

"But she still loves you!" I say. "That's something."

"Does she?" he says simply. "I don't know. I hope she doesn't." When I let out a little cry of protest at this, he says,

"She's married now, Marek. It's all over. I want her to be happy."

The simple dignity of this statement is all the more moving because of its source. I would never have thought to hear something like this from Falko.

"You should forget about her, too, Falko!" I say vehemently, then more teasingly, "A big, handsome guy like you. Forget about your vow. You should find another girl."

"It's not that easy," he says. "And what's the point of renouncing my vow now? As you may have noticed, there aren't any available girls anywhere around here."

What can I say? He's right.

But it's a pity. I would never have believed it, but from the sound of it, Falko could teach even Tristan a thing or two about courtly love.

Imagine my surprise when I have this suspicion confirmed the very next day.

CHAPTER NINETEEN

T he dispatch arrives first thing in the morning.

It promises to be a humid summer day, but it's still early enough that there's a cold mist hanging over the practice field that hasn't burned off yet. I'm stamping my feet and blowing on my hands while waiting on the line to retrieve for Tristan, while Royce is putting the boys through a rather complicated drill that nobody quite understands. He's in the process of explaining the maneuver *again*, for a third time, when the insolent boy who mans the front desk comes out through the stable door, followed by a man in what looks to be a messenger's livery. I have to admit, the idea that I've inherited unique knowledge from my father's expertise has probably made me a little arrogant and I haven't been paying much attention to the lesson, but now I perk up. Royce, though, isn't so happy with the interruption. He simply waves the men down the line and turns back to his instruction, and the others all obediently return their attention to him, except for me. I'm watching as the two of them make their way over to where Taran is standing, and I watch carefully as Taran takes something from the man's hand, thanks him, and retreats to a spot under the eaves to inspect his acquisition.

Even from my distant vantage point, I can see that it's a letter. It must be something quite important, since usually missives are left at the front desk. The messenger must have insisted on delivering it directly into Taran's hands. Curious, I'm craning my neck and trying to cast surreptitious glances back over my shoulder to where Taran is bent over his letter, hoping to get some hint of its contents by reading his expression. But as I should have known, he's not giving anything away, or at least, I'm too far away to read the clues. I'm leaning forward and peering at Taran as hard as I can, as though my intense concentration could make an expression appear on that mask-like face, when suddenly Tristan's voice right in my ear makes me jump.

"Marek, I do believe the butts is this way," he says, taking me by the shoulders and turning me around, and I see with a start that the other squires are already halfway down the field. I'm even more annoyed at having to retrieve immediately and thereby missing my chance to see the effect of the letter on Taran than I am at looking a fool. But to my surprise, when I puff back to the line, he's still sitting under the eaves, in the same position he was in when I left, and he's still staring down at the letter in his hand. Or rather, he looks like he's staring past it. I watch him for what feels like a long time, and I think I'm the only one except for Remy who notices that when he finally gets up, he goes straight back inside the guild rather than returning to practice.

I'm fidgety all through noon mess. Taran and Remy come in late, and so when they squeeze in at the far end of the table where I can't get a good view of them, I can't do anything about it. I'll have to wait until I can corner Remy later back in the barracks and try to get something out of him then. I'm not sure why, but I'm convinced the official-seeming letter must be from Taran's father, and I'm determined to find out what it contains.

Remy, however, turns out to be a slipperier customer than I've given him credit for. We're sitting across from each other on our cots later that afternoon, having both come in from afternoon practice at about the same time (by carefully arranged chance), and as he's pulling off his boots and making to relax a bit before supper, I say casually,

"News from home today?"

Remy's answer is all innocence, but he's giving me a wary look. "What makes you say that?"

"Well, it looked like Taran had a letter this morning, and I just assumed ..." I say leadingly, but Remy simply blinks at me. I'm going to have to be more direct. "Not bad news, I hope?"

"No, nothing to worry about," is all he says.

"It was from his father, though, wasn't it?" I insist.

"I'm going to lie down a bit, if you don't mind, Marek," he says, side-stepping my question. "I've got a frightful headache."

I won't get anything more out of him, but I take this as confirmation. It was from Lord Mellor all right, and whatever it was, Taran didn't like it one bit. The question is: will Tristan like whatever it is any better?

I'm already feeling a little uneasy, then, as I stare down absently at Remy's feet, newly freed from his boots, and what I see doesn't make me feel any better. He's shorter than I am, but his feet look three sizes bigger. His toes are long and thin, with bones that poke out at awkward angles, and there are disturbing black tufts of hair on the knuckles of his toes.

My own feet are as pink and round and smooth as newborn piglets.

I DEBATE MENTIONING THE LETTER TO TRISTAN. I DON'T think he noticed it, and I'm torn. I don't want to bring up his father; on the other hand, I don't want him to be blindsided by news later when I could have prepared him. In the end I decide against it, determined to get some idea of what the letter contains before I bring it up. I haven't decided just how I'm going to do this when the matter is taken out of my hands by Master Guillaume himself.

We're all seated for evening mess, and I've already come back with Tristan's plate before Taran enters the hall. I've been on the lookout for him, and when I see him making his way toward the table, I'm sure my suspicions are well founded. He looks drawn and uptight — or rather, more so than usual — and his manner is particularly wooden. As soon as he's seated, Master Guillaume rises, as though he's been eagerly awaiting Taran's arrival to broach an exciting subject.

"Gentlemen," he says cheerfully, raising his tankard. "We've had a dispatch this morning from sir Brecelyn, and it seems congratulations are in order. Taran, my boy," he calls over to the Journey table, "Come and join me up here!"

So I was wrong. The letter was from Sir Brecelyn. But why would Brecelyn be sending a dispatch for Taran? The whispers begin as soon as Taran gets up from the table, moving so stiffly that it looks a miracle his limbs can bend at all. Everyone else is wondering the same thing.

"What, is the old boy so besotted with him that he's offered him a job, even before he's made veteran?" Aristide jokes.

"Perhaps he simply wished to congratulate the 'fine figure of a boy' on placing *second*," Gilles drawls smugly.

"Ah, here you are, Mellor," Guillaume says, as Taran takes his place next to the master. Putting his arm around Taran, Guillaume raises his tankard, and continues, "I'm sure Taran won't mind my stealing his thunder and sharing his big news with you. Everything has been officially finalized between the fathers, and since they can't be here tonight, I believe it's a master's prerogative to stand in place of a father on an occasion such as this. So let me claim my privilege, and be the first to congratulate young Mellor here on a match well made!"

So *that's* it! Old Mellor has arranged a marriage for him. It should be obvious who he's to be married *to*, but I don't think anyone's quite put it together yet. We're all still so shocked at the thought of Taran of all people becoming engaged.

"No wonder he's looking ill!" Jurian whispers gleefully. "I bet he's imagining having to go through with the wedding night."

"And what a boring night that will be for some poor girl," Gilles agrees.

"He's got to be glad the actual wedding ceremony can't happen until all the trials are over," Aristide adds. "I bet he's never been so glad he's sure to make it into the veterans' competitions! Look at him! He looks like a man sentenced to the gibbet."

At this point, Master Guillaume's voice rings out again. "So please, rise and join me in a toast to Taran and his bride to be, the lovely Lady Melissande Brecelyn!"

Poor Guillaume. His announcement is not met with the reaction he anticipated at all. At the Journey table in particular, you could hear a pin drop in the stunned silence that ensues. To cover his confusion, he pats Taran heartily on the back until we recover ourselves enough to remember that a St. Sebastian's salute is in order. Even then it's a half-hearted affair, and I'm not the only one who's looking more at Tristan than at Taran. Taran himself looks positively ashen, and I doubt it's entirely due to embarrassment. How galling it must be to have one's marriage announcement be such a drab and awkward affair, especially after all of Louvain witnessed Tristan win the affections of his fiancée so publicly and so spectacularly not more than a week ago! Because I was right in what I said to Tristan in the tent at Firsts — when Melissande crowned Tristan, it had to be obvious to everyone watching that she was in love with him.

Tristan's back is to me, since he's at the far end of the table and he's turned to the front of the room. I can hardly bear to see what his face will look like when the announcement is over and he turns back to face the table.

But when he eventually does turn around, it's to share a joke with Jerome. The two of them laugh over some quip, and Tristan looks perfectly composed — amused, even. Initially, relief floods over me, but then my eyes narrow in suspicion. He *does* look perfectly fine. Now he's the one who looks impassive, bored — as cool as a cucumber.

He doesn't look surprised at all.

"You *knew*!" I explode at him later out in the corridor. I've hardly been able to wait to confront him. I don't know how, but somehow, he knew. And when I see his face, I know I'm right. What's more, I bet he's known for a long time.

"I may have heard a rumor or two, yes," he confesses casually, and I have to grab his arm to keep him from merely turning away and continuing on to his room.

"That's why you tried so hard to meet her!" I accuse. "Because she was meant for Taran!" Then something worse occurs to me. "Tristan, is *that* why you love her?"

He pretends to consider this a moment, casting an exaggerated musing expression up at the ceiling, before replying heartlessly,

"Why does anyone love anyone else? Do I love Melissande because she's Taran's? I don't know. Maybe. It's as good a reason as any."

I didn't think I could ever be angry with Tristan again, not really angry, after he did my father's trick. But at the thought of him stalking that lovely girl just to score off Taran I feel fury rising in my chest, made all the hotter by the knowledge that my trick in procuring the rose for him at Firsts played right into his hands. Words flood out of me in such a rush of rage that even I'm surprised by its vehemence.

"She isn't just some prize to be won, something for you to compete with Taran over!" I shout, and Tristan has to pull me hastily into his room and close the door to keep the whole guild from hearing me. But I don't stop.

"You made her love you!" I cry. "That day in the chapel! It *was* a hunt, after all. You hunted her down and shot her with that ridiculous rose as sure as if you'd used a bow. What is she supposed to do now? How can she bear to marry that cold fish, after she's seen you? Did you even think of her at all?" The parade of expressions on Tristan's face during this outburst, from surprised to distressed to outright alarmed, would be comical if I weren't so genuinely angry. I'm getting confused, too, as I rush on, unable to stop, even though I'm no longer sure what I'm really talking about or why I'm really so angry.

"The fever of love! *Ha*! What a joke. What do you know about love? All those fancy words, all that fake show! That's not love. What do you know about really burning for someone you can never have? How will she stand his touch, when what she's longing for is yours? How can she stand to be near you, day after day, and not have it? Do you know what it's like to stand next to someone and to itch to touch them so much, it's like an arrow through your palm? To long to speak, but never to be able to? It's like an arrow, ripping through your throat! And your parting shot, 'dying for love' — what do *you* know about how unattainable love really feels? *I'll* tell you — it's like an arrow, straight through the heart!"

I feel sick now, and I know I'm going way too far. Can I really be using the imagery of my father's death so deliberately and so perversely? But I'm swept up in my own pain, and Tristan always has the effect of driving me to extremes. I had no idea until now how much the strain of it all was affecting me. Even now I can't control myself, and I hear myself adding, "I was wrong! Love isn't the cruelest archer, *you* are!"

"Marek, I didn't think …" Tristan tries to interrupt, both his hands up in the air as if to defend himself from this onslaught, but then a new thought occurs to me.

"Is that why you hate Remy, too? Because Taran loves him?" I rage.

Before he can reply, I have the worst realization of them all.

"Is *that* why you rescued me?" I shriek, my voice quivering. "To have a little rat of your own? Do you have *any* desires of your own at all, or is everything you do dictated by Taran's? Is everything you do motivated by the desire to tear him down?"

At this, Tristan looks as though I've struck him in the face, and I wish I could take the words back. Instead, I turn and stalk out, slamming the door behind me. I haven't been fair; I saw the look on Tristan's face when Melissande put the crown on his head, and I know he can't be as indifferent to her as he pretends. But there's enough truth in my final words to sting us both, and I'm not sure where we stand now. I'm not even sure anymore why he did my father's trick.

What's worse, I doubt he knows himself.

I stay away most of the afternoon. When I've had a chance to cool down, I seek him out. I'm going to have to be the one to apologize, but I don't know what to say. Most of what I said was probably true. I just hope he wasn't listening too hard to some of it, since I can't explain why I made it sound as though Melissande was going to be suffering through being near him every day. But it can't be helped, so I make my way to his room, hoping something will occur to me on the spur of the moment. Tristan thinks I'm infatuated with Melissande myself, so probably I can count on him attributing much of my outburst to that.

When he bids me enter at my knock, I plunge in, but before I can open my mouth to apologize, Tristan looks up from where he's sitting on the edge of his cot, Melissande's rose in his hands.

"Do I really love her at all, Marek?" he asks quietly, and I can tell he's been sitting there a long time. He looks truly distressed, and I have a pang of conscience. My rage at him of course really had little to do with Melissande.

"Maybe I don't. Maybe I just like the idea of her. But the devil of it is, Marek — I like the idea of her, a lot. And it hurts like hell that I'm not going to have her."

"Don't I know it," I say with feeling, and he grins at me. And just like that, we're friends again.

But some of the sting of my words is still there.

THE NEXT DAY, AS WE WAIT FOR EVENING MESS OUT IN the garden where Tristan and Gilles are engrossed in a game of draughts, I remember Taran's insult at the pond. I figure some grumbling about Taran won't be out of place as a way to help patch up things between Tristan and myself, so I pass it along. Only the conversation doesn't go at all as planned.

"Can you imagine it?" I snort, after telling them what Taran said. "A St. Seb's man, with a crossbow?"

"Marek," Gilles says flatly, not taking his eyes off the board, "has it occurred to you that perhaps Taran was being genuine? That he really thought it was a good idea?"

"Ha!" Tristan and I both exclaim at the same time, and I'm gratified by our united response. He sees it for the insult it was. But then Tristan says,

"It's not a good idea — it's brilliant! Absolutely brilliant."

"What?!" I sputter.

Tristan moves his piece carefully, then sits back and looks at me, tipping back his chair. "Of course! It's pure genius. Oh come on, Marek," he says when I frown, "You've got accuracy. But we both know you just haven't got the strength yet to handle the big bow — either to bend it or to hold it steady. With a crossbow, you can show off your aim. Show off your eye, while we keep working on those shoulders."

Gilles has been silent, concentrating on the game, but now he takes one of Tristan's men and sits back, too.

"That's game, old boy. I do wish you'd concentrate. You can't win this game with tricks, you know — the pieces can't be charmed off the board. You make a damned poor opponent. Worse than Pascal!"

"Stuff it, Gilles," Tristan says affectionately.

"I'm not a little boy!" I protest, fully aware of the irony of this statement, but I'm feeling a little hurt. It's not really because of what Tristan's saying; he's right, of course. But they're both being so casual about it. I'd expected some commiseration. "Only weak and infirm old men use crossbows! It doesn't even take any skill."

"That's not true, Marek," Gilles says. "Sure, anyone can use a crossbow. But it takes skill to be good."

"And you can get a reputation with one — look at Guillaume Tell!" Tristan exclaims. He's always going back to Tell. He's fascinated by the guy.

"He's probably no more than a myth," I sniff.

"But he's a famous one!" Tristan insists with a grin. "Mark my words, a crossbow is just the thing for you. It'll be a novelty. Poor old Taran!"

"Tristan," I say, trying not to let some of the anger I felt over the whole Melissande affair creep back into my voice, "is that what this is all about?"

"Whatever do you mean?" Tristan blinks innocently, but he can't fool me. He's going to stick me with the indignity of a crossbow just for the pleasure of seeing Taran's face when his taunt becomes my ticket to passing the apprentice trials. My jab at him the other day in the heat of anger was more accurate than I'd imagined; Taran really is behind every move he makes. And there's nothing I can do about it.

It turns out, Tristan is entirely serious about the crossbow, so much so that he swallows his pride and uses some of the money in Master Guillaume's keeping that his father has provided for him to procure one. Making a crossbow is a complicated affair, so instead of having one made in the shop he orders one, and its arrival less than a week later signals the end of our respite and the beginning of our slow march toward Seconds.

It's time to start training seriously again. The trouble is, I still don't have a plan.

The arrival of a crossbow at St. Sebastian's causes quite a stir. Out on the field, everyone is so eager to give it a try that on the first day, I hardly have a chance to try it myself. At one point, when Falko is grabbing it out of Anselm's hands and some of the other Journeys are gathered around watching as he winds the crank and fits the bolt into the tiller, I notice Taran watching us from his habitual vantage point under the eaves. As usual, I can't read his expression, but if anything, he looks smug. I really hope Tristan is right; I'd better be able to do something amazing with this bow to wipe that look right off his face. I have to admit it: I'd love to score off Taran, too. So I determine then and there that I'm going to do whatever it takes to make it happen. If I've got to be saddled with this contraption, I'm going to find a way to use it to my advantage. I'm going to make Taran sorry he ever heard of one.

My crossbow is the focal point of conversation at evening mess, too. Inevitably, the discussion turns to Guillaume Tell and his famous shot. The boys all start arguing about it, estimating how far the shot could have been to be possible, and disagreeing about whether or not such a shot is possible with a longbow.

"It's not the distance," Charles says. "It's all about nerves. Can anyone be steady when aiming at a loved one? That's the point. He only had one shot to get the apple off his son's head, so he had to make it in one. He couldn't close in on the shot. He had to have dead aim with the first bolt."

"It's not possible with a longbow, at any distance," Aristide agrees. "For one thing, you've got two hands to use to hold a crossbow steady."

"Of course it's possible," says Gilles, predictably.

"It is not, Gilles." Aristide insists. "Not at 100 yards, not at 80 yards, not at 60. You know it, and I know it. Stop being disagreeable."

"Pshaw. I could make that shot, son or not," Gilles replies airily.

"Easily said, since you have no son," Aristide laughs.

"I could make that shot, off Pascal's head, and at 200 yards," Gilles says indifferently, then adds in his most affected tone, "And everyone knows I love Pascal more than any son."

"Gilles," Pascal says nervously from the end of the table, "No one's doubting your skills." Pascal's tone makes me begin to feel a bit apprehensive; he knows Gilles awfully well.

"Hot air, Gilles! That shot is impossible," Aristide insists.

"Just because *you* couldn't make it, Ari, doesn't make it impossible," Gilles replies smoothly.

"Besides," Charles laughs, "you'd be hard pressed to find anyone you cared about enough to make it a real challenge, Ari."

"He'd have to shoot it off his own head," Jurian agrees, as Aristide grows redder and redder. Delighted at Aristide's reaction, Gilles clears his throat.

"Gilles ..." Pascal says warningly, starting to get up, but Gilles doesn't pay any attention.

"How about a friendly wager?" Gilles says, and Pascal groans and falls back into his seat. "At Seconds, we'll both do the 'Tell shot' as our trick. I'll shoot an apple off Pascal's head, you shoot one off Armand's head."

"What?!" everyone says at once.

"It'll be fabulous." Gilles beams. "Shall we discuss terms?"

"Guillaume'll never let you shoot at your squires," Anselm says, but Gilles waves this off.

"Guillaume'd shoot an apple off his own grandmother's head if he thought it would bring in the crowds. He'll love it."

"You aren't serious!" Aristide scoffs, but Gilles gives him a mild look meant to convey that he can't understand why anyone would think he was joking.

"We won't wager anything as common as money. Let's say, the loser has to run the circuit of Louvain from St. Sebastian's along the canal to Porte Charleroi and back at the beginning of morning practice, completely naked."

"You'd lose, just to have the excuse to do it yourself!" Jurian laughs, but Taran says soberly,

"It seems to me, the loser will be busy burying his squire."

"Pshaw," says Gilles again. "Nobody's going to shoot anybody. The loser will simply be the one who backs down."

At this point, everyone starts talking about the details, delighted with Gilles's joke. Everyone knows he's just trying to bait Aristide, and none of us think he's really serious. That is, nobody but Pascal. I notice that he's no longer eating. He's lost his appetite entirely.

The next day, inspired by Gilles's joke, Tristan and I start trying to come up with ideas for Tristan's exhibition at Seconds. He's going to need a pretty good trick, particularly since the crowd will be expecting something big from him after Firsts. Anything that's less than spectacular is going to disappoint them. The problem is, it isn't so easy to come up with a spectacular idea, let alone figure out how to execute it. So we fall back on my old idea of using moving targets. In keeping with Gilles's joke, we decide that I'll throw apples up into the air in rapid succession at a distance (to be determined by the theme of the competition: mid-range for wands, further for clouts) and Tristan will shoot them out of the air. It'll be a good trick, if we can pull it off. The problem is, if he misses even one, the trick will fall flat, literally — and a near miss won't count for anything. Nothing will signal failure more clearly than the sight of an apple splatting on the ground.

The announcement of the theme of the next competition is still a ways away, so we decide to focus on clout shooting; wands is just a combination of distance and accuracy, and Tristan already has the accuracy, so we might as well focus on the distance. Or rather, I decide. Tristan tries to resist, but I tell him that if I've got to learn a new technique with the crossbow, he's got to work on a new technique, too. I've been watching Taran and Falko. Not only is Tristan going to have to bulk up, but he's going to have to work on an entirely new motion. The tricky thing is, I can't just fall back on my father's advice for figuring this motion out; from the techniques he was teaching Jules, it's clear my father was a butts shooter, too, not a clouter. I'm going to have to find an ally, but I have no idea who. The only thing that's obvious is that the one who could help the most is the one I certainly can't ask.

In the meantime, I try to load Tristan up with meat and milk, and both of us work like dogs on exercises meant to build muscles as fast as possible. In Tristan's case it seems to be working slowly but surely; in mine, the extra food just seems to have the unfortunate side effect of returning curves to my body, yet very slowly, I think I see some improvement in my own strength. Maybe, if I really work at it, I'll send that arrow 200 yards with a longbow after all.

I hate to admit it, too, but secretly I'm beginning to love my crossbow. It's taken some time to get used to it, but it really is so much easier to handle, and I think nobody was prepared for just how accurate I'm proving to be with it. We decide to practice

Tristan's trick with it, too — with me shooting down apples that Tristan throws. The only problem with it is how slow it is to load and wind. I can shoot the apples out of the air just fine, but I can only do one apple at a time. I decide to set my mind to the mechanics of it, to see if I can figure out a way to make it faster. That would be a trick, all right.

CHAPTER TWENTY

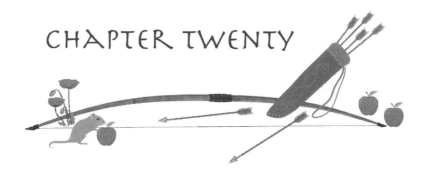

One morning, as I'm pulling on my boots at the edge of my cot, I notice a new arrival in the barracks. It's such a small arrival, I couldn't possibly guess at the time that it would end up causing me so much trouble.

It's a little figurine sitting on Remy's bedside table. Slowly over the course of a few weeks, he's assembled a menagerie of wooden animals next to his cot, and I've become unaccountably fascinated with them. The squires have so few possessions that I notice anything new right away, and since I have nothing at all on my table, I've taken to scanning his table regularly, not wanting to miss any new additions.

They're only roughly carved, but I find them quite charming. The first to appear was a dog curled up with its head resting on its paws that bears a distinct resemblance to old Popinjay. It's so crudely formed it looks almost unfinished, yet in a few quick strokes the carver has managed to capture a look on the old dog's face so typical of the original that the little figure seems strangely life-like: the eyes look up in expectation as though at his master's arrival, and hold a pathetic mixture of hope for affection and certitude of being ignored. I've seen this very expression on Popinjay so many times that the figurine seems almost a reproach, since I'm usually the one ignoring the old dog. It doesn't help that I probably wear a similar expression quite regularly myself.

Other figurines have joined this one at irregular intervals, and in each one Remy demonstrates the same remarkable ability to capture the spirit of the creature while executing the features in only the broadest of strokes. There's a rabbit, frozen with fear but alert and ready to run, a crafty fox, and an obstinate mule whose expression so reminds me of the one who kicked me that I touch my face involuntarily whenever I see it.

After noticing the first figures, I thought of trying to make myself one in the shop. It would be nice to have something of my own on my table, too, but I hadn't thought of making myself something until I saw Remy's animals. After all, I'm good with my hands and I work with wood all the time; if Remy can do it, so can I. I figured it would be easy.

It turned out to be anything but. I managed to carve out something that looked a bit like an animal, but I just couldn't figure out how to indicate the expression the way Remy does, or even what expression to convey. In the end, I was too dissatisfied by the result to do anything but toss it away and reconsider Remy. I've thought before that he was not as simple as he appears, but with each new figurine I've become increasingly surprised by the sensitivity with which he renders them. There must be more to Remy than meets the eye.

Today, the new little figurine is so evocative that I can't help myself. I pick it up. It goes against the unwritten code of the barracks, that the boys don't bother each other's things. There's no privacy in here at all, and so we're pretty strict about protecting each other's rights. It's the only way to have any ourselves. But I just have to get a closer look.

It's a little mouse, sitting up on its haunches, its tail curled around its body. Its paws are up at its face, as though it's smoothing its whiskers, which are indicated only by lines carved into the face. In some ways it's the most crudely carved of the figures, but Remy's put such an intriguing expression on the little mouse's face that I can't stop staring at it, turning it this way and that, trying to figure out what it's supposed to be thinking. The combination of intelligence and introspection he's indicated is extraordinary. When did he make it? I've never seen him whittling in the barracks, and I didn't even know he owned a knife.

Somehow, the thought of Remy with a knife isn't particularly pleasant.

I'm still holding the mouse in my hand when Remy comes in. I know I should put it down, only now it would look furtive anyway, and I can't bring myself to do it just yet. But as Remy approaches, he doesn't look annoyed. He's got the same goofy expression he always wears on his face.

"Do you like it, Marek?" he asks, his voice bubbly.

"Like it! It's …" I can't think of an adjective that captures what I really think about the figures, so I finish lamely, "it's lovely."

"They are good, aren't they?" he chirps immodestly, but he isn't bragging. It's the simple truth.

"Would you like to keep it?"

"What? The mouse?" I can't believe he'd part with it. I know I wouldn't.

"Sure. Or, you can choose a different one. Any one you want." At my incredulous expression, he continues:

"The hard part is getting the right piece of wood. Look: if you take one, maybe in exchange, you could bring me some odds and ends from the shop? You know, some really nice left-over pieces."

I agree readily, and so the little mouse becomes my first real possession since being stripped of all of my old ones. That is, if you don't count the crossbow, which I don't. That's different. This is personal, and as I place the figurine dead center on my table, I feel as though I've now got a new ally in the barracks. I've obtained it from the most unlikely of sources.

On a whim, I press Remy to join some of us who have made a plan to go out together this afternoon; it's the birthday of Falko's squire Pruie, and some of the squires have asked permission to take him out on the town. Remy's been refusing to come along, and now he looks so thrilled by my insistence that I feel a pang of guilt that I haven't made more of an effort to befriend him. After all, Taran's not his fault, and I can't blame him for being loyal. It's time I start trying to figure out Remy.

It turns out to be a big group that assembles for town after noon mess: me, Pruie, Auguste, Rennie, Benoit, Pascal, Armand, Henri, and Remy. Only Turk's squire Andre doesn't come along. As it happens, the Journeys aren't going to miss us. They've got a special session this afternoon on knightly combat, so they're going to be enjoying themselves dressing up in armor and bashing on each other with big sticks.

"There's nothing more satisfying than connecting with a mace," Falko tells me in anticipation, and I'm glad we're not going to be around. I sincerely hope Baylen and Royce aren't foolish enough to let Falko within twenty yards of a mace. When I say as much to Tristan, he replies:

"Don't worry about Falko. For once, he actually knows what he's talking about. He was in service to a knight before he came to St. Seb's, you know, and then he was his father's squire. I think he may still intend to complete training as a knight if he gets cut."

When he sees my dubious expression, he adds with a laugh, "Nobody's going to be using a mace, kid. This is just a tutorial, to give us an idea of what heavy combat entails. We aren't going to really be fighting."

Still, I'm glad Tristan's been bulking up. I don't trust the vets to keep things theoretical, and if anyone ever gets the idea of squaring Tristan and Taran off with weapons, heaven help St. Sebastian's. It's a great day to be getting out of the guild.

As we cut through the garden to make our exit, the unexpected sound of construction out on the practice field meets our ears.

"What's all that hammering?" I ask. "Don't tell me they're actually building lists for this tutorial."

"Gallows, more like," Pascal replies glumly.

"Whaddya mean?" Pruie asks. He's like a big kid. Literally. He's supposedly turning fourteen today, but he looks about twenty. Either he can't count, or he's lying about his age. He's almost as big as Falko, and regrettably, not a lot smarter.

"I think you'll find Gilles is responsible," is all Pascal will say.

Out on the streets, it takes me a while to notice that we're not headed to the Drunken Goat.

"I'm afraid I'm not allowed in the Goat by myself," Pascal says with a blush, and everyone laughs.

"Where are we going, then?" Remy asks, sounding nervous. I've noticed he's getting a bit squirrely the further we get from the guild.

"There's a place across town by the smithies we sometimes go when the Journeys aren't with us," Armand says. "The Fool's Bells."

"Sounds charming," I say sarcastically, but I understand. It doesn't seem right to go to the Journey hangout without the Journeys. But I am sorry that it will mean not seeing Roxanne.

"Sorry it'll mean missing your girl," Pascal says apologetically, as though reading my mind.

"I expect absence will just make her heart grow fonder," I say, trying to sound both disappointed and nonchalant; I'm secretly a little proud of my unexpected reputation as a lady's man, but I'm not eager to dwell on it.

"Isn't the Bells a bit rough?" Remy asks, darting glances down the side streets and sounding even more anxious.

"What could happen to all of us?" Armand says dismissively, but he puts a protective arm around Remy. "We'll look after you."

I sincerely hope he's right. It suddenly strikes me that I will be in a world of trouble if anything happens to Remy. I was the one who insisted he come along, after all.

Fortunately, our trip to the Fool's Bells goes smoothly, but it's anything but uneventful. What happens there is such a surprise, we can hardly contain ourselves when we get back to the guild, but we agree to hold our tongues until evening mess. What a coup it's going to be, that it's going to be the squires who have the real news tonight!

As we file into the great hall behind our masters, we can't keep from flashing conspiratorial smiles at each other, and we're all enjoying our secret knowledge so much that the meal is almost finished before any of us say anything. We've hardly been listening as the Journeys drone on, bragging about their prowess this afternoon with the heavy equipment, and unfortunately for me, I'm the first to break. As Aristide is saying,

"The key is a well-balanced sword. If the balance isn't right ..." I interrupt. I don't know what comes over me, but I can't contain myself any longer.

"You'll never guess who we saw at the Bells this afternoon!"

Aristide stops mid-sentence with his mouth still open and glares at me, but my outburst has the intended effect. All eyes turn to me, and I blurt out joyfully,

"Taran's not the only one who's engaged! *Baylen's* got a girl!"

My stunning announcement is met with complete silence. I feel like Guillaume must have felt when his announcement about Taran fell flat. I can instantly tell that somehow, I've put a foot wrong, though the other squires don't seem to notice.

"Can you believe it?" Rennie is laughing. "Our formidable trainer, with a soft side!"

"You must have been mistaken," Charles says quietly, but Auguste chimes in:

"There's no mistaking old Bayley! Oh, we barely recognized him at first, that's true, what with him being out of St. Sebastian's garb. Why, he was all cleaned up, too! And sitting way off in a corner ..."

"A *dark* corner," Rennie puts in, elbowing Auguste meaningfully. "He didn't even notice us, he was so absorbed!"

"But the hair. The eyepatch. It was Baylen all right," Auguste finishes.

By this point, there's such a tense air at the table that I hope the others have the sense to drop the subject, but Rennie is just warming up.

"Can you imagine Baylen with a girl? Hey, do you suppose he wears that eyepatch to *bed*?"

"Forget the eyepatch! What about the whip?!" Benoit cackles, and he breaks into such a fit of laughter that Auguste has to whack him on the back.

"Boys," Gilles says reprovingly, "I'm afraid somehow you've gotten the wrong idea."

"What's the matter?" I demand, finally getting annoyed. "He can't hear us over here. Are you all so intimidated by him that you don't even have the guts to give him a little good-natured ribbing behind his back?"

"Of course not," Tristan replies sternly, giving me a warning look. "It's simply that there's been a mistake. If it even was Baylen," and he puts up a hand as some of us begin to protest, "then you've simply misunderstood the situation. Let's drop it."

"There's no mistake," I say seriously. "We overheard him talking to the tavern keeper. He referred to the girl as his intended. He's engaged, all right."

The silence that follows this convincing statement is downright awkward.

"That'll mean he'll be leaving St. Sebastian's," Armand says slowly, just putting it together. "I wonder if the masters know. I wonder if that's why he didn't take her to the Goat. Maybe he hasn't told anybody yet."

"Do you think he'll stay to see us through Thirds?" Auguste muses.

"I never thought Bayley'd leave us before Vets. He's always talking about seeing one of the Journeys make Guards. Surely he'll stay 'til then?" Pascal says.

"Of course he will — and just think of the ceremony!" Rennie cries. "The prince's coronation, induction of his new Guardsman, and a triple wedding, all at once: Taran, Baylen, and with all the offers of marriage alliances coming in these days, the prince, to boot!"

All the squires dissolve into laughter, but I'm uncomfortably aware that none of the Journeys are joining in.

As we're leaving the hall, before heading back to the barracks I pull Tristan aside.

"What's wrong?" I ask.

Tristan looks worried, but all he'll say is, "Marek, I wish you'd learn to leave people's secrets alone!"

The next morning, when I wake up I notice that Remy doesn't look very good. I haven't made a particularly early start today, either; I didn't overdo yesterday, but I'm not used to afternoon imbibing. Remy was completely silent during mess last night, and as I think back on it, I seem to recall him having a bit too much to drink at the Bells. The excursion seemed to frighten him unduly, and he must be a nervous drinker. I should have kept a better eye on him. He's shivering, so I throw my blanket over him. I think he's still asleep, but as I tip-toe past, he says sleepily,

"Thanks, Marek. I'll put it back on your cot later. I'm not going out today. Taran told me last night to stay in today. I, uh, must be getting a cold."

I let him save face, and on a whim, I pick up the little mouse from my table, thinking I can tuck it into my waistband during drills for a little companionship. I find it oddly comforting to carry it with me as I make my way out toward the field.

I don't make it that far before Taran catches up with me. When I enter the stables, he's right on my heels. He must have been waiting for me. As usual, the first I'm aware of it is when his huge hand grabs me by the scruff of the neck and yanks me backward.

"What were you thinking, taking Remy to a place like the Bells?" he growls, dropping me heavily to my feet. I'm barely awake and in no state to confront Taran, but I'm also not really awake enough yet to be as thoroughly terrified by him as I usually am, so I mumble,

"I just invited him. I didn't force him to come. It was a big group. We were perfectly safe."

He snorts. "You have no idea what's safe. *If I ever catch you again* ..." he's saying ominously, when suddenly he catches sight of the little mouse in my hand. The angry look on his face is instantly replaced with shock, then pure rage, and my stomach constricts in fear.

I'm wide awake now. I take an instinctive step backward.

"What in the *hell* are you doing with that?! That's Remy's! You *are* a thief!"

He begins to reach for me, and I can tell I'm about to be punched again. It didn't take the little mouse long to turn against me. I fling my arms up in front of my face protectively, and to my disgust, I start to plead with him.

"I didn't steal it, I swear!" I squeak, cowering so low I'm almost crouching. "Ask Remy, if you don't believe me. He *gave* it to me."

To my surprise, this stops Taran in his tracks, and as I peek through my arms at him, a look so dark and stony has replaced the anger on his face that I forget my fear in surprise.

"He gave it, to *you*, of all people?" he finally says, his voice thick with disgust. "Why would he give it to you?"

"I wanted it," I say simply, telling him the truth in my amazement that he's actually asking me anything. "I, uh, just had to have it."

"It's nothing but a wretched bit of whittling," he says blankly. I didn't expect him to appreciate it, but I'm shocked that he'd insult something of Remy's even as he's willing to beat me for it. The injustice makes me mad enough to reply.

"It's not! It's exquisite. Its expression, why, it's ..." and I break off, because I'm staring down at the little mouse in my hand, and at that moment, I see it.

"It's Remy," I say, almost to myself. It's a self-portrait. Why in the world *did* he give it to me? "How could he bear to part with it?" I add, under my breath.

In my confusion, I've almost forgotten that Taran is standing there over me. But not quite. I force myself to look up at him, and he looks so angry again, a new wave of fear washes over me. He looks ready to fulfill his promise in the alley of ripping off my head. Instead he says tightly,

"I guess it's yours, then." But his hands are clenched so tightly, his knuckles are white when he turns and stalks away as quickly as he came. As usual with Taran, I'm too terrified by him to feel the full effects of my fear until after he leaves, so I'm left standing alone in the stables, trembling uncontrollably and staring down at the little mouse. I'm not at all sure what just happened.

"Why *did* he give you to me?" I ask aloud, when I'm startled by a sound behind me.

"Having a rough day too, squire?" says a voice, and I jump as fear surges through me again. But Taran's not back. It's Jurian, coming out of one of the stalls. He must have heard my whole conversation with Taran. I've been trying my best to avoid Jurian ever since that lick. He's never done anything like it again, but I find I'm always steeling myself for something unpleasant whenever I see him. Whenever I catch his eye, he's either looking amused or contemplating me with a curious expression. After my run-in with Taran my nerves are raw, and I'm determined not to let Jurian bully me, too, if that's what he intends. I pull myself together, and I decide to confront him.

"I wasn't the thief!" I say boldly, not sure why I'm going back to this, but somehow, with Jurian, I seem stuck back in the hallway the night we saw each other but said nothing. It seems like the place to start.

But when Jurian steps forward into the light, I'm shocked by his appearance. His usual assurance and insolence are gone. His eyes are red-rimmed, and his gorgeous face is blotchy and pale. The skin under his eyes looks paper-thin. He looks so bad, I even wonder if he got seriously hurt during the exercises yesterday. Only his voice sounds the same as usual, as though he's amused by my ridiculous statement.

"Whoever said you were?" He leans against the stable wall and slips a piece of hay between his teeth like a stereotypical stable boy, though he still looks completely wrong for the part. Even in his haggard state, he looks ethereal, like a precious ornament someone has thoughtlessly dropped in the most inappropriate place imaginable. After a pause, he adds,

"You aren't suggesting *I* was the thief, are you?" he teases, and I snap.

"Why do you hate me so much?" I demand, more tremulously than I intend.

"Hate you?" He raises his eyebrows. "I don't hate you. In fact, I rather like you, Marek." He laughs again, but he doesn't sound very amused. "After all, we have so much in common. Oh, don't pretend you don't know what I mean," he adds silkily, and for a split-second, I entertain the idea that Jurian, too, is a girl in disguise. He's beautiful enough. But it's impossible.

I've seen him in the bath.

He's mocking me again. After all, what could I have in common with a creature as supremely beautiful as Jurian? At my angry and confused look, his tone changes, and he says sadly, "You poor kid. You really don't know what I mean, do you?"

And then he does a thing that surprises me more than anything he's ever done. He puts an arm affectionately around my shoulder, and he reaches down to ruffle my hair with his other hand, exactly the way Tristan does.

I go straight out onto the field and sit down heavily against the butts. I put my head down between my knees, completely befuddled. For the first time since coming to St. Sebastian's, I seriously consider running away. I'm supposed to be the one with the big secret, yet for some reason, I feel like I'm the only one who never has the slightest clue what's going on. First with Taran, now with Jurian — why do there always seem to be undercurrents I can't figure out? Maybe it's because of my sex, and I just can't learn to think like a boy. But I don't think so. Maybe everyone feels this way. Why do other people have to be such a mystery?

I wonder if it's easier when you're older, if you learn to read the clues better, or if when you're older, you just don't care so much anymore. I suspect some of my problem is that I've grown up so isolated, I haven't had much of a chance to learn how to read people, and even the people I did live with, it turns out I knew them so little. Maybe it's like archery: I can improve, with practice. But just like with archery, I'm stuck in a place where everyone else is an expert and I'm struggling to keep up. Too bad there isn't a crossbow for those of us who are weak at interpreting emotions.

Tristan finds me still sitting against the butts when he shows up for practice. He helps me up, and we end up setting up our station together. As his hand takes mine to haul me to my feet, though, I know I'm not going to run away. I'll never be able to bring myself to leave St. Sebastian's. Not willingly.

Later, when we make our way off the field after morning drills, I find Remy waiting for me by Tristan's cabinet. He's never done this before, and Tristan gives me an inquiring look before shrugging and heading off through the garden alone as I finish putting away our gear.

"I just wanted to thank you again, Marek. I folded up your blanket for you, and put it on your bed."

He's so grateful for such a small thing, I feel unaccountably guilty, even though I've done nothing. Yet I feel uneasy. The whole thing with Taran this morning has left me feeling shaky, and I find myself fingering the little mouse in my waistband, itching to ask him why he was willing to give it to me. But I can't. Remy's face looks so open, asking him such a question would be insulting. I can't help but feel there's something I'm missing.

It wouldn't be the first time.

We fall into step together, and we end up sitting next to each other at noon mess. We've been perfectly friendly before, but I feel both Tristan's and Taran's eyes are on us at table today. I don't think either of them is going to take it well if we really become buddies. I suppose the idea that I've been making friends with his squire must be what was making Taran so angry this morning.

We haven't been seated long before Master Guillaume is calling for attention.

"Gentlemen," he begins. When he then pauses long enough to make everyone start to grow uncomfortable, I forget all about Remy. "It is with heavy heart that I must make a most distressing announcement. It seems impossible now to avoid the conclusion that we do indeed have a thief at St. Sebastian's." Murmuring begins immediately, and Aristide isn't the only one who looks down the table at me. I feel the little mouse growing heavy in my waistband. Did Taran decide to use it to get me into serious trouble after all? Maybe that was the real source of his anger: when I told him Remy gave it to me, it robbed him of an excuse to get rid of me once and for all. He must expect Remy to go along with any accusation he might make. To my shame, I even consider that maybe Remy has set me up. But he's looking as surprised by the announcement as everyone else.

"This time, the theft is serious. An expensive flask has been taken from a private room. There can be no question of a mistake. It was present and accounted for just this morning, but by noon it had been removed. The flask is a very valuable item and one of sentimental value to its owner," Guillaume continues, nodding in Baylen's direction, and I'm so relieved that the object in question is so clearly one that I couldn't have stolen, I hardly register surprise that anyone would be so bold or so foolish as to steal something from Baylen's room.

Everyone else is astonished, too, so we all begin whispering among ourselves and looking around even though Guillaume isn't finished yet. That is, everyone but Jurian. I notice he's looking down fixedly at his plate, and if anything, he looks even worse than he did this morning. I don't really think he's the thief anymore, but he knows something. That much is clear.

He looks as though he's been crying, and I stare at him so long and so intently that he finally looks up and meets my gaze. As I've said, I'm not good at reading emotions, so I'm probably wrong, but the look on his face seems almost like pity.

"The penalty," Guillaume says gravely as Jurian and I contemplate each other, "is ten lashes, and eviction from St. Sebastian's. There can be no compassion and no quarter for a thief.

Your duty is clear, gentlemen. If you know anything, your duty is first and foremost to the honor of the guild, and not to the misguided protection of each other. Be forewarned: anyone caught harboring a thief will be subject to similar punishment. Let us hope for a swift and satisfactory conclusion to this unsavory episode, so that we may all return our attention to its proper objective: preparation for Seconds. The selection of the theme for Seconds, as those of you who have been paying attention to our schedule may be aware, is set for tomorrow night."

Everyone is still so stunned by the idea of a theft directly from Baylen's room that even the mention of Seconds hardly registers. There's talk of nothing else through mess, and Remy and I are still talking animatedly about it as we make our way together back to barracks. As we near our cots, Remy's right in the middle of a sentence when he comes to a sudden stop.

"What's that?" he asks, staring at my cot.

"What?" I say, looking around. At first I don't see it, though it's impossible to miss. There's a lump under my blanket, and something's partially sticking out from under its folds. Something silver. Although I've never seen it, I recognize it right away. It's got to be Baylen's flask.

"Marek," Remy says slowly at my sharp intake of breath, "that wasn't here this morning. I was here all morning, awake, on my cot. Then I folded up your blanket myself. I went straight out and found you on the field. I've been with you ever since. You couldn't have taken that. And you certainly couldn't have put it here."

"I know," I say calmly, but inside, I've gone ice-cold.

"What are we going to do?" Remy asks, his voice scared. But I don't have any idea, and before I can answer, there's a loud commotion at the door. The other squires who've come back straight from mess for a rest are all jumping to their feet, as Master Guillaume himself bursts into the room, followed by master Leon and Baylen. They all look decidedly grim, but the look on Baylen's face is especially sinister, and it's made worse by the fact that in his hands, he's twisting his big black whip in apparent anticipation of administering a beating.

I sit down rather heavily on my cot, as my legs give out under me.

"Boys!" Guillaume's voice reverberates down the long corridor. "We've had a disturbing report that the missing flask is to be found here amongst you squires. I regret to have to ask you to line up against the wall next to your cots, so that we may make a search."

I knew it was coming, but on hearing Guillaume's words, I can't keep from letting out a dry sob. It's the end. Nobody will be surprised to find that I'm a thief after all, and there's nothing I can say. I'm to be caught red-handed. It will mean a vicious beating, but that's not the worst of it. It'll mean leaving St. Sebastian's. That's bad enough. But being beaten will mean being stripped, and that will mean exposure. It's to mean total disgrace for me, and probably for Tristan, too. That's the worst: Tristan will find out.

I should have run away yesterday, when I had the chance.

At first, I can't get up. Remy has to help me get to my feet and prop me against the wall, and even then, I slump down so far, I'm afraid I'll fall to the floor and be unable to get up again. My legs are shaking so badly Remy has to hold onto my shoulders to keep them from banging against the wall, and as Guillaume and the others make their slow but inevitable way down the room, my teeth start to chatter uncontrollably, and I taste blood as I bite my tongue in the process.

Poor Remy is deathly pale, too, and his eyes keep rolling back in his head and he's started mumbling to himself. We must look like raving idiots, but I'm past caring. All I can think, over and over, is *"this is the end, this is the end, this is the end of everything."*

Even in my agitation, I can tell that the masters are only making a perfunctory search. They must have been informed of exactly where they'd find the flask, so even though it feels like an agonizing eternity, it really doesn't take them long to get to the end of the room. Just before they reach us, Remy lets out a desperate sound and releases his grip on me. Guillaume has his back to us and he's stripping the blanket off of Rennie's bed, when I realize what Remy's doing. While Guillaume's bent over the bed behind him and obscuring Remy's motions from the rest of the room, Remy grabs the flask, shoves it under his own blanket, then sits down on top of it.

It happens so fast, I don't have time to react before the masters are turning to him.

"Remy, you're supposed to be on the wall," Guillaume says to him, quite kindly. Everyone likes Remy. It's impossible to be anything but gentle with him. But Remy doesn't get up. I don't think he can. He looks utterly petrified, and my own stomach is in a knot. I should say something, I should be brave. But surely, nobody could do anything to Remy? Before I can think what to do, Master Leon is lifting Remy easily to his feet, and Baylen is whipping back his blanket.

The look of astonishment on all of their faces when they see the flask is proof both that they know exactly where it's supposed to be, and that nobody is going to believe that Remy stole it.

"*Master ...*" Remy begins tremulously, then promptly passes out in Leon's arms.

"I can't believe it. Remy!" Guillaume says, as Leon and an agitated Baylen fan Remy and call for water in an attempt to revive him. The other squires have all gathered around in amazement, but out of the corner of my eye, I notice Pascal slip out the door. I don't know whether to hope he's gone to find Gilles and Tristan, or not.

After more efforts, Remy finally comes to, and when he can sit on the edge of his cot unassisted, Guillaume takes a deep breath and addresses him, but it's in a voice that makes it clear that this isn't what he considers a satisfactory conclusion to the problem of the thief.

"Remy, what do you have to say for yourself?"

"It was just so pretty. I don't know what came over me," he says in a quivering voice, without looking up. It's terribly unconvincing.

"What's going on here?" Baylen demands angrily. "You can't ask me to believe that Remy's the thief."

"Nevertheless, he appears to be confessing," Leon says grimly. "Rules are rules. The flask has been found, and in the squires' barracks. Punishment must be meted out. I don't like it any better than you do." When Baylen makes no move, he adds pointedly. "I'm afraid, Baylen, there are always consequences."

I can't stand it any longer. No matter the consequences, I can't let Remy take a beating. It would surely kill him, and I just can't let him take one for me. I force myself to step forward, my heart beating so wildly I'm afraid it will jump out of my throat when I open my mouth to speak.

"Remy didn't steal the flask," I hear myself gasp, and instantly all eyes are on me.

"Marek, are you confessing?" Guillaume says shrewdly. "I've heard the rumors about you, of course, but I'm disappointed to find them true."

"No, sir," I say, trying to find some courage, but my voice is quivering just as much or more than Remy's. "I'm not confessing. I'm not a thief!" I wince at how shrill I sound, but I forge on: "But it's true that the flask ..." I gulp and clench my fists to force the words out. "It was on my cot when we came in from mess. Remy put it on his own cot before I could stop him, because he knew I didn't steal it." I close my eyes to block out the sight of the ring of frowning faces crowding in around me. "You can ask him yourself. He was in the barracks or with me all morning, so when he saw the flask, he knew I couldn't have stolen it. He knew someone put it here to incriminate me. He was just trying to protect me."

"Hmm," Master Leon says coldly. "Be that as it may, I'm afraid that protecting a thief is as serious as stealing."

"But he wasn't protecting a thief!" I cry, alarmed. I can't let my confession be for nothing. "He knew *for a fact* I wasn't the thief. He only did it precisely because he was absolutely certain I couldn't have taken the flask!"

"It's true!" Remy says shrilly. "Marek couldn't have taken it."

"It seems we have a real problem," Master Guillaume says, frowning. "Your defense of each other may be commendable, but as Master Leon says, it remains that a stolen flask has been found in barracks, and on Remy's cot. Punishment must be given. Just what are we going to do about it?"

I swallow hard. The little mouse is still in my waistband, and I know what I have to do.

"The flask was on my cot. Give the punishment to me," I say, as bravely as I can. The effect of the brave words is ruined, however, by the fact that my teeth start to chatter uncontrollably again halfway through this speech.

The squires have all been standing around in stunned silence. Now they begin to protest, and I feel a tear trickle down my cheek, in part out of fear for what's coming, and in part because I'm touched that they all seem so genuinely agitated for me.

Guillaume considers me for a long time, but when he speaks, he's looking at Baylen.

"All right. Given that there is some confusion over who the *real* culprit here is, I propose to commute the punishment to five lashes, to be administered immediately. Both Remy and Marek will be allowed to stay at St. Sebastian's, until such time as clear proof of guilt can be established. In the meantime, Marek will strip and take five on the back. Baylen, as the injured party, will do the honors himself, as a reminder, lest anyone forget: St. Sebastian's punishes its own, and when there's a crime, punishment must be given."

As he says these last lines, it's pretty clear that he's not happy with the whole affair, and I also think he's convinced I'm not the thief. I doubt he'd believe me, but it's hard not to see that Remy's telling the truth. Whoever put the flask on my cot didn't count on Remy staying in this morning, or being willing to stick out his own neck for me. Even I wonder why he did.

"Master," a tentative voice calls out, and Armand steps forward.

"Armand?"

"It's just, well," he begins nervously. "Tristan intends to put Marek up for apprentice status. Lashes on the back will mean he can't practice. They might even permanently damage his arms. Couldn't he take them on the legs?"

Guillaume looks inquiringly at Baylen, who frowns but then gives a curt nod.

"He doesn't like to undress," Pruie adds timidly, and I feel another tear sneak down my cheeks as the squires rally around me.

"What's that to me?" Baylen snaps, but Auguste says,

"Couldn't he just roll his breeches way up? They're loose enough."

Unexpectedly, Master Leon starts to laugh.

"What a farce this is becoming! Just get on with it."

And so I roll my breeches high up onto my thighs with trembling hands, as Armand and Auguste help me, and Benoit and Rennie comfort the now sobbing Remy. I let myself rest against my friends for a moment, petrified by the pain that's coming, but so grateful to them for their kindness and to Remy for saving me from banishment and exposure that facing the lash seems almost a trifle. That is, until I feel it.

When I'm ready, Armand whispers into my ear, "lie down on the ground, Marek. Face down. There's no point in false courage. It'll be easier to take on the back of the legs." And so I do.

When the lash comes down and bites into my flesh for the first time, the pain is so excruciating that I feel as though my bones have been laid bare by knives of fire, and the wretched sound that escapes me can only be described as the high-pitched shriek of a tortured animal.

Or of a girl.

The sound is even horrible in my own ears, and my wild howls, joined by those of the barracks dogs, are still reverberating around the rafters of the hollow hall when I hear running footsteps. Pascal's back, and he's brought a number of the Journeys with him. I can hear their cries and the sound of their rapid approach as the lash comes down a second time, but I think after my first bloodcurdling cry, even Baylen doesn't have the heart to put much strength into it. I wish I could say I was stoic under the lash, but I'm completely hysterical as Tristan falls to his knees beside me and gathers me up into his arms.

"What the devil is going on here?" he demands angrily, turning me over enough to peer searchingly into my face as he tries to calm my still desperate groans, and brushing the tangled ends of my sweat-soaked hair gently out of my mouth and eyes.

There's a confused minute as everyone starts talking at once, but the whole story finally comes out in fits and starts before Master Guillaume puts his hand up for silence. In the meantime, I continue to cling to Tristan, sobbing loudly and bleeding profusely all over the floor.

"Masters!" Tristan says, looking boldly at each man in turn. "Marek isn't a thief, and what's more, everyone in this room knows it. In the name of justice, call this off, I beg you!"

It's Baylen who replies. "Master has already been quite generous. No banishment. Only five lashes. But three more have to be given. The debt must be paid. There's no getting around it."

"He doesn't look like he can take even one more." It's Charles, sounding ill. "In fact, he doesn't look like he could take the two he's already had."

"Nonetheless," Baylen continues coldly. "The punishment is five."

"Then give the last three to me," says a quiet but determined voice behind me. Of all people to come to my rescue, it's Falko.

"Nobody's going to take lashes for my squire but me," Tristan says, handing me gently into Gilles's arms and standing to face Baylen. I'd just about managed to get my convulsions under control, but at the thought of Tristan or the others taking these horrible lashes, I start to shudder violently again.

"And nobody is taking lashes for *my* squire, but *me*," a deep, authoritative voice says behind me. I know that cold voice, but I'm still surprised when I see Taran step forward to stand next to Tristan, so that now all three of them, Falko, Tristan, and Taran, are standing together shoulder to shoulder facing Baylen and blocking me from him. Faced with this unexpected united front, even Baylen loses his taste for continuing the beating, and Master Guillaume clearly has no interest in damaging his best Journeys. He certainly has no interest in beating the son of Lord Mellor for a crime he didn't commit, so he quietly takes the whip out of Baylen's hands and says with an air of finality:

"Blood is flowing in the barracks. I believe the Saint is satisfied. The flask has been recovered. I consider the debt paid, and I fully expect this to be the last we hear of stealing at St. Sebastian's. That," he adds sternly to Baylen, as though challenging him to object, "will be a satisfactory conclusion to this mess." Turning back to look down at me, he adds, "Squires, tend to Marek here, and I expect all trace of this" — he waves vaguely at the profusion of blood — "to be cleaned up before lights out."

CHAPTER
TWENTY-ONE

I spend the next two days lying face down on my cot, unable to move. My legs are burning and there's little to take my mind off the pain, lying here hour after hour, but the amount of attention I get from all the Journeys and the squires alike is hugely gratifying. Somehow, my cowardice when actually taking the lashes has just increased the appearance of my heroism at being willing to take them in the first place, and I've never had so many friends. I think if I weren't in so much real agony, I would quite enjoy myself.

Tristan is exceedingly attentive, but he's not alone. A rather dour barber on call for the guild attends my wounds that afternoon, and though Gilles isn't terribly impressed by him ("What? No leeches?"), he assigns one of his serving boys to be instructed by this doctor on the proper way to clean and dress my wounds three times a day. He sets the other the task of scouring the woods for herbs to make the necessary poultices, since the fear of infection is worse than the actual wounds (at least according to Tristan, who insists that Baylen must not have been putting his weight into the strokes, saying: "the old boy's lost his taste for violence, from the looks of it." They feel plenty deep enough to me). Jerome plays his lute for me; Falko comes by to read me racy poetry; and the squires take it in turns to entertain me when nobody else is around, telling jokes and trying to tempt me into choking something down with tidbits from the sideboard. Remy is so attentive, fussing around me like a mother hen the way he usually does to Taran, that I can hardly get any respite from his ministrations. I don't have the heart to send him away, though, so I take to pretending to fall asleep when my head starts pounding and he insists on flitting around me anxiously.

Of all the Journeys, only Aristide, Taran, and Jurian fail to appear.

On the second day, I wake from one of my frequent fitful naps to find that my little mouse has acquired a companion. There's a new figurine sitting on my table, one I've never seen before. It's not much bigger than the mouse, but it's fashioned into the shape of a hawk or a falcon. It's carved with more detail than the others and it's out of nicer, harder wood, and I feel a pang that I haven't yet had the chance to make good on my promise of procuring scraps from the shop for Remy. But somewhere, he's gotten ahold of some red yew, the same wood I used to make Tristan's bow, and I don't think it's a coincidence. As I inspect the little hawk, I become convinced that the material — the same wood used for our bows — is part of the depiction. Remy's made the bird small but with a defiant look, and he's cleverly depicted it hooded for falconry in such a way that the line of the hood suggests the shape of the scars on my face.

It's clearly supposed to be me, and I know exactly what this is. It's Remy's way of thanking me for taking the beating, and the little creature looks such a mixture of pathetic and brave, proud even, that I can't help but hope that this is how Remy really remembers me facing the lash. It's hugely flattering, since in reality I was writhing on the floor in abject terror, yet somehow I think the depiction is meant to be sincere. This is how Remy really sees me. I love the little mouse, but this instantly becomes my most valued possession. It's the most beautiful thing I've ever seen, all the more so because of the sentiment behind it. Getting it almost makes being lashed worth it. Almost.

When Remy comes in, I'm still clutching the hawk, as though I'm afraid it might fly away.

"I see you found it!" he cries in delight. "Do you like it?" It's exactly what he said about the mouse. How can he ask? The sophistication with which he makes the figurines clashes jarringly with the apparent simplicity of his personality. I haven't figured him out yet at all.

"Remy, thank you," I say solemnly.

"For what?" He blinks. I think of him grabbing the flask and putting it on his bed, even though it's clear he could never have taken even one lash.

"For everything," I say, gently placing the hawk on my table next to the little mouse. As I drift back into sleep, I think what an unlikely pair they make. But whatever Tristan or Taran might think about it, after standing up to Guillaume for each other, it's inevitable now that the mouse and the hawk are destined to become friends.

On the third day, I'm able to get up and walk around. I'm still bandaged up heavily and I have to use a stick for support, but I manage to hobble out to watch the end of morning practice. As the pain has begun to subside, I've gotten concerned that Tristan will use my infirmity as an excuse to slack off, and I'm determined not to let that happen. I shamelessly used pity to wring a solemn promise from him that he'd practice and exercise as usual in my absence, and to ease my mind, he's even assigned Auguste the role of reporting back to me regularly on his activities, but after two solid days in bed, I want to see for myself. So I find a place to lean up against Tristan's cabinet and watch the drills, since I still can't sit down. Tristan is set up between Gilles and Jerome, and I see that Auguste and Pascal are taking it in turns to cover his retrievals for me.

I'm determined to make it to noon mess today, too, so when the boys come in from the field, they express delight at my strides toward recovery, and Tristan, Gilles, and Pascal lead me into the garden and help settle me where I can lean my posterior against a little table in the shade of the jasmine vines to wait with them for mealtime. I missed the announcement of the theme for Seconds, so as soon as the others pull some chairs around to face me, I ask about it.

"Wands!" chortles Gilles. He's by far the best wands shooter, and he's already in first place coming into Seconds. He's got every right to be pleased, but it's good for us, too, so I don't mind. I asked Gilles once about his surprising strength, and all he would say is "Born with it, my boy. The Lejeunes don't bulk. The stronger we get, the stringier." It's probably true, but it means Gilles isn't going to make much of an ally.

Still grinning, Gilles continues:

"It'll be perfect for our trick."

"What trick?" I ask, thinking I've missed something new.

"The Tell shot, of course. It's essentially a wands shot," he says with satisfaction. So he hasn't given up this joke yet. I don't say what I'm thinking — that wands is shooting at a thin, upright target where elevation doesn't matter: hitting anywhere on the wand counts. I wonder how Pascal likes shooting at him described in this fashion. I try to catch Pascal's eye, but he's looking sullenly at the ground. It's rather cruel of Gilles to keep up the joke even when Aristide isn't around to be irritated by it. So I change the subject to something that's been on my mind, for obvious reasons.

"Tristan, who in the world do you think the thief really is?" I ask.

"What?" he says dumbly. I'm a little annoyed he hasn't been worried about this himself.

"The thief! Who do you think really took Baylen's flask? Tristan, I'm really scared," I admit. At his blank look, I rush on, "I'm safe for now, I know. Everybody knows I can't really get around. But once I'm better, well — it was dumb luck that Remy was able to vouch for me. Somebody put that flask on my cot on purpose. Next time, I might not be so lucky."

"There won't be a next time. Guillaume's seen to that," Tristan says dismissively.

"How can you be so sure?" I huff.

"There's no thief, Marek," he says gently. "There never was."

At this surprising statement, I look around at Gilles and Pascal, but their expressions clearly indicate that they agree with Tristan. They even look a little embarrassed for me. Clearly, I'm being slow again.

"Then who took the flask?" I demand.

"Don't you know?" Tristan says, and I think about it.

And I do know. I can explain everything. It's obvious.

"It was Taran, wasn't it?" I say slowly.

"It's always Taran with you!" Gilles says with exasperation, but I continue, ignoring the interruption, as I begin to piece it together.

"He's been wanting to prove I'm a thief, ever since the alley. That's why Remy covered for me!" It all makes sense now. "Remy must have known Taran did it, and felt guilty. Why else would he try to cover for me? There's no other explanation." I notice Gilles and Pascal shaking their heads bemusedly, but I'm on a roll now.

"How bitter for Taran to find that he almost got Remy beaten instead of me! How much more bitter for him, too, that I ended up standing up for Remy. I bet that's why he offered to take the last lashes — he couldn't stand the thought of having to be in my debt for anything, and he caught himself in his own trap! Oh, I almost wish Guillaume had let him take those last three!"

It's so neat, I'm quite proud of myself for figuring it out.

"You do realize," Gilles drawls, arranging his cuff, "that Taran stepping forward when he did was probably the only thing that saved *you* from taking those last three, don't you?"

I don't dignify this with an answer, but turn inquiringly to Tristan. I'm sure he agrees with me. But he disappoints me with his reaction, too.

"Have you been lying in bed for the last two days thinking up that rot?" he laughs.

I sniff. "If it wasn't Taran, then who?"

Gilles and Tristan exchange a look, and then Gilles says carefully:

"Baylen put the flask there himself, of course."

"What?!" I explode. It's the last thing I expected.

"What's more," Tristan confirms, "Just about everyone knows it. Even old Guillaume. He'd never have softened the sentence otherwise. Ordinarily, stealing would mean losing both hands."

"Baylen!" I cry. "Why would Baylen steal his own flask?" I can't understand it. Then something worse occurs to me. "What does Baylen have against me? Are you saying he was out to get me on purpose?" Thought of having Baylen as an enemy makes my blood run cold.

"I warned you, Marek. People don't like having their secrets exposed," Tristan says evenly.

"What are you talking about?"

"It was you who brought up Baylen's girl at mess," Gilles says.

"How in the world would Baylen know about that?" I'm confused again. Tristan and Gilles exchange another glance, and Gilles finally says,

"You might as well just tell him, Tristan. He's apparently supremely stupid, and unable to figure it out on his own."

"Jurian told him, of course," Tristan says, as though it's the most obvious thing in the world.

"Confronted him with it, rather, I imagine. It must have been quite a scene," Gilles adds. At my still blank look, Tristan sighs.

"They're lovers, Marek."

There's silence as I try to process this information. It all makes sense: Jurian's midnight stroll, his wretched state after our revelation about Baylen's engagement, his inside information from Baylen. I guess I also knew such a thing as two men being lovers was possible, but only in the vaguest way. I've been isolated and sheltered, and I don't know much about what people do in private. My father and Jules certainly never talked about it. I suppose if I'd thought about it at all, I imagined it was something rare and terrible, bringing down some immediate curse, like instant leprosy, but I must be wrong. Tristan and Gilles are talking about it quite casually.

"They have been for a long time, ever since Jurian was his squire," Gilles is saying. "Surely you've noticed how frightfully ugly Rennie is. Who do you think chose him to be Jurian's squire? Baylen insisted. Less temptation."

"Oh, don't look so scandalized, Marek," Tristan says, seeing the look on my face. But I'm not really shocked; I'm just trying to figure it all out. Marieke certainly would have been shocked, but I'm a boy now, and as one, I have to admit, the idea of desiring another boy makes perfect sense to me. "It's against the rules, of course," Tristan continues. "No 'fraternization,' I believe they call it. But it happens. It's bound to, with so many boys in close quarters, and so little opportunity for, er, relaxation."

"And we're all so damnably good-looking," Gilles agrees.

"But that's not really the problem."

"What is, then?" I ask, bewildered. I'm quite out of my element.

"Jurian's gone and fallen in love with him, that's what," Tristan answers.

"Some do go for the rugged type," Gilles puts in.

"And according to *you*," Tristan continues, ignoring him, "not only doesn't Baylen feel the same way, but he's planning to leave. And he hadn't bothered to mention any of it to Jurian."

"Surely he didn't expect Baylen never to marry," I say hypocritically, uncomfortably aware that I myself have sworn off marriage.

"Why not? Not everyone marries, after all. Royce has been living here as a trainer for years. Why not Baylen? But I doubt Jurian really thought about the future. And even if he did, knowing something will happen and having it happen are two different things. And making it the joke of the squires' table is another matter entirely."

I think of Jurian's ravaged face in the stables the morning after I made my thoughtless announcement, and I feel deeply sad. Unrequited love for one's master. I can more than sympathize.

"I suppose that must happen now and then, too," I say slowly, wondering suddenly if anyone was in love with my father, when he was here. Tristan seems to read my thoughts, since he puts in,

"Particularly with us dashing, charming types. Say, do you suppose anyone's in love with *me*?" he asks gleefully. He'd love to have everyone in love with him, I'm sure.

"Gilles, are you in love with me?" he asks archly, and I know he's teasing me now.

Without missing a beat, Gilles replies smoothly, "Not at the moment."

"Pascal, are you in love with me?"

"I doubt Gilles would allow it," Pascal says dryly, and Gilles agrees:

"Certainly not! If Pascal decides to fall in love with anyone around here, I'm going to have to insist that it's me."

"A pity," Tristan says, then pretends to brighten. "But surely some of the others must be secretly carrying a torch for me. I'll have to remember to ask Jerome about it."

"Are any of the others, *er*, 'fraternizing,' that I should know about?" I ask seriously, ignoring Tristan, and hoping to cut off his game before he can ask me if I'm in love with him. I've sworn not to lie to him about anything big, after all. Things are complicated enough.

On receiving a negative answer, since they've all been enjoying laughing over my ignorance, I say with as much dignity as I can muster:

"It seems to me that this whole painful episode might have been avoided if you had just seen fit to tell me about this earlier."

They all have the grace to look suitably chastised, so I decide it's the right moment to take my leave. I've decided to skip mess after all. I've lost my appetite and I'm still weak, but mostly I need a chance to think over what I've just learned. I don't know why, but I find it infinitely depressing that Jurian's exquisite beauty hasn't helped him be any happier than I am. Strangely, this more than anything else disturbs me. This more than anything else shakes my belief in how the world is supposed to work.

I even feel sad for Baylen, despite my beating. To have vented his anger and frustration on me so violently, he must be suffering, too. As I close my eyes back on my cot, the image of the painting of St. Sebastian in the great hall comes unbidden into my mind, only this time the saint doesn't remind me of Tristan, but of Jurian. I think of that vast expanse of young, beautiful male flesh in all its eroticism and agony, and I'm suddenly sure that I'm not the only one at St. Sebastian's who can't stand to have that picture looming over him one minute longer.

Later, when Tristan comes in with a tray from the sideboard for me, I ask him something else that's started to bother me since our conversation in the garden.

"Tristan, why did master Guillaume let Baylen give me those lashes, if he knew all about it? If he knew I didn't do anything? He was going to let me take five."

"That's a mighty good question," Tristan says slowly. "Strange as it may sound," he says finally, "if I were you, I'd take it as a compliment."

I ponder over this a minute. "If that's Guillaume's idea of a compliment, I hope he never takes it into his head to insult me!"

When Tristan departs (promising that it's to practice faithfully), as soon as he's safely gone, I force myself to get up. There's one more thing I have to do to put the episode behind me.

I seek Jurian out in his room. The door swings open at my knock, and when Jurian sees the look of sympathy on my face, he ushers me into the room and closes the door.

"So you know," he says tonelessly.

"Yes," I say simply. "Jurian, I'm so sorry."

"You, sorry! I'm the one who should be sorry," he says bitterly, not looking me in the eye. "Believe me, Marek, I didn't know what he was going to do, not until it was too late. And even then, I didn't really know, I couldn't be sure ..." he falters.

"You just knew," I finish for him.

"Yes," he admits, and he looks so guilty and wretched, I say impulsively,

"I forgive you."

Jurian sits heavily on his cot and puts his head in his hands.

"You were almost kicked out. You were beaten. It could have killed you, if they'd given you all ten. How can you forgive me?" he asks. And I decide to risk the truth.

"Because," I say, "you were right. We do have a lot in common."

Jurian's face melts and he puts his arms up around my waist and buries his head against my stomach. This time, I'm the one who reaches down to ruffle his hair comfortingly.

"It'll be okay, Jurian," I say helplessly. "Why don't you find someone else?"

"Why don't you?" he says derisively, and I realize just how meaningless my words really are, and I hug him tighter.

THAT NIGHT I DO MAKE IT TO EVENING MESS, AND I EVEN manage to sit for the meal. I think that's a triumph enough, but then Tristan does something that surprises me. We've all finished eating, and the squires have cleared all the plates away. We're at the point in the evening that everyone likes best, when we're all sitting around talking and drinking, just winding down from the day. It's already late, so even though nobody else has left yet, when Tristan gets up, I think we're leaving. I start to get up, too, when he motions me back down and bangs his tankard on the table for attention.

"Gentlemen," he says, imitating Master Guillaume's voice and mannerisms so well that some of the others laugh. "Certain unfortunate recent events in the squires' barracks cannot have failed to make themselves known to all of you," he says sternly, still imitating Guillaume, and I dart a nervous look at Jurian. I have no idea where Tristan is headed with this, but Jurian just rolls his eyes; he doesn't know, either. "And I think you would all agree that our boys have done us proud," he says, raising his tankard first to Remy, then to me. "Moreover, I think it is safe to assume that there is not one of us now who would dare to accuse our very own Marek here of being a thief." I'm taken aback, and as Tristan looks challengingly around the table, I think at first so is everyone else. But slowly, first Charles, then Jerome, and soon everyone else starts pounding their tankards in assent rhythmically on the table.

Tristan lets the noise continue for a full minute, then he puts up his hand. He's not done yet.

"And so, I think it is safe to return this to him, and I hereby formally present it to him to serve as a sign of his bravery and his honor in defending a fellow member." As he says this, he pulls the medal he took from me in the alley out of a fold in his tunic, comes around the table to stand behind me, and slings it around my neck.

"You've earned it, kid," he whispers in my ear as he pats me on the back, while I slip the little medal safely under my tunic. I think I have earned it, too, and I'm immensely proud of the public show that Tristan's made of returning it to me, but for some reason, the little medal feels heavy around my neck. It feels almost like I've taken up a burden again.

CHAPTER TWENTY-TWO

Ⅰt takes me a full two weeks to recover from my beating enough to resume my regular duties. By this time it's mid-July, and Seconds are only about a month away. I've been itching to get back to practice; I've got my end of our exhibition trick to perfect, and I'm still convinced that I've got to set my mind to figuring out a new approach for training Tristan. I can see a big improvement in his strength, so I'm beginning to think that with a little luck, with Tristan's accuracy we'll probably manage wands well enough, but it isn't too early to worry about clouts. I'm determined to see him all the way through.

On the first afternoon that Tristan lets me come out for afternoon practice, I'm met by a strange sight as I emerge from the stables onto the field. Gilles is directing his two serving boys, who are struggling to roll an awkward wooden contraption out to a mark on the far butts. The thing looks like a platform on wheels, mounted with an upright wooden beam like the mast of a ship. Near the top of the mast, a smaller plank juts forward at a ninety-degree angle. It does look for all the world like a miniature gallows.

"What is that, Gilles?" I ask, making my way over to where he's gesticulating wildly and yelling at the boys.

"Haven't you met?" he asks. "It's Pascal!"

"He's looked better," I quip.

"Just wait a minute, dear boy, and I'll demonstrate."

So I wait, as the boys maneuver the structure across the uneven ground until it's resting at the 200 yard mark and the perpendicular plank at the top is facing back toward the line, and Gilles is finally satisfied with its position.

"Ah, look. Just in time," he exclaims, as the real Pascal appears at the garden gate. We wait as he makes his way over, rather reluctantly, it seems to me.

"Look, Marek. Isn't it clever?" Gilles says. "It's for our exhibition. Show him, Pascal."

Pascal sighs and steps over to stand next to the contraption. The top of the perpendicular plank near the top of the mast is the exact height of the top of his head. Gilles pulls an apple out of his quiver, polishes it on his sleeve, and places it gingerly atop the plank.

"You see? I can practice my shot until it's perfected, without endangering Pascal. Come on, let me show you how it works!"

Gilles is already striding purposefully back to his station, so I follow behind, falling into step beside Pascal, who's plodding along dejectedly.

"He's really taking this quite far, isn't he?" I say merrily. Leave it to Gilles to take a joke to extremes. "I bet it's really getting under Aristide's skin. But you must know what he's actually planning to do at Seconds. Everybody's wondering. Can you tell me? I bet it'll be pretty impressive."

"Don't kid yourself, Marek," Pascal says glumly. "He's really going to do it."

"All right, don't tell me, then," I say huffily.

By the time we get back to the line and Gilles is nocking an arrow, Tristan joins us.

"Oh, good, you're just in time to witness Pascal Number Three's virgin run!" Gilles exclaims. "The last two iterations weren't quite satisfactory. The boys have just finished this one. Let's see how this baby does!"

The serving boys are still hovering around the structure, but when Gilles yells out "Fast!" at them in an exasperated tone, they don't move.

"I don't think they know what that means, Gilles," Tristan says. "They mostly work in the kitchens. Hey, you!" he calls out, "Get out of the way, or he'll have every right to shoot you!"

"Thank you, old boy," Gilles drawls, as the servants go scooting off in two directions in a panic. "Now, watch this!"

And he lets the arrow fly. And it does stick fast — in the main beam, about two inches below the apple, about where Pascal's nose would have been.

"Not bad, for a first try," Gilles beams.

I look around for Pascal, but he's nowhere to be seen. I find him about five minutes later. This time, he's the one vomiting quietly behind a rosebush.

OUR OWN PRACTICE THAT AFTERNOON DOESN'T GO particularly well, either. I still think our idea for a trick is a good one, but I'm out of shape and practicing it is proving problematic. What with our trick and Gilles's, finding enough apples is proving to be tricky. Today Tristan's gotten ahold of a bag of turnips from the kitchen, the remains of which he says he's going to have to return at the end of the day. The thought that later we'll be eating a supper that we've been tossing around the butts all afternoon isn't very appetizing.

It doesn't take long to figure out that the key to perfecting the trick is going to be finding a way for me to throw the apples consistently (or turnips, as the case may be). I'm distinctly nervous about a trick that requires my precision as much as Tristan's, and throwing the turnips accurately is turning out to be quite a challenge. We've agreed that I'll stand about 200 yards from Tristan. For wands, there has to be some distance, but if we're any further apart, we won't be able to read each other's signals correctly, so this is as far as we dare.

"Let's try having you throw the turnips about 60 yards into the air," Tristan suggests, but I can't figure out how to estimate the distance accurately straight up, and I'm having trouble throwing that far. Even when I do give a good throw, I can't replicate it. With the minimal height I manage to get, Tristan doesn't have long to shoot the turnips before they're falling dangerously close to me, and so I end up taking quite a few turnips to the head.

"Try throwing them out from your body, not straight up," he

suggests, and this does help. I take fewer lumps, but I'm getting even less height now, and my throws are even more erratic. I'm getting so tired of having my strength be an issue with everything, and my still throbbing legs get tired quickly from all the bending to pick up the turnips, which are distressingly intact after an hour's work, that I'm the one who suggests we call an early end to it. I'd thought having about a month until Seconds sounded like a long time. Now I wonder if a year would be enough for me to perfect this trick.

As we're coming in, unfortunately we run into Taran and Remy. Taran smirks when he sees the bag of turnips.

"Practicing your farming, duBois?" he sneers. "I suppose it is wise to have a fallback career in mind."

"I hope yours isn't comedy," Tristan says smoothly, and Taran's face reddens. "Actually," he continues, as always encouraged by how easy it is for him to best Taran verbally, "I *was* planning to plant these turnips." He takes one out of the bag. "And if you'd kindly bend over, I know just where to plant the first one."

Remy steps lightly in front of Tristan, so that he's between Tristan and Taran, and says solicitously in his innocent way,

"I do love turnips. Can I help you carry the bag, Marek? You mustn't tire yourself too soon." It's a clever reminder of the beating I took for him, and it works. Taran's nostrils flair and he twists his lips as though he can barely contain himself from making a comeback to Tristan's insults, but instead he sets his lips in a thin line and growls,

"He's hardly an invalid after just two strokes. He can carry his own bag."

And then he's hauling Remy off across the field. Tristan's still got the turnip in his hand, and when I hear him toss the turnip a few times in his hand and start to whistle softly, I catch his eye.

"Don't even think about it," I tell him. He'd be just reckless enough to send it flying right into Taran's receding back. I almost wish he would. But I'm not that foolish.

We go out to the windmill for the first time in weeks that afternoon, too. The woods are hot and humid, full of new smells, making it feel like even longer since I've been out and away from the guild. On the way, we stop at a stream and sit on a fallen log, pulling off our boots to trail our feet in the cool water. It feels marvelous. In fact, it feels marvelous just to be able to sit without too much discomfort. I splash happily, watching the silver water ripple and flow over our toes.

"Tristan," I say slowly. "You are an extraordinarily good-looking boy."

"I sense a 'but' coming. Am I right?"

"Yes. *But* ... you have very ugly feet!"

He laughs. "You sound disappointed."

"You have no idea," I say.

When we make it to the meadow that spreads out below our windmill, I hardly recognize it. It's been transformed by summer. All the red poppies are gone. They've been replaced by cornflowers, so that the meadow now really resembles a sea, shining blue in the hot July sun, as the taller lacy white wildflowers mingled with them sway in the faint breeze like whitecaps on its waves.

"All the wounds are gone," I say stupidly, but I think Tristan knows what I mean.

"If only that were true," he replies.

As we wade through the sea of cornflowers, I ask him,

"Have you ever seen it? The ocean?"

"No. But I'd like to, one day. Maybe, when this is all over, we'll go to Bruges, and find a ship. Sail away for adventure. What do you say?"

"You're forgetting," I tell him. "When this is all over, I can't go with you. You'll be in the Guards."

He laughs, but I think that's the first time I realize that if I do somehow manage to achieve my dream for him, it'll have to mean goodbye.

I'm no better than Jurian. I haven't wanted to think about the inevitable future, either.

When we climb back over the wall later that afternoon, Taran and Remy are still on the field practicing. Of course. The guy never quits. Remy must not be as fragile as he seems, to keep up with him. Tristan's already gone in and I'm splashing myself off at the rain barrels when Remy comes over, looking sweaty and disheveled but as perky as ever.

"Where have you been, Marek?" he asks innocently. "Just where do you two go off to?"

I hesitate. There's no real reason why I shouldn't tell Remy about the windmill. I'm sure plenty of the other boys know it exists. They must have run across it when out in the woods themselves. But I'm torn. After the flask incident, I owe Remy real friendship now, but the windmill belongs to Tristan and me. It feels like a betrayal to mention it to someone else, particularly Taran's squire. But it's so hard to deny Remy anything, and he looks so much like the little mouse figurine he gave me, I find myself telling him all about it. What real harm can it do?

Before long, Remy goes in, too, and I'm alone again, or so I think, when I hear a voice behind me.

"So, I see the hero of the barracks is all better again. How grand."

It's Aristide. I turn around to find him leaning against the wall, looking down his long, aristocratic nose at me with distaste. He's impeccably dressed, and he doesn't look like he's been practicing. I wonder what he's doing here. Then I see his eyes flit out to the field; Gilles is still at the far butts, shooting at his contraption. He didn't come here looking for me. He's been watching Gilles.

"I seem to be the only one who remembers how you came to be here in the first place," he continues, his voice thick with disgust. "Can I be the only one who remembers that you really are a thief?"

When I don't say anything, he smiles. "I'm sure you remember it, though, don't you? I'm sure you remember everything about it." In one smooth move, he pushes off the wall and takes a sudden step toward me, and he pulls back his leg as though he's about to give me a swift kick on the back of my calf with those polished boots of his, right where the second lash whipped me. When I cringe, he pulls up short and laughs out loud.

"Don't worry, Woodcock," he sneers. "I was just jogging your memory." Only it does bring the memory of his boot kicking me painfully in the alley rushing back, and now that I've weathered a worse beating, my indignation makes me foolish. I know he's just a coward, picking on me because he doesn't have the guts to confront Gilles, and so in my anger I blurt out,

"Do you see what Gilles has built out there, Ari?" I think we're both shocked at my daring in calling him by this nickname, and seeing him caught off guard makes me bolder. "It's a gallows, and it's going to be your funeral! It's going to be the disgrace of pluck-buffet all over again, only this time, all of Louvain is going to be watching!"

As I turn heel and march back into the guild, leaving an astonished Aristide gaping behind me, for a moment I feel triumphant. But as I make my way alone along the long, dark corridor toward the barracks, I begin to wonder if throwing a turnip at Taran mightn't have been a less dangerous thing to do. Why can't I learn to keep my mouth shut? I wish Tristan had been there to stop me, as I'd stopped him. The thing is, I *do* remember everything about that day in the alley. In particular, I remember how it was actually Aristide who instigated my beating there in the first place, and it now occurs to me that he might well have been the one who really pushed me up against the wall at the sideboard. Winning so many friends over the past few weeks has made me careless. I should have been more careful not to antagonize an old enemy.

WHEN THE NEXT NIGHT IS DECLARED A FREE NIGHT, IN preparation for our local Saint Margaret's festival the following day, Remy declares his intention of organizing a special outing to treat me at the Drunken Goat. He's been waiting to have the opportunity so eagerly I can't refuse, and I don't want to, anyway. I feel like celebrating. I haven't stopped thinking about how the squires stepped up to defend me: Pascal running for assistance, Armand and Pruie begging the master to let me face the lash dressed, and Auguste and the others helping me gently to the floor. Above all others is the memory of Remy snatching the flask off my cot in the first place. At least something good did come out of the beating; there's a camaraderie in the barracks now like never before.

When I ask Tristan if he's coming, he begs off. "This is a night for you squires, Marek. Enjoy it," he says, and I appreciate the sentiment. It will be different, without the Journeys around hogging all the attention. Still I can't help wishing he was going to be there.

"You'll be glad enough later that I'm not," he insists, when I say so. "I can't help myself, kid. This is your night. You don't want me around upstaging you." And I guess he's right. I must still look petulant, though, so he offers to stand guard while I take a real bath in preparation, but I'm too leery about getting the still-healing cuts on my legs wet to take him up on his offer. I manage to clean up pretty well without submerging, however, and as I survey the results in the polished metal disk that serves as a mirror in the Journey lavatory, I think I look quite presentable. My shoulders look bigger and wider than the last time I really looked at myself, and my face is more weathered and thinner. Armand's given me a decent haircut, too, and today, with a little imagination I can fancy that the scars on my face make me look as though I've been in tough combat and come out victorious. Maybe I will end up looking something like Baylen, in time. Maybe I am a hawk, after all.

The others have all made an effort to look good, too, so when we finally assemble to head off to the Goat, my spirits lift. It's going to be a good night. All the squires are coming, and though we might not challenge the Journeys, we make a pretty impressive crew. Armand and Pascal, of course, could be Journeys themselves, but even Rennie looks cleaner than usual. Everyone's made an effort for me, and I decide Tristan was right. It's squires' night, and we're going to set Louvain on fire.

Well, within reason. I haven't forgotten my last night at the Drunken Goat. I promised myself I'd never get that drunk again, and I mean to keep my promise. Even out with just the squires, I've got to be careful not to give myself away. I make a mental promise not to have more than three ales, or whatever they're serving. What can happen on three?

It's already about the eleventh hour by the time we bust into the Goat, but if we were hoping to cause a stir, we're disappointed. There's not much of anyone here. Apparently, a bunch of squires from St. Sebastian's isn't enough to draw a crowd and our entrance is less than spectacular, but it can't quell our spirits. But as we're seating ourselves at the same table in the center of the room that the Journeys occupied the last time we were all here together, I notice with dismay that we aren't the only ones from St. Sebastian's here.

Already seated at a table in the corner are Aristide, Turk, Falko, and Taran. Falko greets my blank stare with a friendly wave of his cup, but I don't like the nasty smile on Aristide's face, and of course Taran just looks dour as usual. Turk is probably already drunk. It doesn't take much with him.

"What are they doing here?" I ask, rather rudely. Nobody said Journeys weren't allowed to come out on their free night, after all.

"*Tee hee*," Remy titters. "After last time, Taran wouldn't let me come alone. I think he means to keep an eye on me." He sounds rather pleased about this sign of how protective Taran is of him, so I stifle the sarcastic remark that rises to my lips. Besides, even I can't deny it's true. Remy was sick all day after his last overindulgence. Taran has a perfect excuse for being here. Falko can be relied upon to show up for any drinking party, and Turk is innocuous enough.

But Aristide is another matter. I don't like it.

By the end of my first drink, though, I've managed to forget about the Journeys. They're keeping to themselves, and I'm sitting between Remy and Auguste with my back to them, across from the much more pleasant prospect of Armand and Pascal. We've mostly been occupied toasting each other in increasingly outlandish terms, but it doesn't take long for the boys to start teasing me about Roxanne, too. Pascal is particularly vocal about urging me to go find her, and I've noticed he's not on his first drink, by a long shot. He's been throwing them back, and I get alarmed for him when he starts standing up periodically and calling out, "Where are all the girls, for the love of St. Peter?!"

I sincerely hope Gilles hasn't been foolish enough to give him any money.

By my second drink, I'm pretty sure the drinks here are stronger than I remember, so I resolve to keep it to two, but Remy won't hear of it.

"Three, you said, Marek. One for each lash."

"I only took two, Remy," I remind him. He already seems a bit drunk. I begin to be glad Taran's here, after all. Someone is going to have to rein him in soon.

"Well, one for each one you didn't take, then," he says illogically. But he's treating, so what can I say? Just one more won't hurt.

I'm in the middle of the third drink when things start to go wrong. Pascal has gotten quite hard to control, and Armand's taken to sitting almost on his lap to keep him from climbing onto the table in imitation of Tristan. Rosalinde has appeared, and he keeps threatening to demand to see her. I'm about to suggest that we go, when I do catch sight of Roxanne. She's near the back under the stairs, and I have my first pricking of apprehension when I see that she's standing in a group that includes Rosalinde, and of all people, Aristide. I try to catch her eye, but when she sees me gesticulating, she blushes fiercely and turns away. It's Aristide who turns to look me in the eye, and the gloating expression on his face confirms my fears. Something is wrong, and I'm sure I'm about to reap the wages of baiting a bully.

Pretty soon Rosalinde herself saunters over to the table, much to Pascal's delight. He tries to rise to greet her, even though Armand is sitting on him so heavily he resembles an insect squirming under a child's thumb. But Rosalinde isn't paying any attention to Pascal. Instead, she comes over to stand behind me and Remy.

"Evening, boys," she says in a sultry voice that must have taken a lot of practice to get just right. "I hear this is a special evening for one of you lucky young men. Being treated out to a night on the town by his friends. Is that right?"

The squires are all so thrilled that Rosalinde herself is deigning to grace our table that they fall all over themselves trying to be the first to answer and to get her attention. She's being gracious enough, but I feel apprehensive. I can't imagine why she's bothering with us.

"So, let me guess, which one of you is Marek?" she muses, pretending to look us over and size us up. It's just a game, though. She clearly already knows who I am, and I know who's told her (all Aristide would have had to say is, 'the one with the scars'). I just don't know why. She takes her time about it, making it a tease. It drives the boys wild. Pascal has started virtually pummeling Armand on the back in his desperation to extricate himself, but Armand is either too good a friend or too drunk himself to notice. He ignores it.

Rosalinde's been slowly sauntering back and forth behind our bench. Now she comes to a stop behind me, and I feel her eyes rest on me. She puts a hand on my head, and runs her fingers slowly through my hair. It makes the hairs on the back of my neck stand on end. I'm not sure why, but I'm thoroughly frightened now. She leans down, as though to whisper something in my ear, but when she speaks she's using a voice designed to allow the whole table to hear her words clearly.

"This really is your lucky day, Marek. Luckier than you thought! Why, your friends have banded together to get you a little present. A conquest, for the conquering hero! What do you think of that?"

My mouth has gone dry. I'm not entirely sure what she's talking about, but I'm beginning to have a guess. So are some of the others, from the looks of it. Rennie's eyes have gone wide, and Auguste's mouth falls open.

"Lucky dog!" Pascal croaks, and Rosalinde laughs heartily.

"That's right, boys! Tonight, your friend Marek here becomes a man."

She pulls a fat purse out from between her breasts and waves it over the table. Even if I didn't recognize it, I'd know it was Aristide's.

"She's all bought and paid for. And she's waiting for you, upstairs."

Rosalinde gestures toward the balcony, and I can hardly bear to look up, because I know what I'm going to see. Sure enough, when I force my eyes upward, there's Roxanne, peeking shyly out from behind one of the doors at the end of the hall that's open just a crack. My stomach flips over and I feel color surging into my face, and I'm so angry and scared for a minute that at first I don't even hear the babble of excited male voices around me or feel the table shaking under the force of fists pounding on the table.

"What are you waiting for, Marek?" Rennie slurs. "If he's not going to go up, I am!"

"She's his girl, you idiot!" Auguste replies excitedly. They clearly all think this is a wonderful idea. "Don't disappoint her, Marek!" he laughs.

"Yes, Marek," a satiny voice purrs behind me. It's Aristide. He's glided over to enjoy his handiwork up close. "Sorry I couldn't spring for something a little more, shall we say, *decorative*, but I'm a bit low on funds right now. You understand. But in the dark, you won't be looking at that face of hers, will you? And she won't have to look at yours!" He gives a sharp laugh, then leans in so close that his long, twitching weasel's nose is almost touching mine, and adds under his breath, "You do make quite a nice matched pair, don't you?"

Before I can react, he straightens up and smiles around at the boys at the table, raising his arms as though in recognition of public approbation, the way he did when he tossed a purse to our table that other night. I feel sick at the way he's treating offering up Roxanne as lightly as he offered up a drink. I feel even sicker when he says loudly so everyone can hear,

"Oh, don't worry about any *deficiencies*," he drags out the word unpleasantly and looks down pointedly at my lap so that there can be no mistaking his meaning. "Just remember what they say, 'for girls and chicken, you need to use your hands,' and you'll do just fine. I'm sure you can figure out *something* satisfying to do."

This elicits appreciative catcalls from Benoit and Rennie and the others are all wiggling their fingers suggestively, and I just can't believe they can't see it. Aristide isn't trying to reward me. He's punishing me. But Aristide has chosen his audience well. The boys are either too drunk or too young and callow to see what he's really doing.

I jump to my feet and glare at him, shame and rage blazing on my face, but it's the reaction he's been hoping for, and he smiles triumphantly.

"Now if you really feel you can't *get up* for it," he sneers, "I suppose I'll have to fill in. She's paid for, after all."

He makes a move to push past me and head for the stairs, and I make a grab for his arm. I have to do something. He turns to me, his eyebrows raised as if to say, "What's it going to be?"

What can I do? I take a deep breath, and say:

"Nobody's going to go up to my girl's room tonight, but me."

A cheer goes up from the squires as I square my shoulders, throw my head back in a mock attitude of courage, and mount the stairs, as slowly and deliberately as a man headed to the gallows. But Aristide is getting the last laugh, literally. The sound of his laughter follows me all the way to the top step, ringing out loud and clear even above the joyous din the boys are making; it's my funeral, after all.

I have no idea what I'm going to do, of course. I haven't had time to think that far. I just know I can't let them make a joke of us. The boys, well, I know they don't mean anything by it, but I can't let Aristide belittle us. As selfish as it sounds, it's probably his taunts about my ability to go through with it more than his insults of Roxanne that propel me up the stairs. After standing up to the lash (or rather, lying down to it), I won't let him turn the night meant to celebrate my bravery into a farce where what everyone remembers is that I couldn't really act like a man.

But as the door closes behind me and I find myself alone with Roxanne, all I feel is panic.

The shabby little room is sparsely furnished. In one corner, there's a wooden chair and two small tables just large enough to provide a resting place for the smoking oil lamps that light the room, and on the wall hangs a hideous still life depicting a vase of waxy flowers with a dead pheasant lying next to it. None of this really registers.

All I see is the bed.

I suppose it's just the usual size, but it seems to loom out of the half-dark like a crouching elephant, and until my eyes adjust, it even seems to be growing. Roxanne's back is still to me; she's as nervous as I am, and I sense that she's taking her time closing the door behind me in order to put off having to turn around and face me. That suits me just fine. I've begun to pick at my fingers, and the air has grown so hot and stuffy in the room that I even imagine I can smell the cloying scent of the painted flowers so strongly that I feel like gagging. I know just how the pheasant feels.

It seems like I've already been in that room for hours when I finally hear the soft click of the bolt, and Roxanne turns to face me. She hasn't lifted her head or said anything, yet even in the soft glow of the lamp I can see her blush, and there's a trace of a faint, shy smile on her lips as she raises a trembling hand to her dress and starts to slip it slowly down from her shoulder. She's freed both shoulders and is holding the dress up over her chest with both hands before I can find my voice to stop her. There's even a horrible moment when I think I might let her fully undress, and not even because I'm still too paralyzed to speak.

I have to admit, I'm extremely curious. It's true she's small and delicate, but she's nicely curved. She's got what they call a good figure, and this would surely be my only chance to see what the body of a girl my age is supposed to look like.

Shame at the thought that I might let her continue just to satisfy my curiosity and compare her body with my own shakes me out of my trance, but it's only when she's lifted her eyes to mine and said, *"Marek"* in a such a throaty voice that I realize just how selfish I've been. As astonishing as it sounds, she *does* think she's my girl. I guess she knew she never had a chance with Tristan, but without meaning to and just to protect my own image, I let her think she had a chance with me. There's nothing that fuels affection as much as the thought that it might be returned. How unfair I was to chastise Tristan, when it turns out I've done everything to Roxanne I accused him of doing to Melissande! I just did it without any flair or style. Because I know that look. Roxanne's in love with me. Or at least, she wants me to love her. Maybe it's the same thing. And now she's in danger of being hurt more than if I'd just let Aristide come up in my place.

"Marek," she repeats again shyly, her cheeks so red by now that the mark on her face is barely distinguishable on her flushed face. "I want you to know. It's my first time."

Oh God. Can it get any worse?

I give myself a shake. Where's my courage? My knees have started to tremble, and any moment, my teeth are going to start chattering. Facing her is almost as bad as facing Baylen's lash, but it's got to be done. If I'm not quick she's going to drop her dress, and then it will be too late. I step forward and put a restraining hand over hers.

"Don't, Roxanne," I say as gently as I can, but my voice sounds harsher than I intend, and I can hear it crack. "Please, I don't want you to."

We stand there a moment, her looking down and me with my hand over hers, both trembling, and then miserably I see a tear start to trickle down her cheek. I'm startled by the sight of her tears; usually, I'm the one who's crying.

"Please, Roxanne," I say. "This isn't what I want for you. This isn't what you deserve." When she doesn't respond, I can't take the tension any longer. I sit down heavily on the edge of the bed and run my hands through my hair in exasperation. I'm only vaguely aware that it's the first time I've done this move typical of Tristan.

"Is it ..." she falters, putting a hand up involuntarily to her cheek. "Is it my face?" she says bitterly, still without looking at me, and I despise myself. The unfairness of it all finally stirs me to action — not just how Aristide's set us up, but the mark on her face, and the ones on mine.

I reach up and pull her gently down so that she's sitting on the edge of the bed next to me, and I take one of her hands in mine. With the other hand, I lift her chin and tilt her face up so that we're looking at each other, and when she tries to turn away, I don't let her. I let my eyes search her face, really looking at her in a way that I'm sure few people do. I know nobody ever lingered over my face when I was a girl. In fact, she reminds me so sharply of Marieke that I'm suddenly filled with such a strong sympathy for her that I'm sure my emotions must show, and in response, Roxanne's expression softens, a little.

I move my hand from beneath her chin, but now she doesn't try to turn away. Slowly, I run my fingers over the mark on her face, tracing its outline gently, touching each contour.

"You have a lovely face, Roxanne," I say, meaning it. "Every inch of it." Then I find my hand has moved to the scars on my own face, as I say, "Don't wish it away. It's your mark of distinction. Anyone can love an unblemished face. When you find someone who can find beauty in what sets you apart, you'll know you're truly appreciated. You and I, we're lucky. We've had a narrow escape."

I'm not sure what brings these words to mind, but as soon as I say them, I know they're right. Physical beauty hasn't helped Jurian any, or even Melissande, really. But I'm also fully aware that this means little to Roxanne at the moment. My words are cold comfort, since what I'm really saying is that I don't love her, and she knows it.

"It's all right, Marek," she says quietly. "You can just say it. You don't want me." She looks so sad and small, so disappointed, so much like the girl I used to be, that I can't bear to let her down.

This fragile, delicate girl was looking to me to be her champion, and I can't bear not fulfilling her expectations. I suddenly feel like being one.

I feel, in fact, a lot like Tristan.

I drop dramatically down onto my knees in front of her, and clasp both her hands in mine.

"Roxanne!" I cry, in real anguish. "You don't understand. I wish more than anything that I did love you, that I could love you! How much happier I would be! How lucky I would be to win you, to deserve you! But it's impossible. I'm not free to love you. You see …" and now, I think she deserves the truth, too. At least, part of it. "I'm in love with someone else. I already was, when I first met you."

She's been frowning slightly through this speech, but I think the gallantry of it has done something to soften the blow.

"Do you plan to marry?" she asks, a bit unevenly.

I shake my head. Using Falko of all people for inspiration, I say, "Nothing like that. The one I love is so far above me, there's no question of marriage. I can't even declare myself. But," and I fling my head back and use an intonation that sounds suspiciously like Tristan's top–of–the–wall voice, "I've sworn a sacred vow before St. Sebastian himself, to love chastely and from afar, to devote my life to an unrequited love."

It's probably too much, but I think Tristan would approve. The most bizarre part of it is that it's really nothing but the truth.

It seems to have the desired effect. Roxanne is looking distinctly less upset. In fact, as I speak, her injured look transforms into surprise, then, I think, admiration. It encourages me to keep going. I can see how girls spur boys on without intending to; the adoring look she's giving me now is irresistible.

"Ah, my lady," I say, bending to kiss the palm of her hand, "If only I were free! As it is, I implore you, let me offer you my love, but the love of a friend, which I sincerely hope I am already to you! Nay, more than a friend, a sist— er, I mean, a brother!" By now, Roxanne's eyes are positively shining, and fresh tears are flowing down her face. But I'm just getting warmed up. Tristan was right; he's been a terrible influence on me. I pull the St. Sebastian's medal that Tristan returned to me out from beneath my tunic, and I slip it off from around my neck. I put it in her hand, and then fold my own around hers.

"With the Saint as witness, let me swear a new vow, here and now! I swear always to be your protector and servant, if ever you need one, to the best of my ability! I put my life in your hands, to be at your disposal, though my heart cannot fully be so!"

At this, finally, she laughs, and I'm so relieved I laugh, too. I drop the histrionics and plop down on the bed next to her, and with a smile I slip the medal around her neck.

"Can we be friends, then, Roxanne? Real friends?" I ask seriously, and she nods. I've been putting on a performance and we both know it, but there was enough real emotion behind it that I think I've convinced her to see what happened here as something other than a rejection.

"You aren't really giving me this, are you, Marek?"

"Yes," I say, only just deciding it. "It's probably safer with you, anyway. Keep it for me, will you? As a token of my vow."

"Oh, I'll remember your vow, without a token!" she laughs, but then promises solemnly, "I'll wear it always."

I think we must be done, but when I rise to go she stops me.

"Will you sit with me a while, Marek?" she asks, then blushes again furiously. "I don't want them to think, well ..." and she doesn't have to finish. She doesn't want everyone downstairs to think I've rejected her, and frankly, I don't want them to think I have, either, even without Aristide's threat to get his money's worth one way or another. Only when I sit down again, there doesn't seem to be anything to say.

"Tell me about her," Roxanne says at length, so I do. It's difficult, though, and not only because the pronouns give me some trouble; it's hard to explain Tristan in terms that make any sense outside the context of the guild. Yet in the vaguest way imaginable, I try to convey how he saved me, befriended me and gave me purpose, how he gave me a new life that I love even more than the old one I lost. I'm sure Roxanne can't quite figure out how some girl I apparently never see and who is so above me I can't speak to her did all this for me, but I suppose she takes it as typical male hyperbole. How surprised she'd be to know that in this case, it's all true. I end ironically with,

"You could say with truth, that it's this love that first made me into a man."

She rolls her eyes, and I add dramatically, "Yet I never felt more like a man than tonight, with you!"

Roxanne giggles, and this is really all I intend — to make her laugh. But Rosalinde was right, in a way. Maybe I haven't really become a man tonight, but I do feel that here in this room with Roxanne, playing to her expectations, I've gotten a glimpse of what the whole male-female relationship is like from the man's point of view. It doesn't seem any easier from this side, either. But I've had a revelation. Maybe the main difference between men and women is just what's expected of them.

In the end, I stay talking with Roxanne so long that Rosalinde has to come and pound on the door, calling out "Okay, lover boy! Time's up!" to get me to come downstairs again.

It must be about the fourth hour and the boys are all the worse for it, but none of them have left (though I admit I don't see Turk anywhere, but he may have simply slipped under the table. I also notice that Remy is now sitting sullenly with the Journeys). They've all been waiting for me to reappear.

I've been gone so long and I must look like I've been through *something* upstairs — I've been through so much emotional turmoil and the air was so fetid in that little room that my face is red and sweating, and my hair is mussed from my own ruffling of it — and the boys are all drunk, so as soon as I appear on the landing, a general shout goes up from the floor below. Someone starts up a chant of *"Marek, Marek, Marek!"* and to my discredit, I break into a huge grin. I know what they're all thinking, but I *am* feeling pretty manly, and pretty damned relieved — pleased, even, with how I've handled the whole fiasco. So on impulse, I raise my arms in the air and give a bow of acknowledgment in imitation of Aristide. I go to the railing, and look down right at him, and put my hand to my forehead in a gesture of salute, as though thanking him. *Let him eat that!* I think smugly, as I literally strut down the stairs. *Let any of them think I've got deficiencies now* I think, too, not really as concerned as I should be about the fact that these supposed deficiencies are what explains my refusal to undress.

About halfway down the steps, a terrible thought hits me, and I instantly regret the impulse to antagonize Aristide. Haven't I learned anything? It occurs to me that he might still go upstairs, and that my gesture to him might just goad him into it. He's loaded. He can afford to pay twice. Maybe it's even been his plan all along — to humiliate me by using Roxanne himself. Bile twists in my stomach at the thought, but almost as soon as I think it, I realize how foolish it is. Aristide is a coward. It would be a serious breach of comradeship to treat another member's girl so crudely, and I doubt he'd really risk doing something so certain to turn all the boys against him. Not in front of them, anyway. So I resume my good humor, and as I reach the bottom of the stairs and move to join my friends, I let them all rally around me to congratulate me, and I find that I now fully enjoy being slapped on the back. Male bonding really is quite marvelous.

There are only two things that cast a shadow over my enjoyment of the moment, and both emanate from the Journeys' table. One is Aristide's ominous scowl. The other is the extremely speculative expression on Taran's usually impassive face.

CHAPTER
TWENTY-THREE

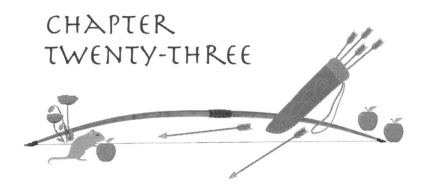

The next day, I can't find Tristan. After our late night, like most of the other squires I've slept in, since the Journeys have a rare morning off from practice for the devout to attend St. Margaret's mass in town at the cathedral, and when I wake up, I'm feeling distinctly pleased. News of my exploits is already making the rounds, and I can't wait to tell Tristan about it. I can't help but feel I handled the whole thing amazingly well; in fact, I secretly think he couldn't have done any better himself.

When I go along to Tristan's room, though, he isn't there. After a quick rap, I open the door and find the room empty except for Popinjay, who squeezes past me and disappears down the corridor as soon as the door opens.

It isn't like Tristan to lock the old dog in. He only does it when he really wants to be alone, like on the morning of Firsts, and it gives me a bad feeling. I didn't think anything of it at the time, but now it seems distinctly suspicious that he didn't say anything to me about what *he* was planning to do last night, and I have a horrible premonition. The only thing that comforts me is the thought that both Aristide and Taran were at the Goat last night, so whatever else he's done, at least it didn't involve killing either of them.

Out in the hall, I run into Auguste, and when I ask him about it, he answers with an embarrassed look,

"Tristan? He's already out on the butts, I think."

He doesn't need to say more. Tristan never starts practicing without me. I've got my squire's pride, and my master is usually very respectful of my prerogatives, as I think of them. But when I get out to the field, there's Tristan, sure enough. He's set himself up at point-blank range without waiting for me, even though this range is the last thing he needs to practice, and he's already shooting, his black quiver slung low on his own shoulder.

When I hurry over to him, he doesn't acknowledge me or even slow his pace. He just keeps pulling out arrow after arrow and shooting deliberately, with a shuttered look on his face, until the quiver is empty. Half the arrows aren't in the white, and despite the close range his last arrow misses the butt entirely. I know enough not to question him when he looks like this, and my foreboding that something happened last night increases. What could have happened to put him in such a foul mood?

When the last arrow is shot and he lowers his bow, I move to go and retrieve for him, but he stops me.

"Don't bother," he says, still not looking at me. His tone is so cold and harsh, a churning feeling stirs in the pit of my stomach. All my assurance from last night fails me, and I don't even have the courage to ask him what's wrong. The idea that I became a man last night is now laughable. Around Tristan, I'm reduced to being a child. *What in the world can have happened last night?* I wonder again, afraid to find out. We stand there for a while, me picking at my fingers, Tristan staring down at the bow in his hands, until finally he breaks the silence and says,

"I heard all about last night. I suppose you're pretty proud of yourself. Got the chance to set the nasty rumors to rest, did you? Well done, Marek." He says this last so sarcastically, I'm stunned. So that's it. For some reason, Tristan is mad at *me*, but I don't know what I've done. It doesn't make any sense. It's so much not what I expected that I don't have time to think it through. It doesn't occur to me to think about what version of last night Tristan has probably heard. His anger and his cold attack are so wounding, it just strikes me as horribly unfair, particularly when I was expecting such a different reaction.

"Maybe I am proud!" I lash out defensively. "After all your talk about girls, I would have thought you'd be proud of me, too!"

Tristan whips his head up and fixes me with a look filled with such loathing and disappointment that I stagger backward a step.

"Did you?" he says icily. "Then you don't know me very well."

It's so unjust, I feel myself getting angry, too.

"Who are you to judge?" I cry, and before I can think, I blurt out accusingly, "Are *you* a virgin?"

As soon as the words are out, I wish I could catch them back. I've been so curious, of course, but this isn't what I meant to ask. What made me say that, instead of just explaining what happened? I'm so embarrassed by my outburst, all I can do is wait for his response. But I know I've veered the argument into dangerous territory. I'm not even sure how we've gotten here.

He's silent a moment, and I'm sure he's not going to answer. Then he says simply,

"No." It's a straight answer, the last thing I expected. It throws me off.

"What right have you to judge me then?" I demand, but my bluster melts when I see his face. He's never looked so angry with me. Despite myself, one hand sneaks up to my throat. I don't think he'd really throttle me, but he's never given me a look like this before.

"Tristan, why are you so angry with me?" I plead, my voice coming out grating and wheedling, like a petulant child.

"You let them make that sweet, gentle girl into a whore."

The word is so ugly, so unlike Tristan, that it hits me like a slap in the face. It stings all the more because I can guess what it costs him to say it. He's used it just to hurt me, and it does.

"But Tristan, nothing happened!" I cry. When his mouth twists in disgust and he starts to turn away, I grab his sleeve. "I swear! Nothing happened. It, it, can't ..." I stammer, shame flooding me, not only because I can't stand his disappointment, but because he's right. I've been preening myself on being so gallant, on thinking I'd pulled the whole thing off in a fashion worthy of Tristan himself, but now I see how sordid it was. I didn't think past the moment, I didn't consider what it would mean for Roxanne.

He looks down at my hand on his sleeve, and I think he's about to thrust it away. Then something goes out of him and his shoulders droop.

"I believe you, Marek," he says heavily, "But it doesn't matter. They all think it did. It's the same thing. What's going to happen to her now? Did you even think about that?"

My hand drops slowly from his arm as tears start falling freely down my cheeks, but Tristan makes no move to comfort me or wipe them away. After a minute, he slings his bow over his shoulder and makes to go retrieve the arrows himself. When I try to follow, he says roughly, "Take the afternoon off."

"Tristan," I plead. "Let me explain. Come out to the windmill with me, please."

He hesitates, but when he replies, his voice is hard.

"Not today. I think we both need a break."

I don't have to ask to know he means he needs a break from me.

I'm so heartbroken as I make my way out over the wall and into the woods that I don't even feel the sharp eyes on me that have been watching the whole wretched scene from a vantage point under the stable eaves.

I'M NOT SURE WHY I DECIDE TO GO TO THE WINDMILL anyway. It isn't really a conscious decision. I simply find my feet taking me through the woods, following the familiar path I usually follow with Tristan. I think I hope that when he realizes where I've gone, he'll soften and come looking for me. I picture him bursting into the little room under the windmill's broken arms, a look of concern on his face that melts with relief when he finds me. But this is the first time I've made the trek without him, the first time I've been in the woods alone since the day I came to Louvain. After expecting his approbation, Tristan's disappointment has made me feel so bereft, so intensely lonely, I can almost imagine it's that day again. Now the woods seem full of alien, threatening sounds, just as they did then. When I reach the little stream where we sometimes stop, its gurgling sounds again like gushing blood; the birds startled from their hiding places in the thickets screech alarms; the rustling of branches in the wind seems to signal the approach of secret pursuers. I know it's my imagination; surely nobody's following me. But I've never longed for comforting arms as much since the day Tristan first found me in the alley, and gave me his.

When I come out into the brilliance of the field of cornflowers and see the sentinel windmill rising beyond it, I feel as though I've reached safe haven.

Up in the little room, though, I can't quite bring myself to open the shutters. I don't want to look out at St. Sebastian's, and the darkness of the room fits my mood. I drop down next to the window and rest my head on the sill, watching dust motes swirl in the thin rays of light coming in through the shutter's slats. I sit there for what feels like a long time, trying to let my mind go blank. At first, I know I'm waiting. I can't stop hoping that Tristan is going to come. Eventually, I have to accept it. Nobody else is coming here today. I'm all alone, and the guild is far away.

At first, all I feel is emptiness. Then slowly, I start to feel unease. It feels wrong, to be here in our place alone. I shouldn't have come. I've acted like a sullen child, running away to try to get attention, to try to force Tristan to follow me. I should know Tristan well enough by now to know that his mood will pass. I should have just given him some time, and then found a way to explain — about Aristide, about all of it. If Tristan's reaction was extreme or even unfair, it shouldn't really have been unexpected. I should have taken Gilles's warning about Tristan's past more to heart. It's my own sense of guilt that's made me overreact, and I've handled the whole thing badly. When Tristan knows what really happened, he'll forgive me, I'm sure. I should be able to forgive him, too, for thinking so badly of me. Maybe this old place *has* given me some perspective, I think, but it's time to go. It was foolish of me to come so far by myself. None of the boys ever venture out this way alone, and for good reason. I'm unarmed. I could have met up with a vicious animal, I could have fallen, and even here, the floorboards could give way. All kinds of accidents are possible. And if Tristan decides to stay mad at me, there's not another living soul who has any idea of where I've gone.

Suddenly, I'm acutely aware that I'm completely, utterly alone.

I'm slowly getting to my feet when I hear a sound that floods me not just with unexpected relief, but pure joy. Just when I'd given up all hope, Tristan's come, after all! He must still be angry with me, because his footfalls on the creaking stairs sound slower and heavier than usual, hesitant, even. But he's come! And now I think I know what to say to make it right between us. My heart is still beating wildly as I scramble to my feet and begin brushing the dust from my breeches in preparation of facing him. When I hear him reach the top of the stairs, as I look down to dust off my hands, I cry happily,

"I'm so, so glad you're here! I'm so glad you came, after all ..."

The words die on my lips, when I hear a familiar, cold voice behind me.

"Expecting me, Woodcock? How gratifying."

I wheel around, and even though I know what I'll find, the sight of Taran standing in the doorway shocks me into silence. He fills the whole frame of the little door, like a giant trying to fit through a keyhole, and I don't think I've ever been more aware of just how big he is. Last night with Roxanne I felt like a man. This morning with Tristan, I felt like a child. Now I feel like an ant. And it's not just his physical presence that intimidates me. It's the look on his face. His wooden look is gone, replaced by a fleeting look of triumph at catching me here, and then grim determination. He looks like he's steeling himself to do something that even he is going to find unpleasant. Whatever it is, I know I'm going to like it even less.

A cold wave of fear washes over me. The thing I've dreaded from the very first, the thing I told myself I could never let happen, has happened at last. I let Taran catch me alone, away from the guild.

I can feel sweat beading on my forehead and on the palms of my hands, which have begun to tremble as my insides writhe like snakes in a pit. But Taran hasn't moved from the doorway. I can't tell if he's savoring the moment, or if there's some chance that maybe he hasn't planned out exactly what he's going to do. Maybe he didn't think his attack through any further than cornering me. At least, now that we're in here together it seems like he's not at all sure how to proceed. Even though he's still across the room, the little airless chamber is so small that he feels dangerously close. Every breath he takes seems to expand and contract the walls of the room around me, until I'm breathing with him, and the tension of his indecision fills the small space so completely it's about to burst the creaky old room at its seams.

It's probably my imagination, but he almost looks like he could be struggling to find the words he wants to say, as though something about confronting me here alone has made him even more tongue-tied than usual.

"T-t-t-aran, I...I...I," I stammer, casting around wildly to find something of my own to say that might sway him, just as he finally says,

"So, what's the big secret out here?"

At the sound of my voice stuttering, irritation flashes across his features. He takes a step toward me, hissing through clenched teeth,

"Unbelievable! Are you *mocking* me?!"

Now he *really* looks like he doesn't know what he's going to do, but the thought doesn't comfort me. If anything, it scares me more, and whatever mood he came here in, thinking I've just taunted him for being inarticulate in the way my master often does has not improved it any.

He balls his hands up tightly into fists and he gives a snort like an angry bull, but he doesn't make another move. He's begun scanning the room as though he's looking for something, and all at once, I can't take the anticipation any longer. So I screw up my courage, stick out my chin, and I demand,

"Well, what are you waiting for?," but before I can get all the words out, Taran's eyes snap back to mine accusingly.

"I'm waiting, *Marek*," he says quietly, "for you to tell me what you're really doing here." And then he takes another step closer, opening and closing the fist of one hand. Whether he's preparing for violence or trying to restrain himself from it, I don't know. I don't wait to find out.

I'm beyond thinking clearly, so my body reacts automatically. I take a step backward, but there's nowhere to go. My heels hit the wall behind me, and the sill of the little window presses into my back. In a flash I twist around, turning my back on Taran, and with one big shove I push open the shutters. I gulp in the fresh air and look out at the clear blue sky. But I don't look down. I already know it's a ridiculously long drop. Behind me, I hear Taran's boots approaching across the creaking floorboards, his voice exclaiming,

"Damn it! What do you think you're doing?"

I don't know if I was really thinking of climbing out the window. I wasn't thinking anything, only that I had to escape, that I couldn't breathe. But at the sound of Taran closing the gap behind me, I don't hesitate. I reach my hands up and put them flat on the windowsill.

"For God's sake!" Taran cries, as he realizes I really am going out the window. "Are you insane?!" Only it's too late. With a leap, I propel myself halfway out the window.

My stomach flips as my feet come off the ground and I pitch forward. Below me the meadow spins, and there's nothing under my torso but air; my hips on the sill are the only thing keeping me from falling. I'm hanging upside down out the window with my arms stretched out in front of me, like a beam with an unbalanced load teetering precariously on a fulcrum.

I flail my arms around wildly, only there's nothing to grab. The windmill's arms are above me, and there's nothing at all between me and the ground — which is an awfully long way down. My tunic's come untucked from my waistband, too, and when it slides down and catches under my armpits, its suffocating folds press against my nose and mouth and I can't even get a breath to scream. Taran's right. I'm about to plunge to my death, and as soon as I think it, with a sickening slide I feel my hips slip, and I'm falling headlong.

My free-fall from the window must last only for a second. But in that petrifying moment when I'm pitching forward with no way to stop myself, I'm seized by sheer panic and I know what true terror is. The ground is rising up, and I'm hurtling down towards it — and as the meadow below me spins faster and I know I'm about to die, all I can think of is my father. My arms stretching out in front of me are reaching out for him, as he was when he lay dying. And as I plummet toward my certain death, I'm willing his arms to fold around me, one last time.

Then I do feel a pair of hands on my waist, firm and strong, hauling me backward through the window. I'm dizzy, and disoriented; but miraculously someone standing behind me is putting me back onto my feet, and I'm flooded by a relief so heady it's almost delirium. My head swims, and when I sway, a pair of big arms folds around me and I know it's Tristan. *He's come, after all!*

Somehow, he's come, and I'm finally in the comfort of his arms, just as I've been longing to be all morning.

I sink back against him heavily, letting my head rest back against his chest, and it's so good to be safely back inside the windmill that I hardly notice what a strange pose we're in, almost like we could be a pair of lovers, clasped in a reverse embrace. My heart is beating wildly, and I can feel his heart pounding, too, in a beat that's pulsing through me in rhythm with my own heartbeat. I can't think beyond how alive I feel, with all my senses heightened, and caught up in this strange moment of relief. I can't think beyond the feeling of the warm hand that's slipping around my waist, steadying me on my feet.

That is, until I feel his mouth so close to mine that his breath ruffles against my cheek, and his deep voice says,

"Well, *that* was a damned stupid stunt!"

It isn't Tristan, of course. It's Taran.

What's more, my tunic has ridden up in my fall. Taran's hand is resting flat against my bare skin.

I would never have thought Taran could have such a light touch, and as soon as I realize it's him, the shock of it sends an electric ripple up my spine and up the skin on my arms, raising the hairs there on end, too, until all my flesh is prickling. The rough callouses of his palm are skimming along the soft hair on my belly, so lightly it's as though he's trying not to touch me, so softly that the tickling feeling it produces is almost as though my skin is rising of its own accord to meet his hand.

And at that very moment, his hand comes to a stop, hovering over the slight swell of my belly, hesitating.

"So you *don't* have any scars here, do you?" he says.

I come back to myself in a flash.

With a jolt, I lurch forward. And when I stumble, Taran makes an instinctive grab to catch me back, and it all happens in an instant — too fast for me to stop it. His hand is still inside my tunic, and as I fall forward, his hand sweeps in a wide arc up across my bare midriff, up and under the now-loose binding around my chest.

"Watch it," he's exclaiming, when beneath the fabric of my binding his splayed fingers clasp the unmistakable swell of my left breast.

"*Whoa!*" he explodes, as he snatches both his hands violently away from me.

Immediately, I hit the floor. Taran's dropped me flat, and my legs are useless under me. He stands there, staring down at me and looking stunned, and I stare up at him, my eyes wide and my pulse racing.

To say that I'm shocked, too, is an understatement. Even though Taran's hand is gone, I can still feel the pressure of it on my skin, stinging like a slap, and it hardly matters that Taran too is holding out his hand in front of him in astonishment, or that he's at a loss for words again.

I'm completely in his power now, and we both know it:

Taran knows my secret.

My cheeks flame hot with shame, not only from the intimate contact of his hand, but also shame at being caught, shame at my failure. *How I wish now I'd made it out the window!* Horror doesn't come close to describing what I'm feeling.

How could I have let my guard down, to come here alone in the first place? How can I have not noticed that Taran was following me? Worst of all, how can I have let myself forget I was in danger even for an instant, just because Taran stopped me from climbing out a window — a window I was jumping out of to *escape* from him!?

I hang my head, and I don't bother to speak. What is there to say now? I've been careless, and I'm reaping the consequences. It's bad enough that it's over. That I'll have to say goodbye to Tristan. But I've let it be Tristan's enemy who discovers me. *How Taran will revel in my humiliation, and Tristan's!* What a fool I was to think I could end my days at St. Sebastian's on my own terms, or that being discovered publicly in the barracks was the worst that could happen! For Taran to be the one to reveal my disgrace, my ultimate betrayal of Tristan — it's too monstrous to contemplate. I really should have run away when I had the chance.

I can hear Taran now moving agitatedly around the room, cursing under his breath, and this time, I can't stand to wait for him to decide to act. I need this to be over. So I raise my head and look up at him. To my surprise, he doesn't look triumphant. He looks thoroughly shaken.

I suppose the reality that he's just been fondling a girl's naked torso is starting to sink in.

"What are you going to do to me?" I manage to ask, trying to sound defiant, but my throat doesn't seem to be working properly, and my breast is throbbing so violently where he held it that it's taking all my concentration to think of anything else.

Taran's stopped by the window to brace his hands on his knees and he's bent over as though he's trying to compose himself, but when I speak, he shoots me a menacing look. I must look as afraid as I feel, because at the sight of me, annoyance flashes across his face, and he says sarcastically,

"What, you don't think I'm going to do something ridiculously melodramatic, like *he* would, do you?"

He can't even bring himself to say Tristan's name, even though we're alone and I'm utterly in his power.

"Like *kill* you?" He gives a pathetic laugh. "Or, *molest* you?" He shudders, as though the thought of touching me again upsets him. It probably does. "Or strip you, and parade you back to the guild in chains?"

But he still doesn't say what he *is* going to do with me, and that's when I know that he doesn't know, either. Wisely, I say nothing, and after a minute he starts pacing around the room as though I'm not there, clenching his fists and muttering to himself and shaking his head.

"I can't believe it! A *girl*!? All right, maybe I *did* suspect it. In the tavern. When I saw your *feet*. But I couldn't really believe it ... I didn't really think ...!"

Then he turns back to me and explodes,

"*How in the hell could he do it?* Even for him, this is too much! How could he bring a *girl* to St. Sebastian's?!? What are you, lovers?" he snorts, but then he shakes his head without waiting for an answer. "No, you're too wretched for that." He starts pacing again. "I didn't think even he would dare go so far! And for what? Just to turn everything of mine to dust! Can't he leave me anything?"

He turns on me furiously, working himself up into a rage.

"What was he going to do, unveil you at Thirds? Or was he going to wait until I made Guards, and trot you out then, to make me a laughingstock, to turn my victory into a mockery? Isn't anything sacred to him? How dare he violate the honor of St. Sebastian's?!"

He flings his arms up in exasperation and resumes his pacing again. As he does, he keeps wiping his right hand on his breeches.

"Isn't there any rule sacred enough that he's not willing to break it? A *girl*. I was right about him all along! He has no honor at all."

He's come to a pause in front of me again, and he's about to start on another rant, when something guilty in my expression stops him. He closes his mouth suddenly, and peers down at me.

Slowly, a look of pure astonishment dawns on Taran's face.

"By all that's Holy! Sebastian and all the Saints! He doesn't know, does he?!" he cries, his voice incredulous and exultant at the same time. We stare at each other, and I know he can read confirmation on my face. Then he makes the most unexpected sound. It's deep and rumbling at first, but then he throws back his head and huge, booming laughter echoes through the little room.

"Hah!" he cries, between gasping for breaths. "How rich! Tristan, the ladies' man! With a *girl* for a squire, and he can't even tell! To hear him talk, he can smell a girl a mile away, and here he is with a girl right under his nose, and he doesn't even know it! Well, not much of one, I'll admit," he sneers down at me, "but what a joke!"

It's not his insults of me that rouse me from my stupor. But I can't stand to hear him belittling Tristan so unfairly, and what does it matter now, anyway? Taran *knows*. I think I'd even welcome a beating at this point. So I lift myself up, first onto my knees, then slowly up onto my feet as I speak, and I amaze even myself at my boldness when I burst out,

"What do *you* know about girls?! Nothing! And what do *you* know about honor, either? Where did you learn about honor, from your *father*?" I jeer at him recklessly. "Well, girls can have honor, too! And I *did* learn about honor from *my* father — who was a greater man than yours! *I'm* not the disgrace to St. Sebastian's. I'm a good squire, as good as any of the others, and what's more, you know it!"

By this time I'm on my feet, and although I may have started off tentatively, now I'm yelling at the top of my lungs. Taran looks completely taken aback. I don't give him a chance to recover himself, I continue the attack. I want to have a chance to have my say. It may be a last stand, but after all my terror today, it feels glorious finally to say what I think, finally to say out loud all I've done and suffered.

I feel a bit like a saint, going down to martyrdom in glory.

"Besides," I rave on, "I've been living as a boy, working as a boy — I do all the same things as the other squires, and more! Can they make bows? Can they fletch arrows? Can any of the others shoot like me? So I'm not strong. There's more to being a man than strength; there's more to being a man than anatomy. I've even won the love of a woman — have *you* done as much? I took a beating like a man, and for your own squire, too!" I thrust my finger out at him defiantly and I can feel my face glowing hot as I take a menacing step toward him. He's so surprised, he even takes an involuntary step backward. But I'm not done yet.

"I claim to be as much of a man as any boy at St. Sebastian's! And as for honor, I claim to have as much honor as anyone at St. Sebastian's, too – and much more than some! More than those who beat me in the street! More than the one who dropped the medal *you* beat me for by the body of my father, the night he murdered him in cold blood! Yes, I've seen my own father shot down before my very eyes, and by a member of St. Sebastian's! How many of the others can say the same? How many of the others could bear it? How many of them would take a knife and cut off their hair, change their sex, and dare to live as a boy, just for the chance of finding out what happened to him? I defy anyone to call me a girl anymore! No, I *did* learn honor from my father — and I swear, I am no girl. No — I am what I claim to be: the son of Jan Verbeke!"

By the time I finish this outrageous speech, I've reached a fever pitch and my voice is high and quivering with emotion, and I've caught Taran so off guard that I've backed him up a few paces toward the door and his hands are up in an almost defensive pose. As I say my father's name, I raise my hand high and throw back my head in a move that outdoes even Tristan, and I promptly pass out, finally, for the second time in as many months.

It's beginning to become quite a habit with me.

When I come to, I'm lying on the floor, and Taran is sitting on the windowsill. He doesn't appear to have made any move to bring me to, but I don't really know what's happened or how long I've been out. When I make a low moan and put my hand to my head, he stands up though he doesn't approach me. Still, the room is so small he's towering over me again, and any pretense at power I might have had during my rant is clearly spent. But his unreadable wooden expression is back. He doesn't seem angry anymore. For a moment there's a strange atmosphere in the stuffy little room that makes me remember Taran pulling me back in through the window that's now silhouetted behind him, and I feel confused.

"All right, *Verbeke*," he says. "I've had a chance to think things over. I've decided it's in my own best interest not to say anything about this just at present."

It takes me a minute to clear my head and remember everything that's happened, and when I do, I'm utterly astonished. Taran isn't going to tell? I don't understand.

Seeing my incredulity, he continues coldly:

"Unfortunately, I've realized that there's no way to reveal your, *er*, secret, that won't bring disgrace on us all. Oh, I'd love to be rid of you!" he says vehemently, wiping his hand distractedly on his breeches again. "And, I'd love to be rid of *him* even more, but I fear we'd all share in the humiliation. There are too many eyes and ears at St. Sebastian's, and it wouldn't take long for all of Louvain to learn of it. I have no intention of letting anyone disgrace St. Sebastian's, not when I'm there! Not ever. Damn it!" he says, losing his cool for moment. "Don't you know what you've done? Don't you know what exposure would mean, for all of us?"

He turns back to the window, and composes himself. "So I'm not going to say anything. To anyone." Then he adds ominously, "For now."

"Taran, I ..." I start to say, not sure how I'm going to finish, but he cuts me off.

"We'll speak no more of *any* of this!" he bursts out angrily, but his voice is strained, and his threats sounds weaker than they did earlier. He's not as composed as he seems, but he gives himself a shake and quickly assumes his usual masklike countenance. My head is pounding and I'm still muddled, yet somehow it registers that this isn't a dream.

Taran really isn't going to tell.

With a grunt of exasperation, he gets up as though to leave and crosses the room without looking at me. His foot is already on the stair when he turns back as though in afterthought, and says slowly and deliberately:

"But, there's going to come a day when I ask you for a favor. And whatever it is, you're going to do it."

With a sinking feeling, I know he's right.

And it was no afterthought. This must be really why he isn't going to tell. There can be no other explanation. He'd never let me stay otherwise. All his talk about not wanting to disgrace St. Sebastian's was a lie. I passed out at just the wrong time. It gave him time to think, and to realize that he's got me wholly in his power now. He's got me right where he wants me, and he's going to enjoy it. And just when it's going to hurt Tristan the most, he's going to call in his favor, and there's going to be nothing I can do but go along. He's going to use me to destroy Tristan, and there's nothing I can do to stop him.

I should let him leave. What more is there to say? Still I have to ask.

"How did you know?"

"I didn't, of course. Not for certain. I just knew you were up to something. I've been watching you," he adds, unnecessarily. Of course he has, and closely, too. Why did I let myself forget it? "Really, I don't know how you've managed to fool the others. You make about the least convincing boy I've ever seen."

"Really?" I say, unaccountably. "If you want unconvincing, you should see me trying to be a girl."

He opens his mouth, then closes it again firmly, and when he does speak, I get the impression he's saying something other than what he originally intended.

As a parting shot, it works.

"Besides," he grins wickedly. "I saw you kiss Pascal."

And then he's gone, and I'm alone again. But my safe haven has proven to be anything but safe. The windmill is ruined for me now. I've brought a viper back to the nest.

Tristan and I will never really be alone here again.

It's after dark when Tristan finds me. After letting Taran get a good head start, I eventually stumble the long way back to the guild, but I can't face either seeking out Tristan or going back to barracks, where the squires would be sure to keep up an unendurable running banter about my supposed conquest last night. Instead, I sneak into the stables when nobody else is around, and I sink down onto a pile of hay in one of the back stalls. At some point one of the stable boys pops his head in, but when I growl at him he scampers off, and he must be the one who ultimately tells Tristan where I am. By the time he appears, though, it's well after dark. I've missed evening mess; Tristan's covered for me, but it must be almost time for lights out.

As soon as I see Tristan's face, I feel wretched for hiding from him so long. He looks utterly tragic. I can tell he's been frantic, beating himself up over our angry words this afternoon. What a fool I've been! I was right. Tristan's mood must have passed swiftly. If only I'd just waited him out instead of acting rashly, this might have all been avoided. But there's no going back now.

I must look pretty tragic, too, because instantly he drops down beside me and gathers me up into his arms, muttering anguished apologies and sighing with relief so deeply that I know he's been really worried about me. I clutch at him shamelessly, and all the emotions of the past twenty-four hours come flooding out of me in a torrent of tears. Violent sobs wrack my body; I haven't cried like this since the day my father's body was found and I clung to Tristan in the chapel in just this way. I know he's thinking the same thing, and blaming himself for causing me so much pain. I wish I could tell him that it's not his fault, that I'm not upset any longer about our argument. I wish I could tell him it's much, much worse. How can I tell Tristan that I've inadvertently delivered him into his enemy's hands? That inevitably, I'm to be complicit in setting him up for a fall?

All that remains is to wait and see how Taran plans to do it. And I already know, Taran can bide his time. It's going to be an agonizing wait.

"Marek, I'm so sorry!" Tristan's saying into my hair. "I've been thoughtless. You're just a kid, after all. It'll be all right. We'll figure something out. Can you forgive me?"

I can't even answer. Whatever else may be true, it's not going to be all right.

"Why, you're ill!" he cries, when at last I break away and he looks down into my face. It's true my whole body is aching and I must look awful, yet it took depressingly little strength for Taran to hoist me back into the windmill. Aside from a few bumps and scrapes against the windowsill, I probably don't have a single bruise to show for my ordeal. But I can't tell Tristan I'm not really ill, unless you can call being sick with shame an illness, and it's not just shame for the future that's weighing on me. It's because Taran *did* leave a mark, just not a visible one. Lying here in the stable, I haven't been able to forget what his body felt like against mine, tense behind me. The imprint of his hand is still burning, the place occupied by each finger scorched onto my skin so deeply it feels as though there must be angry welts where each one rested, and the pounding of my own heart is still beating in rhythm with his.

I can't help it. He meant nothing by it. It was an accident, even, mostly. Still it's the most intimate way anyone has ever touched me, and when it occurs to me that it must have been Taran's most intimate touch, too, somehow, it makes it worse. I doubt any of the others would have given brushing a girl's bare stomach or clutching a breast for a moment a second thought. But Taran didn't take it lightly, and knowing it affected him, too, makes it all the harder to forget.

Tristan helps me back to the barracks, but the whole way, I'm still conscious of the pressure of Taran's arms around me, as though he's still standing behind me, following me down the corridor, as though he's never released me. I make a half-hearted attempt to assure Tristan that I'll be fine after a night's rest as he deposits me on my cot, but he looks worried and distraught, and he finally only agrees to go after telling Pascal that I'm sick and asking him to keep a close eye on me. Remy's overheard Tristan, and so he starts hovering around my cot in concern, too, so I roll over and pretend to sleep. But sleep won't come. Hours later, I'm still struggling to banish the thought of that hand when I finally manage to fall into a fitful slumber.

That's when I have the dream for the first time.

I'm alone in the little room atop the windmill, standing at the window and looking out over St. Sebastian's in the twilight. The shutters are wide open and darkness is already falling outside, but otherwise the room is much as it was this afternoon. I'm dressed as I usually am, too, except I don't seem to have my band wound around my chest.

I'm waiting for someone, and when I hear his long-awaited footsteps, light and quick on the stairs, my heart leaps in relief, but I don't turn around. Instead, I savor the anticipation, and I let Tristan come up softly behind me and wrap his arms around me, enfolding me in a warm embrace. It's what I've been longing for from the moment I first saw him on the garden wall, and my pulse races when I feel him slip his hand up under my tunic and press it against my waist. His fingertips glide across my belly, as lightly and deliberately as if he were running his hand over the curves of a bow, and my whole body is tingling as the rough calluses of his open palm ruffle the soft hairs of my stomach. Inevitably, his big hand sweeps up to capture my left breast in an electrifying arc, his fingers splaying to cup it in exactly the position that was etched there so vividly only hours ago. As it closes in a gentle squeeze, I lean back heavily against his tense body and let my head rest against his chest, listening to the violent beating of his heart. He bends his head low, and when we're cheek to cheek, his lips brush my ear, and I can feel his hot breath on the back of my neck as he parts his lips to whisper one word intimately into my ear:

"*thief.*"

I shoot straight up in bed and come awake with a gasp.

My heart is pounding as revulsion and desire alternately surge through my still-tingling body. I start to shake, but to my shame, I don't know whether it's with relief that the dream is over, or with frustration that I've been wrenched from it too soon.

Light is already streaming in beneath the high rafters overhead, but I make no move to rise. Instead, I roll over and hug the coarse mattress to my trembling body, feeling utterly disgusted with myself. I don't want to get up. I don't want to face anybody.

For the life of me, I don't see how I can face either of them ever again.

CHAPTER TWENTY-FOUR

Out on the field that morning, I feel like all eyes are on me, and they probably are. Between my still recent exploits at the Goat and my mysterious illness last night, there's plenty to be curious about, but instead of the mildly inquisitive stares and kindly looks that the boys are really giving me, to me the stares appear hostile, prying. I can't help feeling exposed, as though my secret has been laid bare for all to see, as though accusations are about to start at any moment. I must still look like hell, too, because when Tristan comes out and joins me at our station, he gets a contrite look on his face and tries so hard to make up for yesterday's quarrel with forced hearty banter that it starts to get on my nerves. He keeps trying to pat me on the back or squeeze my arm affectionately, and every time he touches me, I cringe. I can't help it. I must have dreamed of Tristan many times in the past, but never so vividly as last night, and if I've dreamed of Tristan before, I've managed to put it out of my mind the next day. But this dream won't be pushed aside. It was too real, all the more so because in a way, some of it really did happen. It wasn't all a dream.

There is one person, though, who doesn't seem inclined to look at me today. My days of being watched closely are over. But I don't need to see him to feel his presence, as soon as he comes out onto the field. He's already been standing there behind me all morning, his arm around my waist, his hand sliding over my skin.

"Marek, listen," Tristan says, jolting me out of my reverie, and clearly thinking I'm still upset over the Roxanne affair. I explained some of what really happened with Aristide to him in the stable last night, and we agreed that something has to be done.

"I've thought it over, and I've got an idea. If Gilles will help, and I don't see why he won't, given how he feels about Ari, I think we can set the whole thing right."

"Swell," is all I can manage, side-stepping his hand as it comes in for another comforting pat. When Baylen appears at this moment, I've never been so glad to see him, or for morning drills to start. Baylen even looks nonplussed at the relieved grin I give him. I'm sure he can't account for it. But it's a pure joy to lose myself in the routine of retrieval, and to have no energy for anything but work.

That afternoon I find myself plodding behind Tristan on our way back to the Drunken Goat. I sincerely hope it's going to be my last visit for quite a while, but we have to put Tristan's plan into action. I've got a purse in my hand, supplied mostly by Gilles, but it's also got most of the rest of the money Tristan's father supplied for him for expenses in it. It weighs heavily in my hand.

As we're stepping out into the alley, we run into Falko. When he hears where we're headed, he falls into step beside me.

"Can't stay away, eh, Marek?" he says, prodding me jovially in the ribs. Eyeing the purse in my hand, he exclaims,

"What — not going for another round so soon, you dog?!"

"Don't you have to practice?" I ask rudely. Falko's crude, but he's been a pretty good friend lately. I think of him offering to take three lashes for me, and I regret the outburst. Besides, I can feel Tristan's eyes on me, and I know I have to do the right thing. It's time really to act like a man.

"About the other night," I say, swallowing hard. "Nothing happened with Roxanne."

"Nothing!" he laughs. "You were in there for over an hour."

"We just talked," I admit. "We're friends. Actually, she's quite easy to talk to." As I say this, something occurs to me. "In fact, you'd probably like her. She's delicate."

"She's your girl, Marek," Falko protests, but I shake my head sadly. I'm going to have to say it.

"Aristide was right about me," I confess. "As it turns out, I can't, *er* ..." and I stop. I expect Falko to make some rude jest, but he just puts his arm protectively around my shoulder and says,

"Don't worry about it, Woodcock. It can happen to the best of us."

Even then, I think the inkling of a plan is starting to form in the back of my mind. I'm just too miserable right now to see it clearly yet.

When we get to the Goat, Tristan finds Rosalinde. At first, she seems highly amused with our proposal, but when she sees the size of the purse, she goes along readily enough. So when we leave, it's official. Roxanne is my girl.

I've paid for exclusive rights to her for a full year.

When we return to the guild with the matter settled and Roxanne at least temporarily safe from Aristide's clutches, there's still something weighing heavily on my mind. So I make my excuses to Tristan, and seek the asylum of the chapel. I've got a decision to make, and I don't know how to make it.

I'll admit that I've thought about running away before, but I've never really seriously considered it. Now I must. I know I should do it: I could get away before Taran finds a way to use his knowledge about me against Tristan. I've come so close to being revealed in the past few weeks that I'm beginning to understand what it will mean, and not just for me. And it's not only Tristan that I worry about. How will Remy feel, to have let a girl take his beating? What of Roxanne, if she finds out I'm a girl? Or Jurian? Even Baylen, for that matter? And all the boys in the barracks? Taran was right: they would all share in the humiliation of having it known that a girl has been living and working at St. Sebastian's.

But what about my brave words to Taran in the windmill? Weren't they true, too? Aren't I as good a squire as any of them? I won't believe I'm a disgrace to the guild. The saint accepted my vow, after all, and I swore to see Tristan through Veterans or die trying. And the harm's been done. I *have* been living at St. Sebastian's. It's too late to take that back, and I don't see what running away would serve now. Abandoning Tristan would be a betrayal he wouldn't understand, and so close to Seconds, it would probably destroy his chances as effectively as anything Taran could plan. I have been helping Tristan, too, haven't I? Have I been deluding myself that he needs my help to pass the trials? If there's any way that by staying, I can see him through and fulfill my vow, then I've got to stay, despite the risks. I don't let myself dwell on the other matters, too — how the pressure of being among all these boys is getting to me, how I'm unraveling.

So I sit in the chapel, lost in thought and in a quandary of indecision, deeply regretting the impulse that led me to give my St. Sebastian's medal to Roxanne. I'd give anything for some guidance right about now.

When I hear a gentle sound behind me, like someone respectfully clearing his throat, I turn around to find Charles standing behind me.

"Sorry to disturb, Marek," he says softly. "You looked like you could use a friend."

I'm still a little nervous around Charles, but I can't imagine anyone whose opinion I'd value more right about now, so I smile in relief and motion him down onto the pew next to me.

"Charles, I need some advice," I admit, but then it's tricky. I can't really tell him what's bothering me, so I settle on saying, "I've got an important decision to make, and I just don't know what to do."

"Can you tell me about it?" he asks, and I shake my head. To his credit, he doesn't press. "It must be pretty serious," he says at length, reading my mood.

"It is." We sit side by side in silence a little longer, and then I add: "How do you make yourself do your duty, when all your desires lead in the opposite direction?"

"Well," he says thoughtfully, "if you're going to sacrifice your own desires for duty, you'd better be damned sure you know where your duty really lies."

"That's just the problem," I say in a worried voice. "I'm not at all sure. But I'm not sure if I'm just finding excuses, so I can justify doing what I really want to do."

"We all do that sometimes," he says gently. "I have faith in you, Marek. You wouldn't be worrying about it so much if you weren't really trying to follow your conscience. You'll figure out the right thing to do." I give him a pleading look, and he sighs.

"If you really can't decide, why don't you do what I do sometimes?" He stands up and gestures toward the altar. "Leave it in the hands of the saint."

And so I decide to follow Charles's advice. St. Sebastian blessed my vow, so I mean to keep it. When the saint wants me to leave, he's going to have to give me another sign.

THE NEXT TWO WEEKS OR SO PASS BY IN SOMETHING OF A blur. During the day, I throw all my energy into preparation for Seconds, trying to keep my mind occupied by physical activity. There is one positive thing that comes out of it all. I throw myself into my physical labor so intensely that I really do begin to see some improvement. For once, Tristan isn't the only one getting stronger. It hasn't made much difference yet to my longbow shooting, but I'm getting better with my throws, and accordingly our exhibition trick starts coming along nicely. For the first time, I really start to think that maybe we've got Seconds in the bag.

Still I can't put the episode in the windmill behind me easily. I can't live in constant fear — it's too exhausting, and besides, Taran has proven he is nothing if not patient. But I'm apprehensive. It feels like those first weeks at the guild again, where I was waiting for discovery every moment. Now I'm waiting again, and I don't know for what. Discovery has already come. What's next? There's nothing I can do but wait and see what Taran does.

As the days creep by and Taran makes no move, and as no sign appears from the saint, I begin to relax a little — not because I'm no longer worried, but because it's too hard to keep tense all the time. Taran avoids me so studiously, too, that sometimes during the day as I go through my routine, I can even almost forget about what happened. But at night, when I'm lying in my cot, I can't forget the feeling of his hand on my skin, and the dream of the windmill becomes a recurring companion of my sleep.

And so I wait. And I was wrong about one thing. He tries to hide it, but Taran's still watching me, even more closely than ever.

Almost as closely as I'm watching him.

That's probably why, when Jerome bursts into the archives one afternoon as Tristan is working on translating a passage of Latin for his tutorials (and I'm practicing awkwardly writing my letters under his direction, Tristan having begun to make good his threat of teaching me to read and write), I'm sure the thing I've been waiting for has come.

"Tristan, Follow me! Hurry, you've got to come right away! It's terrible!" Jerome cries, alarm written clearly on his face.

Jerome doesn't wait to see the effect of his words. He turns heel and rushes back down the hall, leaving us to jump to our feet in agitation and follow his receding form down the corridor. I'm positive he's heading to the great hall, where I fully expect to find all the masters arrayed for an inquisition. Instead he flings the door of Gilles's room open and cries out,

"See for yourself!"

I crowd into the doorway behind Tristan, who's come to a full stop and is standing frozen in front of me at the terrible sight that meets him inside the room. From the posture of the two boys on the threshold, I'm almost afraid to look in.

It's Gilles. He's standing in the middle of the small room, with Pascal behind him, helping to adjust a cloak on his shoulders. He's wearing the most outlandish outfit I've ever seen. It's unbelievable, even for Gilles.

He's dressed in dazzling white from head to foot. His legs are encased in luxurious stockings of pure white silk that are so tight and thin, they leave very little to the imagination. Even his boots are white, and he's wearing a matching white linen shirt, jerkin, and long white cloak. But this isn't the worst of it. Virtually every inch of the blinding outfit is trimmed in white fur.

"Gilles, what in the world is that!?" Tristan finally exclaims.

"Ermine!" Gilles exclaims joyfully. "Jerome was right! It's absolutely marvelous."

"No, Gilles, I mean — what is that?" Tristan repeats, gesturing up and down.

"My costume, of course. For my exhibition shot, at Seconds," Gilles replies mildly.

"You can't wear that," Tristan says flatly.

"Why ever not?" Gilles asks.

"For one thing, it'll be the middle of August."

"Pffft. It's going to be fabulous. Pascal, the hat." Pascal obediently bends to the bed and picks up something in his hands that looks suspiciously like a rabbit and a chicken that have died together, horribly mangled under a cart's wheels. As Pascal lowers the disgusting thing onto Gilles's head with a resigned look, Gilles trills:

"Look how well it sets off my red hair! And," he cries, reaching into his sleeve, "how well it's going to set off *this!*" He pulls a bright red apple out of his sleeve and holds it up triumphantly.

Nobody can think of anything to say to this.

"I'm having a matching costume fitted for Pascal. We're going to start a riot! Here, Pascal, show them. Try the hat." Gilles lifts it from his own head and plops it down vigorously onto poor Pascal's bowed head, who looks the very picture of noble suffering.

"If you insist on shooting Pascal," Tristan says wryly, "at least have the decency not to make him die in that."

"Hmm. It's not going to leave much room for this, is it?" Gilles says, ignoring Tristan and looking sadly from the hat to the apple. "Besides, it'd change the height, and I really can't be bothered to have to build a Pascal Number Four. I'm afraid we'll have to forego the hat."

"Well, there's at least some mercy in the world, Pascal," Jerome says. But Pascal just looks dismal. I can't take it anymore.

"Gilles," I say, "Aren't you taking your joke too far? Why don't you tell us what you've really got in mind for Seconds."

"Dear boy," he replies innocently. "If I told you what I really have in mind, you'd never believe me."

He's probably right.

But that night, Pascal looks so wan and pale that I get irritated with Gilles all over again. With Seconds fast approaching, Pascal's started taking some of the boys aside and promising them his prized possessions, "in the event anything should happen to me." So after seeing Gilles's ridiculous get-up, when Pascal pulls me aside on the way into evening mess and tells me he wants me to have his boots, it's the last straw.

"Pascal, if you really think he's going to go through with it, just tell him you won't do it. Guillaume'll never force you to do it against your will."

"It's not that simple, Marek. He'll think I have no confidence in him."

"Well, you don't," I snap. Only Pascal looks so miserable, I add, "It's not a matter of confidence. Anyone can miss a shot. It's utterly ridiculous." But Pascal won't budge.

"You'd do it for Tristan, wouldn't you?" he says.

"Certainly not!" But I wonder. Maybe I would.

During the meal, Pascal just sits and picks disinterestedly at his food, but I notice that Armand is shoveling in his dinner like a farmhand. Aristide has been practicing hitting a small mark at 200 yards, too, though he hasn't had anything built, yet Armand looks entirely unconcerned.

"Armand," I say. "Pascal is petrified. Aren't you worried about the supposed 'Tell shot' at all?"

"Nope."

I can't believe Armand has more faith in Aristide's ability or his nerves than Pascal does in Gilles's, so I ask, "Why not?"

"Aristide's not going to do it."

"I knew they weren't really going to do it!" I cry with satisfaction.

"Oh, Gilles will probably do it," Armand says. "But Aristide won't."

"How can you be so sure?" I ask.

"Because," he replies, munching happily, "unlike Gilles, Aristide is essentially sane."

"I don't know," I say, suddenly worried. "Sanity seems to be in rather short supply around here."

"Yes," Armand agrees readily. "It's not a quality much valued here at St. Sebastian's, is it?"

I ask Tristan about it later.

"Marek, Gilles isn't going to shoot Pascal," he says.

"Can't you talk to him, though, Tristan? Pascal really doesn't seem know what Gilles is planning. Can't you convince Gilles at least to explain what he's going to do to his own squire?"

"Look, Marek. Pascal and Gilles have been together for a long time. If Pascal isn't used to Gilles by now, what can I possibly say?"

I don't know, but I wish there was something. I've begun to wonder if Pascal is going to make it to Seconds at all, and it's only two weeks away.

CHAPTER TWENTY-FIVE

I'm heading in from the workshops the next afternoon when I find that I've forgotten a load of arrows back on my worktable. I'd intended to take them out to Tristan's cabinet before mess, and I curse as I realize I'll have to be fast to have time now. I run back to gather them up, and in my haste I don't get a very good grip on them, so they all tumble out of my arms in the hallway outside the masters' offices. I'm bent over picking them up when I hear voices coming from behind the partially open door of one of the rooms that line the hallway. I'm too intent on my task to pay much attention to them, but when one of the men says distinctly, *"It can't be changed now. I tell you, it's all set for Thirds,"* I stop. Seconds is coming up, not Thirds, so this strikes me as odd and I start listening. I don't really mean to eavesdrop. I just take longer with my task than strictly necessary.

"Move it up. We can't afford the delay," a second voice says angrily.

"It can't be done. It's a question of opportunity. This has been the plan from the first. You know as well as anyone that the wheels have been in motion for a very long time," the first voice insists. It sounds as though they're talking about some of the tests for the trials, and I get nervous. I shouldn't be hearing this, and if I get caught, I'll be in trouble. I start picking up the arrows faster again.

"There's no time to lose. If English troops enter Ardennes, it'll be too late."

"Then you'd better see to it that that doesn't happen. Influence was supposed to be your end. Or don't your men have any influence anymore?"

"It's looking inevitable now, and you know it."

"Then stall! I'm telling you, it's all set for Thirds. We'll do our end. You worry about doing yours."

There's a silence, and I'm afraid they're about to come out. I grab up the last arrow off the floor and scoot back along the corridor the way I came, heading back toward the workshops, so I won't have to pass the door. As I go, I can still hear their angry voices as they say,

"Then you'd better be damned sure your trick comes off without a hitch."

"And just how do you propose I do that?"

"Like anything else. Practice."

And with that, I'm out the door.

When I try to repeat the strange conversation to Gilles and Tristan at mess, they both laugh it off.

"Some of the masters talking about trials, that's all. Talk of a trick coming off without a hitch, you say? They must be trying to figure out how to keep you from doing one of your crazy stunts, duBois," Gilles says.

"Or they've gotten wind of your plan for poor Pascal!" Tristan shoots back.

Only somehow, it didn't sound to me like the men were really talking about the trials at all. Maddeningly, I can't remember exactly what was said, and I wasn't paying attention even to which master's office the men were in. But the whole thing makes me uneasy, and I'm not sure why. Neither Tristan nor Gilles can offer an explanation for the reference to English troops. They think I must have misheard, and I suppose it's possible.

I'm still puzzling over it when Master Guillaume rises to make an announcement that causes such a stir, it quite puts the conversation out of my mind.

"Gentlemen!" the master booms, leaning forward to place his palms flat on the table in a way that signals he means business. "As you know, ensuring quality troops and trainers for our military has always been a central part of our guild's mission, and when called upon, we must put this duty before all other considerations — even the competitions. Such a time is now, men! Because of some recent unrest on our borders and threats from Flanders, the Regent has requested an unusually large conscription of troops, including an order for at least 200 additional archers. These archers must of course be certified through St. Sebastian's. Therefore, I'm afraid that for the duration of the day tomorrow and the next, all areas of the guild, including the butts, will be turned over to the veterans in charge of military certifications, so that the necessary tests can be conducted immediately.

"I know, I know," he says, as the Journeys begin to grumble, and I'm grumbling along with everyone else, because Tristan and I can't afford to miss a day of practice now. "With Seconds so close, the timing is hardly ideal. But sequestered as we are here behind our walls, we cannot forget that the war between France and England is raging around our borders, and the first duty of the guild is to support the crown. However," he grins, as though he's been holding out on us, "we do not plan to leave you men without any way to pass your time. In fact, I think you'll be very pleased when you hear what we have in mind. Our benefactor, Sir Brecelyn, due to his increasingly close *connections* with the guild," here Guillaume looks at Taran, who blanches at this unanticipated reference to his father-in-law–to-be and to his relationship to him, "has planned a *divertissement* of the first order for you boys. Since our grounds will be unavailable to you tomorrow, he's invited all the Journeys and their squires to his estate, to participate in a hunt on his property. One of our own veterans is in service to Brecelyn as his huntsman, and so it will not be entirely a day of rest. Rather, it is another lesson — and as such, it is mandatory. I expect you all to participate, and to show our host every courtesy. Consider it a practicum. Service as a huntsman is a respectable profession that some of you may wish to consider after your Journey days, and this will be an excellent introduction to the art of organized hunting." Guillaume beams at this, and he pretends to be about to sit down, when he suddenly pops up again and booms out, "And it will be a chance for you all to practice your courtly manners, as there will be ladies in the party!"

At this, the dissatisfied grumbling at the table turns to cheers.

The boys have all begun talking excitedly among themselves, when Guillaume unexpectedly approaches the table. He moves around to stand directly behind Taran, but when he starts what is clearly a personal conversation with him, he does it in such a loud voice that everyone at the table can hear.

"Mellor," he says, putting his hand on Taran's shoulder. "You'll be pleased to know that sir Brecelyn is well aware that you have had no chance to meet with Lady Melissande since the engagement has become official. He asked me to pass along to you the welcome news that you will be given the opportunity to have a private interview with her at some point during the excursion."

Taran is usually so formal that it's something of a surprise that instead of replying to this politely he simply grunts. He's put his hand up to his forehead and begun to rub his temple, too, as though he might be able in this way to shield himself from the conversation.

"What's more, this will be an opportunity for you to present the engagement gift to her ladyship for which you have arranged. I've taken the liberty of having it sent on ahead directly to the Brecelyn manor, and it is currently being housed there. Given this unexpected opportunity, Sir Brecelyn has not mentioned it to Melissande, so that you may be the one to give it to her yourself. It's all too fitting!" When this merely elicits another grunt from Taran, with another pat Guillaume takes his leave. There's silence at the table, as everyone burns to start making fun of Taran but nobody dares take the first shot. Finally Gilles says,

"A present that has to be housed! How exciting! Whatever can it be? Do tell, dear boy!"

Taran just glares at him.

"Something fitting for presentation at a hunt," Falko adds musingly. "Maybe it's a stallion!" he laughs. "Oh, I forgot! She's marrying you. She's already getting one! Ha!"

Color has begun creeping up Taran's neck, the way it did when the boys were teasing him at the Drunken Goat, but Remy doesn't seem to notice. He chirps,

"It's not a horse, though it has been in our stables for a while, and none of you noticed! I'll give you a hint. It's being housed in a mews!"

"That's enough, Remy," Taran says warningly. It's the harshest I've ever heard him talk to his squire, but Remy seems so excited about the gift, he isn't paying attention.

"That's right!" he says, bobbing his head, "It's a falcon! A lovely little merlin, the proper bird for a Lady! It's all trained. Isn't that wonderful?"

"An expensive gift indeed," Aristide concedes. "And in the event, well chosen."

"I'm sure Taran didn't choose it himself. His father probably arranged to have it sent," Jurian says, but Remy protests.

"Not at all! Well, Lord Mellor did arrange for it, but it was all Taran's idea, wasn't it?"

"Remy, that's enough," Taran repeats. "Nobody wants to hear about it."

"On the contrary," Tristan says, finally entering the conversation, and I get apprehensive. "I, for one, would love to hear *all* about it. A carnivorous bird trained to drop dead carcasses into milady's lap. What a fitting symbol of your devotion! However did you think of anything so romantic?"

"A girl might have preferred jewels or clothes, it's true," Gilles says mildly, but I can tell he's jumping in to divert Taran's attention from Tristan, particularly since he's giving Tristan a warning look. "Yet I can see the appeal. At least," he says teasingly, "it'll give her something to do, if she's to accompany you on long afternoons when you're out shooting things."

"She'll need to have *something* to do, since …" Tristan starts, but I kick him swiftly in the shins under the table. Not soon enough, though.

"And just what is it that *you'd* give her, Tristan?" Taran asks dangerously, and the table falls silent again. There's a dreadful moment when I think Tristan is going to say something unforgivable, but I grab his arm, and he seems to remember in time that Melissande is Taran's fiancée now. He'd be a cad to say anything, so he just shrugs.

"Wait until you boys see it," Remy babbles, apparently unaware of the tensions at the table. "A beautiful bird, for a beautiful girl." Remy sounds so enamored of the bird that it's clear he's seen it. He must have used Melissande's merlin as a model for my figurine. I don't know why, but this makes me feel a little odd. I don't know how I feel about sharing something so precious to me with her, particularly when it now appears that hers is the original. It feels all too familiar.

"Indeed," says Turk. "To Taran's beautiful fiancée," he says, raising his tankard, but before we can raise our cups in response, Taran snorts. I'm pretty sure he didn't mean to do it. It just came out, as is clear from the fact that more color creeps into his face, as though he's embarrassed by his own involuntary reaction. But it brings Tristan to his feet.

"What are you sneering about? She's your fiancée, man. How dare you insult her! You sound like you don't even love her!" he says accusingly.

Surprisingly, Taran just looks up at him evenly, his face unreadable again.

"Why should I?" he says. "When I don't even know her. Or maybe I should say," he adds darkly, "I don't know her as well as *you* do."

And suddenly, everyone is on their feet. Jerome and Gilles grab Tristan's arms, and I grab him around the waist. It's undignified, but nobody wants Tristan to propel himself across a table at Taran again. But we're all sober and in the guild hall, and Gilles is already declaring,

"Boys, boys. I think that's quite enough. Here," he says, putting a tankard in Tristan's hand and raising his own. "We're on our feet already. Let's drink all together to the very lovely and very *chaste* Lady Melissande Brecelyn."

Tristan and Taran contemplate each other for a long, tense moment, but then slowly Taran takes his tankard from the table and lifts it.

"To Melissande," he says rather unenthusiastically, and we all drink.

Gilles has brought us past the crisis, but I bet it's going to be a long hunt tomorrow.

Taran may or may not know about our visit to St. Genevieve's, but it's clear now that he knows Tristan's purposely set out to court Melissande. He knows there was more to Melissande's expression at Firsts than just Tristan winning the garland, and he's not at all happy about it. Who would be?

When we all settle back onto the benches, poor Remy still seems to be unclear about what's going on, so he turns to Taran and says a bit worriedly,

"Melissande *is* lovely, don't you think, Taran?"

"Of course, Remy," he says soothingly, but unexpectedly, he adds: "But there's more to beauty than a lovely face."

"Like what?" Falko jokes, relieved that the tension has passed. "Don't tell me you're going to say 'a faithful heart,' or something sentimental like that."

"No, nothing like that," Taran agrees, but when he doesn't elaborate, Aristide says:

"Well I, for one, admit to being curious. Just what do you find more appealing than a lovely face, Taran?"

"I doubt our boy Taran has much time to admire any curves except those on a bow," Gilles says. "I'm not sure he'd really even notice a girl that didn't have a bow in her hand."

"You're probably right," Taran agrees lightly, getting to his feet again. "Well, boys, as always, it's been a real pleasure, but it's too nice an evening to spend what's left of it in here. And after talking with you lot, I need some air."

Motioning for Remy to follow him, he bows curtly to the table and heads out of the hall, not going toward the dormitories, but out into the garden. And it's true — as he leaves, Taran does look like he could use some air. His hands must be sweating; for some reason, he keeps wiping his right hand distractedly against his breeches, and his composure seems forced. In fact, for him, he looks distinctly rattled, though I suspect it's less because of his altercation with Tristan than because tomorrow he's got to face Melissande. I bet he's not as unaffected by her as he pretends. His dismissive talk about her looks was just a way of saving face. There isn't a boy alive who can resist a beautiful face, particularly not one as lovely as Melissande's. Taran's simply too proud to admit that he desperately wants Tristan's leavings.

But for some reason, I find it extremely irritating that he never answered Aristide's question.

It is a gorgeous night, and so when Taran's departure signals the end of the meal, I find myself drawn out into the garden along with most of the other boys. There's a full moon, and so the little garden is flooded with muted light, and it's bright enough for us to see without any artificial illumination. Taran's seated himself at one of the little tables under the creeping jasmine, and if he resents our imposition on his solitude, he doesn't show it.

I drop down on the grass next to Remy, and I lean my back up against the same tree against which he's propped himself. The others settle themselves at one of the tables, or on the low balustrade that lines the portico between the garden and the great hall, leaning back against the pillars that support its sloping eaves. I don't know if Taran's pensive mood infects us, or if it's the effect of the moonlight, but nobody says much, and a sort of melancholy falls over us all. The boys were so excited about the hunt just minutes ago in the hall, but out here in the semi-dark, the idea of the girls who will be at the hunt tomorrow has just seemed to make everyone feel lonely. We sit for a while, each lost in his own thoughts, until finally Charles says,

"Jerome, play us something. One of the old songs," and Jerome obliges, slinging his lute down from his shoulder and joining his lilting tenor voice to its soft chords.

"*Tonight, I'll shoot an arrow to the moon*," he croons, and I'm not the only one who recognizes the song. It's a favorite at St. Sebastian's; my father used to sing it, too. Charles joins in with a surprisingly deep baritone, and I close my eyes and breathe in the earthy scents of the garden as they sing:

"*Tonight, I'll shoot an arrow to the moon,*
And with it, I'll set my sorrow free,
And with one hand, I'll catch hold of that arrow,
And pull you up to the moon with me.
Tonight, I'll drink the moon, and drunk with moonlight
Moonbeams will shine out like tears from my eyes,
And when I bend and take you in my arms,
With radiance our embrace will fill the skies.
Tonight, I'll shoot an arrow to the moon,
And with it, I'll let my sorrow free,
For my love, you're promised to another,
And here on earth, you'll never be with me."

They've sung it beautifully, but as they come to the last lines, I can't help but think this song was a spectacularly bad choice for tonight. It seems designed to depress just about everyone, for different reasons. It may just be a trick of the moonlight, washing out all the boys' faces, but Jurian looks particularly pale, and Falko doesn't look much better. The only one who doesn't seem affected by the song is Gilles, or perhaps Pascal, whose evident pallor has nothing to do with the song or girls. He's probably the only one who is still thinking more about Seconds than about the hunt.

I'm feeling sorry for myself, too; I'd been thinking that my unique situation has made me isolated in a way that the others can't understand, but now I realize that most of the other boys are all just as lonely.

When the end of the song is met with silence, Jerome begins to strum a new tune.

"Lightly, my lady, lie your head upon my pillow,
And let your golden hair spread across it wide ..."

"Not that one, Jerome," say multiple voices at once, and one of them is mine.

"Play something lively," Anselm suggests, and in response, Jerome picks up the pace and begins a bawdy jig which does manage to lighten the atmosphere. But from where I'm sitting, it happens that I can see Falko's profile outlined clearly against the dark foliage of the roses behind him, and I see the frown that's still fixed on his face when Jerome finishes the merry tune with a flourish and declares that he's calling it a night.

It gives me an idea.

Or rather, it helps crystallize an idea that's been forming in the back of my mind for a while now. So when we've all crossed back through the great hall and the other squires are crowding into the narrow corridor leading to the barracks, I break away from the pack and follow Falko back to his room instead. It's almost time for lights out, but if I'm quick, there should be just enough time. It's got to be tonight.

I wait for him to go into his room, and when I think nobody else is watching, I cross over to it and give a sharp rap, then open his door a notch without waiting for him to answer.

"Marek?" he asks questioningly as I peek my head around the door.

"Can I pop in for a second?" Again I don't wait for an answer, but squeeze in and close the door behind me. His room seems even smaller than Tristan's, but it's just because Falko's in it. I wonder how he even has room to change his clothes in here. Falko's giving me a rather apprehensive look, so I get right to it, lest he have some idea I might have 'fraternization' in mind. I say hastily,

"I've got a proposition for you," which as soon as I say it, I realize is not the thing to put him at his ease. "What I mean is," I rush on, "I think maybe we could help each other out. Look, this isn't coming out right. Let me explain," I say, sitting down on the edge of his bed, and motioning to him to sit down, too.

"What's this all about, Marek? It's late. Can't this wait?" he says, still looking a little wary.

"No, it can't wait," I insist. "And I'll be brief, I promise. The thing is, maybe you know, Tristan's planning to put me up for apprentice status." Falko nods, relaxing a little but still looking confused. "Well, I need some help," I continue. "I've been working on my strength, but it's not enough. I need real help, if I'm going to have a shot at even pretending to shoot clouts. You're a fantastic clout shooter. I think you could help me. And the thing is," I say when he doesn't respond immediately, "I think I can help you, too."

"Just what are you proposing?"

"If you help me with my shooting, I'll help you get a girl," I say baldly. Put this way, it sounds dangerously close to procurement, so I add, "I mean, I'll help teach you how to talk to girls. We can start tomorrow, at the hunt. You said it yourself, there aren't any available girls around here. Well, there will be, tomorrow. Now's your chance."

He's quiet again for a while, looking down at his big hands, but I think I've got him. I know he already thinks I'm quite good with girls.

"You know, I'm not as stupid as I look," he says unexpectedly.

"I know that," I say. Nobody could be as stupid as he looks. But I mean it sincerely.

"This is really about helping Tristan, isn't it?" he says, and he's got me.

"Does it matter?" I ask finally. When he still doesn't respond, I say gently, "She's married, Falko. It's time to move on. Let me help you tomorrow; I really want to."

And so he agrees, as I knew he would.

"Lesson one," I say as I get up from next to him on the cot. "If at all possible between now and tomorrow morning, take a bath!"

As I close the door behind me, I think to myself with satisfaction: it's a good end to the day; unlikely as he may seem, I've got my ally now.

But the day isn't over yet. As I'm bustling back to make it to the barracks before lights out, Tristan's door swings open down the hallway and he gestures me in.

"Marek," he says, closing the door and fixing me with a steady gaze. "I've been giving it some serious thought."

I have no idea what he's talking about, so I wait.

"You may not think it, but I took what you said the other day to heart. It's about tomorrow. I don't know what the right thing is anymore, so I've decided to leave it entirely up to you." He pauses, and then looking a little embarrassed says, "If the opportunity presents itself to claim my prize from Melissande, should I take it?"

His question catches me off guard, but I can tell he's serious. I open my mouth, then close it. I don't know what to say. I don't know why I didn't think about this possibility earlier; Tristan's clearly been thinking about it all night. I know what I want to say; I want to tell him not to do it.

But I can't. I sigh heavily.

"The damage is already done," I say. "If I were her, I think it would hurt more if I thought you had the chance and didn't take it. It's just one kiss, what can it hurt? If she's got to be married to that barbarian, you might as well give her something she can remember. Give her a kiss, and she can live on it the rest of her life. I know I would."

I trudge back to the barracks slowly, not really worrying any longer about whether I make it before lights out or not. Tomorrow is going to be quite a day.

When I'm lying in my cot in the barracks, trying not to think about windmills, I find myself thinking back to the conversation I overheard in the masters' hallway before mess, and I finally figure out what's been bothering me about it. It's not just the lingering feeling that there was something sinister about it, as though the plot the men were hatching for Thirds was somehow political and about more than just the Journey trials. Something happened on the day my father visited St. Sebastian's — something that changed his mood suddenly. What if he overheard something he shouldn't have that day, too? What if *that's* why he was killed? After all, one of the men said, *the wheels have been in motion for a very long time.*

Maybe the conversation I heard this afternoon was perfectly innocent, and maybe it was just about the tasks for trials. But even so, the more I think about it, the more I think that my father overhearing something in just this way is the only explanation that makes any sense for the change that came over him at St. Sebastian's that day, and I've never been so irritated at my inability to recognize voices reliably.

CHAPTER
TWENTY-SIX

Carriages arrive early the next morning to take us to Brecelyn's estate for the promised hunt. The Journeys are to ride in two carriages ahead, and so I make the trip in one of the squire carriages behind, crammed between the massive Pruie and the narcoleptic Benoit, who falls asleep immediately on my shoulder and begins to drool even though the ride is so rough and bumpy that we bob along the whole way like marionettes.

We ride through Louvain and out into the countryside along the L'île-Charleroi road, just as though we were going back to my old house near the Vendon Abbey. I'm struck by the strangeness of making this reverse trip toward my old house in a carriage with red trim, and I start to wonder what I'd find if I really were on my way back there. What's left of my old home now? Is the house still standing, with the yard overgrown and the workshop in ruins, or has Bellows moved in and appropriated it all? I'm standing there in the middle of the yard, looking the long way down into the well, when I'm jerked out of my thoughts by the feel of the carriage turning off the main road under me. We've reached the turn-off; from now on, all the land on either side of the track belongs to Brecelyn. As we bump along for another good thirty minutes or so, it strikes me that Taran is going to be an extremely wealthy man. I don't know what he's going to inherit from his own father, but Brecelyn has no sons. Once Taran marries Melissande he's going to be Brecelyn's heir, and from the looks of it, half of Louvain is going to belong to him.

Soon enough, we come out of the scattered woods and farmlands to an open vista sweeping down toward Brecelyn manor, which turns out to be heavily fortified, with towers and a large circuit wall enclosing a vast area around an inner keep. It's a castle, really, and I shouldn't be surprised. After all, 'sir' is a knight's title, and I've known all my life that Brecelyn has many troops at his disposal. But I'm impressed anyway. Flocks of sheep dot the expansive lawns that surround the castle, but not far beyond the walls thick forests begin, as the flat land gives way to the rolling foothills of the mountains that rise in the background.

Outside the walls, near where the forest begins to thicken, a colorful pavilion has been set up, and it is in front of this pavilion that the carriages come to a stop. We spill out of the cramped carriages and stretch out after the long ride, looking a rather motley crew. Knowing ladies will be present, the Journeys in particular were annoyed when we were told not to wear our best clothes, but to stick to drab browns and greens, if we had them. It's a hunt, after all, and we need to blend into the forest. Hunting in full regalia would be ridiculous, but I think some of the boys would have worn it if we hadn't been told in strict terms to dress appropriately. I shudder to think what Gilles might have worn. As it is, as soon as he extricates his lanky body from the carriage, Gilles surveys the activity around the tents and exclaims indignantly,

"Where are the girls?!"

There are none to be seen. Instead, male servants bustle about, setting up long tables in apparent preparation for a feast, while other men busy themselves with tasks related to the upcoming hunt. Some sort through piles of equipment or affix dogs to leads, while a number of boys lead mounts over from stables within the castle's walls. In the midst of the activity is a tall, gaunt man dressed all in forest green, who barks orders at the others with a serious expression. I'm surveying the scene when a loud voice unexpectedly answers Gilles's question with a chuckle.

"The ladies will be joining us in due time, boys!" It's sir Brecelyn himself, who's come out of the pavilion at the sound of our arrival, and who is now offering his hand to Master Guillaume.

The master must have been riding in a carriage of his own at the head of our party, along with a few veterans from St. Sebastian's. After the men exchange a hearty greeting, Brecelyn turns his attention back to the Journeys.

"I bid you a hearty welcome, men. It is a great pleasure to serve as your host, and I will see to it that my household extends you every hospitality. You're in for some great sport today! There's no better hunting than here on my estate, if I may be so immodest as to say so. As everyone knows, these very lands were once the favorite hunting grounds of the great emperor Charlemagne himself! So with no further ado, let me introduce to you my master huntsman, a veteran of our own St. Sebastian's. Gentlemen, may I present to you M. Etienne Beaufort, the finest hunter in these parts by far." He gestures to the solemn man whom I'd noticed overseeing the preparations, and he bows slightly to us at this introduction.

"Now, I'm sure many of you boys of the gentry have been on a hunt such as the one we are going to have today," Brecelyn continues, nodding specifically to Gilles and Aristide at this, "but as this is to be a tutorial on organizing a hunt, I will now pass you into Etienne's expert hands, and I'll leave it to him to lay out our plans for today."

He gives a curt bow, which we all return politely, but as Brecelyn takes his leave, he first pulls Taran aside for moment. Unfortunately, he's more discrete than Master Guillaume, so I can't hear what he says, and Taran's face as usual doesn't give anything away. He's regained his composure since last night, and he's got his usual stoic look again. So I turn my attention to Etienne Beaufort, who is already explaining that first, we're to have a lesson on arranging a hunt that coordinates the efforts of horsemen, hounds, and archers.

"Sir Brecelyn has dispensation from the crown to hunt deer on his own lands, and so we're first to have a hunt for red deer. Two fine animals have been sighted in the forests around the manor over the past few days — a five-year hart and a six-year stag, both magnificent creatures. We'll hunt the first we get wind of. I've already sent my trackers out early this morning; as soon as we're ready, we'll follow the trail they've left for us, and it shouldn't take us long to locate our quarry."

This announcement is greeted with much enthusiasm from the boys; I don't think they expected such fine game. St. Sebastian's has a similar allowance, but tracking large game takes time, and I don't think any of the boys have ever gone after deer on an afternoon excursion over the wall. Tristan and I have always stuck to small game like birds or rabbits, and somehow I find the idea of riddling a 'magnificent creature' with arrows this morning distinctly unpleasant.

"Ordinarily," the huntsman explains, "for a hunt for a single beast like this, we wouldn't have such a disproportionately large number of archers. Three is really all we need. None of my own archers will be participating today; we want to leave the glory of the kill to one of you boys. I'm afraid, though, that ten archers are just too many. I'm going to have to ask that the squires not shoot." A ripple of disappointment passes through the crowd of squires, and Beaufort turns to us and adds, "However, I am going to allow you to accompany your masters into the woods. So boys, go quietly." Turning back to the Journeys, he says: "I will also have to ask some of you Journeys to ride instead, too, to lessen the number of archers. I'm afraid handling the dogs is too specialized a task, unless any of you already have experience."

Predictably, Turk volunteers to ride, and eventually Gilles and Aristide do, too, since it seems expected of them. But they do it rather reluctantly. It seems the promised girls have been temporarily forgotten at the mention of 'the glory of the kill,' and I can see that all the boys want to be the one to bring down the poor stag.

"As it is, we're still going to have too many archers," Beaufort continues. "So be careful. One of the most dangerous things about a hunt like this is stray arrows. Shoot carefully, and for God's sake, take your time aiming; not only do we want a clean hit, but we also want to avoid any accidents." He pauses, looking us over, then puts his hands together and exclaims,

"Okay, boys. Let's gear up. I hope you've brought light bows; the lighter the better. Once we spot our animal, you'll want to nock and bend right away, then hold at the ready from cover until your quarry nears and you can get good aim. All right, I can explain the rest as we go. Let's hit the woods!"

As we're getting organized, Beaufort fills us in quickly on the program for the day:

"Brecelyn has a two-part hunt planned for you boys today, with plenty of chances for a little rest and relaxation in between. Once we fell the deer, the ladies will join us for a leisurely midday feast, to be followed by some light shooting in the afternoon. Some of the ladies in the party who shoot will be joining you on the line, where beaters will flush out birds for you to snag from behind a blind."

It's going to be a full day, and the boys have clearly begun to get excited about it, but since I'm not to be allowed to shoot and the prospect of a leisurely feast with a bunch of girls doesn't thrill me much, I start to lose interest. As Beaufort launches into a detailed discussion of how to identify the age of a deer from its droppings, I make my way around to Falko, and at an appropriate pause in the lecture, I whisper to him,

"Be the one to bag the stag, and you're in with the ladies," I say. "At the least, it'll give you an opening."

It's obvious, but I've got to start somewhere. I really don't know how I'm going to follow through with my promise to him last night, but he nods solemnly as though this is a pearl of wisdom.

And so, as we get ready to head out into the forest behind Beaufort, who is now droning on about how to gauge the extent of an animal's wounds from the appearance of a trail of its blood, I fall into step with Falko.

"Just what do I say to them, when I've got an opening?" he asks.

"Keep it light at first," I reply confidently, as though I know what I'm talking about. "Stick to safe topics, like the weather. Or give them some teasing compliments, but nothing too serious," I add, wondering if this is good advice or not. I can't fall back on 'be yourself,' because that clearly won't work with Falko. He's always himself, and I despised him when I first met him.

"Falko," I continue, curious. "Tristan tells me you were in training to become a knight, before you came here." He nods. "Well, doesn't that include some training in the social graces?"

"Oh, I can dance, more or less, and use decent table manners," he replies. "And I've had the proper way to address a lady drummed into my head. But somehow, when I come face to face with one, I get so muddled, the wrong thing just seems to come out. The harder I try, the worse it seems to get."

That doesn't sound promising.

By now, two of Etienne Beaufort's men, along with Turk, Gilles and Aristide, have mounted up. Beaufort's horsemen each have a brace of scent hounds attached to their saddles by long slip-leads, and another man on foot who looks to be a tracker is consulting with the huntsman as the boys choose their bows and sling them onto their shoulders. There isn't much for us squires to do, since the boys are going to carry their own quivers. It really would be quite ridiculous for us to squire them in the woods. When everyone is ready, the horsemen lead the way; the hounds are to follow the scent of the trackers, while we follow along with the huntsman behind on foot, watching for the visual markers of the trail in the form of broken branches that the tracker has left for us.

It's still early, but the woods are already humid and still wet with dew. The moist ground is springy and silent under our feet, and even the horses' hooves make only a muffled sound as we make our way along a narrow track between the trees. When we come to a gentle stream we follow its course, and it isn't long before we cross through a misty glade in the center of which a strangely familiar structure is standing. From its form it's evidently a chapel, and the pinkish hue of its stones reminds me of the walls of St. Sebastian's.

"What's that?" Charles asks Beaufort, and he laughs.

"Don't you recognize it? It's a copy of the chapel of St. Sebastian from your own guild. Sir Hugo had it built here on his estate as an exact replica. A little reminder of the old days, I imagine. A rather nice conceit, don't you think?" Beaufort says, a bit nastily.

I suppose I should take this as a sign of Brecelyn's great devotion, but to me it seems a little arrogant. I'm not sure why. Perhaps sensing that some of us are all thinking the same thing, Beaufort adds,

"It's a good landmark, anyway. If anyone gets separated from the party, just follow the stream back here, and then it's an easy shot along the path back to the lawns. Because from here, it looks like we're going to be leaving the track behind."

He's right. The hounds are straining at their leads in the opposite direction, and soon it takes all my concentration to keep up with the group and pick my way through the thick undergrowth, and accordingly I don't have any spare energy for thought or conversation. We've gone a fair ways from the castle when the horsemen rein in their mounts and pull back on the dogs, and the tracker at the head of the party puts up his hand for us to stop. Beaufort makes his way silently to the fore, then comes back and motions to the Journeys to gather.

"It's the stag," he says in a loud whisper. "Up ahead. It's in pretty thick cover, so we're going to have to flush it out. There's no real open ground around here, but there's a small clearing just ahead where the trees thin out. We're going to leave the horsemen here while we circle around downwind, and I'll station you around the clearing. Then we'll let the horses and hounds drive the stag to us. They'll try to bring it on slowly. If the animal bolts, a shot is impossible; you'll shoot each other sooner than it. Just let it go." He looks around pointedly to make sure the boys understand. When he's satisfied, he continues:

"Good. From here on out, we've got to be as quiet as possible. Deer fear a man on foot more than one on horseback, so stay under cover until you're sure you've got a good shot. Once the animal sees you, it'll startle for sure, and we might lose it all together. So have your bows at the ready, but don't shoot until you're sure you've got a clear shot."

The boys all nod and prepare to follow the huntsman into our places for the ambush, but he's not done. In the darkness of the thick forest, his face looks even longer and thinner than it did out on the lawns, and he's so solemn as he continues that something about the long, irregular shadows of the leaves overhead on his gaunt face and the tone of his voice raise goose bumps on my flesh:

"It's not just a clear shot you need. You need a killing shot. An arrow in the creature's haunches won't be fatal, and a deer can move faster than you think. You want to put your arrow between its ribs, straight into the heart. From behind, aim between the upper ribs on the left or the right. If the stag is facing you directly, you can also go for a shot through the windpipe. An arrow right through the throat will bring instant death."

"Please," I say to myself as I follow Tristan into the hiding place behind a thicket where Beaufort stations us to await the stag a few minutes later, "don't let it face us directly. Don't let it face anyone." If we have to bring the great animal down, don't let it be with an arrow through the throat.

Once we're all in place, we're so tense with anticipation that it seems an eternity before the stag finally arrives. From our place of concealment, I can barely see the others; we've been stationed at large intervals and in a wide semi-circle around the clearing to lessen the risk of stray arrows, and the others are all well-concealed, too, so I sense them rather than see them. If I hadn't seen Beaufort instruct Falko and Pruie to crouch behind the tangled roots of a fallen tree about 20 yards away, I would never know they were there, and I'm not at all sure where the others are. But the air is so thick with tension I can't believe the stag doesn't sense it when finally it steps out from among the trees into my line of vision, lifting its long legs high and stepping with precision, its stately head and magnificent set of antlers bobbing gently over its body as it moves. Its breath comes out in a cloud of mist in the morning air, and I'm breathing so heavily that I imagine my own breath must be visible, too, as I watch it pick its way carefully toward its inevitable death.

Tristan already has his bow drawn to full length as the stag passes, its flank turned to us, and when it's a few feet beyond the thicket, he rises silently and takes a step forward, training his bow on its back and following it with his aim, looking for the killing shot. I rise, too, and I swear, it isn't on purpose when my foot hits a concealed root and I lose my balance. Just as he's about to shoot, I fall heavily onto him from behind, knocking his bow off to the side and sending him stumbling. His bow arm drops, and with a muted exclamation of surprise and irritation, he lurches forward to try to keep from falling. The stag startles, and in two springing bounds it leaps in front of the stump where Falko is waiting, just as an arrow whistles past us.

It goes past so close, I can feel the rush of air it leaves in its wake.

"*What the* ...?!" Tristan mutters angrily under his breath. "Doesn't Falko have the sense to hold his fire?"

But Falko is just now rising from his concealment, and I watch as he comes up in one swift move and shoots the surprised beast right in front of him straight through the heart. The stag rolls its eyes and stretches its neck, and lets out a piteous cry, before it falls to the ground at Falko's feet, breathing out its life in a foam of blood. Standing over the body, Falko gives his own cry, part triumph and part a signal to the others that the quarry's been downed.

Slowly the woods come alive, as the others all rise from their hiding places and gather around to congratulate Falko and gaze down at the fallen stag. Beaufort was right. It is a magnificent creature. Tristan is standing next to me, looking down at it in silence, too.

"I'm sorry, Tristan," I say, trying to feel truly sorry, and trying not to look down at its impaled form. "I ruined your shot. The stag should have been yours."

"I should thank you," he says, but he doesn't sound very grateful. He sounds angry, but not at me. "You probably saved me from being Falko's first kill."

"You don't really think that arrow was Falko's, do you?" I say. I don't see how he would have had time to get back under cover and reload.

"Oh, I don't know. Probably not. But somebody sure jumped the mark. It should have been clear the shot was mine."

In typical Journey fashion, he sounds angrier that he's been denied the glory of taking down the stag than that someone's almost accidentally shot him. But the hunt's over and no harm was done, except to Tristan's pride, so I don't think any more about it. I do sympathize, though. I know Tristan wanted to show off for Melissande, to do something worthy of claiming his prize, should the chance arise.

AT FIRST, THE STAG IS SLUNG ONTO A MAKESHIFT BIER of two long poles with canvas suspended between them, and we take it in turns to carry it back the long way to the castle grounds. There's no need to go quietly now, so along the way the boys are lively, discussing the hunt and going over aspects of it with

Beaufort, and of course listening to Falko describe his shot over and over, and in terms so extravagant they'd be more appropriate for a one-man conquest of Constantinople. As we near the edge of the forest, however, Falko stops us and claims the right to present the deer himself, and despite its size, he lifts it easily onto his back.

I do have to say, Falko does look grand carrying the huge beast along single-handedly, its legs hanging down on either side of his neck and its body slung across his massive shoulders. As he steps out of the woods at the head of our hunting party and onto the lawns in front of the pavilion, a high-pitched babble of appreciative voices rises from a long table set up in the shade near the tents.

The ladies have made an appearance at last.

They're arrayed prettily along the far side of the table, and as soon as we come into view, they all start tittering and clapping at the magnificent sight of Falko holding the deer aloft. Unfortunately, this makes him decide to stride over and fling its dead body down onto the table right in front of them. It lands with a resounding thud, its body giving a gruesome little lurch it lands so heavily. Blood flies from its carcass at the impact, spattering the closest girls with a rain of gory drops. Falko appears not to notice the look of horror on the girls' faces as they contemplate the dead creature in front of them and try to wipe the blood from their hair.

Instead, he puts his hands on his hips and booms heartily,

"It's going to be a stinking hot day today, isn't it, ladies?" and I cringe. "I'm already sweating like a pig. In fact, my ..."

"*Master*," I say hastily, rushing over and cutting him off in alarm before he can mention any more bodily functions. "I believe the butchers are awaiting the stag; let me help you remove it to a more appropriate location."

"Oh, er, quite," he says, snatching up the deer again in a swift move that at least shows off his incredible strength, and as I lead him off to where a group of servants are waiting to retrieve the stag, he says,

"How'm I doing, kid?"

"So far, so good," I say helplessly.

Maybe promising to help Falko get a girl wasn't such a good idea. Getting me to shoot clouts is going to be virtually impossible, but I'm beginning to think I'm going to have the harder part of the bargain.

The boys begin to put down their equipment and to clean up from washbasins that have thoughtfully been provided for them, and they're all still talking animatedly about the hunt, but from the moment we came out of the woods and saw the table full of girls, I know that it's been the real focus of their attention. It soon becomes clear that while Master Guillaume and the veterans will be dining at a table with Brecelyn and his men, the Journeys are to sit with the ladies, lined up opposite them at the table. We squires are to sit at a separate table by ourselves.

"No girls for us," Pascal grumbles, but I don't think any of us expected any different.

I survey the girls openly. Who cares if a squire gapes at them? Brecelyn's been a thoughtful host. There are ten of them, one for each Journey, and although they appear to be various ages, they're all more or less in a range appropriate for the boys. In the center sits Melissande herself. She's wearing all white, and her outfit is as dazzlingly bright as Gilles's get-up for Seconds. The only color is provided by a small circlet of pink rosebuds that crowns her head and holds in place the filmy white veil that covers but doesn't obscure the glory of her golden hair. She looks so stunning, even I can feel the pull of her attraction.

I wonder if she's supposed to look like a bride, or a virgin being offered up for a sacrifice. Maybe both.

It takes me a while to notice the other girls, she outshines them so, and I'm not the only one. The Journeys are all trying not to gape and drool at her, too. I even have a moment's sympathy for Taran. It's clear he's expected to take the seat directly across from her, and I can't see how he's going to keep from being a deep shade of purple throughout the meal. But the worst sight to me is Tristan; I ruined the hunt for him, and now he can't even bring himself to look at Melissande. His expression is such a pitiful mixture of longing and regret that I'm infinitely sorry I ever accused him of heartlessly leading her on.

When I do get around to surveying the other girls, I see that many of them are quite attractive, too. There's a girl with creamy white skin and raven black hair next to Melissande who's quite a beauty in her own right, and I spot a petite creature at the end of the table that I think will do nicely for Falko if I can figure out how to get him back on track.

I'm just pondering this when a hissing sound behind me makes me jump.

It's Gilles. He's apparently just gotten around to giving the girls a good look, too, and when I turn around, I see a look of utter astonishment on his face.

"*'Ods Blood!*" he exclaims fervently, staggering backward and clutching his heart. "She's magnificent!"

For a horrible moment I think he must be talking about Melissande. All we need is another corner on our love triangle. But when I follow his gaze reluctantly back to the table, I see he's looking down to the far opposite end. I don't see anyone even remotely magnificent there.

"What's the matter, Gilles?" Jerome asks with a laugh.

"Whomever do you mean?" adds Charles, and Gilles looks at him with amazement.

"Haven't you got eyes, man?" he says. "Look at her! A veritable Valkyrie! The jutting bosom, the flashing eye! And that magnificent red hair! Why, it's enough to make you want to die in battle, just to be slung over her saddle!"

I look back at the table again, but all I see is a rather large girl with a beetling brow who looks to be significantly older than the others. She's got a rather sour expression on her face, and she's surveying the Journeys with apparent dissatisfaction. She does have red hair, though.

"Get out of my way, boys!" Gilles cries, pushing past Charles and Jerome and making a beeline for the table. "Valhalla, here I come!"

"There's no accounting for tastes," Jerome shrugs with a grin, but when he catches Charles's eye, they both drop their bows unceremoniously and rush for the table themselves.

There's a mad scramble as all the Journeys jockey for position before they finally sort themselves out, some grinning as they win the best spots, others attempting to look courteous as they settle into seats across from the less appealing girls.

At the squires' table, there's nothing for us to do but eat and watch them.

Falko's maddeningly gotten himself at the wrong end of the table from the girl I have in mind for him, but I decide that's a good thing. At least he can't wreck his chances with her entirely over supper. As for Tristan and Taran, from where they're sitting, all I can see is their backs. From their postures alone, though, Tristan seems to be making a valiant attempt to be attentive to the girl opposite him, while Taran is predictably sitting so rigidly he looks like he might sprout roots at any moment. But they're both miserable. For Tristan, it's looking like there will be no chance for him to claim his prize, and for Taran, he must know the threatened private interview is imminent.

Gilles, however, is in raptures. I can see him gesticulating wildly, and reaching out fervently to grab at the hand of the imposing girl across from him. The more she glares at him, the more excited he gets, and when she finally reaches across and slaps his face, he looks ecstatic. Even Jurian looks to be enjoying himself. He's playing along and turning on the charm to a lovely little brunette who clearly looks like she thinks she's hit the jackpot.

As the meal comes to an end but no move is made to progress to the next phase of the hunt, the Journeys and the girls begin to excuse themselves from the table in pairs. They wander through the long grass, the girls picking flowers and handing them to the boys to carry, or they sit and talk on blankets spread out on the lawns. Gilles continues the pursuit of his formidable lady, strutting around behind her like a bantam rooster chasing a plump hen around a chicken yard.

I notice with some surprise that Jurian is still courting the little brunette. They've situated themselves on a blanket near the trees, and Jurian's already got his head on her lap, as she gazes down at him adoringly and playfully feeds him bites of food. He's eating it quite lasciviously, and treating her to quite a preview of that long tongue of his.

I wander over to the serving table that's still heavily laden with food. Brecelyn's put out quite a sumptuous feast, much better than the fare we usually get at St. Seb's, and there isn't really anything else for us squires to do but keep eating, so I've been stuffing myself. Besides, watching Jurian's lingual gymnastics has made me hungry. But before long, Jurian himself gets up and comes over to stand next to me by the table, and starts loading up another plate. I guess they need more ammunition.

"Having fun, squire?" he asks, managing to sound both amused and a bit insolent, but I don't mind. He sounds like his old self, so I'm glad.

"Not as much as you," I say back sarcastically, as he looks over some fruit indifferently and rejects it. Then I add more seriously, "It's good to see you looking so happy and enjoying yourself."

He turns to me and raises one eyebrow, and the corner of his mouth twitches when he replies, "I am enjoying myself, kid. You see, I've decided to take your advice."

"My advice?" I frown.

"Yes," he says smoothly, popping a morsel into his mouth. "As it happens, I've got my eye on somebody new."

I try to hide my surprise. I wouldn't have thought he would rebound so quickly.

"Is it, *er*, one of the boys?" I ask, trying to sound casual, but not sure I really want to know.

Now he raises both eyebrows. "Whatever makes you assume it's a boy?" he says archly. Seeing my confusion, he puts a hand on my shoulder and says,

"You do know I was a stable boy, don't you, Marek? Well, I'm just like the stable door. I swing both ways."

He laughs, squeezing my shoulder and picking up his plate, and then he's sauntering back to the waiting girl, who's watching him with the rapt attention of an acolyte.

I can't believe it. Could he really jump from the likes of Baylen to that soft little creature? I can't really believe he's over Baylen, either. But I'm left there puzzling over it, when it occurs to me that Jurian very effectively side-stepped my question.

He never said it was a girl.

I really have no idea who Jurian's got his eye on. For all I know, it could be Melissande herself.

Or worse, it could be Tristan.

It's already mid-afternoon by the time the ladies retire to freshen up and change into attire more suited to the second round of hunting planned for the day. Some of the girls intending to shoot also need to equip themselves, and so the boys naturally gather around their own equipment, both preparing for the birding to come and comparing notes about the girls.

Without much hope, I sidle over and ask Falko how he made out, as I'd noticed him thrashing around through the meadow behind the raven-haired beauty.

"Terrific!" he says. "You were right, Marek. A few well-chosen compliments really did the trick."

"Uh, what exactly did you say?" I ask with trepidation.

"I told her she looked good enough to eat, just like a ripe peach! Pretty good, huh?" When I don't answer, he adds, "I may have added something to the effect that, given the size of her, it's a good thing I'm such a big guy, with such an insatiable appetite."

Fortunately, Gilles bursts in at just this moment, saving me from the necessity of replying.

"Boys!" he exclaims, rubbing his hands together, "She's the one! I'm going to send to father about her right away."

"Just who is she, anyway?" Jerome asks.

"Sibilla!" Gilles says dreamily, drawing out the *s* in a satisfied sigh.

"Yes, but who is she?" Jerome repeats.

"Some cousin or other. What does it matter? I daresay her blood's blue enough to satisfy the old man."

"Isn't she a bit, um, mature for you?" Jerome insists. "She looks about thirty."

Gilles just glares at him. "An older woman, Jerome, has a little sophistication. And, she's had longer to ripen on the vine! Did you see those hips? We're going to have a whole passel of sons."

"Uh, Gilles," Tristan says, restraining himself from making a comeback to this last. "She didn't seem that keen."

"Oh, she'll be keen enough, when she finds out I'm to be the marquis de Chartrain," Gilles says smugly.

"I give up," Jerome declares. "Pascal, you try. Talk to him."

"Does she have any good-looking servants for me?" Pascal asks.

"That's not helping, Pascal," Tristan says sternly, but Pascal just shakes his head.

"Tristan, if I could talk Gilles out of anything he's set his mind to, I wouldn't be in the fix I'm in now."

But Gilles is no longer paying attention. "Where the devil is Mellor?" he says, looking around distractedly. Upon catching sight of Taran, he puts out his hand to stop him and pulls him into the conversation. "Oh, there you are, Taran. Look, when you get that interview with Melissande, be sure to ask her to bring her cousin Sibilla with her to Seconds. I want her to see me in action. After she sees my exhibition, she'll be keen, all right!"

"I hope she likes fur," Jerome says dryly.

"Gilles, Taran's going to have more pressing matters to discuss with his fiancée than arranging your amours," Jurian laughs.

"Yeah, he's got his own to arrange. That is, if he's going to be talking at all! He may indeed have much more *pressing* matters…" Falko adds suggestively with one of his obscene gestures, letting the implication hang in the air, and the boys all start laughing as Taran storms off.

All but Tristan. When I put a hand on his sleeve, he says to me softly, so the others can't hear,

"Falko's rude, but he's right. Taran's about to get *my* prize, and there's nothing I can do about it."

I don't bother to remind him that she's Taran's fiancée.

It's not long, though, before sir Brecelyn appears with a retinue from the castle and signals the resumption of the hunt, without making any move to provide the promised private interview. I suppose he thinks to make it the crowning event of the day, or else he's intentionally and cruelly putting it off to increase poor Taran's anticipation. But he does motion to Taran as he leads us away from the pavilion and around toward the back of the castle, where a long row of low screens has been set up on the margin of the woods.

It's then I notice that one of Brecelyn's servants is wearing a falconry gauntlet and carrying a bird on his arm. It could well belong to Brecelyn; perhaps he intends to hunt with it, while we shoot. But the bird looks small, not the size I'd expect for a knight to use. There's a strict hierarchy of birds appropriate to each rank, and since this is a clear mark of distinction, most hawkers won't use a bird below their station, at least not at a public gathering such as this. This looks like a bird for a lady, and I know it must be

Taran's gift for Melissande. Brecelyn is going to make him present it to her in front of all of us.

As we near the blinds, the boys again start jockeying for position, trying casually to get next to the girls they've been cultivating. It's harder now, since we squires are going to be allowed to shoot, and we're trying to get to the front, too. Tristan has dropped any pretense at interest in the girl he was paired with earlier, so he joins me on the line, but I see Falko barreling toward the black-haired girl, who when she spots him, snatches up a small bow as though to she intends to defend herself from him with it.

To my disgust, I notice that a number of the girls are armed with crossbows that look only slightly smaller and lighter than mine, and I'm glad I didn't bring mine with me today. Less than half the girls have armed themselves, however; Melissande herself is holding no weapon, and neither is her cousin Sibilla. We're all assembled and waiting for instructions when I overhear Sibilla say witheringly,

"Birds! Filthy creatures."

She's said it very loudly, and I can tell that Taran hears it too. Unfortunately for him, he's now standing next to Melissande and he's taken the falcon onto his own arm. He must be about to present it to her.

"What an auspicious introduction for the bridal gift!" Gilles says to Tristan in a loud whisper, elbowing him in the ribs, and they both laugh. I'm too far away to hear what's going on down the line, but I can see that Taran is indeed now taking off the little falcon's hood and showing Melissande the bird. Tristan and Gilles are keeping up a running commentary, repeating their jokes about the unlikely appeal to a girl of a carnivorous present, but I'm not listening. I'm too busy staring at the merlin.

It's absolutely beautiful. Its head and tail feathers are a soft grey, but its breast is speckled tan and brown, so that even when its hood is removed, the bird's natural colors make it look as though it's still adorned for falconry. Taran strokes its chest feathers lightly with one finger as he holds the bird up for Melissande to inspect, and the bird preens in response, darting its head quickly from side to side in a motion that makes it look alert and intelligent. It's probably because of the little figurine that Remy made for me, but I've been dying to see the bird, and now that I see it, the emotion I feel can only be described as lust. Taran slips the toggle lead carefully from the leather thongs around the bird's delicate legs, and when he jerks his arm up in a quick motion, the bird takes flight.

Instantly it's soaring high on swift wings; it's incredibly fast, and as I watch it climb higher and higher against the blue sky, I feel myself flying free with it. How it must feel, to leave the ground behind, to fly up into the clouds and leave it all behind! How I wish I could pull off my hood of scars, and soar like that little hawk!

It's all because of that little wooden figure. I've been thinking of myself as a hawk because of it, so priding myself on the qualities of the bird that Remy sees in me, that now I feel as though the bird and I are one. Suddenly I can't bear the idea that anyone is going to have it but me. *That bird should be mine*, I think irrationally, and I want it more than I've ever wanted any other possession. Let the boys make fun of it all they want. As a gift, no robe or jewel can touch it.

Soon it darts beyond the line of the trees, and we watch and wait for it to return. In the interim, Brecelyn himself explains how the shooting is to go, but there's really nothing to it. Once the hawk returns, he'll give the signal for the beaters to begin, and then it'll be a free-for-all, with everyone shooting at will. We're on a line, so there's no danger here of shooting each other. I've actually been rather looking forward to this part of the hunt, since I'm quite good at shooting small moving targets, and I'm sure Tristan will have a chance to make a good showing compared to the others now, too.

We don't have to wait long before the merlin is spotted, circling over the clearing, a songbird clutched in its talons. As it circles, Taran lifts Melissande's arm up towards it; while it was gone, he's helped her put on a gauntlet, and apparently they're going to try to get the bird to return to her. I can't help myself — as the bird circles, I find myself reaching my own arm up, too, as though willing the bird to come to me instead. There's no way it will, of course. It heads straight back to Taran, and I wonder when he's had the chance to work with it. It clearly recognizes him as its master. When it decides to descend, it dives down so sharply toward Taran that Melissande shrinks back, trying to lower her arm that's trapped in his hand, and she shields her head up against Taran's chest. I hear Tristan's sharp intake of breath at the pretty picture this makes.

The bird lands obediently on Melissande's arm, and Taran helps her lower the bird. I'm not sure what happens next, as they bend over the bird — probably Taran is showing her how to take the prey from it safely, or helping her replace the falcon's hood, but suddenly there's a sharp cry.

"Ha!" Tristan cries triumphantly. "The wretched thing's *bit* her!" and he and Gilles dissolve into barely concealed laughter again. It's not very gallant; after all, Melissande's been hurt. But the joy of having Taran's gift backfire so spectacularly is irresistible.

"Talk about inauspicious!" Gilles chortles. "What an omen for the marriage! A bridal gift that draws blood," to which Falko adds, "First blood, at that! Zounds, the blasted thing's gone and consummated the marriage for him!"

"We knew the bird ate meat, but we never expected it to eat the bride!" Jerome calls out merrily nearby, and pretty soon all the Journeys at our end of the blind are joining in. And I have to confess, I'm pleased, too. It's gratifying that the hawk doesn't recognize her as its rightful master, either.

There's a flurry of activity around Melissande as her bite is tended to and the bird is whisked away; predictably, Taran seems more concerned about the bird than about his bride-to-be, and to cover the confusion of the moment Brecelyn signals to the beaters to begin. Pretty soon the air is filled with birds. The boys forget all about the hawk as soon as they see them, concentrating on bringing them down. I'd been looking forward to making a good showing, but after watching the hawk, I've lost my taste for killing birds. Instead, I lower my bow, and I watch as servants take the merlin back toward the castle.

I wonder a bit sadly what its fate is going to be as the possession of that lovely girl who doesn't seem to want it.

CHAPTER
TWENTY-SEVEN

With so many shooters, it doesn't take long to exhaust the supply of birds. Servants materialize to fetch the fallen creatures from the field, and as each one is brought back, it's easy to match the birds to the hunters. The Journeys are all using their own arrows, which are marked with their colors. A few of the birds were brought down by the girls, and there's a little more difficulty in assigning these birds, but the girls are using diverse enough bolts that it's a pretty simple affair. I'm pleased to see that Tristan does have a relatively large pile of birds by his feet; our hunting has paid off, and he's clearly better at hitting a moving target now than many of the other Journeys. Gilles has a sizeable pile next to him, too, but he confesses to having been spurred to unexpected heights by Sibilla's outburst before the hunt started. He shot as many of the offending creatures for her as possible.

The day is winding down at this point and I assume the hunting is just about over, so I'm caught off guard when Brecelyn's huntsman Etienne Beaufort suddenly appears again. I hadn't noticed him during the birding.

"Gentlemen," he exclaims, rushing over and then stopping dramatically to catch his breath. "I've just had word from one of my trackers. The hart has been spotted in the woods, close to the spot where we took down the stag this morning. Who's up for pursuit?"

Predictably, all the Journeys start shouting out assent, and without further ado, they start to follow Beaufort back around toward the pavilion where their equipment for hunting larger game was left behind. My heart sinks. Killing the stag was bad enough. I thought it was pretty clear, too, that we were only going for one deer today. I almost decide not to go along; the boys can slaughter the hart without any help from me.

Then I see Brecelyn out of the corner of my eye, putting a restraining hand on Taran's arm, and from the frown that crosses Taran's brow as Brecelyn begins to speak, I think I know what's happening. Brecelyn is reminding him of his interview with Melissande, which hasn't happened yet. Taran is to stay back from the hunt, to meet with her. I don't want to be around for that, so I pick up my pace and catch up with the others, falling into step beside Tristan.

This time, there are to be no horses or dogs. We simply head into the woods behind Beaufort and his tracker, and the two of them lead us back along the same track we took this morning. It's not long before we come to the same stream, and as before, it leads us past Brecelyn's little chapel of St. Sebastian. But from the glen around the chapel, we take a new route, and after a ways, the tracker halts.

"This is where my man saw the hart just a little while ago," Beaufort tells us. "He won't be far. We've got to track him from here, and then set up for the kill as we did this morning."

All the boys have some experience tracking game, but we leave it to Beaufort and his man, and it doesn't take them long to find the hart. I'm a little surprised, though, when eventually we come out into an open place in the woods and I see we've actually circled around to the same spot where we set up to take down the stag earlier this morning. It must be a favorite haunt for game and Tristan doesn't seem to think anything of it. He's been unusually silent the whole way, and I have a heavy feeling that he's determined to be the one to bring down the beast this time. I think he noticed Taran staying back, too, and he knows why. Tristan's out for blood now.

Although I find the thought of Tristan killing the hart unpleasant, I'm determined not to foil him this time. So when Beaufort points us to the same spot behind some bushes as he's arraying the boys in cover around the small glen where the creature's been feeding, I settle in a ways away and tell myself to stay down. There's every chance the animal will go the other way, but if it comes past Tristan, I've got to let him take his shot. What are the chances the quarry will come our way twice, anyway?

I'm just thinking this, when I see that the odds are against me. The hart is coming our way, slowly but surely, and if it continues on its present trajectory, it's going to present itself neatly for Tristan's shot any moment. It may be a little smaller than the stag of this morning, but the creature looks just as regal as it bends to nibble on a leaf only a few paces from where we're crouched. When Tristan begins slowly to rise for the shot, I rise slowly behind him, too, and I'm trembling with fear and anticipation, but I'm being careful. It isn't me this time that makes Tristan stumble. I'm not sure what happens, but unbelievably he misses the shot, and all of a sudden I hear the sound of twanging bowstrings, and then the excited shouts as the other boys bring the hart down. But Tristan's fallen so hard, we both tumble backwards and he lands on top of me in the underbrush.

"I guess that makes us even!" I laugh, relieved that Tristan didn't kill the deer but through no fault of mine. "What happened, did you fall on a root, too?"

As I'm saying this, I'm trying to get out from under Tristan, but he's fallen heavily and he doesn't seem to be making any move to get up.

That's when I see it. The arrow. Sticking out of Tristan's side. He didn't stumble. He's been shot.

"Tristan!" I cry, clutching at him, but he hisses at me, "*Shhh,* Marek! Don't make a sound."

"Tristan, you're shot!" I say stupidly. Of course he knows that. "I've got to call the others. I've got to get help."

"No!" he whispers vehemently, his voice thick with pain. "Help me get under cover. Drag me into the bushes, and fast!"

When I look at him uncomprehendingly, he says urgently,

"Hurry, Marek! I can't let anyone know I've been wounded. Don't you see? I'll be out. I'll be out of St. Sebastian's, if they find out. For God's sake, help me, please!"

I don't fully comprehend, but he sounds so desperate I don't argue. If there's any chance he's right, I can't risk it. I scramble around and put my hands under his shoulders, and heave. Tristan lets out a grunt of pain, but when the sound stops me, he gasps, "Be quick about it!" and I start dragging him again, trying not to hear the muffled moans he makes each time I pull him.

I manage to drag him about five yards from where we were hiding and I crouch down next to him behind a spinney of small trees which masks us from view, while the others are busy over the hart. I expect any moment for someone to look for us, but in the excitement of the kill, nobody seems to notice that we aren't there. I try to question Tristan, but he puts a hand to his lips and gestures toward the group; he'll not say anything until the others are away. I try not to look at the arrow. I can't believe this is happening. Not again.

It appears to have been Charles who brought down the hart. Since we've brought no bier with us this time, he takes the first turn carrying the kill, and from our hiding place I watch him swing the hart up onto his shoulders with quite a bit more difficulty that Falko had this morning. It seems to take them an agonizingly long time to gather themselves up and move out, but before long I can't hear their receding footsteps any longer, and Tristan and I are alone in the woods.

"Tristan, what are we going to do?" I ask, as soon as I dare.

"It's not bad," he gasps. "I don't think it's hit any organs, or bones. It's gone straight through. It's not much more than a flesh wound, really."

With trembling fingers, I reach down and gently tear his tunic from around the wound. Another inch, and the arrow would have missed him. As it is, it's gone through his side at an oblique angle, low above the hip, in an area a less fit boy would probably have nothing but fat. And he's right — the extreme tip of the arrow is just poking out the back, so that it's only skewered about two inches of muscle. It shouldn't be a fatal wound, but it is serious. It's already bleeding freely. Once the arrow is out, it's going to bleed profusely. It must hurt like the devil.

"What are we going to do?" I ask again.

"You've got to get me out of here," he says, speaking with difficulty and pausing for breath between every word. "There isn't much time. They'll be leaving for St. Sebastian's soon. You've got to get me back before they leave. But first," he says, his head lolling back horribly for a moment, "You're going to have to get the arrow out."

"What?!" I cry.

"It's the only way."

"Tristan," I say seriously. "We can't hide this. If you're not tended to properly, you're going to bleed to death. Let me go and get help."

When he starts to shake his head violently, I plead desperately, "One of your friends, at least. Jerome, or Gilles!"

"We're wasting time, Marek. You're the only one I can count on. You're the one I need. I'm relying on you, little brother." He fixes me with such an intense look that I relent.

"Tell me what to do."

"The chapel of St. Sebastian's," he says. "It isn't far. If you support me, I think I can make it. We should find cover and what we need inside. You can remove the arrow in there. Appropriate, don't you think?" he says weakly, trying to make a joke of it, but I can't laugh.

I'm not going to describe the excruciating process of getting him to his feet and dragging him along to the chapel. Mercifully, the door isn't locked, and when we're inside, I lower him to the ground near the font. Working as quickly as I can, I strip off his shirt and cast around for some kind of cloth to use to clean him up and to bind his wound, afterward. There isn't much, but I say a prayer and hope the saint won't mind as I pull down the large altar cloth and use the tip of an arrow to rip it into long strips. With the wound laid bare and the blood wiped away, it looks worse than I thought at first. I have no idea how Tristan's managed to come this far with that terrible shaft in his side. Blood and other bodily fluids are seeping out around the arrow almost as quickly as I can wipe them away, and now that it comes down to it, the stretch of flesh that the arrow is going to have to pass through to come out seems to have increased dramatically. I know I can't put it off any longer; it's got to come out, and soon. But I have no idea how I'm going to be able to bring myself to pull it out.

As though reading my mind, Tristan says gravely,

"You can't pull it out, you know. The arrowhead could come out in the wound, and then it'd be all over. You've got to push it all the way through and out the back."

My eyes widen and my mouth goes suddenly dry, the way it does right before one's sick. Right on cue, a wave of nausea brings the taste of bile up in throat, but I force it down. I can't stop staring at the arrow. It's midday and the only light in the room is coming from daylight pouring in through high windows, but for some reason, I see firelight flickering around the room.

"Tristan, I don't think I can do it."

A flash of agony crosses his face and his whole body constricts in pain, and he reaches out and grabs onto my arm.

"Do it for me, Marek. Please!" And I know I'm going to have to find a way to do it.

"Take some wet cloth and wrap it around the fletching and the shaft first," he says through tightly clenched teeth. "Then, try to be quick, will you? To get it in one try?" His breath is coming quicker now and his face looks grey, and I'm not sure how much longer he can hold on. I can't wait any longer. I've got to do it now.

I leap up and take a small strip of the cloth and bathe it in the font of holy water at the front of the chapel. Then I kneel next to Tristan and wrap it around the arrow.

Thin beads of sweat are forming on Tristan's upper lip and along his brow, and I can tell he's scared. He's trying to give me a courageous look, but I think he's not sure I can do it, either. I'm just not strong. I've never wished I was stronger! *Please, Sebastian*, I pray to myself, *find me some strength for this!*

I roll him gently on his side, so I can get a good grip on the part of the arrow that's sticking through once I've pushed it free — I've got to push from one end and pull from the other to have enough leverage to get it out. As I put my hands in position, I tell him: "Go ahead and cry if you want. I do it all the time."

"So I've noticed," he says, but tears of pain have already started running down his face.

"Just don't pass out!" I cry. "If you leave me here alone, I really will kill you."

"Do it now, little brother," he says, his eyes starting to glaze over. "I can't take much more." But then a flash of his old smile crosses his face, and he says, "It'll be okay, kid — remember our motto, *non me occident sagittae*. If you want to kill me, you'll have to bludgeon me to death."

"That's not funny!" I cry, but I laugh nervously anyway, and while he's still smiling, I throw all my weight against the back of the arrow, and as the arrowhead appears out the back, I grab it and give a violent pull on the front. The sound that Tristan makes as the shaft of the arrow slides roughly through his tender flesh, sticking and juddering as it tears through him nauseatingly, sounds just as terrible as the death cry of the stag in the glen this morning.

But the arrow doesn't come free. I haven't gotten it in one. Tristan's now gasping and moaning so freely that I think I really will be sick, but I grasp the arrow again and give it one last terrible yank free. It makes a stomach-churning wet smack that makes me think wildly of Jurian's tongue as it comes out of his body into my hand.

As soon as the arrow's out, blood begins to pour from the wound, and I have to be quick. Who would have thought one boy could produce so much blood? But he's still breathing. I haven't punctured any organs getting the arrow out, and now that it is, I can see that Tristan was right. He's been extremely lucky. The whole wound is probably only about two or three inches long.

I stanch the blood with wads of the shredded altar cloth, and pressing against them as hard as I can, I work to wrap the long strips around his body to hold the cloths in place. To do this quickly, I have to toss Tristan around quite roughly, and despite my pleas, he finally succumbs to the pain and the loss of blood and passes out.

I don't really think he's going to die. The wound does seem relatively superficial, and it looks like I've managed to stop the bleeding. If no infection sets in, he should be able to recover from it fully. But when I look down at his still body, ravaged by the bloody arrow lying next to him on the floor, and his face looks as pallid and waxy as my father's did as he lay dying in my arms, I have a moment's panic. I gather him up and press my face to his, running my hands through his hair.

I begin to whisper desperately, feeling his shallow breathing coming unevenly from between his slightly parted lips, as I press my own lips down on his:

"Don't leave me, Tristan! Don't leave me," and I forget everything and kiss him with all my longing for the one I've lost and the one I'll never have. I can't lose him. I can't lose him again.

"Did you see? You did it!" I mumble against him incoherently, my tears running down both our cheeks. "You did the trick. You didn't fall. You're not going to fall. I won't let you fall! You're not going to die. Oh, you've worked so hard, don't give up now! You're going to pass Seconds, you'll see. I've sworn it, haven't I?" Why was I ever so foolish as to care whether he loves me or not? All that matters is not losing him. "You're not going to die!" I repeat foolishly over and over again against his mouth, "Don't leave me, Tristan. Don't leave me here alone."

When a soft groan of pain escapes him, I force myself to pull myself together. Hysterics aren't going to help him. It's going to kill him.

I shake myself and try to think, then I leap up and drag him gently into a dark corner in an alcove. Like it or not, I've got to have help. It's getting late — getting him here probably didn't take much longer than it took the others to get back, but our party will be leaving soon. I couldn't get Tristan back by myself, even if he were awake. His clothes are covered in blood, and I've gotten some on mine. How can I possibly hide it? Then there's the mess on the floor in here, too. I can't hide that, either.

I consider my options: Jerome's father is a physician at the University at Meuse, but I doubt even his father has ever seen a patient. It's all theoretical. Besides, I suspect what Tristan was thinking earlier. Jerome's in last place. He's got to pass two boys at Seconds, or he's out. That's going to be a tall order for him, the way he's been shooting lately. It wouldn't be fair to put the temptation of revealing Tristan in front of him.

That leaves Gilles. I've got to find him. Good old Gilles. He'll help me.

As soon as I make my decision, I'm quick. But as I reach the door, I hear voices right outside. With an exasperated curse of frustration, I flatten myself up against the wall, even though the voices are outside, and listen. Unbelievably, it's sir Brecelyn himself. And he's not alone. I hear him say,

"No one will disturb you two in here," and my heart sinks.

They're coming in. "It's fitting, too, isn't it?" he chuckles, and I understand. Of all things, it's Taran and Melissande. They're finally to have their private interview, in here. That's probably why the chapel was unlocked.

I have an agonizing moment's indecision. Here is help, right outside the door. If I step forward and explain, Tristan will have instant care. But it would be a betrayal of his confidence. If he's right, it could mean the end of our time at St. Sebastian's. The end of my time with him. But how long can I delay, without putting Tristan into real danger? I think I've stopped the bleeding, but I'm no doctor. What do I know? If there's any chance Tristan could die, I've got to break his trust. Nothing is worth risking his life.

The door starts to open, and I have to choose. I dart back into concealment beside Tristan in the dark alcove and duck behind a bank of pews. I'll wait and hope the interview is short. At least if Taran is in here, the others can't be leaving for St. Sebastian's. I just hope the boys are all too busy trying to make the most of their last time with the girls to notice that Tristan and I are missing.

"I didn't get a chance to thank you properly for the gift, earlier." Melissande's lilting voice comes drifting back to me, and I shrink down further.

"I'm sorry it frightened you," Taran replies, his voice sounding stilted and cold, even for him. "If you don't like the hawk, I understand. I can get you something else."

"No, it's a beautiful bird," she says sweetly, then she adds timidly: "It did frighten me, though, a little, at first. It's so big and fierce. But, I expect I shall get used to it, in time."

There's an awkward silence, as I suspect they both realize she hasn't really been talking about the bird.

"Whatever made you choose it, as a gift?" Melissande asks lightly, simply to break the silence.

"It's one of my own," he says stiffly. "I've raised hawks since I was a boy. I've always admired them. Merlins, in particular. They're small and delicate as hawks go, but they're tough. Gorgeous and swift in flight, and relentless in pursuit." This is the longest and most eloquent statement I've ever heard Taran make. In fact, he seems about to continue, when Melissande cuts him off, her quiet voice teasing.

"Are we going to spend the whole time in here talking about hawks?" And there's another long silence. It's agonizing listening to them, mostly because Tristan is still lying unconscious on the floor and time is ticking by; I've got to get out of here and find Gilles, but there's no way past them. But I'm also keenly aware that I have no right to be privy to any of this, and if the conversation turns more personal, I'll be mortified. Particularly if they stop talking all together.

Finally Taran says formally,

"What would you like to talk about, my lady?"

I hear the rustling of her gown as she moves, and then Melissande responds huskily, "We needn't talk at all, you know. You might kiss me, if you wish. We're bespoken. It wouldn't be a liberty." Her words are genteel, but they so echo Falko's crude comment earlier about 'pressing matters' that despite myself, I almost laugh out loud, but I'm glad Tristan's out cold. I don't think he could bear hearing Melissande offering his kiss to Taran, or worse. But I don't blame her. She's probably just curious. She's going to be married to him, after all.

The pause that follows this suggestion is even more awkward than the last.

"Forgive me, my lady," Taran replies at last, sounding strained. "But ours is to be a long engagement. It might be more satisfactory to wait, until we know each other better."

I can't believe it. He's rejecting her! It suddenly occurs to me that maybe he thinks Tristan's gone much farther than he has. Why else would he hesitate? He can't really be that shy or uninterested, can he?

"Indeed," he continues, "I beg your pardon, but I believe the day has quite exhausted us both. Please allow me to bid you good day. I will leave you to your prayers, with the assurance that I look forward to renewing our acquaintance in future, at which time I hope that we may continue our interview to our greater mutual satisfaction."

I hear his footsteps receding as he leaves the poor girl cold. He's brushed her off about as callously as he did the girls in the Drunken Goat.

The interview has been mercifully short, but infuriatingly

Melissande makes no move to leave. She's been told by Taran to stay and pray, and I can hear her moving toward the altar. After such a cold dismissal, I can imagine she's going to need some serious spiritual comfort. She could be here for a long time. Every second is taking Taran one step closer back to the party on the lawn, and I have no desire to eavesdrop on Melissande's private devotion. So I make a desperate decision. I'm going to have to trust her.

I stand up and step out of the shadows.

"My lady, please, do not be alarmed!" I say as soothingly as I can, but my voice must sound as desperate as I feel, and it comes out as an urgent rasp. Melissande starts violently and puts a hand up to her throat with a gasp, and I hurry on as she looks around wildly as though she's about to call Taran back to defend her.

"Please!" I cry, taking another tentative step towards her. "I mean you no harm! I'm a squire, Marek — do you remember me, the kid with the scars? I'm his squire, Tristan's squire."

Melissande still looks petrified, as though I'm about to molest her, and I remember that I've got blood on my hands. I shove them behind my back quickly and rush on.

"It's my master, Tristan. Oh, help me, do, my lady! He's been wounded. Shot, by a stray arrow, during the hunt."

Melissande is still standing frozen in a pose of alarm, staring at me uncomprehendingly.

"If you don't believe me, come, look where he lies!" I step back and gesture down at Tristan, and curiosity must get the best of her, because she takes a few tentative steps forward, as though I'm trying to lead her into a well-baited trap. But she can't resist, and when she's come forward enough to see his legs sticking out of the shadows of the alcove, she rushes forward and drops to her knees next to him.

"We must get help!" she cries anxiously. "Taran, or my father — they must be nearby. Quickly, run and get them!"

"No, my lady!" I say urgently. "Oh, listen, do. I know I can trust you! I'm putting my master's fate into your hands. Someone as beautiful and as gracious as you can't be anything but noble and true! And forgive me, but I think, you're not indifferent to him." At this she blushes and looks about to reproach me, but I give her no opportunity. Time is wasting. "Nobody must know he's been hurt. See, I've removed the arrow myself," I say, gesturing to the broken, bloody thing I removed from his body just a few minutes ago. "I've bandaged him, I've stopped the flow of blood. But he's in real danger, my lady. Not, I hope, of dying, but of being out of St. Sebastian's for good! He won't be allowed to compete with an injury like this. The competitions — they're for the best of the best, at the height of their abilities," I say, reasoning it out for myself as I speak. "Even if they did let him compete, they'd find an excuse to cut him. Nobody wants to watch a lame Journey," I end bitterly.

By now, Melissande has Tristan's limp head on her lap, and she's begun to stroke his forehead gently.

"What would you have me do?" she asks quietly, and I sigh in relief. I knew I was right to trust her.

"I've got to get help, and it has to be discrete. A friend. Will you stay with him, my lady, just as you are now? And if he comes around, tell him I will be back soon, and not to worry. Tell him, his secret is safe. It is safe, isn't it, my lady?"

She nods, not looking up from Tristan's pale face, and I add slyly:

"And if I may be so bold, my lady, but under the circumstances … perhaps, you might try to bring him around, with a kiss."

She looks up sharply; she must have realized by now that I was in the chapel when she and Taran came in, and that I witnessed her rejection. I figure it won't hurt to stroke her ego by letting her know that there's someone who would never have turned her away so coldly. "If anything could give him strength, it would be that. He's been living for the day he might dare to steal a kiss, to treasure for the rest of his life!"

With that, I turn heel and run out of the chapel. I've got to get to Gilles before the carriages start rolling and our absence becomes acute. I'm barreling down the track so quickly and with such single-minded intent that I almost don't notice Taran ahead of me on the path until it's too late. My conversation with Melissande mustn't have taken more than a few moments, and he's been in no hurry to get back to the lawns. In fact, when I suddenly spy him only a few yards ahead of me, he's come to a complete stop, and he's leaning heavily on a tree, with his back to me and his forearm raised over his head, his forehead resting against the tree underneath it. The disastrous interview clearly affected him more than he let on; in fact, he looks for all the world like the rejected party. He's in no hurry to get back to the boys and to the good-natured taunts that will surely follow fast upon his reappearance. I suspect he also wants to let some time pass, so that the extreme brevity of the interview isn't instantly clear to everyone. That's probably even why he suggested that Melissande stay and pray: just like me and Roxanne, he doesn't want it to be obvious to everyone that nothing happened.

Whatever the reason, it's to my advantage, and I say my own silent prayer of thanks as I jump off the track into the underbrush and skirt around him, giving him a wide berth. Fortunately, he's so absorbed in his own thoughts that he doesn't seem to hear me even though I'm making quite a racket.

As I near the edge of the forest and see the lawns ahead through the thinning trees, I hope against hope that my luck holds. I can't just burst out of the woods covered in blood and drag Gilles off. From the cover of the trees, I survey the scene: the Journeys and squires are still milling about, either talking with the ladies or helping to gather up equipment. Amazingly enough, it seems as though only a little time has really passed since the boys came back with the hart. Its body is still lying on the ground in the midst of a group of servants, and Charles is still hovering nearby, talking over his kill with some of the men. Only I can't see Gilles anywhere. Just when I think I'm going to have to come out into the open, I spot Remy not far away. He's hovering around peering into the woods anxiously; he must be looking for Taran. It's not ideal, but I have no choice. I make my way over to him, keeping concealed behind the bushes, until I'm only a few feet away.

"Psst! Remy!"

Remy looks around in confusion until he notices me lurking in the bracken.

"Marek! There you are. I've been wondering where you'd gotten to." Of course he has. He doesn't miss anything. "Whatever are you doing in that bush?"

"Remy," I say deliberately, trying to sound calm. "There's no time to explain. But I need your help. Please, don't ask any questions!" I say insistently as he makes to interrupt, "Just get Gilles for me, please. Tell him it's urgent. Tell him to come right away. Just do it for me, will you, Remy? And hurry!" I plead. I know he'll do it. After all, I took the lashes for him, didn't I? I'll figure out how I'm going to explain it all to him later.

Remy cocks his head to one side and looks me in the eye. Seeing my expression, to my great relief he doesn't say anything else, and I watch him scamper off. It's only a matter of seconds before he reappears, with an annoyed Gilles in his wake. As soon as Gilles is within range, I reach out and pull him into the woods, calling out to Remy both in thanks and dismissal. I'll deal with him later.

I'm completely incoherent as I try to explain what's happened to Gilles, but somehow he manages to comprehend the situation almost immediately, and as soon as he does, he takes charge. I knew I could count on Gilles! He darts back out onto the lawns and is back in a flash, carrying what look like a pile of cloaks and a flask. I don't waste time asking him what he intends to do, I simply turn and race back to the chapel, with Gilles following close behind. When we burst in and see Tristan lying limply in Melissande's arms, Gilles lets out a cry of surprise. It's not only the sight of Tristan unconscious that shocks him, though — I've forgotten to tell him about Melissande.

But Gilles is nothing if not poised under pressure, so he recovers quickly, and as he bends over Tristan, I ask:

"Has he come to, my lady?"

"No! Oh, do something! I've been so frightened!" she says, as Gilles inspects the wound and the bandaging job I've done.

"You've done really well, Marek," Gilles exclaims. "Only we'll need something more. If he's going to make the trip back in the carriage, we'll need to bind him tighter. And we've got to bring him around."

Without another word, Gilles opens the flask and empties half of it over Tristan's head, then he gives him a hard slap on the face. With a groan, Tristan's eyes flutter open, and as he slowly shakes his head, his eyes come into focus, looking into mine.

"Marek!" he says, and I move to drop down next to him and take him in my arms in relief, only to find to my annoyance that

Melissande is already there, in my place. All I can do is stand there and say,

"Tristan! You're fine. You're going to be just fine."

Melissande has begun to stroke his head, and now he seems to notice that she's there, for the first time.

"My lady!" he says softly, his voice still weak. "What are you doing here? Oh, I didn't want you to see me this way!"

"Tristan!" Melissande is exclaiming, "How could I not care for you, when you're hurt? Oh, I've been so worried …" when Gilles interrupts.

"Nonsense," he says to Tristan, turning to the pile of cloaks he's brought with him. "Did you a world of good. But now we have no time for a touching scene. Tristan, you're drunk," he says sternly, pouring some of the wine onto Tristan's discarded and stained tunic nearby, using the liquid to wash out some of the blood and to disguise the stains that remain with new ones. "Very, very drunk. It's ungentlemanly, but understandable. When lady Melissande here was with her fiancé, you couldn't bear it." When Tristan tries to protest at the bald way Gilles is talking about his feelings for Melissande, Gilles cuts him off. "Look, this is no time for mincing words. We've got to explain your state and the stains on your clothes somehow. Master Guillaume won't be happy, but if we time it right and get you back just as we're getting into the carriages, maybe he won't take much notice. It's a story the boys will at least understand; everyone knows you're crazy about her."

At this, Melissande blushes prettily, but she smiles shyly and I can tell she's thrilled, and Tristan doesn't really mind, either. Gilles is doing a splendid job of wooing Melissande for him, actually.

"Come on, there's no time. Tristan, do you think you can stand?" he asks.

"I don't know, but I'm going to have to, aren't I?"

Between the two of us, with Melissande flitting around behind, we get Tristan to his feet, but he has to lean heavily on me to stay there.

"Just as I thought," Gilles says. "The binding is good, but it isn't enough." He looks around the room, but there's nothing else to use, or I would have already used it myself.

"My lady," I say tentatively. "Would you be willing to lend your veil?"

It's a lovely sight when she reaches up and removes the circlet of roses, and pulls the veil away to lay her head bare, letting loose the splendor of her hair. Tristan sways and I almost think he's going to pass out again, though I doubt it's from his wound. How could he not be affected deeply by the sight of his beloved in all her beauty sacrificing her veil for him?

When we've got the veil tied tightly around him and Tristan has drunk some of the wine, Gilles and I manage to get Tristan's soiled tunic, now reeking of wine, back onto him, hiding his binding just as my tunic hides the one on my chest. Gilles throws one of the cloaks around Tristan to obscure the worst of the bloodstains, and I wash my hands with water from the font, and throw the other cloak over me, to hide my own stains. Melissande assures us that she has faithful servants who can be enlisted to clean up the chapel without asking questions; I'm sure it will be the talk of the servants' hall, but there's nothing we can do. As long as sir Brecelyn doesn't get word of it, we should be safe.

As Gilles pulls Tristan further up onto his hip and I slip my arm gingerly around Tristan's waist to support him back to the lawns, he puts up a hand to stop us.

"Melissande," he says throatily, and as she turns to gaze deeply into his eyes, I'm reminded of the day in the chapel of St. Genevieve, when Tristan pretended to be sick with love, and Gilles and I supported him past Melissande's pew. Only now, it's all true. This time, though, Tristan's flowery words escape him, and he seems to be at a loss as to what to say. But the need for words is past, and Melissande leans in, oblivious to me and Gilles though we're holding Tristan so close on either side that it's like a four-way embrace, and she kisses him lingeringly on the lips, before turning and sweeping down the aisle of the chapel, her shining head a flood of molten gold leading us out behind her.

So he's gotten his prize, after all. And all it took was an arrow in the side to get it. He probably thinks it was a small price to pay.

WE WAIT WITH TRISTAN ON THE VERGE OF THE FOREST until we see through the cover of the trees the carriages roll up that are to take us back to St. Sebastian's. As we support Tristan the long way from the woods, past the pavilion, and to the waiting carriage, it seems to me that it must be obvious that there's something much more wrong with Tristan than just being drunk. He's gone markedly pale again and sweat is beading on his forehead, and I doubt all the boys are fooled. But if they suspect something, they don't say anything, and they act willing to accept Gilles's lies. In particular, I think we're extremely lucky that Taran is still preoccupied with his own misfortunes. In fact, I don't see him around anywhere. He's usually so watchful, and he's told me directly he'd love to be rid of Tristan. Whatever the other boys might do if they knew, Taran would be sure to tell.

We manage to avoid taking Tristan past Master Guillaume. Though it will surely be considered rude, we dump him into a carriage without taking him past sir Brecelyn, and Gilles climbs right in behind him, not offering the expected thanks to our host, either. I have to make the return trip with the squires, and the whole way back I feel every bump in the road in sympathy with Tristan in the carriage ahead, and I hope he hasn't passed out again from the agony of being jostled along so painfully. When Remy comes up to me as I'm climbing in and says,

"Everything settled, Marek?" in a blandly innocent voice that strikes me as anything but innocent, I reply lightly,

"It's all okay now, thanks, Remy. And thanks for your help. Tristan had gotten himself quite drunk, you see," I say, falling back on the explanation Gilles provided, "and I needed Gilles's help. Tristan's quite fond of Melissande himself, you know."

At this, Remy looks distressed, as though it's the first he's heard of it. "That's unfortunate, isn't it, Marek?" he says seriously.

And I say just as seriously back, "Very."

I can't help adding maliciously, "And how is Taran feeling, after his interview?" But if I hoped to get a reaction out of Remy, I'm disappointed. All he says is, "I don't know. He was talking so intently with sir Brecelyn just now, I didn't get a chance to ask. But the interview, it was quite long, wasn't it? They must have had quite a lot to talk about."

Back at the guild, I help Gilles get Tristan into his room, and we survey the damage together. Tristan's remained conscious during the trip, but just barely, and he feels dangerously hot. I know the risk of infection is the biggest danger he faces, but there's nothing we can do tonight. We can't bleed him ourselves, and we can't call for the barber, either. So we settle for unbinding the wound completely and washing it out again, then binding it up again with fresh wrappings. We leave only Melissande's veil as an outer layer, for good luck, and because Tristan won't hear of taking it off.

Luckily, we're well versed in caring for wounds because of my recent lashing, and Gilles promises to send one of his serving boys out for herbs again the next day to make the same poultices we used on me to draw out the infection. I bathe Tristan's forehead with cool water, but then I have to leave him and go back to barracks. I want to stay with him all night, but after the incident of Baylen's flask, I can't risk being caught out after lights out. I can't stand leaving him all alone, though, so I search around on his table and find my manuscript page, and I press it into his hand. It's appropriate: he's had a narrow escape, all right, and it will remind him of Melissande and how she cared for him on the floor of the chapel. I can't help it if it will also remind him of the kiss.

CHAPTER
TWENTY-EIGHT

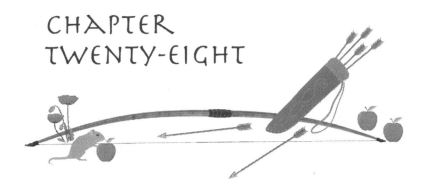

T he next morning brings fresh troubles, but not at all as I expect. Tristan seems in fact to be much better, but I find my vow to him is to face a second test, and this time, it's much harder than the first.

I hasten to Tristan's room as early as I dare, and I'm overjoyed to find him cool to the touch, though his color is still poor. Fortunately, there's no practice again today since the certifications are still in progress, so Tristan can stay in bed all day on the pretext of being hung over. Hopefully nobody much will notice. I bring him some food and force him to eat; then I go in search of Gilles's servants. By late morning we've applied the first poultice and the wound appears to have stopped seeping.

"Just a flesh wound, I told you," Tristan says, trying to sound cheerful, when I express my satisfaction with how the wound is coming along. But we both know the situation is serious. Because of Gilles's help and quick thinking, we've managed to get him back with no one the wiser, but tomorrow he's going to have to take the field again or questions will be asked. I don't see how he's going to be ready to practice, and even if he can fake his way through the next few days, Seconds is coming up fast. I have no idea how long it takes to recover from a puncture wound like the one he's sustained.

Reading my thoughts, Tristan takes my hand.

"Marek, it's going to be fine."

"I hope so, Tristan."

To my surprise, he says, "I know so." When he sees my dubious look, he says,

"I had a vision, Marek. In the chapel. A lady came to me."

"That was no vision!" I scoff. "She was really there. You remember, don't you? Or were you delirious? Lady Melissande held you, she stayed with you. Surely you remember." I don't mention her interview with Taran.

"No, Marek," he says, shaking his head. "I remember Melissande. That's not what I mean. There was a girl. I didn't see her, I just heard her voice. She kissed me, Marek."

"That was Melissande," I say, getting worried. Tristan seems better, but if he really can't remember what happened in the chapel, he must have been in worse shape than I thought.

"No," he insists, looking tired. "Oh, I can't explain it. I wouldn't try, to anyone but you, little brother. But I wasn't delirious. It was real. She kissed me, Marek. So tenderly. I can't describe how it felt. She told me I wouldn't die. That I'd make it through Seconds. And I believe her. I think, it must have been a saint."

Color has begun to creep into my cheeks as he speaks, as the memory of my rambling protestations against his lips comes back to me. I'd forgotten all about it.

"St. Irene, maybe," I joke, forcing a laugh to cover my embarrassment. But he shakes his head.

"Don't make fun of it, Marek. I thought you'd understand." He gets a wistful, faraway look on his face. "That kiss. There was something about it. You accused me of not knowing what love is really like, and maybe you're right. But I could feel it, in that kiss. It was love. It was a saint, all right, a saint's blessing. She promised she'd see me through Seconds, and I believe her." This speech has taken all his strength, and mercifully he drops back onto his mattress and rolls over in preparation of sleep, and there's no need for me to reply.

"I sincerely hope you're right," I say to myself as I tuck his blanket around him and tiptoe out. The kiss Tristan is talking about was no vision, but if thinking it was will get him through Seconds, I'm not going to disabuse him. I wouldn't, anyway, and St. Sebastian couldn't have sent *me* a clearer sign yesterday than the sight of Tristan with an arrow in his side. There's no longer any doubt in my mind about where my duty lies. There can be no running away; I've got to stay. But keeping my vow never to reveal myself to Tristan just got harder, knowing that he did get a kiss he can't forget in the chapel yesterday, and that he's counting on the memory of it to pull him through. Only it wasn't Melissande's kiss, it was mine.

I shake it off, reminding myself that I also know Tristan very well; he's enjoying the romanticism of it. The reality of a girl with scars would be an entirely different matter.

There's no question of Tristan coming to noon mess. Since it's a free day the masters don't seem to notice, and I put off the few questions I get about it from the boys with some jokes about the effects of wine and melancholy. I hastily take him a plate and stay with him long enough to force him to eat, but what he really needs is rest, so I take my own meal back in the great hall with the others.

After noon mess, most of us wander out into the garden. We can't go out to practice, since although the certifications are winding down, they aren't done yet, but it's too nice a day to spend it locked up inside. Gilles settles himself at one of the small tables and spreads a manuscript out in front of him, while Pascal and Armand start a game of dice on the grass. Some of the squires have brought out mending or other work to busy themselves with, and Jerome predictably starts to strum a tune on his lute. It would be a wonderful lazy afternoon, if I weren't so worried about Tristan. It would look suspicious if I were constantly running off to his room, though, so he's told me only to check on him sporadically. I'm trying to sew some cloth marks and concentrate on the words of Jerome's song when Turk saunters out of the great hall with a draught board under his arm and plops down in the seat next to Gilles.

"Fancy a game, Gilles?" he asks.

"Not now, my boy," he answers distractedly, and Jerome stops playing and laughs.

"Just what are you doing over there with such concentration, Gilles? Drafting that letter to your father?"

"Whatever do you mean?" replies Gilles innocently.

"Lady Sibilla," Jerome says, but Gilles just blinks at him with apparent incomprehension. "You were going to write to your father about her."

"Oh, that," Gilles says airily, waving his hand in dismissal. "That's all over. I've given her up."

"What?!" a chorus of voices cries. I'm shocked, too, after Gilles's raptures the other day. These Journeys certainly are fickle. "What happened?"

After a pause, during which I notice Pascal hang his head, Gilles replies coolly, "I seem to have been mistaken about the lady's character."

"Come on, Gilles!" Jerome insists. "Tell us what happened."

"I'm afraid she had the nerve to insult Pascal," Gilles sniffs, and I shoot a look at Pascal, whose head is now hanging down so far it's almost in his lap.

Everyone is interested now, and Turk calls out, "What exactly did she say?" and Charles asks, "What, did she try to order him around like a common servant?," while even Aristide adds, "Ladies these days! No respect for a squire's rank," and the other Journeys all add their voices, urging Gilles to give us the details and expressing indignation that anyone would dare to insult one of their squires. It's all rather rich coming from them, since they order us around like dogs every day, but I wisely don't say anything.

Finally, Gilles says, "It's Pascal's affair. It's up to him to tell or not," and instantly everyone turns on Pascal and begins to badger him for details. But he won't budge. We finally drive him from the garden, his head still hanging and his face burning.

Whatever she said, it must have been pretty bad.

Not long after Pascal makes his escape, old Albrecht totters out into the garden to tell us that the certifications have finally ended and that the field is ours again. This news brings everyone to their feet, and as the garden empties, Gilles comes along with me to look in on Tristan, though I can tell that he too is eager to get back to practicing. I tactfully refrain from mentioning Sibilla.

When Gilles proclaims that Tristan is making good progress and excuses himself, I take my leave, too. Tristan needs sleep, but if there's any chance for us for Seconds now, I can't take the day off. So I go out to the field by myself, intending to take advantage of the daylight that's left to practice my end of our exhibition trick. I can at least perfect throwing the apples, even if I now have no idea how Tristan will be able to shoot them down.

I haven't been at it long before Falko finds me.

"What in the world are you doing?" he asks me jovially.

When I explain, he snorts: "That's ridiculous! Come on, if you want to train. That's a waste of time. It's my turn to hold up my end of the bargain."

"I'm not sure I really helped you much, Falko," I say honestly, but he replies merrily, "Well, I don't think I'm really going to be able to help you much either, so we're even. But a bargain is a bargain."

And so I get my bow, and follow him out to the clout field.

"First," he says, leaning on his bow and contemplating me once we get out to the line, "there's not much I can do about your strength," and I droop visibly. If he can't help me with that, what's the point?

"I told you," he continues, seeing my disappointment, "I probably can't help you much. But the thing is, it's not all about strength. You and Tristan try to muscle the long shots through with your arms, but that's not going to work. With the right motion, you should be able to get more distance with the strength you've already got. And as for building strength, you're going about it all wrong, too. You don't want to bulk up. Bulging muscles will just get in the way."

I fix him with a withering stare. He's nothing but bulging muscles.

"Okay, okay, having a strong physique is crucial. That's not what I'm saying," he says. "I've got a lot of big muscles, but that's because I'm naturally big. The key isn't to grow uselessly big muscles, but to get the maximum strength from your muscles for your body type. And it takes the whole body, not just the arms and shoulders. You've got to have strong legs, a strong stomach, and a strong back, too. I mean, look at Gilles. He's lean as a whippet, but his whole body is a mass of nerves. He's got great distance."

I think about it; he's right.

"Or, look at Taran. Have you ever taken a good look at Taran's body?" he asks. When I don't reply, he says, "Well, do. He's big, all right, but he's big all over, and he's not bulky. Everything is in perfect proportion, every muscle defined, and he's hard as a rock. His size is a definite advantage, but only because he's made the most of it."

"Okay," I say, eager to change the subject. "So if you can't help me with strength, how are you going to help me?"

"Well, I do have some suggestions for different kinds of exercises you can do on your own to work on total body strength, but mostly, I'm going to help you with your motion. Here," he says, putting my bow in my hands.

For the next fifteen minutes or so, he coaches me about using the whole body and leaning back into the shot, but each time I pull back the bowstring, he shakes his head in frustration.

"No, no, no!" he says for the hundredth time. "Aren't you listening? It all starts from the legs. Sit back!" I really think I've been doing exactly what he's telling me, so I start to get frustrated, too.

"This isn't working, Falko," I say finally, lowering the bow.

He glares at me like I'm a recalcitrant child, and I glare back.

"Okay, I guess I'm going to have to force you through the motion myself," he says, pushing my arms back up into position. "Come on!" To my surprise, once my arms are up and I've got the bow in position to bend it, he steps behind me, puts his arms around me, and puts both his hands over mine on the bow.

"Just what are you doing?" I ask nervously.

"Relax," he says. "I'm going to do the motion with you. Just lean back against me and follow me."

I'm dubious, but game. So I lean back, and suddenly Falko is sweeping down and back so far I'm sure we're going to fall over in a heap. Instantly I see why he's been so frustrated with me. The motion is much, much more exaggerated than I'd imagined. But it catches me by surprise, so I lose my balance and we stumble. Falko rights us and we're about to try again, when I'm startled by Taran's voice behind us.

"And just what are you two supposed to be doing? Dancing?"

I feel my cheeks flame, since Falko's got his arms around me and is hugging me to him quite tightly. Falko's not the least bit embarrassed, but he doesn't know I'm a girl. Taran does.

"Oh, Taran, hullo," Falko says, letting go of me and turning around. "Lucky you came by. I'm just helping Marek here with his motion for distance shots, and having quite a time getting him to understand. Say, you're the expert. How about having a go at it? Maybe you can explain it better than I seem to be doing."

I can't see Taran's expression since I haven't dared look him in the face, but out of the corner of my eye I see him start violently. He recovers quickly enough, and he sounds perfectly calm as he says ironically,

"You seem to be making out just fine. Marek here seems to be benefitting immensely from your ministrations."

"Oh, come on!" Falko insists. "He's going for apprentice, didn't you know?" Falko's still babbling when Taran's voice interrupts in a tone I can't quite place.

"Is that true?" he says quietly, and I nod miserably, without looking up. Letting me stay on as a squire is one thing, but apprentice status is a step toward trying for Journey. I can't imagine Taran ever standing for that. He'll never let it go that far. I guess he was bound to find out sometime, but I wish it hadn't been when I was standing right next to him.

"Of course it's true," Falko's continuing, oblivious to the tension between us. "He won't make it without more distance. You can afford to help him out, just this once, can't you? After all, he's no threat to you." Then he adds slyly, "I'd think you'd see it as your duty to help a fellow member, when he's no competition to you. Come on, Taran, where's your sense of duty?"

I could kick Falko. Maddeningly, he seems to know exactly what to say when girls aren't around.

"It's all right, Falko," I say, finding my voice. Searching around wildly for something to say to put Falko off, I blurt out the first thing that comes to mind. "I'm sure Taran has more *pressing matters* to attend to."

It's a damned unfortunate choice of words. I don't remember where I've heard that exact phrase recently, and from Falko himself, until it's too late. I curse under my breath as Falko laughs heartily, thinking I've purposely made a lewd joke at Taran's expense.

Taran clearly thinks I have, too, because he suddenly says, "You're right, Falko. We're all friends here, aren't we?," but his

426

voice sounds malicious. "Maybe I should help out a fellow member, just this once."

I look up into Taran's face in alarm, to find him glaring down at me, his neck red, and for once I think I can read what he's thinking. He's going to punish me now for sure.

I open my mouth to protest, but before I can think of anything to say, Taran's taking my bow out of my hand and putting his own into it.

"What are you doing?" I say stupidly. "I'll never bend that."

"You're not going to," he says ominously. "I am."

When all I do is gape up at him, he says "Pick it up," in a voice so menacing I do it without thinking. "Now hold it as though you're going to shoot."

With Falko standing there nodding encouragingly, I can't refuse. I lift it up around the middle with my left hand, and grasp the bowstring with my right hand.

"What are you waiting for?" Falko asks, so I turn my back to Taran and step up to the line in preparation of taking a shot. Silently, Taran steps up behind me, just as Falko did, and when I sense him right behind me, despite myself, my heart starts racing. Taran's huge left hand folds over mine on the bow shaft, completely engulfing it, and his right hand closes over mine on the bowstring. As his hands cover mine, his body presses up hard behind me, just as it did in the windmill that day.

He's going to punish me, all right. He already is.

My knees start to tremble, and my hands under his start to shake so violently on the bow that I feel thoroughly humiliated. How he must be enjoying having me in his power again! How he must be reveling in my discomfort! But if he's thinking about the windmill, too, he gives no sign, and when he hisses in my ear,

"For God's sake, relax. I'm not going to hurt you," I'm so relieved that he thinks my reaction is due entirely to fear that I do relax, a little.

I feel him take a deep breath, as though he's steeling himself, then he says, "Lean back onto me."

"I think I can follow the motion fine, just like this," I reply in a small voice, and he tenses angrily.

"For the love of St. Peter, just do it!" he commands in a

strangled voice, so I do. I slump heavily back against his body, trying not to think about how Falko described it just a few minutes earlier. Taran bends his head down to mine and begins to explain the motion to me in a tight voice, but even though his mouth is so close to my ear I can feel his breath on my cheek, I hardly hear his words. I'm leaning on him of my own accord and his arms aren't on my waist, yet our position is so like the one in the windmill that I imagine at any moment his hand is going to come sliding over my belly, and I can't concentrate. All I can do is feel it, slipping upward in an arc across my flesh. Despite myself, I lean back against him harder, not sure if it's because I want to, or because my legs aren't working properly anymore.

Vaguely, I'm aware of him saying in a voice so low and deep it's almost a whisper, "The motion starts from the ground, and it takes your whole body. Push hard off from the ground, and sit back into the draw. Way back. Give yourself over to it." As he says this, he pushes off and leans back, pulling me with him as he bends his back leg deeply and the world tilts under me. We move as one, sweeping back in a motion that's almost a swoon.

"Feel that?" he says roughly, pushing upright again but not letting go of me. All I can do is nod weakly as I try to keep from swaying. "That's the sit. You've got to go all the way back."

Falko, who's been watching the whole thing, of course, chimes in:

"That's what I've been trying to tell him, but he just won't sit back far enough. They never do. That's what I told him. You've got to feel it to understand just what a deep motion it is."

"Got it now, Woodcock?" Taran asks softly in my ear, and I mumble something again, my face even redder than before.

"Now we add the arms," he says, not waiting for my response. "But it's not just the arms. It's your whole body, too. This time, as we sit back, we're going to bend the bow. Really push on the bow with your left arm. Remember, they call it bending the bow for a reason. You're bending the bow, not the bowstring. But the motion comes from your legs, your stomach, your back, all working in concert with your arms and shoulders. And you've got to bend it all the way — you've got to draw the whole arrow to get maximum distance. You've got to take the whole length of the shaft."

When I give an involuntary lurch at the unfortunate way this sounds, he falters, seeming to realize what a suggestive image he's just used. He recovers quickly, but his voice is strained and thick when he says,

"Ready? Remember, put your whole body into it. Give it everything you've got," and before I'm ready, he's moving again, as he pulls me back and pushes my arms apart, forcing my body in opposite directions as it follows his through the motion. We push off and reel back until I think again we're in danger of falling, but at the same time we push the bow out and away, and up in such a high, sweeping arc that I think we might really be aiming to bring down the moon. We're straining so hard in so many directions at once that only the violence of the opposing forces keeps us balanced. His bow is so big that my arms are much too overextended under Taran's hands as he pulls the bow into its full extension. But as I spread them wide, I feel like the hawk taking flight, with my head thrown back against his chest and the vast vault of the sky a brilliant vista above me. At that exhilarating moment, he cries out "Let it fly!" and I open my hand under his, and I feel something of myself fly out with the arrow into the blue as it speeds from the massive bow.

I half expect Taran to drop me at that moment, just as he did in the windmill. Instead, as the arrow is released, he pushes off with his back leg and we rock forward. My own back leg comes up off the ground with his as we're propelled forward, as though our bodies are hurtling forward with the arrow in its flight.

Falko was absolutely right. The motion is nothing like anything I've ever done before, and I was never going to figure it out by myself. But I'm never going to forget it now. It's like nothing I've ever felt, but Taran's burned it into every muscle of my body just as surely as he did the invisible imprint of his hand on my breast, which I'm acutely aware began to throb vividly about halfway through the draw.

"What a beauty!" Falko roars. "Why, that looks to be well over 450 yards. What a shot!"

It takes me a moment to realize that even though the arrow's long gone, Taran is still holding me up against him, his breath hot against my ear and his body tense and rigid under mine. He seems to realize it suddenly, too, as he slackens his grip and repeats roughly,

"Got it now, Woodcock?"

All I can do is nod again weakly, and I know he's about to let me go. But to my surprise, for a split second he squeezes me tighter and jeers in my ear, so softly that Falko can't hear,

"So, what are you going to do now? Run off and do it with Tristan?"

Then he does release me, so abruptly that I stumble backwards and have to catch myself on the bow for support.

"What do you say, Falko? Can I go now?" he says sarcastically. "I believe I've fulfilled my *duty*. Let him practice it on his own. Let him replicate *that*."

"Yes, yes, thanks, old man," Falko says, completely ignorant of my shattered state and of Taran's barely contained anger. "Come on, Marek! Let's see it. Let's see you try it yourself now."

I bend over shakily to pick up my own bow, as Falko blathers on innocently: "You'll never get the same range with your bow. It hasn't got nearly the draw weight of Taran's. But I bet you'll be surprised with the distance you get."

But I'm not listening. As I prepare to go through the motion again alone, all I can hear is the sound of Taran's steps retreating in the distance.

It takes me a few tries to get the motion down when doing it on my own, but I was right. It's part of my body now, and once I manage to replicate it, I can tell instantly by the feel of it that I've got it right. Falko was right, too. To my amazement, my fourth arrow soars past a wand at least 250 yards from the line.

As I trudge back toward the stables not much later, I should feel exultant. In one afternoon's work, I've gained more than 50 yards. Instead all I feel is drained.

At the stable door, I run into Gilles.

"How's the patient?" he asks, and I'm feeling so wretched and sorry for myself that for a confused moment, I think he means me. I'm about to say something rude when I remember Tristan. I can't believe I've forgotten all about him. "Oh, uh, I've been letting him sleep," I stammer, "but I'm going to check on him now. Want to come?" But Gilles shakes his head.

"Later, dear boy, later," he says, holding up his bow. He's apparently just getting around to practicing. He's about to head off to the field, when he pauses and cocks his head to one side.

"I see you've been getting some pointers from Taran. Is it my imagination, or are the two of you becoming friends?"

"It's your imagination," I say firmly. What happened on the field just now was anything but friendly. "A fluke," I add, when he gives me a disbelieving look. "An idea of Falko's."

"I see," he says, sounding like he doesn't see at all. "Fluke or no, he seems to have helped you, quite a lot."

"Gilles," I say abruptly, brushing this annoying comment aside by asking something I've been wanting to ask anyway; of course, Gilles doesn't know that what Taran was really doing was reminding me just how far I fall physically below the standard of the likes of him, and how ridiculous the idea of apprentice status for me really is. "Just why did Lord Mellor sponsor both Tristan and Taran? Why would he set them up, to compete against each other?"

"I couldn't possibly know, Marek," Gilles replies lightly. "But I can guess. He wanted a son in Guards, and he was going to get it. I think he was hedging his bets."

"That's terrible," I say slowly. "Can you imagine how Tristan must feel, knowing his father set him up to fail, just so he'd have a back-up for his favored son?"

"You're so sure Taran can beat him, then, are you?" Gilles asks pointedly, and I blush.

I spoke without thinking; I didn't mean to be disloyal. But after this afternoon, I'm sure. If he were whole and sound, I think Tristan could surely get through Seconds. I might now even get him past clouts, and into Veterans. But if it comes down to the two of them, Tristan will never beat Taran. After all, that was what Taran was just trying to show me, wasn't it?

"Lord Mellor isn't a bad man, Marek. Oh, I'm not defending him, but he was young and he made a mistake. He's tried to do the right thing by Tristan. But try looking at it this way: he's sponsored his dashing, smooth-talking bastard son, against his stiff and inarticulate heir, just so he can be sure to have a son in Guards, one way or the other. And he doesn't seem to care much which one it is. Can't you imagine how that must make Taran feel, a little, too,

Marek? Can Taran be so sure which one his father really hopes will win, of which of the two old Mellor is setting up for failure?" Gilles says.

But I'm in no mood to have any sympathy for Taran right about now. Not while I can still feel him pressing up behind me, his voice mocking in my ear. No, Taran wasn't trying to help me.

How I'd like him to be humiliated, the way he's just so deliberately humiliated me! I only wish Tristan could find a way to beat him.

Evening mess that night seems endless, and as I lay down on my cot, I'm a mass of nerves. I'm worried about what tomorrow will bring, when Tristan has to take the field. And I'm even more worried about what dreams might come during the night. There are no experiences from the past few days I care to relive. I'm lying there putting off sleep, listening to the familiar sounds of the other boys getting into bed and settling in on their cots, when the lights all go out. Tonight, the sounds I once found so irritating are comforting; the boys are my friends, and their familiar sighs and rustlings help keep my thoughts at bay.

The room is finally settling down into sleep when Rennie's voice breaks the silence, calling out,

"Okay, Pascal. It's just us now. Come on, won't you tell us what the old cow said to you?" and instantly others start to add their pleas. I do, too, glad of the diversion.

"I don't want to talk about it," is all Pascal will say.

We keep at him for about ten minutes, but to no avail, and I figure we're never going to find out. As the barracks begins to fall quiet again, Auguste begs one last time,

"Tell us what she said, Pascal! What could be so bad?"

But it's not Pascal who answers, it's Armand. "It wasn't so much what she *said*, it was what she did!"

"You know!" cries Auguste, and instantly we're all at it again, begging Armand to give, while Armand prods Pascal to tell us himself.

"Come on, Pascal. Tell them. It's actually terribly funny!"

"I said I don't want to talk about it!" growls Pascal.

"If you're not going to tell them, I will!" Armand finally cries, and when there's no reply from Pascal's cot, Armand announces,

"You want to know what happened, boys? She reached out as bold as brass and gave him a big fat pinch right on the buttocks, that's what!"

The whole barracks is instantly rocked by laughter, and I can feel Pascal burning with embarrassment in the dark. I'm grinning from ear to ear, too. *Good for Sibilla!* I think. It serves them right, all running around in those form-fitting tights. I've been dying to goose one of them myself since the first day I set foot in St. Sebastian's.

As the laughter dies down to a few last sputters, Auguste manages to say between giggles,

"You didn't, *er*, do anything to encourage her, did you, Pascal?

"I should say not!" comes the indignant reply.

"Well," Auguste says, "I'd make damned sure Gilles knows that when he puts that apple on your head!"

CHAPTER TWENTY-NINE

The next morning I get up early, even for me. I've tossed and turned most the night, so it comes as a relief to be able to get up and abandon the pretense of sleep. I hurry out to set up as quickly as I can, knowing I've got to have time to go back inside and help Tristan up and out to the field. This is going to be the real test, if he can make it through practice today, and it could go either way.

I'm the first one out today, but the other squires make an early start of it, too. Everyone's eager to make up for our recent days off, so soon Auguste appears and starts to set up Jerome in his usual spot next to me. I am surprised, though, when Rennie is the next to appear, since he's usually not very diligent. I'm distinctly annoyed, too, when he drags Jurian's stand over and sets up on the other side of me. I'd been counting on having Gilles next to Tristan as usual, for moral support if nothing else. Why today of all days did Rennie have to take Gilles's spot? Besides, Jurian usually shoots at the other end of the line, down with Taran by Charles and Turk.

When I tease Rennie about it, not entirely good-naturedly, he says,

"Jurian's been after me to get an earlier start. Nag, nag, nag! He's been wanting me to set up near Tristan. I just never get out here fast enough. Besides, this way we can be together; you're more fun than Andre."

I scowl. Whatever Rennie says, today is going to be anything but fun, and I don't like what else his words might imply. But I don't have time to worry about it now. I've got to go and see what shape Tristan's in.

I'm practically running when I reach the stables, so I almost knock poor Remy over as he comes out the door in the opposite direction. I'm apologizing and making to push past him, when I notice he looks entirely miserable. Despite my haste, it brings me to a stop.

"Remy, what in the world is the matter?" There are dark circles under his eyes, and his hands are twitching, but instead of answering me, he jerks his head furtively back and forth, as though looking to see if anyone else has overheard.

"Remy! Are you all right?" I ask again, really worried. He's never looked so fragile. He opens his mouth and closes it again, as though unsure whether or not he should tell me something he clearly wants to. I decide for him.

"Remy, tell me what it is!" I insist, and he caves.

"Oh, Marek," he says, his voice quivering. "It's terrible. It's Taran. He's been utterly wretched. I can't stand it! I've never seen him in such a state."

So that's it. He's finally had a chance to find out how the interview went. Leave it to Remy to take it so seriously. I relax visibly, relieved that's all it is. But then Remy says something so awful that when he's done, I think I must look as bad as he does.

"It's the hawk, Marek, Melissande's little merlin. It was such a beautiful thing!"

"The hawk?" I repeat dully.

"Don't tell the others, will you? They might tease him, and I don't think he could stand it! But when we were out hunting the hart, sir Brecelyn, he ..." his voice falters, then he sobs, "Oh, Marek, he wrung its neck, for biting his daughter!"

I can't believe it. The image of Brecelyn's hands on the bird's neck flashes before me and I feel sick. Why would he do such an ugly thing? I saw his servants carry it back to the castle. Perhaps killing it in anger would make sense. To go back later and coldly twist the life out of the poor thing, it makes no sense at all. I try to block it out, but in my head I hear the sound of its small bones cracking, I see its head hanging limp and lifeless. Brecelyn must be a vindictive man, indeed. I can't believe that soaring, free thing is dead.

I can't think of anything to say.

"My little hawk. It's a copy of the merlin, isn't it?" I finally find myself asking.

"Yes," Remy admits sadly, and I'm afraid I might start crying, too, so I put my hand briefly on his shoulder and give it a squeeze, and then hurry out of the stables and down the corridor to Tristan's room. I know why Remy didn't want to tell me about the bird. How Tristan and the others would love to learn the fate of Taran's bridal gift! Tristan in particular would revel in gloating over the fate of the hawk. I can almost hear Gilles's voice making some new quip about how much more inauspicious the whole thing was than he'd thought. I bet Falko could even find a way to make it into something lewd. But I can't laugh about it. I'm not going to tell Tristan. I'm not going to tell anyone. I wish I didn't even know it myself.

When I reach Tristan's door, concern over what I might find on the other side pushes the thought of the hawk to the back of my mind. But when I open the door, I find Tristan already dressed and sitting up on the edge of his cot, grinning. He's clearly immensely proud of himself, and as soon as I enter, he says,

"What do you say, Marek? Do I look a new man?" He actually looks a bit grey, but I don't say so.

"Ready?" I ask instead.

"As ready as I'll ever be."

"Then let me see you get up by yourself."

He manages it quite credibly, with only a slight jerk and wheeze at the initial effort. He makes it all the way out to the field entirely on his own, too, without my support, though we take it at such a leisurely pace that any casual observer would surely think we were philosophers out for a stroll rather than archers taking the field. As we approach our station, Gilles catches up with us. With his usual spot taken, Pascal's set him up at the other end of the field, down by Falko and Taran. I curse Rennie again; once practice starts, Gilles will be too far away to be of any help.

"Why didn't you boys wait for me?" Gilles asks irritably. "I went along to your room, and you weren't there."

"I had to come out on my own, Gilles," Tristan says, but Gilles shakes his head.

"You should have waited for me to bind you up properly this morning. The wrappings were loose for the night. You'll need more support for practice," he scolds. "You'd better take it easy, or they're never going to hold."

"Glad you reminded me, Gilles," Tristan says sarcastically, "or I'd have really tried to push it today." But I'm worried. Gilles is right. We should have redone his binding this morning, and now it's too late. Baylen is already striding out onto the field, and to my dismay, right behind him is Master Leon. It seems he's finally decided to take a hand in training the boys himself.

"Just watch yourself!" Gilles snaps as he moves off to take his place on the line, and practice is upon us.

The next three hours are agonizing. I feel like I did on my first day as squire, only now it's Tristan who is woefully out of shape and struggling to keep up. With Master Leon watching, the boys are intent on their own shooting, so I don't know if any of them notice at first how awkward and stiff Tristan is. Mercifully his wound is on his left side, away from his pulling arm, so his general weakness seems more of an issue than the actual wound, but his shots are slow and tentative, and many of them don't even make it to the embankment. It's pretty obvious, since I have to bend down and pull the arrows out of the ground, so eventually Jurian says,

"What's with you, Tristan? Master Leon throwing you off?"

To which he replies lightly, "Just experimenting with something new."

But he looks worried, and I can tell he's already getting winded even though we've only been at it for about thirty minutes. I try to take my time retrieving to give him more time to recover between rounds, but when Baylen calls me on it I have to hustle, and when Master Leon calls for speed shooting, I hope nobody notices that Tristan is only shooting one arrow for every four of the others. My only consolation is that Jerome doesn't seem to be doing much better than Tristan today, for some reason. Strangely enough, he seems to be trying to avoid taking all his shots almost as assiduously as Tristan is.

After about an hour, Tristan's looking pale and his face has a pinched look every time he has to shoot. So we play a little farce, where Tristan pretends to offer me his bow on a lark, to see how I'll do. By this time we've moved to the far butts and we're shooting at about 260 yards, and the look on Tristan's face is priceless when I try the new motion I learned during my training session the previous day — and my arrow not only reaches the butts, but sticks about a foot below the target.

"Let's see that again!" he says, not just playing at wasting time now, so I nock another arrow. Only this time, when I rock back and strain to pull Tristan's bow to its full extent, as I spread my arms wide, I feel a jab of pity as I think of the merlin spreading its wings and soaring over the forests of Brecelyn's estate. How I wish it had flown away, and never come back! I hear Taran's voice in my head, saying *'I've raised them since I was a little boy. I've always admired them.'* As the arrow flies from my bow, in my mind I see a lonely, sullen little boy, stroking the breast of a merlin with one finger, trying to model himself on the bird he so admires. For the first time, I do spare a thought for how Taran must feel; about how he must feel about all of it.

"If you can do it a third time, I'll really believe it!" Tristan jokes, pulling me back from the thought with an exclamation of praise. So I prepare to shoot again, this time determined to give it everything I've got. And this time, as I push my body through the motion that Taran showed me, my momentary sympathy for him is swept away by a rush of shame, remembering how I responded to the feel of him under me. I feel his body again behind mine vividly and I hear his soft, mocking voice in my ear, "Got it now, Woodcock?"

I still feel sick about the little bird, but I could gladly wring Taran's neck myself.

After that, I don't want to shoot again, and three arrows is all we can really get away with, anyway. Tristan's got to keep shooting, and though he's clearly done very poorly today, by stalling, dawdling, and other similar maneuvers we manage to get through the rest of practice. I'm not sure what the masters think; from Baylen's expression whenever he looks our way, I get the impression he thinks it's some prank of Tristan's, which suits me fine.

The final half-hour of practice is the worst. Tristan has been holding up admirably, but he's looking drained and his arm that holds up the bow on his wounded side is starting to shake visibly. I don't like his color, either. What makes it worse is that we're so close to the end. Every time there's a pause, I think it's over and so does Tristan, but our relief is then cut short when Baylen calls for another round. Finally, though, I think it really must be over. We've made it through, and I'm already starting to pack up our gear with a grin at Tristan, when Baylen's voice calls out,

"To attention, men!" and I fall into line next to Tristan, apprehensive.

"With Seconds so close upon us, Master Leon would like to see for himself how you boys are progressing. Please line up, and resume shooting at 260 yards. The master and I will make our way down the line, inspecting each of you individually, and offering personalized corrections and criticism. When we have passed your station, you may go in."

Master Leon, who's been lounging in the shade of the stable eaves all morning, now rouses himself to join Baylen, and they head down to the far end of the line, where Falko, Taran, and Gilles are stationed.

I turn to Tristan with a heavy heart, and I try to sound encouraging. "It's just a few more shots, Tristan. We'll make it. Take your time, until they get close."

But he doesn't even lift his bow, and Jurian says jokingly,

"Can't you even be bothered to finish the set?," and even Jerome adds, "That must be quite a hang-over, old man, to last two days!"

"You've got no idea," Tristan says with a ghost of a smile, but it isn't funny. We just stand there silently next to each other, Tristan swaying a little, while Baylen and Leon work their way down the line, absorbed in their critique of the other boys. I notice that Gilles doesn't go in, even though he was near the beginning of the line and other boys after him are already long gone. He stays lounging near the stables, leaning on his bow and pretending to confer with Taran about something, but I know he's purposely delaying, and that he's worried about Tristan, too. I wish there was some pretext I could use to call him over, but I can't think of anything.

Jurian's been shooting steadily and keeping up a running banter the whole time, but as Baylen and Leon get closer, I notice that he isn't really paying attention to Tristan. His banter has been for his own benefit, to distract himself. He and Baylen have been avoiding each other lately, for obvious reasons, and I can tell he's getting nervous as Baylen approaches for his personal inspection. I'm sure I was right; he's not over Baylen by a long shot.

When Jurian's turn to be critiqued finally comes, with the masters so near Tristan has to resume the pretense of shooting. But as he nocks an arrow and lifts his bow stiffly, I see with horror that a bloom of fresh blood is showing on his side. Gilles was right. The binding hasn't held, and Tristan's opened his wound. Blood must have been seeping through the bandages slowly for a while, and now it's soaked through the binding and onto his tunic. Stupid, stupid! Why didn't I wait for Gilles? Why didn't we think this might happen, and dress Tristan in something darker than dull grey linen?

It's not really that much blood, but it is blood, and it's unmistakable. I didn't notice it before because Tristan's arm was down. Now with his arm raised to shoot, there's no missing it. I'm blocking the view of Tristan from the boys still to come on the line, but as soon as Baylen and Leon turn from Jurian and step over to inspect Tristan closely, they can't help but see it.

It's only a matter of seconds after I notice the blood that I hear Baylen say, "Okay, Jurian. That'll do," and I know the masters are about to turn to Tristan.

There's no time to think — it's time to panic.

So I do the first thing that comes into my head. I grab up one of the arrows I've stuck point-down into the ground near my feet to be ready to hand, and I step up right into Tristan, while saying to him in a low and urgent whisper, "Tristan, I'm going to foul your shot!"

"*What are you talking ...?*" he starts to say uncomprehendingly, but before he can finish, I take the arrow in my hand and shove it as hard as I can into my own forearm, biting down hard on my lip to keep from crying out. If I thought pushing that arrow through Tristan's body was hard, pushing one through my own is even harder. In fact, as soon as the point breaks my skin, I can barely force myself to do it, and I don't manage to get it in very far. It isn't even the pain, which I don't really feel yet — it's the nauseating resistance of it, the horrible way it slips and slides against the soft tissues that makes me gag. But I've got to get blood, so I force myself to drive it in again as hard as I can, twisting it with all my might and willing it to bleed.

"Marek, what the devil?!" Tristan exclaims in shocked surprise, and as he does, I let out a cry of pain that's entirely genuine, too, grinding the arrow in further and then clamping my hand over the wound, trying to sop up as much blood as I can. As Baylen pushes Jurian aside and strides around him to see what's going on, I sway and grab onto Tristan for support, making sure to smear him with my bloody hand in just the spot where his own blood is beginning to show.

"What in the blazes happened, kid?" Tristan mutters, and I lean so heavily onto him that in his state he almost loses his balance, but in the process I whisper desperately in his ear, "You're bleeding through your shirt! Play along!"

Surprise then comprehension flash across his features as he drops his bow and we each try to support the other.

By now both Baylen and Master Leon have come over, as have most of the other boys who are still out on the field, and I'm holding the bloody arrow and bellowing bloody murder.

"What happened here, boys?" Master Leon demands, sounding more annoyed than concerned. "Haven't shot another one, have you, duBois?"

"It wasn't his fault, master!" I gasp, really feeling the pain now. "It was mine. I didn't realize he was about to shoot, and I put my arm out at just the wrong moment."

"And just why would you do that?" Leon asks reasonably, making no move to help me or even look at my arm. I already know from the barracks he's one cold bastard.

"I don't know," I say truthfully. It doesn't make any sense, but I have to say something, don't I? "I got distracted and forgot I'd already given him an arrow, I guess," I say feebly, as Leon looks at me skeptically. I'm sure he doesn't believe me, but I don't think he knows what's really going on.

"Master," Tristan interrupts, sounding desperate, "Permission to attend to my squire!"

"Are you sure you want this boy squiring for you, duBois?" he drawls. "He seems to be inordinately accident-prone."

"This was his last accident, I promise," Tristan says.

"See to it that it is," is all Leon says, looking down at me with the same look he gave me in the barracks when I took Remy's lashes. I know he suspects something, but he also looks a little amused. "Permission granted," he says sardonically, without much interest. "And, for Pete's sake, somebody, clean up this mess!"

As Tristan and I lean on each other and make our way back into the guild past an astonished Gilles, I say to Tristan through clenched teeth,

"Well, that killed two birds with one stone, didn't it? It hid the blood, and it got you out of shooting for Master Leon!"

"Next time," Tristan replies heavily, "Try not to mangle yourself in the process, eh, kid?"

Tristan takes me straight back to his room, not to the barracks, and Gilles soon joins us there. It hasn't taken him long to figure out what must have happened.

"That was quick thinking, squire!" he says enthusiastically, as he binds Tristan up again, then turns to tend to my now throbbing arm. But Tristan isn't at all enthusiastic.

"It was outrageous, Marek!" he storms. "You should have just let them see the blood, and let me take the consequences. What were you thinking? You could have hit a nerve, and lost the use of your hand! You could have hit a bone. Then the arrowhead would have had to be cut out. You shouldn't have done it!"

But I don't mind. I let him rant for a while, pleased by his concern.

"Are you done?" I ask finally, as he runs out of things to say. "Stop fussing so! It's barely a scratch. I only managed the slightest of cuts. If they'd have looked closely, it would have been obvious the blood couldn't have all come from it. Most of the blood was yours. In fact, with it bandaged up, I could even return to practice now." Tristan looks a bit mollified by this; I can tell he's feeling guilty. But then Gilles says soberly,

"That's not entirely true, Marek. You're right, your wound isn't very serious. You should heal up nicely. But it's pretty deep. It took a lot of courage to do that to yourself, and Tristan's right. You could have easily done some permanent damage. Not many of the other boys would have done it."

Without knowing it, Gilles has just paid me the compliment I most want to hear, so instead of making a reply, I bask in it while Gilles turns back to Tristan.

"You've actually come through today relatively well, too, I think. The wound's only reopened slightly, and if you did that well today with a loose binding, you should be fine as long as we get you wrapped more tightly tomorrow. I'd say you should be on the road to recovery in about a week's time."

None of us say what we're thinking — that in a week, it will be only a few days before Seconds.

When Gilles goes out, Tristan turns to me soberly.

"Marek, there's no way I can thank you for what you did today."

"Yes there is. You can make it through Seconds," I say lightly.

"About that," he says slowly. "I don't like to ask, not after what you did. But ... do you think you can do something else for me this afternoon?"

I'm surprised, but I don't show it. What can be so important to him, that he's thinking about it now?

"There's no point pretending we're going to go out and practice," he continues. "So, if you're up for it, there's something you could do for me. For us. But only if you really feel up to it."

"What is it?" I ask, curious after this lead-up.

"I want you to go into town, to the square. To the cathedral. I want you to buy a medal of St. Margaret, for me to wear around my neck along with my Journey medal. I think she must really be looking out for me, Marek."

I don't reply. What can I say to that?

Taking my silence as assent, Tristan reaches for something on his table, and soon he's putting some coins in my hand.

"This is the very last of my money. Take it to buy the medal; buy one for yourself, too, if you want. Do you think you could do that? If not, it can wait." He sounds so serious, and solicitous, too, that I don't hesitate.

"Of course I can do it. It's not like I have to walk there on my hands. Besides," I lie, "my arm doesn't even hurt anymore."

"Good!" he says, relieved. "See? The saint is looking out for you, too, already."

I don't say what I'm thinking, that if St. Margaret is really looking after me, having me shove an arrow through my own arm is a rather funny way of doing it. Besides, it should be perfectly obvious who it is who's really been looking out for him.

And so after noon mess, I find myself crossing through the garden on my way out of the guild. Before I make it to the gate in the wall, however, Remy catches up with me under the vines, wanting to ask me about my arm, so I invite him to come with me.

"Oh, uh, thanks, Marek. Maybe another time," he says, and I assume he's got to practice with the insatiable Taran. But when I say so, he disabuses me. "No, Taran's not practicing today," he says, frowning. "It's not that. It's just, I don't like to go outside, by myself."

"You wouldn't be by yourself, you'd be with me. And it's just to the cathedral."

"Still, I'd rather not," he insists. "And if I were you, I wouldn't venture out by yourself, either. There are some rough customers around Louvain, you know, who'd like nothing better than catching a squire outside the guild by himself."

I refrain from saying that his master is one of them.

As I cross the little bridge over the canal that skirts the market square, I think guiltily how long it's been since I've set foot inside the great cathedral. I didn't even attend mass here on St. Margaret's own feast day, since my disastrous quarrel with Tristan and confrontation with Taran in the windmill swept all thought of it from my mind. As soon as I step inside the great church and feel the cool, austere air inside, I'm instantly sorry it's been so long, and I feel guilty for being scornful of Tristan's desire for guidance from the saint. He's right. We could both use a little guidance, and for Seconds, we can use all the help we can get.

I go straight to a little room at the side of the narthex and buy Tristan his medal from an old woman behind the counter, then I count the remaining coins. There are just enough for one for me, too, and for five candles. This time, instead of lighting the candles in the side alcove where Marieke used to light them, I take them up to the front altar, and I light them at the feet of Margaret herself: one each for my mother, my father, Jules, Berthal, and Tristan. It's depressing how many of them there are. My candles alone let off quite a blaze.

It's still not long after high noon, and at this hour the cathedral is quiet. Only a few other patrons light candles or pray in the various chapels that line the sides of the church, so I sit down in a pew a few rows back, off to the side, and watch the flames of my candles from a distance, and think. My father was right: the arrows do just keep coming. But I think even he would be surprised at how many of mine have involved literal arrows! I suppose that's what I get for taking refuge in an archers' guild.

As I stare at the flames that represent my misfortunes, my eyes blur and the flames run together, and all the arrows begin to blend together in my mind; the ones that struck my father, the ones that felled the deer, the one in Tristan's side, even the one in my own arm, and the ones bristling from St. Sebastian's body. I can't help but feel that they're all connected, somehow, if I could just puzzle it out.

And lame Journeys: there's another recurring theme. Tristan and I are going to be quite a pair at Seconds. Here in the quiet church, with its atmosphere that invites introspection, thinking of Tristan's accident inevitably reminds me of my father's. I haven't wanted to think about it, ever since Tristan told me he thought my father's fall was no accident. I haven't let myself. But now, looking at the candle I lit for him burning away accusingly, I do have to wonder. Why would anyone have wanted to hurt him, so long ago? Did they mean to kill him, even then, or just ruin his trick? His accident can't have had anything to do with his death, can it? No, it must have just been rivalry among the Journeys.

Yet even as I think it, it doesn't seem enough. None of the Journeys I know would do such a terrible thing, not even Aristide or Taran, though they all want to win badly. It must have been something more than the competitions, something personal. And the man who killed my father; I can't remember now exactly what he said, but I do remember his cold, mocking voice. He sounded like an old enemy, and the words he said as he shot him, they sounded personal, too. But if someone had tried to kill my father with that saddle and failed, why would he wait so many years to try again?

There's something about that thought that disquiets me, as though I should be remembering something, but I can't think what it is. So many years *did* pass, and my idea that my father overheard something at the guild, that has to be right. That he had an accident at the guild years before must just be a coincidence, and not even a very surprising one. Accidents seem to happen to me at St. Sebastian's all the time.

Feeling dissatisfied, I look up for inspiration from the candles to the image of St. Margaret that rises above them. It's another gruesome painting of a saint, but this one fortunately isn't as evocative as the one of St. Sebastian. For one thing, she's fully dressed. It depicts the virgin grappling with the Devil in the form of a dragon, and she's got a hammer in her hand, ready to bash her enemy.

If only I could recognize my own enemies as clearly, I think, or even know how many there are.

I sit there for a long time, lost in thought. After what must be at least an hour, I'm about to rise to go when I notice a boy step out of the shadows of a side chapel. It's odd, because I've been sitting here for so long, and I didn't see him come in. He must have been praying at that chapel for a very long time. It's rare for someone so young to be so devout, so I watch with mild curiosity as he comes into the light. To my infinite surprise, I recognize him. It's Jerome!

I'm about to call out, when I see his face. It's dry, but I can see the tracks of recently spent tears clearly on both cheeks, as though he's been weeping profusely and has only just wiped the evidence away. Jerome is always so even-tempered and cheerful, the sight of him shocks me into silence, and I shrink back down in the pew and let him go past without a word. I feel dirty, as though I've purposely been spying on him. From the looks of it, his troubles are worse even than my own.

I'm still watching Jerome's receding back so intently that when I'm suddenly grabbed and pulled backward into the shadows of a side aisle by a huge hand, I start guiltily, as though I've been caught in something. The timing of it, being caught in my surreptitious surveillance of Jerome, makes my heart jump erratically, but of course, I also know instantly who it is. Who else would it be? I've never had a conversation with Taran that didn't start with him grabbing me in just this fashion. Remy as good as warned me that he was out and about. Why didn't I pay any attention?

As usual, I'm instantly gripped by fear as soon as I realize it's him. Only this time, it's not fear of being hurt. Not even Taran would dare assault me in a cathedral. Still all my senses are on high alert. No, even he wouldn't beat me here, but I'm instantly afraid — afraid my body will betray me again by responding to a man who despises me, and I'm not wrong. As soon as I know the touch is his and I feel him leaning over me in the darkness, a thin flame begins burning along under my skin, radiating out from his hand. I was right: it really is all about expectation. That's why his touch affects me more than those of the others. I should have known it would feel different to be touched by a boy who knows I'm a girl, whatever we think or feel about each other otherwise. Particularly when he's touched me before. That's the only explanation that makes sense, isn't it?

"Just what do you think you're playing at?!" he demands angrily, only inches from my face.

As so often with Taran, I have no idea what he's talking about, and he's caught me so off guard here where I least expected to see him that I couldn't respond anyway. When I just stare at him dumbly, shaking with what must seem like abject fear, he lets go of my arm suddenly and steps back, and says accusingly,

"The arrow. I saw you shove it into your own arm."

Of course he would. He *is* still watching me closely, and he was standing there talking to Gilles the whole time.

I don't bother to deny it. Taran has a way of finding out all my secrets, it seems. He already knows most of them, anyway. What's one more?

"Tristan was bleeding," I stammer, still flustered and confused at finding myself so unexpectedly in such close quarters with Taran. "He was wounded, at the hunt. His wound opened again during practice, and if the masters had seen the blood, he might have been out. I had to do something, to hide the blood."

As soon as my words are out, I see what I've done. I haven't just told Taran my secret, I've told him Tristan's. Did I really just hand Taran the means of ridding himself of Tristan once and for all, just because I was more intent on hiding my reaction to him than on protecting Tristan from him? With a horrible sinking feeling in the pit of my stomach, all I can do is wait for the inevitable exultation

Taran is sure to express. I hang my head, waiting to hear that booming, triumphant laughter that filled the windmill. Instead, he growls:

"That was a damned idiotic way to do it!"

"I had to do something," I say stupidly, as he takes hold of me again and gives me another angry shake.

"You little fool!" he hisses, sounding close to losing control again. "Don't you know you could have hit a nerve, or a bone? That the arrowhead could have come out in your arm?" His words are such a strange echo of Tristan's earlier that I almost laugh absurdly. I can't figure out why he's so angry. What's it to him? But it's true — Taran's eyes are flashing with emotion, and I begin to wonder if I was wrong that he wouldn't assault me in here, so I repeat nervously,

"There was no time to think. I had to do something."

At just this moment, a family appears out of the shadows, making its way down the aisle toward us. With a grunt of frustration, Taran shoves me roughly back behind a pillar and out of view, but he doesn't let go of my arm. His other hand is clenching and unclenching in that move I suspect is meant to try to keep himself from further violence.

"You're a fraud!" he hisses at me when the others have finally moved away. "All that talk of yours, the son of Jan Verbeke! And I believed you. But you're not doing this for your father, are you? You're not at St. Sebastian's to find out what happened to him. This isn't about your father at all! It's about *him*, isn't it? *Isn't* it?!" he repeats louder, squeezing my arm harder. "It's all about Tristan!"

Even if I couldn't feel the heat radiating from him, I'd know how angry he was simply by his use of Tristan's name. But I surprise him and myself by my calm, miserable response.

"Why am I here? My father? Tristan? What does it matter? I'm not sure I can tell the difference between them anymore."

I can't seem to stop telling him the truth.

Whatever Taran expected me to say, it wasn't this. He drops my arm with a look of consternation on his face, which is quickly replaced by frustration. He puts a hand up and for a moment I think he's going to strike me, but instead he runs it through his hair distractedly in a move that's so like Tristan that for the first time I can see that the two are brothers.

"What do you expect to happen?" he asks roughly. "Do you think when you reveal yourself, he'll love you for your sacrifices? This isn't some romantic ballad, you know. You don't think he really believes any of that stuff he spouts, do you? You think he'll fall into your arms, with some of his drivel about how he now understands the mysterious feelings he's been having? He's not going to love you when he finds out you're a girl. That's not how this is going to end."

It doesn't occur to me to wonder what business of Taran's this is in the first place. The only thing I notice is that he's talking about Tristan finding out about me, and I can't let that happen. I take it as a threat. Taran's talking about revealing me to Tristan.

"He's never going to know!" I cry out, alarmed, my eyes wild. "I'm never going to tell him!" And to my disgust, suddenly I'm begging in a way I didn't even in the windmill. "*Please*, Please, Taran! Don't tell him!"

"What do you mean, he's never going to know?" he says, irritated. "You can't live as a boy forever."

"Oh, yes I can!" I almost yell, and I'm aware my voice is echoing through the high, empty vaults above me. "In fact, I've sworn it!"

All at once the same melodramatic impulse that always seem to overcome me in Tristan's presence gets the better of me, and I drop down on one knee and put my hand over my heart. It's probably the worst thing I could do; it's so like Tristan himself I'm sure it's just going to enrage Taran further, but I can't stop myself. I even hear myself using Tristan's top-of-the-wall voice as I cry:

"I've sworn a sacred oath by St. Sebastian to keep my secret from Tristan forever, or die trying! To live the rest of my life as a boy, to devote myself to being a valiant squire, and to doing everything in my power to see Tristan through Veterans. I've *got* to see him succeed, where my father failed! And he sent me a sign! The saint has accepted my vow!"

But when I see Taran's face frowning down at me, my bravado fails me, and I start groveling in earnest.

"Please, please, don't tell him! Never tell him! I'll die before I let him find out! Please, don't tell the masters he's been wounded, oh please! Let me fulfill my vow, I beg you! Oh, I know you want to be rid of him! How glad you must be to have a way to do it, and so easily, now ..."

I'm about to continue begging when his voice, as sharp and cold as a shard of ice, cuts me off:

"Is that really what you think of me?" He says it so softly, I almost don't hear it. "Do you really think I'd want to win, that way?"

He puts a hand up to his temple and briefly squeezes his eyes shut, and when he resumes, his voice sounds pained. "The things you said to me that day ... you were wrong about me, you know. I *do* know what honor is."

Whatever comes over him is gone quickly, and the irritation is back in his voice as he spits vehemently at me, "*I*, at least, would never threaten to rat out a member!"

When he puts it this way, I believe him. Taran would never want the others to think he'd ratted Tristan out. And he doesn't need to reveal Tristan. He's going to beat him anyway, and I bet he's looking forward to doing it publicly, and in front of his father, and in front Melissande, too. Now that I think about it, Taran is probably the least likely person of all to tell the masters about Tristan's wound. It would deny him the pleasure of beating Tristan fair and square. I suddenly feel foolish that I didn't recognize it sooner.

Some of the anger seems to go out of him when he sees my thoughts clearly mirrored on my face, but he doesn't move, and I'm still on my knees in front of him. I'm feeling spent from my outburst and rather embarrassed by it — why in the world did I tell him of all people about my squire's oath? — and he's now looking more frustrated than angry, but he makes no move to leave. I'm feeling very confused now, too, as I begin to wonder just what we've been talking about, and why Taran followed me here in the first place. It was surely no coincidence.

Just when I think we're starting to look ridiculous and that I'm going to have to say something just to break the silence, he says flatly,

"So, you're planning to live as a boy forever?"

"Yes," I reply, trying to sound confident. There's another pause, as he looks down at me. At length, he says:

"Forever is a very long time."

With that, he turns to leave, and I don't know what comes over me. I call him back.

"Taran," I say, "I'm so sorry, about the hawk."

His back is to me, but I see his shoulders tense, and when he responds, he's really talking to himself.

"It was my own fault. The boys were right. It was no gift for a girl."

"No," I hear myself protest. "The bird was perfect. She just didn't deserve it."

I scramble to my feet and bolt down the aisle before he can say anything, with the strange sensation that like Melissande at the hunt, I'm not really talking about the hawk, either.

Once outside, I slow my pace and take my time getting back to St. Sebastian's. I wander down a side-street, ignoring the stares of the townspeople, always eager to gawk at an inhabitant of the guild. I circle around slowly, not wanting to run into Taran on his way back, either. When I come back out onto the canal, I sit down on the low parapet wall that follows it and dangle my feet over the edge, and I watch the oily black surface of the water glide by, trying to think things over. I'm in such a foul mood that when a swan wafts past, I throw a pebble at it to drive it off, saying "Birds! Filthy Creatures!" in imitation of Sibilla.

Taran says he's not going to tell about Tristan, and I believe him. He's got selfish reasons not to. But why hasn't he told anyone about me? Is he just waiting for the most devastating moment for revelation, as I thought, or could I have I misjudged him, at least a little? Would any of the others have let me stay on so long, knowing I'm a girl? I try to think back over everything I know of him and turn it over in my mind, confused. As I do, snatches of the things he said to me in the windmill repeat in my mind: *"Are you two lovers? No, you're too wretched for that,"* and *"A girl! Well, not much of one, I'll admit."* For some reason these cruel truths seem to hurt more now than they did then. I must have been too afraid at the time to take much notice, or something else has changed, but now this low opinion and the cruel tone he voiced it in make my face burn with shame, when I think of how I felt when he leaned over me in the cathedral. I finger the newly acquired medals, slick in my sweaty hand. *Oh, how nice it would be to really be St. Margaret*, I think again, *and to know just who your enemies really are!* But eventually I have to pick myself up and head home, even though instead of finding answers, I seem to have simply found more questions.

CHAPTER THIRTY

My first thought is to take Tristan his medal, but when I rap on his door and open it cautiously, in case he's asleep, to my annoyance I find the room empty. He was supposed to be resting! Where can he have gotten to now? I can't imagine he's really foolish enough to have gone out to practice, but when I look in the archives, the kitchens, and the great hall and I don't find him, I head out to the field, just to be sure. The field is busy; most of the boys have been putting in long hours with Seconds coming up, but I don't see Tristan or Gilles anywhere.

I catch sight of Jerome fiddling with something at his cabinet, but after the sight of him in the cathedral, I can't bring myself to go over to him. I'm about to turn to go, when he sees me and calls me over. As I approach, I'm relieved to see he looks like his usual self, if a bit strained, so I ask him if he's seen Tristan.

"Sure," he says. "He's out there, on the clout field." He nods vaguely in the direction of the far field, but when I turn to look, I don't see Tristan.

"Where?"

"Out there," Jerome insists. "Back by the wall. Positioning that wicker butt."

I look again, but I still don't see Tristan. There is someone out there, pushing one of the moveable butts back into line, only it's not Tristan. It's Baylen. I suppose there is some vague resemblance. They've both got black hair and Baylen is wearing a tunic about the color of the one Tristan had on this morning, but that's about as far as it goes.

"Jerome, that's Baylen," I say. "Unless Tristan's grown out his hair and taken to wearing an eye patch since this morning."

"Oh," he replies, sounding embarrassed and ducking his head to peer at the figure in the distance. "I guess I didn't look properly. Sorry."

Whatever's bothering Jerome, it certainly has him distracted. He may look better than he did in the cathedral, but something is seriously wrong. I wonder if it can be just the stress of Seconds. After all, Jerome is in last place.

I'm pondering my next move when one of the serving boys comes out of the stables and scans the field. When he sees me, he comes over in a hurry.

"Marek, there you are! The master has been looking for you." I assume he's talking about Tristan, so I fall into step behind him to let him lead me to him. But when he leads me all the way down the Journey corridor and past the barracks, I frown. When we turn into the hallway where the guild offices are located, I stop him.

"Where are we going?"

"I told you. Master Guillaume wants to see you."

I don't like the sound of this at all. What in the world can Guillaume want with me? I didn't even think he remembered my name. But by now we're outside Guillaume's office, and the boy is knocking. I hear Guillaume's deep voice beckon from within, and the boy swings the door open.

Although it's still afternoon, the interior of the office looks much as it did the only other time I've ever been in it, on my first night at the guild. There are no exterior windows, and the dark wood of the walls smothers what light is coming in through the open door. Guillaume is seated at his massive desk just as he was then, too, and again the room is lit only by a single candle resting next to him. He must keep the room just like this always, aware of how intimidating he looks seated behind that single light, like a giant spider in the midst of a dark web.

I step into the room past the boy, who departs and pulls the door closed behind me without waiting to be told, and I stand at attention in front of the master.

"You wanted to see me, *master?*" I say in a crisp tone meant to sound military and respectful, and I fix my eyes on a point about a foot over the intimidating man's head. But I can feel his eyes surveying me, as he sits back and says,

"Ah, Marek. There you are. Yes, I did want to see you. I hear you were wounded this morning. Fouled a shot of duBois's, was it?"

"Yes, sir!" I bark. "It was entirely my fault, sir!"

"Hmm," he says, sounding amused. "Well, I wouldn't expect you to say anything less, would I? Not after the whole flask fiasco, anyway," he laughs. "Oh, relax, squire. I'm not interested in asking questions. Frankly, if he did shoot you on purpose, I don't want to know." When I start to protest, he puts up a hand to stop me.

"I hear the wound isn't too bad. Can it be fully concealed, for Seconds? That's what matters."

"Yes, sir!" I reply, relieved. "It's just a scrape. Even if it still needs a bandage by then, my tunic will cover it. Or if that's not enough, it's the left hand. A bracer or a gauntlet wouldn't be out of place."

"Good, good. Quite adept at deception, aren't you?" he says speculatively, and I blanch. I doubt he really brought me in to talk about a scratch. I have a feeling he's getting around to his real purpose now.

"You know, I've been watching you," he says. *Is there anyone here who hasn't?* I think wildly. But I don't reply, and I force myself to keep my eyes fixed over his head.

"You must know I wasn't very enthusiastic about welcoming you here, at first. I heard the rumors, and let's just say that duBois can be trying at times, can't he? But I have to admit, you've proven to be very ... *interesting.*"

The way he says it, I don't know if it's a compliment or not. The last compliment he gave me was a beating.

"Sir, yes sir, thank you sir!" I bark. It's probably too much, but what the heck? I don't know what to say anyway.

"In fact," he continues, his tone almost teasing, "you remind me very strongly of someone. Yes, the resemblance is uncanny. You could be a young version of him. Surely you know who I mean?"

The room spins around me. I do know who he means. It's obvious. Somehow, he's found out. Maybe even Taran has told him.

I steel myself to hear my father's name, my stomach tying itself in knots. It's come out of nowhere, and I can't think what this is going to mean for me, or what exactly he must know. I don't even think about the inevitable punishment that must follow. All I can think is that I'm about to find out whether or not Guillaume is really my father's friend. I'm almost glad — glad that it's all coming out, glad that I can finally find out if Guillaume is going to be an ally. But as I sway forward and sweat starts to pour down my back, he says,

"Yes, you're his spitting image! You could be a younger Baylen."

"What?!" I squawk, taking a step forward and forgetting myself in my astonishment.

"Of course! The scarred face, the austerity, the posturing. It's all the same! Even down to the fact that you're both better at coaching than at shooting. Oh yes, I've seen what you've done for duBois. Just grow another foot or so and pack on some pounds, and you'll turn out to be another Baylen, for sure."

He gets up and comes around from behind his desk and puts a hand on my shoulder. "And if you turn out to be as good with that crossbow as they say, there might just be a permanent place for you here at St. Sebastian's, down the line, when Baylen is gone. Think on that, boy."

And I do, all the long way back down the corridor as I leave the master's office, stunned. Me, another Baylen? It's such a strange thought, this time, I don't even ask myself whether or not the master means it as a compliment. I picture myself straddling the prostrate form of some hapless squire, a bloody whip in my hand, and I know that another Baylen is the last thing I want to be.

I finally find Tristan and Gilles lounging in the garden, predictably playing draughts. When I chastise Tristan for being out of bed and I give him his medal, he looks sheepish.

"I couldn't sleep any longer, Marek. I'm not doing anything but lying here, I swear, and the fresh air will do me good," he says, taking his Journey medal off from around his neck and stringing the St. Margaret medal onto the same string with it.

"How does it look?" he asks Gilles, who simply nods approvingly without much interest. "Thanks, Marek. I hope it wasn't any trouble getting it."

"No trouble at all," I lie. Guillaume was right about one thing. I am getting disturbingly adept at deception. Yet for some reason, I don't feel like telling them about my meeting with the master. I have even less desire to mention Taran. So I simply settle myself in a chair and wait for them to resume their game.

As Gilles makes a move, he says casually, since there's nobody else about,

"By the way, old boy. I never did ask. Just which unfortunate Journey shot you?"

"You know," Tristan says wonderingly, pausing with the game piece he was about to move in mid-air. "I never thought to ask. Who was it, Marek?"

"How should I know? I didn't see him."

"But you must have seen the arrow," Gilles says. "I didn't think to inspect it myself."

"The arrow?" I repeat.

"Yes, the arrow, stupid!" Gilles drawls. "Whose colors were on it?"

Gilles is perfectly right. All the Journeys were shooting with their own arrows. The arrow I pulled from Tristan's side should have been marked with one of their distinctive colors. And I did see the arrow, up close, and much better than I wanted to. Only there were no bands of color on it. It was unmarked.

When I say as much, the boys scoff.

"In the stress of the moment, you must not have noticed," Tristan says. "There was a lot of blood, after all." But I insist so much that finally they have to believe me.

"One of the boys must have been out of arrows, and he grabbed a few unmarked ones from somewhere. That'll be the long and short of it, I expect. I guess that means we'll never know who the careless Journey was."

But it doesn't make any sense, and none of us are satisfied. All the Journey arrows are always marked, by force of habit.

"If it wasn't one of the Journeys, who could it have been?" Gilles says reasonably. "Only Beaufort and his men were there, and they weren't shooting."

"Unless it wasn't an accident," I say in jest. "And one of the Journeys planned the whole thing, to cut down the competition, literally!" When Tristan and Gilles both laugh, I'm encouraged to stretch out the joke.

"And I know just the one! After the way you two went at it in the great hall the night before, I'd be willing to believe Taran purposely brought along an unmarked arrow or two, in the hopes of finding an opportunity to shoot you down! He looked like he could have been planning murder out in the garden that night. But, sadly, he wasn't at the second hunt. A perfect theory, shot down!" I start to laugh really hard at my own joke, but Gilles is frowning.

"What do you mean, he wasn't there for the second hunt?"

"He stayed back from the hart," I say, "to meet with Melissande." Yet as I say it, something's off. Taran didn't actually meet with Melissande until after the hunt, as I have every reason to know. Just where was he, when we were hunting the second deer?

"I saw Brecelyn pull him aside," I continue weakly, almost to myself.

"No, I'm pretty sure he was there. Brecelyn did pull him aside, but he caught us up," Gilles insists, and there's a terrible silence. Taran could have shot Tristan, after all, and it's the only explanation that makes any sense. And I know exactly why he did it, too.

But Tristan shakes his head in disbelief.

"No. It's fantastic! Taran, commit cold-blooded murder? I don't believe it. I might buy him going after me in one of his rages, but an ambush? It's not his style. No, Marek. I've told you, if he ever goes for me, it'll be out in the open, with an arrow straight through the eye. Besides," he adds bitterly, "he's the last Journey who needs to resort to tricks to beat me."

It's true, of course. I thought it myself. But that's not why he did it. It was the oldest motive in the world: good, old-fashioned jealousy, over a girl.

"Tristan," I say carefully, my voice trembling a little, "I'm afraid, I think, no — I *know* Taran thinks that, uh, you took things further with Melissande than you did."

He just gapes at me. "How in Hades do you know that?" he asks at length. "Did Remy tell you so?"

"No," I admit. And now there's nothing for it but to tell him the whole sordid story. "I overheard him with Melissande." I have to tell him about the interview, and worst of all, I have to tell him about her offer to Taran, and his cold refusal. I can't explain without it.

When I'm done, Tristan looks stony, like his face is carved from solid granite. I don't know what makes him angrier — that it now seems indicated that his half-brother tried to kill him, or that he got his kiss on the rebound. Both are serious blows.

"Oh, Tristan!" I exclaim, frightened. "What if he tries it again?" As I say it, my own thoughts at the cathedral come back to me, the ones that bothered me at the time, about my father's accident. I remember thinking it odd that if a culprit's first attempt failed, he wouldn't try again. That's when I realize that the arrow in Tristan's side *was* the second try.

"The stag hunt! He *did* try twice!" I explode, to the confusion of the others. "Tristan, the first arrow! Falko never shot it, I'm sure," and I tell Gilles all about the narrow miss we had during the first hunt.

"I didn't think to look for that arrow," I say angrily, "but I'd bet anything it was unmarked, too! One stray arrow, right at Tristan, I can believe. But two?" It's too much of coincidence. Not even Tristan and Gilles can laugh it off.

Gilles is looking particularly grave, and I know he still doesn't want to believe it. Only this time, he can't think of another explanation. It all fits. I can believe it all readily enough, though. Taran would never want the others to think he'd ratted out a member, sure, but I was right: his famous sense of honor counts for nothing in secret. What a fool I was, to have been thinking I might have misjudged Taran, just because he likes birds, and put his hand on my breast! Am I really so desperate to be touched that I could be swayed so easily? Did it take so little to make me forget that brutal punch in the face, or the way he's been threatening and terrorizing me?

But I *did* misjudge him. I never thought he'd do anything as bad as this. He's even worse than I thought. Instead of bothering me, the thought gives me a strange comfort. I don't have to be confused anymore. Now I do know who my enemy is, and it couldn't be clearer. But I try not to admit to myself that I'm particularly willing to believe the worst of Taran, because one of the phrases I haven't been able to get out of my head all afternoon is still echoing in the back of my mind: *you're too wretched for that.*

It's so much easier to be despised when you can despise in return.

That night as I lie down on my cot, I think perhaps my new clarity will finally break me from the tyranny of my recurring dream. Yet as I drift into sleep, the dream begins again, just as it always does, with me standing at the window in the abandoned windmill, looking out over St. Sebastian's. It progresses as usual, too, with Tristan's long-anticipated arrival, and his sensual caresses. Only this time, when his hand slides slowly up by body, it creeps all the way up to my neck. As he's stroking the soft skin at the base of my throat, the air in the windmill grows hotter and hotter, until it's cloying and stifling, and his hands start to push harder, until they're hurting me and I feel trapped.

I break free and run to the window. As I stand gulping for air and drinking in its sweetness, I look down into the meadow of cornflowers, to see a great stag standing rigid and still in the moonlight below. Its huge head holds its magnificent antlers high, as its hot breath comes out in a cloud of mist on the cool air. I reach down silently, unable to stop myself, and I bring up my bow. With trembling hands, I nock an arrow and shoot. My arrow rips straight through the stag's throat, and I watch with satisfaction as it breathes out its life in a gurgle of blood.

CHAPTER THIRTY-ONE

When I wake up the next morning, it's with a feeling of relief, although my wounded arm is throbbing painfully and it smells funny, as though it might be beginning to fester. But when I sit up on my cot and inspect it, I find it functional enough, and things have shifted back into a shape I can recognize: I've got Tristan to see through Seconds, and Taran is safely my enemy again. I don't dwell on the fact that if I really believed deep down that Taran tried to kill his brother, what I should be feeling is not relief but abject fear that he'll try it again. Instead, I push the thought away; it's time to focus all my energies on Seconds. All my questions from the cathedral will just have to wait.

As I'm about to rise, despite my renewed sense of purpose I do have a moment's disquiet as the little figurine of the hawk on my bedside table catches my eye. I don't want to look at it, but I can't bear to get rid of it, either. I quickly pick it up and turn it face down, so I won't have to see its expression. It's appropriate, anyway. The little hawk is dead.

Remy's started moving on his cot, too. He's had one of his bad nights, I know. I could hear him tossing and turning, and occasionally letting out a low moan or mumbling something distressed in his sleep. He's always a restless sleeper and he's prone to nightmares, but it seems he's been having bad nights more often lately. I narrow my eyes and watch him for a minute, wondering. Maybe he knows more about what happened at the hunt than he's let on. When at last he rolls over, stretches and sits up on the edge of the bed, rubbing his eyes and exclaiming sleepily but as cheerfully as ever,

"Morning, Marek!," I feel a stab of guilt at suspecting him.

We both stand up at the same moment, and suddenly I have an entirely different reaction. Remy's noticeably taller. When did that happen? Has he grown, in just a few days?

"What's the matter, Marek?" he asks, seeing my expression.

"Remy, you're as tall as I am," I say, stupefied. "What's happened to you?" As I say it, I look at his face. The strain of recent events is evident in his features, but that's not the only thing that's different. His face looks older, more mature.

"I'm growing into my feet!" he exclaims happily.

It's not my imagination. He's changed, and quickly. I'm sure it hasn't really been over night, but he's losing that elfin appearance. Even his chirpy voice sounds deeper to me today, and there's a disturbing shadow that looks suspiciously like incipient facial hair on his upper lip. I look wildly around the barracks, trying to remember what the others looked like just a few months ago, when I first met them. Are all the squires transforming, except for me? I look down at Remy's feet, not yet encased in boots, and my heart sinks. Remy's going to be very tall indeed, if he really grows into them.

"Wait till it happens to you, Marek," he says. "My bones have been aching something terrible." I don't answer. Why bother telling him it's already happened? I'm not going to get any taller. Instead, I reach down to my table and turn face-down the little figurine next to the hawk, too.

Remy's not a mouse anymore.

Unbidden, Taran's words from yesterday come back to me: *you can't live as a boy forever.* I give myself a mental shake. I can't think about that now. All that matters right now is Seconds.

I make my way slowly out to the field, worrying about the smell coming from my arm, and worrying about Tristan. We agreed that he should come out to the field by himself today to keep up the appearance of normalcy, and Gilles promised to stop by his room on his own way out and help bind him up tight, to avoid a repeat of yesterday's debacle.

As I'm making my way to Tristan's cabinet, I pass Gilles's wooden Pascal resting against the garden wall, and I stop to inspect it. There are a disturbingly large number of holes in the main beam, just beneath the plank where the apple is to rest. Out on the field, I catch sight of the real Pascal, and to my delight I see that he's already setting up Gilles's station in its usual spot next to where I always put Tristan. I'll be glad to have Gilles on hand, in case anything goes wrong today.

Pascal is bent over loading Gilles's quiver, his rear end in its tight grey hose resembling nothing so much as a full moon, and in need of diversion, I sneak up behind him and give him a big pinch. All of us squires have taken to pinching Pascal whenever possible, ever since Armand told us about what happened with lady Sibilla. It's juvenile, but really a lot of fun. Out of respect for Gilles, we only do it when we think no Journeys are watching, and after an initial reluctance, I've become one of the worst offenders. Poor Pascal! He's been caught so many times, last night at mess he looked like he could hardly sit down.

"Oof! Marek," Pascal yelps, slapping a hand defensively over his posterior and turning on me. "I'd have thought at least you would take pity on me and lay off."

"If you don't want to be pinched," I sniff, "don't keep presenting such an easy target."

"Ouch!" Pascal cries again, as Rennie comes up behind him while we're talking and gooses him again.

"Morning, gents!" he says. "Marek, is that stench you?"

"What are you doing out so early again?" I ask him irritably, wondering how he can smell anything over his own habitual body odor. To my dismay, I see he's got Jurian's bench in his hands and he's preparing to set it up on the side of Tristan's station opposite where Pascal's putting Gilles. That makes twice in a row. Before I can question him about it, though, some of the Journeys start to come out onto the field, so I hustle back to Tristan's cabinet to get out the rest of his gear.

As I'm reaching in for Tristan's bow, Anselm comes over and stops next to me.

"Morning, Marek," he says, hovering. "How's the arm?"

"It stinks," I say. But I'm sure he didn't stop just to ask me about it, so I add, "Something on your mind?"

"Well," he says nervously. "I *was* wondering; if you can't practice today, what with the arm and all, I thought maybe you'd watch me shoot this afternoon. Give me some pointers, the way you did before. You know, I never did really thank you properly, but it was a big help."

I like Anselm, and he's always been decent to me. But this time, there can be no helping Anselm, and I tell him so. Tristan's got to beat out two boys at Seconds, and Anselm is one of the most likely candidates to be one of them. It's cold, but somebody has to lose, and I don't want it to be Tristan.

I feel like a heel as I make my way back to our station, and my mood isn't improved by the sight of Jurian strutting over, rubbing his hands together and grinning wickedly.

"Jurian," I say, in a voice that's an accusation. "Just what are you doing over here again, anyway?"

"What a greeting! Anyone would think you weren't happy to see me this morning, Marek," he replies, chuckling. "My, my, somebody's in a mood, before the cock's even crowed." He slaps the back of Rennie's head, rather hard, and circles around behind me. To my surprise, he puts his hands on my shoulders and starts to massage them.

"Tsk, tsk, you're carrying a lot of tension here. You're a bundle of nerves!" he says, as I try to whip around. "Relax!"

I shake him off and turn on him, but he just laughs. I lean in and hiss at him, "Whatever you're up to, I don't like it!"

He just raises his eyebrows at me in the way he does and smirks. "Who said I was up to something? Or that you have to like it?"

I'm saved from having to respond to this by the appearance of Gilles and Tristan, and mercifully Jurian behaves himself for the rest of practice. It's probably because Baylen doesn't make an appearance; it's occurred to me that perhaps Jurian has some thought of making Baylen jealous. It's an old ploy, but effective, and I don't like the chances of any boy that Baylen should take it into his head is his rival. But Royce runs the practice today by himself, and since he's usually laxer than Baylen, it's good for Tristan, too.

In fact, Tristan does much better today, and his tighter bindings hold. No blood comes through, though he's taking no chances; he's dressed in a dark black tunic.

Like yesterday, Tristan and I work in concert to stall, delay, and generally take practice as easy as possible without being too obvious about it. By the time morning drills are over, I'm greatly encouraged. Tristan's still weak, but the shots he does take are good; the wound hasn't seemed to affect his aim. If we can just keep the wound closed, I'm beginning to think we just might have a shot at limping through Seconds.

There are only two things that disturb me during practice. One is my own wound. It doesn't get in the way of my work, but Rennie was right. It really is foul. By the end of the morning, the smell is getting oppressive. I know I'm going to have to do something about it, and it won't be pleasant. The other is that I'm distracted. It's never been so hard for me to keep from looking down the line to where Taran is taking his long, deliberate shots, each one hitting the mark.

I find myself watching him, forcing myself to picture him taking aim at Tristan. It has to be true, doesn't it? It all fits, even his anger over my self-inflicted wound. I've finally put it all together. Taran may not have wanted to risk his reputation by being the one to tell that Tristan was wounded, but he must have known his arrow found its mark. He must have been watching us closely at practice, hoping that Tristan would give himself away. No wonder he was so angry that my rash act kept Tristan from being discovered. Yes, it's very neat. It explains everything. I push away the nagging thought that this doesn't really fit with what Taran actually said to me in the cathedral. I watch him lift his huge bow and bend it, and I picture the arrow flying from the bow and striking Tristan in the side. Yes, he must have shot Tristan, and I'm glad I can hate him for it.

But what I'm really thinking as I watch him rock back in that sweeping motion of his is, *you're too wretched for that.*

Back in the barracks, I unwrap my arm, and I find what I'd expected. The wound is clearly infected; there's a big pocket of pus forming under the skin. When Charles's squire Henri sees it, he insists on fetching Tristan right away, and when Tristan sees it, he convinces me to go to the master.

"Won't it mean I'll be out?"

"He already knows you're hurt, kid. And there's a big difference between a scratched squire and an impaled Journey. But if that isn't seen to, it could be serious."

And so we make our way to the master's office, and when the door swings open at our knock, we find that Master Guillaume is not alone. He's in the middle of conferring with Royce and Baylen, probably about the Journeys' progress. Baylen's leaning up against the desk with his arms crossed over his chest when we come in, and I do a doubletake when I see him. Needless to say, I've been giving him a wide berth lately; I did, even before my beating. It's distinctly unpleasant being in such cramped quarters with him. He doesn't look too pleased to see me, either, but after an initial frown, he listens with what can only be described as a smirk on his face as Tristan explains about my wound and Master Guillaume inspects my arm.

"You'd better take him along to the barber, if he's going to be in shape for Seconds," Guillaume concedes, eyeing my arm with dissatisfaction. "Otherwise, the smell alone will drive the crowd away." When Tristan nods and moves to usher me out, he adds,

"Not you, duBois. From all reports, you can't spare the time away from practice. Baylen'll take him."

This snaps Baylen out of his complacency, and as he jumps to his feet and looks about to protest, I groan,

"Can't we just let it fester?"

It just slips out. Guillaume laughs, and motions to Baylen, so there's nothing we can do. Tristan gives me an apologetic look over his shoulder as he goes out, and I have to follow the rigid Baylen as he storms out of the office in front of me.

In the narrow corridors of the guild, it's not unreasonable for me to walk behind Baylen. When we come out into the alley, however, I start to feel ridiculous, since I'm almost trotting along trying to keep up with his long, angry strides. He's clearly eager to be done with this task as quickly as possible and with minimal interaction with me. But when I hustle to catch up with him, almost breaking into a speed-walk to do it, he suddenly turns and grabs me up by my shirtfront, and shoves me up against the outer guild wall.

As he leans in with his nose inches from my face, I think *"here we go again."* Really, is this the only way these clout shooters know how to converse? It gives me more respect for Falko, who seems to be the only one who can resist constantly throwing his weight around.

"Got something to say to me, squire?" Baylen demands, an ugly scowl on his face. I guess he's been thinking my silence is accusatory, or else he's just feeling guilty (as well he should!). But of course I wasn't planning on saying anything about the beating, and he catches me off guard. In my fear, I say the first thing that comes into my head.

"I hear congratulations are in order."

Oh, God! What made me say *that*? I can hear Tristan's voice in my head urging me to learn to keep my mouth shut. I can't think of much I could have said that would have been worse, and predictably, Baylen's forehead wrinkles and he screws up his lips in what looks like the beginning of an angry sneer. But to my surprise, when he bares his teeth, it's in a grin, and he throws back his head and laughs.

"You may have taken the lash like Guillaume's grandmother, but you've got guts, I'll give you that!" he roars, amused. He pulls me back onto my feet, and gives me a casual slap on the back of my head, hard — just the way I saw Jurian do to Rennie. He doesn't expect a response, since he's already turned and is stalking off again, which is good, because I'm speechless. I follow him the rest of the way to the barber's in silence.

It's not long before we come to a house with the typical white and red pole out front. I don't mind the white for bandages, but I'm less enthusiastic about the red for blood, particularly when it's going to be mine. We're ushered into a small room in the front of the house that serves as the surgery, and after inspecting my arm, the barber declares,

"We'll have to drain the wound," as he looks over an array of small but very sharp-looking knives laid out on a table nearby. He looks them over for a minute, running his hand over them lovingly and crooning to them in a disturbing manner before he picks out a particularly nasty looking little number. Giving it a wipe on his rather filthy sleeve, he puts out his hand, and I've got to stick out my arm and let him cut. In the meantime, Baylen's settled himself against the wall to watch, his arms crossed in the same pose he adopted in Guillaume's office, and with much the same smirk on his face. It turns out, my arm is so rotten by now that the incision itself doesn't actually hurt, but in the wake of the knife, such a disgusting flood of thick yellowish-green putrescence the consistency of rancid clotted cream bursts out with a stench worse than a canal full of rotten fish that even Baylen looks queasy. I'm so relieved it's over when the barber finally wipes away the last of the oozing matter that I literally sigh, but then he says:

"Now for the actual cure," and my heart sinks. It's not over.

"The proper cure," he continues, "depends on the source of the evil. Infection like this, young man," he says sternly, looking down his nose at me, "is usually a manifestation of sin. Look to your soul. Is it pure?"

I scroll through the seven deadly sins in my mind, and I don't like the result. I can honestly say I'm free from sloth and avarice, but that's probably only because I don't have any possessions or any way of acquiring any. As for the rest: pride. *Check.* Envy. *Check.* Gluttony, Wrath. *Check, check.* Don't even ask about lust. I don't include my deception at St. Sebastian's in my sins, though. The saint accepted my vow. I'm safe there. But I look down at the red, inflamed wound on my arm, still giving off a faint odor, and I know I've got to do better. Seeing my guilty expression, the barber continues:

"If sin is the cause, we must drive it out by cauterizing the wound."

"Cauterizing?"

"The application of heat," he clarifies.

"He's going to stick a burning poker in your arm," Baylen puts in, looking like he's beginning to enjoy himself.

"Sometimes," the barber muses, ignoring Baylen, "these things can be the result of an imbalance of the humors. Too much blood, too much bile. If that's the case, cauterization won't help. The application of leeches is in order." He looks at me shrewdly. "So, which is it to be?"

"Are you kidding?" I blurt out, as Baylen says, "Give'm the rod."

"Take it yourself! Give me the leeches," I cry.

But when I see him lifting the first fat, squirming body of a leech from a jar and feel its greedy sucker of a mouth latch onto my skin, I wonder if the rod mightn't have been better.

We make the trip back to St. Sebastian's in silence, just as we went, with me trotting along a few paces behind Baylen, feeling light-headed and holding my freshly bandaged and bled arm out in front of me. If anything, Baylen seems to be moving even faster than before, and I notice his back twitching now and then as though he's thinking about something irritating intently to himself. When we're only a few feet from the gate in the garden wall, he comes to a sudden stop, but he doesn't turn to face me. From the set of his shoulders and the tilt of his head, I even think strangely enough that he's steeling himself to apologize to me for what happened in the barracks, or at least to offer some explanation. But when he does speak, he says,

"You know, squire, I'm hard, but I'm a good trainer. You have to be, to be good, and I'm the best. Guillaume knows it. Seeing a boy you've trained win, knowing you've made the difference, knowing you found something in him he didn't know he had, that's a real victory. It's the best victory. But there is something that would be even better than that."

I think he's going to say winning yourself. Instead, he says,

"Training your own son to win."

Without turning around, he takes the last steps to the gate swiftly and disappears inside the guild, leaving me standing alone in the alley. I guess it was an explanation, of sorts. As I slowly follow him in, thinking over all he's said, I decide that maybe I could do worse than becoming a Baylen.

Only I think I'll forego the whip.

By the next day, Tristan's doing much better and my arm has reacquired something close to its usual odor, and we decide to put in an appearance on the field in the afternoon to give the semblance of practicing, since it's now only a week to Seconds. By unspoken consent, we don't try our exhibition trick. I don't think either of us wants to witness the sight of that many apples falling. Instead, we just horse around, taking random shots when anyone is looking, and we try to figure out what some of the others are planning for their exhibitions. Most of the Journeys are being pretty cagey about their tricks this time, so it isn't easy. We aren't particularly worried about Turk, since he isn't to have a horse, and Falko seems to have some crazy scheme involving fire, which is more worrisome, but not necessarily because it's going to be so good. He's likely to send the grandstands up in an inferno. From what I can tell, though, most of the other tricks don't look to me to be as impressive as Tristan's, if he can pull it off. Except, of course, for Taran's.

Predictably, only Taran doesn't seem to care if everyone knows exactly what he's going to do. We watch as Remy sets up a long line of wands, spacing them at intervals of about 10 yards, and placing them at various distances from the line. I notice with despair that all of the distances are quite far. Taran then takes up his quiver and proceeds to run lightly down the line shooting at each wand, alternatively crouching to shoot and standing upright. He does it incredibly fast, and he hits every wand. There's nothing gimmicky about it; in fact, it's all the more impressive because it looks practical. He looks like he could cut through a wide swathe of an enemy army all by himself.

As we're about to call it a day and go in, I notice Jerome out on the far field with Auguste. They've got three wands set up next to each other, and although Jerome is shooting, Auguste is standing down the field by them, about 10 yards off, and after each shot, he gesticulates wildly back to Jerome.

"What in the world is that all about?" I ask Tristan, but he can't figure it out either.

"They must be trying to practice without giving their trick away," he says, frowning, but it's odd.

"Tristan, something is wrong with Jerome. Do you think it's just Seconds, or could something else be wrong?"

"He is in last place, Marek. And 'just Seconds,' what does that mean? If he's out, that's the end."

"Do you know what he'll do, if he's cut?"

"Probably go back to Meuse. He's got a girl waiting for him back home, I think. He'd make a good scholar. Maybe he'll try to follow his father at the University. It could be worse."

"And Auguste?" I ask, worried.

"I don't know, Marek. I doubt Jerome can keep him."

"Tristan," I say, making up my mind. I tell him about seeing

Jerome at the cathedral. "And at drills, he's been trying to avoid shooting, too. If I didn't know who was wounded, I might even think it was Jerome, not you."

"You know, it *is* odd, Marek," Tristan says slowly, his forehead creased in thought. "When I first got here, Jerome was golden. I thought to myself, he's going to be one of the boys to beat. But instead of getting better with all the training, he's getting worse."

I nod; it's true. It's strange that I never thought about it before. I guess I've always been too caught up in Tristan to notice the others much.

"But you know him, he's easy-going," Tristan continues. "It can't be the pressure. I wouldn't have thought he felt it at all, if he weren't falling apart. After all, I'm not sure he really cares about archery that much. I think he'd be just as happy reading in the archives all day, or strumming on that blasted lute."

"Competition or no competition, you've got to talk to him, Tristan. He's your friend."

And so we agree to dawdle by the cabinets and wait for Jerome and Auguste to come in from practice. When they do, Tristan takes Jerome into the garden. I've been assigned to distract Auguste, so he and I head back to the barracks together, and I have to wait until that night to find out how the conversation went.

"What did he say?" I ask Tristan as soon as evening mess is over and we're saying goodnight outside Tristan's door. He knows immediately what I mean, but he doesn't respond right away.

"He told me he's been thinking of going to the master," he says finally with a frown, "to tell him he can't go through with Seconds. He's been thinking of quitting."

Questions start spilling out of me too quickly for Tristan to respond. "Quitting? Now? So soon before Seconds? You talked him out of it, didn't you? What did he say? Why?"

"He wouldn't tell me why, but he was serious. And I don't think it's just because he knows he isn't going to pass."

"Is it that certain, then?" I ask soberly, not sure if I should be pleased or not. After all, Tristan has to pass two boys, and in his state, that isn't going to be easy. I'd rather have Jerome out than Tristan.

"If he doesn't pull it together, I'm afraid even I'll have an easy time beating him," he says, and I feel a surge of pride that he sounds so upset about it. At least Tristan is nobler than I am.

"What did you say to him?"

"I think I convinced him to go through with it. You know — to go out with a bang. To give them something to remember him by." And I do know; it's the thing Tristan's said to me so many times, and I know it's what he's thinking he might be going to do himself. I hate that he's so clearly thinking about going down in glory again, and when we part for the night, we're both depressed, for different reasons.

As that last week before Seconds creeps by, though, I begin to brighten, as Tristan seems better and better each day. He's regaining his strength, and all the hard training we did before his accident has clearly paid off. He fatigues easily, but underneath it all he's stronger than ever. A few days before the competition we decide it's time to practice our trick again, and when I come past his room after mess to collect him for our afternoon practice, he pulls me in, closes the door, and pulls a big bag out from under his bed.

"Look!" he exclaims, opening the bag proudly and grinning as I look in. It's brimming with apples.

"Where did you get all of those?" I ask, impressed.

"I seduced some of the kitchen maids. Don't tell Marta! And don't tell Gilles, or he'll be at it himself, and then our supply will dry up. Come on, let's get them out to the field and see what we can do. It's now or never."

I take this as a good thing; he must be on the mend, if he can be up to his usual tricks.

Out on the field, the first practice run of our exhibition trick is a disaster. Then slowly, as we work through the bag, we get into rhythm. The original plan was to shoot ten apples, in five groups of two. For each two, I'd throw the apples in rapid succession, so that they'd both be in the air at the same time, making it more impressive when Tristan shot them down.

It *is* damned impressive, but after the first attempt, I see that we're going to have to revise it. Trying to get two shots off that quickly is straining him, and we're going to have to abandon the idea of having two apples in the air at once. It's still a good trick, though, and when after a few attempts we manage to run through it twice in a row without a hitch, Tristan's so overjoyed at hitting every apple that he runs across the field and despite his wound he picks me up, swings me around in the air, and we fall to the ground together, laughing. We lie there on our backs side by side laughing and joking for a long time, and now and then Tristan throws one of the few remaining apples from the bottom of the bag up into the air over us and makes me shoot it down with my crossbow, so that the pieces of shattered apple rain down on us and make us laugh even harder.

The trick must be starting to look pretty good, because when Tristan finally gets up and pulls me to my feet next to him, I look up into his face, both of us still laughing, and over his shoulder I notice Taran standing by the stables watching us, with a mighty displeased expression on his face.

After the long lead-up, the day before Seconds dawns before I'm ready for it. At morning practice, Tristan is shooting smoothly and evenly; it looks like Gilles was right about the time it would take his wound to heal. It hasn't completely closed yet, but it probably would have, if he'd been able to rest. With the constant training it's opened slightly over and over again, but with proper binding, it should hold.

That afternoon, Tristan wants to go out to the windmill. Since he's been wounded, the trek through the woods has been out of the question, and I've been spared having to go back since Taran caught me there. I don't want to go now, so I try to put Tristan off, but he's insistent.

"If I can't take a leisurely stroll through the woods, I've got no hope for Seconds anyway. Come on, Marek, for good luck. It's tradition. It'll do us good."

I can't tell him that it will certainly not do me any good, so I follow him out over the wall. It had to be faced sometime, but as we pick our way through the stalks of now-dead cornflowers, I half expect to trip over the lifeless carcass of a stag moldering in the decaying weeds. My own feet sound heavy and hesitant on the stairs as we climb up to the little room, and as I pass over the threshold, I know I was right. We're not alone. Not really.

My legs are trembling a little as I lower myself down to the ground, while Tristan settles himself at his usual spot by the window. He seems happy as a lark to be back here in our place again, and I'm glad he seems oblivious of my mood. After bantering for a while about this and that, most of which I confess I don't really hear, he turns quiet. Looking out the window, he says soberly,

"You know, Marek. I've been thinking. If things don't work out tomorrow ..." and I try to cut him off with a protest, but he shakes me off. "If things don't work out tomorrow," he continues determinedly, "I'm sure you could stay on, with Marcel in the shop, as I said. But I've been thinking. When we do have to leave, what do you say we stick together? We could find a way. We make a good team, don't you think? I could look out for you, and you, well, you could look out for me. Strike out for adventure, like I said."

"You could help me be extraordinary, and I could keep you from getting yourself killed?" I say sarcastically, to hide my emotions.

"Exactly!" he grins. And I think he really means it. But I know it's never going to happen, and not just because I'm determined to see him pass Seconds. It can't happen. I don't know why, but ever since Taran confronted me in the cathedral, I can't stop hearing his voice in my head. Maybe I hear it now, because he's been here in the room with me since I stepped inside. This time, though, what I hear is, *that's not how this is going to end.* I can't think about the end, not now. Not with Seconds to win tomorrow. But I'm going to have to think about it, soon enough.

That night, we leave evening mess early. Tristan wants to have time to pray in the chapel before bed, and he's asked me to help him bathe. With his wound he can't risk using the Journey lavatory, so I'm to do what I can with a sponge back in his room. We've been washing out his wound regularly, but it's been a long time since Tristan himself had a wash and the boys are supposed to look their best for the competitions. So I fetch a bucket from the kitchen and a sponge from the lavatory, and when I meet him back in his room, he's already undressing.

I close the door hastily behind me with one foot lest anyone out in the hall catch sight of the binding around his middle, and as the door swings closed, the cramped little room seems to grow darker and smaller, as it always does when I'm alone in it with Tristan. A single candle is burning on his bedside table, and the light flickering around the dark room and across Tristan's naked chest reminds me sharply of the first time I was ever in here with him, when I thought for a wild moment he was about to embrace me. I know better now, but even after all this time, I'm not unaffected.

I stand nervously up against the wall as Tristan slowly removes all of his clothing until he's standing naked in front of me, except for the bandaging around his waist. I've bathed him before, of course, but it's always been in the lavatory, never intimately like this, and I feel beads of sweat start forming on my upper lip as he stretches out one arm to brace himself against the wall, since he's to remain standing so we won't soak his mattress. I look up at his handsome face, bent down toward me to let me reach his head, with his hair falling forward over his forehead, his lips slightly parted, and I abandon any pretext of dignity. I almost lost him. After tomorrow, he may be cut; we'll have to leave St. Sebastian's. I've kept my vow; I've not given myself away, and I never will. Taran was right when he sneered at me in the windmill, telling me I was too wretched to be desired. No one will ever be my lover. But there's no point denying that I'm Tristan's lover, or at least, that I love him desperately. If lust is a deadly sin, I'm going to have to take the consequences. I can almost feel my arm starting to fester again already.

I kneel nervously at his side to unwrap his wound and inspect it carefully before getting to his bath proper.

"It looks good," I say unsteadily when the wrappings are off, taking a deep breath and putting a hand that trembles slightly on the places in front and behind where the arrow penetrated. "Really good. I think it's finally going to hold." I'm actually not at all sure, but the holes look closed now and he needs confidence for tomorrow. But I can't put off the bath any longer, so I stand up shakily.

"Ready?" I say, my voice catching a bit as I look up at him, and when he nods, I dip the sponge into the bucket and wring it out, and I raise it to his head. I give the sponge a gentle squeeze, and as the water drips down over him, I let myself run my hands through that thick hair of his as I've wanted to do so often, massaging the water through it. It feels so glorious, he finally laughs and says,

"That's half the bucket on my head alone, kid! Leave something for the rest of me," and his laugh is delicious, rippling under my hands, and I laugh, too. I dip the sponge again.

For modesty's sake, as I have to move lower, I skirt around behind him, and I run the sponge over each muscle of his broad shoulders and down along his back, watching as the firelight plays over his wet skin as he stretches and moves in response to the touch of the sponge. Every inch of him is beautiful, more beautiful than any work of art, and even in the dim light he dazzles my eyes, just as he did when I first saw him on the garden wall. I'm filled with such a sudden, violent surge of love for him that it threatens to bring tears to my eyes, and I slip the sponge gently around his waist, not caring that it's dangerously like a reversal of the pose from my dream. I glide the sponge across his stomach, listening to his soft breathing, my face only inches from his shoulder, resisting the urge to lean in and rest my cheek against it.

My hand hesitates over his belly, just as Taran's did over mine in the windmill, just as Tristan's does in my dream. And for a moment, I even wonder what would happen if I let it slide *down*. Would Tristan say anything? Would he object to a little innocent 'relaxation' between friends, a release of tensions before Seconds? But I don't really want to find out. It's not just that I don't want to risk it. It's that it's not what I want it to be like between us. I won't deny that I'm aching so badly to toss the sponge away and feel his body under my hand, for him to turn around and take me in his arms, to press those parted lips to mine, that I'm sick with it. But only if when he did, I could see my beauty reflected in his eyes, only if they were shining with that stunned look he had when he first laid eyes on Melissande. Without it, his kiss would turn to ashes on my mouth. Even if somehow, incredibly, he might want it, might want me as I am, if he knew, I know I wouldn't do it. I don't want to be the ugly stain on the illumination, the thing that mars the beauty of the picture, the rightness of it. And there's just no picture of Tristan that's perfect with me in it. I accepted that long ago, and Tristan and I don't dwell on impossibilities. So I slide the sponge up across his chest, letting the water drip down, and I force myself not to think beyond the moment. It's my last indulgence, I promise myself. Because I do want Tristan and me to love each other, but in the only way we can that's possible, in the only way that doesn't make me ugly, the way that's right between us: as friends.

"Bath's over," I say roughly, handing him the sponge. "You can get the rest yourself."

"You've no idea how good it feels, Marek," he says by way of thanks, "to finally be clean again. How I hate to have to put that bandage back on."

"Leave it off for the night," I say, swallowing hard. I do know how good it feels. "Let it get some air. We'll get it back on in the morning."

CHAPTER THIRTY-TWO

A s I join the crowd of squires around the cabinets the next morning and I drag Tristan's equipment across the road and over to the exhibition grounds to set up for Seconds, I don't bother to gawk at the mad scene already in full swing there. I feel like an old hand now, and the bustle of activity around the booths and the grandstands doesn't hold any fascination for me this time. I've got other things to worry about.

The set-up is virtually the same as it was for Firsts, and so I stock Tristan's tent as quickly as possible and then hasten back to the guild to help him get ready. I've got to get Tristan bound up as tightly as possible; fortunately, I don't need to worry about his clothing, since his regalia is all black, with a touch of red. I just hope the only red today is going to be the lining of his cloak.

Tristan insists that I wrap Melissande's rather soiled veil around him as the outer layer of his binding, and so when I've finally gotten him ready to my satisfaction, he's got two tokens to take with him into competition this time: Melissande's veil, and the medal of St. Margaret. He's going to need them both. He looks well enough; I don't think anyone could tell to look at him that he'd been shot just two weeks ago, but I know he's not going to impress anyone with his flair or style today. I tell myself that's okay. He's in third place going in; he has room to fall. All he needs is just not to fall too far. I don't let myself dwell on the fact that it's Jerome's unexplained and rather precipitous breakdown that's opened the door for Tristan. He's only got to beat two boys, and with Jerome down, that leaves only one more.

A few well-worded questions to Remy during the past week elicited the welcome news that Lord Mellor and the Guards are not to be in attendance today, but otherwise when we make our way through the crowds already packed into the exhibition grounds and we emerge near the bleachers, we see a similar array of dignitaries near the grandstands. Sir Brecelyn is again to serve as one of the judges, only this time I don't notice Taran out with him on the field beforehand. He must not be eager to shake the hand that wrung his bird's neck.

Or maybe it's Melissande he's hoping to avoid. I see her already seated in the box set aside for the ladies, as lovely as ever in a sea-green gown and a filmy veil that floats like foam on the waves of her hair. This time I recognize some of the other girls around her from the hunt. They must be girls she knows from St. Genevieve's, since a number of stern older women in the box behind them look to be nuns.

"Look, Tristan. Melissande came through after all. Isn't that lady Sibilla?" I say. She's seated next to Melissande and she's got the same imperious look on her face she wore through most of the hunt, but she's fidgeting and she looks nervous.

"I doubt Gilles will thank her for it. What can have put him off her so quickly?" Tristan responds absently, and I grin to myself. The squires have all kept Gilles's secret. "She seems to be scanning the crowd down among the tents rather intently. Maybe I was wrong, and she is keen, after all."

"No doubt she's looking for Pascal," I say, without explaining, while noticing that Tristan only takes the quickest of glances at the box. He doesn't seem inclined to gaze at Melissande the way he did at Firsts. I can't resist; I ask him about it.

"I can't flirt openly with another man's fiancée," he says, rather wistfully. I bet he would, I think, if he thought he could get away with it. But then he says, "And if you're right, there's been enough talk already. I've been foolish, Marek. Taking an arrow in the side, that was one thing. But I've done more damage than that, if I've ruined her reputation," and I'm ashamed of myself.

Today Tristan isn't inclined to linger on the field, either. We go straight to his tent, and we wait there in nervous silence for the horns to signal the commencement of the competition. He shows no interest in peeking out through the tent flaps. He simply sits with his head bowed, and I see him fingering the medal of St. Margaret as his lips move in silent prayer. For all his talk about striking out for adventure if he fails today, he desperately wants to pass and he's not at all sure he can. He's going to have to give it everything he's got, wound or no, and so I bow my head, too, and add my prayers to his.

"She told you you'd pass, didn't she, Tristan?' I say. "Have a little faith." And he grins up at me.

"I've got your bow, too, little brother. But I'm afraid, even with it, I'm not going to be very extraordinary today."

"Don't worry, they already know what extraordinary means. They saw you last time. They won't forget." Yet as I say it, I know it isn't true. A crowd is fickle thing. It won't take it long to turn against him.

We're both startled when the sound of the first fanfare blasts outside, and the competition is underway. Guillaume is already making his announcements and we're sitting in nervous silence when the tent flap flips open and Gilles appears.

"Gentlemen!" he says cheerfully, and I grin. Good old Gilles.

"Gilles! I wasn't expecting any social calls," I laugh, and he slaps me on the back.

"Ready, old boy? Marek here got you bound up tight?" he says to Tristan.

"As ready as I'll ever be," he smiles back. "I'm in good hands."

"The best," Gilles agrees, with a nod to me. "I can't wait to see what they've got in store for us!" Gilles really does sound excited, and he's got every right to be. It's going to be his day again, I'm sure.

"Whatever it is, it's going to be brutal," Tristan says. "After all, St. Sebastian's punishes its own."

Gilles laughs, and then with a soberer look, crosses quickly to Tristan and embraces him warmly. "Good luck out there, duBois. If it was anyone but you, I'd be worried," he says, then steps back to the entrance. "I'd better get back, before Pascal has a fit. And you, my boy," he says, pointing to me with a wink, "Keep your eye on the apple!"

Somehow, Gilles's visit has dissipated the tension, and when we're called out onto the field almost as soon as he disappears, I think Tristan was right: we're as ready as we'll ever be. As the herald calls Tristan's name and we stride out of the tent to take our place on the line, I find myself looking over the other boys just as I did at Firsts. Only this time, instead of thinking how magnificent they look, I'm coldly figuring which two we can hope to cut.

As with the first trials, Seconds is to consist of three main tests, to be followed by the boys' exhibition shots in place of the mounted exercises. Also like Firsts, the actual tests themselves are rather simple affairs; the difficulty is not the complexity of the task but the quality of the competition, and the first test proves to be extremely straight-forward. It's pure wands. Each Journey has a 2-inch thick willow wand set up in front of his station, at 260 yards distant. Each boy then has five arrows to hit the wand, and this time, instead of shooting all at once, the boys are to take each shot in order, one at a time.

After seeing the boys at Firsts, the crowd already has its favorites, and so it's louder in its cheers and taunts than at the first competition. There are sure to be many bets placed on the boys, too, and when Tristan steps up to take his first shot, the noise from the bleachers is deafening. Everyone clearly expects great things from him, and after his tricks last time, he's the audience darling. The cheers don't encourage me, though; all I can think is, *how they're going to hate him when he doesn't deliver!* Particularly if they've got money riding on his performance.

It's something I didn't think of before — that Tristan's success during Firsts is just going to increase the pressure now, and I'm not wrong. His first arrow misses the wand. When his second does, too, the disappointed silence of the crowd turns to murmurs, then to hisses when his third also misses. What's more, Tristan looks tired already, after only a few shots. He'd been holding up so well during practice lately, I didn't expect it to happen so quickly, but I didn't factor in the effect of competition. He can't hold anything back here, and I worry that he's wrenched himself with one of his very first shots. He looks in pain. But maybe it's just the pain of missing;

I can't tell, and I don't bother to ask him. There's nothing I can do about it either way.

So far, Gilles hasn't missed a shot. Taran's already gotten at least two in the wand, too, and by now, everyone but Jerome and Turk have hit the wand at least once. Tristan's only got two more arrows; he's got to hit the wand before the end of the round, or his chances don't look good. To make it more of a show, we squires are sent down to retrieve our masters' arrows between each round, and as I run back with Tristan's third missed arrow, I try to think of something to say to give him some encouragement. I can't think of anything, but I have to say something anyway, so as the boys down the line from him take their shots, I say:

"Tristan, you can make this shot. Come on! You took an arrow in the side for this chance. I pushed it through your body myself, so you could have it. I stuck an arrow in my own arm for it! Don't let all that be for nothing. Look down there and put the next one right in Taran's eye."

And it's his turn. He laughs, and says, "You're right, little brother. We've been through too much to fail now, by God!" and he shoots, sweeping back in a powerful move that holds nothing back, even though I'm sure now he really is in pain. But the arrow hits the wand, and so does his next one. When the round is over, Gilles has incredibly hit his wand with all five arrows; from what I could see of the others between retrievals, I think Taran is tied or close behind with four, and Aristide and Jurian each hit theirs with three. Tristan, Charles, and Falko all made two, while Turk and Anselm hit with one each. Jerome missed every shot.

"So far, so good!" I say cheerfully once we're safely back in the tent between tests, but Tristan shakes his head.

"I've come open."

I drop instantly to my knees and get to work pulling up his tunic to see to the binding. But he doesn't mean his binding is loose, he means he's ripped his wound open again. I feel the thick, sticky slick of blood on his tunic as soon as I touch it.

"It happened on the very first shot," he says.

I hasten to help him down into a chair, and I prepare to assess the situation. This time, we've at least thought ahead. Anticipating that his bandages might need reinforcement, I've brought extra strips of material over from his room, stuffed down into a quiver. Only when I get his tunic rolled up, I see that it isn't just a little blood that's seeping through. He's done serious damage.

"How in the world did you manage to do this, when you've held up so well during practice this week?" I ask, dismayed.

"I guess I tried to give it some of the old Verbeke flair," he quips, but I notice he's breathing heavily, and he's started to sweat.

"Look," I say evenly, though I'm starting to panic. "Do you remember how you made it through the forest, into the chapel, and how you took it when I shoved that arrow through you? Compared to that day at the hunt, this is going to be a snap. I'm going to bind you up tight again, and you're going to go back out there, and wow them all over again. Who knows? You might even get another kiss."

I try to make light of it as I quickly unwrap his bindings. I try not to react when I see what he's done. His wound is bigger and more ragged in the front, where the back of the arrow with its fletching first came through, and here the flesh has torn open and it's now bleeding freely; what's worse, some other fluids are coming out, too. All I can do is stuff a wad of material into it as hard as I can and hold it there, as I wrap fresh strips of cloth around him as tight as I dare without cutting off his wind. I just manage to get him patched up when the horn sounds for the second test.

Mercifully, the next test doesn't involve speed shooting. But by the time Tristan's finished shooting 10 arrows at wands arranged at intervals up to 300 yards, I can see the dark stain that's creeping across the front of his tunic and the color that's draining from his face, almost as though it's draining straight through him and out onto his clothing. Only the dark color of his costume and the distance hide the stain from the other boys and the crowd. Each time he lifts the bow, I wonder if it's going to be the last time he's got enough strength. I don't bother to pay much attention to whether his arrows hit or not, or how the others are doing. I'm just willing him to stay upright.

As soon as we get back to the tent, I lower Tristan straight to the ground. I don't unwrap him; this time, I'm going to wait to change his bandages to the last minute, because otherwise he's going to bleed through them before we even take the field. He's looking so pale now, though, that I risk leaving him alone to rush out among the booths and get him some wine and bread. He needs something. As I'm barreling through the crowd, pushing my way rudely to the front of the line, I see some of the other squires out of the corner of my eye, but when they try to hail me, I ignore them and dart back to the tent as quickly as I can. I force some of the wine and food into Tristan, and then I set about binding him up again. To my relief, I see that the wad of material I stuck in the wound succeeded in slowing the bleeding; in fact, it looks a little better.

"Just one more," I whisper to him, as I add fresh wrappings. "Can you make it?"

"I don't know," he says, "but we're going to find out. I'm not going to quit. They're going to have to carry me off the field."

"That's the spirit!" I say, hoping fervently that his words aren't prophetic.

When we're called back out to the field, we find that they've saved the worst test for last. I don't know why I should be surprised; it's pretty typical of Guillaume. The last test is in fact a lot like what Taran has planned for his exhibition. It's a course of 10 wands, set up at 20-yard intervals, at random distances back from the line. Each Journey is to make his way down the line as quickly as possible, taking one shot at each wand. Not only are we going to have to stand and watch the others do the course, but as the competition begins, I see that many of the boys are going to take the course at a run, stopping only to shoot.

"Can you run?" I hiss at Tristan, who shakes his head.

"Maybe I can roll," he says back, but it isn't funny.

It's pure torment watching the others do the course, knowing that every minute Tristan has to stand immobile is draining what little strength he has. His face is pale and drawn and he's begun to sway slightly as Taran takes his turn. It's the unfortunate luck of the draw that Tristan's going to have to follow him. Unsurprisingly, Taran's performance is flawless, since the test is so close to the trick he's been practicing, and it can only be demoralizing Tristan even further.

When his turn comes, I wonder what he can possibly do to cover for his lack of speed. I'm trying to think of something to suggest, but it's too late. He's already stepping up to the mark, and hailing the crowd. He gives them one of his dazzling smiles, and then he has to start. I can hardly bring myself to watch.

He doesn't try to run, or even jog or trot. He knows it would just look ridiculous, even if he could manage it. He just swaggers up to the first wand, and he makes a show of taking his time and giving one of his exaggerated shots. He pretends to be insolent, arrogant, and to saunter along as though he thinks his shooting is so beautiful that he doesn't need to try to hurry to impress them, and although at first I think this angers the crowd (and I can't even bring myself to look over at the judges' table), after a while he gives such a good performance and his shooting is so accurate that the crowd begins to play along, a little. I can see the effort he's making, though; for this to work, he's got to hit the wands. And he does — all but the last one. It's a bad one to miss, but then he does something unexpected. He shrugs his shoulders, walks out to the wand, picks up the arrow, and sticks it into the wand with his hand, then turns and bows deeply to the crowd. The stands erupt in laughter and applause, and I think he's won them over with his charm, at least enough to keep him alive, I hope. But I doubt Master Guillaume is impressed.

"That was damned risky!" I whisper to him when he makes it back to his spot next to me on the line to watch the remaining Journeys make their runs; then I see that his hair is wet with the sweat that's pouring down his face and he looks almost yellow.

"What choice did I have?" he snaps back, but he's smiling, and so am I. Some of the others have tried too hard for speed on the course, and as a result, they've missed a number of the wands. Surely Tristan's got to be ahead of at least two of them, even though his insolent performance must have turned most of the judges against him. He's sure to have fallen in the ranks, and probably very far. It'll put him in a terrible position for going into clouts, but that's a problem for another day. I think he's going to squeak past.

We just have to make it through our exhibition.

Unfortunately, I'm well aware that the exhibitions shots are going to count for more this time than they did at Firsts. The mounted exercises were simply a way of showing off Turk, but this is different. These are pure archery displays, and the boys have been working hard at coming up with stunts that are going to be pretty impressive. I know Tristan's going to have to do more than just stay upright during the exhibition. He's going to have to do a credible job of it, if we're to pass.

"Tristan," I say back in our tent when the third test is finally complete, and as I change his bindings yet again in preparation for our exhibition, pleased with how they've held up. "We don't have to do all ten apples. If you feel you can't, put up your arm like this to signal you want me to bring the trick to an end early, and I'll send up the last apple." I put my arm straight up in the air, and he nods. We've both always known that letting even one apple fall will be a disaster. Better to do fewer apples than to risk having one splat to the ground.

The wound now seems to be holding well, but Tristan's strength is almost gone. So as the exhibitions start, a plan begins to form in the back of my mind. A plan 'just in case.' We don't go out and watch the others. It's going to be a long wait until our turn, since each exhibition requires individual set-up, and the masters are in no hurry for the competition to end. Instead, we stay in our tent where Tristan can rest and we listen to the crowd's reaction, trying to gauge the success of the tricks that way. Without a horse, Turk seems to falter; there's only a smattering of applause when he's done. Falko's trick turns out to be extremely popular, but probably not quite in the way he expected; peasants love a near disaster. There's a rather long interval between his trick and the next as a crew of veterans struggles to put out the fire he starts with a stray flaming arrow (later he explains that the plan was to ignite a wand drenched in oil. Apparently, he did do it eventually, but not before setting off a chain reaction that left more than half the wicker butts lined up at the end of the field burned to a crisp. Leave it to Falko to set up a trick involving fire near a stockpile of flammable materials. "Who could have anticipated the effect of the wind?" he says, and I refrain from saying, "just about everyone").

By the time Taran's turn comes, Tristan is looking a little better. He's had a chance to sit and rest, and he's had some more of the wine and bread I brought for him before the last test, but we listen in silence to the cheers of the crowd as Taran goes through his exhibition. His trick may be very similar to the third test, but nobody seems to be holding it against him. If anything, his course is harder than the test, and he's clearly doing it superbly. With the applause for him still ringing in our ears, the fanfare that marks the announcement of the next competitor blares, and the herald calls Tristan's name. It's our turn.

I let him step out of the tent in front of me, as I turn to gather up the things we'll need to set up our trick: the bag of apples, Tristan's bench to lay them on in readiness, and over my shoulder, I sling my crossbow.

Tristan stops at the line and strikes his pose to wait for me to set up, but when he sees me go past wearing the crossbow, he asks curiously,

"What's that for?" He hasn't turned his head to look, since he has to hold his pose for the crowd.

"I just thought it would look good on the bench; you know, add a little color," I say as I hasten past him and make my way down to the 200-yard mark.

I set up the bench and line up the apples, ready to hand. I bend over, and with my back to Tristan I prepare the objects on the bench to my satisfaction. Then I square my shoulders and turn to Tristan, to give him the sign that I'm ready. As I do, I reach down and lift the medal of St. Margaret to my lips, and I kiss it for luck. Despite the distance, I see Tristan do the same, and I wonder if he's thinking about the kisses he thinks the saint gave him in the chapel. I hope he is.

Tristan raises his hand to the crowd. Then turns to me and raises his hand to the side, signaling for me to throw the first two apples. I grab them up and throw, up and away, one after the other, in more rapid succession in my nervousness than I intend. Both apples are in the air at once; it's inadvertently like our original plan. Tristan takes it in stride, and shoots the first apple, then quickly nocks and shoots the second, to the astonishment of the crowd. The audience has been seriously disappointed with Tristan up to this point. At this, it begins to sit up and take notice. None of the other boys have tried to shoot a moving target, let alone two at once. Hearty applause rings out, and we're off to a good start.

Two down.

Tristan motions to me to throw the next apples, and I get a little cocky. I decide to throw two quickly again. He did it once, didn't he? And the crowd loved it. They'll love it even more if he does it again. So *boom, boom*, I throw them up, high and away, and I see Tristan whip the bow up and shoot. He gets them both, again, and the crowd begins to stomp in the stands.

Four down. It's going beautifully.

But then I see Tristan list to the side, and he puts his hand straight up. It's the signal for the last apple; he's not going to make it to the end of the trick. He wants to end it. I'm disappointed, since he's been doing so well, but I'm not a fool. Five apples, that's a decent trick. It'll be enough. But as I release the last apple, when I look back to Tristan, I see that he's now bent partially over, his hand at his side. He hasn't even lifted the bow. As I watch, he drops it entirely, and doubles over. He looks about to fall himself, and the apple is reaching the top of its arc. Any minute, it's going to drop. If either of them drops, it'll be all over. He'll be cut for sure.

There's no time to think it over. I have to act. There is one thing about a crossbow that's superior to a longbow. You can have it loaded in advance. And of course, that's what I did. With my back turned, I cranked the bow and slotted an arrow into the tiller, and I put the bow gingerly on the bench where it would be ready to hand, just in case.

So I snatch it up and shoot the apple out of the sky myself.

Then I drop the bow and run to Tristan, my arms spread wide in triumph, and I embrace him, before he can fall to the ground. I try to make it a performance, as he would, as though the whole thing has been an act, a little drama we worked out ahead of time to amuse the crowd. Though he's surprised and in pain, Tristan's smart enough to play along. With great effort, he grins and springs upright, as though to show the audience it was all a bit of fun, and we take exaggerated bows while the crowd claps in appreciation. We stand arm-in-arm for a while waving at the cheering throng in the grandstands, and when we leave the field, it's still with our arms around each other's shoulders, as though we're celebrating in solidarity. In reality, I'm supporting Tristan's weight with difficulty, and we're lucky to make it back to the tent before I collapse under the effort.

As soon as we're safely inside the tent, Tristan's knees buckle under him and we both fall to the floor. Tristan begins instantly to make a wretched wheezing sound under me that scares me to death, and just when I'm sure we've pushed him too far, that's he's really in danger now, I recognize the sound. He's laughing.

"Marek!" he says, gasping for air, "If I live to be a hundred, I'll never see anything as beautiful as that shot!"

"Well," I say, rolling off him and blushing, "Gilles told me to keep my eye on the apple."

"And thank God you did!" he says, lying flat and not trying to get up.

"Do you think it was enough? Do you think you made it through?" I ask, wiping the sweat off his forehead and preparing to check him for damage again.

"No," he says gallantly. "But I think *we* did." After a pause, he grins wickedly and says, "Remind me to thank Taran, won't you?"

"For what?" For a moment, I think he must have found out I told Taran that he was wounded, and that Taran hasn't told. But then he says with great satisfaction:

"For suggesting I get you a crossbow, of course!"

Somehow, I'd managed to forget that the crossbow was Taran's idea in the first place.

We spend the duration of Charles's trick patching Tristan up again, though it soon becomes evident that he's mostly just exhausted. When he assures me that the wound is stable and that all he needs is rest, I agree to let him come out and watch the remaining exhibitions. I'm not really sure it's safe, but Gilles is next, and I have no intention of missing whatever he's got planned. I don't care what it looks like; I pull a stool out in front of Tristan's tent and make him sit on it to watch, and then I settle in next to him as Gilles is announced.

As threatened, Gilles has changed into his white ermine-trimmed outfit, but when he struts out onto the field, followed by Pascal in a matching get-up, I have to admit that what looked ridiculous in the close quarters of his room looks pretty stunning out here in front of the crowd. It is fabulous, and I start to get excited about the trick. I've been waiting so long to see what it's going to be. The ermine *does* set off his red hair, and if he's sweating under the stifling weight of it, I can't see it from here. Pascal looks handsome, too, but he's so pale his skin looks even lighter than his robe. When he passes by our tent, he raises a hand in a sad gesture that looks for all the world as though he's bidding us farewell, like a gladiator saluting the emperor after getting the thumbs down.

The crowd has come to its feet for Gilles. He was in first place coming into the competition, and from what I can tell, he's done nothing but confirm his superiority by his performance today. Everyone wants to see what he's going to do, and we're not the only boys who come out to watch. All the Journeys and squires have come out of their tents to watch Gilles's trick, too. But he's in no hurry to do it. He's going to take his time, and milk the moment for all it's worth.

First, he swirls his cloak, and makes a show of taking it off and handing it to Pascal, who drapes it over Gilles's stand. Then Pascal swirls his own and takes it off, too, laying it with similar ceremony next to Gilles's.

"I see they've foregone the hats," I mention to Tristan, as Pascal then pulls out three bright red apples and holds them up to show them to the crowd. "Oh Look! Three apples," I say smugly. "I knew Gilles was holding out on us. Do you think he's going to throw them, too? Ha! If he does, we'll beat him by two!"

But Tristan doesn't respond, and soon Pascal is heading down to the 200-yard mark, as the crowd falls silent in anticipation. When he reaches the mark, he turns to face Gilles, and to my dismay he balances one of the apples on his head, then stretches out his arms to either side of him, holding them perpendicular to the ground, with an apple resting on each open palm.

"What's he going to do? Toss the two, then snatch the one from his head and throw it? Isn't this taking the joke way too far, even for Gilles?" I ask Tristan, confused, but Tristan still doesn't respond. He's sitting very tensely on the edge of his chair. Even the silence of the audience has changed from anticipation to apprehension as Gilles lifts his bow.

As a murmur starts to go through the crowd, Gilles steps quickly to the line, and he grabs up one of three arrows he's stuck point down into the ground. He nocks it rapidly and shoots, and the apple flies off Pascal's right palm. I'm shocked, but before anyone can say anything, he swiftly nocks the second arrow, and shoots the apple off Pascal's left palm. By now I'm thoroughly alarmed, and I can hear the other Journeys starting to talk at once, but Gilles smoothly grabs up the last arrow, and as Pascal crosses himself, he takes his last shot.

He shoots the apple clean off Pascal's head.

I can't believe it. Pascal was right all along! The sodding bastard did it.

The astounded crowd erupts in thunderous applause as Pascal drops gracefully to his knees in a fervent prayer of thanks, and out of the corner of my eye, I see lady Sibilla up in the stands, one hand at her throat, dropping much less gracefully into a dead faint.

"Tristan! You said Gilles wouldn't shoot Pascal!" I cry accusingly. Tristan just says mildly,

"I didn't say he wouldn't do the trick. I just said he wouldn't shoot Pascal, and he didn't."

By now Pascal is running full tilt at Gilles, and the two of them embrace in front of the appreciative crowd, pride beaming on Pascal's face. I'd been thinking I'd done a lot for my master today, but really, this is too much. If anything, Pascal should be punching Gilles in the face, not congratulating him, but from the look of him, you'd think the whole trick was Pascal's idea in the first place.

"All I can say is, I'm glad I didn't know," I finally say, as I watch the two of them in disbelief. "And, I'm even gladder it's over!"

"Unfortunately, it's not over yet," Tristan says, and I look at him inquiringly. "Have you forgotten whose turn it is next?"

And the thing is, I had forgotten.

"You can't mean *Aristide* is really going to try it, too, can you?!"

It's unthinkable. Yet as soon as I say it, Gilles and Pascal are already leaving the field, and the fanfare signaling the next competitor is starting. It's Aristide's turn.

As Aristide and Armand come slowly forward, all the Journeys are on their feet. I don't know how many of them really thought Gilles would go through with the trick, but now that he did, I can tell we're all petrified that Aristide might try to go through with it, too. Even Tristan is on his feet now, and I don't bother to try to get him to sit down again. Instead, I'm remembering how I taunted Aristide outside the stables as he watched Gilles practice the trick, and I instantly regret it. What if this *is* pluck-buffet all over again?

Aristide missed every shot. Gilles has that effect on him, and Gilles has sustained the joke for so long and goaded Aristide so hard, he probably thinks he has to go through with it now. Poor Armand!

'Tristan, we've got to stop them. We can't let Aristide try it. He's got no nerve at all. He'll kill Armand. We've got to go to the master and tell him to put a stop to it!"

"If Guillaume doesn't stop it himself, there's nothing we can do about it now. If nothing else, there's no time."

And so we watch in appalled silence as a pallid Armand makes the long march down to the 200-yard mark, turns, and places an apple on his head with a hand that's trembling so hard it takes him quite a while to get it to stay balanced there. There's no ceremony about this performance, no swagger, and the audience seems as appalled as the Journeys. This time they know what's coming, and they seem to have as little confidence in Aristide's ability to pull off the shot as Aristide does. I can't believe Master Guillaume is just sitting there watching, making no move to stop it. Aristide hasn't bothered to salute the crowd, and his face looks as pale and clammy as Armand's. There's no way he's going to make the shot, though it's apparent he's going to try.

I can't watch. I just don't want to see another arrow sticking out of a boy's body, and certainly not one as nice as Armand's. As Aristide nocks his arrow and takes aim, I turn away and hide my face against Tristan's chest. Then suddenly Aristide lets out a loud curse, and I peek out, and see him swiftly lift his bow high over his head and aim almost straight up into the air, in the opposite direction, away from Armand. The arrow comes down and sticks into the ground about 20 yards behind Aristide with a dismal thud, and Aristide lowers his bow in an attitude of defeat.

I think I'm even more amazed than I was when Gilles took his turn. Aristide's purposely muffed his shot. He'll be out for sure. He's put himself clean out of the competition, because he wasn't willing to risk hurting Armand. Armand, on the other hand, didn't wait to see if Aristide was going to falter; as soon as he heard the twang of the bowstring, he dropped to the ground in the fakest faint I've ever seen.

The crowd begins to hiss and jeer as Aristide turns tail and starts to stalk dejectedly off the field. It's the end of his career as a

Journey. I even feel sorry for him. It seems to me that people should be cheering. What Aristide did took real courage. I didn't think it possible, but I feel a rush of admiration and even affection for Aristide. Armand was right about him. He is essentially sane. I never would have thought it.

As Aristide is trudging off, suddenly Gilles darts forward unexpectedly and runs out onto the field to the place where Armand is now getting to his feet. When he sees Gilles, Master Guillaume rises to his feet, too, but he hesitates and then doesn't interrupt. So far, it's good drama, and he's going to wait to see what's going to happen.

"Aristide Guyenne!" Gilles calls out in a loud voice, and an expectant hush falls over the stands. At the sound of Gilles's voice, Aristide stops, too, but he doesn't turn around. His shoulders go back, as though he's waiting to hear Gilles's inevitable taunts, and from his posture, he not only expects them but thinks he deserves them.

"Turn around!" Gilles commands, and slowly Aristide turns, throwing out his chest and steeling himself for Gilles's vaunting speech. But to everyone's amazement, Gilles has no intention of teasing him.

"Come on, Aristide, my old friend!" Gilles shouts, much to my surprise. As Aristide looks on dumbfounded, Gilles bends down and plucks up the apple from where it's fallen a few feet from Armand, who's wisely taken the opportunity to duck off the field and disappear back inside Aristide's tent. Raising his voice even higher so that the whole audience can hear, Gilles calls out again,

"I, for one, know you can do it!"

He takes a big bite out of the apple, leaving only slightly more than half, and with his mouth full, he steps to the spot where Armand fell and puts what's left of the apple on his own head.

"Come on, Ari! Let's show them all what we Journeys can really do! Take the shot!"

The audience comes to its feet, delighted, and the cheers and calls from the bleachers completely mask whatever it is that Master Guillaume now begins desperately shouting as he starts to wave his arms and rush out from behind the judges' box. I suppose letting the Journeys publicly kill their squires is one thing, but letting the future marquis de Chartrain get shot in front of all of Louvain is too much even for the master.

It's too late. As Gilles spreads his arms wide and cries out again in a voice that booms over the noise of the crowd, "Come on, Aristide, my friend! Show them what we mean at St. Sebastian's when we say, *Arrows won't kill me!*," Aristide pulls an arrow from his quiver with a determined look and shoots the half-eaten apple right off Gilles's head.

Both Gilles and Armand were perfectly right. Aristide *could* do it. And Gilles is completely insane.

As the apple flies off his head, Gilles jumps in the air with a whoop and runs straight for Aristide, just as Pascal did to him a few minutes ago, and the two embrace on the field like long-lost brothers. With their arms draped around each other, they turn to the grandstands to acknowledge the deafening applause that greets them. There's no doubt about it. They're the undisputed kings for the day.

Stunned, I turn to Tristan.

"I thought they hated each other."

"Oh, they still do. I expect they'll be back to acting like it by tomorrow," he says smoothly.

Boys. Will I ever fully understand them?

After Aristide's performance, it feels so much like the end of the competition that I start to go back into the tent, when Tristan reminds me that there's still one Journey left.

Jerome.

He's been doing so badly that I don't want to watch (even though I've been curious about the strange trick we witnessed Jerome and Auguste practicing the other day), and neither does Tristan. Instead, I help Tristan back into the tent, only vaguely aware of Auguste setting up wands around the 220-yard mark, and then hovering down by them as he did the other day on the field. We haven't been inside long when we hear the exhibition start, and from the sounds of grumbling and hissing that start to float in to us from outside, it's clear Jerome isn't doing any better now that he has all day. Tristan and I haven't said anything. It's painful to hear, particularly because we have the added burden of guilt at the knowledge that Jerome's failure is to our advantage. But when there's a sudden scream from the field and an eerie sigh like a collective intake of breath from the spectators in the stands, we look up into each other's eyes and without a word rush outside the tent.

Everyone in the stands is on their feet, only this time it's not in appreciation. The judges' stands have emptied, and all the Journeys, squires, veterans, and masters are running down the field to where the wands Jerome was shooting at are standing. Instantly Tristan and I are running, too; what he couldn't do for the test he's doing now out of dread.

When we've pushed our way to the front of the crowd that's now gathering around a distraught Jerome, we find what I know we both expected: the writhing form of Auguste on the ground, an arrow sticking out of his thigh. Jerome's shot him.

So a Journey did shoot his squire at Seconds, it's just not the Journey anyone would have expected.

THE ATMOSPHERE BACK AT THE GUILD THAT NIGHT IS nothing like the festive mood after Firsts, for obvious reasons. Although Auguste's wound shouldn't be fatal, it's serious. The arrow hit the bone, requiring full-scale surgery. Not even the insertion of an arrow spoon could pull the arrowhead out, and it's unlikely he'll recover full use of the leg. Needless to say, Jerome is out. Even without shooting his squire, he was in last place. But I don't think he's thinking about that. After carrying Auguste into the make-shift surgery hastily set up in one of the guild offices, he refused to leave Auguste's side throughout the procedure, and when the operation was hailed a tentative success, he announced his intention of dragging in a cot and staying by Auguste's bed all night.

Nobody's quite sure what really happened, but Jerome is devastated, and their misfortunes set the mood for the night. It doesn't help that throughout the surgery itself, there was no place in the guild to escape the awful sound of Auguste's tortured cries. I can tell Tristan feels guilty, too, about convincing Jerome to compete, though there's no way he could have known it would end this way. Only Master Leon seems unaffected by the tragedy. As the Journeys sit sullenly at evening mess, this time still in regalia not because of the desire to celebrate but because no one's thought to take it off, he gets up with a cold smile and a leisurely stretch to announce the standings after Seconds, and I think I'm the only one who's actually interested in hearing about it.

Not surprisingly, Gilles is still in first place, followed closely by Taran in second. After almost putting himself out of the competition entirely, his trick with the half-apple has pulled Aristide into third place, just ahead of Jurian and Charles. Despite the mishap with the flaming arrow, Falko has moved up to sixth place, and miraculously, Tristan is in seventh, just ahead of Turk, Anselm, and the unfortunate Jerome. Anselm and Jerome will be cut; that'll leave Tristan in second-to-last place going into clouts. It's a terrible position to be in, but who cares? He's through, that's what matters, though I think that even wounded, he did better than some of the boys now ranked ahead of him. Our exhibition went over much better than Falko's, for example. But it's clear the judges didn't like Tristan's antics, and I can't really blame them. How were they to know we had no choice?

The next morning, after a night's rest and a fresh bandaging job, Tristan declares he's feeling fine and ready for morning practice, but he doesn't fool me. He's just as eager as everyone else to see what's going to happen, so I don't say anything, and I let him come out. We've all gotten an early start, and some excitement about getting past Seconds has started to filter through our concern for Auguste. When Jerome appears out on the field, too, looking exhausted but encouraged, to tell us that Auguste came through the night well, it seems like permission to celebrate. Jerome's so relieved himself as to be almost exuberant, and whatever disappointment he must feel at being out of St. Sebastian's is at least temporarily pushed aside by relief that Auguste survived the surgery and that he appears likely to recover.

Nobody's really anxious to practice, of course. We're all waiting to see what Gilles and Aristide are going to do to settle their 'Tell shot' bet. Neither of them has appeared yet, and Pascal and Armand haven't come out to set up for them. When even Master Guillaume himself wanders out, trying to look as though his appearance on the field at this hour isn't entirely extraordinary, it just fuels our anticipation. Before long everyone's out except for the four of them, and even some of the veterans who have nothing to do with training have lined up along the stables. Taran was right; there are a lot of eyes and ears around St. Sebastian's, and clearly everyone has heard about the wager.

Finally, the stable doors burst open, and Gilles and Aristide parade out, arm-in-arm, grinning like idiots and waving to us regally as we start to cheer. Behind them come Armand and Pascal, also arm-in-arm, and they stop behind their masters and take a bow, bending low and grinning just as broadly. After the fact, from the way they're acting, you'd think Pascal and Armand thought shooting apples off their heads was a fantastic plan, the best idea they'd ever heard.

When Gilles and Aristide come to a stop in front of us, Pascal and Armand break apart and move around to stand at attention next to their masters. Gilles and Aristide face each other and give each other a deep bow, and without a word they both begin to strip, slowly and deliberately taking off one item at a time and handing it to their squires to fold. When both Gilles and Aristide are completely nude, they grin at each other again, and then they're off, racing across the field toward the garden. Over our calls and cheers we can hear them thrashing through the garden and swinging open the gate in the wall, on their way to make the circuit of Louvain together.

A second after they've gone, Pascal looks at Armand, and before I know it, they're stripping, too, only with no ceremony. They throw off their clothes and with a laugh they race off after their masters, and the next thing I know, I hear Tristan next to me shout out *"what are we waiting for, boys?"* and he's ripping his clothes off, too, not caring now that the competition is over that he'll reveal his bandage and everyone will see he's hurt. I don't bother to ask him how he thinks he's going to run all the way around Louvain today when he couldn't run 300 yards yesterday; I am beginning to understand boys. Pretty soon, all around me the Journeys are stripping down, and then so are the squires, and in a raucous pack — laughing, tripping, and still throwing random articles of clothing off behind them — they all dart off across the field, buck naked, to give the inhabitants of Louvain the thrill of a lifetime.

I'm left standing there alone on the field with the masters, watching them go. I've never thought it before, but what I wouldn't give right about now to have the necessary equipment to join them!

It does cross my mind to wonder if in all that spectacle anyone is going to notice that the outer layer of Tristan's wrappings is embroidered with tiny pink rosebuds.

THIRD
TRIALS

PART THREE

CHAPTER
THIRTY-THREE

After the running of Louvain, it's clear to everyone that Tristan is wounded, and that he was during Seconds. Not long after the boys get back, Tristan is called into Master Guillaume's office, and he's in there quite a long time. I don't have to ask to know they've had one of their rows, but there's no point in kicking Tristan out right after he's managed to pass Seconds anyway, and I think Master Guillaume is secretly rather impressed with his performance now that he knows the circumstances under which he gave it. It's more than two months until the final competition, too, so Tristan will have plenty of time to recover for Thirds, but the master is taking no chances. Tristan is under strict orders not to lift his bow for at least a solid week, and this time, the barber who is still in attendance on Auguste is called in to sew up the ragged front end of the wound properly to make sure that it really heals.

This should all be good news, but there is one aspect of it I don't like. With Seconds over and Tristan unable to practice, I'm going to be at loose ends. It'll give me plenty of time to think, and that's the one thing I'm not eager to do.

While Tristan is being seen by the barber, I go along to Anselm's room to say goodbye. It's a little strained, given my refusal to help him these last days, but he's pretty philosophical about the whole thing. I think he made it further than he thought he would, and he thanks me nicely for helping him do it. As I've said, he's a very decent guy. Saying goodbye to his squire Benoit back in the barracks is harder, since we've been living together for so long now, but the loss of Auguste hurts the most. Of all the squires, with the possible exception of Pascal, he's been my closest friend, and the uncertainty of what awaits him when he leaves makes it harder still.

I've not been allowed in to see Auguste since the accident, but Tristan gives me a hopeful report when he gets back from being patched up himself, and we decide to go see Jerome together.

When we get to his room, we find Gilles and Pascal already there, but somehow we all manage to cram ourselves into the tight space. After commiserating in general terms for a while, Tristan finally asks what we've all been wanting to know.

"What happened, Jerome? What was Auguste doing down by the wands?"

"He was signaling back to me, to help me adjust my shots. To help me narrow in on the marks. It was absurd, I know, but I never thought I'd shoot him! I must have misread one of his signals. I've never come close to hitting him before."

"Signaling for you?" Gilles repeats, and Jerome sighs.

"I've been losing my sight," he confesses. "I don't know what's happening, but it's been getting harder and harder to see the targets, particularly the ones far away. Everything just looks blurry. I guess it started even before the Journey competitions, but I just thought I was tired, or the sun was in my eyes. Only now it's been getting progressively worse, and fast. At this rate, I won't even be able to shoot on the near butts soon. If it keeps up …" he breaks off, and Gilles puts a hand on his shoulder.

"I've been praying every day, and I've spent all my money paying for penance, but it doesn't seem to do any good. I guess my sins are just coming home to roost."

Tristan frowns. "If blindness is a punishment for sin, you should be about the only Journey who can see at all."

"What are you going to do?" Gilles asks quietly.

"Master's going to let me stay on, until Auguste is better and he's sound enough to travel. Then we'll go back to Meuse, and we'll figure it out. I'll find a way to take care of him. You know, I'd planned to study music theory at the university, if I was cut. My Latin's good, and at least that's something I've still got a chance of doing. I can still see the distance of a book ..." he breaks off, before ending dispiritedly with, "for now, anyway."

There's nothing we can say to that.

I'm on my own in the afternoon, since the ministrations of the barber leave Tristan weak and he has every excuse now to get the rest he needs. He suggests I make a trip out to the Drunken Goat; I'm supposed to visit Roxanne on occasion, to keep up appearances and to make sure that Rosalinde is keeping up her end of the bargain, but I haven't been back since the day we made the deal. To my surprise, as I'm settling Tristan in for the afternoon, he says,

"Look, Marek. Don't go all the way down there by yourself. Take someone with you. There are some tough costumers in Louvain, particularly around the taverns. All we need is for you to get jumped by some of the thugs that roam the streets right about now."

"I suspect I can handle myself," I reply, not liking to seem too much like Remy, afraid to go out alone, but he insists.

"Some of 'em love nothing better than giving a St. Seb's boy a licking. And they know we've usually got some money. If nothing else, they'll go for the medals. Take somebody with you. Ask Falko. He's big, and he'll go for sure."

And so I do, even though it means listening to an endless recap of his stunt with the flaming arrows on the way. But Tristan's right. With Falko clumping along next to me, nobody's going to bother me.

When we get to the Goat, I ask for Roxanne, but since Falko is along we don't go up to her room. Instead, she brings us some ale and we all sit at one of the long tables. As I make the introductions, I notice that Falko seems perfectly relaxed in Roxanne's company, since he still thinks she's essentially my girl.

We've been drinking and chatting away about Seconds amiably for a while when Falko notices the string around Roxanne's neck.

"What've you got there?" he asks, and she pulls the St. Sebastian's medal out shyly.

"Marek gave it to me."

"Then what's that you're wearing?" Falko asks me, pointing to the string around my neck. I pull out the medal of St. Margaret for him to see.

"Hey, that's funny!" he exclaims. "You two should switch, since you're the archer and she's the ..." and then he comes to an abrupt halt, his face red, as the unspoken word 'virgin' hangs over the table.

Falko really is hopeless! It's an indelicate word to allude to in front of a girl in any event, particularly when it's in reference to her own sexual status. It's even worse when you're sitting in what is essentially a whorehouse and you say it to a girl who has supposedly only recently joined the profession. But in addition to all of this, Falko isn't supposed to know that nothing has actually happened between me and Roxanne.

To my surprise, Roxanne laughs. "That *is* funny!" she giggles, and it occurs to me that a girl who works in a brothel might just be used enough to crudity to appreciate Falko. "You're right!" she says, and she reaches up and pulls the medal from around her neck and hands it to me, while holding out her hand for mine, and we exchange medals. I just can't seem to get St. Sebastian off my neck.

As we make the switch, she continues:

"Only I don't have a hammer. Can you picture me trying to swing one at my enemies?" At the opening to talk about swinging things at enemies, Falko jumps in with:

"It'd be just like swinging a mace. You know, there's nothing ..." and I finish with him, *"more satisfying than connecting with a mace!"*

"Have you really used one?" Roxanne asks, sounding genuinely fascinated. "They look so heavy. You must be terribly strong."

And they're off. They spend the rest of the afternoon talking animatedly about combat, while I sit and stare off into space. Falko does most of the talking, and he's actually quite eloquent when talking about something he knows so much about. Roxanne keeps up her end with a tireless string of appreciative noises and leading questions. It's all very easy. By the end of the afternoon, with really little work on my part, it's clear to me that though they may not know it yet, Roxanne is destined to be Falko's girl now. I wonder what his father would say, if he knew.

The next morning, I forget that Tristan's not to practice, and out of force of habit I get up early and head out of the barracks to set up Tristan's station. As I cross the corridor, I hesitate as usual on the threshold of the great hall, and think to myself, maybe today I really will take the shortcut through the garden. I'm just about to do it, but then I see something that stops me. This time, it's not the painting. It's the sight of Taran at the far end of the hall, his back to me, hunched over in intense consultation with Albrecht. What in the world is he doing up so early, and in here? When I notice that Albrecht looks distinctly nervous, and that he's bobbing his head back and forth and trying to cast furtive glances back into the room over Taran's shoulder as though he's worried about being caught, I step back into the shadows with a frown, before turning to head out down the Journey corridor as usual.

Out on the field, I come across Pascal bent over Gilles's bench, but I don't disturb him, though he's presenting the perfect opportunity. After what he did for Gilles, none of the squires are going to pinch him again. I'm already dragging Tristan's bench out of his cabinet when I remember that he's not to come out today. As I stash the bench back in the cabinet wondering how I'm going to spend my morning, I see Remy come out, so I wander over to him. After offering a greeting, I try to sound casual as I say,

"If you're looking for Taran, I saw him just a few minutes ago in the great hall, with Albrecht. I wonder what he could have been talking to him about at this time of the morning."

Remy frowns, but doesn't say anything, so I make a direct attack.

"Do you know what that was all about?"

"I suspect he was asking more questions," he says. "It's quite odd, but he's been asking around a lot, about that man. You know, the one who had the accident, a long time ago. You know the one I mean."

"Jan Verbeke."

"That's the one," he confirms.

"Do you know," I ask, licking my lips and trying without much success to sound only marginally interested, *"why?"*

"He seems determined to find out what happened to him. He must have been a great friend of his father's."

Determined to check up on my story, more's like, I think. But it is odd, and I'm still puzzling over it so intently as I make my way back inside that I'm twisting my hands together and looking down at them as I come around the corner of the archives into the

Journey hallway, just as Taran himself is coming out to the field in the opposite direction.

I run right into him.

I've been avoiding him more assiduously than usual ever since our encounter in the cathedral, but when I literally rebound off his chest, we can't pretend that we don't see each other.

We both come to a sudden stop in the cramped space, and after looking up at him in my initial surprise, I drop my eyes and stand there stupidly, wondering how I'm going to get around him without looking at him again. There's a pause, then somewhere above me he says in his clipped voice,

"Nice shot."

For a second I think he means my crashing into him, but he must mean my shot at the apple. When I don't respond, he adds tonelessly,

"So you've managed to save him. Again."

I don't like the implication: that Tristan should have failed. So I whip my head up defiantly, and retort:

"Tristan says to thank you for him, for suggesting the crossbow!"

I fully expect this to enrage him, and I prepare to take the consequences, but when all he does is say "anyone can use a crossbow," I see he's decided to content himself with insulting me instead of resorting to his usual violence.

But when he adds, "but it takes real skill to be good," I'm too surprised to do anything other than gape as he pushes past me roughly and disappears down the hall.

It's almost exactly what Gilles said when I first told him about the crossbow. If I didn't know better, I'd almost think this was some sort of compliment.

I spend all morning out in the shop, ostensibly working on a batch of arrows, but really thinking about what Remy told me and debating whether or not to confront Taran about it. If my father and his really were friends, maybe Taran does think it his duty to find out what he can about what happened to him. Maybe he'd try anyway, since he seems to think it's his duty to uphold and defend the reputation of St. Sebastian's all on his own; maybe that's even the real reason he's never told about me, just as he said. *Would a boy who's willing to shoot down a member himself really care why someone else did the same thing? Or can I really believe after all that Taran shot Tristan?* I can't decide. But I suspect that if Taran really tried, he could find out more about my father than either Tristan or I could. After all, he's the son of Lord Mellor; he probably already knows more about my father's past than I do. If I want to know what Taran knows and what he's found out, I'm going to have to swallow my pride and ask him. After this morning, that doesn't seem quite as impossible as it once might have.

By the afternoon, Tristan is well rested and in a fine mood. By now everyone knows he's wounded, and so after mess, he holds court in the garden to tell the boys the whole story. Just about everyone comes out to hear about it, since Tristan is such a good storyteller, and even though I already know what happened, even I'm eager to hear his recitation. He's going to make quite a show of it, I'm sure, and of course, I'm going to get to be the hero, at least in part. I can't imagine Tristan giving anyone but himself the starring role.

As he settles himself into a chair under the jasmine vines and we all scramble to find a comfortable place from which to watch and listen (since he's sure to act out some of the more dramatic moments), Gilles sits down next to me, as is appropriate. We're both part of the cast, as it were. When everyone is ready, Tristan begins, starting from the beginning of the hunt and going through the whole story in such dramatic fashion and with so much embellishment that periodically I forget I was actually there, I get so caught up in his narration. I let myself get lost in the pleasure of listening to him; he really could charm the leaves right off the trees if he tried.

He plays up the arrow that narrowly missed him during the first hunt splendidly, but when he gets to the second hunt, there's no need to embellish. What happened was fantastic enough. I'm glowing with pride as he describes my valiant efforts to conceal him and to drag him to the little chapel in the glen, and when he reaches the point in his narrative where I push the arrow through his body, it hardly matters that what he plays up most of all is his own stoicism and suffering. He gives me my due and my bravery shines through, and I can tell all the boys are duly impressed.

I'm not prepared, though, for him to tell them all about his supposed vision. He'd said he wouldn't try to describe it to anyone but me, but he's gotten caught up in the story and before I know it, I hear him saying,

"And as I lay there, hovering between life and death, on the very threshold of the pearly gates, what do you think happened, boys?," and then he's telling them about my kisses, describing how they felt, and repeating some of the things I said to him with disturbing accuracy. I can feel heat surging up my neck and I will myself not to blush, because at the same time, I can feel one particular set of eyes burning into the back of my head. I'm sure there's at least one person who knows whose kisses those really were. I wonder if he's figured out the timing of it yet, too. If not, it won't be long now. He's going to figure out pretty soon that Tristan and I must have already been concealed in the chapel when he met with Melissande there.

Tristan himself wisely leaves Melissande out of his recitation. The other boys won't notice; none of them probably knows where Taran and Melissande had their interview. But I'm no longer enjoying the story, and as Tristan goes on to describe (or rather invent, since he was out cold) my summoning of Gilles and our efforts to disguise his state, all I can do is wait impatiently for him to finish, so I can make my escape without attracting too much attention.

When he's finally finished and everyone's still busy exclaiming over the events and expressing their admiration for all of us, Charles is the first to ask the inevitable question.

"Say, Tristan. Just which one of us was it who shot you?" he laughs.

"Actually," Tristan says, in such a studiously casual tone that I have a terrible premonition, "the arrow was unmarked." He looks around appreciatively at the surprise this pronouncement elicits, and I know he's not going to let it alone. He's just pausing for effect.

"Tristan …" I say, trying to get up, and feeling all of a sudden a lot like Pascal, but even as I try to get his attention, I know it's no good. He's going to tell them. I should have known that this is actually what he was leading up to with his telling of the story all along.

It doesn't take Tristan long to confirm my fears.

"Marek here actually has quite an interesting theory about it. Why don't you tell them, kid?" he says recklessly, and all eyes turn to me. My stomach constricts and I suddenly feel as though I could gladly punch Tristan right in the face. He's setting me up! But I bet he thinks I'm enjoying it, too. After all, I've wanted to score off Taran just as much as he has, haven't I? I bet he thinks we're working in concert again, making a terrific team. When I don't say anything, he continues smoothly,

"Come on, Marek. Don't be shy." When I still don't reply, he ignores my warning glare and continues: "Oh, all right, I'll have to tell them myself. It seems Marek here doesn't think it was an accident. He's of the opinion there's one of you here who hates me enough to plan the whole thing ahead, down to coming prepared with an unmarked arrow, just to take a dirty shot at me." As he says this last, he narrows his eyes and looks pointedly behind me, to the place where I know Taran is lounging against the portico.

Unexpectedly, Aristide laughs, taking it as a joke. "I hate you enough to take a shot at you, and I bet I'm not the only one."

"He didn't mean you, Ari," Tristan says evenly, holding Taran's gaze over my shoulder.

"Of course not! There's only one of us who really hates you enough for that!" Turk laughs, and everyone joins in. Nobody's taking the accusation seriously, and here in the harsh midday light of the garden, in front of everyone, it suddenly does seem more than ridiculous. I feel thoroughly humiliated, though clearly none of the boys think I really believe the outrageous accusation, either. They just think Tristan is taking the opportunity to try to irritate Taran as usual.

But I suspect there is one person who believes I was serious, who has reason to believe I'd think him low enough to resort to murder. *Is that really what you think of me?* I hear Taran's quiet voice in the cathedral, and I want to cry out in protest, to think of anything to say to defend myself. But there's nothing. I did think it. And I did try to convince Tristan and Gilles it was true. What can I say now? I can't jump up and declare that I wanted to believe it to comfort myself. What a scene *that* would make, if I jumped up and threw myself at Taran's feet, and confessed in front of all of them that I only believed it, to defend myself from lusting after him!

Whatever he's done, accusing Taran of murder is unforgivable. At least, he'll never forgive it. I'm just lucky the others think it's a joke. Tristan is looking so pleased with himself, I almost hurl myself across the little table and try to rip his handsome head right off.

"I'm afraid there's one flaw in your theory." I don't have to turn around to know Taran's voice, or to know what expression I'd see on his face if I did turn around. I can hear the cold disdain behind his deliberate words. "If I'd tried to kill you, I'd never have missed you with the first arrow. And when I got you with the second, I'd have put it right through your eye."

"Funny," Tristan calls out happily, as the sound of Taran's retreating footsteps echoes in my ears. "That's exactly what I told him myself!"

There's no point making a retreat from the garden after that. I sink miserably back down onto the ground and wait, eyes downcast and unheeding of the lingering jokes and conversation, until the garden is finally empty.

Then it's my turn again to vomit behind the rosebushes.

THAT NIGHT, I DON'T THINK I CAN FEEL ANY WORSE, when we're hit with more bad news. We're just settling into our cots when Henri bursts in, agitated, to tell us that Auguste's leg has become seriously infected, and there aren't enough leeches in Louvain to do anything about it. The barber's on his way; the leg is going to have to come off.

I'm not going to describe what it's like, huddled outside the room with the other squires listening to the animal cries that ring out from within as the men work to saw off Auguste's leg, or the sight of Jerome, convulsing in tears, collapsing into the supporting arms of the Journeys. I'm particularly not going to describe seeing the severed limb carried from the room to be thrown onto the rubbish heap in the alley, or smelling the burning flesh as the remaining stump is seared to stop the bleeding.

Miraculously, Auguste lives through the gruesome procedure, though the concoction of poisons given to him to dull his senses for it probably should have killed him. It's past the third hour when he slips into a drug-induced stupor that allows him to rest in relative peace, and we slink to bed in a state that's somewhere between relieved he's alive and traumatized by what he's been through.

When I wake up the next morning at the sound of Remy stirring restlessly in his cot (the events of last night having induced some of his accustomed nightmares), I sit up on the bed and rub my temples, trying to clear my head and drum up the energy to face the day. With Tristan still unable to attend morning drills, I'm rudderless, but I can't just drift through the days until he's well. Any thought I might have had yesterday about confronting Taran about my father is obviously out of the question now, too. The image of him Tristan painted in his story yesterday was of a coward with no honor at all, and I was supposedly the one spreading this rumor around the guild behind his back. Any grudging respect I might have won from him as a squire has surely been replaced by pure hatred. Somehow, knowing that he now must think me 'not much of a boy' hurts even more than being judged wretched as a girl. I'm not sure why I should care. We hate each other, don't we? But I guess the shocking idea that I might have been beginning to win some glimmer of respect for my skills from my worst critic makes losing it again hard. So I determine to go out to the field to watch practice. I can at least begin to size up the remaining competition; it's not too early to start thinking about Thirds. At least, I don't want to think about anything else.

Having settled on a course of action, I bend down to pull on my boot, when I notice something odd on my table. Someone's set the mouse and the hawk back upright and placed them next to each other.

I look across at Remy. He must have done it, and he must have meant something by it. I've suspected he must be angry with me, too, after yesterday. I don't know if he thinks Tristan's comments in the garden were a joke or not, but he's so protective of Taran, he can't have been pleased. I wonder if this is his way of letting me know he doesn't believe the theory Tristan spouted in the garden really originated with me. I'm just glad he doesn't know that for once, Tristan is entirely innocent. I can't blame the sordid story on anyone but myself.

I wait for Remy to wake, and when he finally stops stirring and sits up, I give him a minute or two before I ask,

"Are the mouse and the hawk still friends, then?"

I probably haven't given him long enough to wake up fully, because he looks confused, and replies rather drowsily,

"What's that, Marek? A mouse and a hawk can't be friends." I don't like the sound of that. Either he's really mad, or he doesn't know what I mean. So I nod at the figurines on the table.

"The merlin?" he says, and I nod again.

"The merlin's dead, Marek," is all he says, as he bends down to get his chamber pot and take it down to the end of the room.

Either that's an unlikely threat, or Remy really has absolutely no idea what I'm talking about. I put my head down between my knees, wondering if it's too early to go back out behind the rosebushes again.

I SPEND THE REST OF THE MORNING OUT IN THE SHOP, but by afternoon I don't have any taste for more fletching and I'm in no mood for company, either. Most of the boys will be out on the butts practicing at this hour, so I grab up my crossbow and head out for the horse pasture, thinking I can do some shooting by myself out there. I make it through the stables and across the yard without meeting anyone but a few stable boys, but when I get out past the outbuildings, I find that I'm not alone after all. Turk isn't practicing, either. He's out riding, whipping across the field. I can't very well shoot while he's out there, so I sit down by a fencepost and watch him. As I do, I turn the crossbow over in my hands idly. It doesn't have the same beautiful shape as a recurve bow, or a longbow. Running a hand over it isn't the same satisfying experience as handling one of those. In fact, the whole shape of it is entirely unsatisfactory. When Turk slows his horse to a canter and then pulls up alongside me, I'm lost in thought.

"Have you finally decided to learn to ride, Marek?" he asks, slipping off the horse in a fluid motion and leaning on the post next to me. "I could teach you, if you want."

"I wouldn't want to keep you from your preparation for clouts," I say sarcastically.

"Oh, clouts. I'll never pull up in the ranks on clouts, and you know it, kid. What's the point of practicing?" Turk's in last place, and he's the smallest Journey. He's right, so I don't insult him by demurring.

"I'm afraid of anything with hooves. Hooves are for the Devil," I reply instead, and he laughs.

"What are you doing out here, then?"

"I've been thinking about this blasted crossbow. It's just so slow. I've been trying to figure out how I could adjust it, so I could load and shoot it faster. But it's impossible."

Turk strokes the horse's nose, then after crooning something in its ear, he slaps it lightly on the rear and it trots out into the field. Then he drops down onto the ground next to me and picks up the crossbow.

"It is clumsy, isn't it?" he says. "But you're awfully good with it, Marek. That was quite a shot at Seconds."

I try not to preen at this praise. "It just seems to me there ought to be a way to improve it."

He frowns for a minute, turning the bow over in his hands now, too, and then says slowly, "You know, I remember my grandfather showing me something once, when I was little. A weapon from the east — a novelty. Something recovered from one of the barbarian invaders. It was a long time ago, but it was a sort of crossbow, I think. A repeating crossbow."

"Repeating?"

"It was small and light. It could only shoot light bolts at short range, nothing that could penetrate armor. It wouldn't be very practical in real battle, but it was fast."

"How did it work?" I ask, feeling a prickling of excitement down my spine. But he shakes his head.

"I don't know. I don't remember it very well."

"Try!" I cry in exasperation, rather rudely. So I add, "Can't you remember anything about it at all?"

He frowns in concentration, still shaking his head, then says, "I remember thinking it was clunky, not much to look at. It had a sort of a long, thin box on the top, where you could load the arrows."

"And?" I say encouragingly.

"Somehow, a single pull of a lever pulled back the bowstring and dropped a bolt from the box into the tiller. All you had to do was keep pulling to nock and release arrows, until the box was empty. I don't know how, exactly."

It's enough for me. I know what I'm going to do with myself, while Tristan heals. If it's humanly possible, I'm going to figure out how to build a repeating crossbow for myself. Who cares if it isn't practical, if it wouldn't be effective in battle against real knights? I don't need it for battle. I just need it to make an impression. I haven't forgotten that apprentice trials are at Thirds, and I'll need a trick of my own. A repeating crossbow. What a trick that'll make! If they liked it when I shot down one apple, wait until they see me do a dozen!

And so the week passes quickly, and stretches from one week into two, and I spend every day out in the shop, thankful to have found work to be absorbed in again. By the end of the second week, Tristan has fully recovered. His wound is sufficiently healed, and he's so bored of lying in bed, reading in the archives, or sitting in the garden that he even takes to coming out to the shop with me. The one thing he doesn't do is watch the others practice. He knows his position going into clouts isn't much better than Turk's. By the end of the second week, Auguste has also healed. At least, he's as healed as he's going to be. His stump is closing up nicely, and he's begun to practice walking with the help of a stick. The only thing that hasn't made real progress is my repeating crossbow. Try as I might, I can't figure out how to produce one.

"Turk was having you on, kid," Tristan laughs at me, as he watches me struggle with my latest model. It's a dismal failure, and I have to admit that Tristan is probably right. Now that Tristan is well, it's time to get back to our real work. I've got to figure out how to make him into a crack clout shooter in less than two months, and I'm going to have to pass the apprentice trials without relying on gimmicks. There's to be no repeating crossbow for me after all. I'll have to pass on skill alone.

"Tristan, just what are the apprentice trials like?" I ask the afternoon before Tristan's set to start practicing again as usual, as I realize that I don't even really know what will be expected of me. I've been putting off thinking about them so assiduously that it never occurred to me before to ask about it. Deep down, I'm not entirely sure I should be trying for apprentice status, anyway. I haven't let myself think about just how far I'm really willing to go. A girl squire is one thing, but apprentice status means eventually trying for Journey. I'm not sure how St. Sebastian would feel about that.

"It's nothing like the Journey trials," Tristan assures me. "All you're doing is earning the right to train next year. You've just got to show the masters that you've got potential. It isn't a competition. All the squires can get apprentice status, if the masters think they're worthy."

"Are any of the others going for it, do you know?" I haven't thought about it before. All of us shoot, but I've never really seen any of the others practice much.

"Pascal and Armand, probably," Tristan says, without much interest. "Maybe Henri, too. I doubt any of the others. Oh, and Remy."

This surprises me quite a bit. I've never thought of Remy as an archer. He's certainly never played pluck-buffet, and I don't think I've ever seen him shoot. I've just assumed he was too small even to lift a bow. But then I catch myself. He's stronger than I am. I saw that on my first day as squire. And he's not so small anymore. He's been growing before my eyes. He's probably taller than I am by now.

"Is he any good?" I ask. I'm not sure why, but I find the thought that he might be better than I am distinctly unpleasant.

"He's got Taran to coach him. What do *you* think?" comes the disquieting reply.

I GO ALONG TO THE MASTER'S OFFICE THAT'S STILL serving as Auguste's room on my way to evening mess that night. Auguste has been making such good progress, it can't be long before he's declared well enough to travel, and I'm acutely aware that he may not be with us much longer.

I find him in good spirits. He's up, hobbling around the room in circles, practicing with his stick. As I skirt around him to sit down on his bed and watch, he says excitedly,

"Look, Marek! Look what a tight turn I can make, with my new stick!," and he does a little maneuver that looks depressingly clumsy to me, but he seems so proud of it that I try to smile. As I watch, I see that he does indeed have a new stick. It's not just a simple crutch, either. It's a lovely thing of polished wood, carved cleverly to resemble the body of a snake with two heads, which branch to form a support under Auguste's arms.

"I know who made you that," I say, with a knot in my stomach. I've felt uncomfortable thinking about the little animals after finding them set up on my table. I'm not ready to think about what my conversation with Remy might mean. "I recognize the carving."

"Yes! Isn't it beautiful? And such a clever design. It really supports me much better than that old one. And it must have taken such a long time to make! I have to admit, I was surprised. I mean, it's not as though we've been particular friends."

I swallow hard at this. He and Remy have been friends, so I have to ask.

"Remy *did* bring you that, didn't he?"

"Of course!" he confirms, and I relax. I hate it when I don't know what's going on. "And Marek, I've got the most wonderful news! Master Guillaume, he feels so bad about what happened, he's invited me to stay. He's going to let me stay at St. Sebastian's!"

"Stay?" I repeat stupidly. What can Auguste do here now?

"He's going to let me man the front desk! He's going to send that idiot who works there now down to the kitchens. Isn't it great?"

I am glad that Auguste won't be leaving. But it doesn't sound very great to me. I can't imagine being happy sitting at the front desk, after being a squire. It's a distinct demotion. I don't know how I could stand to watch the others taking the field day after day, knowing I could never join them. Unexpectedly, I feel a sharp jolt of pain at the thought of my father. I suddenly have a flash of what it would be like, having been at St. Sebastian's, and never being able to bend a bow again. But Auguste sounds thrilled, so I try to be happy for him. I guess I'm not the only one who will never leave St. Sebastian's willingly.

We end up heading to the great hall for mess together. It's the first night Auguste has taken a meal with us in the hall since his accident, and his appearance is greeted with great enthusiasm. But it's also to be the last night Jerome is with us. With Auguste set to stay at St. Sebastian's, he's to leave for Meuse in the morning.

"Don't think you've seen the last of me!" he tells Tristan. "I have every intention of coming back, to see you win Thirds."

"I sincerely hope you do," Tristan says, and we all know he means more than just that he hopes he'll pass.

After mess, we linger for a long time in the garden. It's Jerome's last night at St. Sebastian's, and nobody wants it to end. For me, Jerome is the first Journey to go that really hurts, and I think the others feel the same way.

"Play us something, one last time, Jerome," Charles asks, and we all add our voices to his request. When he slings down his lute to comply, I feel tears pricking behind my eyes.

"What do you want to hear?" he asks quietly, and when nobody replies, after a minute, Remy says, "How about *the hawk and the hart? Do you know that one?*"

It's not one I know, but somehow, I don't like the sound of it. I suppose it could be worse — it could be the hawk and the mouse. But Jerome nods, and as he begins to play softly, his voice is bittersweet:

A hawk spied a hart, once in the leafy green
from where it circled high,
And against its nature it loved it so,
it hovered ever nigh.

I was right. I don't like this song. I shoot a suspicious glance at Remy, but he's looking as innocent as ever. He seems entranced, and as sad as everyone else that this will be the last time Jerome plays for us, so I try to relax and enjoy the song.

The mighty hart, distracted
by the bird's soaring flight,
mindless of danger in the woods
kept the hawk ever in its sight.

But in cover of the greenwood,
an archer hid nearby,
and taking aim at the beast,
shot it straight through the eye.

As we're making our way back to the barracks later, I fall into step next to Remy.

"Whatever made you suggest that song, Remy?" I ask casually.

"I've always liked it," he smiles back.

"It's rather depressing, isn't it?"

"Very," he agrees happily.

CHAPTER
THIRTY-FOUR

Tristan makes a triumphant return to practice the next morning. Despite being idle for two weeks, now that's he's sound again he's stronger after all our work for Seconds, and his aim is as good as it ever was. It won't take long to get him back to top form. That is, top form for a butts shooter. Getting him ready for clouts is going to be another matter.

I've been eager to get back to my old routine, too, so it's with excited anticipation that I drag Tristan's bench over to set up his station. The only thing that mars my enthusiasm is the sight of Rennie fast approaching with Jurian's equipment. He's going to set up next to us yet again. It's clear to me that it's as I feared. Jurian's got his eye on Tristan, and I can't ignore it anymore. I'm going to have to say something about it. I can't let Tristan become fodder for Baylen's whip.

As the boys begin to come out to the line, I see that something has changed while Tristan and I have been out. With apprentice trials coming up at Thirds, some of the squires have brought bows for themselves out to the line. We're going to be allowed to participate in drills now, alongside the Journeys (though I soon see we have to retrieve both for ourselves *and* our masters). Accordingly, each Journey takes two spots, so that if desired, he and his squire can shoot at targets on either side of their station. Tristan was right, too, about which squires are in contention: Pascal,

Armand, Henri, and Remy all have bows. So I grab mine out of Tristan's cabinet.

It's been an awfully long time since I practiced with a longbow. I've been working so hard on my crossbow, I've neglected practice. It's not just Tristan who is going to have to get back in shape.

We start out on the butts, but with clouts coming up it isn't long before Baylen and Royce move us out to the far field. It's here that I get my first inkling of just what Tristan is going to be up against. Taran is untouchable, of course. But Falko isn't far behind. The two of them are unbeatable at clouts. Gilles has good distance, too, and he's in first place. There's no beating Gilles, either. In fact, the only one Tristan can outdistance easily is Turk. Charles, Aristide, Jurian — he's going to have to better one of them to make it through. I know who I'd like it to be, but Aristide is now in third place. I can't see how Tristan can improve enough to pass him, but frankly, Charles and Jurian both seem stronger than Tristan, and clouts is almost entirely about distance. I hate thinking in terms of shooting one of the boys down, but that's the reality. Tristan's got to pass one of them, somehow.

I'd be lying if I said I wasn't also watching the squires shoot with great interest. At close range, after getting back into the swing of things, I think I make a good showing on the butts. I've got better accuracy than the others. Out on the clout field, even with my demoralizing tutorial on the clouts motion, I'm still a disaster. With extreme difficulty, I manage a few shots over 250 yards, but that's my limit. I hate to admit it, too, but I can't really bring myself to try my best to replicate the motion Taran showed me. I don't want to remember it, and I certainly don't want to feel it. I haven't been able to make myself look down the field to where he's shooting, but I can tell he hasn't looked down at me, either. He isn't watching me anymore. Not after my accusation. I'm so used to being watched that somehow, the knowledge that my surveillance is over makes me feel distinctly lonely.

None of the squires can make the distance of the Journeys, but most of them can eke out 300 yards with enough accuracy to drop down within about 10 or 15 yards of the mark. Henri is particularly strong, and though his shots tend to go quite wide, he can send an arrow down the field, all right. Both Pascal and Armand make a decent showing, too. But Remy is quite remarkable. For his size, he's got great distance, and his accuracy at long range isn't at all bad. I watch him covertly for a while, trying not to see his master, eyes narrowed. Clearly, being coached by Taran has been a big plus.

"Jealous?" Tristan whispers in my ear, seeing my look. "Cheer up, kid. When it comes to clouts, we're both not the golden boys anymore."

We're exhausted by the end of practice, so after splashing off at the rain barrels, we drop down against the wall under the eaves, too tired even to go inside or out to the garden to wait for mess. Gilles joins us, though he looks as fresh as ever. It's never irritated me more.

"Don't you sweat, Gilles?" I grumble.

"I'm afraid I'm too genteel for that. Aristocrats don't sweat. Just ask my father," he replies sweetly.

"If he didn't sweat in that get-up for Seconds, he's not going to sweat after just a little practice," Tristan adds.

"Just what's become of that outfit anyway, Gilles?" I ask.

"He's having it stuffed," Tristan says, and I laugh, hoping it's a joke.

Just then, Jurian struts over, strips off his tunic, and starts splashing himself off in what can only be described as a deliberate display of his physique. When he catches my eye, he bends his head to his arm, as though he's about to lick his arrow welt again, but at the last minute he grins and winks at me. With a last languorous rub of his belly, he throws his tunic over his shoulder and heads inside. I decide the time has come to do something about Jurian. So I tell Tristan and Gilles about what Jurian said at the hunt, about how he's got his eye on somebody new.

"That's unlikely," Tristan says dismissively.

"He's going to try to make Baylen jealous, Tristan. Do take it seriously!"

"It doesn't sound very serious, Marek. What's that to me?"

"The one he's got his eye on, it's you!" I say.

"That's even more unlikely!" he scoffs.

"Why?" I ask. It seems perfectly reasonable to me, and I'd have thought he'd agree. I still think him ready to believe everyone's in love with him.

"Because I'm not his type. I'm too much like him." Leave it to Tristan to compare himself with the sublimely gorgeous Jurian with absolutely no self-consciousness. But he's right. "Besides," he adds, "I'm pretty obviously interested exclusively in girls."

"I doubt elegant aristocrats are to his taste, either," Gilles says, when I turn to him.

"Then who?" I ask.

"It's probably not true at all. He's crazy about Baylen," Tristan insists lazily. "He's just teasing you, Marek. But if he really has set his sights on someone new, you've got to look for his type."

"Which is?"

"Somebody tough, rugged, and not interested in girls. Somebody like Baylen."

To my dismay, I realize that there is somebody at St. Sebastian's that Jurian has every reason to think is uninterested in girls, and who Guillaume himself said is just like a younger Baylen.

Me.

When I venture to say as much to Tristan and Gilles, I think Tristan's in danger of busting his gut wide open again, they laugh so hard. It's really terribly unflattering.

That afternoon, when Tristan and I take the field for our first solo practice session, I know what I'm going to have to do. I've known it for a long time, but I still feel apprehensive, now that the moment is finally here. I'm going to have to teach Tristan the clout motion that Taran showed me. There's really no other way. And I'm going to have to teach it to him in the same way Taran taught it to me — by taking him through the motion myself. I'm not looking forward to it, and not only because I can hear Taran's sneering accusation, *what are you going to do? Run off and do it with Tristan?* It's also because when I step up behind him and take Tristan in that embrace around the bow, I'm going to have to let myself really feel that motion again. And I know there are going to be three of us in that embrace, just as in my perverse dream of the windmill. *If only I could ask Falko to do it for me!* But it's one thing for him to know that I'm planning to help Tristan. It's another thing entirely to ask him to help Tristan directly himself, now that the competition is getting tight. No, I'm going to have to do it myself, but one thing is certain:

I've got to do it somewhere I can be absolutely sure that Taran won't see us.

When I suggest to Tristan that we take our bows and go around to the horse pasture to practice, he thinks at first that I'm kidding. It takes me a while to explain, and even then, I do it so incoherently that I'm not sure what he makes of my ramblings about helping Falko with girls in exchange for tips on clouts. I don't mention Taran, but that's an omission, not a lie, isn't it? I manage to convince Tristan to give it a try, and that we're going to look strange enough in the process that we'd be better off trying it in private.

Fortunately Turk isn't out this afternoon and there are no veterans doing certifications out here, so we have the place to ourselves. But when it comes to it, I find that taking Tristan through the motion isn't going to be as easy as I thought. It's distinctly different to have to be the one to pull Tristan through the motion. I'd forgotten that I'm not particularly strong, and I'm shorter than Tristan. The first time I have him lean back heavily onto me, I'm surprised by how heavy he is and we fall right over backwards before we can even get started. There's no way I'm going to be able to support his weight while pulling him back into the sit. We try switching positions, so Tristan is behind me, and I try pushing him through the motion instead. This works a little better, but it's certainly not fluid and I can't reproduce the feeling that the motion gave me when I did it with Taran.

Try as I might, I just can't replicate it with Tristan.

In the end, I have to fall back on explaining it, and this eventually works, more or less. It's a struggle to get Tristan to abandon the idea of muscling through with his arms, and the motion is so different from his habitual form that he feels as though he's sacrificing all his grace and style to do it. But after about two hours or so, I'm able to get Tristan doing something that looks like a real clouter's motion. I'm pretty satisfied with the result, so we call it a day, after doing some of the exercises together that Falko suggested. They do leave my whole body feeling sore, but it's not just the exercises that give me this effect. I've had to demonstrate the motion myself so many times that I'm thoroughly fatigued, but that's not the whole reason, either. It's been unsettling feeling that motion again, and though I hate to admit it, there's also a part of me that's disappointed at not getting to feel that three-way embrace, after all.

It's still relatively early when we go in. I assume most of the other boys are still out practicing and there's nobody much about, but Tristan is tired after his first full day back in action, and so am I. I don't feel much like sitting around in the barracks by myself, and I can't sleep. It's still August, and it's hot and stuffy inside in the afternoon, or it just feels that way to me after two solid hours of thinking about rocking back against Taran, so I wander out into the garden.

Out here, I don't feel any better. It reminds me too much of Tristan's revealing of my interpretation of the hunt. Suddenly the guild walls that were once so protective seem claustrophobic; there doesn't seem to be anywhere inside them that's free of associations. I lean up against the wooden garden wall and rest my hand on the top of the broken little gate leading out to the practice field, lie my head back, and close my eyes.

I think I might really have fallen asleep right there, upright, with the faint scent of decaying jasmine in my nostrils and the buzzing of flies in my ears, if I wasn't jolted awake by a familiar voice, disturbingly close by.

"My, my! What's this? A faun in the garden? How delightful!"

It's Jurian. I almost jump out of my skin.

"All alone out here, Marek?" he says, and to me, it sounds dangerous. My eyes fly open to find him leaning up against the wall right next to me, one of his amused smiles on his face.

"Jurian," I say warningly, looking over his shoulder in the hopes that he's not alone. But he is. There's no one else in the garden. Even though we're right next to the gate and it's hanging open as usual, the field and any boys who might still be out in it suddenly seem very far away.

"Marek, Marek," he says, pretending to smile sadly. "It really is demoralizing. You might at least pretend to be glad to see me these days. I did rather think we were becoming friends." I can tell he's enjoying himself.

"Look, Jurian," I say sternly. "When I told you to find someone else, I didn't mean me!"

At this, Jurian's eyes widen, then he throws back his head and laughs just as hard as Tristan and Gilles did when I suggested the same thing to them. He laughs so hard, he has to put a hand to his side and double over. Catching sight of my red face, he pulls himself together and puts a hand on my shoulder.

"Sorry, kid. I guess I deserved that. I have been teasing you, haven't I? No offense, but don't tell me you really think I'd go from him, to *you*?" He leans up against the wall again, even closer to me than before.

"I'm sure I don't know," I say with as much dignity as I can muster. "But it did occur to me that you might try to make, *er*, someone jealous." I can't bring myself to say Baylen's name to him directly, particularly when he hasn't used it himself.

"Did you, now?" he says speculatively, looking off over my head for a moment. Then he turns on his side to face me more directly and leans in, saying softly, "would that be such a bad idea? To make *someone* jealous? Who knows, it might even be fun."

Before I can reply, he pushes gently off the wall and swings around, and steps in close in front of me. To my astonishment, he puts one hand against the wall behind me over my shoulder, and with his other hand, he takes mine and pushes it up under his tunic, so it's resting against his stomach, where the line of soft hair under his navel begins. I look up at him in alarm, and I know I should pull away — only for some reason, I don't seem to be doing it.

"Jurian, what are you doing?" I whisper unevenly. It's all I can manage. He's still holding my hand, balled into a tight fist, up against his skin when he bends down so that his mouth is almost touching mine, and replies softly,

"Don't tell me you haven't been dying to know what it feels like. Do you want to know what *he* feels like, Marek? Why don't you open your hand, and find out?"

Then he laughs, but it isn't one of his mocking laughs. It's a low, purring sound, and it feels so good rippling through him under my hand that despite myself, I feel it open. I have been dying to know what it feels like, and there's no denying Jurian is absolutely gorgeous. Or that he's a lot like Tristan. But I don't mean to do it. It's just so hot in the garden, he's so close, and I've been feeling so frustrated.

"Don't you want to know what he feels like?" Jurian is repeating in a low, teasing voice, as he guides my now open palm up over his belly and across his chest. He bends in lower, until his lips are just touching mine, and still moving my hand slowly over his body, he whispers against my mouth,

"Don't you want to know what he *tastes* like?"

To my shame, I'm parting my lips and reaching my mouth up to his, eager to find out, when I'm suddenly grabbed by the back of my tunic and flung forward across the garden, to land in a quivering heap in front of the rosebushes.

"*What in the hell do you think you're doing*?!?" an enraged voice bellows over my head, and I shrink down further.

"Don't get in a twist, Taran," Jurian answers smoothly. "Just giving young Marek here some instruction on proper form. A rather belated education. Nothing that's any of your business."

"Touch him again, and I'll kill you!" Taran roars.

"My, my. How dramatic," Jurian drawls. I haven't looked up. If anything, I've rolled myself into a tighter ball, willing myself invisible. I've never felt so humiliated, which is saying a lot, since I've been humiliated plenty lately.

"Just get out of here, Jurian!" Taran snaps, then regaining his composure he continues in a more even voice: "And don't let me catch you breaking the rules at St. Sebastian's again. I won't tolerate it!"

Jurian readjusts his tunic with a shrug, and I hear him sauntering off, but not before calling merrily over his shoulder, "Oh yes, the *rules*!"

Taran just snorts angrily at this, as Jurian's echoing laugh recedes down the portico.

I haven't looked up, but as soon as Jurian's gone, inevitably I feel one of those huge hands reach down and pluck me up from where I've been cowering on the ground. Taran pushes me roughly back up against the wall and leans in over me, one hand thrust against the wall over my shoulder, so that we're strangely in about the same position that Jurian and I were in when he interrupted us.

"And *you*!" he snarls, letting go of me but still leaning in close. He starts clenching and unclenching his fist in that motion that signals he's trying to keep himself from violence.

"Just how far were you going to let that ... that ... *Lothario* go?" he snaps. The word is so ridiculous, I almost snicker, but it isn't funny. My face is burning with shame, but Taran's is burning red, too. His eyes are flashing, and I can tell he's about to lose control.

"What were you going to do when he put his hand in your breeches and didn't find what he was looking for? Did you think of that?" He breaks off with a grimace, then bursts out again angrily, "Are you so desperate to touch a man that you'd bring St. Sebastian's down around our ears, just to feel up the likes of Jurian?!"

I haven't been able to say anything to defend myself, and there's nothing I can say. I'm guilty as charged. I have been desperate, and if Taran hadn't appeared, I probably would have let Jurian discover my secret right then and there. I'm so miserable I start to tremble, but I will myself not to cry. I can't do that again, I won't! But the tears start to form anyway. I know I must look even more wretched than ever.

He stares down at me with exasperation, but there's something else there, too, that I can't place. He reaches up and runs his hand through his hair and gives himself a shake, but then another surge of anger washes over him and he really does lose control. Suddenly he leans in dangerously close, and gripping my arm painfully, he says roughly,

"So you want to know what a man feels like!?," and his body moves swiftly down toward mine, and I think he's going to do as Jurian did and pull me into an embrace. But instead of being afraid, despite myself all my senses leap up in me and begin straining for it, and suddenly I do feel what I vainly tried to replicate out on the field all morning, that exhilaration as I let my body fly. Although I'm standing frozen in place beneath him against the wall, I feel as though everything in me is flying toward him, and every inch of my skin is straining for the moment it touches his, not caring that he despises me and that he will even more when he feels how desperately my mouth opens under his. Just when I think I've reached a fever pitch and I can't wait another second for him to reach me, I hear the shattering crack as he hurls his fist against the garden wall inches above my head, roaring,

"Next time you want to know what a man feels like, ask someone who already knows what you are! Ask *me!*"

I slide slowly down to the ground as he stalks off still fuming through the rosebushes, a hole a foot wide gaping in the wall above me.

"Well, that went well, don't you think?" a voice says not far away. It's Jurian coming in through the open gate. He's apparently circled around to come back and see the results of his handiwork.

"Yes, very satisfactory!" he exclaims, looking at the huge hole in the wall and reaching a hand down to help me up. "Didn't I tell you it would be fun?"

I DON'T BOTHER TO REPLY. I DON'T THINK I COULD, anyway. When Jurian sees the look on my face, he has the grace to look repentant. I'm sure he did think it all just a bit of fun. But I suddenly can't stand to be in the garden one second longer, or anywhere in the guild for that matter. I push past Jurian and head right out the door on the opposite side of the garden that leads out into the alley, not sure where I'm headed. It doesn't matter. I've got to get away.

I just start walking, head down. I'm probably headed for the canal, where I can sit and watch the water flow by, like I did the other day.

Or throw myself in.

I don't even know what I'm feeling. The humiliation is still there, burning furiously, but I'm also reeling. After that fleeting second of feeling like I was about to take off and fly, the disappointment is so sharp I feel just like one of the apples from our trick that's splatted to the ground.

I wander aimlessly down a side street, not paying attention to anything around me, not noticing that I'm heading for a part of town I've never been in before. When I bump heavily into a man carrying a load of wood and it spills out into the road, I hardly notice. Because now I know I've got to do the one thing I've been avoiding. The thing I've been putting off.

I've got to think.

I've got to think about how this is going to end, because it's never been more obvious that I can't stay at St. Sebastian's indefinitely.

For one thing, I can't freeze time around me. All the other squires are growing up. I won't be believable as a boy much longer. Just how long can I get away with it? Will I be believable for another whole year, long enough to see Tristan through his veteran competitions, if he makes it that far? I don't know. Maybe. But that's not the real problem. The real problem was made crystal clear to me in the garden. I just don't see how I can control myself around the boys that long.

It's just lust. But it's turning out to be a more powerful force than I'd bargained for. I was a fool to think I could conquer nature. Taran was right. I was about to let Jurian discover my secret, without a thought, even though Jurian is nothing to me. I was probably desperate enough to have had a go at any male who happened to wander into the garden. I probably would have even let old Albrecht have his way with me. Or even worse, Aristide.

And what of Taran himself? How much longer can I stand the indignity of wanting to be touched by a boy who hates me, just because he knows I'm a girl? It doesn't take a genius to figure out that the insulting things he was raving in the garden were really all about me, not Jurian, and knowing I've only sunk lower in his estimation just makes it worse. My only consolation is that so far I think I've managed to keep him from seeing it. If he ever realizes how I feel when I'm around him, what added scorn he'll have for me! My humiliation will be complete.

But I'm not just thinking about myself. I really don't want to bring St. Sebastian's down. I don't want to be discovered, and certainly not in that way. I refuse to be a disgrace to the guild. I want to be able to end it all on my own terms, so it's time to figure out just what those terms are going to be. It's time to stop being distracted, and to think about what it is that I really want, about what 'just possible' really is for me. And I know I'm not going to like it.

By this time, I've taken so many turns that I'm hopelessly lost, but I don't care. Out here the streets aren't cobbled, they're no more than narrow dirt lanes twisting between tightly packed hovels, and if I were paying attention, I'd probably have noticed that I've been past some of them more than once. I'm going in circles, but it seems appropriate. So I just keep going.

After about a half-hour of stumbling along, I come to a hard conclusion. Staying at St. Sebastian's much longer is an impossibility. Of course, the things I want most are all impossible: I want Tristan. I want to stay at St. Sebastian's forever. And I want my father back. But I've got to deal in possibilities. Nobody can have everything they want. All I have to do is think of Baylen to know that, and I've already done more than I once could have dreamed. I've been inside St. Sebastian's. I've lived there, I've been a member of sorts, and I've taken the field with the Journeys. What I've done is much more than Marieke could ever have imagined. It should be enough for me.

The problem is, as Marek, I can imagine a lot more, and I can no longer see what can possibly come after St. Sebastian's for me. Like Auguste, I'd rather lose a leg and sit at the front desk than leave the guild. I don't want to be a boy away from St. Sebastian's, and I don't want to be a girl again, period. Particularly not 'not much of one.' What would be possible for me as a girl now? I could be a kitchen maid, if I'm lucky, or more likely, a drudge in a field. Even if by some miracle I could be a girl as privileged and lovely as Melissande, how could I stand to sit in the bleachers and watch the boys compete, when I've been out there with them myself?

Suddenly I do know what I want, and it's as much of an impossibility as anything else. I pull out of my memory the image of Tristan being crowned at Firsts that I've tucked away in my mind and examine it closely again. This time, though, I don't picture being Melissande. This time, I'm the one on my knees, looking up, transfigured by what I see above me. But I'm not looking at a lovely face, or a flow of golden hair, and maybe Tristan wasn't, either.

I'm looking at the garland.

What do I really want? I want to be the son of Jan Verbeke, I want to be my father all over again when he was young, charming, at the height of his abilities, and I want to win. In short, *I* want to be Tristan. I want to be the hero myself.

I come to a stop under a low-hanging willow tree, and sit down heavily in the dirt in its shade. I can't be Tristan, but I've helped invent him, or at least, a version of him that's part what he already was, and part my father all over again. In a way, Tristan is part me, then, too. We *are* a team. I remember what Baylen said, about how seeing a boy you've trained win is the best victory. So I make my decision: I've got to find a way to hold it together through Thirds. That way, I'll keep my vow, at least most of it. I'll see Tristan earn veteran status, using what I've taught him of my father's skills, and that will be my victory and my redemption of my father, too. That'll be my possibility. It'll be more than that: it'll be a triumph. It'll be enough for me to live on, after. I know I said I'd move heaven and earth to see him make Guards, but I don't think I can make it another whole year. I've got to get myself under control, so I can go out on my own terms, as a boy, without ever letting Tristan be the wiser. Thirds is as long as I think I can make it.

I get to my feet again slowly, resolved. After Thirds, I've got to force myself to leave St. Sebastian's. What I'll do then, I don't know. It doesn't matter, because I'll have attained my goal. When I get back to the guild, I'll go to the chapel and ask the saint to give his blessing to my decision, and to help me see it through, because I just don't see how I can bring myself to do it. Plus, he's going to have to figure out what to do with me after that, since I can't picture anything beyond St. Sebastian's. It doesn't really matter, though. When I have to leave the guild, when I have to leave Tristan, Marek will be as good as dead. I'll just have to hope that Tristan is right, that it's worth it, as long as you go out in glory.

As I'm dusting myself off, I know there's only one flaw in my plan. I haven't had much success keeping my urges under control so far, and I'm not sure how I'm going to do it now. One thing's clear, though: I've been concentrating so hard on stifling my feelings for Tristan that I let them spill over onto the others; I forgot to watch myself with them. I can only hope that being aware of the danger is going to make me more vigilant. It's only two more months. Surely with effort, I can make it until then? Maybe I should stop by the cathedral and ask for St. Margaret's help, too. This problem might be more in her line.

As I pass a very familiar-looking pigsty for what seems like the third time, I look up into the sky to try to gauge my direction from the position of the sun. It must already be late afternoon by now. I have no idea how long I've been wandering around Louvain. It may even be approaching time for evening mess. I can't hide out in the streets any longer. I've got to go back and face them all. Besides, what's a little more humiliation, compared with facing the inevitability of losing St. Sebastian's? Knowing I don't have much time left there suddenly makes me desperate to get back.

It's with great relief, then, when I strike out in a new direction and I come around a corner to smell the tinge of putrid water in the air. I'm getting close to the canal, and I recognize where I am. I must be only a few blocks from the Drunken Goat.

I pick up my pace, glad to be back in familiar territory, but as I do, I hear the unmistakable sound of footsteps behind me that quicken to match my pace. I've been so lost in thought I haven't been paying attention to anything around me. Now I get the distinct impression that I'm being followed. From the sound, it isn't just by one person, either. I feel a prick of worry along my spine, as I remember Tristan's admonition not to go to the Drunken Goat by myself.

I don't turn around or look over my shoulder. Instead, I put my head down and try to hurry, but I hear the footsteps behind me catching up, and pretty soon I'm surrounded by a pack of scruffy-looking boys. They aren't very big, but there are a lot of them. When I try to keep going, they circle around me, so I can't even see exactly how many of them there are. They aren't any older than I am, but that doesn't comfort me. They all look very tough. They're unkept and undernourished, dressed in ill-fitting and filthy clothes, and from their battered faces, they've been in plenty of brawls. They must look a lot like I did when I first showed up outside St. Sebastian's, in fact. One of them, a bigger boy whom I take for their ringleader, steps in front of me, blocking my way. He's got a mean expression on his face, and an even meaner-looking stick in his hands. At the sight of the stick, my apprehension turns to fear. I have a feeling I'm about to find out what it's like to be beaten by somebody who really does have absolutely no sense of honor.

"What's your hurry, Moneybags?" he says, holding up the stick and tapping it against his hand. When I don't say anything, he says,

"Those some mighty nice boots you got. 'Bout my size. Mind if I give 'em a try?" and he swings his stick and whacks me painfully in the thigh. Pain shoots up my leg, and when I bend forward at the impact with a cry, my St. Sebastian's medal swings out from tunic.

"Well, well, well!" he crows, as the others crowd in. "Look what we got here! It's one of them high and mighty St. Sebastian's toffs! Runt of the litter, aren't you?"

"Hey, I recognize that face!" a snot-nosed kid with a dirty face next to him says. "It's one of them squires. I saw 'im at the trials."

"Out without your *master*?" the older boy sneers, and the others laugh. I'm too frightened now to say anything. I try to take a step around the boy, only there's nowhere to go. Two other boys step up to block my way as the stick swings out again and catches my other leg, and the bigger boy commands,

"Bow down to *me*, then! *I'm* your master now!" and the others laugh.

The blow catches me on the back of my knee, and my leg buckles underneath me. I fall to my knees heavily, though I hardly feel the pain. I'm in too much of a panic now. The boys are all around me, leaning in, eager looks on their faces, and there's no hope of escape. The boy with the stick looks like he's just warming up, and I know that anything I might say would just make it worse.

"*Bow!*" the boy yells again, and I put my arms up defensively as he swings the stick, hitting me hard across the side of my head. I go down, my head ringing and blood gushing out from somewhere below my ear. I'm vaguely aware of the boy tossing the stick aside and starting to search me with rough hands, and the others are now all on me, too, kicking and punching, and there's no defense. Most of the blows aren't very hard, but there are just so many of them. I cover my head and try to roll into a ball, but they just keep coming, harder once they figure out I don't have any money. Just as a hand reaches down and pulls out a big handful of my hair and another grabs onto the twine around my neck to try to pull off my medal, there's a loud cry from down the street. It's a voice I never thought I'd be glad to hear. Now it sounds like the sweetest thing I've ever heard.

"What are you trash doing there? Haven't I told you to stay out of my sight?," then more urgently, "What the devil? That's Marek! Get the hell away from him!"

It's Aristide. He must be coming home from the Drunken Goat. I've never been so glad that he's not above visiting prostitutes.

The blows stop immediately, and it doesn't take me long to figure out why. Falko's with him, and in two big strides he's come over and snatched up the stick. After he catches the nearest boy with a brutal swipe to the gut and turns to tower over the rest of them, the street boys wisely scamper off like rats, while Aristide calls after them,

"Next time, remember! Nobody beats a St. Seb's man with impunity!"

"Marek!" Falko cries, dropping the stick and bending to pick me up like a rag doll. I try to smile up at him, but I can't. My jaw isn't working where the stick hit it, and I'm nauseated by the pain from all the blows. Blood is flowing from the place where the hair was torn out by its roots from my temple, and it feels like someone caught me on the lip, too. Fortunately for me, some of the boys were small enough that they couldn't do much damage, but not all of them, and that stick did its work all too well. I manage to open my mouth, but words don't come out, just a trickle of blood. On seeing it, a look of panic crosses Falko's face, and he gathers me up effortlessly in his arms and calls to Aristide:

"He's hurt. We've got to get him back to the guild. Come on!"

Falko carries me all the way back to the guild bundled up in his arms like a little child, and even through my pain I can feel how tense he is. Even Aristide seems upset. When we get back to the guild, it's just the hour when mess is about to start, and the boys have started spilling into the great hall. Aristide throws the garden gate open, and Falko follows him across the garden, down the portico, and directly into the great hall, where he bursts in with me in his arms, limp and smeared with blood.

My eyes are unfocused and blood is running into them, but I'm vaguely aware of everyone coming to their feet at once and rushing forward, and there's such an outraged din of voices that I can't make out what's being said. Everyone's talking at once, demanding to know what happened, trying to ask me questions, and I hear voices calling for Tristan. He's been out in the corridor waiting for me to show up, since masters go in for mess with their squires.

"We found him down by the Drunken Goat," I hear Aristide explaining. "There must have been ten of them."

"By the time we came along, he was already down. They were beating him with a stick," Falko says, talking over him.

A voice with a hard edge cuts through the others. It's Taran. "Tell me you got them, Falko."

"They ran off as soon as they saw him," Aristide laughs, but it's a harsh laugh.

By now the boys are lowering me onto an empty table, and finally Tristan's here. He takes one look at me and lets out a curse, and picks me up again. My whole body is aching, but once I'm in Tristan's arms, I feel better. The places where the stick hit are the worst: my knee, my thigh, and the side of my face.

"I'm okay, Tristan," I manage to say, but I think the sight of my bloody teeth belies my statement, and Tristan looks stricken. So do all the other boys leaning in around him. I see Gilles looking pale, Pascal grimacing behind him, Turk wringing his hands, and even Falko's squire Pruie looks ill. I'm feeling light-headed, and the looks of concern on everyone's faces gives me a warm feeling (or maybe it's just the after-effects of being punched in the gut), so I say,

"I guess it's not just arrows that won't kill us at St. Sebastian's. I can't even be bludgeoned to death!" But nobody laughs.

"Marek, whatever possessed you to go down there by yourself?" Tristan asks in distress, wiping the blood off my face with his sleeve. "Don't you know what could have happened if Ari and Falko hadn't happened along?"

"I ... I ... don't know," I say. I can't tell him about the garden. "I just wanted some air. To clear my head. I guess I got it cleared for me, didn't I?" I try to joke again. But just then Jurian pushes forward, looking almost as miserable as Tristan.

"Marek!" he says gently, stroking my hair out of my face. "Bloody hell, kid, I'm so sorry!" I know he thinks he's the one who upset me, and I don't want him to feel guilty. He couldn't have known this would happen, and he's not really the reason I was so upset, anyway.

"It's not your fault, Jurian," I say, a dribble of blood creeping out of the corner of my mouth, and I think maybe I unintentionally put some emphasis on the word *'your,'* because the next thing I know, I hear Taran asking Falko quietly in a tight voice,

"Just where did you say this happened?"

It's Aristide who answers: "Just a few blocks north of the Goat, in the alley with the big fig tree. You remember the place, I'm sure."

I can't see what happens next, but in a moment Charles calls out, "Looks like Taran's going to get them, boys! Who's coming?" and there's a sound of shuffling and boots ringing on the stone floor as a pack of the Journeys follow him out. They're probably going to get in trouble for missing evening mess, but I don't think they care. And I don't care for the chances of anyone they manage to find. I should know.

By this time some of the veterans have started to wander in, and as they do, they come over and start asking questions and expressing concern. Someone's already sent for some kitchen boys to bring water and a cloth to clean me up, and it isn't long before Master Leon wanders past. He gives me only the most perfunctory of glances, and mutters, "I thought you said he wasn't going to have any more accidents, duBois!" before heading off to eat his supper. I fully expect to hear him call back, "And somebody, clean up that mess!"

Tristan and Falko carry me back to the barracks between them. After patching up my face, Tristan wants to inspect my ribs, only I won't let him. I think one might really be broken, but I can't let anyone help me with it, so I have to grind my teeth and pretend it doesn't hurt. Maybe the thick binding around my breast protected me enough that it's only bruised, anyway. I'm going to have a patchwork of bruises as it is tomorrow, but nothing else is broken, so I've been lucky, I guess. Falko really did come by before much serious damage could be done. As he's lowering me down onto my cot, I wheeze to Falko,

"I was sure lucky you came by, big guy. Just what were you doing at the Drunken Goat?" and he blushes. He doesn't have to tell me he was hoping to see Roxanne. I'm just gladder than ever that I introduced them.

I know I'm in real trouble, though, when Tristan finally decides it's safe to leave me alone to sleep for the night, and despite my aching jaw and the burning patch on my temple where the hair was pulled out, the thing that I'm actually thinking about as I drift off to sleep is how that soft line of hair on Jurian's stomach felt under my hand. I have to admit, Jurian was right: I *had* been damned curious to know how it felt. And the devil of it is, it felt absolutely marvelous! Controlling my urges is going to be even harder than I thought. It's going to be much harder than taking a beating.

The next day, I'm not sure whether to be sorry or glad when I learn from Turk's squire Andre that the Journeys who set out to avenge the honor of the guild couldn't find any of the boys who jumped me. I want to put the whole episode behind me. I've promised myself not to get distracted. My beating is hurting enough, and not just literally. When I gingerly prod my ribs in the morning, I decide that nothing's broken after all. Yet I'm sore enough that it'll be at least a week before I can bend my bow again, and I'm intensely aware that the blows and the ripped hair have left me even uglier than ever. It's not supposed to matter, but I'm sure the masters will take my appearance into account at least to some degree when judging me for apprentice status. I'd really like to earn it, before I go. I think Marek deserves to go out with it. I almost consider finding some way to poke out an eye, to have an excuse to wear an eye patch.

I've also got to figure out some new strategy for Thirds. I'm going to have to admit that my own tutorials aren't going to be enough to make a difference with Tristan. He's stronger than he was, but I'm out of my element with clouts. I'm contemplating this and thinking about the eye patch when I have an idea. A dangerous idea, to be sure, since Tristan really is about the same type as Jurian, but I can't think of any others. And getting individual instruction from someone who knows what he's doing obviously makes a big difference: just look at Remy. But there's only one person at St. Sebastian's who knows as much or more about shooting clouts than Taran.

So I screw up my courage, telling myself that I've faced the lash and the stick now, so surely I can face knocking on Baylen's door.

Besides, he owes me.

I'm still thinking about just how I'm going to do this when I get to Tristan's room, and I think he's surprised when I insist on going out to drills with him. Beating or no beating, I'm not missing another minute of the time I've got left here, and I can at least watch. In the cramped corridor I'm walking a few paces in front of Tristan as we head out to the field, and as I come through the stable door, Taran steps right in front of me. He does it so quickly, I get the impression he's been waiting for me.

"Look …" he says urgently, and I instinctively shrink back, shocked by finding myself at close quarters with him so unexpectedly and so soon after my embarrassment in the garden. Shame at being caught with Jurian, at my accusation, and even just at risking exposure so carelessly floods over me, and I must look stricken. He seems to be steeling himself to say something when Tristan steps through the door behind me. Taran clearly didn't expect him. He clamps his mouth tight shut in irritation and steps back.

Taking one look at the dismal expression on my face, Tristan steps protectively in front of me and says angrily,

"Back off, Taran! Can't you see what he's been through? I'd have thought even you would lay off him today!"

Taran leaves without a word, his mouth set in a grim line, and without another glance at me. I don't know whether to be grateful to Tristan for saving me from another painful encounter with him, or not. But as the day wears on and Taran makes no attempt to seek me out, I don't feel very grateful. I get the distinct impression that with all that's happened, just like my days at St. Sebastian's, my encounters with Taran are numbered, too, and the thought doesn't comfort me the way it should.

It's after evening mess and almost time for lights out before I manage to work up enough courage to go through with my plan for Thirds. At my knock, Baylen gives a sharp bark, and when I tentatively swing open his door, I find he's already got his tunic off and he's stripping down for bed. Without his shirt he's every bit as big and muscled as I'd imagined he would be, and I know I've come to the right place.

"Oh, for the love of St. Peter! What are you doing here?" he says, looking exasperated. I notice his whip lying on his bed next to him; the boys were right, he really does take it to bed with him. I can't help myself, instead of saying what I meant to, I blurt out:

"Do you sleep with that eye patch on?"

An incredulous look passes over his face as he roars, "Please don't tell me you've come here to find out!"

I quickly disabuse him of this by telling him directly why I've really come. "I want you to coach me and Tristan at clouts."

"You're asking *me*, to help *you*?" he says gruffly, surprised. "You really do have guts."

I ignore this. "Will you do it?"

A suspicious look crosses his face, as though he thinks maybe I'm going to try to blackmail him by bringing up my whipping, and he says, "Just why do you think I should train you?"

"You're the best. You said so yourself. And I want the best. For myself," then I pause, and I let my emotions show in my voice. "And I want the best, for him."

We stand there staring at each other for a few minutes, but I don't look away. I hold his gaze, and I think we understand each other. Finally he says slowly,

"Tomorrow afternoon. After noon mess. Tell him to meet me on the clout field."

I know it was what I was hoping for, but I'm still stunned that he's agreed. When in my surprise I don't respond or make a move to go, he says sardonically,

"And now I'm going to take off my pants, so I suggest you leave. Unless you really do want to find out how I sleep."

I take my cue and leave.

Unexpectedly, it turns out to be harder to convince Tristan to go along with my plan than it was Baylen. As we're heading out for morning practice the next day, I bring it up casually as we're passing the archive room, and he comes to a full stop.

"Baylen? Train us personally? This afternoon?" He squawks out the disjoined phrases just like a talking parrot.

"Yes. We're to meet him out on the clout field after mess." Actually, Baylen told me to tell *Tristan* to meet him, but I have no intention of leaving the two of them to train together without me. Even though my ribs are still too sore for me to shoot, I'm going, too.

"Marek," he says sternly, "Just what did you say to him to get him to agree to that?" I know he thinks I've blackmailed Baylen, too.

"Does it matter?" I reply. I can't tell him why I suspect Baylen is really helping us, and I'm not even sure I know, anyway.

"He's rarely given individual instruction to anyone, except Jurian. This isn't going to make me very popular, kid. It's certainly not going to make me very popular with Jurian."

"Is that why you're here? To be popular?" I reply, but Tristan's frowning, so I say more seriously,

"I know, Tristan. It isn't ideal, and I am sorry about Jurian. But this is Thirds. It's the big one, the big prize. It's veteran status. Isn't that worth it? Isn't that worth anything?" When he still doesn't reply, I add:

"If I could think of something else, I'd do it. But Baylen can help us, I know he can. And I need the help, too." It's low, but I've got to convince him.

"Baylen and I don't like each other much. He's never bothered to give me any corrections during drills. He finds me irritating, and frankly, I'm not sure I'm ready to forgive him for setting you up. Have you already forgotten your lashing? Are you ready to forgive him for that?"

"I'd forgive him anything if he helps you win," I say simply, hanging my head. He still hasn't said anything, but I think he's wavering. "Tristan, listen," I say, still looking down. "You and I both know I'll never make Journey. Or as you say, even if by some miracle I did, I could never win Veterans. But you can, I know it. If I help you get there, then I win, too." I look up at him now. "And I want to win."

"I want us to win, too," he says quietly, then he puts his arm around my shoulder. "Okay, kid. You've gotten me this far. I'm not ungrateful enough not to admit that. So if you say we need Baylen, we need Baylen. I'll meet him. But if he's got his whip, I'm going back in."

"Fair enough," I agree.

Our first training session with Baylen starts out less than auspiciously. I think we're both a little surprised that he actually shows up. After about a minute, I can see that Tristan's right. He really does irritate Baylen. Tristan's nervous, so he's being even more verbose than usual, and although I find his steady string of banter thoroughly entertaining, Baylen doesn't appreciate the idle chatter. He's all business. As Tristan is starting in on yet another of his florid statements, Baylen lets out an exasperated roar and hits him on the back of the head, hard — just the way he did to me in the alley, only this time it doesn't seem at all affectionate. But it's effective. Tristan stumbles a few steps forward and shuts up, and he remains silent and sullen for the rest of the session.

It doesn't help that most of the Journeys are watching from a distance. Tristan was right. The sight of Baylen giving personal instruction causes quite a stir, and I'm sure everyone is wondering how it came about. Baylen won't have to explain himself, but there are going to be plenty of questions for us. I'm particularly aware of Jurian's eyes on us, but I try to block him out and concentrate on what Baylen's saying.

When I do focus and hear what it is, I don't like it one bit.

"What's that flimsy thing? What's its draw? 130? 140?" he's saying to Tristan, pointing at the bow I made for him for Firsts. "That's part of your problem right there. You need a bigger, heavier bow for clouts. That much should have been obvious, even to you." He grabs my bow out of Tristan's hands and throws it on the ground behind him.

"Here," he says, putting his own massive bow into Tristan's hands. "This has a draw of around 190 pounds. That's what you'll be using in competition. You've got to practice with a bow like this. You can't just step into competition and bend the heavier bows."

I know he's right, but it means Tristan can't practice with my bow any longer, or use it in the final competition. It's almost symbolic. I'm not what's going to get him the rest of the way.

They work together for the rest of the afternoon, with Tristan using Baylen's bow. I try to follow along, so that I can use the techniques Baylen is suggesting myself when I'm back in shape to practice, but after a while I stop paying attention to the content of his criticisms, distracted by the way he makes them. Guillaume was right. He is a good trainer. He sees things that seem obvious after he points them out, but I never would have thought to mention them myself. He's gruff and not very encouraging, but when he does give praise, it's sincere. That was always what I appreciated about my father. I can tell that after getting the first compliment after about an hour's work, it spurs Tristan on to try harder than ever to get more, even though the extra draw weight of the bow is a struggle for him, at first. By the time Baylen finally calls it a day, Tristan's dropped all his affectations and I think he's surprised Baylen by his serious effort, and as I head in to put away the equipment, they're still out on the field deep in conversation about some point of technique. I've already taken a few trudging steps back when I remember my bow lying forgotten in the dust, and I pick it up rather dejectedly to stow in the back of Tristan's cabinet. He won't be needing it now.

I haven't been at the cabinet long when Jurian appears out of nowhere, leans up against it, and with a nod out to the field, says accusingly, "So, was that *your* idea? What is it, pay-back, for the garden? I thought you could take a joke."

"It's not like that, Jurian," I say, hoping I'm right. "It's just archery."

"That's rich, coming from you," he replies. "It's never just archery."

He turns to go, but I put a hand up to my temple, to the still juicy patch of skin where my hair came out. This isn't about what happened in the garden, but I find I am still mad about it, and there's something I want to know.

"About the garden. You knew Taran could see us, didn't you?"

"Of course. I saw him over your shoulder. He was at his cabinet." He smiles. Taran's cabinet is right on the other side of the garden gate. He must have been able to overhear the whole thing. "Otherwise, it wouldn't have been any fun, would it?" he adds wickedly.

He's gone before I can think to ask him just who he intended to make jealous with his stunt, and why.

CHAPTER
THIRTY-FIVE

"I have to admit it, kid. You were right."

It's a few days later, and Tristan and I are on our way out to the windmill after another training session with Baylen. Tristan's in a fine mood. He's been slowly improving at clouts under Baylen's tutelage, and he's been doing Falko's exercises so diligently that he's in danger of starting to look like Falko — all bulging muscles. I've started practicing again, too, but only half-heartedly. There isn't much of my body left that hasn't suffered since my arrival at St. Sebastian's: the back of my legs are still scarred from the whip, my forearm is a mess from the arrow, and my face will never recover from its beatings, old and new. But this isn't really what's bothering me. I'm jealous. I do want Tristan to win, but when he does, I want it to be our victory — his and mine, not his and Baylen's.

Climbing up the stairs of the windmill does nothing to improve my mood, so when we're seated, Tristan finally asks me what's the matter. As soon as he does, the idea of voicing my thoughts makes me realize just how petty they are, and I can't do it. I just sit there miserably, but Tristan's smart enough to have figured it out for himself.

"I want you to do something for me, if you will," he says. "I need a new bow. It's a tall order, but do you think you could make me one, with a heavier draw weight, in time for me to practice with it, so I can use it during competition?" I don't reply. He's throwing me a sop, to make me feel better. But then he says quietly,

"Marek. Do you think I don't know who's really helping me? Who got me through Firsts, and Seconds, too? Who helped me in the chapel, who covered for me, who shot down the apple? And now, who got me Baylen? If Baylen helps me, even a little, that's because of you, too. Baylen's a good trainer, but that's all he is. He's not my friend. And he's not my squire. You are, and you're the best that's ever been at St. Sebastian's. None has ever done more for his master, I'll wager."

Tristan always knows exactly what to say. But what makes his words so right is that I know him well enough to know when he's being completely sincere, and I feel like he's banished a ghost that was threatening to hover between us. In fact, his words make me feel so warm that I think they could almost banish all the ghosts that linger in this place. Yet even as I think it, I feel something warmer. The pressure of an open palm, burning against my left breast, and I know it isn't true. There is still one ghost here, and he's still standing behind me, his hand lingering over my belly, his fingers sliding upward across my skin. I give myself a little shake, willing it away.

It's only after his speech pulls me out of my own thoughts that I notice that something's bothering Tristan. It was only my foul mood that made him seem so cheerful by comparison, or else something about being here in the windmill is making him contemplative, too.

"Okay, Tristan," I laugh. "If you get me the funds, I'll make you the bow. The biggest you've ever seen. I'll make you one so big, even Taran can't draw it." I mean it as a joke, but as soon as I say Taran's name, I see I've made a mistake. For some reason, Tristan's been thinking about Taran, too. So I have to ask.

"Tristan, what's wrong?"

"It's just, I've been thinking. About Melissande."

I'm surprised. He hasn't brought her up for a long time. I'd almost managed to forget all about her, but he clearly hasn't.

"After what you told me, about what happened in the chapel, I've been trying to forget her." He pauses, and I think, *of course*. He's cooled on her after he found out she offered to kiss Taran. But again I've misjudged Tristan, because what he says next is:

"I didn't want to hurt her more. But, the thing is, if I really love her, Marek, how can I let her marry Taran? If you're right, if Taran really thinks I've taken things too far, he won't forgive her. I can't let her marry him, if he really thinks the worst of her. I'd be letting her in for an awful fate."

When he puts it this way, he's right. I hadn't thought about it before. I suddenly remember wondering what the fate of the little hawk would be as the possession of someone who didn't want it, and the gruesome result: it got its neck wrung. Would Melissande fare much better in Taran's possession, if he really believes Tristan got to her first? Taran is not the forgiving type. But it's one thing for Tristan to win Melissande's affections. It's another to win her hand, particularly when she's already engaged to his own half-brother, and let's face it, he's a bastard.

"Couldn't you just explain to Taran that nothing happened?" It's weak, I know, and Tristan is rightfully disdainful.

"Just what do you suggest I say? *'Look, old boy, I didn't deflower your fiancée, and by the way, here's her bridal veil back?'* You don't think he missed seeing that I was wearing it, do you?"

It's a problem, I'll admit, and the more I think about it, the more convinced I am that Tristan's right. He's going to have to find a way to win her from Taran. And although it's painful for me to picture them together, the more I think about it, the righter it seems to me. I've determined to leave after Thirds. I won't have to see it. But I do want it all for Tristan. I want to win for him everything I can't have myself, and that's more than just the competitions. The hero always wins the girl in the end, doesn't he? That's the happy ending, and I suddenly want it for him with a stab of longing that's partly the longing I feel for having him myself. I want to believe the whole scene from my illumination is possible. Like it or not, the picture of Tristan that's right, the one that's perfect, has Melissande in it. If I want to be able to share in Tristan's victories, then I have to help him win her, too.

But Melissande really is one prize beyond Tristan's reach, and even I can't think of a way to help him get it. I determine to set my mind to it, anyway. Besides, I can't leave that lovely girl to Taran, can I? For some reason, I don't like picturing her with Taran much, either. The image of them together seems terribly wrong to me.

It's getting late, but Tristan hasn't made a move to rise.

"There's something more, isn't there?" I ask.

"You know me awfully well, kid." He smiles ruefully, but then his mouth droops back into a frown.

"Is it about Melissande?" I press, and after a minute or two, he admits:

"It's that kiss. My prize, in the chapel. I know, I know, it sounds silly. But I can't help but feel, it wasn't quite what it should have been. It wasn't everything I was expecting. It wasn't, well, extraordinary."

"You were hardly in a state to appreciate it," I say, trying not to sound too pleased. "You'd just had an arrow shoved through your side."

"I suppose that's it. But, I think, I know how it should have felt," he says, and I don't ask him what he's talking about. I don't want to know. I'm determined not to get distracted from my goal this time, not even by Tristan.

"Wait and see. The next one will be better," I say lightly, not sure if I really hope I'm right or not.

It's late afternoon by the time we get back to the guild, and Tristan asks me to fill his splash basin in the lavatory so he can shave. None of the serving boys are around, so I have to fetch the water myself. It's been a while since I've had to do such a menial task, and so I'm rather annoyed as I duck into the stalls in the stables looking for a bucket. I'm muttering to myself as I swing the low half-door of the last empty stall open and step inside. Suddenly there's a flurry of straw next to me as a large figure leaps up in alarm from where he's been lounging in the hay. It only takes me a second to realize with shock that it's Taran. I can't imagine what he's doing out here.

I almost turn and dart straight out. Whatever he's doing here, I don't want to know. Suddenly I am glad Tristan saved me from confronting him the other day, as I feel a fierce blush of embarrassment snaking up my neck and cheeks. He's clearly thought better of it, too, since he hasn't even looked my way since then. But even as he rises to full height in front of me and I'm taking a step backward, I determine not to be the coward, and I force myself to stop and face him. If I'm going to make it through Thirds, I've got to clear the air. I throw back my head bravely and look up at him, to see him staring with a pained look at the lurid scab where my hair was ripped out. I'm sure it does look quite disgusting.

"Look ..." he says tightly, then he falters, as though caught off guard and searching around for what he wants to say. No wonder he usually just grabs me. He seems incapable of having a conversation any other way. So I cut him off. My voice is quivering, but it can't be helped.

"About the other day in the garden," I say, and he flinches, running his hand through his hair in an exasperated fashion. I raise my voice, afraid he's going to interrupt. "You were right. I disgusted myself, and I deserve what I got." At this, he makes a strangled sound and for a second, his hand comes up and I think he's going to take hold of me, but when I continue hastily with a step backward, he drops it.

"I *don't want to disgrace* St. Sebastian's. *I won't*," I say bravely, determined to have my say, though I feel myself losing courage and my eyes slip from his. He's been looking distinctly unhappy about being reminded of the garden, and he has that unreadable look on his face. "So I've decided. I'm going away, before that can happen. Right after Thirds."

I've been standing stiff and rigid, with my hands clenched at my sides, but now that I've gotten out what I wanted to say, I go limp and turn around quickly, ready to bolt.

"Going away? Where?" he says blankly behind me.

"Does it matter?" I reply bitterly, without turning back to face him. "You'll be rid of me. Maybe I can join the thugs on the street. You said it yourself, I'm too wretched for anything else." At this, he grasps my upper arm and swings me around to face him. His face looks stricken as I say, "Then if you ever run into me, you'll have a perfect excuse to beat me again!"

It's not fair. I know he went after the street boys because of what they did to me, because they dared touch a member of St. Sebastian's. If I'm really fair, I can probably even guess why he went after me in the alley in the first place. But I don't want to be fair. I'm feeling too miserable. Taran looks terrible, too — confused and upset. His mouth flies open, but no words come out, just inarticulate noises.

Before he can formulate anything to say, I see he's holding something in his other hand.

It's a knife.

My eyes go wide and fly up to his, and my mouth pops open wordlessly, astonishment and fear writ plainly on my face. When he sees my fear, Taran looks down at the knife, and the other emotions that were on his face a moment ago vanish, leaving only anger. Without releasing his grip, he lifts the knife so I can see it better and sneers:

"*Afraid?* That's right, how could I forget? Pretty careless, to get caught alone in the stables with a would-be killer, aren't you? What do you think, that I'm on my way to sneak into Tristan's room, to ... what was the phrase? ... take another *dirty shot* at him?! By God, I'd like to!"

His eyes flash, but then he just looks disgusted, and finally he drops my arm, pushes past me, and stalks off.

I don't try to say anything to stop him. From the moment I saw the knife, I've been too upset to move. And I am genuinely afraid. But it's not because I think he'd use the knife on Tristan, or on anyone else, for that matter. It's because as soon as I saw it, I knew instantly what Taran was doing out here, and what he does use that knife for.

I stand there for a long time, then I slowly make my way out of the stables and turn heavily down the corridor to cut through the great hall. As I go past under the painting of St. Sebastian, I look up at it and really look at it for the first time in a long time. The saint's expression, that mixture of ecstasy and pain, is almost more than I can stand today. I go out through a door that I never use, the one on whose threshold I stood when I first saw the painting, the one that communicates directly with the entry vestibule. I've got to see Auguste, just to be sure.

He's looking smart, seated at the big desk, and he's so pleased to see me that I'm sorry I haven't come to visit him more often. It's just that I rarely come in and out of the guild through the formal entrance, and somehow, much as I hate to admit it, now that he's no longer a squire, Auguste and I just don't have as much in common anymore. I've become a terrible snob, worse than any Journey.

"Auguste," I say, after nervously exchanging some pleasantries. "You told me that Remy made you that stick." I nod to his crutch where he's propped it up in the corner behind his desk.

"No," he frowns. "I'm pretty sure I didn't. Why would I? Remy didn't make it." As he says it, I know it's true. He didn't say Remy had made it, only that Remy had brought it to him. I phrased my question very carefully at the time, but now I've got to know.

"Just who did make it for you, then?"

He laughs. "You told me you recognized the carving! I thought you knew Taran made it."

Of course he did. He's the one who carves, not Remy. I think I knew it the moment I first saw the merlin take flight. But I didn't want to believe it.

No wonder Taran was so mad that Remy gave me the mouse he'd made for him, and that I'd seemed to want it so much. How galling it must have been at the time that I valued it more than Remy did, that I was the one who saw what he could do and recognized it as a portrait of Remy. Remy really didn't know what I meant when I asked him about the mouse and the hawk. There's no mystery to Remy. He is as simple as he seems. It was Taran who gave me the hawk. He was the one who saw some of the qualities of it in me. And I repaid him by accusing him of having no qualities at all.

I slink back to the barracks with hardly a mumbled word to Auguste, and throw myself down on my cot, despising myself almost as much as Taran must.

I think I'm beginning to understand just how Tristan feels about him.

It's only much later that I remember Tristan waiting in the lavatory for a bucket of water that's never going to come. I feel like I could use a bucket of cold water myself.

TRISTAN AND I SPEND THE NEXT WEEKS TRAINING HARD, either by ourselves or in periodic sessions with Baylen. Tristan's come in for quite a bit of ribbing because of it, none of it much to Jurian's taste, I might add. But it's helping. I try to concentrate, but

I'm distracted. There are too many things on my mind. As we march through September, the days are getting cooler and shorter, leaving less daylight for practice, and I feel irrationally that the season is trying to rob me of my last precious time at the guild. As finals approach, with each passing day I'm more acutely aware that I'm in a countdown, both to the last hurdle to clear for Tristan to earn veteran status, and to my departure from St. Sebastian's. As our training progresses apace and the final competition nears, I'm increasingly hopeful that Tristan is going to pass, yet at the same time, I think ironically just as I did about my father, that if Tristan does pass and we win, how cruel it will be that our best day is to be our very last.

It's only about a week before finals when we first get some inkling of what Thirds is going to entail. The masters didn't bother to announce that the final competition would be clouts, since it was obvious, and none of us thought that there was really anything to say about Thirds that we didn't already know. We were wrong.

As we're coming into the great hall for mess one evening, Turk spots sir Brecelyn already seated at the masters' table, deep in conversation with Master Leon.

"Look, Taran. Daddy-in-law's here!" he cries merrily over his shoulder. "Why don't you nip off to the archives and compose a love letter for him to carry back for you?"

"Nah, there's no time. It would take Taran all night to compose even one sentence!" Aristide says.

"Don't worry, old man!" Falko cries happily, "I'll compose one for you!" He clears his throat, then recites: *"Roses are red, violets are blue, my bird pecked you, now I will, too!"*

While everyone's laughing, I sneak a look at Remy. I don't dare look at Taran, and Remy's the only other person who knows what happened to the hawk. I'm a bit startled to find that when I do, Remy's looking right at me. I wonder if he regrets telling me about it, or if he thinks I told some of the others. Surely, though, he doesn't think even Falko insensitive enough to joke about the bird if he knew what happened. Things have been rather cool between Remy and me since Tristan voiced my accusation, so I'm not surprised when he looks away as soon as I catch his eye.

As I take my seat after serving Tristan, I'm still thinking about sir Brecelyn's hands on the hawk's neck and hearing the crack of bones when Master Guillaume rises and calls for attention.

"Gentlemen, I'm sure it has not escaped your notice that we have a special visitor with us tonight, and one who needs no introduction to you," he pauses to nod to Brecelyn. "Yet I think you will be surprised when you hear the reason for his visit. He comes to us straight from L'île de Meuse, bearing most welcome news. It seems that we are to be graced with a very distinguished guest at Thirds. The most distinguished guest possible, in fact. *Gentlemen!*" he booms out suddenly, in a louder voice, "It is my great pleasure to announce that the royal court will be in attendance at our final competition this year." At the astonished murmurs that meet this pronouncement, Guillaume drops some of his formality and cries,

"That's right, boys! The prince is coming to Thirds!"

All the Journeys come to their feet at once with a boisterous cheer, and the rhythmic pounding of tankards on the long wooden tables reverberates loudly through the hall. The boys all love the prince, or as Tristan would say, at least the idea of him, and I'm as excited as everyone else. Seeing Tristan win permanent membership in the guild in front of the royal court is going to be sweet indeed, if he can pull it off.

Guillaume lets us go on for a long time before he puts up his hands for silence, and even then, it takes us a while to quiet down enough for him to continue.

"That's not all, men. Since the Black Guard will be escorting the prince as usual, they've agreed to give a public exhibition as part of the ceremonies immediately following the competition. It's going to be a Finals never before witnessed in Ardennes, boys!" he cries out again in glee, unable to contain himself. It really is a big honor, and we've all started talking again at once. I look apprehensively at Tristan, since the attendance of the Guards will inevitably mean the presence of his father, and I know how that affected him before. But he looks just as thrilled as everyone else, and I think after winning the garland at Firsts, he's put the demon of performing in front of his father to rest.

Guillaume pulls himself together again, and continues in a more serious tone:

"Accommodating our exalted guests will require some

adjustments on our part, and some of them may not be to everyone's liking. First, we will be dropping the individual exhibition shots from the competition. I know it's a disappointment, but it can't be helped," he says, but I don't feel disappointed at all. I feel overjoyed. Needless to say, with clouts as the theme, we haven't been able to think of an exhibition shot for Tristan. "There just won't be time, if the Guards are to perform, and ..." the master breaks off, and I think I know what he means. I doubt he wants to risk having anyone shoot his squire or start a fire with the prince watching. The individual stunts can't be closely controlled. He certainly doesn't want to run the risk of anyone accidentally shooting the prince. "Well, they're just going to be dropped," he finishes. Guillaume makes to take his seat, only to pop up again in the way he does when he thinks he's saved the best for last.

"And Gentlemen!" he beams, "because of our unprecedented guest, this year we will have an unprecedented change of venue. For the first time in the history of the guild, Thirds will not take place on the grounds of St. Sebastian's. In the interest of space and security, and to provide accommodation worthy of His Majesty, sir Brecelyn has agreed to host the final competition on the grounds of his own manor! What do you say to that, boys? Isn't a St. Sebastian's salute in order for our benefactor, sir Hugo Brecelyn?"

As we all begin to stomp and whistle, still stunned by this unexpected announcement, Brecelyn slowly rises to his feet to shake hands with the master. When the applause shows no sign of abating, Brecelyn eventually puts up his hand to silence us, and as the last calls die down, he says by way of acknowledging our appreciation for his generosity,

"Boys, Boys! *No, Don't try to thank me. It's my pleasure.*"

I don't remember sitting down again, or anything the boys say in their excitement during the rest of mess. The room has frozen around me, and I don't hear anything but that cold voice. *Don't try to thank me.* I picture Brecelyn's hands on the hawk's neck, twisting the life out of it. *It's my pleasure.* Twang! I hear the crack of a bowstring, and with startling clarity, I recognize that voice. I've heard Brecelyn speak many times before, but this time he's saying the exact same thing he did when I watched my father die, and I know without a shadow of a doubt that Hugo Brecelyn killed my father. And I think I know why. My eyes dart up to the painting of St. Sebastian, bristling with arrows, and it's all I can do to keep myself from leaping up and hurling myself at that sick, self-satisfied snake who's sitting there calmly underneath it.

By the time the interminable meal is over, I've figured everything out. Or at least, as much as I can without knowing anything about politics. Guillaume was right: Brecelyn certainly intends for this to be a final competition unlike any other. And whether the master likes it or not, somebody *is* going to shoot the prince at Thirds. That's the whole plan.

I've been waiting with mounting agitation for supper to be over so I can tell the whole thing to Tristan. As soon as he rises from the table, I grab his arm and attempt to drag him out in my eagerness to get away and explain everything, but to my extreme annoyance Gilles calls down to him before we've left the table and suggests a game of draughts in the garden before bed. I follow them out, wringing my hands, but I just can't contain myself. I can't wait for them to finish the game. In fact, I can't even wait for them to start. I'm going to have to tell him in front of Gilles and Pascal, who's trailing along after Gilles, too. It can't be helped, and after all we've been through together, if I can't trust them, I can't trust anybody. So as soon as the board is spread out on one of the little tables and Tristan and Gilles have seated themselves in position to play, I push Pascal out of the way and blurt out,

"Hugo Brecelyn killed my father! I'm sure of it!"

Needless to say, all three of them look up at me with astonishment. When Gilles gives Tristan an inquiring look, Tristan says calmly,

"Gilles, Pascal — I don't believe you've been formally introduced. Meet my squire, Marek Verbeke."

It takes quite a while after this for us to answer their flood of questions, and I leave most of it to Tristan. I'm too agitated, and I can hardly wait for him to finish explaining who I am and what happened to my father before I'm trying to explain my new theory.

"I recognized his voice."

"I seem to recall you thinking the voice was Guillaume's, then

Baylen's, not to mention a few other veterans'," Tristan says, a disbelieving look on his face.

"Oh, I know," I say dismissively, "I've thought I recognized the voice before. Only this time, I'm certain. It all fits!"

"What all fits?"

"Listen. Brecelyn must be plotting with someone here at the guild to assassinate the prince, at Thirds!"

"Marek," Gilles says smoothly. "I think you've been spending too much time with duBois. Your sense of the melodramatic is beginning to exceed even his."

"Just listen, Gilles!" I insist. "Don't you remember, I heard men plotting something here at the guild, at least once before? They were talking about something that had to happen at Thirds, without a hitch! Something that needed to *practiced*."

Gilles nods, and Tristan looks thoughtful, but I can tell they're humoring me. Pascal just looks confused.

"Well, I said at the time it sounded political. I just can't remember exactly what they said, and it wouldn't mean anything to me, anyway. But doesn't it seem a coincidence that the prince is coming to Thirds? That Brecelyn clearly had something to do with arranging for it? And that Thirds is going to be *at his estate*? You heard Guillaume say it was unprecedented! Isn't all of that rather remarkable?"

"Just because Brecelyn's invested a lot in this competition doesn't mean he intends to kill anybody," Tristan says reasonably.

"Come on! Isn't it enough just to hear 'plot at Thirds' and 'prince' to suspect I'm right? And that's not all. When I heard the men talking, that was before the hunt. The hunt at *Brecelyn*'s place, too, just like Thirds is going to be. And do you know what we learned at the hunt? Just how easy it is to explain away a stray arrow, when there are lots of young archers around! How easy it would be to shoot someone at the competition, with all those arrows flying. We all assumed it was a Journey who shot Tristan at the hunt, didn't we? It'll be so easy to blame one of the boys for any accident."

"But the Journey arrows are all marked," Gilles objects, and I turn to him, ready with an answer:

"All the easier to place the blame, then!"

"The boys will be shooting individually, with a huge audience watching. It won't be that easy to disguise the origin of a shot in the competition," he replies.

"I don't know exactly how it will be done, do I?" I snap, frustrated. "But that must be why the competition is to happen away from the guild. Somewhere allowing for cover for the real shooter, somewhere where the whole thing can be orchestrated to come off without a hitch." Turning to Tristan, I add, "It wasn't a Journey who shot you at the hunt, after all. It must have been one of Brecelyn's men, maybe even Beaufort himself. And do you know why?"

"No, Marek. Inform us," Tristan says with an indulgent smile, and I know none of them believes me.

"Practice, just like they said! Practice, to see if it would come off, if it would be thought an accident. And they *did* practice. When they missed you during the first hunt, they arranged for a second. I thought it strange at the time that we went after the hart although the hunt was really over, but even then, I didn't suspect anything!"

"But why shoot at *me* both times?" Tristan says with a frown.

"It had to be someone, didn't it?" I say. "And, I can think of a reason Brecelyn might have chosen you. Oh, I thought it was just luck that the prey came past you first both times, but I was wrong! Brecelyn as much as told us Beaufort is the best hunter around these parts. He knew just where to station you, just how to bring the deer on so they would pass by you first!"

"So, why me?" Tristan repeats, as Gilles drums one of the draught pieces against the table with a frown.

"The man who shot my father had known him for a long time. He hated him. I don't know why — maybe he hated him from old times, at St. Sebastian's. Maybe it was no more than what Royce said, they were all jealous of him. I heard him taunting my father, reveling in his misfortunes! Then you did my father's trick. He can't have liked seeing my father's trick redeemed. That alone might have been enough to make him choose you as the test case, to see if we'd believe a stray arrow. After all, they had to have a target. Why not you?"

Gilles clears his throat.

"Gilles?" Tristan inquires, his eyebrows raised.

"Possibly the familiar look Melissande gave you at Firsts didn't escape his notice, either."

"Don't tell me you believe any of this?" Tristan asks.

"I don't know," Gilles says lightly. "It's all rather much to take in after supper."

"You know, Marek, I don't mean to be insulting," Tristan says, proceeding to insult me, "but you've been absolutely sure of a lot of things that turned out not to be true. If I recall, you thought Taran set you up with that flask. Then you were convinced *he* shot me during the hunt. Now you're on to Brecelyn. What's next?"

"There is no next. Oh, Tristan! This is it. The day my father died, I saw one of Brecelyn's carriages, one with red trim, parked down by the guild business entrance. He was here, at St. Sebastian's, that day. My father must have overheard him, talking to whoever is in on this with him at the guild. Brecelyn might have been an old rival of my father's, but that's not why he killed him. I think my father overheard something about this plot, way back then. After all, the men I overheard said it had been in the works for a very long time. My father overheard something, and he was killed for it!"

I've gotten so hot and distressed talking about my father that I've started to yell, and seeing how upset I am, Tristan gets up and puts an arm around me.

"Okay, kid. Calm down. Look, I guess it's possible."

"But why would Brecelyn want to kill the prince?" Pascal asks.

"How should I know? You're the ones who claim to know so much about politics! Isn't there always a reason to kill someone in power? What are the usual reasons — rewards, political intrigues, power, money?"

"Only according to your theory," Gilles puts in, "it's not just Brecelyn. It's also someone at St. Sebastian's." I can tell this part is the most unpalatable to him.

"Maybe much more than that! Maybe, it's even the Black Guard." As I say it, I think we all think the same thing. Sir Brecelyn has recently become very chummy with at least one member of the Guard, at least enough to make a marriage alliance with him.

Nobody makes a joke of it. After all, I'm talking about the murder of my father. That much is true. That certainly happened, and this is the first Gilles and Pascal have heard of it. I can tell it's upset them. But I don't think I've convinced anyone. I do have to admit that I've been wrong about a lot of things, so I can't blame them.

"If it's all as you say, Marek," Gilles says slowly, "and Brecelyn's men made such an effort to shoot one of us at the hunt, to see if a stray arrow would be believed, then why not call attention to Tristan's wound? Why not go looking for him, when he went missing?"

I'm so caught up in my theory that it takes me a while to understand what Gilles means. When I do, I have to admit I can't answer that.

"Well ... they missed once, didn't they? Maybe they just assumed they'd missed again." But it doesn't sound very plausible, and I begin to waver.

"Look, kid," Tristan says kindly. "You've had a big shock. It can't have been pleasant to hear those words again. But this is all rather fantastic. If you were telling me this after the first time you heard Brecelyn's voice, well, that would be one thing. As it is ..."

He leaves the sentence hanging, and I feel confused. Am I just reacting to the phrase, and a rather commonplace one, at that? Would it really be such a coincidence for someone to use it again? I remember how foolish I felt in the garden, blaming Taran for shooting Tristan. But this feels different. I can still hear that cold voice saying *"it's my pleasure,"* and this time, I'm sure.

But I've been wrong before.

"Look," I say, and I think I'm being very reasonable, considering. "I don't really expect you to believe me. I probably wouldn't, myself. I'm not even sure that I believe it. But if I'm right, this is the thing that got my father killed. I can't avenge him, but maybe I can keep his killers from getting away with it! All I'm asking is for you to keep your eyes open at Thirds. If there's any chance the prince is in danger, isn't it worth considering?"

"You have my word," Gilles says solemnly. "My eyes, in any event, are always open."

Good old Gilles.

I look inquiringly at Tristan.

"We're a team, aren't we, kid? Besides, I've always fancied myself the type to save a prince."

I don't doubt it. Despite everything, I grin up at him.

"Who knows? If you foil a plot against the prince, you might just win the girl, after all!" I don't explain how that would work, since if I'm right, the one doing the plotting is the girl's father.

When I lie down on my cot that night, I know sleep won't come. It's not just that I won't be able to block out the memory of my father's death now. It's that I'm still puzzling everything over. Out in the garden, I was so sure my theory was right. Here in the dark room, with the familiar sounds of the other squires moving in their cots, it seems like just another example of my overactive imagination getting the better of me. It is too fantastic, too much like a story Tristan might make up. He was probably right. The phrase upset me, nothing more, and with a sinking feeling, I suspect that this is all my attempt rather unrealistically to find a way to put everything to rest at once. I have to accept the truth: I'll be leaving St. Sebastian's soon, without having accomplished my original goal in coming here. I'll never know what really happened to my father. Anyway, it's much too late to save him, isn't it?

CHAPTER THIRTY-SIX

It's hard to describe my mood during those last days before Thirds. Hearing Brecelyn's voice has thrown me off, and I can't decide whether it's because there's any chance my outrageous theory is true, or simply because it's stirred up my sadness over my father all over again. My uncertainty about the whole thing has just fueled my nervousness. Yet at the same time, a strange and unexpected calm has settled over the Journeys, and somehow, despite my anxieties, I find myself sharing in it. I would have thought we'd all be a bundle of nerves and at each other's throats, particularly now that we know the scale of the arena in which we'll be competing. Instead the boys seem to be taking a fatalistic view, and rather than intensifying the rivalry, the approach of the final competition of the year has only renewed our sense of camaraderie. The elimination of exhibition shots means that there can be no relying on tricks or stunts. It's going to come down to pure skill, and it feels right. This is the last competition. The best boys should win.

I also think Tristan is ready. He may not pass; all the boys are ready, too, and he's got to pull up in the ranks. But we've both done everything in our power to get him in top form, and this time, there'll be no distractions or injuries to impede him. It's time to see what he can do. He's put in the work, and I can almost feel that no matter what happens, that'll be triumph enough. He'll make a good showing, the best he can. That's a victory.

But I still want him to win.

As for me, I'm as ready as I'll ever be for the apprentice trials. I may not look like much, but my close-range shooting is good. I've got accuracy. I've even improved my control of the bow at longer distances. But even with Baylen's help, I can't compete with the boys in strength. It's not just because I'm a girl, even. I just wasn't a very strong girl to begin with. So I'll have to wait and see what the masters think. If my lack of distance puts me out of contention, there's nothing I can do about it.

Even Baylen seems impressed with our progress. On one of the last afternoons just a few days before finals, when we come out to meet him on the field, he announces that he's done coaching us. He's done all he can. The rest is up to us.

"I have to admit it, duBois. You surprised me," he says, shaking Tristan's hand. "I thought you were all talk. But you've worked hard."

Tristan looks a little stunned. I think it's the first time I've seen Tristan truly at a loss for words, so I jump in.

"Does he have a chance, Baylen?"

"I don't know. Taran, Falko, Gilles … they're sure to pass. But Charles, Aristide, Jurian," he wavers as he says Jurian's name, and I notice he doesn't bother to mention Turk. "I don't think I have to tell you that Jurian won't be easy to beat at clouts." Of course not. Baylen's tutored him personally, too, and for a lot longer than he did Tristan. I also know Baylen wouldn't have helped Tristan if he weren't sure Jurian could beat him. "It's a tough field, and you're down. But you've got a shot. That's all anybody has."

It's a good indication of my mood when Baylen offers to treat us to a drink at the Drunken Goat in lieu of a final practice session, and I beg off. I've only got a few more days at the guild, and I don't want to miss one minute of them, not even to be with Tristan. Besides, nothing good ever happens to me at the Goat, and I'd probably be expected to spend most of my time visiting Roxanne. Much as I like her, that would probably mean sitting in that stuffy little room talking about Falko all afternoon, which doesn't sound very appealing to me. So I let them go off together.

I don't feel like practicing, either, and nobody much is about. It's a strange afternoon. Summer's really over, and the air has that crisp and cool quality it has in the early fall, though the sun is bright overhead. It's like summer is lingering on, not wanting to die out just yet, trying to hang on a little longer, though the end is near. It so matches my mood that I almost feel responsible for the weather, but I think that sense in the air that something's about to end has infected all the boys.

I wander around aimlessly for a while, trying to memorize every inch of the place, and letting a sort of nostalgic melancholy infect me. At first Popinjay follows me, but even he tires of dogging my heels, and after a while he slinks back to the barracks, no doubt to infest my cot with more fleas. I run across Aristide in the archives, and though it isn't what I had in mind for the afternoon, I know there's something I have to do.

"Aristide," I say tentatively from the doorway, and he looks up inquiringly from a manuscript he's been reading.

"About the other day," I say. "I never thanked you properly. So thanks. If you hadn't come along, I'd have been in serious trouble."

"It wasn't personal, Marek," he replies, with his usual sour look. "I'll not let anyone beat a St. Sebastian's boy." Ever since Seconds, he's been enjoying the unfamiliar feeling of being the hero, and it's gone to his head. I wonder if gaining the respect of the boys was enough to turn him from his bullying habits, but then he adds, "Particularly not when I'm saving that pleasure for myself." I don't know whether to believe him or not. But I notice he didn't call me Woodcock.

Out in the yard, past the stables, I run across a number of the squires watching Pascal and Armand wrestle. They've stripped down to breeches and are grappling rather inexpertly in the dust, while the boys egg them on. I spot Auguste, waving his stick and taunting Armand. He must have put a sizable bet on Pascal. I watch for a while, but they're so evenly matched neither can make much headway, and since I've got no money riding on the outcome, I lose interest. I feel like each moment I have left here is precious, and I can't find something to do that seems worth wasting even one of them on. I wander back inside, then out to the garden, then out to the field again. Few of the Journeys seem inclined to practice today, and in fact the only archer I see out on the field is strangely enough Remy. After never having noticed him practice before, all of a sudden I seem to see him shooting all the time. He's taking the apprentice trials very seriously, though from what I can see, he's going to pass them easily.

But that's not really what catches my attention. He's alone. That means that Taran is lurking somewhere in the guild, and in my fragile mood, I just can't bear the thought of running into him. So I decide to go out after all, just not far. I'll take the opportunity to nip out to the mill pond by myself, to get a proper wash before finals. I'm in no danger of being disturbed there; the luxury-loving Journeys will all be asking for heated water for baths in the lavatory, but the sun should be warm enough to dry me and I'm tough enough now to stand a cold emersion. It'll feel good to be clean, to go out looking presentable, if nothing else, and it'll be nice to have this typical St. Sebastian's experience for myself once before I go. So I climb out over the wall unseen, and make the short hike to the pond.

When I come out into the open glade around the pond, I see I was right. Nobody's here. Despite the cool air, the sun is strong and I'm sweating inside my woolen tunic. It's been so long since I washed, I virtually rip off my clothes, eager to feel the water slide over me. It's been even longer since I was completely nude. I've still got my bow with me, so I prop it against the trunk of a large beech tree, and I throw my clothes in a pile next to it before plunging into the pond. It feels marvelous to shed my dirty rags and to let my bound body free, and after the initial shock, the cold water is invigorating. It feels so good finally to be entirely clean!

It's too cold for me to stay in long. I climb out quickly and stretch out on my back on the ground to dry, reveling in the unaccustomed feeling of being free from my restrictive clothing. I'm in no hurry to put that binding back on. The sun is so bright, though, that after a few minutes I reposition myself so that my head is resting in the shade of the beech tree, leaving the rest of my body to warm in the sun's rays. Even then, the sun filtering through the tree's leaves hurts my eyes, so I bring up my left arm to cover my face, strangely aware that I'm placing the scars on my forearm down on the scars on my head, scars covering scars. I'm lying on my back, so the scars from my beating on the back of my legs are concealed, too. Lying this way, with my face covered and my scars hidden, my binding shed, I can almost feel new again, like I might have felt if I were still Marieke, but a Marieke never kicked by a mule. Would it be so bad to be a girl again, if I could be this girl? I wonder. If the kind of girl I'd be would be one someone could desire? I don't know. But I let myself consider it.

The soft grass tickling against my bare skin and the sun warming it from above feel so delicious, so sensual, I let my free hand roam slowly over my body, caressing it. And why shouldn't I? The boys indulge themselves all the time. I hear them in the barracks at night, not caring who hears them, but I never do it. And I don't really now, either, but my hand feels good, and it's a safer way to vent some of my urges than others I've indulged in recently. I let myself imagine it's a boy's hand touching me, and I wonder what a boy would make of my body as it is now — an unusual combination of hard and soft, of male and female.

I don't dare think of any one boy in particular. Instead, as my hand slides over my belly, I think of them all, a sort of composite of what's best of all the Journeys: the curl over Charles's collar, Pascal's clean, sweet-smelling neck, Falko's broad shoulders, Gilles's sinewy arms, and that line of soft golden hair on Jurian's stomach. As I do, I almost feel as though I'm saying goodbye to them, as though I'm taking them all in a farewell embrace, the embrace of friends who are a little more than friends.

The only one I don't let myself think of is Tristan. It's not out of loyalty, or even because of my vow. It's because it would be too painful. I know that way danger lies. Yet inevitably, try as I might, that composite image begins to shift, and all the perfect pieces come together in Tristan's form against my will. My heart constricts as I picture his lean body and his handsome face smiling down at me, his eyes sparkling with mischief and that one thick lock of hair tumbling over his forehead. Just as inevitably, my hand slowly begins to glide upward toward my breast, following the same arc that Taran's did in the windmill, the same one that Tristan's does in my dream. And as it does, I think of Taran, too. What does it matter? He may be cold and inarticulate, brutish even, but let's face it. He's as gorgeous as any of them and built like a brick wall, and there's no point in pretending that his isn't the only boy's hand likely ever to touch me, or that I've been able to forget what it felt like. Or that I haven't wanted him to touch me again. Anyway, it has to be safer than thinking about Tristan, doesn't it? Isn't that exactly why I think of Taran so much, because he's safely my enemy?

As my palm opens to enclose my breast, my fingers spread to cover the exact spot each of Taran's fingers found. I see him in my mind, with the fierce expression on his face he had the day in the cathedral, when he raged at me, *"What do you think you're playing at?"* and though I may not know what emotion moved him then, his expression was anything but cold. Despite the chill in the air, I feel myself burning hot, and a low sound escapes me, floating off over the pond. It isn't a groan or a moan, exactly, but it's a sad sound. It's the sound of someone who's been lonely and untouched for too long. It's the sound of someone who can't bear to let any of them go.

By the time I force myself to bind up again and dress, I'm feeling more at peace. The swim has done me good, and I do feel that some of my tension is gone and I've begun to accept the inevitable, even though that inevitability is that I'm destined to be damned lonely. For now, I'm clean, and as I climb back over the wall, I see more of the boys are out on the field. I can at least be glad it isn't quite time really to say goodbye to them yet. Turk's riding around in the pasture again, Charles and Henri are practicing on the butts, and Aristide is splashing off at the barrels. It's business as usual. Still I can't shake the bitter-sweet feeling that came over me at the pond.

As I wander back across the field toward the guild buildings, I see that there's still a crowd of squires out behind the stables, so I go over to see what's going on now. Incredibly, Pascal and Armand are still at it. They've been wrestling the whole time I've been gone, and neither has been able to get the upper hand. They're still grappling with each other, only they're so exhausted by now that they look less like they're competing and more like drunks who are clutching each other for support. Rivulets of sweat are running down through the thick layers of dirt and grime that cover their bodies, and they're so dirty that at first I have a hard time telling them apart. Just as I approach, they take a few stumbling steps and collapse together in a heap in the dust, at which point all the other squires crowd forward, arguing over which one hit the ground first and not making any move to help them up.

I don't stop to help them, either. Instead, I head inside, looking for Tristan. As I'm passing the archive room, I notice Falko sitting at a table bent over a page of parchment with a frown on his face. I know Falko can read and write, but I'm surprised to see him in the archives when he doesn't have a tutorial. As far as I know, he doesn't spend one minute in the archives more than absolutely necessary. So I stop.

He's got a quill in one hand and he's bent over what looks to be an almost blank page with such a look of furious concentration on his face that it's almost funny. He's so intent, he doesn't notice me standing in the doorway for a full minute or two, until he throws the pen down in frustration and exclaims,

"Damn it all! Oh, Marek, I didn't see you there."

"Lessons giving you trouble, too?" I commiserate. I've been finding it rather harder to learn to read than I'd anticipated.

"Not exactly," he admits, and then to my surprise, he blushes. "It's, well, a bit awkward, actually."

"Falko, just what are you doing?" I ask sternly, taking a few steps into the room and coming around next to him.

"Well," he says guiltily, "After the other night, I thought maybe I'd try my hand at a letter."

He doesn't have to tell me he means a love letter, or to whom he intends to write it. I suppose it should be awkward.

"Just don't really start with *roses are red*," I suggest sarcastically, but sarcasm is wasted on Falko. He looks up at me eagerly and says,

"Actually, I could use a little help." So I lean over his shoulder to peer down at the line he's already got scribbled across the page, but his writing is cramped and my reading isn't what it should be, so I ask,

"What've you got so far?"

He clears his throat and recites:

"*Dear Lady, what raptures divine 'twould be indeed ...*" and I cut him off. I've been looking down trying to make out the words on his page and I see that somewhere further in the text he's got the phrase 'sweet nectar,' and I just can't listen to any more. I shudder to think what Falko's idea of imitating Tristan's purple prose might be and I don't want to hear it.

"Listen, Falko," I say. "I'm sure that's very lovely and all, but that sort of thing ... well, that could be for any girl. Why don't you tell her simply what you really want her to know?"

Falko just looks glum, so I elaborate: "Imagine that you were dying, say, and you had just one last chance to tell, uh, this girl how you really feel, what you'd want her to know before it's too late."

"I can't tell her that," he says flatly, to my surprise. I shudder to think what it is that Falko wouldn't say, but I ask anyway: "Try me."

"Well," he says, sneaking a look at me, "I'd want her to know that her face isn't ugly, to me."

We sit there in silence for a while. I already knew he was talking about Roxanne, of course, but it's another thing for him to make it clear to me that he's courting my girl behind my back, so I suppose I have to act as though I care. Eventually, though, I just agree quietly,

"No, you can't say that."

But what I'm really thinking is, if someone said that to me and really meant it, it would make a pretty good love letter, after all.

"You could try to get the same idea across, a little more diplomatically," I suggest. Falko's silent for another few minutes, and I can almost feel him thinking. It does seem to cost him an enormous effort. But when he finally speaks, I'm sorry that I thought so little of him.

"How about this," he says slowly. "When I look at you, all I see is beauty."

"Perfect," I say, and on impulse, I bend down and kiss the top of his head.

"Hey! What was that for?" he growls.

"When I look at you, buddy, all I see is beauty, too!" I say with a laugh, and then I slap him on the back of the head, hard, before wandering off in search of Tristan again.

Tristan's got to be back by now, so I set about trying to find him in earnest. When I do, he's huddled in the garden with Gilles, and the two of them are sharing a private joke that they don't seem eager to share, so I go in without bothering them. I'm fully aware of where Tristan's just been, and I'm in no mood to hear anything that might be about girls. I'm even less eager to hear anything that might be about Baylen. I think maybe I'm finally learning to leave other people's secrets alone.

When Tristan meets me in the corridor for evening mess, he's looking very pleased with himself. He slaps me jovially on the back, saying,

"I hope you've got your appetite, Marek! It's going to be quite a meal."

Not unreasonably, I don't like the sound of that. I'm always suspicious when Tristan is this happy. When Gilles shows up, the two of them smirk at each other across the crowd hanging around in the doorway, but when we start to file in, I notice that the two of them are at pains not to sit next to each other. In fact, I'm about to sit down next to Pascal when Tristan plucks me up and moves me down to the other end of the table, and I get distinctly suspicious. They're up to something.

My suspicions are confirmed about halfway through the meal, when Tristan rather conspicuously clears his throat and calls casually down the table to Gilles. Since they've arranged themselves at opposite ends, any conversation they have will by necessity involve the whole table, and I'm sure now that was their intention. I settle myself in, prepared to enjoy whatever they've got cooked up. From Tristan's expression, it's going to be good.

"So, I hear you had quite a hunt this afternoon, Gilles," Tristan says. "Catch anything?"

"No, no," Gilles says smoothly. "I'm afraid our quarry quite escaped us, didn't it, Mellor?" He leans back and turns to Taran, who I now notice is seated next to him, but he doesn't reply. It's pretty clear already that whatever they're going to do, it's going to involve teasing Taran. I don't mind. I hope they humiliate him. Irrationally, I hope they pay him back for catching me with Jurian in the garden.

"But it was worth it, wasn't it?" he continues with a wicked smile.

"How mysterious!" Tristan exclaims, as though he doesn't have any idea of what Gilles is talking about, and all the boys are paying rapt attention now. It's not hard to tell that they're setting up one of their performances. "Do tell!"

"Ah, the boys don't want to hear about a boring hunt, do they?" Gilles asks disingenuously, looking around the table and inviting everyone to urge him to tell the story, and of course we do. So he continues:

"Well, Taran and I weren't out in the woods for long before we were on the trail of big game, boys. The biggest! A great big stag, right outside the guild wall!" I don't like the sound of this, either. I don't want to hear about killing another deer, but I can't see how the boys could have brought back a stag without anyone being the wiser, so I relax again. This must be some story about how Taran screwed up and let the deer get away. All the Journeys seem thrilled, and Gilles has some trouble shutting up Falko before he can divert the conversation into a recap of his own triumph at the hunt.

"We weren't expecting it so close to the guild, and I'm afraid we startled it. It led us a merry chase indeed, out past that abandoned windmill — you know the place — and then back again. We'd lost sight of it and were about to give up, when we came upon its trail again, and we tracked it through the woods."

So far, the story *is* quite boring, and I can't figure out why Tristan is sitting next to me with such smug anticipation. Then I hear Gilles saying something that gives me a horrible sense of foreboding.

"It must have thought it had shaken us, and it was heading for a drink."

"I thought you said your quarry escaped you," Charles protests.

"Patience, Charles," Gilles replies, resuming his tale. "The creature was picking its way silently through the glen by the old mill pond. We crept up on it as quietly as we could as it neared the water's edge, but it bolted before we could get too close. We never did catch it."

Gilles looks around the table, beaming, while the boys just look confused. I'm looking straight down at my plate. I know where this is going now, and there's nothing I can do.

"Too bad, Gilles," Turk says dismissively, turning to start a new conversation with Jurian, but Gilles cuts him off.

"That's not all, boys! The stag may have gotten away, but he led us to even better game!" He says this with such glee that the others finally get it. They're always hoping to catch some girl bathing at the pond. Some of the kitchen maids go there, and some girls from the village, but so far, they've had little luck actually disturbing one there.

"Why, you lousy dogs caught one!" Falko cries out, and Gilles breaks into such a big grin that it's instantly clear Falko's right. I sink down lower on the bench until my face is only about an inch above my plate. I feel Tristan elbow me in the ribs, as though to say, "Wait until you hear the rest of the story," but I don't want to hear anything else. The only thing that makes it bearable is that it's clear they don't know the girl they caught there was me. I do some quick calculations: my head was in the shadows, covered by my arm. All my identifying scars were hidden. Even my clothes and equipment were in the shade. There's no way they could have known it was me. It's not a total disaster. But it's bad enough.

"Come on, tell!" Aristide is saying, as Falko asks "Who was it? The miller's daughter?" and Turk demands,

"Was she naked!?"

Gilles lets them all dangle for a beat, then crows, "*Stark!*" As a cry goes up from the table, Gilles continues loudly over them, "And stretched out on the ground as a veritable feast for our eyes, boys!"

"Who was it? What did she look like? Oh, I bet she was a beauty!" they all start demanding, as my nose sinks down into my parsnips.

"Unfortunately, her lovely face and hair were completely in shadows," Gilles admits, and as the boys make disappointed noises, he adds slyly, "But … it was quite clear, she was a brunette!" And they all roar again.

"And," he cuts in again above the din, "I know exactly who she was."

At this, my heart literally stops. I wonder what they would all say if I died right there, face down in my dinner. But Gilles can't know it was me, can he?

"It was Diana, the goddess of the hunt herself!" he cries, and I start to giggle quite hysterically as the other boys laugh. The whole thing is so absurd, but my heart is beating wildly, and if Gilles doesn't stop soon, I'm in danger of passing out yet again. I'd hoped to leave St. Sebastian's without doing that again. I can feel my whole body growing hot with embarrassment, but I will myself not to blush. I can't give myself away.

"Gentlemen," Gilles says seriously, "I do not jest. Her face may have been hidden, but her glorious body was on full display, and what a body! No mortal girl ever looked like that. Strong, lean, muscled — an archer, indeed! — but round, full, and soft where a woman should be round!" Gilles breaks into a leer and uses his hands to suggest a curvy silhouette, as Falko whistles appreciatively.

"I tell you," Gilles resumes, "when I peeked out through the trees and saw that miraculous form, I was thunderstruck! No mortal man was meant to gaze on such immortal beauty. Thank goodness we had no hounds with us, or surely like the poor Actaeon from the story, we would have been set upon and devoured by our own dogs for the sin of surprising the goddess at her bath! Why, I'm sure I even saw the outline of a bow resting against the tree behind her."

Just when I don't think it can get any worse, Tristan licks his lips, puts a hand on my back, and says,

"Pray tell, just what did *you* make of her, Taran?" and it doesn't take much to see that this is what Tristan's been waiting for. He's hoping to score off Taran with this story somehow.

I think it's only then that I remember just what I was doing at the mill pond when the two of them must have seen me.

"Boys," Gilles exclaims happily, taking his cue and slapping Taran on the back. I haven't lifted my head from my plate, but out of the corner of my eye, I can tell that Taran's been looking down through most of this, too. "If I was thunderstruck, it was nothing compared to our young friend here! Why, he was absolutely rooted to the spot! *Rooted!* His eyes bugged out, he began drooling like an idiot, and his tongue lolled out so far, it was almost dragging in the dust! He looked so hot, I thought his hair was about to catch on fire!" Gilles slaps the table with a hearty laugh, and all the boys join in. "Didn't I tell you Mellor would only be interested in a girl with a bow? Well, when I'd recovered myself enough to remember common decency," he pauses suggestively, and I'm sure that he didn't remember it very quickly, "Why, I had to *drag* him away, literally! It took all my strength. And when that gorgeous, nubile young thing began to move, to caress her own body sensuously ..." he begins moving his own hands in an exaggerated imitation, but he doesn't get any further, since all the boys begin to hoot so loudly at this that Guillaume looks over from the master's table in annoyance and pounds his tankard on the table for silence.

When they've quieted down, Gilles leans over the table and all the boys do, too, and he continues in a lower voice,

"When she *slid* her hand up to *fondle* her own *breast*, why, I thought Mellor here was going to faint!" Gilles cackles, and I sway on the bench. Tristan slaps me on the back, thinking my motion is from humor and that I'm enjoying the story, but what I'm really thinking is, *"it can't last much longer, it can't last much longer. Thank God, thank God, they don't know it was me."* But now Gilles is throwing his hands up in the air to deliver the punch line:

"And what a strange noise he made, boys! He let out an ardent groan, just like the bellow of a wounded beast! I thought the game was up, we'd be discovered for sure. But by providence we were saved. The sound was masked by another, even more desperate, coming from the divinity herself!" Gilles finally dissolves in such a fit of laughter that he can't continue and has to drape himself on Charles's shoulder for support, and fortunately all the boys are laughing so much that nobody can hear the equally desperate noise that escapes me now.

"Come on, Taran!" Aristide teases. "Gilles is done for. Tell us about it yourself!"

"Yeah, whaddya say, Taran?" Falko says, and they all start to tease him. Tristan is having a marvelous time. But I think he's more surprised than anyone when instead of turning red or stalking off, Taran suddenly looks up and says evenly:

"I have to admit, boys ... it was quite a revelation," and they all give him a cheer.

"Come on! Give us some details!" Falko cries, and there's a pregnant pause. Just when I think to my relief that Taran isn't going to respond, he says in a slow, deliberate voice,

"I did notice one thing in particular. She had very lovely ... *feet*."

"Ha! Leave it to Taran to have a naked girl spread out in front of him, and be looking at her feet!" Falko laughs.

But I'm not amused.

Despite myself, my head shoots up in dismay from where it's been resting virtually in my lap, to find Taran staring right at me with a smug look on his face. Our eyes meet across the table, and for an instant I feel as though the rest of the room has receded and we're sitting there across from each other, alone.

Then he does it.

Very slowly, he closes one eye, and gives me a great big, exaggerated wink.

I was right. Taran really can bide his time. He's paying me back in spades, for my wink at the Drunken Goat. It's payback, all right, because he's letting me know two things at the same time with that wink: that he knows it was me this afternoon at the pond, and worse, that he knows exactly what I was thinking about.

I can't help myself. I pass out again, face down in the stew.

WHEN I COME TO AGAIN, I FIND TRISTAN'S TAKEN ME back to barracks. A few of the other squires are hovering around, too, and I'm particularly aware of Remy lurking in the background, looking distraught. I think he feels guilty for being so cold to me lately, and when he sees my eyes flutter open, he gives me a tentative smile over Tristan's shoulder.

"What in the world came over you, Marek?" Tristan asks, wiping some remains of the stew out of my hair.

"I really couldn't tell you," I say honestly.

"The stress is getting to be too much for you, I imagine," he says, and he's right, but not in the way he means. "It'll be over soon, one way or another, kid. It's just one more day till Thirds. And when it's over, well, it'll be okay, whatever happens. Understand? I'm going to take care of you, Marek," and I nod. He's right. It'll be over soon. I just have to hang on a little longer.

The thing is, after Tristan leaves and I'm left there on my cot, still smelling of roasted meat (how quickly the effects of my bath have been obliterated!), I don't see how I'm going to make it even one more day. I thought what happened in the garden was bad. This is worse. Taran knows I was thinking about him. I'm not just humiliated, I'm mortified. And from the look of satisfaction on

Taran's face, he's not going to let me forget it. He's going to revel in it. And suddenly I'm tired, more tired than I've ever been. I'm tired of being bullied. I can't let Taran ruin my last days at St. Sebastian's. I won't skulk around the guild anymore, afraid of running into him. I've run scared from him for too long. This is the last straw. It makes me realize that there is one loose end, one thing I didn't think about: how it's all going to end with Taran. As always, I've been focused on Tristan. But I want to go out on my own terms with Taran, too. I can't let him beat me. If I'm going to make it successfully to the end, I've got to confront him. The only problem is, I don't see how I'll have the courage.

The next morning, as soon as I wake up, I steel myself to do it. It's got to be done in private, and that's not easy to arrange at St. Sebastian's. All morning during drills I'm distracted by thinking about it. As I set up Tristan's station and as the other boys begin to come out onto the field, I'm so nervous about the thought of seeing Taran again that I'm a wreck and I feel completely embarrassed, as though I'm standing there naked in front of all of them. When Gilles comes out, it gets worse. When I remember how he described me, I blush even more. But when Taran finally does come striding out, to my eyes looking very smug and self-satisfied, I break. All my embarrassment turns to anger. Over the course of practice, I work myself up into such a rage of righteous indignation that I think if I can ride this wave of anger, I might actually be able to go through with confronting him after all.

I finally get my chance after noon mess. Tristan's gone to lie down for a while, when I notice Taran head out through the garden. He must be on his way into town somewhere, so I follow him at a safe distance. When I see him go out the gate into the alley, I let myself out and settle in to wait for him. I'll catch him on his return, before he can get back inside. It's better to do this outside the guild wall, away from all the eyes and ears of St. Sebastian's. I settle myself in on the crates next to the gate, and as the minutes drag by and Taran doesn't reappear, I'm reminded strangely of the first day I came to the guild, when I waited here with little hope for the gate to open. In fact, it takes Taran so long to come back that I start to worry, thinking perhaps he's come back in by another entrance, and I've missed him. I won't be able to wait much longer. Tristan will be looking for me soon, and after all this time, I've started to lose my nerve. I haven't even figured out what I'm going to say to Taran, either. What if I just make a fool of myself, and humiliate myself further?

I'm just thinking that I must have missed Taran and that it's probably better that way, anyway, when I see him round the corner into the alley. He's strolling along slowly, smiling to himself, and I suddenly lose all my courage. What in the world was I thinking? What could I possibly say to him? Why didn't I think it through before rushing to confront him? I shrink back against the crates, unsure whether to try to go through with it, or bolt.

Just when I decide to turn tail and run, he looks up and sees me, and it's too late. Irritation at him for catching me before I can run away makes me angry enough to step out boldly in front of him, only in my nervousness I misjudge it, so my brave act falls flat. I step up too close, and then take a quick step backward to keep from being trodden on. What was supposed to be an attack starts out inauspiciously in a retreat.

Taran pulls up short and comes to a stop with a surprised look on his face. But if I'd hoped to startle him, I'm disappointed. Though he comes to a sudden halt, when he sees it's me his surprised look dissolves into something that looks to me a lot like a smirk, and he looks as cool and composed as ever. Against my will, color creeps into my cheeks, as the anger that helped propel me into the alley is replaced by acute embarrassment. If I had a plan at all, faced with his imposing form inches from me, I've forgotten it. All I can remember is Gilles's voice, describing to all the boys how I touched myself while he and Taran watched, and I have to lash out.

"How dare *you* call *me* a fraud!" I screech, trying to drown out the memory of Gilles's voice with the sound of my own. "You're the one who's a fraud! You said you knew what honor meant! Honor!" I spit the word out, the way he did to Tristan that first day. "You don't even know what decency is!" I'm shrieking hysterically, my voice shrill, my eyes focused on his stomach, too much a coward to look at him directly. Even so, I can tell that his amusement is gone when he replies steadily,

"I'm not the one who brought it up. I didn't know Gilles was going to say anything. Just how do you propose I could have stopped him?"

"That's no excuse!" I scream irrationally, though I know exactly what happened. Tristan and Gilles staged the whole thing last night to embarrass Taran. Tristan couldn't have known that scoring off Taran was going to be at my expense.

Taran hasn't moved, but I suspect he's thinking the same thing, that this is actually all Tristan's fault. At the idea that he's reading my thoughts, my embarrassment turns to fury again. *It isn't Tristan who humiliated me, it's you, and you're going to pay for it!* I think, just as he's saying:

"Whatever you may think to the contrary, I would never knowingly cause harm to a ..." and I snap.

"Don't you dare say it! Don't you dare call me that!" I scream, clenching my fists and looking up at him defiantly, to find him watching me with a look on his face more intense than any I've ever see there.

"Are you still going to try to tell me seriously that you don't have the feelings of a girl?" he says quietly.

And then suddenly there's a tension between us, and I know we're both thinking about the real reason I'm so angry with him. I could almost be standing here naked, sliding my hand up to my breast while he watches. I can feel the tension mounting, and the intense look on Taran's face suddenly makes me register how Gilles described him when he watched me by the pond, knowing I was thinking of him. I've been so focused on my own embarrassment, I haven't really thought about it before, but now I hear Gilles's voice saying *"he looked so hot, I thought his hair was about to catch on fire!"* and all at once I feel hot, too, and I'm acutely aware of how close we're standing to each other. I open my mouth to reply, but I can't. There's nothing I can say, and the tension is building. And now it feels as though it's Taran's hand running lightly up across my belly, and the tension is getting so thick, I have to do something to stop it. I have to do something to get control again, to get the upper hand.

So I do the first thing that comes to mind.

Something outrageous.

I punch him as hard as I can right in the face.

As I duck back through the garden gate and make my escape before he can react, my own hand is killing me. My knuckles feel like they've hit a brick wall, and I doubt my fist hurt him much. But the look of sheer surprise on Taran's face was priceless, and for the first time, I know I've gotten the better of him. This time, I hold my head up high as I make my way through the garden and into the guild to find Tristan. I've gotten a bit of my own back. There's a certain satisfaction, too, that by chance I leave Taran in the exact spot where I first encountered him. Only this time, it's his blood that's staining the alley.

Quite by chance, I found the perfect way to go out on my own terms with Taran after all.

But I still feel like I could use that bucket of cold water.

CHAPTER THIRTY-SEVEN

The morning of Thirds dawns cold and chill, and as I gather up our equipment and help pack it into the wagons designated to carry our gear to Brecelyn's estate, I'm glad that cloaks are part of our regalia. Once again, we squires are to travel in our own carriage, so I won't even get to make this last trip with Tristan. As I prepare to leave the barracks for the last time, I don't even bother to bring anything away with me. I don't have anything, anyway, except for my bows, which are coming with me in any event. But as I dress, I tuck my St. Sebastian's medal down into the binding around my breast as usual, to keep it from swinging around, then I start to slip my little wooden figurines into my waistband, too. I can't just leave them behind.

"What are you doing, Marek?" Remy asks, seeing me. "You don't think anybody will steal them while we're gone, do you?"

I don't know what to tell him. "I just thought they might bring me luck."

"You don't need luck, Marek. You're sure to pass."

"You too, Remy," I say, handing him the mouse. "Still it never hurts to have a little insurance. Why don't you take this, for luck?" I figure I might as well return it to Remy. After all, it was supposed to be his.

He looks down at the mouse in his hands. "A hawk. That might be a talisman to help an archer. You know, to help the arrows fly. But a mouse? How will that help me?" He puts it down on my table again dismissively. I leave it there, an offering for the next inhabitant of my cot. It seems appropriate.

Even the little mouse and the hawk are destined to part company today.

We're to get an early start, but even before we're on the road, as soon as I look out through the guild gate it's clear that the competition will never start on time. The roads are overflowing with carriages, wagons, and foot traffic, and there's such a crowd streaming into the L'île-Charleroi road that even out at this end of town we'll only be able to inch along. With the prince to attend the competition, visitors from all over Ardennes and beyond have been packing into Louvain over the past week, and now the flood of traffic trying to make its way out to Brecelyn's manor is clogging the small streets. I seem to be the only person in all of Ardennes not eager to get there.

It's not just because when I see the line of carriages with red trim lined up outside the guild wall, I can't help but feel a prickling of unease. Even if my outrageous theory about a plot at Thirds is wrong, I'm not anxious to return to the scene of Tristan's wounding, or to the estate of the man who wrung the little hawk's neck. But what if my theory is right, at least in part? Over the past days I've managed to dissuade myself, and it really is too fantastic. Still I can't shake a niggling worry, and as I climb into the carriage designated for us squires, all I can hear is that cold voice repeating, *it's my pleasure*. I can't help it. I've got a bad feeling about the whole thing. Somehow, after punching Taran in the alley, I feel as though I'm receding into the past, as though things are coming full circle. It could even be that day I first visited the guild with my father again, when I stepped out of the guild and saw a carriage with red trim parked outside.

That's not the only reason I'm in no hurry to leave for Thirds. As I step out through the garden gate and into that little alley by the chapel, I'm leaving St. Sebastian's behind for good. I've decided to cut out straight from Brecelyn's place. What's the point of returning to St. Sebastian's? It will just make leaving again harder. I'm not sure where I'll go. I have some thought of making my way back to my old home, at least to see what's become of it, and we'll be on that side of town. Then I'll probably go to the abbey. It might not be too late to take Abelard up on his offer to help me. Maybe he could help me find some menial position somewhere with few questions asked, but it doesn't really matter. As the carriage door closes behind me and I get my last glimpse of the walls of St. Sebastian's receding behind me, I feet a sharp stab of pain at leaving. It's the worst arrow of all.

There's virtually no conversation in the carriage on the way to the competition. We're all too nervous, particularly those of us up for apprentice status. I've been picking furiously at my fingers the whole way, and before we're even halfway through our journey they're a bloody mess. Even when Henri gives me a look of disgust, I can't seem to stop. The silence and tension in the carriage begins to grow oppressive as the carriage rolls closer to our destination, since even the squires not competing themselves are dependent on their masters' performances, and I know I'm not the only one who doesn't want to leave the guild. Turk's squire Andre looks particularly bleak, since there's little chance Turk will pull through, but I must look the worst. I'm the only one who knows that my departure today is a certainty.

I'm not just worried for myself. I'm worried about Tristan. This is the final test, the culmination of everything we've worked for. Today will determine whether Tristan is really a St. Sebastian's man or not, and after all we've been through, I don't think I can bear it if he's cut now, not when we're so close to the end. Somehow, the thought of leaving St. Sebastian's myself isn't as hard as the thought of St. Sebastian's going on without Tristan.

I raise my eyes from my hands to look around the carriage, wondering whose cots will be empty in the barracks along with mine when the final test is over. Pascal and Armand have little to worry about, and Remy in particular looks as cool as a cucumber, as though he's adopted the usual attitude of his master.

Remy, of course, has absolutely nothing to worry about at all.

He's sitting directly across from me, and I watch him for a while, wondering if I'll miss him, or not. He's changed so much over the past months that I hardly recognize him. It's been gradual, but today I really look at him, and I'm disturbed by what I see. It's not just that he's taller. If I hadn't known him all this time as a little boy, if I'd just met him today, I'd have to admit that Remy is distinctly handsome, with his thick black hair and big, lopsided grin.

In fact, the eye color is wrong, but he's beginning to look a lot like Tristan.

I was right. It's definitely time for me to go.

When we reach the turn-off for Brecelyn's estate, the foot traffic is so thick that the mounted veterans escorting us have to ride out in front of the carriages and clear the way. Even then the crowd presses in, hoping to get a close-up glimpse of some of the Journeys, and everyone is so caught up in the event that even when it becomes clear our carriage holds only squires, it doesn't seem to matter. At one point, a particularly pushy woman who reminds me distinctly of Berthal makes a grab at Pascal's arm, and we have to grab him back to keep her from pulling him right out of the carriage. After that, he insists on changing places with Rennie, and once he's next to the window, we don't have any more trouble. Still we're all feeling mobbed and mauled by the time the towers of Brecelyn's castle come into view, and completely overwhelmed.

I've never seen so many people gathered in one place. As we pass the long open fields that stretch out in front of the castle, all the flocks of sheep that were grazing there when we came for the hunt have been replaced by flocks of people. A large area has been blocked off right in front of the castle's outer enceinte to serve as the competition grounds, and an equally impressive grandstand erected alongside it, perpendicular to the walls near the place where a great portcullis forms a grand entryway into the fortifications. These wooden bleachers extend the entire length of the right side of the field, but even so they look only big enough to hold a fraction of the crowd. Gaily colored tents and booths surround the competition arena, but smaller and shabbier tents dot the landscape over a wide area radiating from this center where people have been camping out in anticipation of the event, probably for several days. It's as though an enemy army has encamped in front of Brecelyn's walls and settled in for a long siege. Rising behind this impressive scene are the equally impressive and colorful walls of the castle, which today sport royal banners and the banners of St. Sebastian's interspersed with the colors of Brecelyn's house. From the top of the central keep a huge pennant is flying emblazoned with Brecelyn's crest: a rampant boar.

"How appropriate! The filthy swine," I say under my breath, when I see it.

Our carriage rolls us right up to a large, long tent provided to accommodate the Journeys. It lies within a barricaded area on the left side of the competition grounds, directly opposite the grandstands. Apparently the boys aren't to have separate tents, so it will mean no private preparations or pep talks between tests, but I think we're all glad we'll be together today. In a nod to the usual set-up, the tent has eight flaps which open onto the field, and over these flaps the colors of the Journeys still in contention are flying. As we climb out, I notice another large tent set up next to the Journey tent, but this one is solid black. I don't need to see the flag flying at the top, a black field with a single silver arrow below *a fleur de lis*, to know that this tent must be for the Guards who are to perform after the tests are over. As we approached, I already spotted a number of Guardsmen out on the field. Since they've been here all night as Brecelyn's guests at the castle, they're all dressed and ready.

"Are all the Guards here?" I ask Armand, as we begin to unload our gear from the wagons parked nearby and carry it into the Journey tent.

"Not all, no. Somebody's got to be on guard at L'île de Meuse, right? But I think there must be at least thirty or so," he replies. "Have you ever seen them?"

I think he means have I ever seen them shoot, so I say no.

"I have, once. It's going to be fantastic! They did something called 'shower of arrows,' where they were all shooting at once, and so fast! Their arrows blocked out the whole sky. Oh, I hope they're going to do that today." So do I, and I say so.

"Oh, they're sure to do it. It's their signature trick," Henri says. They seem to know all about the Guards.

"Who's your favorite?" Pascal asks him, and I move off to busy myself with organizing Tristan's things before he can ask me my opinion. I don't know who any of the Guardsmen are, except Lord Mellor, and somehow, I can't bring myself to claim him as my favorite.

It's not long before the Journeys start to filter in. Their carriage left earlier than ours, but they were taken directly to meet with Brecelyn and some of the other dignitaries, so they're just making their way to the tent now. It's taken us squires so long to get here, though, it's already time for the Journeys to start getting ready for the competitions. We all dressed back at the guild, but the Journeys are to dress in here. I've got Tristan's regalia in a bundle with me, and so as soon as I see him, I begin to unpack his outfit and shake it out. Although the tent is big, with all the squires and Journeys packed in and trying to change, the space feels cramped, and I begin to regret that we'll all be together after all. I've not yet figured out just how to say goodbye to Tristan, and as I'm jostled from behind by Rennie, I realize that whatever I say to him is going to have to be done here, in front of everyone. I'm to be robbed of a proper goodbye to him.

Just as this unpalatable thought is occurring to me, Tristan spots me and comes over, smiling.

"Marek, there you are!" he says heartily, putting his hand on my shoulder. When he sees my bleak expression, he says more gently,

"Nervous, kid?"

"No," I say bravely. "You've worked so hard. I know it's going to pay off."

"Nervous for yourself, maybe?" he says, even more gently. But I just shake my head. There's so much I want to tell him, but I can't think how, particularly not with Rennie bustling around behind me and Falko raving in the background about his misplaced tights. It's not the place for a touching scene, and anyway, Tristan hates sentiment. The air is so thick with the smells of tightly packed boys that it's even more cloying in here than in that little room in the Drunken Goat, and the disappointment that I'll never be alone with Tristan or have the chance to say anything privately to him again weighs on me so heavily that I feel suffocated by it. What could I say, anyway? There's nothing. There isn't anything I could really say that would tell him how I feel. But even as I think it, Tristan leans in and says goodbye for me. His smile fades, replaced by a serious expression, and he moves his hand from my shoulder to the back of my neck, and says so the others can't hear:

"Whatever happens today, Marek, I want you to know. It's been a hell of a ride, and I'm glad we did it together. I couldn't have done it without you."

I don't care if everyone sees us. I step in close and hug him tight, burying my head against his stomach, and he reaches down to ruffle my hair one last time, as I knew he would.

When I turn back to our equipment to compose myself, I notice something stuffed down into Tristan's quiver, and I start to pull it out when Tristan puts a restraining hand on mine.

"What's this?" I ask, my hand still down in the quiver and touching a length of fabric. Tristan looks around the tent and leans in closer.

"It's her veil!" he whispers. I finger the material, and sure enough, it's soft and filmy.

"How are we going to wrap that around you in here with nobody seeing?" I hiss at him, angry with myself for being annoyed that he wants Melissande's token with him today.

"We're not!" he laughs. "You're going to help me figure out how to give it back to her." I start, and he gives a covert glance around the room before continuing quietly,

"It won't be easy, I know. But she returned the rose, didn't she? I ought to return the favor, and besides ..." he breaks off, but I already know what he's going to say. "I need an excuse to see her. I've got to find out. After the tests, it may be too late, if I'm cut. Now when I'm well and sound, I've got to claim my prize. My real prize, when I'm in a condition to appreciate it."

I knew it was coming, still I can't believe it. With his veteran's status at stake, what Tristan's thinking about right now is a kiss.

"With the court here, that's going to be impossible! I can't just saunter over to her box, past the Black Guard, and throw something into the stands!"

"Of course not. But surely between the two of us, we can think of a way. It has to be 'just possible,' doesn't it? Besides, I've already got an idea. Look." He bends over his pile of discarded clothing lying on the ground, and from the bottom of the stack he lifts up the edge of a garment, making sure to block the view of it from the room with his body. I peer over his shoulder to see the corner of a black cloak, emblazoned with the silhouette of a castle encircled by silver *fleur de lis*. It's a Guardsman's cloak.

"Oh, Bloody Hell! Where did you get that?" I cry, and my curse is so loud that despite the commotion in the tent, some of the boys look over. We're crammed in so closely, it's impossible not to be in each other's business, and the Journeys never give each other any privacy anyway. After shushing me and stuffing the cloak back under the other clothes, he looks up with one of his winning smiles.

"I seem to have been a little confused about which was the Journey tent earlier, and wandered into the wrong one. The Guards were ever so nice about it."

"Oh, Tristan! You can get in real trouble for stealing that!" If the penalty for stealing at St. Seb's is usually losing both hands, I'd hate to think what the penalty for stealing from the Guards might be. It would be a real pity for anything to be cut off of Tristan's body.

"We're just going to borrow it for a while."

"Tristan," I say, with a knot in my stomach. "You aren't going to ask *me* to wear that, are you?"

"No," he says, and I relax, until he adds, "You're too short. We're going to have to borrow Pascal again."

Before I can respond, a boy in livery bursts into the tent and calls out in a loud voice,

"Which of you is Mellor?" and we all turn to see what's happening. Taran's been dressing at the far end of the tent, but he steps forward now, and as he does, the boy says loudly,

"Parcel for you, from your father."

He hands Taran a leather satchel, and after Taran thanks him politely but with little visible interest, the boy departs again. On hearing 'your father,' I dart a nervous glance at Tristan, but he hasn't looked up and I can tell he's trying to feign disinterest, so I don't say anything. I'm openly curious, though. But Taran simply tosses the satchel next to his gear without making a move to look inside, as though unaware that everyone in the tent is watching him. When he turns back to adjusting a gauntlet on his arm as though the boy never appeared, Aristide asks rudely,

"By the Saint, aren't you going to open it, Mellor?" and it's what we're all thinking. If I thought Taran had a sense of humor, I'd think he was purposely teasing us, he's tossed it away so casually and he's now so studiously avoiding touching the bag or meeting anyone's eye.

"It can wait," Taran says dismissively, and before Aristide can prod him further, Baylen pops his head in and bellows,

"About ready in here, boys? We're already running late, and the crowd's starting to get unruly. We can't bring out the prince's entourage until the competition is ready to begin. For the love of St. Irene! DuBois, aren't you even dressed yet? Lejeune — what in the hell is that?"

All eyes now turn to Gilles, to see him sporting the hat he commissioned for Seconds but never got to wear. When he opens his mouth to reply, Baylen cuts him off with a sharp bark:

"Lose it, Gilles. Pascal, I thought you could control him!" and he's gone again, and I turn my attention back to Tristan and hasten to help him into his regalia, cursing my bloody fingers and trying to keep my hands from shaking as the time for competition nears. When I've finally managed to get his jerkin adjusted and his cloak fastened at his shoulders, I take a step back and I survey him critically. I want him looking his best today. Reading my thoughts, Tristan asks with a smile,

"How do I look? Will I pass?"

I frown, and shake my head. Then I reach up and pull down that unruly lock of his hair so that it's curling over his forehead at a rakish angle, so he looks again like that beautiful boy from the top of the garden wall.

"Now you're ready," I say, satisfied. "Now, you're ready for anything."

Behind me, I hear Gilles exclaim suddenly, *"You're* not going to turn any heads today, Mellor! What in the blue blazes happened to your eye?" and I jump, but I don't turn around. I don't have to be curious about that. I know exactly what happened.

"From the looks of it, he got in a fistfight, with Melissande!" Falko laughs. "Or, did your bird peck *you*, too?"

"Possibly," I hear Taran say evenly. "If so, I may have deserved it."

Despite myself, I grin. But there's no time to dwell on his words, because at this moment Falko's squire Pruie, having located the missing tights and helped wedge Falko into them, peeks out through one of the tent flaps and exclaims,

"Baylen wasn't kidding! It looks like they're starting to get underway out there. The Guards are already taking their seats."

I hurry over and peek out with him, anxious to see the set-up. Directly across the field from our tent, in the place of honor, an elaborate box stands empty. This must be where the prince and his courtiers are to sit. Surrounding the royal box is another area of special seating, and it's here that the Guardsmen are starting to settle themselves. It's a clever arrangement. The Guards will entirely encircle the prince, adding to the spectacle, but also providing protection. Another line of Guardsmen is standing along the front of the grandstands directly below the box, bows in hand, and in front of them is the judges' box, which is also beginning to fill. I spot Lord Mellor talking to Master Leon, and with an involuntary shiver, I notice sir Brecelyn standing behind them. I force myself to look away; I won't let myself be distracted today, not even by him.

There are so many distinguished visitors here today that additional special boxes are sprinkled throughout the stands, and when Pascal comes over to peek out through the flap next to us, he points out Gilles's father, who's made the trip to see his son win veteran's status. Down at the far end of the bleachers I spot a box set aside for the noble ladies of Brecelyn's house, and I see with some satisfaction that with the prince in attendance, it's been relegated to the sidelines. Melissande won't be taking center stage this time.

"Ooh!" Pruie exclaims, just noticing the box himself. "Here come the ladies! They're filing into their box! Oh, Taran — you've got to see! Melissande looks just ravishing!"

I follow his gaze to where Melissande is indeed now entering her box, and I see he's right. She's wearing a dress that looks made of pure gold, and despite my comments to the contrary in the past, she looks every inch a prize to be won. Out of the corner of my eye, I see Taran move to the closest tent flap and look out, but I can't see the expression on his face, and I don't want to, anyway.

Suddenly there's a fanfare louder and more elaborate than any at the previous trials, and the huge crowd in the stands rises as one.

The masses of spectators lined up around the perimeter of the field begin jostling against the barricades, and it's all that the horde of veterans enlisted to help Brecelyn's men can do to keep them from spilling out into the field. The prince is coming.

Now all of the boys crowd around the tent flaps, too, eager to get a good look at him. I think only Gilles has ever seen the prince before, and maybe Aristide, and at his appearance, the cheers of the crowd are so loud that I can't hear the announcement of the names of all the members of his court. It doesn't matter, though. I wouldn't be paying attention, anyway. I'm too mesmerized by getting my first look at the prince, despite the fact that he really isn't terribly impressive. I can recognize him instantly from his splendid clothing and crown, but he's younger than I anticipated. He looks rather like one of the smaller squires who's been dressed up beyond his rank, but as I've said, it's all about expectations, so I'm as thrilled by the sight of him as the others. Beside the prince is an older man who would be impressive even in rags, and I also know instantly that this must be the regent, the prince's uncle Reynard. His thick mane of auburn hair and Roman profile remind me distinctly of Gilles, and I'm not surprised. These nobles usually are all related. It's also clear that he's really the one in charge, as he leads the prince to his seat and settles him in like he would a little child. For some reason, what I notice the most is that seated like that in the grandstands, the prince makes an awfully small mark. It would take an experienced marksman to hit him.

Tristan seems to be thinking along the same lines, because he surprises me by turning back into the tent and announcing loudly,

"Listen, boys. There's something important I've got to say." I think he's going to offer them all luck or make some encouraging speech, but instead when the boys have all turned to him, he says, "I can't explain, and there isn't time, anyway. But Marek and I have reason to think that there might be an attempt on the prince's life at some point during the day."

I can't believe it. Tristan seemed entirely unconvinced when I outlined my theory to him in the garden, and even a little scornful. I shoot him a covert glance to see if this is just one of his pranks, but he looks perfectly serious, and I notice that he both gave me credit for the idea and included himself in it so as not to leave me open to ridicule. I feel a surge of gratitude to him, for taking me seriously. He looks so dashing, standing there in his regalia warning the others, that I indulge in a romantic fantasy and imagine him as the captain of the Guard, ordering his men and leading them in the defense of the prince. With his charisma, he's perfect for the role.

At Tristan's pronouncement, all the boys have started talking at once, but to my amazement, none of them seems scornful, either. They're caught up in the atmosphere, too, and I have to admit, here with the prince looking so young and vulnerable and sitting in the open in a box amidst such a huge throng, my theory doesn't sound quite as ridiculous to me, either. Tristan puts up his hands for silence, and as the questions die down, he continues rapidly,

"What better place for an accident with a stray arrow, than here?"

Before he can continue, Taran cuts him off. "Don't tell me you think *I'm* going to try to kill the prince."

"Fortunately not! We all know you wouldn't miss! Besides, nobody ever *really* believed you'd shot me, did they, Marek?"

A small 'no' is all I can manage, looking fixedly at the ground. But Tristan hasn't waited for my answer.

"There isn't much time, so just be on the lookout, boys. Maybe we're wrong. I hope we are. But if we're not, well, we all want to be Guardsmen, right? We're all St. Sebastian's men, and that's what we've been training for, ultimately, isn't it — to protect the prince? But it won't be easy to spot. This place offers a lot of places to conceal an archer. So if we think we see anything suspicious, we tell each other, despite the trials. We work as one, agreed?"

I don't know if any of them believes what Tristan's been saying, but they all nod. The heady atmosphere's affecting all of us, I guess.

From across the field, Master Guillaume's voice booms out in the usual announcements and introductions, and Thirds is officially underway. At the sound, the boys disperse again to take up their bows and see to their final preparations, and I put a hand on Tristan's sleeve.

"I didn't think you believed me, Tristan. I might still be wrong."

"Frankly, I don't really know if I believe it or not, kid!" he says with a laugh, "But I wasn't kidding when I said I'd rather fancy myself the type to save a prince."

Tristan seems so relaxed, I don't want to jinx it, but I have to ask him about it. I'm a bundle of nerves myself, and this is the big prize. Losing out now, when he's so close to veteran status, would almost be worse than being cut at Firsts. I ought to know. Coming so close only to lose was thrown back in my father's face all his life, and seeing Tristan so calm makes me apprehensive.

"I'm not being defeatist, Marek, don't worry. It's just too late to worry now. It won't do any good. Between you, Baylen, and the Verbeke method, if I'm not ready now, I never will be. And it's not just that. No matter what, I want to go out and do it my way, and I can't do that tense and worried. I've done that twice, I'm not going to do that again. Now I'm going to go out there and show them all what I can do, and if it's not enough for them, well, it'll be enough for me."

And I think he really is ready. But I'm still a nervous wreck.

As the sound of Master Guillaume's voice introducing the judges drifts through the tent, the central flap flies open and Baylen strides in again.

"Men, this is it!" he says, rubbing his hands together and addressing the room. "I want you all to know, it has been a privilege to train with you, and I wish you all the best of luck." He then proceeds to make his way around the room, shaking hands with each Journey. This is the warmest and most encouraging he's ever been, and I can tell that the timing of it makes his words all the more meaningful to the boys. I secretly wonder if this is why he's never been very encouraging before, because he knows what an impression it will make now when it really matters.

To Gilles, he says, "You're on top, Lejeune. Stay that way."

"Pshaw. Oh, it's been fun to be in first," Gilles drawls modestly. "But we all know who'll be on top by the end of the day."

"You'll be through, that's what counts," he responds, and I notice with some distaste that he doesn't bother to disagree with Gilles. When he reaches us, Baylen takes Tristan's hand in a firm shake and says,

"You can go the distance out there, duBois. I'm looking forward to giving you a hard time next year, so don't deny me the pleasure."

"Does that mean you'll be staying on, to see the survivors through?" Tristan asks, smiling.

"If you can stand it, so can I!" he laughs, and slaps him on the back. To me, he says,

"Good luck to you, too, squire. I'll admit it. DuBois here may have surprised me, but you ..." he shakes his head. "Nobody's ever surprised me more, and I don't mean just about archery, either."

"Is that a compliment?" I ask, trying to look serious but smiling, too.

"Hell if I know!" he laughs, already moving on to the next boy.

We've all been eavesdropping, wanting to hear what Baylen has to say to each Journey, but when he makes his way to the corner of the tent where Jurian has been studiously bent over his equipment ever since Baylen entered, his back to everyone, we all pretend suddenly to busy ourselves over our own equipment. In reality, we're all eavesdropping even more.

Out of the corner of my eye, I see Baylen put his hand on Jurian's back and say something to him intently in a voice too quiet to be overheard. At first, Jurian refuses to turn around and tries to shrug off Baylen's hand, but as Baylen keeps talking insistently, eventually Jurian turns to him and Baylen pulls him into a close embrace. Neither of them seems to care that we're all watching, as Jurian clutches at Baylen desperately and Baylen puts his hand around the back of Jurian's head, pulling it down to his shoulder, then rests his own head heavily against Jurian's. Finally he gives Jurian one last tight squeeze and kisses him fiercely on the temple, and then he's gone. We didn't need to hear, though, to know what he was saying to Jurian. He was saying goodbye.

As soon as Baylen's gone, a new trumpet blast rings out, and it's time for the first test. It's the beginning of the end.

Tristan turns to me and slings the new, heavier bow I made for him over the past week up onto his shoulder. He asked me to make him one, and so of course I did, but this time I couldn't make it all by myself. It was too big, with too heavy a draw weight for me to work into its bend alone. Marcel gave me a strong piece of yew he had already seasoned and helped me tiller it into shape out in the shop, then I worked it down in concert with Tristan as he practiced with it, shaving down the belly as needed to get the proper draw. It's not as lovely as the first bow I made for him, but that's appropriate. Neither of us is really a clouter, and a clouter's bow is never going to be Tristan's weapon. Besides, it's not a beautiful bow that's going to get Tristan through Thirds. This is his day, to win or lose, with no crutches or tricks. He can't charm his way through today.

As he shoulders the bow, I shoulder Tristan's quiver and we take the field, emerging from the tent into the crisp October air to meet the roar of the crowd. Standing next to Tristan as the rest of the boys come out and join us on the line, it's Firsts all over again, and my emotions are the same as they were then, when I looked down the line at the Journeys and I loved them all. Only this time, it's not just a reaction to the moment. Now, it's really true. As I stand before the teeming crowd as one with them, with all of Ardennes watching, I think I wouldn't trade this one moment as a St. Sebastian's squire for a lifetime as Melissande.

The first test of any trial is usually the simplest, and today proves no exception. As Baylen directs us to our place on the line, I see two rows of small catapults down at the far end of the field in front of the façade of the castle. They're lined up parallel to each other and to the stands, to form a lane about 15 yards wide between them leading up to the castle entrance. Since the competition is taking place in front of Brecelyn's fortifications, the conceit is to make the tests look like military maneuvers in some vague way. That doesn't bother me. What does bother me is the distance. The whole set-up doesn't even begin until about 380 yards distant from where the Journeys are stationed, and that's clearly meant to mark the minimum point at which a shot will count. That's over 100 yards further than I've ever shot an arrow. Predictably, this test is going to be all about distance.

As I'm contemplating the set-up with disfavor, Baylen steps forward and in a loud voice addresses both us and the spectators.

"Gentlemen. For your first test, you will each shoot exactly one arrow. There is no mark. As long as the arrow hits anywhere within the lane delineated by the catapults, it will count. The longest shot will win. That's all there is to it. Squires," he adds, turning to us. "There will be no retrieval. Simply collect your Journey's arrow during the break between tests."

I should be happy that the performance of the squires is clearly not going to be crucial in the tests today. The distances are too far for retrievals, and it's fitting, too. This is the final competition, and it should come down to the skill of the boys, not of the squires. Instead, the whole set-up makes me distinctly nervous. First, because ever since we came out on the field, I've been feeling unaccountably vulnerable. It's occurred to me that if in fact my outrageous theory is right and there's to be an accident blamed on one of the boys, Tristan is likely to be the boy in question. Even though I'm not the intended victim, out on this vast, unfamiliar field, with all these eyes on us, I can't help but feel as though we're targets. Try as I might, I can't keep my eyes from darting to the judges' box, where I know Brecelyn is seated. Second, because the very first test is going to make or break Tristan. There's really little accuracy involved. It's time to see if he can go the distance or not, as Baylen said.

Once the boys start shooting, it becomes evident just how close the competition really is. The differences between them have always been small; they're the best of the best, after all, and they've been training together for months. But now we're down to the best boys, and I'm acutely aware that they all deserve to win. As the arrows start flying, they land so close together that it's hard to tell from here whose arrows go the furthest, they end up clustered so close together. In most cases, it looks to me to be a difference of feet, not yards, between them.

Aristide is up first, and his arrow sails an impressive 470 yards. He's followed by Charles, who betters him but by just a little. Next is Turk, whose arrow falls short of both of these. Gilles and Jurian both manage to edge out Charles, though from here it looks like Gilles is now in front, but it's a close thing. Then it's Tristan's turn.

Before he takes his shot, he turns his head to me and gives me one of his dazzling smiles, and something about the gleam in his eye makes me worry, so I blurt out,

"Tristan, don't fail with style!"

"No, Marek," he replies. "Today, I intend to *win* with style!," and he takes his shot.

As he does, I have a moment's qualm. Although he rocks back far onto his back leg into a real sit, he's doing a different motion than the pure clouter's move he's been working to perfect. Instead, it looks something like a combination of the move that Baylen and I tried to teach him and his old style, and I think it's going to be a disaster. Yet as he moves through a unique mixture of grace and power, I forget to worry about how far the arrow will fly. I'm too intent on watching him. He's made the motion into something high and light, he's infused it with his personality and made it his own, and it's as exhilarating as any shot he's ever taken. With a surge of pride, I realize he wasn't just spouting off earlier — he really is determined to win or lose shooting his own way. Without even looking down the field to see where the arrow lands, as soon as the arrow is away, I exclaim,

"What a beauty!"

"How's that for a little Verbeke flair?" he grins.

"No," I grin back. "That was pure duBois!"

Miraculously, when I finally look down the field, I see that his arrow has bettered Charles's, and it even looks to have equaled Jurian's. I'm so elated, even when Falko's arrow sails past the 500-yard mark, it can't dampen my joy. Tristan has bettered or equaled four of the boys!

Taran is to take his shot last, and I'm sure that can't be the luck of the draw. I'm sure Guillaume rigged the lots, to save Taran for last. Sure enough, when he steps up to the line and bends that massive bow of his, the stands fall quiet, and for the first time during any of the trials, I really watch him as he takes his turn. As soon as he releases his arrow it's clear he's going to outdistance them all, and the audience in the stands comes to its feet again. Even the prince rises to see just how far the arrow is going to go. But from the reverberating cries in the grandstands when the arrow lands, I think I must be the only one who isn't surprised that it surpasses even Falko's shot by at least 40 yards.

As we file back into the tent for the break between tests, the boys are all still busy congratulating Taran on his ridiculously long shot.

"I bet few of the Guardsmen could outdo it!" Gilles says with enthusiasm. "I bet they're all rethinking their exhibition right now," he chuckles.

"Might as well get comfortable, boys," Turk says, throwing his bow down and plopping heavily onto a stool next to his gear.

"They've got some serious entertainment planned between the tests, so we're likely to be in here quite a while."

I'm about to plop down somewhere myself, when Tristan pulls me aside.

"Come on, Marek. There's no time for resting now. We've got to find Pascal. I just hope this break is as long as Turk says."

"Tristan," I snap angrily, voicing the thoughts now that I didn't when Tristan first brought up his intention of returning Melissande's veil. "Everything we've been working for is on the line! After all the sacrifices we've made, how can you be thinking about anything else? I thought you were serious, when you told me you wanted to win!"

"I was serious, kid. I do want to win, and I'm determined to do it," he replies evenly. "But I also meant it when I said I won't let this trial get the best of me. What good will it to do sit here stewing, getting more and more nervous, while we wait for the next test? I want to do this thing with confidence and flair, or it's no good. I can't do that nervous, or if I overthink it. Besides, you saw what the promise of a kiss did for me at Firsts. Just think what an actual kiss will do!"

"It's damned risky, Tristan," I say sullenly.

"That's what's going to make it worth it!" he exclaims. "And after all, there's more to life than archery."

"Not for me," I mumble, but I dutifully follow Tristan over to where Gilles is already lounging on a camp stool, with Pascal and Armand chatting away behind him. Maybe Tristan is right. If this is to be a long break, sitting around worrying won't do us any good.

Without any preliminaries, Tristan begins to explain his plan to Pascal in a low voice, not caring that Gilles and Armand can hear the whole thing, but making sure none of the others do. I can't imagine what my face looks like once Tristan starts to outline his plan, but I'm sure an impressive parade of grimaces crosses my countenance. Before he can finish, Gilles puts up a hand.

"I'm sorry, old boy. I'm going to have to stop you right there. I really do wish you luck with your affairs, Tristan, but I'm afraid I can't let Pascal risk his neck for them." For a moment, I think Tristan is going to say something rude about how Gilles seemed perfectly willing to risk Pascal at Seconds. Instead, he says wistfully,

"I suppose you're right. I probably wouldn't let Marek risk his neck for your romances, either," and it occurs to me to mention that he seems perfectly willing to let me risk my neck for *his*, but I don't. "But it's too bad! It really was a beautiful plan."

"Why don't you do it yourself?" Gilles suggests, but Tristan shakes his head.

"It wouldn't be the same. Besides, Journeys aren't supposed to leave the tent between trials. As it is, I'll have to risk leaving once. Twice ... well, that'll sure to be noticed." But I think his first reason is the real one. He's modeling his return of the veil on my procuration of the rose, and he wants to stick to his original idea. To him, it's the one that's right, and I know he wants everything to be perfect, this time. Just when I think he's going to be disappointed (and I'm going to be unexpectedly saved), to my surprise, Armand says,

"What about me? To hell with Aristide. I'll do it." Just my luck, Armand turns out to be a budding romantic. I think he's been wanting to be in on some of Gilles's and Tristan's antics for a while now, but this is going to be quite an induction.

"Excellent!" Tristan cries. "There's no time to lose, then. Come on, boys!" and before I know it, Tristan is leading me and Armand over to where he has the Guard's cloak stowed with his gear. As Armand stuffs the cloak under his arm and hides it under his own cloak, Tristan slings his huge bow over my shoulder and helps me shove Melissande's veil up under my tunic.

"Remember not to give it to her now, just flash it so she sees it. You understand where to tell her to meet me?" he asks.

"Around behind the north tower, at the gazebo in the gardens," I say hollowly. Tristan apparently noticed the spot from the carriage, a place near the competition grounds but out of view, and just the kind of evocative place for a tryst.

"Be careful, boys," Tristan warns. "The Guards are going to be paying more attention to the royal box than to the ladies, and thankfully their box is quite a ways down from where most of the Guardsmen are stationed, but don't run any risks. If you think anyone is on to you, Armand, abandon the plan, ditch the cloak, and deny everything!"

We duck out of the tent as inconspicuously as we can, though nobody is paying much attention. Many of the squires have already left to bring back refreshments from the booths, so our departure goes unnoticed, I think. As soon as we're out of the tent, we go around a corner and Armand slips the Guardsman's cloak on over his own, pulling the hood up over his head so his face is in its shadow. He's tall enough to pass for a Guardsman, and surely nobody here can know them all. I may not be as convincing as a Guardsman's squire, but with Tristan's big bow and quiver slung over my shoulder, I hustle along with my head down a few paces behind Armand, who is now heading around the perimeter of the competition ground as quickly as he can. We're going to skirt around to the far end of the grandstands and cut onto the edge of the field down there, and then work our way back along the front of the bleachers. Hopefully this way we'll avoid most of the real Guardsmen and the judges' box.

Armand strides along quickly and purposefully, and at first nobody tries to stop us or question us. We have a moment's panic when another Guard hails us and asks Armand where he's going, but Armand keeps his head down, keeps going, and calls back in a gruff voice,

"Errand for Mellor," and the man doesn't question us further.

We make it all the way around the field and over to the bleachers before we run into trouble. Just as we're looking for a good place to attempt entry through the barricades, a man steps in front of me and grabs Armand from behind, hissing loudly in his ear,

"Just where do you think *you're* going, imposter?"

Armand jumps guiltily, and I know there's no hope. Armand isn't a good enough actor to pull off impersonating a Guardsman when confronted by an accuser, and there's nothing I can do. I'm just contemplating throwing myself on the man so Armand can make a run for it when the man suddenly slaps Armand on the back and laughs.

"Marek, what in the world is Tristan up to now?" he asks, turning to me, and I see — it's Jerome! He's made good on his word and come to watch us at Thirds. I should have noticed the lute slung over his shoulder.

"Jerome, you bastard!" I cry happily, as Armand bends over

gasping for breath in a very unGuardsman-like fashion. "How did you of all people spot us? And what in the blazes is that on your face?!"

Jerome's now slung one arm around Armand's shoulder and he's grinning at us broadly, while holding up to his face the strangest little contraption of wires and glass I've ever seen.

"It's a pair of *occhiale*! My father got them for me from a colleague in Italy. These little lenses of glass magnify everything. They're really for reading, but through these, I can see every shot you boys make! But even I could see through you two without any help from them. What on earth are you up to? You're going to be caught, for sure."

"Not if you keep your voice down!" I say, as Armand tries to recover from the shock. Armand's just not as used to this sort of shenanigan as I am, so I hasten to fill Jerome in while he composes himself, and after a minute or two, Jerome accompanies us, determined to help.

When we see a likely spot where only a few of Brecelyn's men are on guard, Jerome steps up to them, waves his lute around and starts asking for directions to the musicians' tent. It's ridiculously easy for us to cut in past the barricade and onto the field. The men are distracted by Jerome, but they simply stand aside for a Guardsman anyway without giving Armand a close look, and when I squeeze in with him, calling out *Master, wait for me!,* they don't seem to think anything of it.

Once we're inside the competition arena, though, I start to get nervous. We're not really out on the field, we're just skirting along the front edge of the bleachers, yet I feel exposed. Mercifully, nobody is paying any attention to us. Out on the field there are at least five different troupes of acrobats performing, and everyone is watching the dancing bears and fire jugglers, and Tristan was right: nobody looks beyond the cloak.

Unfortunately, these two things — the performers and the cloak — are what cause us some difficulty when we actually find ourselves at the foot of the box housing the ladies. None of them is paying any attention to us, either. We've been counting on the resemblance between Pascal and Armand to help us, but Melissande's handmaiden is so enthralled with the jugglers that we can't get her attention. It's Lady Sibilla who first notices our furtive gestures. She peers down at us inquisitively, and Armand pulls the hood of his cloak down off his head far enough for her to see something of his face. Then he points back and forth from Melissande and to me, and finally Sibilla prods Melissande in the side. After a few whispered comments pass between them, Melissande turns to look down at me. When I point to the scars on my face, recognition and surprise cross her face, and I quickly pull the veil a little ways out from under my tunic, just far enough for her to see what I've got. Seeing it, she flashes me a shy smile, and I start pointing urgently at her handmaiden and then back to the end of the bleachers. After a while, she nods tentatively and I hope we've communicated successfully, because we're beginning to get some strange stares from some of the Guardsmen down by the royal box, and it's time for us to go.

Armand and I beat a hasty retreat, and as soon as we're past the barricade, Armand pulls the Guardman's cloak off his head and shoves it under his own cloak, relieved. When Melissande's girl shows up I make short work of arranging the rendezvous for the next break, and after a few hasty words to Jerome, we head back to the Journey tent in triumph. I think we did have some idea of returning the cloak to the Guards' tent, but in the end we simply leave it in a wad on the ground near the tent flap, unwilling to risk actually tossing it inside.

When we cross back into the Journey tent and we know we're safe, we both start laughing so hard, I know all the boys can figure out we've been up to one of Tristan's tricks, but I don't care. I was right. It was damned risky, and I'm just so relieved that we pulled it off. The thing that *does* bother me, though, is just how easy it was for us to get onto the field in disguise, and within a stone's throw of the royal box. The idea that a bunch of boys could really do anything to protect the prince in all this throng if someone is determined to harm him is patently ludicrous.

Tristan and Gilles have been waiting anxiously for our return, and as both Armand and I talk over each other describing our exploits to them, I can sense the other boys trying to listen in. It's just as Tristan said. They've all been waiting in here with nothing to do but get increasingly nervous, and they're eager for some diversion. Tristan seems more relaxed than the others as he listens with delight to our recitation and to the news that Jerome is here, so maybe the whole scheme was worth it, I think, if it took his mind off the next test.

We've just about managed to get the whole story out without letting the others hear when Aristide catches sight of Armand and comes bustling over.

"There you are, blast you! Where have you been?" he exclaims, but in his haste, he stumbles and has to clutch Armand's arm for support. "Oof! Watch your gear, Mellor! Get this blasted parcel out of the way. I keep tripping over it."

At the reminder of the mysterious package from Taran's father, Falko calls out,

"Come on, Taran! Aren't you ever going to open that? What can it be ... a Guardsman's cloak, already? Ha."

The four of us smirk to ourselves, thinking how surprised Falko would be if he knew we'd just had one in our possession, but Taran just bends to pick up the package calmly.

"It can wait," he says again maddeningly, just as before. Only this time Remy reaches out for the bag in that innocent way he has, and before Taran can stop him, he squeaks in delight,

"Oh, Taran, I know what it is! It must be the new ... *er, the other,* gift!," and before Taran can say anything, he's opened the bag and he's pulling out a length of shimmering fabric.

Everybody is watching now, and in particular, Gilles and Tristan exchange a glance over my shoulder.

"*Another* bridal gift?" Aristide drawls. "My, my, what ardor! What is it, a veil?"

"Somehow," Taran replies, looking up straight at Tristan, "I thought she could use a new one."

So he did notice. The veil still barely concealed in a bulge under my tunic now feels entirely conspicuous, and I wonder if our antics have really gone as undetected as I thought. I wonder even more what kind of message this new gift is meant to send to the bride.

I try valiantly to look uninterested as Remy pulls the veil from the satchel and spreads it out so Aristide can see it.

"Very pretty," Aristide declares, putting out a hand to feel the fabric. "Expensive, too, I'll wager."

He never misses a chance to talk about money. But he's right. I can see even out of the corner of my eye that it is pretty. As Aristide holds it up, I drop all pretense and gawk openly at the veil. I can't help myself. It's a light sea-foam green, the color of the dress Melissande wore for Seconds, and it's so thin, I can see Aristide's hand through it. It's shot through with fine gold threads in a random pattern, yet as I stare at it, they seem to resolve into figures that slip away when I try to focus on them. I can almost make out knights and ladies, with banners flying as though at a tournament, but I can't tell if it's just my imagination. The lines are so abstract yet suggestive that I'm reminded of the figures Taran carves, where he indicates so much with so little. It's a ridiculous comparison, since Taran can't be responsible for this. He can't have picked it out himself, or even ever have seen it before.

But there it is. Unlike the flimsy thing with the simpering pink rosebuds still stuffed under my tunic, this veil is absolutely beautiful.

"So you do appreciate a lovely face, after all," Aristide is saying, still fingering the fringe of the veil, "to want to set it off with something as stunning as this. You know, you never did tell us, Mellor," he muses. "That day. You were going to tell us just what it is you find more compelling than beauty."

I suddenly find it impossible to pretend not to be interested. My ears are burning. To cover my confusion, I turn to busy myself with Tristan's quiver, waiting nervously to hear if Taran's going to answer.

"That was a long time ago," he says quietly, and to my frustration, I'm sure he's going to avoid answering, again. "I'm sure I can't remember what I might have been going to say, what I might have thought, then."

"He wasn't going to say anything, boys," Tristan calls out dismissively, staring at the beautiful veil with a frown on his face. "He was just bluffing. Trying to sound superior." Then he adds in a taunting tone, "Or if he did have some answer in mind, he remembers it, I'm sure. He's just afraid to tell us, for fear we'll laugh at him. Am I right?"

A tense silence falls over the tent as the boys wait anxiously to see if Taran is going to rise to the bait. Everyone's nerves are so raw, we all half expect a fight to break out, but after a moment in which Taran seems to be debating with himself and coming to some decision, finally he slowly turns to Tristan and responds deliberately,

"You're right about one thing. I do remember. But I'm no coward." He takes a deep breath, then says carefully, looking fixedly down at the veil in Aristide's hands in front of him:

"What do I find more attractive than a lovely face? I was going to say ... a defiant look."

"Whatever's the matter, Marek?" Tristan says sharply, as I give an involuntary cry of surprise.

"I've caught myself on the tip of an arrow," I mumble.

"Do be careful, kid."

But it's much too late for that.

At just this moment, the fanfare for the second test blasts through the tent. As I'm gathering up Tristan's equipment with trembling hands, Remy puts a hand on my back.

"Are you sure you're all right, Marek?" he asks solicitously. "You really should remember, even the smallest of barbs can be dangerous."

Don't I know it.

CHAPTER THIRTY-EIGHT

A s I follow Tristan back out onto the field for the second test, I don't know what I'm feeling. As I step up to the line, I find myself searching out Melissande in the stands. If Tristan has anything to say about it, she's going to get two veils today, and I've just helped him arrange to accomplish it. Looking at her now, I know Taran's is the veil that best fits the picture she makes, glowing like an exquisite vision in gold. But I suspect she's going to enjoy the process of getting her old, soiled veil back from Tristan more. I can't help but wonder which veil she'll value most. It's a harder choice than I once would have thought.

The sound of Baylen's voice describing the next test wrenches my attention out of the stands and back to the field, where it should be.

"Men, our second exercise will test both accuracy and speed at long range. You each have fifteen arrows, and before you, you each have three marks four spans wide, set at increasing distances from the line." I look down the field to see three large, white cloth-marks about three feet in circumference lying flat on the ground in front of each Journey. The first mark is at 350 yards distant, the second at 400, and the third at 450. "You have one minute to loose fifteen arrows, dropping five arrows down onto each mark. Time will be measured on a water clock at the judges' bench. At my command, you may begin. When time is called, you must cease fire. You may shoot at the marks in any order you wish. Understood?"

Again, there's nothing for us squires to do but watch. I've lined up Tristan's arrows point down in the ground ready to hand, but that's all I can do for him. All my agitation and confusion over other matters disappears, or rather it transforms and merges with my anxiety over the test, and as Baylen cries out *"Fire!,"* I'm a mass of nerves.

But I've underestimated Tristan. I guess I've never seen him shoot in competition when he didn't have some handicap to hold him back; today he really is ready, and competition always brings out the best in him. Watching as he pulls the arrows smoothly from the ground and lets them fly, I'm taken back to the day on the butts when I saw him shoot for the first time and thought him the most beautiful archer I'd ever seen. His grace and style are there, but he's stronger now, and his accuracy doesn't fail him. As I watch him now through the eyes of a crowd seeing him for the first time, his form looks to me to have more beauty than ever before. He hits the white with all five arrows on the nearest mark, with four on the middle mark, and he even puts three in the mark at 450 yards. What's more, he does it so fast, he's done with time to spare. It's a fantastic showing. I haven't been watching the others, but this performance has to pull him up in the ranks, and I don't know what makes me happier: that Tristan's on his way to passing, or that he so clearly deserves to.

Back in the Journey tent, I'm immensely relieved. Not only did Tristan do extremely well, but the second test passed without incident. My idea of a plot at Thirds seems increasingly unlikely, and only one test stands between Tristan and all my goals for him. Tristan himself is elated, and at first I think it's entirely because of his performance on the field. Then I remember what he's got planned for this interval. He's going to get his prize.

"Coming, kid?" he whispers to me almost as soon as we're back inside. "I might need someone to run a little interference."

"Why not?" I agree. After all, this is part of what I wanted to win for him, too, isn't it? If it's got to happen, I might as well be part of it. Besides, Tristan was right. With only one test left, I can't bear the thought of sitting in the stifling tent through the long interval with nothing to do but feel the tension mounting.

As Tristan opens the front flap and makes to exit with me on his heels, Aristide says, "Just where do you think you're going, duBois?" and all eyes turn to us.

"Just going to relieve myself," he says smoothly, but Aristide won't drop it.

"You need your squire for that?" he sneers.

"I can't let Gilles be the only one who has an entourage to the lavatory!" Tristan replies with a grin, and at that, Armand pops up and exclaims,

"One's not an entourage. I'm coming with you!" Armand clearly wants to witness the results of his earlier efforts. Tristan's been a terrible influence on him, too! Before Aristide can object, Armand is ducking out of the tent, while Pascal calls out,

"Wait for me!" and much to the amusement of the other boys, we all rush outside in Tristan's wake. Poor Pascal's been feeling left out, and now that there's no danger for him, Gilles can't object. He's not going to miss out on any more of Tristan's stunts.

"You know, boys, I wasn't really planning to have such a large audience for this," Tristan says as we follow him quickly around the grandstands.

"Don't let it put you off," I say sarcastically.

"On the contrary! I'm sure it will spur me to greater heights," he says, and I don't doubt it.

As we circle around behind a protruding tower of the castle, a small garden nestled up against the castle wall comes into view. It's so tucked away I'm surprised Tristan noticed it, but then he must have been watching carefully from the carriage for a likely spot for a rendezvous. I see instantly that it really is perfect. Though it's October and only a few flowers are in bloom, the formal little garden is lovely, but it's the folly at the center that must have caught Tristan's eye. It's an elaborate wooden affair, set high enough off the ground to require a set of steps leading up to the platform that serves as its floor. A series of arches form wide openings before rising to meet in a circular domed roof. The whole thing is whitewashed and trailing with vines.

Melissande is already there. She's settled herself in one of the openings so that she's framed prettily by one of the arches, her long hair loose around her shoulders and mingling with the vines. I notice she's come prepared to play her part. She's taken off the veil she was wearing earlier, in anticipation. She looks just like a damsel poised on a balcony for a love scene in a stage play, and I guess she is.

When we near, Tristan pulls me aside.

"Marek, let's really do this right. You approach first, and soften her up. You know, sort of give me an introduction."

It's the chapel all over again, but I don't object. I wanted to be part of it, didn't I? At least, this way I can share it in. It's the only way I'll ever share in a romantic tryst, so I might as well try to enjoy it. As Tristan conceals himself with Pascal and Armand, I step up below the gazebo and clear my throat.

"M'lady, do you remember me?" I call up, in my best dramatic voice. Melissande gazes down at me rather fondly, and for a moment I can't speak. She really is stunning, and standing there looking down at me from among the vines, she's perfect. I can't imagine what it would be like to be that beautiful. I suddenly wonder if Tristan didn't send me out before him because even he's intimidated to confront so much beauty.

"Marek, isn't it? Of course I remember you. How could I forget?" She gives a little laugh, a sweet, tinkling sound that hovers on the breeze. I stand there stupidly listening to it, as transfixed by her as Tristan ever was.

"It's my master," I say at length, recovering myself. "He begs an audience, mistress. To thank you, for your kindness, and to return something to you, if you'll have it."

"And where is your master, pray?" she laughs gently.

"He dares not show himself until he knows he's welcome, lest he transgressed against your courtesy when last you met, and until he knows you'll accept what he has to offer."

"And what is it that he's offering, little squire?"

"He wants to return what you so kindly lent him, but not quite as you left it! Now, it's soaked with his heart's blood, poured out for you! Let him return it to you, as an emblem of what he really has to give you... his whole heart! Take it, mistress, for you already have its blood, so away from you, it can no longer beat!"

Okay, it's pretty sappy, but it's the best I can do. Melissande seems to like it, though, and as an answer, she blushes and nods her head. Seeing her nod from his vantage point in the bushes,

Tristan leaps out, and accordingly I recede back into the shadows of the vines at the base of the gazebo where I belong. I take it as a compliment to me that Tristan doesn't bother to add any of his own blandishments to my speech. He strikes a pose under the balcony and fixes Melissande with a searing gaze, then proceeds to climb up the vines to reach her, even though there's a staircase right there.

As I watch from under the vines, he unwraps her veil from where he's fastened it around his waist, throws it over her shoulders, and pulls her to him with it. Dry leaves are scratching my face and thorns catching in my hair, but I don't feel any of it. All I can feel is the hollow place where my own heart should be, and this time, when their lips meet, it's in a kiss that shivers down the vines and tingles along my skin from my toes to my fingertips, more vividly than any lick of Jurian's. It's everything he could want, I'm sure. It's perfect. But try as I might, I can't be happy for him.

At just this moment, before I can feel too sorry for myself, lady Sibilla steps out from behind the gazebo. Apparently Tristan wasn't the only one to come to this tryst with an entourage. By this time Pascal and Armand have come out of hiding and they're standing next to me, blatantly watching Tristan and Melissande, too, with wistful looks on their faces, and she catches us completely by surprise.

"So what about it, boys? Any of you fancy a kiss?" she demands boldly.

Before I know it, Pascal's scampered off with a yelp, while Armand and I fall over each other trying to step backward. Only Armand isn't fast enough. Sibilla reaches out and grabs him with a scornful glance at Pascal's retreating form, and saying "I suppose *you'll* have to do!," she pulls him into an embrace. At first poor Armand is so shocked he just stands there stock still while she plants a big kiss on his mouth, but when after a moment she steps back and moves to release him, with a little cry of surprise he suddenly catches her back up enthusiastically, twines his hands through her hair, and gives her back just as good as he got. I have to admit, I really am becoming quite fond of lady Sibilla.

When Tristan finally climbs back down to where I'm standing rather awkwardly at the foot of the gazebo, we have to pry Armand's hands from around Sibilla's neck and drag him off, and even then he looks quite stunned. In fact, he looks almost as stunned as Tristan. I don't bother to ask Tristan if the kiss met his expectations this time. From the looks of him, it's evident that he finally got a kiss extraordinary enough even for him.

As we make our way back, I try to shake a deep sense of sadness that threatens to envelope me, and not just for the obvious reason. I can just imagine what Pascal is going to have to say to the squires back in the barracks tonight about Armand's encounter, and it hurts that I won't be there to hear it. To make up for it, I make a few half-hearted attempts to tease Armand about it now, but we're moving so fast and he's still so distracted that it's too hard and I give up. In fact, the actual tryst has taken us a lot longer than the arranging of it, and so as we skirt back around the grandstands, the musicians and dancers who have been performing are already making their way off the field. We get back just in time, and as we step into the tent through the front flap, Baylen bursts in through one of the flaps facing the field. A moment later, and Tristan would have been caught out. As it is, we have no time to recover from our outing before the final test is upon us.

"All right, boys," Baylen says gravely. "Guillaume's about to start. For this last test, you'll be called out one at a time. Squires: bring just one arrow. Your biggest, heaviest bodkin point."

He doesn't have to tell us why. I'm pretty sure we can all guess the nature of the final test. Bodkin points are known for their ability to penetrate armor.

"Can you give us any sense of the standings so far?" Charles asks nervously, and Baylen hesitates. I'm sure he isn't really supposed to tell us anything, but we all crowd around him anxiously, and he relents.

"I'm sure you can all tell who's ahead, but ... for those of you near the bottom, it's a close thing. I'm afraid, as far as I can tell, it's pretty much going to come down to this last single shot. So make it count."

This statement is met with complete silence. Master Guillaume really knows how to put on the pressure. It's outrageous. Cruel, even. How can all our months of training and practice come down to one shot? Even Baylen looks distressed, and when I glance at Tristan, he's looking down with a frown on his face. Despite all his efforts at distraction, the stress of it all is finally getting to him, as the enormity of what's riding on this last shot sinks in.

"Guillaume's making his final announcements out there, so it won't be long now," Baylen says, wishing us all good luck one last time and disappearing out onto the field again. But the boys are all too numb to say anything, and since Baylen's departure they've been standing around in a group looking at each other in silence. It's so quiet that I can hear Guillaume droning on in his usual fashion in the distance, and I know Baylen was right. It won't be long now.

"Might as well get ready, boys," Falko finally says, turning to his equipment and pulling out a long arrow. He gives it an exaggerated kiss, and says heartily, "Come on and do it for me, baby!" with one of his crude gestures, and this finally breaks the tension. As the boys laugh and turn to attend to their own gear, I notice Taran fingering an arrow of his own with a frown. He can't really be worried, but I remember what Tristan said before Firsts, that anything can happen in a competition.

I know the fanfare calling us out to the field will come at any moment, but I realize that there is one last thing I've got to do, if there's time. I was wrong in the alley the other day. I haven't yet ended things on the right note with Taran. So while Tristan is busy fastening his cloak back onto shoulders, I slip down to the other end of the tent. Remy's gone to peek out the tent flap, and Taran is now standing facing the tent wall, running his hand lightly over his bow. I come up behind him and clear my throat nervously. When he turns around, I put out my hand to him.

"I'd wish you good luck, but you don't need it," I say solemnly, offering him my hand to shake.

He looks quite surprised, and the slight frown that was creasing his forehead deepens as he takes my hand and shakes it, quite gently, for him.

"Why are you saying this, now?" he asks, not letting go of my hand.

"Because despite what you may think to the contrary," I say, mimicking the words he said to me in the alley, "I do think you have honor …" I hesitate, but now it's time for the truth. After all, this is my goodbye to him, so what does it matter? I might as well acknowledge to myself the real reason I've hated him so much all this time, and been attracted to him, too, ever since that first day I watched him shoot. "Besides," I admit grudgingly. "You're the best."

I drop his hand suddenly and turn to go, but he grabs my hand back quickly and says urgently,

"That's not what I mean. I mean, why *now*? Just what are you planning to do? Look, Wood ... uh, Marek ... Damn!" he breaks off and runs his other hand through his hair. "I can't call you that! It can't really be your name."

"Everything all right?" a solicitous voice says behind me, and Taran instantly drops my hand as Remy sidles up, an inquisitive look on his face.

"Fine," I say, not feeling very fine at all. "Just wishing you both luck," I say, as the fanfare blasts, and I have to scurry to get back to Tristan.

Turk is called out to the field first. Although his shot can only really take a matter of minutes, it feels like an eternity as we wait for him to reappear. We're all lined up ready to take the field, even though no one can see us, and although it would be easy, nobody tries to watch through the flaps of the tent. We're so silent that I even think I hear the crack of the bow as Turk takes his shot, though it must be my imagination. From the smattering of applause from the audience that finally rings out, it's obvious to us Turk's arrow didn't do it for him, but when he bursts back into the tent, he looks mostly relieved. He knew he wasn't going to pass, and at least now it's over.

As Guillaume's voice cries out *"Aristide Guyenne!,"* Aristide takes a deep breath and follows Armand out of the tent, and Jurian asks Turk nervously,

"Just what is the test, Percival?" It's the first time any of them have ever used Turk's proper name, yet somehow, it sounds right. I think Jurian means it to be respectful, but it's appropriate. Turk's not really one of the boys now. He's not a Journey anymore.

"There's a dummy in a suit of armor set up on the ramparts of the castle. You know — the full deal. Mail, plate, helmet. The distance isn't marked, but it's damned far! Well over 400 yards, I'd say. You've got one arrow to give it a killing shot. I didn't even hit the cursed thing! My arrow bounced off the parapet a few feet away. It was pretty ugly," he admits, with a bitter laugh. Nobody says anything, and we all pretend not to see his squire Andre sit down in a corner and begin weeping openly.

It's not long before a cheer goes up and Aristide comes back in, looking more pleased.

"Got it in the leg," he tells us, as Jurian is called out. Even though each Journey's turn is short, it's interminable waiting through them, particularly since we have no idea of the order in which we're to be called out. We have to wait through Jurian, Gilles, and Charles before it's finally Tristan's turn, and the knowledge that they all hit the target doesn't help. Charles hit an arm, and Jurian and Gilles both got it somewhere on the legs. Tristan's got to make a decent hit to pass, since there's no chance Falko or Taran will miss.

Our walk out to the line is the longest of my life. Time seems to slow down around me, and as I lead Tristan out, I relive all the months since my father's death in my mind: the night in the brewery and the morning Marek was born there with the cut of a knife, my beating in the alley, and Tristan's appearance on the garden wall. All the long days of drilling, practicing, and making Tristan's equipment in the shop. I see myself on my knees in the chapel of St. Sebastian, vowing to see him through Thirds or die trying. I see it all again, and over all of it, I see Tristan smiling down at me. It's all come down to this.

I stop at the line, and Tristan steps up next to me. Whatever happens, this is going to be the last time I stand on the line with him. I try to block out the sight of the hundreds of faces watching us from the stands and the sounds of the calls and cheers that fill the air, and imagine we're back at St. Sebastian's, practicing alone together. I know I should be making this a performance for the crowd, but I can't do it. Ironically, this is my last minute alone with Tristan. When I take out the single arrow from his quiver and hand it to him, he sees the tears in my eyes. Taking the arrow, he nocks it, but doesn't raise his bow. For once, he isn't paying any attention to the crowd, either. Instead, he says to me quietly,

"This is it, Marek. Any words of encouragement? You always know what to say."

I don't have anything ready, and I know I should be quick. The audience is waiting. But I'm going to have my say, anyway. Let the prince wait.

"You don't have anything to prove to me, Tristan. To me, you've already won. You did my father's trick. You redeemed him, for me. But now you can win for yourself what was robbed from him, so long ago. We've worked hard, both of us, together, and we *are* a team. Only it's up to you, now. They're all watching you: all of Ardennes, your father, Taran, Melissande, and even our prince. But don't do it for any of them. Do it for me. Do it for him. And do it for yourself. Use that style that's a combination of us all, and give that dummy of Brecelyn's a fatal wound!"

Tristan smiles down at me, that dazzling smile I imagined just moments ago, and does something completely unexpected.

"You're right, little brother. It's time we won," he says, as he takes one hand from his bow and pulls me to him briefly, putting his hand on the back of my neck and resting his head lightly on the top of mine before planting a kiss on my temple, just as Baylen did to Jurian.

I'm still dazed as he quickly steps back, raises his bow in one swift, thrilling movement, and lets his arrow fly. I'm soaring, too, as the arrow rips through the air to lacerate the effigy on the wall.

Tristan's shot it, right through the heart.

I let out such a shout that it can be heard even over the noise of the crowd, as Tristan falls to his knees in a prayer of thanks to the saints who saw him through. Even I no longer doubt that both Sebastian and Margaret are on his side today, and I don't even care if it was Melissande's kiss that gave him the confidence to pull it off. With that shot, he's got to have made it through. He's sure to pass. He's a veteran of St. Sebastian's now.

Tristan tucks his medals swiftly back into his tunic after giving them a fervent kiss, and rises to acknowledge the resounding cheers of the audience. Before we turn to head back to the Journey tent, he lifts me up and twirls me around exuberantly, unable to contain his joy. We burst back into the tent grinning like idiots, and we don't have to tell the boys for them to know he's outdone himself. As Falko is called out to take his turn, the others crowd around to congratulate us, and I'm so moved by the generosity of the boys that the atmosphere in the tent that was stifling a few minutes ago now seems like a warm glow.

As the sound of renewed cheers meets our ears a few minutes later and Falko reappears with a beaming smile, I'm the first to clasp him in a congratulatory embrace. Once again, Guillaume's saved the boys destined to do the best on this test to the end, and Falko didn't disappoint. He got the dummy in the throat. It takes me a minute to realize that somehow, old Guillaume knew Tristan was going to pull it off, to have placed him so close to the end.

There's only one Journey left to shoot, and this time, when Taran is called out to the field, none of us stays in the tent. We're probably not supposed to, but we all follow him out, and as he and Remy make their way to the line, we line ourselves up in front of the Journey tent to watch. It's not just that his is to be the last shot of the competition, of the whole year of competitions. It's because we all want to see him make the shot that's going to win it all for him. None of us doubts that he's going to do it. We all know exactly what he's going to do. After all, Taran isn't one for empty boasts. But I want to see the shot for myself, the one that will make him the undisputed master of the Journeys. And just like Falko, he doesn't disappoint. He doesn't even bother to go all the way to the line. He stops about 60 yards out, and raises his huge bow in that inimitable motion of his, the one that lets everything in him fly. I share in the exhilaration along with everyone else, as all of Ardennes comes to its feet to watch as he sends his arrow through the narrowest of slits in the helmet's visor, to stick straight in the dummy's eye.

Back in the tent, it's pandemonium. The boys are all wild, worse even than when they're drunk, and I feel just as light-headed. Everyone is talking all at once and without listening, boasting and congratulating each other in equal measure, and I've started going around hugging everyone shamelessly. It's wonderful to have a perfect excuse. I think I hug Pascal at least four times. Tristan's just lifted me up onto his shoulders and started parading me around the tent when Baylen appears, hauling what looks like a big metal cauldron, at the sight of which a cheer goes up from the Journeys. Tristan pulls me down and puts me on my feet again, and he starts to unpin his cloak, while all the other Journeys begin to strip eagerly, too.

"What's all this?" I laugh, and Gilles explains. "It's branding time, again!" Apparently veterans get a second arrow, on the other arm, and Baylen's going to give it to them right here.

"You wanted to know if it hurt. Watch and see!" Falko says happily. "If girls like one, they're going to love two!"

Baylen's started to kindle a fire in the big brazier, and I now see that he was carrying the arrow brand under the other arm. As the coals heat, he pulls Charles aside, and from the look on their faces, I know what they're saying. In my excitement for Tristan, it didn't occur to me to wonder which of the other Journeys didn't make it, and now I can't believe it. Charles, who was to me the quintessential Journey, is out. The others are too busy pulling off their shirts and stripping down to notice, but suddenly the celebration in the tent seems all wrong.

Charles quickly ducks out of the tent, with Henri close on his heels, and I don't blame them. I can't imagine what it would be like, to watch as the others go through this bonding rite that will mark him as an outsider. But it pulls me up short, too. The competition is over. Tristan's made it. My vow to him is complete, I've fulfilled my purpose at St. Sebastian's, and now, while the others are all preoccupied, it would be the perfect time to go. Nobody would miss me. Charles isn't the only outsider now. It's time for me, too, to leave.

I cast a last look around the tent at all of them, wanting to remember them as they are now, laughing and smiling, the young and radiant Journeys as my father described them, with 'that certain something.' He was right — they all have it. As I make that one last scan of all their faces, my eyes meet Taran's across the tent. He's looking at me with a curious expression on his face, and I suddenly remember that I told him I was planning to leave right after Thirds.

I must look guilty, because he frowns, and starts to push past Aristide as though he might be trying to come over to me. I'm not sure why he would, but I can't let him stop me, if that's what he intends. He decides for me. There's no time for more goodbyes, and I've said my goodbyes already, anyway. There's never going to be a better time, and it's never going to be easy. So I slip out of the tent as quickly as I can, and as soon as I'm out among the booths, I break into a run, heading for the forest's edge.

When I near the place that I emerged from the woods on the day of the hunt, I slow my pace. Nobody's following me. I was wrong. Nobody is going to try to keep me from leaving. I know where I am, too. Brecelyn's chapel of St. Sebastian is only a little ways down the path leading into the woods that stretches out in front of me. It would be an easy thing to hide there tonight, and then make my way through the woods at my leisure tomorrow. Only somehow, I can't make myself step into the woods.

I'm hesitating, looking back over my shoulder at the scene of the competitions, when I notice Charles and Henri. They've also separated themselves from the crowd, and they're actually not far from the little garden where Tristan got his kiss not long ago. Charles is leaning heavily up against the castle wall, and Henri has his arm around Charles's shoulder. I know he's taking it hard. Unlike Turk, Charles had every hope of passing. I probably shouldn't intrude on their disappointment, but I can't help myself. Charles was my first Journey, and I can't leave without saying something. So I backtrack, and as I approach them, I cough loudly, since Charles is bent over with his head hanging down, and Henri is leaning in to whisper something consoling in his ear.

"Sorry to intrude," I say, giving Charles a hesitant smile when he raises his head at the sound of my voice. "But you look like you could use a friend."

He has the grace to smile back. "Thanks, Marek. But the better men won. Tristan was brilliant today."

I acknowledge his graciousness with a nod, though I can't help looking sad. Seeing my expression, Charles adds,

"It's okay, Marek. It hurts, but it was to be expected. I've never been one of the stars of St. Sebastian's."

"You have been, to me," I say, putting out my hand to each of them in turn, and we shake.

I wonder what Charles would say, if I told him how I felt the first time I saw him, standing there on the landing, his arm raised in greeting, a single curl of hair brushing his collar.

As I move away, I have no more excuses to delay. I can't put it off any longer. Yet as I reach the edge of the woods again, I still can't make myself go in. It has to be now, I tell myself. If I can't leave now, at this culminating moment, when Tristan's won and he's on top, when I've reached my goals for him, I'll never be able to do it. How can I stay any longer, and risk exposure at every turn? How can I bear to keep standing in the vines, watching while Tristan claims his prizes? How can I stand one more second of that little space that's between us? That's what it all comes down to. How can I stand either to leave Tristan, or to stay with him? Both are intolerable.

I know I was right to determine to leave. It's what I've got to do. It's what's best for Tristan, and for me. I promised the saint I'd leave after Thirds, and I refuse to risk disgracing the guild. But I think of the apprentice trials starting, and of Tristan looking for me. I think of my cot, standing empty in the barracks, of Tristan's cabinet in disarray, and of Tristan himself, trying to figure out why I left him. Most of all, I think of never seeing him again, and I know I've been right all along. I've been fooling myself. I'll never leave him willingly. How can I?

I sink to my knees, facing the direction of the little chapel of St. Sebastian that I know lies not far out of view, and I say the most fervent prayer I've ever prayed, begging the saint to help me. As tears stream down my face, I ask him to help me find the strength to leave.

"Help me, Sebastian! Help me do what I can't do alone."

When all my tears are spent, I rise shakily, and I do feel some renewed strength. The saint has renewed my purpose, I think. Yet when I start to move, despite myself I find that I'm running in the opposite direction, away from the woods, and back toward the competition grounds. Back to Tristan. It's not what I intend, but I can't stop myself. New tears of frustration start flowing down my cheeks, but I can't seem to turn around. I don't stop. I just run faster. Maybe I can get back before he even notices I'm gone. Maybe I won't even miss seeing him get his veteran's brand. Maybe I will bring St. Sebastian's down around me, brick by brick. It doesn't matter. Nothing is going to keep me away. When it all crashes down, I'm going to be with Tristan in the rubble. I'm staying with him to the bitter end, even if I have to suffer through witnessing a hundred kisses to do it.

As I near the north tower, a flash of light coming from up on the ramparts momentarily blinds me and I stumble to a stop. I drop instantly to my knees, filled with dread and awe at the apparition. I know what it is! It's an epiphany. Saint Sebastian is answering my prayer. He's appearing at last, to help me leave.

I'm so grateful, so relieved, I call out the saint's name in fervent thanks, and I put up one hand to shield my eyes from the dazzling light, to see if I can see the saint's form, wanting to see again that glorious boy rent with rays of light that appeared to me on the guild wall. As I do, the light disappears, only to flash out again a moment later.

It's no vision. It's the sun glinting off metal. Someone is moving up on the tower.

It must be one of Brecelyn's men, stationed up there overlooking the grandstands as extra security. But it's odd that there would be only one man. As I'm getting to my feet, I hear trumpet blasts coming from the arena, and after a moment's confusion, I realize what they must herald. The Guard is taking the field for its exhibition. I'm going to have to hurry to get back before my absence is detected, but I waver. Even if it wasn't really the saint, that light was a sign, a warning. I look back over my shoulder to the darkness of the forest, a bleak black expanse stretching out before me. That light was a reminder, and the saint is right. It's time for me to leave, and I know I've got to make myself go. I want to do it, I really do. Still I can't bring myself to turn back to those woods.

I'm in an agony of indecision, torn again between my duty and my desires, unable to bring myself to move either forward or back, when another fanfare rings out and the light flashes out from the tower again. Finally, I put the obvious together. The Black Guard is about to perform, with its shower of arrows. So many that they blot out the sky, as Armand said. A lone figure, concealed on the tower, with something metal glinting in the sun: a weapon. *Of course!* Why didn't I think of it before? Gilles was right. It would be hard to disguise the origin of an arrow during the Journey competitions, but during the Guards' exhibition, so many arrows will be flying, nobody will notice the origin of one more.

Unbelievably, my wild theory was right. And it's all going to happen right now.

All my indecision is swept away, and if I was running hard before, now I'm virtually flying. I race around the end of the grandstands, not caring who or what I knock over on my way. When I barrel into the Journey tent to the smell of burnt flesh and to Aristide's loud bellowing as Baylen applies the brand to his arm, I'm so out of breath I can barely gasp out my news to Tristan. He's already been branded, and he's standing nearby bare-chested and nursing his arm. I was right. He hadn't noticed I was gone.

"A man!" I wheeze. "On the tower." Another wheeze. "A weapon."

"Oh there you are, Marek. Wherever have you been? What are you on about? Hey, watch the arm!" Tristan says, as I clutch him for support and try to catch my breath.

"There's no time to explain! It's happening, just as I said! Follow me!" I pick up his discarded shirt and throw it at him, then dart toward the entrance again. It's almost as an afterthought that I call back to him, "and bring your bow!"

I'm in such a panic that I don't even remember to grab up my own bow, and I don't look back to see if Tristan is following. He's faster than I am; he can catch up. Instead, I run full tilt again back around toward the tower, wondering how we're going to figure out how to get in. It's not long before Tristan joins me, puffing hard, with his huge bow and quiver slung over his shoulder, his shirt on inside-out.

"What's this all about, Marek?" he demands, and I simply point. I've seen the flash of metal again, and this time, when it gleams out brightly, Tristan sees it, too, and I don't have to explain.

"We've got to get up there! Come on!" he exclaims, darting ahead of me to where a small door looks to open into the interior of the tower. Behind me I'm aware of the voices of some of the others calling to us. I think I hear Gilles and Falko, at least, but there's no time to wait for them or to stop and explain. Tristan's shouldering the door open, and we rush inside, clambering up the narrow stairs beyond as fast as we can. Even with the heavy bow and quiver Tristan can easily outdistance me, but out of fear I manage to keep him in sight as his back comes in and out of view as we spiral upward. When he reaches the top of the stairs, he's slowed by having to open a heavy wooden trap door that must give access to the ramparts. I catch up with him just as he's disappearing through the door, and I scramble out into the open air and onto the fortifications right behind him. We're only on the first rampart of the tower, a narrow landing surrounded by a low parapet. Above us, the tower narrows but continues to rise to higher fortifications, but from here there's a perfect view down over the bleachers, and at this height, we're in clear bowshot of the royal box.

Fortunately, the sounds of our arrival are masked by another loud blaring of trumpets from the competition grounds below, signaling to the Guards to begin their performance. As I step up next to Tristan, I see a man crouching behind the crenellations of the parapet about 20 yards away, a bow in his hand, an arrow already nocked.

It's what I expected, yet I can still hardly believe it. The man hasn't heard us, but before I can think, he rises up slowly and aims down at the crowd. All of a sudden, the field below and the stands go quiet; it must be the moment for the Guards to begin. Now I can hear the scuffling of some of the other Journeys opening the trap door behind us, but before they can reach us, the man settles into his final aim, ready to make the killing shot. At just the same moment, beside me Tristan pulls an arrow from his quiver, nocks it rapidly, and into that expectant silence he lets out a huge warning cry. The sound of it reverberates across the tower and down to the field, and cries of alarm start to rise up to us from the stands. Some of the spectators have noticed what's happening, but there's no time to turn to look. It happens so fast.

The man startles at the sound of Tristan's voice, and as he turns his head slightly toward us, Tristan shoots. It's one of his best shots — he shoots the bow right out of the man's hand. The would-be assassin takes a stumbling step or two forward as his bow falls over the edge of the parapet, surprise writ clearly on his face. A second later, a shower of arrows from below strikes him, as the Guards redirect their trick up to the wall and bring the man down.

He falls forward heavily, and his body follows his bow tumbling down from the tower amid shrieks from the grandstands. Tristan grabs my arm and presses me up against the back wall of the tower out of the range of the rain of arrows, but the man was far enough away and the Guards good enough shots than none of their arrows come close to us, and we're in no real danger. As he does, Tristan lowers his bow and drops it gently to the ground next to him, looking shaken. I don't think it's entirely because he can't believe he's just saved the prince. To his credit, I think he's disturbed by being part of bringing the man down, though his wasn't the killing shot. He aimed it carefully, and I can tell that Tristan doesn't have a taste for blood. I'll admit, the sight of a man falling headlong from a tower is one I don't care to see again, either.

"Tristan!" I say, stepping up next to him and taking his arm. "You were right! You *are* the kind to save a prince!" As I say it, I hear Gilles's voice from the top of the stairs; the others are finally emerging up onto the landing behind us.

"What? Another show-stealing shot, duBois?" Gilles exclaims, still only half-way out of the trap door. "Just couldn't let Mellor have his day, eh?" he chuckles, putting his palms flat on the stone floor to lift himself through the opening. Then he cries out suddenly in alarm, "What the devil?! Tristan!," and I turn around to see what he's looking at behind me.

There's another man.

He's been concealed a little ways further along the tower, crouched low behind the first archer and hidden from our view by his body. With the first archer gone, he's exposed. There's no other way down from the tower than the way we came up, and now that so many of us block his retreat, he must realize that he can't hope to escape. There's no hope for him of completing his task, either. If he rises up, the Guards will surely shoot him down. But he doesn't move to rise, and he doesn't take aim at the grandstands, either. In that split-second as I turn at Gilles's alarm and I spot him squatting there, he doesn't move from his crouch. Instead, he raises his bow, arrow nocked, and aims it straight at Tristan, a look of pure hatred on his face. It's Etienne Beaufort, Brecelyn's huntsman, intent on taking out Tristan to vent his rage at finding himself trapped.

There's no time. I don't even have my bow, and Tristan's put his own bow down. Gilles isn't through the trap door yet, and the others are all behind him. I take a step toward Beaufort, almost as though I might be able to reason with him, but it's already too late. He's loosed the arrow, and it's headed straight for Tristan.

Twang! I hear the crack of the bowstring, I see my father fall, and I do the only thing I can. I step lightly in front of Tristan, my back to him, as the arrow meant for him pierces my heart.

I'm only vaguely aware of what happens after that. Blinding pain sears my chest and I fall back heavily onto Tristan, as the full force of the arrow at point-blank range throws us back against the wall. Tristan cries out in surprise, clutching me to him as we slide down to fall in a heap at the base of the wall. Gilles darts forward, bow in hand, followed by Falko, then Taran. From the sound of it, they all get off arrows before Beaufort can shoot again, and I know with a certain satisfaction that Brecelyn's man must be dead. Gilles, Falko, Taran — three arrows, as it should be.

None of this registers much, though. All I can see is the arrow sticking out of my chest. St. Sebastian certainly doesn't go in for subtle signs. I guess it really is time for me to leave St. Sebastian's. It serves me right for asking the saint to help me do it. And I have to admit, this is the only way I'd ever go.

Suddenly I know it's the right way, too. I've always known there's nothing for me after St. Sebastian's, and despite the pain, I feel a surge of gratitude that the saint has finally come to my aid after all. I won't have to step into that dark woods; I can stay with Tristan to the bitter end, and feel his arms around me as I go. But as I do feel Tristan's arms close tight around me and his cheek press hard against mine, and as he begins to rock me back and forth, making inarticulate sounds, it's a hard thing to die. I still can't bear to leave him. But nobody gets everything he wants, and I know this is right. Me, in Tristan's arms, the arrow meant for him in my chest: that's the picture of him that's right with me in it. It's the picture that makes me beautiful.

"He's shot Marek!" I hear Jurian cry.

"No," Gilles says, his voice astounded. "He shot Tristan. But Marek stepped in front of him. He took the arrow."

"Oh, Bloody hell!" Falko yells.

I must be in shock, because as the boys crowd around, I look up at them and say quite wryly,

"I guess this means I won't be getting apprentice status."

But then suddenly I start to really feel the pain, and when I cry out, Tristan clutches me tighter and starts to sob, while the boys look on in grief.

"It's all right, Tristan," I say, trying to smile, but it comes out as a grimace. "This is the way it had to end. You said it yourself, it's inevitable. I don't mind, not really. I'd do it again."

"Don't try to talk, kid. You're going to be fine. You're going to be fine," Tristan mumbles, starting to rock back and forth again, but I can tell from the faces of the others that none of them thinks it's going to be fine. They all know I'm dying. There are some wounds you don't survive.

"You did it, Tristan!" I say, looking up at him wonderingly, though I have to pause for breath between each word. "You saved him, didn't you? They all saw you. You're a hero. Nobody can deny you anything now. You'll go on to win it all, now, won't you? Guards, the girl — everything. I know you will. And we stopped them! We stopped them, together, didn't we? You'll figure it all out now, won't you? And I ... don't you see? I finally learned it, the grand gesture. Going out in glory. You can't tell me now I don't know how to fail, with style. I get to be the hero, too. I've finally outdone even you!"

But Tristan isn't listening. He's bent over me, one hand smoothing back my hair, and he's begun to ramble protestations that strangely echo those I made to him when he was lying wounded in the chapel in the woods below:

"Don't leave me! You're not going to die, I won't let you!"

"It's too late, master," I say, as the pain gets sharper, and I'm starting to have trouble focusing my eyes.

"It can't be too late! Listen, Marek! Do you remember what you said, at Firsts? It's all true. You're my friend, you're my brother, my family. You're all I have in the world to love. Don't you dare leave me now!" Tristan's being as maudlin as I ever was, stroking my hair and hugging me to him, but I can't be happy about it. He's so wretched, I can't bear to see it, but after a while, with a little shake, he pulls himself together and turns to the others.

"Falko, Gilles, hurry! Help me get him up. We've got to get him down from here, to get him help, before it's too late. Help me see to the wound! Hurry, help me get this tunic off!"

"*No!*" I cry out in alarm, as Jurian and Gilles bend down to help Tristan try to pull off my tunic, so loudly that despite his desperation to get at my wound, Tristan pauses to clutch me up again. Only I'm more desperate than any of them. I can't let Tristan find out about me, not now! Not when I've made it this far. I've got to see my vow through to the end, or it was all for nothing.

"Please!" I plead in real agony, so wretchedly that tears start to form even in the other boys' eyes. "Tristan, let me go out with dignity! I don't want you to see me. Not after all this time. Please!"

"The devil with that!" Tristan cries, starting to tear at my tunic again. "I'm not going to let you die, kid, not for anything!"

The pain is blinding now, and I have no strength left. I try to struggle, but I'll never be able to stop Tristan by myself. Wildly, I do the only thing I can.

I cry out to Taran. I know he's here somewhere.

At my vehement outburst and at hearing me call Taran's name, Tristan looks utterly shocked and confused, but I have no choice. I have to hope I was right, that Taran has honor after all.

It takes all my effort to lift my head, and even then I can't hold it up and it lolls forward, but it's enough. My eyes meet Taran's, where he's lounging against the parapet, looking on with what can only be described as annoyance. He doesn't look distressed for me at all. In fact, he looks like he's irritated that it's taking me so long to die. There's a squeezing sensation in my chest and I suddenly feel foolish for thinking that he meant to stop me from leaving earlier, for thinking ... well, for thinking a lot of things, really. He must be glad finally to be getting rid of me, just as he said. From the look on his face when he opens his mouth, I half expect to hear Master Leon's voice come out, saying,

"Somebody, clean up this mess!"

Instead, he says rather dispassionately, "It's too late for him. But he sacrificed himself for a member. That makes him a St. Sebastian's man in my book. That should give him the right to his dignity."

"Tristan, Please!" I beg. For whatever reason, Taran's kept my secret for me all this time, and I think he intends to help me keep it now, if only to save himself from sharing in what he would think of as my disgrace. It hurts, but that's all I really need from him now.

"He doesn't have much time left, Tristan," Gilles says gently, putting a restraining hand on Tristan's shoulder; when Tristan shrugs it away roughly, Gilles adds softly, "Let him rest quietly."

Tristan looks up at Gilles hopelessly. "How can I just let him die?"

"Look, duBois," Taran cuts in again, with a sharp edge to his voice. "Your squire owes me a favor. It looks like I won't be able to collect it from him, so I'm going to demand it from you. The kid doesn't want any of you to see him. So I'm going to have to ask you to give him to me. I'll take his body from the tower. I'll see to it. I don't think he cares what I think of him."

"Are you crazy?!" Tristan cries, but I jump in. "Yes! Yes, that's it." I clutch at Tristan with what strength I've got left, and as he turns back to me, my eyes search his. "Promise me, Tristan. I don't want you to do it. I want you to remember me as I am right now, as we've been together. Oh, Tristan! I don't want you to remember me as the sorry thing I am, but as the boy I've tried so hard to be, for you! Promise me! Promise me you'll let Taran take me down from the tower. He can take me to the Vendon Abbey. The monks there are my friends. They can bury me. Oh, *promise* me!"

Tristan's still angry and hurt, but when he sees the desperate look on my face, he softens.

"Does it mean so much to you, then?" he says softly, and I nod.

"It means everything. Swear it," I say, my voice breaking, from emotion and from pain. "Swear it, on St. Sebastian." All the fight suddenly goes out of Tristan, as he finally realizes that I'm really going to die, and there's nothing he can do. He slumps down and rests his head against mine, and whispers,

"All right, kid. I swear."

My desperation to keep my secret safe has been helping me hold on, but now I can't fight anymore either, and I feel myself slipping slowly into unconsciousness. Although I know Jurian, Gilles, and Falko are all huddled close around us, I'm alone in Tristan's embrace, and I find I was wrong. I am to have a chance to say a final goodbye to Tristan, and one where I'm justified in being as sentimental as I want. Only I'm not ready. I'm not prepared. I'm worse than Falko, sitting in the archives struggling to find words, and there's nothing I can say. There's really only one thing left to say between us, the only thing that matters, but it's the one thing I can never say. The weight of it hurts more than the wound in my chest, it's heavier than the arrow pressing on my heart. But it's a burden I'll have to take with me. I've carried it so long already, and it's with a sense of triumph that I know I've managed to keep it to the end. I get to die a St. Sebastian's man, to the last.

Slowly my vision blurs, and even the pain begins to recede, as though I'm slipping away from it, too, and no matter how hard I struggle, I can't fight back to it. I look up at Tristan, and the image of him before my eyes swims, rippling and transforming, until I can't tell if I'm looking at him any longer or at my father, and as I gaze up at that handsome face that's both of theirs for the last time, I start to ramble incoherently, desperately,

"Did you see? You didn't fall! I saved you, this time, didn't I? I *did* save you, at last."

And now I can't see any of them any longer, they're all already far away, and the arms around me could be my father's again. I'm floating somewhere high above the walls of St. Sebastian's, looking down at a familiar image, the image of a beautiful boy rent with arrows. His face still holds that disturbing mixture of pain and ecstasy, but the expression holds no more mysteries for me, because this time, his face is mine. I can still feel Tristan's cheek on mine, his ear close to my mouth. I've only got one last chance, one moment to say all that's left unsaid, to say one final goodbye, and not just to Tristan. To all of them, to all of it. But of all the things I could say, of all the things I've been longing to say and that come bubbling up in me now, as I slip away, strangely enough what I hear myself whisper in Tristan's ear with my dying breath is,

"non me occident sagittae."

EPILOGUE

I wake up alone in a room so spare and white my first thought is that I must be in heaven. I put up a tentative hand to my chest to find the arrow gone, and I know I'm right. I'm whole again, on a soft mattress, with a simple white nightdress like an angel might wear covering me.

Then I feel a stab of pain.

It's out of place, it doesn't fit. Confused, I lift my hand gingerly up to find its source, and my fingers brush the edge of a bandage wound tightly around my left shoulder. With a frown, my hand slides down, to find bare flesh. The binding around my breasts is gone.

I'm not dead.

Even worse, I'm a girl again.

A NOTE FROM THE AUTHOR

The Archers of St. Sebastian I: Journeys is more fiction than history, and it would be more appropriate to say that this story was inspired by late medieval Belgium than that it actually takes place there. There was never a principality called Ardennes; although the forested region of the same name is undoubtedly real, the country at the heart of this story, its institutions, and its attitudes are all fabrications. The Louvain in this story is not Leuven; that city lies well to the north of my fictional Ardennes, whose borders I imagine as corresponding roughly to those of medieval Wallonia. The real towns and rivers of this region, too, have been altered to suit the story, and even the basic topography of southern Belgium as it is described in my book is probably more convenient for my purposes than it is accurate.

Likewise, although there were many longbow and crossbow guilds throughout northern Europe during the 14th century, my archers' guild of St. Sebastian, its operation, inhabitants, and competitions are all the products of imagination. Nonetheless, I have endeavored to avoid glaring anachronism in the telling of my tale whenever possible, and to present an image of medieval archery that is detailed and compelling. But I have also taken it as my guiding principle that the needs of storytelling should always trump the demands of strict historical accuracy, and so I hope I can be forgiven if on occasion I have stretched the truth a little. In particular, I have no doubt exaggerated some of the distances; for example, although there is some debate about the effective range of a longbow such as my Journeys are shooting, in truth it is highly unlikely that an arrow could penetrate anything but the flimsiest of armor if shot from more than 200 yards distant. For the basics of medieval archery, fletching, and hunting, I relied heavily on *With A Bended Bow: Archery in Mediaeval and Renaissance Europe* by Erik Roth, Spellmount Publishers Ltd., 2012; all errors, misrepresentations, and flat-out embellishments are of course my own.

It would be disingenuous, however, if I did not admit that the glorious city of Bruges provided the inspiration for this story. Indeed, the seeds of it were planted long ago, on an idyllic afternoon spent wandering lost through the backstreets of Bruges with my father, searching for a park purporting to contain a statue of Jacque Brel's Marieke (the Judy Collins version of the song being one of his all-time favorites). I still have the picture I took of my father once we finally tracked down our quarry, holding the statue's hand and pretending to skip along with it — just as somewhere there is a picture of a youthful me, sitting in Bruges's archers' guild of St. Sebastian earlier that same day, and staring up at a beautiful painting.

... *and a plea:*

If you enjoyed *Journeys* (and even if you didn't!), please consider leaving an honest review of the book on Amazon or Goodreads. I'm always interested in constructive feedback, and independent authors like me depend on ratings from readers like you to give us visibility. Your support is greatly appreciated, and if you can think of anyone who might like the book, please do recommend it to them! 'Word of mouth' is my marketing department.

I'd love to hear from you; visit me at www.jeanneroland.com if you have questions or comments, and if you're interested in keeping up with my latest projects, please consider signing up to get my newsletter. **Don't forget to request a sneak peek of the next book in this series, *the Archers of St. Sebastian II: Squires!***

ACKNOWLEDGMENTS

Writing this book has been the greatest adventure of my life. To list all of the people who have helped me along the way would be a true impossibility; if you read a draft of the book, offered advice, listened to me talk about it *ad nauseam*, or provided much-needed emotional support, you know who you are and I thank you from the bottom of my heart. But I would be remiss if I did not mention by name those individuals without whom this book could never have been completed: first and foremost, my super-sister Sue, who has been with me from word one with unflagging support and enthusiasm, my truest champion; Mimi, my first and best fan, and the best amateur editor on the planet, or perhaps in the solar system — had I been able to bring myself to take her advice at every turn, the book would surely now be much better!; Sam, a fountain of strength who never lets me give up, or cave in, and her husband Paul, who gave me hope that the book could appeal to men as well as to women; Laura and Nadine, my oldest friends, and Nadine's daughter Ayla, my first teen reader; Melissa, and her wife Naomi — both of whose support has gone far beyond simply reading and commenting on my story.

I'd also like to give a special thanks to my agent Victoria, for all her hard work and assistance, and for her generous acceptance of my decision not to modify my text in the obvious ways that would have made it more marketable; I'm indebted to Sally B. for introducing us, and to Victoria's assistant Gabry, for her painstaking readings of the text and for all of her thoughtful comments. To all my early readers — those listed above, Tim, Kara, Michelle C., Sarah M., and many others — your encouragement bolstered my resolve, and gave me courage to pursue publishing.

I also owe a big thanks to my family, both here and in Greece, for patiently putting up with my obsessions and my moods, and for allowing me the time and space in which to write. S, C, and V — I know it has been a sacrifice, and I love you all the more for making it so graciously for me.

Last but not least, I want to thank my mother, for being an exemplary model of what women can achieve, and my father, for never losing the ability to see the world through the lens of childlike wonder, and for teaching me that a life filled with passions and lit by intellectual curiosity is the best life possible. If anyone ever embodied Socrates' phrase *"not to live, but to live well,"* it was he.

ABOUT THE AUTHOR

Roland hails from northern California, where she spent most of her youth lounging at the pool, soaking up the sun, and daydreaming. She had a key ring that read *I'm running away to join the circus*, and her favorite moment of the day was when the local movie theater went dark, and the slogan *escape to the movies* appeared on the screen. As an adult, her passions include all things melodramatic and beautiful — everything from classic movies, British romantic poetry, ancient tragedy and epic, to Italian opera. She is now a professor of Classics in a small midwestern town, where she lives with her Greek husband, her fraternal twins, and a Bernese mountain dog named Franco Corelli.

To find out more, visit www.jeanneroland.com

SNEAK PEEK OFFER

Squires: The Archers of Saint Sebastian II is on its way! If you enjoyed *Journeys*, why not start on it today?

To request your complimentary complete first chapter of *Squires*, visit the *Squires* book page under 'browse my books' at www.jeanneroland.com.

ILLUSTRATION CREDITS AND CITATIONS

All illustrations in this book were created for Nepenthe Press using Canva fonts and graphic elements licensed under the Canva Pro license, illustrations and vectors licensed under the Shutterstock standard license, Herculaneum font, and public domain artwork for which source files have been made available under a Creative Commons license. A comprehensive list of all the source files used herein is as follows:

Cover:

Canva Pro graphic elements (arrow, arrow hole, poppies, frame) and fonts, plus: background image: *"Still Life with Poppy, Insects, and Reptiles,"* Otto Marseus van Schrieck (Dutch, Nijmegen 1619/20– 1678 Amsterdam), ca. 1670, oil on canvas, 26 7/8 x 20 3/4 in. (68.3 x 52.7 cm), Rogers Fund, 1953, Metropolitan Museum of Art AN 53.155, Open Access image https://www.metmuseum.org/art/ collection/search/436976, accessed September 1, 2021, and inset image: *"Saint Sebastian Expiring,"* François-Xavier Fabre, ca. 1789, oil on canvas, 77.9 in x 58.4 in., Galerie des Colonnes, Fabre Museum AH 825.1.62, Don François-Xavier Fabre in 1825; this painting is the Public Domain in its country of origin and other countries and areas where the copyright term is the author's life plus 100 years or fewer; photograph image file shared by Finoskov 2018-01-07 15:42:46 under the Creative Commons Attribution-Share Alike 4.0 International license via Wikimedia Commons, https://common-s.wikimedia.org/wiki/File:PeinturesMuséeFabre182_Fabre_St_Sébastien1789.jpg, accessed August 1, 2021; the image has been slightly cropped, and graphic elements (arrow, arrow hole, frame) superimposed.

Title page:

"View of Bruges old town and Belfry tower, postcard as watercolor drawing," from Bruges, Belgium, Shutterstock illustration ID: 1830944432 By Savvapanf Photo.

Dedication:

"Doodle Red Poppies," Shutterstock vector ID 1238279428 by Ollisia; poppy color has been modified.

Section divisions:

Canva Pro graphic elements (poppy, scrolls), plus the following artwork: *"Festival of the Archers,"* Master of Frankfurt (ca. 1460 – 1533), ca. 1490, oil on panel, Height: 176 cm (69.2 in); Width: 141 cm (55.5 in), Royal Museum of Fine Arts Antwerp AN 529, Public Domain image via Wikimedia Commons, https://commons. wikimedia.org/wiki/File:Frankfurt_master-Archers_festival.jpg, accessed September 15. *"Hunting arrows collection,"* Shutterstock vector ID 194942657, by Tribalium 88.

Chapter headings:

"Poppy flowers collection on white background," Shutterstock vector ID 386473642, by Stockakia;*"Medieval Bow 3D illustration on white background,"* Shutterstock ID 1810862491, by PixelSquid3d *"Hunting arrows collection,"* Shutterstock ID 194942657, by Tribalium 88; *"Different mice,"* Shutterstock ID 1484129015, by A788OS; *"Vector red apple icon,"* Shutterstock ID 659128897, by Eva Spsheneva; *"Set of predatory bird cute adult falcon cartoon animal design birds of prey character flat vector illustration isolated on white background,"* Shutterstock ID 1817468843, by Alfamaler; *"Quiver and arrows,"* Shutterstock ID 517555045, by Elsbet. Shutterstock ID 194942657, by Tribalium 88.

Squires unofficial cover:

Canva Pro fonts and graphic elements (arrow, arrow hole, frame, poppy, shapes), and the following artworks: background: *"Peacocks,"* Melchior d' Hondecoeter (Dutch, Utrecht 1636–1695 Amsterdam), ca. 1683, Oil on canvas, 74 7/8 x 53 in. (190.2 x 134.6 cm), Gift of Samuel H. Kress, 1927, MMOA AN 27.250.1, OA Public Domain image, https://www.metmuseum.org/art/collection/search/

436671, web accessed September 1, 2021. Inset: *"The Plague in Rome,"* Jules Elie Delaunay (French 1828 – 1891), oil on wood, ca. 1869, 14 7/16 x 18 1/16 in., gift of Mr. and Mrs. Atherton Bean, Minneapolis Institute of Art AN 72.128, Public Domain, https://collections.artsmia.org/art/1913/the-plague-in-rome-jules-elie-delaunay, accessed September 30, 2021.

Made in the USA
Las Vegas, NV
12 November 2021